UBLIC OF PANAMA

RUINS OF OLD PANAMA

PANAMA

CEMETERY

CUCARACHA MT.

CAMP ELLIOTT

BALBOA

ANCON

PEDRO MIGUEL

PARAISO

POST OFFICE AT LA BOCA

S OBISPO

CULEBRA

EMPIRE

RIO

A

PANAMA CANAL ZONE - 1905

┼┼┼┼ = PANAMA RAILROAD

‑ ‑ ‑ = PROPOSED CANAL ROUTE

= PROPOSED GATUN LAKE

Panama Passage

A NOVEL BY DONALD BARR CHIDSEY

Panama Passage

DOUBLEDAY & COMPANY, INC., GARDEN CITY, NEW YORK

MCMXLVI

To
GINNIE

THE WAGON MOVED with a sluggishness positively saurian; and mud mixed with garbage, mud that was feculent and stank, rose on the wheels to slip off with a loud plop at the apex. The wagon was a dray, sideless and without tailboard, merely a platform. Its load was a rectangular box painted black, with two brass handles on either side. One horse pulled it. In the seat, unblinking, apprehensive, as alert and twitchy as a ready-to-bolt rabbit that sits by the side of the road, was a driver whose nationality was anybody's guess. His eyes were gooseberries, his mouth a slit of slate. Nevertheless, and without looking at it, pauselessly he beat the horse. This did no good. The driver cursed in a voice unexpectedly shrill, a carrying voice. The mud—it was a terrible effort—rose with each wheel, and lengthening, thinning, let go and slapped back.

'What's he saying? Or shouldn't I ask?'

Madeline gave him a quick sideways smile. They talked hastily, for they knew that the rain would soon start again.

'No, you shouldn't ask. Really, I can't get all of it myself. I am proud to say that there are some words I don't know.'

He feared that he was blushing, and knew that he marveled. The ease with which Madeline met such questions amazed him. She was never embarrassed. She never pulled herself up haughtily, stiffening her back to an unnatural curve, at a decision to ignore something. Oh, she was a lady! Knowledge of this fact, however, did not seem to haunt and pursue her. Harry wondered fleetingly whether all Frenchwomen were like that, and decided that they weren't. He reasoned: They couldn't be. Madeline was the only Frenchwoman he had ever known.

'Gives you the creeps, the way they hustle them off.' He nodded to the wagon, which would be passing for a long time. 'And it's awful the way they thrust 'em in. I went to Art Crowell's burial last night. He probably had as many friends as anybody on the Isthmus, but I was the only one there besides the driver. This same driver. I read the service, and he was shoveling in the dirt before I was half through.'

'I'm sorry. I did not know that he had died. You liked him?'

'Yes. Very much.'

'I did not know that he had died.'

'You can hardly keep track of 'em nowadays, they're burying 'em so fast. You'd think people could catch yellow jack from the corpse!'

'Some people still do think that.'

'Yes. . . . Every morning at the mess you go to breakfast and look around and say "Well, who's dead today?" You don't say it to be funny. You really want to know.'

The waiter brought them preposterous little cups of coffee, and the rain started again, a gray roaring rain, javelins, not drops, which blotted every other sound and curtained even the wagon.

When the rain slackened the wagon was halfway down the block and Madeline was staring strangely at Harry Kellems.

'Monsieur——' Sometimes she called him that, half playfully, but more often it was 'Arry or, when she remembered, aspirating heavily, Harry. 'I'm sorry about your friend. But that is not what troubles you this morning.'

'No, you're right. It's something else.' He drew a cablegram from his coat pocket. 'I—I'm afraid our Spanish lessons have got to end, ma'mselle.'

She was hurt, and even shocked, but she did not show it. She only shrugged and said something noncommittal in French. He watched her as she stirred coffee. He had never known what to make of Madeline Desmoulins. He did not know when she was acting, or whether she never was or always was.

The Café de Jesus, a malodorous dump with dark circles under its eyes, seemed astonished to find itself open at noon. Madeline and Harry, according to their custom—her father was crotchety and might be cross with visitors, especially Americans, and of course Harry could not take her to the place he shared with eleven others—had strolled Las Bovidas along the old sea wall of Panama City through the course of the Spanish lesson. Rain had caught them on the way back, in a side street in which the buildings were not arcaded, and they'd leaped into the Café de Jesus. Soon, after finishing the coffee, stuff as thick as the sleech that bottoms a slow river, a ropy goo, black and viscid, they would scurry on: Harry had to rejoin his pyrethrum squad, Madeline had to get home and prepare lunch for her father. It was not raining now, though it would rain again soon. There was a mumble in the sky, a padded but filling sound like the drumming of God's fingers upon a gigantic table top. The joint, musty, smelled like wet hay exposed to the sun.

'My wife is coming down here' blurted Harry.

2

There was nothing for which to reprove him. He had never pretended to be single, he had never made any flirtation with her. All the same, she was obliged to tighten her throat to keep from sobbing. Not until this moment had she known how fond she was of Harry Kellems.

'That will be nice.'

'But don't you see? She can't come here!'

'Why not?' She nodded toward the wagon. '*That* can't go on forever.'

'It can return! As long as there are fresh batches of laborers arriving who aren't immune, it *will* return! As long as they don't give Dr Gorgas a decent appropriation to work with! He could clean this place up the way he cleaned up Havana, but they won't give him a chance! Do you realize that there are still people, people higher up too, who control the funds, who go right on refusing to believe that yellow jack's spread by mosquitoes?'

Madeline spoke quickly, politely, asking his wife's name.

'Phil. Well, her real name is Phyllis, but everybody always calls her Phil.'

'And when is she coming?'

'Now! On the *Allianca!* Gets here Saturday! She just took matters in her own hands and packed her things and got on board!'

'So. Don't you think that's rather admirable?'

'I think it's rather crazy! Every time I write her, every week in the ten months I've been here, I've warned her that she mustn't dream of joining me yet—not the way things are here. I suppose she can't believe that. She can't believe that Americans could do such a poor job as we've been doing, so far. I'll bet the papers at home aren't telling about conditions the way they are! But she could at least believe *me!*'

He had been writing to her every week, all along, Madeline thought. Immediately afterward she thought: Well, why shouldn't he?

'It's true I didn't ever tell her how horrible it was here, because I didn't want her to worry about me.'

'Perhaps she would not worry if she was with you?'

'She *can't* stay in a place like *this!*' Desperate, he waggled his hands, and the hands spoke of mud and filth, of malaria and yellow fever and trachoma and hookworm and dysentery, of misunderstandings, misfits, changes, uncertainty, red tape, of appalling, excruciating inefficiency. 'She was brought up in a decent home. Her folks are practically the richest people in Paterson. She's never been away before—except once to go to Europe, after finishing-school, and then she had all kinds of

3

companions and guides and chaperons and so forth. Don't you understand? This place would *kill* her!'

No, Madeline did not understand.

'Why?' she asked.

He shook a gloomy head.

'She's stubborn, too. Of course she'll want to go right back, as soon as she gets one look around, but I think she'll probably refuse to go back unless I go with her. Which means I'll have to resign.'

'You will not be the only one.'

'No,' bitterly. 'No, they're running out like cockroaches from a fire, aren't they?' With haste he begged her pardon, she did not understand why. 'Only thing is, I hadn't thought I'd have to run out with them. But I guess I will. I don't really know Phil very well, but I know her well enough to know that she's going to insist upon getting out of this place—and unless I want to let her stay here and die out of sheer stubbornness, I'll have to go with her.'

Interested, Madeline also was puzzled. She was too polite to suggest, simply, that a wife's place is by her husband's side.

'Is—is she ill then, 'Arry?'

'Oh no! Oh, Phil's healthy enough, as far as that goes! But she's been protected all her life, she's never had to face anything like this. She lives in such an elegant house. I remember when it was built and I was asked to a party there, a kids' party. Gosh, what a big place! I was scared. There was a man opened the door for us, in a kind of uniform, and they had hardwood floors and a telephone. It was the first time I'd ever seen hardwood floors and a telephone. The party was nice enough, I guess, but I was scared.'

The rain had stopped; it only dribbled off the eaves in an uncertain curtain. Madeline should have hurried on, but here was a problem. She leaned forward.

'Please do not think that I am—fresh, you call it?—such a curious word!—but still I do not understand, 'Arry. Once you say that you knew her when you both were children and you lived in the same city, and then you say that you do not know her well?'

'Well, I don't, really. I knew her when we were kids, yes. When she still went to public school. But then her father got to making a lot of money and they took Phil out of public school and sent her to a private school. A finishing-school, they called it. I didn't see much of her then, naturally. And after the finishing-school was over she went abroad to visit Europe, and by the time she came back, with a lot of fancy French

4

gowns and everything, I was in college. But I used to see her week ends then, at parties. I was always invited to the parties.'

'Because of the friendship of childhood?'

'Well, that had something to do with it, of course.'

'Or because you sing so well, 'Arry?'

Surprised, he grinned briefly.

'Well, all right. That was the real reason. I knew it at the time. I was no fool. I used to sing in the Episcopal church—that's kind of the fashionable church in Paterson, where the nicest people go, or at least the ones with the most money—and I was the soloist and I got plenty of invitations that I wouldn't have got otherwise. I couldn't go to the very swellest parties because I didn't have a full-dress suit. That's the way it was at first, anyway. Then after a while, when I was in the glee club at college, then I had to have a dress suit or else I couldn't sing at any of the concerts we gave, and they said they needed me and they bought me one. It came out of some kind of expense fund. They said to look on it just like a business proposition, as far as they were concerned. It was only a secondhand one, but it was in pretty good condition. Then after that I used to go to *all* the parties. Sometimes I sort of hated myself for it. I never felt very easy at those parties. I guess I'm not cut out to be a society man. But I did like to sing, and I used to tell myself that I was meeting the right kind of people who might help me when I got through college. And another thing: they always gave you plenty to eat. Not that I ever went *hungry* in those days—I still had a little of the insurance money my father left—but I used to come pretty close to it sometimes, and every little bit helped. And then Phil was practically always at the parties. She used to accompany me. She plays the piano beautifully.

'As a matter of fact,' he went on, 'I guess you could say it was my singing that was the reason we got married. I don't believe her parents ever thought a lot of me. They were nice, but I guess they were looking for somebody with more, uh, background. But Phil used to invite me there lots of times when there wasn't any other company at all, and we'd just play and sing, mostly hymns and ballads. When there were other people we'd sing ragtime and silly songs mostly, but when we'd be just together we'd sing the nicer songs, like "Sing Me to Sleep," and "When the Sunset Turns the Ocean's Blue to Gold"—she always used to say that reminded her of afternoons on board the steamboat when she went to Europe that time—and "Mighty Lak a Rose"—that was a big favorite with both of us—and best of all, the one we both liked most, "Jest Alongin' for Your Smile."'

5

Madeline thought that it was good to hear him talk, even though he talked of this Phil; and she wondered what Phil was like.

'Then one night her parents had gone to the theater in New York and she invited me over and we sang for hours, and after a while I put a hand on her shoulder, the hand I wasn't using to turn the pages, with. I remember she had on a blue dress that I guess she'd brought from Paris. It was the prettiest thing I'd ever seen. Phil's a mighty pretty girl, anyway. We sang "Jest Alongin' for Your Smile" clear through three times, and after that we went out to the conservatory. They've got a regular conservatory in that house that's all glassed in, and it's just like part of the house itself, like in the rest of the house. This was wintertime—it was a year ago the sixteenth of last January— but it was just like summer in there, with all the plants and flowers growing. I can remember how they smelled, kind of close and heavy, it almost made you dizzy, and you could smell all the earth too, like being in the woods on a warm night. They've got steam heat in that house.

'We ran away. I guess you could practically say we eloped, though as a matter of fact we only went as far as Passaic, which is right near Paterson, and there I got hold of a friend who got me a ring somehow —I never did know how—and we went to a justice of the peace. Phil certainly looked lovely in that blue dress. It was after one o'clock in the morning when we got back, and her folks were home from New York and they were wild. But they hadn't notified the police, because they had been afraid it would start talk.'

Madeline asked if they had in fact become man and wife.

There was no mistaking her meaning, which jolted Harry. It brought his chin up, and he felt his face go hot; but he resisted the temptation to glare at her. Sure, he was aware of her shady reputation. He had always discounted it. In the first place she was French, and French-women were supposed to be bad, though he didn't himself see any reason why they should be worse than other women. She was almost the only unmarried white female on the Isthmus, the only one without a job, and the only good-looking one. Her father, that cantankerous high-nosed old hold-over from the French company days, had a poor enough clerical job, as everyone knew, a job which would not even last much longer: he was engaged in translating certain old engineering records. Madeline kept house for him, and she always looked trim and in a quiet way stylish. She was better educated than anybody else he had ever met. She had learned English at school, in France; and in six years here in Panama she had easily acquired Spanish. Why

6

shouldn't she pick up a little pin money by giving Spanish lessons? It graveled him, it always had, the way the boys at the mess, sniggering, referred to his 'Spanish lessons' with stress on the 'Spanish.' His own opinion was that Madeline Desmoulins was an honest girl, and straightforward, and clean. True, she was sometimes disconcertingly outspoken, though he had never heard her say a bad word, unless she did so when she talked French. He attributed this partly to her foreign upbringing and partly to the fact that, like him, she had lost her mother early. It was always pleasant to talk with her.

Nevertheless her question was a shock. He was not indignant, as he might have been. He was too embarrassed to be indignant. To his own amazement he heard himself answering with haste but quietly.

'Well, yes and no. What I mean is, we used to see one another, of course, whenever we got the chance, mostly when I was back in Paterson week ends, and as much as we could we tried to be together, and sometimes that was possible for a little while. But we never—well, we never really lived together. Day by day. I mean, we couldn't set up housekeeping, the way we wanted to. We figured that that would have to wait until I had finished college and made enough money for us to really get a start.'

'D'amour et d'eau fraiche' she murmured.

'Huh?'

'It's part of an old saying. But go ahead.'

'Well, it was pretty terrible waiting. But of course we had to.'

'But 'Arry, you have said that her father was rich. Did not you arrange something with him? I don't know your word in English: a *dot* we call it. If he was rich and prized his daughter——'

'Do you think I'd take any of his money?' He was angry, for a moment. 'What do you think I am? A fancy man or something?'

'I am so sorry! In France——'

'I wouldn't have touched a cent of his money, even if he'd offered me it! I shouldn't have gotten married until I was ready to support a wife—maybe not in the style to which she was accustomed, but at least support her. But since I did, the thing for me to do was to settle down and make some. I had practically nothing left of my father's insurance. And then I'd had to dress up so many times: that meant bigger laundry bills. And I'd paid my friend for the wedding ring he got us—four and a quarter, which is just what he said he'd paid for it himself, and I believe him. I kept on at college for a couple of months, but I knew I wasn't doing the right thing. She stayed home, naturally, and she couldn't have been very happy. She's an only child.

'Then all of a sudden, out of a clear sky, came this offer to come down here as some kind of an engineer—they weren't very clear what kind—and the pay would be twice what I could hope to get even after I had my degree, and the government promised to supply living quarters besides. That was May of last year, when they were just getting ready to send the first ones down here, just after we'd assumed control of the Zone. I had to take it or leave it, fast. I took it. It meant quitting college when I had only two months more to go to get my degree, but we talked it over and we figured that I could come back later and make up those two months. Meanwhile I'd get some practical experience in engineering, which wouldn't do me any harm. Of course,'—*he* could be frank too!—'I supposed then that I was going to have something to do with machinery. I didn't know I was going to be put to work covering rain barrels and cleaning out gutters and fumigating houses and dumping disinfectant down the holes in privies.

'We talked it over, and we decided that I'd come down here and save enough to set up a decent home for us and then she'd come down and join me. A couple of years, we figured, would be enough. Then we could go back to Paterson and we'd get a regular home and I'd finish my course at Stevens and set up as an engineer.

'As soon as I got here I realized that I couldn't let her come. She naturally supposed that any place where Americans were would be all right, the way I had thought myself until I got here. Well, things haven't got any better. Matter of fact, they've got worse, especially now with this yellow fever. I didn't want to tell her about all the disease and so forth, and the kind of job I had, because I didn't want to scare her or disgust her. But I did try to tell her, in letters, enough so that she'd realize she ought to stay where she was. She's been pretty impatient, I could tell from her letters. Her folks have probably been making sarcastic remarks about the kind of man who marries a girl and then goes away to a foreign country and doesn't even try to support her but lets her stay at home. Phil would hate that. It would make her wild. Oh, I knew she was getting impatient! But I never thought'—he tapped the cablegram—'that she'd do anything like this.'

He sighed, putting the cablegram away.

'It simply means that I'll have to get her return passage somehow. And you know what that means, with all the rats scrambling to get off the sinking ship. Weeks—maybe months! And I'm sure I don't know where we can find a place to live in in the meanwhile. I can't let her go to one of those hotels or boardinghouses, even if I could find a room for her. It wouldn't be decent. I'll just have to quit my job and ar-

8

range to go back with her. After all, I'm responsible. It's because of me that she's coming here.'

Madeline thought: And it's because of her that you came here. She said nothing. But she stiffened at his next remark.

'This damn place!' explosively. 'Of *course* she can't stay! This is no place for a decent white woman to be in!'

Immediately afterward, knowing that he had offended her, he was apologetic.

'I'm so sorry! It—it must be worrying so much that's got me half crazy!'

She smiled forgiveness, but rose. They had lingered too long. Soon it would rain again. Until the Plaza, where they were to part, she said nothing. There, when they faced one another, she asked if the Spanish lessons were to continue.

'Oh, sure! As long as we can, anyway. Tomorrow, sure. After all, Phil doesn't arrive until Saturday.'

She put a hand on his arm, an act which flustered him there in a public place.

'Please do not worry too much, Harry. I am sure that it will be all right.'

'Thanks. It—it was nice to talk to you. Well, see you tomorrow.'

'No!'

'Eh?'

He turned back, startled, a whit frightened.

'Digalo en español.'

He chuckled.

'Absolutely. Well, hasta luego, señorita.'

'Adios, señor. Hasta mañana.'

He stood and watched her, her quick smooth walk, her unlumpy figure, the way she held her skirt, the easy set of her head on her neck. When she had left the Plaza and entered a side street he still watched her awhile. There the sidewalk was narrow, and men stepped right and left to give her passage. All the men looked at her the way spiggoties do look at a woman who's alone—for the only time a señorita should show herself in public is late afternoon, and even then she should be guarded by a duenna—and a few simpered or started to touch their hats; but she paid them no attention, walking serenely with head high. Oh, she was a lady all right! She was the cleanest non-American thing in Panama, he reflected, and one of the nicest. He felt like a skunk for having offended her—for he knew by the way she'd said

9

good-by, somehow, that he *had* offended her. He couldn't have explained it, but he knew by the way she walked.

'I ought to be kicked' he muttered when at last she was out of sight. 'I wish I hadn't said that "damn," damn it!'

When the work was over, Harry Kellems went to the office, to his boss, whose name was Simpson, and told him that he would probably have to resign soon. Simpson was a small person with the manner of a harassed field mouse. He was marvelously pale; and rolls and cushions and blobs of pale fat, which should have departed long ago, hung listlessly and haphazardly to his person, as though they had long since lost all interest in him as in everything else. He sweated a great deal, so that the armpits of his shirt always, even first thing in the morning, were grayly half-mooned.

He looked at Harry, not saying anything. That look was the look of one stricken by a pain more than physical, and Harry, uneasy, feeling hot guilt inside, was reminded of the assassination scene in *Julius Caesar*, which he'd had to read in high school.

Trying to laugh: 'You're going to say "Et tu, Brute," I suppose?'

'I wasn't going to say anything' Simpson replied with weariness. 'Except that I think you ought to see the Chief about it. I'll telephone him. He'll be home now. Always is at this time.'

'Now listen, I don't want you to think this is because I'm afraid of yellow jack!'

Simpson did not acknowledge the protestation, but went to the walled instrument and took off the receiver and spun the crank. He gazed at the ceiling, perhaps to keep from looking at a funeral which was passing the office window.

'Central? Central?' he shouted presently. Now he looked hard at the mouthpiece, his eyes popping. 'Hello, Central? . . . I want Colonel Gorgas's residence on Ancon Hill. . . . Yes, Colonel Gorgas, on the hospital grounds. . . .'

'Say, don't call him up just because of *me!* Why, he's the busiest man on the Isthmus, especially at a time like this!'

'Don't be silly' Simpson said wearily. 'He thinks a lot of you.' He shouted again: 'Hello? Hello? Is this Dr Gorgas? . . . This is Simpson. . . . Simpson, yes. At the office. . . . Listen, can you hear me? . . . Kellems is here' he shouted. 'Harry Kellems, he says he's going to quit. . . . Yes. . . .'

'I didn't say anything of the kind' Harry cried. 'All I said was that because of a personal matter it might be necessary for me to resign.'

'That's right, he says he's going to quit' Simpson shouted. 'Yes, Harry Kellems! . . . Yes, that's what I thought, I thought you'd want to. . . . When, now? Right now? . . . All right, I'll send him up. . . . Good-by, sir' he shouted.

'You live up that way anyway' he said, and flumped back into his chair, a jelly. 'I don't know whether I'm coming or going. You tell it to the Chief. He says he wants to see you.'

There was a dray climbing the hill, three long cases on it, each plain and black, each with a couple of brass handles on either side. They would be empties, shipped over from Cristobal, being carted up to the morgue just inside the hospital gates. Harry, who had worked hard and was wet and very tired, caught the back of the dray and vaulted to a sitting position; but the mud was slick and the bumping forceful, so he scrambled up to sit on the backmost box.

'D'you mind?' he called. 'Esta bueno if I sit here?'

The driver turned. It was the same one, the one with gooseberries for eyes. He said nothing, only shrugged, and went back to beating his horse.

Of other things they might be short, but of these at least, of coffins, they had plenty. Dr Gorgas had asked the commission for some sort of emergency fund; and that request had been treated as an impertinence. You never knew what you might get or not get. Dr Gorgas, admittedly the world's leading sanitarian, had asked for twenty field inspectors—and had got eight. He had asked for one hundred female nurses—and had got, or sooner or later would get, forty. He had asked, five months before, for twenty-five hundred square yards of wire screening to save lives—and this was cut to five hundred yards, which hadn't yet arrived. You were not supposed to press the Old Man of the Sea too hard: it was Dr Gorgas's own name for the lace-curtained admiral who was chairman of the commission, and Harry, like everybody else in Sanitation, had taken it up gleefully. You filed your requisitions and hoped for the best, though you knew that there were no Aëdes aegypti in Washington, no, nor any Anopheles either, nor, for that matter, any pellagra or beriberi or leprosy or dengue, and not even any mud worth mentioning. You filed your requisition with your boss, Simpson say, who got it endorsed by Dr Gorgas, after which it went for another endorsement to the governor, who sent it to the chief disbursing agent, who after a while sent it by mail to that commission in Washington; the commission in time gave it to one of its own committees, which studied it, and perhaps o.k.'d it, though not uncut, and then presented it to the full commission, which acted upon it; if the commission left anything of it, bids were advertised for and awards were made, and what remained of the requisition was filled under the supervision of a purchasing agent who might have been all right in his own way but who knew nothing whatever about surgical or medical supplies or about tropical sanitation; and the stuff was shipped to the Isthmus, probably by sailing schooner in order to save expense; and eventually the chief of the bureau of material and supplies, to whom it was consigned, notified the disbursement officer, who notified Dr Gorgas, who notified Simpson, who notified you; and after that it was up to you to go to the quartermaster to arrange for transportation of the supplies, if you still needed them and if they were the right size—which meant only two vouchers in the unlikely event that he could help you, but six separate vouchers if you had to hire a cart. American efficiency! was Harry's bitter thought, while his buttocks thudded the rearmost box. Christ Almighty! But there were always plenty of coffins. The aged supervisors in Washington had been thoughtful, very liberal too, in the matter of coffins.

It came to Harry after a while, on the slow, wet, uncomfortable trip up the hill, that there was a song which had been going through his head all afternoon. He wished he could get rid of it, if only for a few minutes. He wished that, all ache as he was, he could stop thinking of Phil for a little while.

> *'Jest alongin' for your smile,*
> *Jest to make my life worth while. . . .'*

The mud that clung to the wheels rose, swung in flabby obscene stalactites, thinned, lengthened, and slapped back into the mother mud and filth; and the driver lackadaisically thrashed his horse, screeching Spanish curses; and it began to rain again.

All manner of white workers, including Harry himself, lived inside the grounds of the Ancon Hospital, a splattering of inherited buildings on the side of a hill, and Harry was familiar with the St Charles, the building the French had reserved for their white employees of the hospital. Harry knew it because it was in the main hospital office downstairs that they used to hold impromptu Protestant services Sunday mornings. Upstairs, in apartments, lived Dr Gorgas, Dr Carter, and several other of the more eminent medicos.

The St Charles stood a little back of the center of the grounds, facing northeast, toward Panama and the bay. A macadam road ran before it, and beyond that was a grass plot and a retaining wall, and in the grass plot was a spectacular row of royal palms planted by the French, who had imported royal palms and coconut trees and flowering shrubs even though they hadn't done much about running water. You got a wonderful view from there. Back of it, for some four hundred steep feet, covered with jungle so dark a green as to show almost black, rose the rest of the mountain.

William Crawford Gorgas, colonel, U. S. Medical Department, was dazzling in white, a benign man, breathlessly handsome, with white hair and exquisite silky white mustaches. No go-getter, you would say. A gentleman, surely; but not a go-getter. He beamed at Harry.

'Come on up. Sit down. Nicest time of day here. Except maybe the dawn. Sun comes over the bay down there. Something to see. Drink?'

'No, thank you.'

'Why not? It's good for you. You're wet, son.'

'Well . . .'

'Sit down and enjoy the scenery. I'll be right back.'

Harry was nervous. He had not expected a reprimand, but he had expected to catch a glint of reproach in those celebrated blue eyes. There was none. Dr Gorgas went into the apartment whistling—whistling slowly and very badly: the man could never carry a tune.

'Marie!'

'Yes, darling?'

'Where did Tranquilina put the whisky, d'y' suppose?'

'Right where she always does, darling.' And presently, when the whistling was resumed and glasses were clinking: 'What are you worrying about, darling?'

'Me? Worrying?'

'I always know you're worrying about something when you whistle.'

Harry heard the great man grunt.

'Why, I'm worrying about being replaced, my dear. Whispers of a movement afoot have reached me. . . . They want a practical man, somebody who isn't cracked on the subject of mosquitoes and who'll spend less money. Believe it or not, my dear, the successor they've got all picked out for me is an osteopath!'

'You'll stay' she called serenely.

He chuckled.

'Oh yes, I'll stay. There's *some* sense in the government, and fortunately it's at the top. Teddy will keep me here. No, what I'm really worried about, darling, is that the telephone will interrupt me while I'm enjoying the sunset.'

'I'll listen for it. I'll be out of here soon.'

The sun itself was beyond sight, but it threw spears that skittered across the hilltop behind the house and lit the palm tops and made the shadows fantastically long. The fronds of the palms clacked softly, like thin slats of wood striking together: there was an apologetic breeze.

Harry, when the colonel returned to the veranda, was watching a tug which chuffed around some floating piles of lumber, mother-henning them, far below, off the mouth of the Rio Grande. He grinned sardonically, knowing the reason. For months frantic calls for lumber had gone unheeded; but recently out of a clear sky no less than five ships had appeared from Oregon—La Boca could accommodate only one at a time—with twelve million feet of the stuff. The ships couldn't wait. The lumber had swamped the single small dock. Some had been carried ashore on the backs of Negroes, who waded, and had been stacked on the muddy riverbanks. Some had been lashed into rafts and anchored; but there was a twenty-foot tide at the mouth of the Rio Grande, and many of the rafts broke their anchorage, giving all sorts of trouble. Dozens of the rafts had floated out to sea.

'Brilliant planning, eh?' The colonel carried the drinks to a burlap-covered kerosene tin which hung in a corner of the veranda where it would catch the breeze. Above this hung another tin, from the bottom of which water dripped, keeping the burlap around the lower tin wet. He removed the burlap and dumped water from the lower tin. 'They say the housing men are getting it any old way, regardless of what they'd asked for. Not measured, some dressed, some undressed, six-by-sixes instead of two-by-fours and the other way round. And of course plenty of them won't get a stick.' He brought the drinks over to where Harry sat. 'Here we are. Be nice if we had ice, wouldn't it? But that dingus keeps the water tolerably cool.' He sank into a chair. 'I'm fighting every way I know how. But there isn't any profit in grinding your teeth and making faces. Cigar?'

They lighted up, and the colonel fell silent, sipping sometimes, sometimes puffing, mostly just looking out over the veranda rail. The hill was streaked with shadows, but the bay still gleamed in sunlight, iridescent, opalescent, like the neck of an immense pigeon. Around neat little Taboga a thousand pelicans, doubtless squawking, dived and dived.

The silence was flattering. Dr Gorgas, his eyes half shut, acted simply as if he was glad to be in the presence of an old friend. He worked, Harry knew, fifteen, sixteen hours a day; but this particular hour, when he had his drink, was a special one.

'It'll get better' he said quietly, after a while. 'We're a funny nation,

Harry. We go into everything all excited, slapping ourselves on the chest, telling everybody how good we are. We go into things without any preparation at all. And after a while, when we've got everything as wrong as it can possibly be, *then* we get good and sore. *Then* we really go to work. Did you meet Dr Reed when he was here, in February?'

'No, sir.'

'A pity. You'd have liked him. He's chairman of the legislative committee of the American Medical Association. Well, he was here two weeks, and now he's publishing his report, and it's very good reading for men like you and me, Harry. For one thing, he tells about the X-ray expert, a very expensive man, who was hired to come down here. He was in Washington while they were purchasing the apparatus, and he dropped in to suggest that he himself select the Crookes tubes, since nobody in the world was better qualified to do that job. They told him certainly not. That would be highly irregular! There wasn't any authorization for them to accept suggestions! They knew best! Well, he came on down, and in due time the X-ray apparatus followed him on another ship, and the Crookes tubes were all wrong. Not the slightest use with such an apparatus. They had to be sent back and another set ordered—the kind he'd tried to ask for in the first place. Meanwhile this high-priced expert, through no fault of his own, has been sitting here for four months, fuming, talking about resigning—and drawing his pay—while we have no X-ray service. Reed told that one. And he told about LaGarde and the nursing bottle. You heard that, Harry?'

'No, sir.'

'You know Major LaGarde, of course? Superintendent here. Yes, of course. Well, this is the sort of thing that's happening all the time, as you and I know, but this particular story just happened to strike them right. Seems to have caught the public's imagination.

'There was an insane woman with a baby she couldn't nurse, and the nurse applied to LaGarde for a bottle and a rubber nipple. There weren't any. This was February, and LaGarde had put through a requisition last September, but it hadn't been filled yet. So he made out an emergency requisition. They do permit us to spend a *few* pennies on our own responsibility. He had to bring the emergency requisition to me to be endorsed and then take it to Mr Tobey, the Materials and Supply chief down in the city, for another endorsement. Then it went to a clerk to be copied and engrossed. Finally the clerk was formally authorized to go to a drugstore and purchase the bottle and the nipple, which he did. They should have cost less than twenty cents; but Reed figured that because of the time of everybody involved in making out the economy forms, that bottle and nipple actually cost the government six dollars and seventy-five cents.'

The telephone rang. They heard Mrs Gorgas tell somebody that Dr Gorgas was not at home but that she expected him soon.

Dr Gorgas, nodding, breathing again, swiveled his eyes back to the bay.

'Odd how things turn out' he mused. 'You know, Harry, I only took up the study of medicine because I couldn't get into West Point. It was the only way I could get into the Army. So I studied medicine. And I must say I've enjoyed it. I certainly never thought when I used to drive out in a sleigh, in a blizzard, at Fort Randall in North Dakota, fifteen-sixteen years ago, wrapped up in blankets, half frozen—I never supposed then that someday I'd be ordering the whole town of Siboney in Cuba to be burned. Yes, I did that, Harry. It seemed the right thing to do at the time. To get rid of yellow fever. That's how much we knew then. Back in those days people used to take whisky and brandy and smoke a lot of cigars and carry things around with them to sniff all the time—camphor, a tarred rope, a sponge soaked in vinegar. They used to fire off cannons, thinking that that did something to the air. And I burned Siboney. . . . I issued that order myself. It was just before Walter Reed's commission went to work.'

He nodded down toward the bay.

'A pump barge down there, attached to the quarantine station, has been named after Walter Reed. There's immortality for you! Jenner and Lister and Pasteur died rich men, loaded with honors. But we're a funny nation, Harry. We forgot to raise Walter Reed's rank. He was just a major when he died. The Lord in heaven above only knows, Harry, how many millions of dollars that man saved us, not to even mention the human suffering. But Congress had to do quite a bit of talking and fussing before they got around to granting his widow fifteen hundred a year pension. And of course there aren't any monuments or statues. But still,'—his lips curved as he drew on his cigar—'still we've recognized him down here, anyway. We've named a pump barge after him.'

They drank somberly, watching the shadows stretch. They had met, these two, on the *Allianca* coming down from New York ten months before, the *Allianca* on which Phil herself even then was coming. They had been part of the first group of workers—Dr Gorgas indisputably the most important part, Harry Kellems probably the least—sent to rip a groove through a mountain range in order to join two oceans.

'I know you never expected anything like this, Harry. You never

16

dreamt that you'd find yourself doing work that was so dirty and dis-agreeable—and dangerous too. And of course you'll never get any glory for it. All the same, the work has to be done.'

Harry burst out: 'Listen, sir, please don't think that this is because I'm afraid of——'

The telephone. Dr Gorgas moved only his eyes, gazing sideways at the door. He held his cigar a few inches from his mouth. He was not demonstrative; but when his face sagged like this, worriment claimed it. After all, the man bore a stupendous load of responsibility.

'No, I'm sorry, Dr Gorgas is not here now. . . . Oh yes, Mr Hattle-son. . . . Yes, I'll see that he calls you as soon as he comes in.'

Mrs Gorgas appeared in the doorway and saw Harry.

'Oh, hello. I didn't know it was you. Sorry you have to overhear me telling all those lies, but this man,' pointing to her husband, 'must be kept an hour a day from trying to kill himself. Though you wouldn't believe it now, would you? You'd think *he* ought to be named Tran-quilina, not the criada.'

'My dear,' reproved Dr Gorgas, 'I am an executive. I do not do, I direct. And so smoothly does my system function that there is no need for me to stir. Instead I just sit here and drink.'

He drank.

'What he's really graveled about' Marie Gorgas told Harry 'is the fact that he never has any time now to try to learn how to dance. He's been trying for fifteen years, off and on, and he never will learn, of course. He's the worst dancer in the world.'

'Darling, you haven't tried every one of them. You're not qualified to say.'

'He has positively no sense of rhythm, bless his heart. But he keeps right on trying.'

When she went away Dr Gorgas followed her with his eyes.

'By God,' he whispered reverently, 'I certainly love that woman.'

Harry was hasty, starting, spilling some of his drink.

'And I certainly love *my* wife too, sir! Don't you understand?'

The celebrated sanitarian was all host again. He put his cigar into a tray. He opened his eyes very wide.

'Why, see here! It's the first time I ever even knew you were married, Harry! Tell me about it.'

Harry told him about it. He told the story in spurts, clumsily, talk-ing much more than he had supposed he could. Here was a perfect audience. The mouth beneath the white mustaches never smiled. The warm blue eyes were steady and kind. Only once did Dr Gorgas interrupt, and that was when Harry mentioned his singing.

'I should think she *would* fall in love with you if you sang to her, son! Why, Marie in there, she's in love with you right now. Never known her to be so devout before. Gets downright fidgety toward the end of the week. Just can't wait for the services to start.'

Harry explained why he felt that he had lured Phil into something practically against her will. He said that he couldn't bear the thought of being the cause of her coming to a place like Panama, where her life would be in danger and where she'd be so far from the things she had always known and loved. He tried to point out that he had undertaken marriage, he had vowed a vow, and so he must see the business through. That was very important. He must see it through.

'I've got to be the kind of husband she expects me to be!'

The colonel asked quietly if he knew what kind of husband that was. Then, without waiting for an answer, the colonel smiled.

'I knew it must be something like this, Harry. I knew an old shipmate like you wasn't going to be scared of anything *personally*. That's why I wanted to see you and find out. You know how our turnover's been. Don't be too concerned with the fact that you aren't really an engineer. You're a darned sight more valuable to me, here, than many a man who is. I'll admit I was thunderstruck when Simpson told me about you. I—I think I even got a little sick there for a second, Harry. My heart sort of went qu-*wop*-up. Well, it's all right. I can't help you. I'm not going to try to give you advice. You've got to make up your own mind. But it's all right. I feel better about it now. And you will too, soon.'

He looked at the rest of his highball regretfully. He tossed it off. He rose.

'Where're you going to put her? She'd never be able to get back right away anyway. You know that.'

'Yes, I know it. And I haven't any idea where we can live. Even with everybody trying to get away, there isn't any room. Not for a lady. And of course I wouldn't rate married quarters.'

'Why not? But there aren't any ready yet anyway, as far as that goes. But wait a minute——'

He went to the rail, looked around the darkening grounds. His fingers jiggled. He began to whistle very badly, very low.

He snapped his fingers.

'Say—that old storehouse back there! Why didn't I think of it before? The supplies it's supposed to be stored with haven't come, and

Heaven knows when they will. You don't rate it, but we'll fix that. We'll make you a physician for the occasion, or a major. Something, anyway. It'll be all nice and illegal. But before anybody discovers it and starts to make out all the forms and vouchers and so forth to eject you—why, by that time there might be steamer accommodations, or else we'll have something else ready for you.'

'Oh, hey, I can't let you do that!'

'Why not? The place is no palace, mind you! There's no plumbing, and you'll have to move a heap of junk around to make room for the furniture. What furniture? Just thought of that! Oh well, Marie can scrape you up something, a piece here, a piece there, and I'll send Tranquilina down to do some scrubbing and put the finishing touches to it—you know, the woman's hand. Don't tip her. She's overpaid already.' He raised his voice. 'Marie, darling! Oh, here you are.'

There she was, in the doorway, holding his coat for him and smiling. His hour of peace had ended.

'Thank you, dear. Come along, son. You ought to get those wet clothes off anyway.'

He took the umbrella his wife handed him. It was going to rain again soon: they could feel that.

He kissed his wife, bustled his visitor downstairs.

'We'll see you at the services Sunday morning, won't we?' Marie Gorgas called after them. 'I want you to be sure to sing "I Love to Tell the Story." Mrs Carter was asking for that too.'

'Who—me?' Colonel Gorgas shouted back.

'Don't be ridiculous, William!'

He chuckled as they hurried along the macadam road, and he had a hand on Harry's shoulder.

'I told you she was in love with you, didn't I?'

That night they ate in their underclothes, for trousers, shirts, and socks hung, steaming, before a charcoal fire. A few even sat naked. This was not unusual; and it was a custom of which Bertram persistently if soundlessly disapproved. Bertram was their cook, a staid Jamaican who spoke some French, having waited on the French in Compagnie Nouvelle days, and whose English was their delight. Bertram's English was grammatically superior to that of the college-educated men upon whom he condescended to wait. It was scintillatingly polysyllabic; it was circuitous; almost courtly, it was anything but curt. 'More, more, Berty-boy! Seconds!' somebody would shout, clanging a fork on his plate; and Bertram, emerging from the kitchen, would bend disapprovingly over the container: 'You implied, sir, that it is

19

your desire that this should be replenished?' Ed Snyder said that he talked like the Boston Boy. A sunburned Limey was what Georgie Walsh called him. He wouldn't be hurried and he wouldn't be sassed —'I am a British subject, sir'—and he deplored the manners and crude speech of his employers. 'I shall return with alacrity, sir' he would say as he'd start for the kitchen. He was unbelievable, and a very poor cook.

After the meal there was poker. There usually was. Three male nurses dropped in, dripping, and then an intern; and soon the clothes of these men too hung steaming around the fire. A bottle of rum was opened.

'Gulp, Harry? Do you good.'

'No, thanks.'

'Do you good. Wash the taste of Berty's swill from your mouth. Dear Jesus! I wonder if I'll ever taste fresh meat again!'

'No, thanks' Harry said. 'I still taste a little of the whisky I had before dinner, and I don't want to spoil that.'

Whisky? The table's eyes were all at Harry. Where the hell had he got hold of any whisky?

He told them that he'd had a drink with Dr Gorgas.

'Oh, fawncy that!'

'Pahdon my glove!'

'That's what it means to have a good tenor voice. Sing us something, Harry.'

'Nope.'

'Ah, go on, sing us something!'

'Nope. I'm going to bed.'

He had not told them about Phil, and he decided that he should not do so—not until the last minute. He liked them, by and large, but not tonight. Tonight he was worried, and he wanted to pray, but he wanted to pray on his knees and not lying flat on his back in a bunk. But it was pouring outside.

He sat on the edge of a bunk—the game took all chairs—and talked with Georgie Walsh for a while. Georgie came from Pittsburgh, and he was a Pirates rooter. Was there anything in the whole game that could compare with Hans Wagner? Challengingly he thrust his face toward Harry's.

'You wait till old Mike Donlin gets socking 'em' Harry threatened. 'And Roger Bresnahan.'

'You and your Giants!'

'Me and my Giants, all right! And how 'bout Bill Dahlen? And as far as your wonderful Hans Wagner is concerned——'

'He led the league, didn't he?'

'—he's going to swing like a sand-lot kid when the ol' Iron Man gets hurling 'em in!'

'I hope he's better than Red Ames!'

'Red Ames is all right. He gets a little off his game sometimes, but when he's throwing 'em just right he's something to try to hit!'

'When is that?'

'And Mathewson. You watch *that* slinger come up!'

'You and your Giants!'

After a while Harry quit. Georgie Walsh would have argued all night, but Harry was tired. The poker game was getting noisy, the players shouting above the thunder of rain on a corrugated-iron roof. Two more bottles had been opened.

'Don't give that Giants fan a drink! He don't touch crude stuff like that. Nothing but Scotch whisky for him, the lucky bastard!'

'Keep it for yourselves' Harry agreed.

He squirmed out of his underwear and pulled a nightshirt over his head. When Prendergast re-entered by the back door and called 'Anybody want it before I put it down?' Harry called 'Me!' and took the umbrella and went back to the outhouse.

From there, afterward, pausing a moment, he looked through the downpour toward the gate of the hospital grounds. He could distinguish the wagon as it drew away from the morgue. There were two boxes on it. It started down the hill—and the unremitting gray rain fogged it.

Sure, rain or shine, day or night, in a climate like this you had to get rid of them promptly. Half the time a man had been buried before you heard he was dead. Preferably at night—lest the sight of all those funerals cause panic—but night or day, any time, when they were going as fast as they were going now.

Harry trod the plank walk carefully, for the planks were rotten and you had to know just where to step or you'd plunge into mud. Outside the back door he paused. Not likely that anybody else would be wanting the umbrella just yet. And there was a space under the eaves that was almost dry. Hitching up his nightshirt, he knelt there, the umbrella more or less over him.

'Dear God, watch her at sea on that ship——'

'Push the bottle down here, somebody.' . . . 'See your three and

raise you three, and what are you going to do about *that*, kiddo?' . . .
'What am I going to do about it? Why, I'm going to call, sweetheart.'
. . . 'Pass that bottle.' . . .

'Take care of her always, dear God, and give me the strength always to be kind and good to her. I ask it in Jesus' name. Amen.'

2

THERE WAS A DECK CHAIR next to hers the second morning, and for a moment Phil was angry; for she'd picked the spot carefully. She meant to read a lot on this trip, and to think a lot. She had four novels—not light, trashy novels, but heavy ones, one of them by Hall Caine, in addition to a book entitled *Spanish Self-Taught*. She meant to spend one hour each morning and another each afternoon with the Spanish book, and to read all of the novels; though most of the time, she planned, she would stretch out lazily and look at the ocean and dream about Harry.

The spot, though amidships and on the main deck, was secluded, being between a ventilator and a large white wooden locker in which life belts were stored. She herself had found it, and she'd directed Sid the deck steward to place her chair there; and if she hadn't actually asked Sid, in so many words, not to put anybody *else* there, at least she had cooed with delight about how nice it would be to get away from the crowd. From that place she could watch everybody go by, as they walked around the deck—a brass plate said that fourteen times around was a mile—and yet not have her feet tripped over, and not be obliged to listen to somebody else's conversation. Not that looking at the others was likely to be very edifying. From what she'd seen of her fellow passengers, so far, they were a common lot.

A chair alone in that cubbyhole had been comfy. Two chairs were crowded. Of necessity they were so close together as to suggest the chairs of honeymooners. Well, this *was* a honeymoon for Phil, in a way; but she did not have Harry with her. Whether man or woman sat there, Phil would have to talk to him. If he or she breathed heavily or made stomach noises or picked his nose or sucked his teeth, anything vulgar like that, Phil, while wishing to study Spanish or to sit entoiled in dreams, would be obliged to hear and to shudder.

No, no! She had found this place, it was hers, and she'd have it to herself or know the reason why! Sid would either move the other chair or her own, but probably, she reflected grimly, the other chair. She looked up the deck for him, she looked down the deck; he was not in sight. He'd be along soon, though, with the bouillon. She would have it out with him then. She spread her steamer robe, got into it, pulled it across her legs. She retied the veil under her chin, making it tighter, so that it held the pancake firmly in place. She was rather proud of that pancake. It wasn't from Paris, no, but she had bought it in a very stylish shop on Fifth Avenue, New York, and there probably wasn't anybody on *this* tub who wouldn't take it to be Parisian. Held by the chenille veil, it pressed firmly against her pompadour. True, she couldn't get the steamer robe to fall into place below her feet, so as to cover her shoes, even though repeatedly, with feet pressed together, with knees stiff, she lifted her legs; but this did not greatly matter, for it wasn't chilly, and the shoes, as it happened, *were* Parisian: they came almost to the calves of her legs, and though of course nobody would ever see the tops of them, the heels were high and wonderfully slim—the sort of thing, she told herself, surveying them with a pleased sigh, that only the French could make.

She had *Spanish Self-Taught* with her, but at the moment she did not feel like studying. She lolled, closed her eyes, and felt the thrill, the delicious thrill of being alone for the first time in her life, really alone, her own mistress, answerable to no one. The trip to Europe had been different. It had been exciting, of course, and she'd had fun, and she'd gotten a lot of culture on that trip too; but all the same, everything they'd done had been so conscientiously scrutinized, everywhere they'd gone they had been so assiduously attended, and she'd kept a diary—they all had—and had been committed to write home at least a short note each and every day. This was so different, now. Not that the *Allianca* was much of a ship as compared with the liner she had crossed and returned on; but if it lacked elegance, it held, for her, adventure. Now she was on her own. She had been entitled to this for a long while; but they'd always held her down and fussed about her. Now there was nobody to regulate her life, to tell her what to do and what not to do (mostly what not to do), and to say sarcastic things about her choice of friends—and of a husband. Mother and Dad had been furious. Well, what of it? She wasn't going to remain their darling daughter, coddled and cuddled, all her life. She was a married woman now, a matron. 'Where did you ever get the fare?' Triumphantly: 'Saved it out of my allowance!' There had been nothing they could do.

Somebody was coming, and she opened her eyes, opened too the Spanish book. However, Mr McCormack, interrupting his promenade, was not to be put off by a book. He was an insistent, garrulous, pushingly pleasant man, very old, thirty-five at least, who waddled, a large bland Buddha-bellied man with a face all innocent of hair—or for that matter, of expression.

'Ah, there!' His gaze had fallen upon the empty chair. 'Cozy, eh? Saving that for some lucky fella?'

He came closer. She looked up from the book and gave him a smile —she could hardly do less, since he was at her table—but when she answered, her voice was chill.

'I'm saving it for Sid, the deck steward, who wants to take it some-where else. If you should see him you might send him here, please. Thank you.'

She smiled again, briefly, and returned to the opened-at-random *Spanish Self-Taught*.

Mr McCormack wavered, shuffled, but eventually departed.

Others passed, and she did not look up; but neither did she study much Spanish. An increasing irritation shook her, a growing anger against the man or woman who was entitled to have that chair next to her, the chair everybody who passed glanced at meaningfully. Who-ever he or she was, he or she wasn't going to stay there long. Phil would see to that. When Sid came with the bouillon——

He *or* she? Pricked by curiosity, Phil turned to read the name on the card slipped into the little slot on the back of the deck chair next to the one in which she sat.

The card read: MRS KELLEMS.

Good heavens! She was in somebody else's chair! If that other per-son came along right now, there would have to be all sorts of explana-tions and apologies, and an acquaintanceship so volubly begun would be bound to involve unending jabber. Phil dropped her book, she swung her legs out, she started to pluck at the steamer robe.

Sid came.

'Sid, I'm in the wrong chair! I didn't notice it till just now. I never thought that——'

'That's all right, ma'am. One chair's the same as the other. We'll just change these——'

He put down the tray of boullion and with deft fingers transposed the name cards. Phil, who could have done that herself, felt a shade foolish. She was sharp with Sid when she took the bouillon. He was inclined to be fresh anyway. He didn't have the nice manners of those English stewards or the waiters in those dear little French and Italian cafés.

'Sid, didn't I ask you not to put anybody else here?"

25

'No, ma'am, you didn't,' respectfully but firmly.

'Well, I don't want anybody else here. I want to be alone.'

'Well, you see this was——'

'I don't care who it is! I wouldn't care if it was the President of the United States! I want to be——'

She had turned, while she spluttered about not caring who had the next chair, and naturally she'd looked at the card in that chair. Now she stopped.

The card said: CAPTAIN WRIGHT.

'Oh' said Phil.

She glanced up. Sid was watching her shrewdly, and he began to grin. Instantly, to put him in his place, she froze.

She did not stay frozen. There was something she wanted to know.

'Sid, did he *ask* to have his chair put here?'

'Yes, ma'am, as a matter of fact he did. And I figured you knew him, of course.'

'Why "of course"? I don't happen to have the honor of an acquaintance with Captain Wright, nor have I any desire to start one.'

'Well, all the ladies seem to flock around him, and I naturally thought—Mrs Landis, she's in your cabin, isn't she? Well, I see her talking with him every time she gets a chance, so I figured——'

'Did he *tip* you to have his chair put here, Sid?'

'Well, yes. What's wrong with that? We're allowed to take tips.'

'Pantherine' was the mot juste she had already selected for Captain Ward Wright, or Captain Macklin, as he was more often called by fellow passengers, for the man surely could have been Richard Harding Davis's hero in the flesh. 'Pantherine,' yes. In the Browning Club of Paterson, Phil had always been a crier for the mot juste; nor was this, as Madge Nichols had been heard to say, because she wanted everybody to remember that she had been in France and could pronounce it. She used to amuse herself by seeking for the mot juste for each of her friends. It was not always possible to find this. She had none for Harry himself, for instance. 'Earnest' perhaps most thoroughly described Harry, but it was hardly inclusive enough to call a mot juste; and there were times, and especially when he sang, when she would have preferred a more ecstatic adjective. But 'pantherine' . . . that was perfect, in addition to being a lovely word in itself.

Grace Landis, her cabin mate, hardly a companion Phil would have picked out, but good-natured enough, was more outspoken about Captain Ward Wright. Gracie, indeed, making no attempt to conceal

26

her excitement, had talked Phil to sleep on this subject the previous night, talk-talk-talking from the lower bunk while the stolid *Allianca* swayed and squealed.

'Gawd, but wouldn't he be a sight in riding pants!' she would exclaim. 'Or for that matter, in a bathing suit.'

A woman of the world, and not stupid, she made no idol of this hero. 'He likes himself plenty. Oh, he's very fond of himself! Notice how whenever he stops to talk to anybody that's in a deck chair or anything, he always stands with his feet spread wide apart? He knows he looks better that way. Dashing.'

Phil was more inclined to esteem that stance a wise one, adopted not because of its appearance but because of the *Allianca's* unpausing roll. But even she admitted that it did become the captain.

But then, everything became him, even the jaunty linen cap he wore.

'I don't usually hurl these fading charms of mine at just anybody,' Grace Landis said, 'but that one could ask me for the limit, and I don't think he'd even have to say "please." I love my husband, but oh you kid!'

What he was a captain of, nobody seemed to know. Anybody could tell that he was a military man. It was whispered that, like the Richard Harding Davis character again, he had connections in Latin-American republics, that he was associated with riots and revolutions, a man to be called in when something violent was about to happen. He looked the part. He was tall and lean, a straight man, with hard flat muscles, a man, you would have said, who would age, of course, but would never soften. His hands and wrists, though slim, were steel-strong; there was a lift in his step; his dark brown eyes were clear and bright. He wore light clothes, and everything about him suggested residence in the tropics: his hands, face, and neck were heavily tanned: he would have fitted neatly underneath a sun helmet. His stiff hair was so dark a brown as to show almost black, and this fact, together with the tanned features, which set off dazzling teeth, suggested Latin-American blood. His mustache, however, made him look an Englishman. It was not a long wavy soup strainer all wisp-shredded at the ends. It was trig, perky, exact, the shortest mustache, both as to its own length on the lip and the length of the hairs composing it, that Phil had ever seen. Its owner from time to time brushed it, a futile gesture, with his right thumbnail on the right side, with his left thumbnail on the left side.

The handsome, the captivating, the pantherine Captain Wright. Not only Gracie Landis but half the women on the ship screamed without sound when he passed.

'As a matter of fact, he told me outright he was getting rushed around too much.' Sid waxed chatty. 'And he said he'd looked 'em all over and that you were the only one he really wanted to know.'

'That will do, steward!'

'O.k.' caroled Sid, picking up the tray. 'I just thought you might be interested.'

Captain Wright did not appear on deck that morning. Phyllis Kellems, reading steadily, looked up to smile only when some acquaintance hailed her in passing; and this was not often, for she knew few fellow passengers and didn't think she wanted to know many more. Once a man appeared before her.

'Is this chair taken?'

She looked up. He was smallish and stringy, wearing a gray suit, and he had eyes in which sad blue water seemed to slosh back and forth like the water in a bucket that's been jogged.

'I'm afraid it is. At least, I understood the deck steward to say that.'

'Oh, excuse me.'

After lunch she went to her cabin to lie down a little while. She was glad that Gracie was not there: Gracie was probably out on deck making a fool of herself in chase of the captivating Captain Wright. Phil rested in the darkened cabin; and afterward she put on her parrot-green traveling dress, a different pancake, a yellow one, held down by a white-dotted veil, and an ostrich boa. She took a novel to the deck chair and pointedly read in order to show that she was not to be considered available for shuffleboard.

The sun had the sky to itself, and the sea, no longer green but blue, was a lake. The *Allianca's* prow swooshed rose point, and somewhere far below her engines thumped and thamped.

'Ah, here it is! So the steward's put me here, eh?'

It was Captain Ward Wright. She looked up to nod slightly, with her eyes rather than her head, but she did not smile. She went on reading. He flopped into the chair beside her, exhaling, putting his head back, and stretched long legs and with thin brown hands emphatically slapped the chair's arms.

'A nice place. Nice and quiet. Probably that's why you settled here?'

'Yes' she said, not looking up.

'It wasn't why I came. I came because of you.'

28

Now she did look up.

'Well, I——'

'Why not? It's a simple matter of self-protection. In your company I'm sheltered from those saber-toothed tigresses who stalk me everywhere else. You wouldn't deny a man sanctuary?'

'I'm afraid I don't know what you mean.'

'Why, of course you do. If I walk with any woman, or sit and talk with any woman, another one is sure to come along and try to cut in. They're all flirting like mad.'

'But I don't see what I have to do with that?'

He answered dispassionately: 'Why, because you're so much the best-looking woman aboard, you're so easily head and shoulders above any of the others. No woman in her right mind would try to cut *you* out.'

'That's very nice' she said coldly. 'Thank you.'

She returned to her book. But in a moment: 'Except that I must say I never in my life before heard such a conceited remark.'

'I am conceited, yes. A pity, isn't it? But then I always have been. I suppose that makes it less offensive than if I'd just gotten that way, don't you think so?'

'Perhaps. I hadn't thought of it before.'

Determinedly, again, she returned to the novel. He was silent for a while. He did not fidget but sat motionless, his head back. Some of the time, she sensed (she would not give him the satisfaction of catching her stealing a covert glance), he had his eyes closed, and some of the time, she suspected, he watched her sideways, with amusement in his slitted dark brown eyes.

'You like Hall Caine?'

'Very much,' without looking up.

A little later: 'I do hope you don't think me rude. I don't mean to be. On shipboard, you know, everybody sort of talks to everybody else. You don't need an introduction. It's quite proper.'

Now she sat up and turned to face him.

'I'm perfectly acquainted with the customs that prevail aboard ships, Mr—uh——' She looked deliberately at the card back of his chair. 'Captain Wright. I have traveled before.'

Surely when she looked at the card there had been a glint of amusement, of droll gentle mockery, in his eyes. But his answer was swift and respectful.

'Oh, I'm sure you have! I knew that as soon as I saw you and saw how much at home you were here. I'd have known it even if I hadn't happened to notice you when you came aboard with those valises with all the stickers on them.'

It softened her. She even smiled a little.

'Though I must admit' she added graciously 'that I've never before been on a boat like—well, like this.'

'It's not much' he conceded. 'The liners that go to Europe, I guess they're much better. I've never been to Europe.' He sighed. 'Always wanted to go. It must be very interesting?'

'Well, I've always found it so. Yes. It—it's very interesting, yes.'

'The Leaning Tower of Pisa. Napoleon's Tomb. Westminster Abbey. I've often wished I could see them. And the Louvre. I suppose you can spend hours in the Louvre?'

'Oh, hours and hours.'

'It would be hard for me, in a way, because I can't speak French. Spanish, yes, but not French.'

'Oh, you'd soon pick it up.'

'You speak it yourself, of course?'

'Oui, oui, monsieur. Mais absolument.'

He sighed again and shook his head, as he stared past promenaders, past the rail, to the great silver tray that supported them. He seemed lost in wistful thoughts. Suddenly he looked at her.

'See here, I didn't mean to interrupt you! It's so refreshing to talk to somebody who has really traveled and knows something about culture. My work has always brought me into association with some pretty rough characters, and I—I'm afraid I've missed a heap of the finer things in life, like art and so forth. But if you want to read——'

'Oh well' said Phil.

Day, as day will, had sombered into night, before the gong brought them struggling stiffly to their feet, and Phil scarcely had time to change before dinner. After dinner they met on deck and by unspoken agreement made for the chairs once more. They sat very close together, as necessity dictated, and gazed out over the Atlantic while the moon rose with a shrug of weary graciousness as though doing the world a favor.

Phil brought her husband into the conversation very early that night. There was to be no misunderstanding! In the afternoon people had passed constantly, and the sunlight had been upon these two, and moreover they'd talked mostly about cultural matters and it had been a conversation which Phil herself easily led. Moonlight made everything different. Warily she eyed that moon, a gibbous low-hanging one. Captain Wright must not be permitted to get any false ideas. The others on this ship might cheapen themselves to fawn upon him, to grimace and simper before him, but he must learn, and promptly, that Phil was not such a woman. The passenger list she knew had her properly as Mrs Harry Kellems, and she wore her ring of course, and the card behind her chair read MRS KELLEMS, and twice that afternoon Captain Wright himself had so addressed her. Nonetheless there were married women and married women. Gracie Landis, to mention only one, like Phil herself was going to Panama to join or rejoin a husband; but Gracie made no bones about her susceptibility. He could think Phil a widow, perhaps, if she did not set him right. He might even think her a divorcee.

'We've talked a lot about Paris and Florence and Rome, Captain. It hasn't been fair to you, really.'

'I've enjoyed every moment of it! You made it all seem too real to me, and so close!'

'Suppose we talk about some of the places *you* have visited? I know from what I've heard about you—oh, you're well known!—I don't have to tell you that the women are all chattering!—I know, or at least I understand, that you have spent a great deal of time in Central America?'

'Well, yes.'

'I told you that you were famous!'

'Notorious might be better. Why?'

'Why, I was wondering if you had been to Panama. You see, I'm going there to be with my husband, who's an engineer on the canal they're building, and so naturally I'm interested. Harry Kellems. Perhaps you know him?'

'I'm afraid not. I'd like to—even though Oscar Wilde says that the husbands of beautiful women belong in the criminal classes.'

'But you have been to Panama?'

'Oh yes. Many times. In fact, I live there.'

'Tell me about it.'

She looked at the moon, and he looked at the moon, and the moon was unbelievable. The night was warm.

'Well,' he said at last, 'Panama's Panama. It's a good deal like the other places down that way. Except that it won't be now, for a little while, now that they've started to dig this canal.'

'Why do you say "for a little while"?'

He shrugged.

'I don't think they'll ever finish the thing. They've made the worst possible start. And as a matter of fact, they shouldn't have started at all, in the first place. Panama's not the right spot for a canal. They should have built in Nicaragua, if they were going to build at all.'

'You mean to tell me that you think the United States is going to start something it won't finish?'

'Well, I don't know. I suppose I'm as patriotic as the next man. But they certainly have begun it all wrong. It's three months since I've been there now, and from what I hear things are getting worse all the time—and they were an unholy mess when I left, if you'll excuse my language. You see, we went at it without any preparation at all. Our engineers said in the first place that there ought to be at least two full years spent in making soundings and surveys and so forth. But did we do that? Oh no! We started digging right away. The newspapers said that everybody wanted to see the dirt fly, and the politicians had to have something to make speeches about, after such big appropriations, and so they started digging. They don't know yet what type of canal it's going to be, or exactly where it's going, and all they're really doing is just taking mud from one place and dumping it into another. I'm no engineer, I admit that. But I think I do know something about the Latin-American temperament. That sounds pretty fancy—"Latin-American temperament." But anyway, there is such a thing.'

'And just what have we done that's wrong, Captain?'

'Everything, so far. For one thing, we've made every spiggoty down there hate us.'

She stiffened a trifle. She was not sure of that word.

'That's slang' Captain Wright said quickly, sensing her perturbation. 'It's what all Americans down there call the natives, just like they call us gringos. Spiggoties. Or sometimes just spigs. Supposed to come from "No spika da English"—though as a matter of fact no Spanish-speaking person would ever say it that way. But anyway that's how it's supposed to have originated. I wouldn't know.'

'This is very interesting, Captain. How have we offended them, do you think?'

'Big talk. Pushing 'em off the sidewalks, figuratively and literally too. The sidewalks are narrow there, when there are any, and in Panama City the streets slant quite a bit and the sidewalks go straight and then there'll be four or five steps down or up and then another level stretch. That means that if you get shoved off the sidewalk just above a set of steps you've got some little distance to fall. The spigs don't care for that. And there are other things' he continued. 'We slap our own tariff on the Republic of Panama, just like any other country.

The Dingley tariff. But the Canal Zone doesn't come under that. People in the Canal Zone can buy things from the commissary that are duty-free. You can imagine how much the Panamanian merchants love that! It only costs two cents to send a letter from the Zone to the States, but it costs five cents, the same as any other foreign country, to send one from the Republic of Panama. What's the result? Every Panamanian just goes across the street—that's about all it amounts to —and mails his letters in the Zone. And the Republic gets cheated out of all that revenue, which it really needs. There are a heap of things like that. Petty things. Petty to us. But the Panamanians don't look at them that way. And the Panamanians aren't very likely to forget, either, the way we grabbed the Zone in the first place.

'What's even more important is that we don't put on a show for them. We don't make a big fanfare about the business, the way the French did. Whenever the French dedicated a new building or broke ground on some new part of the canal or did practically anything at all, they staged a fiesta. Had bands playing and flags flying. Set off fireworks. Made speeches. Opened champagne. Do we? No, indeed! I happened to be in Panama last May when we officially took over the French company's properties. What did the ceremony amount to? Absolutely nothing. The governor wasn't even there, didn't show up until a couple of weeks afterward. All that happened was that an army lieutenant—a *lieutenant*, mind you!—we couldn't spare them a general, or even a colonel!—well, this lieutenant simply signed the necessary receipt and said thanks. If he remembered to say thanks. That was all.'

'I can't see that that should make such a difference.'

'To the Panamanian it does. He likes a display. It's all he's got to live for, practically. It means a lot to him. And when we don't beat the drums and open the bottles he gets the idea that maybe we're not on the level—to use a slang expression. It wouldn't do us any harm, would it, to hand a few gold-laced officials a few highballs—a big nation like us? It wouldn't cost us very much to let a few thousand men send letters to the States for two cents instead of five cents, would it?'

'Yes . . . I see what you mean.'

She snuggled lower. This was most gratifying. She had feared that Captain Wright was going to be what he appeared, a flirt, a masher; and now he was turning out to be not only a perfect gentleman but also a man with some very sound and edifying ideas.

'Uh, getting back to my husband.'

'Yes?'

'I, uh, I don't really know my husband very well, Captain.'

'Ah?'

He sounded not merely polite but sympathetic. She told him something about Harry and how they'd married so suddenly. She was dignified about it. She did not tell him—she had scarcely even told herself—about her aching need for Harry, for marriage day by day. She did not detail personal matters. She didn't impress upon him that for the first time in her life she felt that she was going to really *live,* to expand, and be herself. But she did tell him something, giving him a rough idea.

'And that's why I'm so interested in Panama, you see? After all, we're going to live there for a year or two, I suppose. I've brought some furniture and things. I've even brought along my piano as a surprise for him. He loves to have me accompany him.'

'A piano!'

'Why not? It's mine. It cost quite a sum to have it crated and moved —it's right on the ship with us now—but after all, I want to make Harry a real home. What's wrong with a piano?'

'Why—why, nothing. The only thing is, it's not very usual down there. Guitars are about the only musical instruments they go in for very much. I'm afraid a piano wouldn't stay in tune very well down there. It's frightfully hot, you know, and wet. Things get unglued. Things are practically always damp. Ordinary furniture isn't much good there, the kind we'd use in the States.'

'Oh.'

'I certainly don't mean to discourage you. I think it's very admirable, the attitude you're taking. But I'm afraid that you're going to find housekeeping in Panama a lot different from housekeeping at home.'

'Well, of course at home I never really did any housekeeping, so maybe I won't notice the difference' she suggested brightly. 'What *about* servants, by the way?'

· 'Well, they're cheap. But if I told you how bad they are you wouldn't believe me. One of them would cost you about half as much as a reasonably shiftless servant in the States, but she wouldn't do a quarter as much work. The Jamaicans are best, if you can get one. They take their time, and you have to treat them like duchesses, but they're clean. That's the big thing.

'Your biggest job will probably be trying to keep things dry. Mold forms on everything. Overnight. And if you let it go, it falls apart. Anything. You see, Panama's awfully wet. There's a rainy season and a hot season, but it's rainy in the hot season too, just as it's hot in the rainy season. In the rainy season, nine months of the year, practically everybody has malaria. The other three months practically everybody has dengue, which they call breakbone fever. And of course there's likely to be an outbreak of yellow jack any old time.'

'You don't make it sound very pleasant.'

'Well, it's pleasant in some ways. You have to get used to it.'

'*You* seem to have thrived on it, Captain.'

'It's different with me. I always have gotten along best where things were worst. I just seem to be born for trouble.'

'From all I hear you don't go out of your way to avoid it!'

He shrugged. 'It's my living' he said, not boastfully.

She steered the conversation back to Harry. She wasn't going to forget Harry—or let Captain Wright forget him.

'You know, my husband didn't really want me to go down there, Captain. He always wrote that it wasn't a fit place for me. I got sort of—sort of provoked about it. Do you suppose,' banteringly, 'that he's leading a double life?'

'Does he drink?'

That startled her. 'Well, Harry takes a highball now and then. He never drinks much, certainly.'

'It's a bad place for a man who drinks much.'

Still lightly: 'I wasn't worrying about that. Like a good wife, I was worrying about something else. Tell me, Captain, are these señoritas as lovely as all you hear?'

'No.'

'Ah, you men all stick together!'

'I wouldn't worry about the señoritas.'

'Well, of course I'm not, really. But what about the white women?'

'There aren't any. Or practically none.'

'There must be some nurses. I understand we have some very fine hospitals we took over from the French, and my husband is a sanitary engineer, you see, and works under Colonel Gorgas there. They must have some nurses. That's what I'm really losing sleep about.'

He caught her tone, her mood. 'You wouldn't, if you'd ever seen them. There aren't many of them, in the first place, and I'll tell you what they say about them. They're old army nurses mostly, and they say that some of them were with the boys in the Philippines and some were with Gorgas at Havana, and then somebody's sure to add that, yes, but most of them must have been with Washington at Valley Forge!'

They had a good laugh at this.

They walked around the deck several times, listening to the woosh of the sea along the sides, and for a little while at the stern watched the hurly-burly of the wake, where he pointed out the phosphorus, which she said (though she wasn't certain of it) that she saw. He went up her corridor with her, and they said good night outside her cabin door. The surge and thump of the *Allianca's* engines was pronounced in the still night. Captain Wright bent over her hand when she offered it, and for an instant, with a catch of breath, she thought that he was going to kiss it. She'd had her hand kissed twice, in Europe.

'I've enjoyed this so much' he said earnestly.

'And so have I. I've enjoyed it too, Captain.'

'We must see one another again in the morning.'

'In the morning' she smiled. 'Good night, Captain.'

'Good night.'

That was all. She went inside the cabin, wondering whether she'd wake up Gracie if she snapped on the electric light. Gracie herself settled this question. *She* turned on the light. She was sitting up in bed, a purple wrapper around her.

'Ain't you the smarty, though! Here all the rest of us are spraining our ankles running after him, and you just sit tight and he falls into your lap! Tell me all about it.'

'Captain Wright was very nice' Phil admitted.

'I'll bet he was! You made a hit with him, did you?'

Phil smiled deprecatingly. She was undressing.

Gracie, accusingly: 'Know what time it is?'

'Oh well, we can sleep as late as we want in the morning. I think maybe I'll have breakfast in bed anyway. They always do that in France.'

'Never mind about France. Tell me about—you know.'

'He was very nice' Phil said again. 'He was a perfect gentleman.'

'Say, he *was*, honestly?' Gracie shook her head, settling back in the bunk. 'Oh well, he'll get over that, kiddo. There's four days yet.'

They were to dock at noon, and Phil, when she was packing, swallowed hard at the sight of the Hall Caine book. She had read a chapter and a half of it. She had not touched any of the other novels, nor had she studied much Spanish.

She was frightened. This was not a thing she liked to admit to herself, and surely she would never admit it to anybody else; but the fact was there: she was frightened. The hand that held the book above the opened valise trembled—no, it wobbled. Furious, she jammed the book into the bag.

'You're worried, dearie?'

'I?' Gracie was vulgar—oh, concede that!—but there was something comforting about her very vulgarity and in her voice. Phil didn't turn. 'Why should *I* be worried?'

'Well, for one thing, you're going to meet your husband pretty soon.'

Phil was a ramrod. 'And what's that got to do with it, pray? Do you think I'm afraid to meet my husband?'

'Nope. I don't think you'd ever be afraid of very much, kiddo. Anyway, not anything like what we're talking about now.'

'And just what is it we're talking about now?' not moving.

'You know that as well as I do. Hell,' Gracie burst out, 'don't get it into your head that I'm sore! You're much better-looking, even if you are skinny, and of course he'd go your way. Only thing is, you're worried. I don't blame you. You're not used to it.'

Phil whirled as though she were a mechanical thing, a marionette, set on a pivot. Her shoulders were well back.

'See here, Grace Landis, let's get this straight: Is there anything you can say against me?'

'Not a thing, dearie. And if there was, I wouldn't say it anyway. You still think I'm sore, don't you? Uh-uh! I *envy* you, sure. But why shouldn't you hook him? I told you that before.'

In a coarse way Gracie herself was good-looking. She was no more than thirty, and some men wouldn't have called her fat. She had huge floppy breasts, tremendous buttocks. Yet socially she was a straight sort of woman. She certainly wasn't a lady, and things she said sometimes revolted Phil; but she was straight, and straightforward, if cuttingly honest.

'I got to go and do a Number One. You peek, dearie. You're all dressed.'

Phil unlatched the door and looked out and listened and then said 'All right.' Gracie yanked the purple wrapper around her; Gracie brushed back her hair; Gracie plunged at the door, giggling, and scurried to the toilet. Phil returned to the open valise—and to the Hall Caine novel.

Yes, of course she was afraid. 'Pantherine'! That word hit hard at her nerves now. No longer a mot juste, it was a disagreeable, very sharp article, turned and turned around inside of her. 'Pantherine'! He was surely that. Panthers were cats, weren't they? They loved to torture smaller animals, the way cats did at home?

37

He had been quiet. He had not been pushing. But there was a velvet-lined assurance about him which touched her with panic. He had seemed to know all the time that he could do as he wished with her. He was smart. She fussed and worried, she said things she hoped would awe him, she brought up Harry's name, she talked about Europe; but Ward, quietly, with a feline slow certainty, pushed on to what he wanted. He had never wavered, he had never shown hesitancy. The shade of a mocking smile on his lips and in his eyes, he had listened to what she had to say; and now he controlled her. You could tell it just the way he moved, and the way he looked at her.

Could others tell it? She caught her breath. Had she and Ward been obvious? So far as she could recall, they had never touched one another or even stood close together when people were around; but you couldn't be sure on a ship.

Gracie came back into the cabin.

'You're crazy if you worry, kiddo. Not likely any of these people will ever get to meet your husband anyway. And what could they tell him if they did? None of 'em ever saw anything. And as a matter of fact, there probably never *was* anything, was there? I don't know how, anyway. I don't know where.'

Phil cried, chokingly: 'Grace Landis, if you don't stop talking like that I'll have to——'

'D'y' mind, dearie?' She had wriggled into her corset and done the front, and now she offered the back to Phil. 'There's not too much time, you know. We're supposed to dock at noon.'

Furious, Phil started to lace. It was an automatic action. Yet she wished that she could strangle Gracie Landis.

'I want to get this business straight right now! What do you mean by indicating that you think that there's anything between Captain Wright and me? Explain yourself, please!'

'Dearie, I *don't* think there was anything! That's just the point! I figured it out, we all figured it out, and we figured there just wasn't any place where you *could* have! There aren't any empty staterooms: the chief steward told me so. You couldn't have come in here without me knowing about it. You couldn't have gone to Captain Wright's stateroom, because he shares it with a man who's been seasick the whole trip and's never even got out of bed. So we all figured that——'

'You mean to tell me that other people have been discussing this too?'

'Why, of course, dearie! There's not much to do on a hooker like this, naturally. And you can't play shuffleboard at night. You and your beau have been the talk of the voyage, of course. What'd you expect? You can pull them a bit tighter, dearie. Thanks.'

Phil sobbed a little, but deep in her throat; her eyes, though blazing, were dry. She yanked the corset strings viciously, making Grace emit thin involuntary squeals. Those precious hours, those silvered walks, and the kisses under the shadow of the bridge, all had been spied on! Those dearest of moments, when she and one other had seemed to exist alone in a glad world, in fact had been peered at, squinted at, gloated over in the darkness. Each caress a silent simper elsewhere, a vicarious thrill. Each clasping of hands the signal for sweaty excited hands to be clasped in a dark place near by, perhaps behind some ventilator.

'Listen, kiddo, I want 'em tight, yes, because I want to look my classiest for Gus. But you don't have to tear me in half.'

'I'd like to!'

'Now, now, dearie, you don't really mean that. I told you once already, didn't I, that I never did believe that anything happened? I wouldn't even go round looking at the lifeboat covers with the rest of them. They have those canvas covers over them, you know. But I told them they were wasting their time—and they were, because not a one had been disturbed. I told them I was in the same stateroom with you and I knew you well and I knew you wouldn't do it in a place like a lifeboat anyway, you're too refined.'

Chokingly, after a last angry tug: 'There! Now please put your petticoat on and get out!'

Gracie was not offended. Gracie liked Phil and felt sorry for her.

'Haven't got my rats in yet, dearie. But I'll hurry. I know you want room to pack.'

'I want room.'

She didn't cry, even when Gracie had gone. It called for a mighty effort; for after the first flush of rage had a little subsided, tears almost irresistibly pushed themselves hot upon her eyes; but she did not give way. The ship would be in soon. She ought to be up on deck right now: they might be near enough so that she could see Harry on the dock.

Angrily she pulled something over the Hall Caine novel and the *Spanish Self-Taught* and closed the valise. Ward had been impressed by all the hotel labels on that valise the first time he saw her, had he? He'd said he had. He'd said a lot of other things. . . .

She didn't cry, but instead she went to the washstand and folded it up against the wall, causing Gracie's dirty water to cascade into an unseen slop jar. She stood at the mirror there. It was not much of a mirror: it was narrow and its surface was uncertain. Head back, shoulders back, she looked at herself for some time, until once again, in spite of everything, she began to admire herself. A smile, a whit sardonic at first, but twitchy with triumph, caught at the corners of her mouth. Her eyes shone dry and hard.

Here was a lovely woman to see. She knew it; and why not? Phil stared at this woman and loved her. Charles Dana Gibson must have loved her too, he drew her so often. The forehead broadish but not bulgy, not overintellectualized, so that the chin seemed in fact even tinier than it was. The same minute mouth. The same imperturbable eyes, downcast not in humbleness but because it was becoming. And the pompadour, the grand high full pompadour, every strand of it her own, padded only by combings from her own cup. Phil's hair was a honey-colored brown, but a brown of which nobody could speak with finality, since there were times when in sunlight it glittered a Lorelei yellow, as there were times when it showed curiously dark and when glints of red appeared and vanished and reappeared in it. It was soft and full and thick hair, with just a hint of a wave.

I can handle it, she whispered to herself, staring at her reflection, her chin high. Maybe I've been foolish. Well, I have a right to be foolish, haven't I? He won't hurt me any more. And Harry's waiting for me, and I really love Harry.

'I really love Harry!' she said aloud, passionately, leaning forward with outstretched hands, forgetting that she had folded the washbasin back. 'I really love him!'

There was love in her. There was a great deal of love in her, and it moved and shook her. Harry. . . . *He* was good-looking too, not sensational, no matinee idol, but handsome, eager, fresh, earnest, with clear fine eyes and such a lovely susurrant voice. He would be waiting there, on the dock, very near now. He'd be waiting, loving her. And how she would love him! Perhaps he was worried about that? Her recentest letters had not been notably warm. She'd been cross, uncomfortable, even humiliated by her position as a dependent at home, and no doubt this feeling had found its way into the lines she wrote. Well, it was different now. Harry was going to get a pleasant surprise. She smiled into the mirror, and there was no hint now of harshness in the smile.

'I really love him!'

She pinned a pancake on, a yellow one, uptilted and pert. She was wearing brown ribbed silk with coffee-colored lace, and there was a swooping osprey in her hair, yellow tourmalines screwed to her ears. Her waist was boned in, as Gracie Landis's never could have been, to show how stylishly curved was her figure. She tossed a brown boa over her shoulders.

She closed and locked the valise and examined the tag on it. She nodded. She opened the door, and in the doorway turned for another, farther-away look at her reflection, over her shoulder. Again she nodded, again smiled a little. Yes, she could handle this matter. And oh, what a wonderful surprise Harry was going to get! She still was smiling as she swept out.

SHE SAW when she reached the deck that they were near the shore which half an hour earlier had been a blur. They were no more than a few hundred feet away from it, and already the *Allianca's* engines were in reverse, causing the ship to vibrate.

She ran to the rail.

She paid scant heed to the remote outline of this country to which she'd come to make a home. Indeed, she couldn't see far anyway. Briefly she had glimpsed mountains, and then these were lost from sight behind something grayish and filmy. Rain? It had rather suggested fog. The town itself held her attention no longer. She was aware only that it was appallingly dirty. Anyway it was some distance to the right of where they were about to dock.

The dock itself was crowded. There was some rain here, a light, gay, golden, glittering rain, through which the sun shone, and those on the dock who held umbrellas were able to hold them high and to tip them back, looking up to the *Allianca's* deck. One of these must be Harry! Breathless, she leaned far over the rail, scanning faces too fast, so fast that she knew she'd probably have to go back and start over again, as the ship sidled closer to the dock.

Then the rain, the real rain, came. There was a great hollow roar —and it was there. It was everywhere. It and it alone, you would have said, existed; for it blotted everything else from sight, nor could there be any sound to go through its thunder.

One minute a peaceful scene, a scene of greeting, with people already recognizing other people, and waving, and calling things, a pleasant and happy scene, sunlight upon it, the rain no more than an amiable, brightly lit drizzle. The next moment it was as though Phil herself had been plunged into the sea: she couldn't have been more cut off, she couldn't have been more confused and frightened.

The part of the deck on which she stood was roofed. Nevertheless the rain was so full and hard, and it came down so violently, lashing the rail, that in an instant she was wet. She staggered back toward the place where she knew the social salon was. The air was all spray, and she couldn't see a thing.

Her shoulder blades met the deckhouse, and there she stood, trembling, gasping, filled with dismay.

She had been so near to Harry there for a moment or two, and perhaps had even seen him, looking right past him, not noticing that he was waving to her. She had been, after all this time, and in this exotic place so far from home, that close, that very close to the comfort and goodness of Harry. Then the rain. Without warning, stunningly, the all-obliterating rain. And now where was Harry? A curtain had been drawn between them. Phil, throat-lumped, could not even see the rail for the mist, much less the dock. The *Allianca* shuddered and thumped with engines furiously in reverse.

Phil Kellems was often to forget but as often to remember again that moment when she pressed, frightened, against the deckhouse. It was like a horrible experience a child has in the dark, an unaccountable, unfight-against-able experience, an urgent awareness of danger combined with the paralysis of a nightmare. Frozen, fascinated, she stood and stared. There was that curtain, so suddenly drawn between her and Harry. There was that veil not to be pierced.

Once she felt an arm against her upper arm, a hand upon her wrist. She moved away; and though she had seen no more than a hazy gray blur, she knew that this was Ward Wright. How could the man find her in this mist? Did he have *eyes* like a cat, too? She heard no sound except that of the rain, and she shivered as she moved away from the person who had touched her. She was afraid of Ward Wright, no denying it. That posing in front of the stateroom mirror, that Gibson Girl posing, which ordinarily settled her mind and brought her chin up to where it belonged and strengthened her so that she could face anything, this time had been futile. Its effect had passed. It might have been all right at home; but here in this strange steaming land, here in the presence of such a man as Ward Wright, something more was needed. Yes, she was scared. Harry would have comforted her; but where was Harry? Somewhere the other side of that curtain was like saying somewhere in a different, unreachable world.

Abruptly, though not as swiftly as it had been lowered, the curtain rose. The rain did not stop, but it slackened greatly, so that the air was cleared, and the sun came out, almost with a click, almost like the snapping on of an electric light. Truly the only sounds in the world were the confusion of voices, the squeal of hawsers, the hasty muddy torrents and cascadings everywhere, the swift dribble-dribble-dribble from the upper decks; but the recent roar seemed to linger in the ears, indeterminately, as the roar of the sea is supposed to continue in a shell.

Phil ran to the rail.

The ship was close. Hawsers had been thrown to the deck and were being made fast, and steam winches had set up a terrific racket. Phil saw Harry almost immediately. He was directly below her.

'Darling!'

'Phil! Phil! Oh, are you all right?'

'Ah, it's so good to see you, darling!'

Head tipped back, he grinned, and she remembered again how nice-looking he was, especially when he grinned like that. She smiled to him.

It was not only that Harry was nice-looking. More important was the fact that he was Home. He was Paterson, N.J., and school, and parties. Why had she ever supposed, even for a little while, even in the lovely light of the moon, that there could be any joy sitting beside a pantherine soldier of fortune, a story-book hero, and in talking to him—who himself offered no contribution to the talk, being reticent about his past—of Paris, of art, and cathedrals and towers? What did culture have to do with it? Ward had never been interested in culture anyway! He'd only led her on by pretending an interest in it, at first.

But Harry, Harry down there, grinning up at her, his eyes shining, *he* loved her! *He* would take her into his arms, and talk quietly to her, and make her feel safe.

Delighted, she beamed and beamed.

Phil had noticed the crowd's size only because its greatness made difficult the finding of Harry. No more than she had noticed in detail the far mountains so swiftly erased by rain, or the squalid town, did she heed the crowd's curious restlessness. Here was much more than should be expected to greet the arrival of a steamer from the States. Some, like Harry, were occupied with waving, and shouting to certain passengers, but many more were pushing and surging back and forth, jostling one another, so that in fact the crowd on the dock almost resembled a mob. Phil however did not remark this—until the first man started to climb a hawser.

Two hawsers had been thrown, one forward, one aft, and it was the forward one, still slack, and dripping with water in the middle, that the man started to climb. He was a roughly dressed man, and he had a straw suitcase slung over his shoulders by a cord. Clumsily but with a desperate earnestness, with a strength lent him by fear, he shinnied and struggled up the hawser the winches were drawing taut. A police-man on the dock tried in vain to reach him.

'Come back here, you God-damn——'

There were two sailors near the hawsehole, and an officer yelled to them to prevent the man from boarding, but they were startled, and the man was frantic. The man got aboard, somehow, despite the sailors, and flopped to the deck, suitcase and all.

'This is where I *stay!* You can't put me off! Ticket or no ticket, got the price in my jeans and I'm going to *stay* here!'

Another tried to get out on that same hawser, and the policeman clutched him, and they struggled. Meanwhile no less than three others had fought their way to the aft hawser and were climbing it monkey-like, their packs swinging from their shoulders.

Still more vigorously agitated was the crowd around the spot where the gangplank soon would be lowered. Phil noticed now that many policemen were there.

Yet Phil had but one thought, which was to get to Harry. She gave him a last reassuring wave over the rail, and turned, and hurried to the deck below, the deck from which the gangplank was being run out.

They swarmed up the gangplank even before it had been made fast. The policemen, working hard, weren't able to stop them. It was like an invasion by pirates; and for a little while Phil and other frightened passengers really did think that the ship was being stormed by des-peradoes. These were white men, and most of them were reasonably well dressed; but they were wild-eyed; they were sweating, yelling, swearing, panting, gasping, fighting every moment, and against all who would stop them, to get aboard the *Allianca*. An officer shouted from the bridge, and sailors tried to run the gangplank up again, but it was too late. The policemen too did what they could, some of them using clubs. The mob surged ahead. The gangplank was black with humanity; and each man had panic in his eyes, a bag or bundle of some sort over his shoulder or under his arm.

Once aboard, however, they showed no propensity to rape or may-hem. Rather they seemed concerned with getting out of sight as quickly as possible. Butting and shouldering through the passengers and crew, running where running was possible, they scattered to seek out remote corners of the deck or to pop below like gophers popping into their holes at the discharge of a shotgun. Only one of them paused at the head of the gangplank. He was a huge panting man, streaked with sweat, disheveled, heavily tanned by the sun, but obviously American. His protuberant eyes, screeching his fear, surveyed the huddled, bewildered passengers.

'You mean to say you're going *ashore?* In *this* hellhole? You must be crazy! Not me! You couldn't get me to put a foot on that place again for a million dollars! Why, don't you know that——'

A sailor confronted him and grabbed his coat. 'Off you go! You got no ticket, you got no right to——'

'Ticket be damned, brother! I stay *here!*'

The big man lurched back, at the same time swinging loose the valise that hung from his shoulders. An end of the valise struck the sailor in the face, causing him to lose his grip. The big man ran.

'Not *me!* No, *sir!*'

'*Get that fellow!*' an officer shouted. '*Throw him in the brig!*'

It was a full ten minutes before some semblance of order was restored. Some of the passengers had fled to their staterooms and locked themselves in, some had returned to the upper deck, but Phil and perhaps a dozen others lingered anxiously near the gangplank. The officer in charge there, clearly acting on the captain's orders, was eager to get them ashore as soon as possible, as indeed they were eager to go. They had been cleared by quarantine, the Sanitation men having come aboard previously by means of a launch. No tariff was imposed upon Americans in the Panama Canal Zone, and these were all established Americans. Their bags, boxes, rolls, trunks had been properly labeled and piled. There would be rough work aboard the *Allianca* soon, when the brash determined stowaways must be pushed ashore, and no doubt the captain thought that the fewer the passengers there were left at that time the better.

So it was that Phil at last, trembling, horribly mussed, and realizing with a start that rain still fell, found herself stepping gingerly down the gangplank toward an ocean of faces. She could no longer see Harry; she had not seen him since she'd left the upper deck; but she was sure he was there somewhere. The purser gave her a harried smile and took up the balance of her ticket, and a policeman passed her through rapidly yet gently, saying 'Just get off the dock as soon as you can, lady, that's all.'

This crowd was white. It was not a crowd of ignorant natives. The men—there seemed to be only men—were ordinary artisans, by the looks of them, plumbers, carpenters perhaps, switchmen, steam fitters, engine men, foremen. From their clothes, from their general appearance, as taken in at a glance, you would have supposed them to be everyday self-respecting Americans, as indeed previously they had

46

been and elsewhere they soon would be again. But now they were packed with terror, drunk with fright, and unpredictable. They were lost to all sense of order and decency. They knew only that they wanted to get away from Panama.

Scarcely had Phil entered among them, whispering urgently, when they were seized by another spasm. The cry rose that the gangplank was about to be pulled in and that the *Allianca* would retreat to the middle of the bay. Heedless of everything, even of their own personal safety, certainly heedless of the young woman who pleaded to be permitted to pass, again they surged against the police; again they fought and swore and howled and were clubbed.

She was a cockleshell tossed in a tempest, and if she wasn't squashed it was only because of her very lightness and fragility. Unnoticed, her sobs and little cries unheard, she was elbowed and shoved away from the gangplank—but not toward the street. She found herself getting closer and closer to the edge of the dock. With tiny fists she beat the back of a man, then that of another man, but neither even turned. Step by step she was forced back. The police now were countercharging, trying to clear the dock. They had forgotten her.

Perhaps she screamed. She heard Harry's voice, though she could not see him.

'Let me through here! My wife—— Say, I'm not trying to get on that ship! Please let me past! Damn it, I tell you my wife——'

She teetered on the very edge, and glanced once, foolishly but humanly, behind her and down. Sickness rose to tighten her throat while it loosened her breast and stomach, and she closed her eyes. A man was swimming down there in the slit of dirty water between the *Allianca* and the dock. Well, not swimming so much as floundering like some confused, frightened, amphibious beast. He had a pack on his back. Probably he had been pushed off one of the hawsers. Sailors who held clubs now lined the rail where the hawsers were made fast on deck.

'Let me through, I tell you! You son of a bitch, let me *past!*'

At last Harry was with her and had an arm around her, and he was trying to hold her away from the edge and at the same time to push against the backs of men retreating from the police.

The police could not see them. The police couldn't know that one of the passengers, a female too, had been caught in an eddy and whirled to a dangerous spot, and that they themselves were forcing the crowd against her. Harry shouted and fumed. He had lowered and folded his umbrella, which was badly torn, and with this lustily he belabored the heads and backs of men who seemed all unaware of his very existence: he was a horsefly.

Ward Wright was more than a horsefly. He appeared suddenly, dramatically, bellowing, swinging his fists.

'Get out of my way, you skunk! Don't you know there's a lady back there! Don't you know——'

A man cried: 'I don't care if there's a——'

Ward Wright punched this man, very hard, in the mouth, so that blood fairly sprang from the lips to slobber over the chin. The man, choking with rage, started to lift his fists. Ward Wright kicked him in the shins, and the man doubled over, screaming in pain.

'I got no time for fist fighting now, Jack. You stay still—or I'll kill you!'

He meant it. His dark brown eyes were blazing, his teeth showed white.

But when he looked up at Harry, across the small clearing his violence had created, he smiled. He even thrust out his hand.

'Are you Kellems? Sorry I didn't get here sooner.'

Harry muttered 'Thanks' and asked no question.

'I think we'd better push out of here as soon as we can' said Ward Wright. 'They're likely to start another rush, and the cops might try to shove the whole pack into the drink. What do you say to working around a little to the left here? Can you keep close to your wife, Mr Kellems? That's fine. Only, don't let me get too far ahead.'

There was little for Harry to do then. Ward Wright was no stranger to rough-and-tumble, and if he was thin he was marvelously quick and strong, and with long arms he had a long reach. Using elbows, knees, fists, occasionally even butting with his head, and all the while keeping up a stream of curses and warnings, some in English, some, when he remembered Phil, in Spanish, he was a cyclone to clear a path. Harry held Phil's arm, leaving his own right arm free, and they simply walked behind Ward Wright. *He* never hesitated. He never asked, he demanded; never pushed, but furiously punched; never squirmed or wriggled, but kicked. Once he flashed them a smile over his shoulder, to encourage them. Once, near the street, a mauled man wanted to fight him.

'Hey, you can't do that to me!'

'I'll do a whole lot worse to you, brother, if you don't get out of this lady's way!'

Wright only put his hand under his coat. Neither Harry nor Phil, behind him, could see what it was he touched there; but afterward they deduced that it had been a revolver. The man stumbled back, his mouth open, his eyes a couple of ping-pong balls.

When they reached the street it was Harry at least who got the hack. 'Coche! Here, you cochero!' It was by all odds the dreariest vehicle Phil had ever seen, all mud and moth-eaten cushions, with a sogged fringe from which all jiggle had gone, and it looked as though the weight of a child would make splinters of it; but they all got in; whereupon the driver, without anger or even interest, lashed the nag, so that they squealed away. Ward Wright must have been enjoying himself: he was laughing, and his eyes glittered with excitement like those of a boy at a carnival. As soon as he conveniently could, and before either Harry or Phil had properly caught breath, he halted the hack.

'I'm sure you two want to be alone. And I do hope that Mrs Kellems won't think too harshly of Panama after such a welcome. I am delighted to have met you, sir. Well . . . hasta la vista.'

'Hasta la vista' muttered Harry; and Ward Wright puddle-leaped for cover.

'Well, I must say' said Harry 'you seem to have made some mighty convenient friends!'

They looked at one another, not breathing, each with wide eyes, and with lips a bit open; and then he put his arms around her and kissed her on the mouth. It embarrassed both of them, and when he released her they didn't look at one another for some time, though she did not reprimand him.

'Well! Well . . . I got here.'

'Yes, you got here.'

'Well, you don't seem very enthusiastic.'

'Oh, I am! I really am! The only thing is—— Well, I wish you'd written me first that you were going to come.'

'If I had, you'd have written to forbid it. What else was I to do? Ah, Harry, don't start finding fault with me right away, just as soon as I've arrived and I'm so glad to see you and everything. I should think *you'd* be glad to see *me*, too!'

'Oh, say, I am! Positively I am!'

'The rest of the population of this country' Phil remarked, adjusting her pancake, 'doesn't seem to feel that way. What in the world were all those hoodlums doing there anyway, darling?'

'They aren't hoodlums. They acted like it, I'll admit, but they

49

aren't, ordinarily. They're just workmen who want to get away. No matter what happens, they want to get away.'

'Well, I certainly hope they succeed! Why are they so anxious to get away, dear?'

'Yellow fever. Oh, it's a lot of things, more than I could tell you about if I talked all day. But mostly yellow fever. There's too much of it. Only yesterday one of my best friends, Georgie Walsh, came down with it. And everybody's scared.'

'Are *you* scared, darling?'

Somberly: 'I'm scared for you. I don't think you should have come, and I really think you ought to go back as soon as you can.'

'Well, I like that! Here I spend my own money for a ticket to travel two thousand miles to surprise you, and the first thing you tell me is that I ought to turn right around and go back!'

'Now wait a minute, Phil! Please don't twist that around, what I meant to say!'

'Well, that's what you *did* say, isn't it?'

'Oh, in a way I suppose it was. But what I really *meant* was that this is really no decent place for a white woman to be in. It isn't clean. It isn't safe.'

'But I thought Dr Gorgas—I thought you were in the Sanitary Department yourself, darling——'

'I am. But do you know how many men we've got for all the work that ought to be done? About two hundred. And they're dying and quitting on us every day. Two hundred! We could use two thousand —and more! They won't give us any money. They won't send us enough sulphur. And screening! The only way to keep anybody at all safe from disease here is to keep them screened up, but that bunch in Washington——'

She shook her head swiftly and put a firm hand on his arm.

'I know, dear. But let's not talk about that now. After all, we'll have everything fixed up pretty soon, now that we're together, won't we?'

'You really oughtn't to be here at all. I'm worried. But there's no way I know of that you can return until the *Seguranca* comes back the second time, three weeks from Monday. Not unless you want to try to climb a rope, the way those men did when they couldn't get tickets.'

'I haven't the slightest intention of going back. What do you think I came here for?' She looked around, wincing a bit. 'So this is Panama?'

'No, dear, this is Colon. Panama's the other side of the Isthmus.

That is, Panama City. Where we're going. In—in some ways it isn't quite as bad as here.'

'Well, I should hope not!'

All this while, from the time Ward Wright had halted the cab, they had been motionless. The driver never turned, but sat as though unaware of the rain. The rain wasn't heavy now, and it made little noise. It fell like fine oil; and the very mud, where it wasn't scattered with sewage or garbage, seemed oily. There was no pavement. In places a rickety rotten board sidewalk stripped dubiously before some house or some Chinese shop; but mostly there was only that same mud and garbage, mud and garbage, and mud. The shops and houses, all unpainted, seemed falling apart from sheer weariness. What few two-story buildings there were had balconies, and these sagged precariously, showing, like the houses below them, so little strength and spirit that you wondered that the very rain didn't cause them to collapse. The stink suffocated *all* your senses, not merely your sense of smell. The rain cleansed nothing, washed not a thing away: it only made things more sodden, and collected in pools. Colon's lack of plumbing was evident in the nature of Colon's architecture, not to mention the contents of many of the puddles. Little wooden bridges led to the backhouses, which stood on little wooden stilts in yards that were swamps; but many of these bridges were broken—broken from decay, not from use. Even as Phil looked around, aghast, a Negro came out on his crazy veranda and without troubling to turn his back urinated over the crazy railing.

'But do we have to come to a slum section, Harry?'

'My dear, this isn't a slum section. This is the center of town. This is the Herald Square of Colon. Welcome to Panama. Viva Panama!'

'Please don't try to be funny. We can't stay here.'

'No.' He spoke to the driver, and after sufficient whipping the horse hauled them suckingly away. 'I've arranged for you to use a friend's room, in his boardinghouse, while I get your baggage to the station. Things ought to be straightened out down on the dock by now. This isn't any palace I'm taking you to! But you'll only need to be there an hour or so. The landlady speaks English, and she's really not bad. My friend has some bottled water there, so you can have a drink, and the landlady will get you some water to wash in too. But I wouldn't——' He looked away. 'Well, I'd—you know—I'd sort of wait for the rest, if you can. Until we get to the other side of the Isthmus. I don't think it would be safe here.'

She asked him while they slogged slowly on, and the hack dipped and lurched, why, if Americans had charge of sanitation in the cities of Colon and Panama, there wasn't running water. He told her that it was different in Panama City. They were installing a water system there, and it would be ready pretty soon, in a month or so; and they were paving some of the streets there too.

'But here it's different. They haven't done anything because they're not sure yet whether this really is going to be the Atlantic end of the canal. They may decide to locate that at Porto Bello.'

'You mean to tell me that we've been digging this canal for almost a year and we don't know yet where one end of it's going to be?'

'That isn't all we don't know. We don't even know whether the canal's eventually going to have locks and be fifty, seventy-five, maybe ninety feet up in the air, or whether it's going to be cut through at sea level. It will make all the difference in the world as to what kind of engineers and equipment we want.'

'But if we haven't made up our minds about matters like that, what are we *digging* for?'

'Sometimes I wonder.'

Señora Morales did in fact speak some English, interspersed with a great deal of Spanish; but it all might have been Spanish as far as Phil was concerned. The woman was fat and solicitous, and she jabbered incessantly. She lived in a side street somewhat narrower and more squashy than those thoroughfares which came together to form the Herald Square of Colon. The street was quiet; yet partly because of Señora Morales and her delight in the exercise of her astounding English, and partly because of the absence of shades in the windows, it lacked privacy. The windows were tall and faced directly out upon a tiny veranda almost flush with the street itself. True, there were lace curtains, dirty curtains, but these were so sleazy and so very full of holes as to offer no protection. How did Harry's friend ever dress and undress in such an exposed place? was what Phil wondered as she washed. Under his nightgown, perhaps?

Phil refused an invitation, extended largely by means of sign language, to visit the outhouse. She sat down, tired. She knew she looked a fright. Her clothes were damp. Her osprey, her boa, were without spring. She felt a headache coming on.

Señora Morales prattled indefatigably, and after a time Phil made only the scantiest pretense of listening, of nodding, sometimes smiling. She wished that the woman would go. She wondered why Harry had acted the way he had.

Harry loved her, she was sure of it. She would never worry about that. He had told her that he'd loved her since they were kids together, and Harry was a man who wouldn't lie. She could be certain of him. But she wished that he had been a little more thoughtful when he greeted her. Almost his first words had been a reproof. Well, possibly he was right. Possibly he had common sense on his side. But in matters of love, where was the use of common sense?

Señora Morales at last stopped talking and went out of the room, and Phil was almost sorry about this, so eerie was the stillness that followed. The street was deserted except for a dog of disgusting skinniness, a mongrel hairless because of mange, and with great nasty sores on its flanks, which snoofed in search of garbage.

She didn't want to think of Ward Wright; and she was fair-minded enough to know that a comparison of Ward with Harry, this morning, was not just. Fighting was Ward's own specialty, his line of business: it wasn't Harry's. Harry had done well, and certainly he had never shown fear or hesitancy. All the same, she could not help admiring Ward Wright. She had decided that she did not like him, in fact even disliked him, and distrusted him. Nevertheless he had thrilled her when he pushed those men aside. Nor could she help remembering how silly Harry had looked as with his folded torn umbrella he beat a futile tattoo on backs which twitched no acknowledgment. She giggled at the remembrance; and then severely stopped giggling, ashamed of herself; and looked up.

There was a man in the street, a colored man, she thought. However, he did not look like any sort of Negro she had seen at home. He was lank and long, and wore smudgy white clothes, and he picked his teeth as he gazed at her. Right through those once-lace curtains he gazed, which was easy enough.

There was nothing about his stare which was in itself offensive, and certainly nothing threatening, as well as she could recall it to memory later; but the circumstances were everything; and suddenly she was frightened again. Where *was* she? She rose, her hands instinctively going to her breast. She swallowed hard. Why call for Señora Morales? This was absurd! She sat down with a flump, vigorously. She glared at the man in the street.

He had not stirred. Still he looked at her and picked his teeth. It seemed to her that already they had been looking at one another for a long, long while. She froze her face. She knew how go-awayey she could show. A gentleman would have departed some time before; and even this man ought to shuffle on. He didn't.

She stirred with restlessness and started to drop her eyes, and changed her mind, looking instead to one side. A dropping of the eyes could suggest interest or even fear. For a long while she studied, scarcely seeing it, a ridiculous garish saint picture on the wall: Señora Morales would be a Catholic, of course. But when Phil looked back, the man was still there.

A scream would be undignified. And after all, where was the need to scream? You kept screams for perilous situations. This was broad daylight, middle of the morning. She fixed the man again with eyes that were outthrust icicles, and then carefully again she looked away. She was determined not to look out of the window another time. She did not let her gaze rest upon any one thing in the miserable room, but rather let it stray round and round, while an hour might have passed, though more likely it was but a few minutes.

At last she looked again. She had to. The man was gone.

When Harry came back, half an hour later, she wondered what in the world had been the matter with her for a little while there.

She rose, and smiled straight at him, and made the corners of her eyes crinkle, the way she knew he liked to see them.

Harry had kept the hack, and in addition he now had a dray upon which were piled the various trunks and bags Phil had brought, all covered with a tarpaulin. There was one thing he hadn't been able to get immediately, because, he reported, it was still in the *Allianca's* hold. It.must be a big thing? She told him that it was the piano.

'The *piano?*'

'Yes, dear. It's mine, you know. It never did belong to the family. It was given to me when I was a girl.'

'But—but, you brought the whole *piano* down here?'

'Well, you wouldn't have me bring just four or five keys, would you?'

He stood flabbergasted, and she went to him and slid her hands up his chest. Señora Morales was not there at the moment. What, Phil asked, was wrong with bringing the piano?

'You see, I figured you must be lonesome, and the piano always did mean so much to us, and I figured that if we're going to be really happy together—and we certainly are, aren't we, darling?——'

'Why, yes, of course!'

'Well, I figured that maybe we wouldn't have much to do here, out here in the jungle and everything—I mean, nights and Sundays and holidays, when you aren't working—because of course I understand that you *do* work most of the time—but anyway I love to play it sometimes just all by myself anyway.'

She slid her hands up to his shoulders.

'Sundays and times like that, was what I thought, we could have some music, the way we used to. You could sing things like "Mighty Lak a Rose" and "Jest Alongin' for Your Smile"— I'll bet you'd like to sing "Jest Alongin' for Your Smile" right now, if I accompanied you, wouldn't you?'

The amazement did not leave his eyes, but he was able to talk and to move. He touched both sides of her face with his fingers.

'Why—why, darling, if you accompany me in anything at all, it's all right.'

'That's what I thought. That's why I brought the piano. See?'

'Why, *darling!*'

He kissed her very hard and held her tighter than she would have enjoyed if she had not loved him so much, and the voice of that genie Señora Morales was a sword to splinter and to hurt.

'Ah, el amor, el amor! Que hermoso!'

'Oh hell!' cried Harry.

'Darling!'

4

RAILROADS, she had supposed, were American. Good railroads any-way. Everybody knew that if we hadn't actually invented them, at least we had made railroads what they were. American trains were clean; they went fast and even, and on time; they were fancy—Wagner cars, Pullman cars, palace cars; and even the day coaches were comfortable. She'd been on some trains in France and Italy, in Germany too. She knew the difference.

Not in Germany or France or Italy, however, had she known such a railroad as this one.

The station stank. Even in her mind, for this occasion, she was obliged to admit that word. To say that the station was permeated by an unpleasant odor was not to tell the whole truth. It stank. Nobody seemed to know where anything was. And on the train, no window worked: those that were shut could not be opened, while those that were open could not, when the rain came again, be shut. Cinders lay everywhere: all surfaces were gritty. Peanut shells, orange peel, even cigar butts littered a floor stippled with spittle. The seats were damp and lumpy, and their backs were mottled with what appeared to be some sort of particolored fungus growth. The conductor, who smoked a cigar, noisily and somewhat contemptuously took cash from Harry, and this cash he stuffed into a pocket, without offering a ticket or a receipt, without speaking thanks. The conductor sauntered on.

'That man ought to be discharged!' came like an explosion from Phil.

'Yes' Harry said.

The conductor turned only his head and inverted the cigar twice to get its sponginess up to a corner of his mouth.

'Want the job, lady?'

Phil was speechless.

Phil was speechless, however, for a very short time. She grabbed Harry's arm.

'Are you going to let him talk to me like that?'

'What's *he* going to do about it?' the conductor asked.

There were nine or ten persons in the car. They leaned forward or frankly turned, grinning. They were all men.

Harry sighed. Phil heard that, and resented it, and thought to herself that once again Harry was going to fail her. No, that was unjust! Harry had not failed her on the dock! He had done everything he could be expected to do. It was only because——

Harry sighed again, not too heavily, and said in a voice intended to reach the conductor: 'Let him alone, dear. The government needs men like him. Men who have had yellow fever before, so that they're immune. And who haven't any life in their blood anyway, so that malaria doesn't mean anything to them. And who like to get twice as much pay as they'd be able to get back in the States. And who think they can talk to ladies the way this greasy ham just talked to you.'

Then Harry lifted his head. 'Go away' he said. 'Get out of this car.'

The conductor's balance tipped toward his heels. Belligerency to him meant loud words, yet Harry had been quiet.

'You can't get me fired!'

'I can hurt your face with my fists' Harry reminded him.

Everybody waited. Everybody watched. Harry leaned across his wife and pointed out of the window.

'This is roughly where the Culebra Cut begins, where we have to tear a chunk right straight out of a whole mountain range. It's not much to look at. Not yet. But I want you to watch it when we come along.'

Somebody snickered, which stung the conductor. The conductor took four steps down the car toward Harry. Phil, who was watching him, gasped. Harry looked up.

'I don't want to fight with you' Harry said coldly. 'You've got your money, now go away. If you mean business, come here. If you don't, beat it. Never mind about your job. I'm talking about your teeth.'

The conductor went away.

Nobody in that car was as astonished as Phil. She had never questioned Harry's courage. Harry was the man she loved, and so of course he was brave. But—but—(there was that thought!) he had done this as well as if he'd been——

'See, now, here it comes. See? It's going to be the hardest part of the job. The French did a heap of work here, of course. See those things with all the little pails that keep going round and round, scooping up dirt? Those are French excavators. We're supposed to have some new-type steam shovels pretty soon, but right now these excavators are the things we're digging with.'

Weakly: 'I didn't know we were using any French machinery.'

'What did you think we were digging with?'

'Well, from what everybody at home says, we just threw away money when we bought out that French company. Forty-two million dollars. They say we just threw it away. That's what Father says.'

'He wouldn't say it if he was here. Look at those locomotives.'

'I have been looking at them. They look like toys. They look like something you'd see in a nursery.'

'All the same they do a lot of work. And it's just as well that they do! Washington doesn't seem to be sending us those big nice grand American locomotives we've been promised, so we use French ones. Look at those drills. Do you know which ones are the drills?'

'Why, of course, dear.' She didn't. She was still marveling at Harry.

'Look at those flatcars. We're supposed to be getting thousands of them. Good big forty-ton ones, not these dinky things. But *these* things are the things that're doing the job—such as it is—now. Talking to a divisional engineer the other day, out at Bas Obispo. He kidded me about the fact that we couldn't get enough screening, so I came right back by asking where all his American machinery was, and particularly his American flatcars. "There ain't any" he said. "Know where we get our cars now when we need more?" he said. "We just send some of the boys back into the bush and haul out those French jobs that were left over. You put a little oil on 'em," he said, "and they work fine. We got a saying out here" he said "that a car in the bush is worth two in the States." That's the way he put it.'

She thought little enough of what was outside the window. It was historic, she supposed; but it was dull. Only the preposterous little locomotives diverted her, and those but briefly. It was an inglorious scene. It was a muddy, unspeakably depressing scene. Yet it seemed to excite Harry. Harry! He talked on and on, telling her about the way they had to scoop dirt up and the way they didn't have the right dumps for the dirt—which he called 'spoil'—and the way the railroad couldn't handle all the work. What did she care about 'spoil' or flatcars? What was it to her how many cubic yards of rock some newfangled steam shovel, which wasn't even here yet (was *anything* here?), worked? It would be more in keeping with the occasion if Harry sat very, very close to her and talked to her in a whisper of how happy he was that she had come. It would be better if Harry—— Which Harry? The man who'd just spoken to that horrid conductor? She looked at that Harry, who was busy explaining to her how a seven-dollar-a-day engineman *and* a six-dollar-a-day craneman could be held up for two, three, sometimes four hours by an eighty-cents-a-day West Indian nigger. What of it? she thought. The way Harry had—— Why, Harry was——

A man was talking to Harry. One of the other passengers.

'Excuse me, sir. I heard you give it right from the shoulder to Napoleon, and if the wiff will excuse me for saying so, why don't you ride up and down on this line all the time?'

Harry grinned.

'All right' Harry said. 'Only, you don't mind if we forget about it now, do you? Didn't mean to get sore. Ordinarily—all right. But I've got something better to do right now.'

'Meaning you've got something better to do than talk to me?'

'Yes' Harry said, smiling, meaning the smile.

'Sure, I know.' The man was deferential. Phil, smiling politely, gathered that he was the representative of the others in the car. They had talked it over. This man, not sober, but not a fool, had been named the spokesman. 'Sure, but the point is, we've all wanted to say that for a long while. And you did. Holy smokes! Let joy be unrefined!'

'I did what?' Harry asked.

'Flummoxed him! Flummoxed him to beat the band! Ah say, I shouldn't be here talking to you—I know maybe you'll tell me to go roll my hoop—but, brother, that was the sweetest skiddoo anybody ever gave that old—uh——'

He paused, holding the edge of the seat, swaying with the swaying of the train, though surely he would have swayed anyway. He had stopped before a word, a forbidden word, and his eyes grew large as obviously he thought of what Harry might have done to him if he'd *said* that word. He all but trembled. He was a plump and patently decent man.

'All right' Harry said, laughing a little.

'What I really meant, Captain. What I really meant——'

'All right' Harry said. 'You don't mind if I talk with my wife here, do you? She's just come.'

'What I really meant, Captain, is some of us have been talking and sort of figuring things out, and we sort of thought——'

'Ah, come on' cried Harry. *'Please!'*

'You aren't sore, are you, Captain?'

'Don't call me "captain." I'm not the captain of anything. Forget that conductor, will you? I want to talk to my wife.'

'Sure, o.k., Captain. We just thought that maybe—well, you *are* Captain Ward Wright, aren't you?'

'No, I'm not Captain Ward Wright, whoever he is.' Harry was glib and good-natured, but firm. 'Now run along, huh? Everything's fine.'

'*Aren't* you Captain Wright? We heard he just came back on th
Allianca.'

'No, I'm not Captain Wright. Now *please* go. Twenty-three skiddoo

The man went back to his seat, lurching toward others, assurin
each that this *was* Captain Ward Wright. Some reason he didn't war
to say it, the man explained. Captain Wright kind of man always ha
to be secret. Some revolution, maybe? Harry, who had not listened t
this, was talking to Phil, who had.

'They load, and how long does it take 'em? Maybe forty minute
Forty-five at the most. Then they sit there, the whole crew sits there
the engineer, the craneman, and all those dark-skinned nitwits wit
shovels. They sit there. And sit. For how long?'

'I give up' Phil murmured.

'An hour and a half anyway. *An hour and a half!* Doing *nothin*
And why? Because there isn't the right place yet to dump the spoil

Harry had been mistaken for another man, but not that fact but th
name of the other man clanged against his awareness when they g
out at Panama City. Phil, sufficiently twitchy anyway, and confused
asked him if they couldn't have a hack and get right to somewhere
Harry said certainly. Harry nodded, and spoke Spanish to a dusty bo
who didn't seem to understand, and yelled for a coche, and patte
Phil's shoulder, promising her that everything would be all right. The
Harry turned the name over in his mind. He chuckled. He appeale
to Phil.

'Say, no wonder! That fellow who was drunk, you know who h
thought I was?'

'Captain Ward Wright' she answered tonelessly.

'Yes, but do you know who *he* is?'

'I should. I introduced him to you this morning.'

'Oh ho! *That's* the guy? Say, he certainly did handle that crow
beautifully! Say, the way he took care of those men——'

'It's his business, after all.'

'It's his—— Well, never mind even if it—— *Say!*'

He was leaning toward her, and she thought that at least this plac
appeared to be dry, and oh for heaven's sake, oh, Harry, please, please
Harry, don't say what you're going to say——

'Never saw anything so slick in my life. Sure, I've heard of him, no
that I think of it. Ward Wright, sure. He's some sort of politician an
military expert all mixed up. They say he's like a lawyer, he'll wor
for either side that offers him money. I don't know. But I *do* know h

can certainly take care of himself!' Harry chuckled. 'And of us too, for that matter, eh?'

'Darling, must we go on talking about that unfortunate business?'

'Sorry. But I can't help laughing when I think that somebody mistook *me* for *him,* that's all. Pretty funny, isn't it?'

'Yes' said Phil.

The coche arrived; but before they could climb into it, Harry Thompson also arrived.

He was tall, lank, all bone ends, and had a horse's face with droll brown eyes. He was homely, perhaps even ugly until you got used to him. There was a gawkiness about him, the air of a hayseed. He grinned expansively at sight of Harry, and his greeting was loud.

'Hi, there! Harry K!'

'Hi, Harry T! Say, you're just in time to meet my wife I told you about. But none of your long fancy speeches now.'

'Ah, there!'

Harry T yanked the straw hat from his head and held it over his heart, and outswept his right arm, the palm up, while he made a leg.

'Say, I cawn't tell you 'ow delighted I am to—— Sa-a-ay, Harry K, you never let us know what a peacherino your wife was! Knowing what *you* are, we all expected some wall-eyed, fish-faced, measly old crab, but, uh—oh my! Pawdon my glove! You see,' directly to Phil, 'he kept very quiet about you, didn't tell the rest of us poor bachelors that used to live with him, until practically the last minute. So naturally we wondered what all the silence was about. We'd begun to think that maybe he was a little ashamed of you and didn't have much to show off. But—oh my! What a mistake *that* was!'

He whistled through his teeth a couple of lines of 'Tell Me, Pretty Maiden, Are There Any More at Home Like You?' and did a step. Then he looked up and laughed at Phil, who was blushing. He flipped his hat back on and struck a comic attitude.

'A mere bag-o'-shells' he tut-tutted. 'A mere bag-o'-shells. You should see me when I first get up in the morning.'

He would have told them a story, something about two chorus girls, but Harry K cried a laughing but undeviating no, and Harry and Phil climbed into the coche. Harry T made them a mock-ceremonious bow, brushing the dust with an imaginary hat plume.

'You'll hear it yet, Mrs. Kellems' he promised.

'I'm sure I will' she said, smiling.

When the carriage had drawn away—Harry T standing at stiff

salute—she remarked to her husband that she must say that *he* seemed to have made some mighty *in*convenient friends.

'Oh, Harry's all right. He's not any polished gentleman, I'll admit that. But he isn't as crazy as he seems at first. You get to like him, after a while.'

'I see' said Phil.

Panama City depressed her as much as Colon. True, it was dry, and bright with sunshine, so bright indeed as to hurt the eyes; there was not much garbage in sight—at least, not enough to attract buzzards, as before; and as Harry had told her, some of the main streets were being paved. Nevertheless it was a dreary place. The people walked, wandered rather, without spring or snap, or else they stood, weak and seemingly bloodless, with no expression in their faces as they watched the carriage pass. Even the children did not play loudly or run back and forth; and though they were naked, they were not quaint, only dirty: many of them, too, had horrid sores around their eyes. Unfed dogs, all ribs, mooched listlessly. The very flies, which could be numbered by quadrillions, hummed and flew not avidly but as though discouraged. Phil thought: I'll never like this city. It was picturesque, technically, and she knew that it had a long and colorful history, and she supposed that she should have been excited; but she was not excited.

The air cleared as they climbed, and a certain hint of breeze was there, kicking up tiny whirlpools of dust which sometimes wafted languorously halfway across the street before sudden collapse caused them to vanish. Looking back, Phil could catch slits of triangles of the Bay of Panama.

She had been looking back when the carriage struggled between the main gates of the hospital, so that when she straightened in her seat she found the grounds all stretched before her and above.

She gasped. This was not so much because of the appearance of the hospital buildings as because of the grounds. The buildings indeed were trim and neat, if not imposing; they were wooden structures, and practically all were one-story; at least they looked clean, a novelty in this land. They were painted a sort of greenish gray, a saucy alert color, and were roofed with bright red tile. The grounds, on the other hand, were heartbreaking. There was no gaiety. Why, this place was even more depressing than the city had been, or Colon; for there hung over it an air of beauty departed, of desolation, decay, and choked grotesque death.

Not long ago the grounds must have been glorious. A great deal of loving work had been done on them. The side of the hill, scattered with hospital buildings, once had been an extensive garden. It rose in graceful terraces to the jungle line near the summit. Here and there, as for example before that two-story house near the center of the grounds, were rows of tall dignified royal palms giddily atwitter in the breeze, in the sun. There was no other vegetation. There *had* been other vegetation: it was this fact which lent such horror to the scene. There had been hedges and flower beds, vine-covered sanctuaries, plots around sundials, shaded paths meandering nowhere. Now there were only raw gaping holes, or the stumps of shrubs which had been hacked with a machete. It was as though a blight had fallen upon Paradise. Half a dozen pottery rings marked a triangle where flowers once had danced in geometrically spaced but doubtless carefree vigor; but there were no longer flowers, and the pottery rings had been deliberately and it would seem insultingly flipped upside down. Jagged stumps of oleander bushes, scant inches high, surrounded a column upon which once a birdbath had rested; the birdbath was overturned on the ground. A saint had presided over a cool shaded bower, where once conceivably convalescent patients or tired overworked nuns had been used to go for a little repose. The saint, uncloistered, unenclosed, still stood—but in the center of a blank terrace, drenched in merciless sunshine, lashed by merciless rains, and with its upraised hand granting benediction to nothing now but raw dirt, it looked a thing outraged and then contemptuously forgotten.

'Oh, Harry! It—it's—— Why, who in the world could ever have *done* anything so horrible?'

'As a matter of fact,' said Harry, 'I did it.'

When she turned to him in wild unbelief, yet moving a little away from him, he called to the hackman to stop. He spread his hands.

'At least, I superintended the job. I left what I could, and maybe some of the stumps will grow later. I hope so. It was a beautiful place here, Phil. Oh, a lovely place! You should have seen it the way it was when I first came! The French may not be much on plumbing, but they certainly know how to make gardens. They brought all these palms. They brought a lot of coconut trees too. And they brought the flowers and bushes my men dug up or cut down—brought 'em from all sorts of places, France itself, and North Africa, and French Guiana, and Martinique, and Guadeloupe. They did the thing right. You never saw such a happy spot.

'But you never saw such an unhealthy spot either. It's up on a hill, but it might as well have been in the middle of a swamp. Because of the umbrella ants the French had brought in hundreds of those pottery rings, of all different sizes. Had them around every bush and tree and flower bed. Filled them with water, of course, so that the ants couldn't get past them. Well, the mosquitoes loved that. There were no screens then, remember. And inside the wards themselves they'd put cans of water under each leg of each bed, to prevent ants from climbing up. The greatest breeding place of yellow-fever mosquitoes in this whole world, I suppose it was. If people didn't have yellow jack when they were brought in, they sure enough caught it before they'd stayed long!

'It's the malaria mosquitoes the bushes and flowers were cut down for. The Anopheles, they call them. They breed outside, not like the yellow-jack mosquitoes. They breed in swamps and places like that, and then they fly in. But they can't fly far without stopping in some shady place to rest. About two hundred yards of straight sunlight—and they're dead. Result is: strict orders from Dr Gorgas himself that there can be no flowers or bushes within two hundred yards of any government building. It's got to be done that way. And it's part of my job to see that it is done.'

Stunned, she shook her head. He slipped an arm across her shoulders.

'I know it seems awful' he whispered. 'It seemed awful to me when I did it. Some of those Sisters of St Vincent de Paul used to come out and watch us. They were still here then. They wouldn't say anything, wouldn't ever try to stop us, but they'd just watch us, and sometimes they'd be crying. I can't tell you how awful it made me feel, Phil. Here they'd fussed with these gardens for years. And in just a few days we made the whole place look—well, like this.'

She shuddered, closed her eyes. But she got nearer to him. She put her head under his shoulder.

'It—it'll be like living in a cemetery' she whispered.

Harry must have signaled to the coachman, for she felt the carriage start. After a while she opened her eyes. She was looking straight up the hillside, to where the jungle's edge lowered, a tottering mass, a reaching mass which would creep down over this hillside if it were permitted to do so, blackening everything, squeezing the life from everything. Phil closed her eyes again. She had glimpsed that same jungle as they came across the Isthmus in the train, while Harry was pointing out excavators and rock drills. In places it had been so close to the track that she'd heard it brush the car's very sides, and it had smelled of heavy wet decay. Black-green, an abode of packed shadows, where silence and spongy death lurked, the jungle had frightened her then as it frightened her now. What a realization!—that here in Panama, no matter which way you turned, the jungle was always somewhere near you, just behind you, reaching and reaching . . .

The hack stopped.

'Here we are!'

It was a small square wooden building, up on posts several feet from the ground, as the others were, but unlike most of the others it had not recently been painted. It had no veranda, and its front door and steps were wide, presumably in order to permit the passage of bulky objects. Some of the tiles of its roof were broken. The hedge of false coffee close around it, which might once have hidden some of its ugliness, had been slashed off almost at the roots. But every window was screened with bright new copper screening, and the door was screened too. Standing in the blazing sunlight, she could see nothing of the interior, even through the screen door. Timidly she opened that door.

Then Harry, who had paid off the coachman, picked her up and carried her over the doorstep.

With a foot he kicked the door shut. With a knee, still holding her in his arms, he threw the latch. It was dark inside, so that she could scarcely see him, and it was cool after the sunlight, though her face still stung and her body throbbed from the heat of the drive. Harry's face too was hot as he lowered his head to kiss her.

'Never mind, darling. It'll be all right in a little while. We're not going to be here long anyway, and it'll be all right.'

5

THEY WERE OF ALL SORTS, the young Americans who first went to Panama, and they went for many reasons. Some had always wanted to visit a foreign country and never could afford it: now they could head for the tropics at the government's expense. The pay was fifty to eighty per cent higher than pay for similar work in the States, with an eight-hour day; free quarters too, a full month of vacation every year plus travel time, and big discounts on the steamer fares. There were those who had not proved much good at anything else, and thought, Why not try the Canal? as well as those who, like Harry Kellems, saw in the project an opportunity not likely to knock a second time. There were those whose friends or families didn't know what else to do with them. There were at least a few fugitives from justice and no doubt many fugitives from wives. There were the born loafers and third-rate bullies who supposed it would be wonderful to just sit in the shade and boss a gang of niggers around. There were the gamblers, the pimps, the touts. Also there were those whose imagination was stirred by the immensity of the task and who wanted by all means to play some part, however humble, in an unprecedented historical undertaking: patriotism was strong in these, who never had forgiven their parents for having produced them too late to get into the Spanish-American War, that inglorious national frenzy in which, being then in their teens, they had been able to participate only as discussion-listeners, and later, when the boys came marching home, as singers, shouters, and envious flag wavers. If a generation which has fought a war is a marked generation, one which has been prohibited from doing so because of tender years is no less marked. It is less remarked upon, that's all. The war makes as great an impression upon it. The battles it fought, most of them in bed before sleep would come, or while watching the bulletin boards, or listening to the men at the livery stable, were not a whit less real than the noisier battles historians have recorded. The medals it won in its daydreams, and so could not wear, to its members are as solid as those that clink on the breasts of orthodox acknowledged heroes. Such a generation is one consisting of men outraged because they were not accepted as men when the stupendous moment came. It can have no confidants above or below; for those below it are mere kids, while those above are honest-to-goodness veterans. It is told, with maddening frequency, that it was lucky. It doesn't agree. It thinks it was cheated, and, resenting this, it is restless.

As a matter of fact, those youngsters who were first at Panama could be likened to the men of a wartime army. This would be an army of non-coms and officers; for the actual spadework was done in the beginning by West Indian Negroes, and later in addition by Spaniards, Italians, Greeks, Russians, Frenchmen, Armenians, Rumanians, and others, comprising the most heterogeneous aggregation of laborers ever assembled since the putting up of that notably less successful structure, the Tower of Babel. Very well, an army of officers and non-coms. Yet they thought and behaved like privates. They went forth as volunteers to a strange and terrible country; and they were pitifully young; and when they found themselves titillated by the prospect of hardship and danger, and stirred by patriotism, they did what they could to conceal this feeling by means of cynical, contemptuous talk delivered out of a corner of the mouth. They were badly and for a time it seemed hopelessly scrambled. Clerks found themselves track superintendents, mechanics measured coal, plumbers checked supplies, horse dealers were startled into becoming nurses, and engineering students supervised the fumigation of houses hundreds of years old. They were exposed to all kinds of weather. They slept where they could find places to sleep, in barracks, in moldering mansions, in freight cars, often in tents. They lived without women, and that is never good. They worked hard; and when payday came they played hard in the groggeries and tinseled brothels of Panama City and Colon. Like soldiers, they complained without pause, though not always without justification, about favoritism, toadying, remote political control, the indifference of the folks back home, a million exasperating unfairnesses, and, most of all, the food. Only a soldier who is asleep fails to complain about the food.

Like soldiers, too, they were bored. They had moments of exaltation which it would have embarrassed them to mention. They had hours and days of personal inside fear, of a loneliness that hurt like wounds, when they believed that the world had forgotten them. But most of the time they were just plain bored.

Oh, there were differences! The chief difference was in discipline. Soldiers are trained not only to do their work but to do that work *with other soldiers*. They might suffer physically, but they are not often obliged to make decisions. The answers are ready for them. If you're in the Army, and you get frightened, or tired of fighting, you don't just go home, do you?

'There are three things wrong in Panama' declared Big Smoke Stevens. 'Malaria, yellow fever, and cold feet. And the worst of these is cold feet.'

The pioneers were not experts. Passing the new civil service examination—*snivel* service, the bosses called it—could scarcely have been difficult. The ineptitude of some of the newcomers was breath-taking. Examples were snorted about. Only one: eighteen so-called track foremen were sent by request, and two of these had had some slight experience in street railways; none of the others had had any experience at all. The sixteen were sent back on the next ship, while the two kept over eventually were used by the medical department as clerks. John Findley Wallace, the chief engineer, complained often and bitterly about the sort of ten-thumbed ignoramuses the commission sent. So did his assistant, Walter Dauchy, who had charge of the work when Wallace was in Washington, which was a lot of the time. So did Big Smoke Stevens, when he took over. 'Am not running a training school to teach boys engineering and construction' Stevens snarled by cable. 'What I want is men who can go to work when they get here.'

Good, good. Yet when you stop to think of it, Americans are intelligent and adaptable. In a little while those in Panama knew how to trip a dump cart, how to lay a compressed-air line, spread oil, tamp the detonating cap into dynamite, swing crane arms, watch the gauges, dredge the channel. What they did not know—and God Himself wouldn't have expected them to learn this quickly—was how to live in a place like Panama AND how to work together.

Not bombs but a microscopic germ brought about the panic. The panic might have spent itself had it not been that at this time—just about the time Phyllis Kellems went to join her husband—the commanding general ran off the field.

John Findley Wallace knew his business; he was one of the best; and he had objected vehemently and properly to the seven-man commission which issued commands at a distance of two thousand miles. At the end of the first year, 1904, in Washington, he had proposed to the Secretary of War, Mr Taft (who had immediate charge of the whole project, under the President), that the commission be reduced to three. Taft o.k.'d this, and on January 13 President Roosevelt proposed such a reform to Congress; but Congress never did get around to doing anything about it. Now this Teddy was renowned as a cutter of red tape. Gruffly he requested the resignations of the com-

68

missioners, and after consulting Wallace he appointed a new commission which necessarily (since the law had not been amended) consisted of seven men; but Teddy made it clear that they were to appoint three of their number as an executive committee to stay in Panama and really handle the job. He named the three, too. They were the chairman, Theodore Perry Shonts, a practical, impatient, disagreeable, and brilliantly efficient man with a bulldog jaw and eyes habitually baleful behind glittering pince-nez; the governor, Charles E. Magoon, a fat fellow with a big black mustache, an amiable, tactful, affable teller of good stories; and Mr Wallace himself. Now it would seem that Mr Wallace should have been satisfied with this arrangement. He returned to the Isthmus in June of 1905, when the yellow-fever epidemic was at its height. He saw what Phyllis Kellems had seen. In less than two weeks he was on his way back to New York and writing his resignation.

Mr Wallace thought of the thing as a job, like any other job. He did not think of it as a holy crusade. He was an engineer: he wasn't Richard Coeur de Lion. He had a family. The Westinghouse people were offering him seventy-five thousand a year, exactly three times what the United States paid him. So he resigned.

The Secretary of War, that man who never carped, never talked behind a back and loved to laugh with his eyes, his mouth, his great fat cheeks, his whole huge fat body—the Secretary of War, for once truly graveled, returned a tongue-lashing which remains a classic in the history of American politics.

It was everything that Mr Taft could do. Mr Wallace was not in the Army. He had a perfect right to walk out if he wanted to.

Three days later John Frank Stevens, 'Big Smoke,' another railroad man, was appointed chief engineer. This genius never shouted or stamped. Anybody could talk to him. He smoked a large cigar, and he was at any given time ahead of his schedule.

Well, these three men, Shonts and Magoon and Stevens, went to Panama to take over the job. They went to try to turn back an army which was in full retreat (men everywhere, in Panama as at home, were saying that the Canal would never be built anyway, that it couldn't be) and to renew a broken-off battle. This is the hardest work a general can have. Shonts, Magoon, and Stevens.

Phil was of two minds when she came out with the fan. It was a handsome enough fan, and, though too flimsy and heavy to be of any use *as* a fan, it would look well, opened, she thought, and fastened to their bedroom wall: it was that kind of fan. The figures were lovely and the colors teased; but she was sure that the handle was not real ivory and that she had paid too much. Also, though she had given American gold, the change was in Panamanian silver. You were always cheated that way when you bought anything in the stores. Clerks would shrug and mutter that pesos and centavos were the only change they had. A lie, sure, but what could you do about it? At least, Phil reflected a little grimly, as she went out with the fan, it was nicer being cheated by a Chinaman than by a native. The few upper-class natives she had met were charming and had beautiful manners and spoke perfect English; but the average Panamanian resident of Panama confirmed Phil's first impression of him as a smudgy, surly, slightly arrogant man. Even the non-oriental shopkeepers were like that. They waited on you as though they were doing you a favor. They didn't seem to understand your Spanish, and few of them made the slightest attempt to speak English: the Chinks at least *tried*.

It was amazing, Phil thought as she walked slowly—she had learned to walk slowly—over to the Plaza. It was amazing that these men could continue to be uppish when anybody could see that three quarters of their business came either from the Americans or the people the Americans had brought here. No matter what they might think of us personally, you'd suppose, wouldn't you, that they'd be glad to treat us right so long as we had money to spend? The truth was, they ought to be eternally grateful to us. Nobody ever would have heard of their silly little country—which in fact wouldn't *be* a country but only a state—if it wasn't for us.

Only the other day, the Fourth of July, the Panama City water system had been opened; and my! the saluting and the speeches! You'd have supposed that they had done it all themselves, though everybody knew that the materials, like the engineers, had come from the States, and that, left alone, Panamanians never would have achieved anything so up to date as a municipal water system. The same thing was true about the streets, many of which were already paved while others were being paved or being surveyed for paving. She looked across the Cathedral Plaza, which a little earlier had been either a morass, a mosquito breeder, or else, less often, a dazzling baked stretch of dust and dried mud. Now it was smooth and hard; and though there had been rain twenty minutes before, no mentionable puddles formed in the Plaza. There was a concrete foundation—for lesser streets macadam was used—and on top of that a layer of fine hard vitrified brick. And where did the vitrified brick come from?

From Peoria, Illinois. And how did it come? In American ships. And who had laid it? Americans.

Phil paused at the curb, irresolute. Except when she forgot, she no longer did anything in a hurry. She had learned to take her time. Now she wanted to go to the other side of the Plaza; and her instinct suggested simply that she go there, by the most direct route, the center of the Plaza containing no more at that moment than a few flea-bitten hacks and horses, a few lice-ridden cocheros. To go around under the arcades would be to walk twice as far. On the other hand, you never knew when a rain might come up. She'd hate to get caught in the middle of the Plaza and be obliged to scamper in an undignified manner while loafers looked. They looked at you too much, anyway, these Panamanians, who seemed to think that any female under the age of fifty who ventured out alone was a nymph du pave, a fille de joie. So it was that Phil paused.

Still undecided, she was hailed. Gracie Landis and a small fast-bobbing man pattered toward her. Gracie's face was red and shone frankly with perspiration. She waved to Phil, and long before she reached Phil she started to shout.

'Dearie, it's good to see you again! Where've you been keeping yourself? Wasn't that *awful,* the way those men were at the dock there when we came in? Say, you know, I was telling Gus just the other day—'scuse me, dearie, but this is Gus. This one here. Silly little thing, ain't he? But all my own. Meet the better half, Mrs Kellems, Mr Landis, Phil, Gus. Phil and me roomed together in the same state-room coming down.'

'Oh, say, that so? Say, that's fine!' Surely this was the most extraordinary coincidence Gus had ever encountered. 'Say' he said. 'Say!'

Back to back in their bare feet, Gracie Landis and her husband might have been the same height. But he seemed much smaller. Partly this was a matter of heels. Partly it was a matter of hair: Gracie had her hair padded higher than ever, whereas Gus, Phil saw when he snatched off his hat, was virtually bald. Also, Gus, though plump in cheeks and neck, and with a startlingly large tummy, elsewhere was thin. He had toothpick legs and arms, and his chest was a trivial thing, his shoulders meager. Gracie boomed. She must have put on ten pounds, though she weighed too much on the *Allianca.* The upper part of her breasts, bulging over the top of the corset, waggled jellylike: it was really disgusting. Her cheeks shook when she chuckled.

Gus beamed. He looked a happy little man.

'What have you been *doing* with yourself, kiddo? My husband's a steam fitter. Is there a lower hole in the world than this one? Have you found a drawer you can open yet? *Where* could that many cockroaches have come from? Talk to me, sweetie!'

Phil told some of the story—about their little house, the skimpy but serviceable furniture Dr and Mrs Gorgas had somehow obtained for them, and Phil's own decorations that helped to make the place more homelike, and all the trouble they'd had getting the piano across the Isthmus.

'It's not a bad little place' she finished, smiling. 'I'm getting very fond of it. There may not be much to sit on, but there's usually a breeze. Of course the roof leaks, but on the other hand we get a lovely view of the bay.'

She had expected a laugh to greet this—Harry's friends all laughed at it—but she hadn't expected a bellow. Gracie put her chin up and roared, so that startled white-clad men shied away from her, passing on the far side of the walk, and those ahead turned, astounded. Even little Gus laughed, cackled rather, a higher and less voluminous noise than that made by his wife, but a noise of great penetrating power. Phil was embarrassed. They were really very common, both of them.

Yet she liked Gracie. You couldn't help it. Coarse though the woman was, and vulgar, still there was something *straight* about her, and certainly she was amusing. Phil even thought that she might like Gus Landis if she ever got to know him well enough. But she wasn't going to invite them to the housewarming party. No, that would be an error. It would only make everybody uneasy.

'Roof leaks but we get a lovely view of the bay! Oh my! Oh my!'

'Maybe the roof *does* leak, but we get a beautiful view——'

Phil smiled, pleased in spite of herself at the warmth of this reception. She had half a mind to ask them to the party anyway. It might shock Harry. But no, Harry the unpredictable might like them. And that would be certain to spoil the party. Not, she reflected, that Harry's friends were such polished cavaliers. She almost giggled when she thought of Harry *T* and Gracie together, Harry *T* bowing low, saying 'At thy service, O queen. The name's Thompson. T-h-o-m-p-s-o-n, with the accent on the "q" as in "cucumber,"' and Gracie guffawing an admonition for him to get away from those swingin' doors. This was a fancy, however, which she kept to herself. Now, to quiet the Landises and keep them from attracting so much attention, she went on about how nice the Gorgases had been and the Carters and Major LaGarde and the others.

'Say, you're right in with the Four Hundred here already!'

Phil told them about Rosina, a cousin of Tranquilina, through whom her services had been obtained, and about how Rosina was clean enough and willing to work, but stupid, and slow, and about how it was so difficult to teach her English—especially difficult since Phil herself knew scarcely a word of Spanish.

'I never learned that spiggoty language myself' Gus Landis declared. 'If they can't learn to talk right I don't want to talk with 'em anyway.'

'Harry doesn't feel that way' Phil said, and smiled. 'He's very serious about it. Says we owe it to these people to learn their language, if we're going to live here.'

'Great Scott! Imagine us owing the spiggoties anything! Why, it's *them* owes *us*! It ain't our fault if they ain't educated.'

'When in Rome do as the Romans do, is his motto. Though I must say, from what I remember of them I wouldn't want to be classed with most of the people of Rome that I saw.'

'She's been in Rome' Gracie informed her husband. 'Rome, Italy, I mean.'

'Is that so?'

'He takes three lessons a week, noontimes, when he's working here in town. Sometimes he's out along the Line. But when he's here he spends half his noon hour studying Spanish with this Frenchwoman. I haven't met her yet. Well, anyway, it saves him making that long trip up the hill and back again in the middle of the day.'

The thought of Mademoiselle Desmoulins was not a happy one. Harry had said that she was going to call on Phil some time soon, and that meant that Phil would practically have to invite her to the house-warming. Phil didn't like teachers, never had. They were skinny un-stylish women with flat breasts and sour eyes; and either they were garrulous and aggressive or else they were filled with humility, as though they realized that their very presence in the midst of non-teachers tended to make for gloom and the remembrance of unloved things: it was a question which type was worse. But she supposed that if the teacher *did* call she'd have to ask her. Goodness knows, they needed women! Phil felt guilty all over again at the thought that she was not inviting Gracie.

They were drifting past the bishop's palace, opposite the cathedral. The bishop, as everybody knew, lived upstairs: the ground floor was occupied by the offices of the national lottery, and on either side of the door were racks of gaudy tickets. Gracie, perhaps from laziness, nudged her husband with her eyes rather than an elbow.

'Gus, you really ought to go take a good look at them, so's you'll be perfectly sure never to buy one.'

'You women' he grumbled fondly and went to the racks like a dutiful boy.

Phil knew what was coming even before Gracie rolled her eyes.

'Well, have you seen our friend since you been here?'

'Why, no. Except for a little while when I first came ashore. This is only the second or third time I've been down in the town, as a matter of fact. Mostly I've been busy getting the house in shape. But Harry's met him several times. Harry likes him. He's asked him to come up and call on us.'

'Oh-oh! I wouldn't advise that, dearie!'

'Now see here, Grace Landis, I thought we both perfectly understood that I'm not going to——'

'Don't get sore, sweetie. I just thought I'd tell you that he's here, in case you were interested. He's hanging around Panama, the Lord knows what for. But I happened to run into him the other day, and he's got a flat on a little alley called the Calle de San Martin, over back that way, over near La Boca. Snug little lair. Regular spider web. He actually tried to lure me into it.'

'Well, from all you've said, from the way you talked on the ship——'

'You don't suppose I'd consent to go into a man's flat alone with him, do you?' cried Gracie in a voice so shrill that Phil glanced toward Gus: *he*, however, went on studying lottery tickets. 'And besides,' Gracie added, 'there were too many people around.'

Phil could not help laughing. She didn't even want to talk about Ward Wright, to whom, in the past two weeks, she had scarcely given a thought; but Gracie was irresistible.

Gracie rattled: 'Though I don't think there would be people there usually. There was a fight of some kind going on at that time. Ordinarily I'll bet it would be very quiet and you'd hardly see a soul. I guess that's why he rented it.'

She rolled her eyes, grinning, and then called her husband.

'Come along, Gus-er-ino!' (She talks to him like a dog! marveled Phil.) 'Mama's getting hungry for lunch.' To Phil: 'Why'n't you come along with us? The food's just as bad no matter where you eat it.'

'Thank you, no. I've still got so much shopping to do. And I must be home in time for tea. I'm expecting Mrs Gorgas.'

'Oh-oh! You and your society friends! Well——'

74

The Calle de San Martin was little even as Panama streets went—an alley, as Grace had said, though it was two-ended and not a cul-de-sac. Phil stared at the sign with reproach, as though she thought it had no business to be there, or, being there, at least no business obtruding itself upon her attention. She had been simply wandering from store to store, window-shopping where there were windows, looking for some souvenir she could send home to Father and Mother, since she'd left the Landises in the Plaza; and while she had known in a general way that she was getting down toward the La Boca section, she told herself that she had not consciously been looking for the Calle de San Martin. She told herself that several times. She didn't usually notice street signs. Come to think of it, here in Panama City there *were* very few such signs. This one looked new. Perhaps Ward himself had caused it to be put up.

Well, it would do no harm to stroll past the place, now that she happened to be there. She glanced down the Calle de San Martin. It was deserted. Less than a hundred and fifty feet away was another street, a larger one. Clearly the Calle de San Martin bisected a small block. She drifted down it.

On the left was a warehouse or tobacco factory, a two-story building with windows only on the second floor, and those boarded. To the right, halfway down, on the street level, was a single door; above this were three long, open windows at which canary-yellow curtains struck a note of almost jarring gaiety in that otherwise dim place. There was no doubt of the occupant. A trig sign held the words 'Ward Wright' fairly in the center of the door. The curtains were not stirred by a breeze, and there was no sound in the alley.

At the other end of the Calle de San Martin, Phil turned right, and she turned right again at the next street, a comparatively broad one. She found a café. Its name was disconcerting, the Café de los Dos Diablos, but it didn't look sinister. On the street it showed only an arcaded entrance: the tables, she could see, were in a patio behind the building.

She knew that Harry would not like her to eat in the town. He did it himself, to be sure; but then, he knew the right places. But it should be safe enough now, now that the new water system was in operation. She would be careful what she ordered. She *was* hungry. Moreover, there was an undeniable thrill in the thought of going into a café. She had felt it in Europe. She knew that here, as in Europe, a café was a restaurant; a true cosmopolite would take this for granted; but Phil could not so readily shake off the influence of Paterson, N.J., where a café was a saloon, a barroom, to which no woman, much less a lady, ever went.

She was stared at; but she was getting used to this. The patio was comfortably filled with the more prosperous sort of Panamanians, who ate and drank dreamily, smoking a lot, not talking much. She esteemed it picturesque. It must have been in the center of the small block, for each of the four sides was a separate two-story building, and each second floor had long windows opening upon a balcony. An Indian rug tossed over one or two of those balcony rails, some dried onions hanging below them, and somebody strumming a guitar somewhere: *that* would have made it a delight—provided there was no rain. Yet even rain had been anticipated. A sadly blue, canvas awning, rolled two ways to the center, could quickly be made to cover the whole of the patio which was not under balconies.

No word of the handwritten menu could she decipher, and she knew the names of few native dishes, but the waiter, a droll fellow with a twinkling eye—*he* could have been one of the two devils!— assured her, she believed, that he would bring her something nice. She asked for water, agua fria. The waiter looked askance at her; but after a while he brought a glass of some semitransparent, slightly yellowish fluid. Water? She didn't know, and she decided that she'd better not try it. She asked for a flask of wine. Red wine. Vino rojo. The strange dish he had brought made her thirsty, but she didn't drink much of the wine, which was so sharp and sour that it hurt her mouth.

Conscious that men were looking at her from time to time, not directly, and to give them credit not rudely, but with persistence, she addressed herself to the mess on her plate, trying to forget the wine. She felt rather little and mean. She should not have treated Gracie Landis that way, and of *course* she should have invited Gracie to the housewarming. Another thing: Why under the sun had she excused herself by telling Gracie that she expected Mrs Gorgas in for tea? She didn't expect Mrs Gorgas in for tea. Mrs Gorgas was a charming lady who had been very sweet and who'd helped her and Harry in more ways than could be counted; but Mrs Gorgas was not coming to tea. The truth was that the hour for tea was the very hour when Dr Gorgas had his quiet drink on the veranda and wouldn't see anybody; and Mrs Gorgas wouldn't dream of not being somewhere near him then. Everybody knew that. Gracie could call her a liar any time Gracie cared to check up. Not only a liar, a snob.

Yet there was something to be said for her claiming the Gorgases as friends. Dr Gorgas was a very important person on the Isthmus; he

76

was a very important man by any definition, a distinguished man; and he liked Harry: sitting in the Café de los Dos Diablos, eating a strange hot concoction of peppers and meats, Phil could swell at the knowledge that Dr Gorgas thought highly of Harry. There had never been a question about it. You could see it in the way Dr Gorgas talked to him —not merely the way Dr Gorgas called him by his first name, a thing the eminent sanitarian might do to almost anybody, but the way Dr Gorgas smiled when he saw Harry coming, and even the way that Dr Gorgas greeted *her*, Harry's wife. Harry was valuable. Harry was somebody. Phil did not yet know the reason for this; but she did know that her husband, low though his position might be on the pay roll, was a personage. They trusted him. Why, of course! Harry had always been a man you could trust. She leaned back, smirking a little. She wondered how some of her friends in Paterson would feel, and for that matter how Father himself would feel, if they knew how intimately she and her husband knew the Gorgases. She had written something about it in her letters to her mother: she had mentioned that Dr and Mrs Gorgas had furnished their cottage for them (she called it a cottage in the letters) and had arranged to get them a criada, which, she explained, was Panamanian for maid-of-all-work. She had written this. She'd write it again. But still, leaning back, she wondered whether they would believe it. She was very happy, not caring. She half closed her eyes. But she opened her eyes very wide when she saw Ward Wright.

Not for an instant had she tushed in her mind her position. She was in a patio and directly facing the balcony which led off Ward Wright's apartment. She knew that. She had known it when she came to this place. Nevertheless his appearance stupefied her.

Ward stood very straight, not stiff, his head up, not considering the patio but rather the sky—actually not looking anywhere—like a man who seeks a word, a name, an address. He wore a dead-white shirt which could have been silk, and which had a collar attached. This collar was carelessly open, unbuttoned. He did not wear a necktie. Yes, he stood the way he used to stand on the *Allianca*, feet apart, tipping now a little to his heels, now a little to the balls of his feet, but always sure of himself. His knuckles were at his hips. He wore fawn-colored riding breeches. He smoked a long thin blue cigar.

Well, why didn't she call out? She sat with a fork in her hand.

He blinked. Unexpectedly, at nothing, he smiled. He seemed to nod. The muscles under his cheekbones twitched, and lazily he took a hand from a hip and lifted the cigar. Blue choppy small rings of smoke one-two-three'd between his circled lips.

Why didn't she call out? He was no more than a few yards from her, a little above.

There was the time when she had been walking the deck (fourteen times around was a mile, remember?) and she'd paused to watch the group just below her. Those men had been almost the same distance from her, below her on another deck, as now she was from Ward Wright. They had been trying to persuade the great Captain Wright to shoot at some sea gulls, which swooped and swayed and sometimes inanely screeched, for this was in the Mona Passage, near Cuba. Some man, somebody she knew, whose name she didn't remember, had held a shotgun. The scene was clear in Phil's eyes as she sat in the Café de los Dos Diablos. This man (whose name she couldn't remember) was offering the shotgun to Ward, and Ward was, clearly, saying No, thanks. The man asked, Why not? Ward, whose upraised voice had reached her, replied that it wasn't sporting. What'd he expect? the man had asked. He didn't expect, on a swaying afterdeck, to hit such birds with a *rifle*? Oh no, Ward had said.

She remembered now how he had looked, with his feet spread wide, with his left fist on his hip, as he brushed his mustache with his right thumbnail. And the *Allianca* rolling back and forth. And the birds, squawking stupidly, now near, now upwinding far away.

Suddenly Ward had cried 'Why a rifle, even?' and had drawn a fancy pearl-handled revolver with a long shiny barrel. Phil had closed her eyes. The last thing she had had in her mind's mirror when she closed her eyes was Ward steelily balanced, that bright weapon in his hand. She had heard the shots, but they'd been that many pips, meaning nothing. Pip-pip-pip-pip—she didn't know how many. Afterward everybody had told her, Gracie Landis most of all, that Ward had fired five times and had made exactly five birds swump-oo into the sea. Then Ward had whuffed the wisp of smoke from the muzzle and had made the revolver disappear. Phil had heard the story many times. 'You got another shot in that gun, ain't you, Captain?' 'I always save one cartridge' Ward had answered. Easy, sure of himself. He had whispered to her later that he was ashamed of the display, and afraid that she, a woman who had traveled, and who knew all sorts of people, would think badly of his showing-off; but, he had whispered, the temptation, that man holding a *shotgun* there, had been too great. Did she mind?

Did she mind!

Up there on the balcony stood Ward Wright, setting heavy white regular teeth into the cigar.

Why in God's name was a woman, any woman, as silly as this? The man was nothing but a strong, very handsome man, and probably not half as good as Harry, really.

She remembered the time when Mr McCormack had come apologetically to the place between the ventilator and the lifebelt locker and had informed Captain Wright that the passengers were trying to get up a little sort of entertainment, to pass the time away, the night after the next, and would he co-operate. Ward had smiled.

'Well, as a matter of fact I have no parlor tricks. Now Mrs Kellems here——'

'Mrs Kellems has been kind enough to promise us that she would lend her talent. She's going to play the accompaniment while her cabinmate Mrs Landis sings "Down Where the Wurtzburger Flows." Mrs Landis, you know, is very entertaining.'

'Yes, I know.'

'Mrs Kellems has been very kind about offering to help. But we wondered about you, Captain. We hoped you might maybe tell us some stories about your adventures?'

'I'm sorry' Ward had replied. 'I don't ever talk about them.'

He had said it rather solemnly. Mr McCormack had cried that the Captain shouldn't be so modest.

'It isn't modesty. It's good business.'

Back through the canary-yellow curtains went Ward Wright from the balcony, and Phil, who had not cried out, rose. The waiter said something, she didn't know what, and she gave him money. The change of course was in Panamanian silver. Hardly a doubt that she had been cheated. Why hadn't she called? He'd have heard and been right down. What if she was the only woman there? What if everybody in the place had sneered and winked?

She thought afterward that this should be the low point in her life, her leaning, actually leaning against a lamppost. Absurd. Funny in a cartoon, some drunken man in evening clothes, with crisscrosses for eyes. Not funny when you did it yourself.

'Señora, servidor de Usted? Esta Usted enferma? Puedo llamar un coche?'

She didn't know what was being said. From the tone she gathered that kindness was meant. She didn't want help, though. She could handle this herself. She had no intention of confessing that those tubes which a little earlier had been her legs were long flat things now filled

79

with warm turning-around air; surely she was not going to explain to just anybody why the wife of a man who after all was very close to Dr Gorgas should be leaning against a lamppost; and she was not going to faint. She got her chin up.

'The sun' she muttered. 'I'm sorry.'

Whoever he was, he didn't understand her. That was all right. At least he did seem quiet and gentle. She tried to make out the words he said. Only 'coche' had caught at her ears.

'Yes' she said. 'Please. Si, si, coche. Si.'

Even seated, and even after the cochero had whipped the horse and they'd started to jolt, she was bewildered. She wished she had been more polite to that man, whoever he was. No matter. The point was, she'd lost all control of herself for a little while there. Why? Because of Ward. Yes, because of Ward. Yes, admit it!

Was there nothing more to a woman than that? Was there no more than that to a decent, well-brought-up woman? Just the *sight* of a man —All right, he was good-looking! Harry was good-looking too. Harry was her husband. Harry would take care of her. Harry——

'Where are you going, driver?'

'Until this juncture, ma'am, you have desisted from divulging your destination.'

'I have—— See here, are you trying to be funny?'

Some of them couldn't speak any English at all, and others, she remembered Harry telling her, spoke an English that even an Englishman would have to look up in the dictionary. 'They're not insulting you' Harry had told her. Harry! 'You'll think they are, but they're not. It's just their way of talking.' Harry! Where in the world *was* he?

'Take me to the Cathedral Plaza.'

'Ma'am, I shall disembark you at that point of establishment.'

Now the Cathedral Plaza happened to be the only direction she could give a driver; and though she did not want anything there, surely she could straighten herself out there, get her bearings, and perhaps walk a little, and breathe, and then hail another coche, and after that she could drive up to what she still liked to call (kidding Harry) the Cemetery. But first, air. First, a moving around. If only she could have Harry to get close to and talk to and——

She got out of the cab; and not ten feet away was Harry, talking to the prettiest woman Phil had seen in years.

Harry lay in bed thinking about Georgie Walsh, the Pirates fan. He had been permitted to see Georgie two days before Georgie died.

But the man was dead even then, for all practical purposes. Harry had been obliged to stand outside the screen cage. Laughing uneasily, trying to cheer him up, Harry had pointed out that the Giants were at the top of the league already, had asserted that they were going to stay there too, had asked where Pittsburgh was, had answered his own question by saying that Pittsburgh was so far down in the league that you wouldn't even be able to make it out if it wasn't for all the coal smudges on the uniforms, and had added that as for Honus Wagner *he* couldn't hit a basketball with a board. Afterward Harry had wept a little. Georgie Walsh, looking right at him, had shown no anger or excitement, not even any interest. In Georgie's eyes there had been room only for pain; and it was then that Harry gave up hope. 'You must go out now. He's beginning to retch again.' Georgie in fact was vomiting when Harry tiptoed from the ward. Black slimy stuff. That's what the Panamanians called yellow jack: el vomito negro, the black vomit.

Harry, gazing at the ceiling, thought of this.

Phil was taking off her shoes, unlacing, unlacing. There were some women in Panama who said that low shoes were all right in a climate like this, where the sensible thing was the most stylish, or should be. They were practical women, nurses in fact. Phil of course wouldn't be found dead in low shoes; but there were times—indeed there was one such time each morning and one each night—when she did wish that the fashion would change. And if you broke a lace, then you could count on losing at least half an hour.

'You never told me your Spanish teacher was such a stunner, dear.'

'Eh? Oh. She is nice-looking, isn't she? Yes.'

'Why, she took the breath out of me! I always thought of teachers as crabby old maids who squinted at you.'

'Well, of course she isn't really a teacher. She just does that for pin money. Her father hasn't got much of a job. And her mother's dead. Her mother died of yellow jack here five-six years ago, and that was when Madeline left the convent where she was studying in France—you know, not a nun or anything, she was just like a pupil in a boarding school——'

'I know how they do in France, dear.'

'She left, and came here to be with her father.'

'Did she tell you all that in Spanish?'

'Oh well, she talks English too. Though as a matter of fact, you two talked French most of the time, didn't you, when you met her this afternoon?'

Phil gave a little laugh. She got the second shoe off at last and gratefully slid her hot feet into mules.

'Well, what *she* talked was, of course. But I'm afraid my own French is pretty rusty.'

'Well, it all sounded the same to me, as far as that goes. I'm glad you like Madeline.'

'Oh, she's very nice. I should think she'd be rushed off her feet in a place like this, a woman as pretty as she is, where there are practically no single white women at all.'

'Oh, I guess she wouldn't have any trouble getting a husband, if it wasn't for her father.'

'What does he do? Sick a bulldog on them when they come sparking her?'

'Worse than that. He insults all Americans every time he gets a chance. He's not right upstairs. Bats in the belfry. Doves in the dome. He thinks all Americans are wicked. I imagine from what I've seen of him, and from things Madeline has said, that he was a very brilliant man at one time. But he's certainly gone to pieces.'

Phil squirmed out of her skirt, untied the drawstring of her petticoat and stepped out of the petticoat, unbuttoned and slipped off her corset cover, started unhooking her corset. She wondered if Harry was watching.

'What is it he doesn't like about Americans?'

'Everything. You see, he had a lot of money at one time. They were a very aristocratic family. And then he lost a lot of it and he sank the rest in the De Lesseps company that started to build the canal here twenty years ago. Every penny he had.'

'Every centime might be a more accurate way of putting it.'

'Well, anyway, they made him an official of the company, and he came out here to live, and brought his wife and two sons with him, because that was considered the thing to do. The idea was to show the workmen that the higher-ups weren't afraid of diseases. Otherwise they'd have had to pay impossible prices.

'Well, he stuck it out all through the bankruptcy and the reorganization and everything, and he was still here when the U.S.A. took over. But his wife and two sons were dead by that time. Yellow fever. That was why Madeline came over to join him.'

Phil gave him a sideways look and was disappointed to see that he wasn't watching her undress, as he usually did. Well, he would watch her when she did her hair. He couldn't resist that sight.

The corset extended almost to her knees. At last she unclicked the bottommost hook and unfastened the garters. She pulled her under-shirt over her head, and swiftly, with a little cry, snatched and put on her peignoir. It was a bright blue thing and became her. It was cer-tainly a peignoir, for she'd bought it in Paris, hadn't she? It made her fume to hear Harry refer to it as a wrapper.

'Why doesn't he go back to France, if he doesn't like Americans?'

Under the peignoir she had started to work off her drawers and her stockings. Still Harry stared at the ceiling.

'Used to the place, I suppose. Maybe fascinated by it. It does hit some people that way, you know. And what would he do back in France? He's got a job here, at least, even if it is a temporary one. He's translating some kind of engineering records. Actually he gets his in-come from the U. S. Government, but all the same he hates Ameri-cans. Claims we're upstarts. Madeline says you never know when he might explode on that subject. That's why she doesn't dare have any-body at her house.'

'I see.'

Phil was hanging up her underwear. She was proud of that under-wear, especially of the shirt and corset cover, which were pink. The drawers had a pink ribbon worked through them, but the corset cover and shirt were all pink. Phil remembered how her mother had raged at sight of them. 'Why—why only *fancy* women wear colored under-wear! Only *bad* women!' 'Not nowadays, Mother. Anybody can wear them now. In fact they're very stylish. Bett Haviland told me the other day she'd seen pink and baby-blue corset covers both, at Stewart's.' A snort. 'Well, I'll bet she never saw them at *McCutcheon's?*' 'No-o, she didn't say *that*.' Phil wished that Harry had been looking at her when she took off that underwear: then he would be sure to want her. Well, he would anyway.

'Somehow he's got it into his head that the Americans are respon-sible for the French failure. That's crazy, of course. If it hadn't been for us, the French outfit wouldn't have even salvaged that little matter of forty million. But anyway that's what he thinks. And he says he wants to be here when *we* fail. He's sure we're going to.'

'A lot of people seem to think that.'

'Yes, I guess a lot of people do.'

'A lot of people think that we ought to have built the canal at Nic-aragua, too.'

Ward Wright thought that. She remembered how he had given his opinion, the first afternoon they met; and she winced at the memory. 'Yes.'

'What do *you* think, precious? *You* think it'll be finished, don't you?'

'It'll be finished' Harry said.

She sat at her dressing table, lifted over the hairpin tray, opened the combings box; and then, sure that he was looking at her, with languor she lifted her hands to the back of her neck, where she broke the eight.

The rats she removed swiftly and dropped them into an open drawer. They were all made from her own hair; but at best a rat was an unromantic article. She took out combs, barrettes, pins. She shook her hair loose and thrilled to feel it tumble around her shoulders, down her back. She started to brush it.

She no longer talked; and this was not because she was absorbed in her task, but because she feared that conversation would haze the picture. She brushed slowly, with deliberation, with long strokes. A pity the hair never crackled down here, the way it sometimes did up north. Hair here kept its luster, but it had no snap.

She studied her reflection as she brushed. She even put her head a little to one side, flirtatiously. What a humiliating exhibition that had been this afternoon! She felt her cheeks go hot at the memory of it. She was not going to let anything like that happen again. It had been simply disgusting, and the only good thing to be said about it was that at least nobody else knew of it. Why, she had been as weak as a kitten for a few minutes there! It was almost like being unfaithful to Harry. But she'd make up to Harry, in a little while. She was always warm with him anyway, for she loved him; but this night would be something special, when he would learn how truly wonderful she could be. He wouldn't know the cause, but he was going to find the effect very pleasant indeed, Phil determined as with cocked head, smiling a little, she combed and combed her hair.

At first she thought to plait it and tie the ends with ribbon, as she ordinarily did, but then it occurred to her that it would be more exciting for Harry—if he needed any more excitement after watching her all this while—if she just let it hang loose.

She rose, turning her back to the bed, resisting the temptation to peek at him. She slipped off the peignoir, and very quickly, exposing her nakedness only for an instant, pulled on her nightgown. She patted down its collar, adjusted its cuffs. Then, her back still to the bed, and with a gesture she knew Harry would love, she raised both arms and dexterously swished her hair so that it fell outside of the nightgown. She turned, smiling.

Harry was sound asleep.

84

6

THE PIECE OF ICE from Boston might even cost more than the bowl Harry had borrowed from a nurse. Goodness knew why that nurse had brought a punch bowl to the Canal Zone; but then, people did bring all sorts of odd things. As far as Phil and Harry were concerned, the bowl cost only an invitation gladly given. Miss Hoffman wasn't any Lillian Russell, but she was a woman. The sugar cost a sum not small. As for the fruit: 'Seventy-five cents a dozen for oranges! Why, I never paid more than sixty in *Paterson!*' Harry explained that the Panamanians didn't grow much, only what they thought they could eat. The rum was the cheapest ingredient.

The ice cost six dollars for a two-hundred-pound cake *on the schooner.* By the time it had been repacked, wrapped in burlap, hoisted to the dock, drayed to the station, checked to Panama City, and carted up Ancon Hill, it cost almost three dollars more.

'Imagine Americans without ice! It's disgraceful!'

'Well, of course this is a pretty funny place, and we're not used to it yet. They're building an ice plant over in Colon. They say we might get deliveries the end of the year.'

'And all the way from Boston! How do they ever keep it from melting?'

'Sawdust. It's nowhere near as hot in the hull of a wooden schooner as it is belowdecks on a steel ship. Took 'em a little over three weeks. The Boston Ice Company. Does seem silly, doesn't it? But those slow-sailing boats don't need much of a crew, and of course no fuel, and they get cheaper, heavier cargoes.'

He grinned at the ice before covering it again.

'Remember how you used to jump up on the back step of the wagon and swipe a chunk? It was all steamy back there, and the floor was all big spongy wet dull splinters, and there was a rack for the ax and a hook for the tongs. And remember the scales? You ever swing from those scales, Phil?'

'I started to, once. But the iceman came back.'

'He was always coming back at the wrong time, wasn't he?' Harry put the ice over near the door. 'Almost nine bucks. Used to be we'd get a five-cent piece and it would last all day, and it was almost a quarter as big as this one at that.'

'We always got a ten-cent piece every day' said Phil.

For the fourth time she looked at her right breast and remembered that she was not wearing a shirtwaist and so not wearing her watch. She had on the green gown from Paris: it was old, but nobody here had seen it. She went into the bedroom and found her watch in a trunk tray. Seven-thirty. They would be coming soon.

It might be clear, she reflected as she looked out a window, and it was a pity Harry wouldn't hear of Japanese lanterns on what remained of the French lawn. Harry's veto had been prompt and emphatic. The mosquitoes! Nighttime was just the time the malaria spreaders liked. True, there wasn't any shrubbery near by; but why take a chance? Nobody was certain yet—though they were making experiments—how far the Anopheles really could fly. Malaria was not yellow jack, no, but in the long run it was more serious. Get yellow jack—and within a few days you were either dead or recovering. Thereafter you were immune. Nobody ever got yellow fever a second time. You suffered hideously; but if you came through you were all right. On the other hand, get nipped by an Anopheles which had previously sucked somebody who was malarial, and you came down with chills and fever, which, if not as sensational as yellow jack, was sensational enough. Malaria was not often fatal, but it kept coming back, two, three, four, even five times a year, each bout taking a little more from a man's corporal and spiritual strength. The natives were immune to yellow fever, presumably because they'd all had mild unnoticed attacks as children; and so they did not help to spread this disease. But practically every Panamanian, man, woman, and child, habitually was malarial. They walked around with it all their lives.

No, no Japanese lanterns. No garden party. That was final! Phil had submitted meekly enough.

She was not pleased with the house. Yet it was so *very* shacklike, as she'd told Harry, that it was droll. At least it didn't pretend to be anything but what it was.

Chez Kellems, as she called it, consisted of four square rooms of identical size, each square, each leading to the next by means of a narrow doorway in which no door was hung, so that they formed a row. There were no closets, there was no bathroom. They did not have a veranda. They had electric lights, though! One light, one wan bulb hanging from a wire wrapped in flypaper, was in the exact center of each room.

The first room, which faced the bay and really did afford a breathless view, they had made into the parlor. The second room was their dining room, the third their bedroom, the fourth their kitchen and washing room. The actual toilet was in a tiny house some yards back of the kitchen, and it was a horrid place where the air was choky with disinfectant. Electric lights but no running water—in the year 1905 in an American home! Rosina, a hunchback who seldom spoke, and never stopped working, brought water in a pail from a nearby tap. In a corner of the kitchen Harry had rigged a shower. It was worked by a wooden lever which tipped water from one kerosene tin into a second, upright one, suspended from the ceiling. In the bottom of the second tin holes had been punched, and through these the water spiraled upon the person beneath. Some of it went just anywhere; but Harry had worked carefully with a spirit level before selecting the site of the shower, and he was pleased when most of the water, like a housebroken dog, went to the back door. You could open the door just before you stepped under this lowering Damoclean device, and then everything would be all right—except that Harry worried about that door being ajar, even for a few minutes, with waste water forming a little pool outside. You couldn't be too careful about mosquitoes. After each shower, whether it had been his or his wife's, Harry went around with a flyswatter.

Phil sighed. She would never be able to tell in letters what it was like to keep house in a place without water, without inside doors, without closets, and in a land of merciless heat and rain. People in Paterson would never be able to understand how everything came apart in air which neutralized glue; how, contrariwise, all manner of drawers and sliding things refused to be budged.

Still it would be all right tonight. Everybody tonight understood. She tilted her chin a bit and smiled at her reflection.

Harry passed through on his way to the kitchen. 'You look swell' he called. She smiled the broader; but soon the smile settled back to fixedness as she studied her reflection. She *was* nervous, no denying. She had been hostess before, but never in her own house. It was different here, with only one servant, and her a girl Phil could scarcely understand; without Father and Mother; with the guests virtual strangers. Yet why should she be nervous about receiving such people? They were all right, these associates of Harry, and some were even rather nice; but except for Ward, and Darl Winter, and perhaps that French girl who taught Spanish, there was nobody with whom in Paterson she would even be likely to come in contact, much less entertain. As for the house, if it was strange, that was not her fault. *She*, as a matter of fact, had done wonders with it. And she could laugh at it. 'Be it ever so humble' she whispered, practicing the laugh.

She looked around. It would be awkward, asking men and women alike to leave their hats and things here. Well, there was nothing else to do. The closet for clothes was a curtained-off corner.

Harry's coat and vest, and his collar and tie and cuffs, the links in the cuffs, were on the bed: he meant to don them at the last moment. It was his blue serge suit, the only good one he had, and fortunately light for serge: it was impossible to buy alpaca or linen or seersucker in Panama. Phil had begged him to wear his full-dress suit, but he'd refused. None of the other boys had full-dress suits, he had said. 'Captain Wright wore his every night on the ship.' 'That's different. These boys—after all I used to live with them—and I happen to know that nobody brought the soup-and-fish—if they've even got them at home.' 'Yes,' she undertoned, 'if they've even got them at home.'

. It annoyed her, when she stopped to think of it, how often Harry overrode her. He was good-natured; but time and again, pleading his greater knowledge of conditions on the Isthmus, he got his own way. She could remember ever so many occasions in the past few weeks. . . . Abruptly she went to the kitchen.

Harry and Rosina were making sandwiches, Harry maintaining a patter of what was no doubt barbarous Spanish, Rosina, as always, tittering. Harry got on well with Rosina. Phil did not believe that the girl understood a tenth of what Harry said, whereas Phil herself spoke slowly and carefully and with gestures, so that the servant could grasp the simple orders. But Rosina just liked Harry. She brightened when he came home.

'It's sweet of you, dearest, but do you mind not spreading that butter so thick? Forty-two cents a pound! And it's canned!'

'Oh, sure. We'll be careful.'

Phil glanced at the punch bowl, half filled, lacking only ice. The ice was an ungainly moist bundle of burlap on the floor near the door, where it would be benefited by whatever movement of air there might be.

'They're likely to start coming any minute now. Don't you——'

'Absolutely!'

She wandered back through the various rooms, set end to end, 'the bridal suite' they sometimes called it. Troubled about her slippers, she side-glanced at the cheval glass she'd brought. She noted no mold.

Shoes and slippers were even worse than clothes in this country. Mold overran them in a matter of hours, and if they were neglected they were ruined. You had to brush them hastily and put them out in the sunlight every time there was a lull in the rain. If the sun never did show, then you had to place them around the ever burning charcoal stove. Nor could you do this just before Harry came home, for his clothes were sure to be wet.

The dining room was bleak. They simply didn't have enough furniture, or enough pictures for the walls. However, tonight the lack of furniture might be an advantage. The punch bowl would be in the dining room, and Phil knew that men preferred to stand around it, scorning chairs. Why did men like to stand up when they drank? The dining room would have been even more bleak without a dozen gorgeous roses which had arrived late in the afternoon. Harry had not been home; and Rosina, summoned to question the native messenger, had only giggled. Phil had smiled at the messenger and had put her right thumbnail to her upper lip to brush back an imaginary mustache, and then her left thumbnail to her left upper lip. The boy had nodded, snickering, and had run away before Phil could find a cinco-centavo.

Harry had been pleased by the roses.

'Say, he certainly thinks of things, doesn't he?'

'Well, we don't really know, dear.'

'Oh, it's Wright all right! Yes sirree! Where do you suppose he got them? Where in the world——'

'Yes, I guess it would be hard to find roses here.'

'*Hard?*' He had looked at her. 'Why, it's *impossible!* At least——'

'Oh. You looked, then?'

'Well, sure. Government time. I felt pretty guilty about it. But this man Wright—— *Where* do you suppose he found them?'

'I don't know' Phil had answered, sighing and laughing at the same time. 'And I don't care. Because I love you so much!'

All the same, Phil thought now, looking at those roses, Ward *had* found them. And they certainly helped the dining room.

She went into the parlor.

This was her triumph. She could honestly say to herself that she had made this room comfy. If it was not like a parlor at home—it was more a sort of den—at least it held objects calculated to make the beholder know that people of taste lived here. The efforts of Colonel and Mrs Gorgas and their friends had resulted in enough articles of furniture, chairs and tables and rugs, to make the storehouse habitable; but anybody could see that it was the touches Phil had given it which made the parlor what it was. Touches. Little things here and there. And some things not so little: those four Maxfield Parrish prints would add something to any room, and on the bookshelf there were books you didn't just pick up anywhere—'I love to read,' Phil used to tell people, 'but somehow nowadays I never seem to have the *time!*' Granted, the window seat was packing cases; but Phil had spread a Navajo blanket over them, a real Navajo, which Father and Mother had purchased in New Mexico the time they took the train to California and back; and at either end were pillows, one an Indian head, the other Niagara Falls, both burned by Phil herself and better than most such pieces.

And—there was the piano.

It was a Chickering. Back of the lyres that made up its façade, dark blue silk was tastefully pleated. Over an end of it was a Spanish shawl she had bought in Marseille. She had never reached Spain; but Marseille was near Spain. Phil used to describe the shawl as a thing she'd picked up in Europe.

Even though Rosina was a good worker, there was a lot for Phil to do here; and when she'd get tired and lonesome she would come into this room and look around, and sometimes sit down and play a little. Oh, it wasn't Paterson! When she had received guests previously it was with a deep rug under her feet, a servant at the plate-glass door, and behind her the staircase and the grand mahogany figure of a woman upholding a spray of yellow electric bulbs. But that had never been her own home. Then she had not been Mrs Kellems.

She began to get nervous again.

She heard Harry place the punch bowl on the dining-room table, and heard his step; and then she felt his arm snake around her waist.

'Now please, darling, don't muss my hair! You've got to——'

'I won't muss your hair.'

'But you've got to remember that——'

'A man can kiss his wife, can't he?'

A man did. Afterward he held her a little away.

'Look, sweetness. I've been awful busy with one thing and another, and I never really have had a chance to——'

'Dear, this isn't the time for anything like that!'

'Any time's the time to tell you I love you, isn't it? Ah, Phil, you wonderful girl! It isn't only that I love you, it's that I *admire* you so much! Gollys, darling, you came here finding me in a dump like this, and I tried to tell you to go away and you stuck to me, no matter what happened you stuck to me——'

'Harry precious, the reason is—— You know, Harry——'

She felt like crying, but of course she didn't dare to. He patted her with large slow hands.

'Sure, I know you figure I never do think of how much you've sacrificed and all that. I do, though! Why, Phil darling, time and again it comes to me what a lucky man I am! Phil, listen, sweetheart—*I* know it isn't very nice here. *I* know that the men are sort of rough and not like what you—well, you know. Listen, Phil, it isn't the way you and I should do it, and it isn't the way we *will* do it, is it, my little sweetness? It—it's hard to explain how I feel. But if maybe I could tell you that I have every confidence in the world in you—— Hell, that sounds dippy, doesn't it?'

'*Harry!*'

'I'm sorry, dear. I'm excited. I mean, I'm excited telling you how much I love you.'

Forgiving him, she blubbed against his chest: 'There is no reason why you should feel that way, dearest. Why *shouldn't* I be with you? I'm your wife, aren't I?'

'There's every reason in the world why I should feel that way! You didn't have to marry me in the first place, you didn't have to come down here, and once you saw how it was——'

He was trying to kiss her, and she raised her head, and the brass collar button, dangling insipidly, clamored for attention.

'Harry! You haven't put your collar on yet! Or even your cuffs!'

'Sweetest, let me tell you first about——'

'They'll be *here!*'

Beyond the screen was blackness, but the sound of a carriage came clear. Harry released her.

'Gollys, I'm sorry! Won't take me a second! If you'll just——'

'*Hurry!*'

She could hear the people getting out of the hack. She put her chin up, carefully lifted her arms, with her hands touched the pompadour and then the eight, and lowered her arms and straightened her back. How do you do? Harry would be all right. Everything would be all right. How do you do? After all, these people were not very important. It's so good of you to come!

The masculine tendency to gather around a punch bowl was unfortunate on a party where there were sixteen men and three women.

Dr and Mrs Gorgas did drop in, as they'd promised, but they stayed only a few minutes. Saturday night was like any other night to Dr Gorgas. 'More than two months since he's been home before the wee sma' hours' Mrs Gorgas told Harry. Harry knew too that Dr Gorgas was up and out on his first visit to the wards soon after seven each morning. 'He'd give anything to stay and hear you sing, Harry. But you know how it is?' 'It'll get better.' 'Why, of course it will' she replied. 'William will clean it up.'

The colonel's temper was unruffled, his suit was unwrinkled, his eyes shone. He slipped away for a moment, to have a drink with the boys. He exclaimed about the precious wonderful ice.

Somebody was humming 'Under the Anheuser Bush,' and that reminded Harry T of a limerick. It was a beer limerick, he announced, glancing archly toward the parlor. He wasn't sure whether he ought to repeat it in the presence of a colonel. He didn't know how colonels felt about limericks. Colonels loved them, Dr Gorgas gravely assured him. Well then, it was a beer limerick—

> 'There was a young girl from Anheuser
> Who swore that no one could surprise 'er.
> But Pabst took a chance,
> Found——'

From the doorway Mrs Gorgas said that she was sorry to interrupt, for doubtless they had been discussing some technical phase of the canal venture? Oh yes, they cried, smirking. Mrs Gorgas said that she knew that her husband was interested in technical problems of that nature, but also she was sure that he wouldn't want to keep Major LaGarde waiting, and it was after eight now.

'Quite right' Dr Gorgas said. He finished his drink. He made a solemn semicircular bow. 'We will continue this discussion at some later date, I trust, gentlemen? I may say that I have found it extremely interesting. *Extremely* interesting.' He turned. 'My dear?'

When he had gone they simpered fondly after him. They listened to him speaking an impeccable farewell to host and hostess. Then they readdressed themselves to their drinks. Harry K appeared with two empty punch glasses.

'Hey, you louts! You're supposed to be in the parlor.'

'Absolutely. Only thing is, there's one little piece of unfinished business before the house——'

'It's a beer limerick' Harry T said. 'It's about beer.'

'Friends, Romans, countrymen, I'm lending you my ears' Harry K intoned, and filled the two glasses, and looked up expectantly.

'How nice of you' somebody said.

> *'There was a young girl from Anheuser*
> *Who swore that no one could surprise 'er——'*

'Cheese it, the cops!'

'No, not the cops, only me' Phil said from the doorway.

'We're coming right in, Mrs Kellems! Absolutely!'

They sang 'In the Evening by the Moonlight' and 'Way Down Yonder in the Cornfield' and 'In the Good Old Summertime,' and twice they sang 'By the Light of the Silvery Moon.' They praised Phil's playing, and four of them struggled to turn sheets for her. Harry T called plaintively for 'Bedelia, I Want to Steal Ya' and 'Always Leave Them Laughing When You Say Good-bye,' but they sang 'Under the Bamboo Tree' and 'Wait Till the Sun Shines, Nellie.' Harry T wailed that what he wanted was 'Everybody Works but Father,' but they sang 'In the Shade of the Old Apple Tree' and 'Good-bye, Dolly Gray.'

'All right, Harry T' Phil called, and without a pause she swung into 'You Can't Play in Our Yard' and then 'Alexander, Don't You Love Your Baby Any More?' and then

> *'Coax me, go on and coax me,*
> *I'll be your tootsie-wootsie if you coax me.'*

She stopped, and they all laughed, and somebody asked for something else, and somebody handed her a glass of punch; but she said no, one other thing first.

'This is special for my better half' she warned, and played the first line of the chorus of 'Mighty Lak a Rose' and then vamped.

'Come on, Harry! Let's hear it!'

'Come on!'

'The guys that don't go to church have got a right to hear you *some* time, haven't they?'

So he sang it. Nor would she let him go with just that. She played the first line of the chorus of 'Sing Me to Sleep,' and again the demand was vociferous, so that Harry sang the whole thing through, both verses, both choruses. It made him feel good to sing like this, among friends, among people who really enjoyed it.

Carmichael had tears in his eyes at the end of the song, and so did Harry T. They were all quiet.

'Gosh, now I catch on why you married him, Mrs Kellems' Ed Lester said. 'Up to this time we'd all wondered.'

Harry himself never understood the feeling people had when he sang. He liked to sing, and he was glad that people liked to hear him. He knew he had a good voice. More immediately he knew that Phil loved to have him sing, even when she wasn't showing him off, as she was now. But he did not think of himself as musical. When people talked about classical music he got embarrassed. He knew very little about music. If you were rich, he supposed, and had plenty of time, it would be fun to learn about such things. Phil, for instance, had been to the opera in New York. Harry didn't savvy things like opera. He had the conviction, always, that if real music started up, if people were present who knew what music really was, he would look and sound ridiculous. He was always afraid that somebody would learn that he was no De Reszke. They never seemed to.

Phil finished, whirling, laughing, and clapped her hands.

'What about some more punch? And Harry, I *think* we might have something to eat in the kitchen, if you'll just poke up that friend Rosina of yours.' She told the others: 'You know, I can't do a thing with Rosina, but all Harry has to do is just look at her and stammer some gibberish I'm perfectly sure the poor girl can't make head or tail of—and she'll do anything he asks!'

'Ah, there! You'd better watch out! He always did have a bad reputation among us D.M.s, you know!'

Except for Ward Wright and Phil and Madeline, and of course the glum non-co-operative Miss Hoffman, these were the same persons Bertram waited upon, the same poker players, the sweating steaming joshers who called themselves the D.M.s. It was ordinarily interpreted as Disgusted Millionaires, though there were other explanations, mostly derogatory.

However, they were not to eat yet. Since nobody else appeared to think of it, and since Phil herself so clearly wanted to be asked to play something serious, Madeline spoke the request.

'Oh, I don't play at all well' Phil answered, laughing. 'Won't *you* play something for us, mademoiselle?'

'No, with thanks. I no longer have a piano.'

'Ah, that must be hard! A piano can be such a consolation when you're feeling blue! See here,' impulsively, 'I understand how you feel about being rusty and not wanting to disgrace yourself, but if you should feel like just practicing a bit, or even playing, why don't you come up here and help yourself? I mean that! We won't call it a visit unless you happen to feel sociable. You simply come and sit down and play as long as you want, any old time. I'll act as if you weren't here.'

Madeline was astounded. It was a kind offer. Madeline could think of no friend, here or in France, who would be likely to urge such an interruption to her household routine.

'Thank you very much.'

'You'll remember that, now, won't you?'

'I will not forget it' Madeline said. 'But yourself, madame? Didn't I see some Chopin on the top of the piano?'

'Oh, do you like Chopin? I just adore his things!'

Madeline only half listened, studying Phil's back and arms. She was glad that Darlington Winter, and not one of the others, was her companion. Of them all, excepting Harry, Darl was the most sympathique. You didn't even have to speak to him, if you did not feel like it; and you could be sure he wouldn't thrust himself upon your thoughts. Darl Winter was no oaf. He was quieter and better educated than the others, and he had the air of a man who came from a good home and had known prosperity. He wore glasses, but his aspect was one of determination and even grimness.

Madeline, enormously interested in her, had seen Phil only twice. The first meeting, in the Cathedral Plaza, had been brief, and clearly at that time Phil was laboring under some mental stress. This was the second time, tonight. In the Plaza, Phil had not been happy; and Madeline was astonished at her appearance at the housewarming. 'There' Madeline had said to herself 'is a contented woman, malheureusement.' Madeline since that moment had been less sure of the appraisal. *Was* Phil happy? In the immediate present, at least, she was having a good time. She was pleased with herself, with her husband, even with their odd house. 'Be it ever so humble' she had said several times, making fun of the place. Well, what in the world did she want? As quarters in Panama went, this was a palace.

Madeline, however, was not interested in the house but in its mistress. *Was* she happy? Madeline believed that Phil was a woman of tactile emotions, who might exercise charm when she wanted to, who had wit and fire and even talent when things went her way, but not a woman who could endure monotony. She could be strong and if necessary cunning. Adversity would spine her: tell her that she should not do a thing or must not have a thing, and she'd work and fight without pause or scruple to do it, to get it. But in the ordinary affairs of life she needed an audience, Madeline decided. A woman who needs an audience, when for a little while she doesn't have one, can be as erratic, as dangerous, as moody and unpredictable as any dipsomaniac deprived of alcohol, or a cocaine fiend whose supply has been cut. Right now this woman playing the piano was placid. But there was no telling what she might do when lonesomeness set in.

Madeline knew lonesomeness. Not in five years, since she had left the convent, had she had a confidant. Her father, crazed by grief after the loss of his fortune and family, was often incoherent, always a whit eccentric; and since the coming of the Americans he had been almost unbearable. He had his moments; and behind it all, and much as he cursed almost everybody else, he was personally kind to Madeline. There were times when the two were positively gay together. She respected her father, and sometimes even admired him; but he was not an intimate companion. There were few Frenchwomen left on the Isthmus, and none of her own age or class; nor did the Americans appear to be bringing women. The Spanish lessons gave her something to do and kept her in spending money; but with only two pupils, Harry Kellems and this same Darlington Winter, at her side, was she at all close. Well, she could not tell Harry how she loved him. He would be shocked. He would refuse to see her again. As for Darl, she believed that he was more than half in love with her, or supposed himself to be. To tell him how she felt about Harry would only be to wound him. So she told nobody.

She studied this woman Phyllis. Everything depended upon Phyllis.

Phil played two preludes and the Nocturne in E Flat, and the applause was loud.

'What do you think?' Madeline asked Darl under their clapping hands.

'Terrible. Too much soul. She thinks those pauses are dramatic, but all they sound like is just that she's trying to figure out how to form her fingers for the next chord.'

'And now' cried Phil 'I really *do* want those refreshments! My, I'm starved!'

It was Phil's night, and she enjoyed it; and Madeline, watching her, knew that she was seeing the woman at her best. The D.M.s, including Harry, 'the graduate D.M.' Ed Lester called him, were enthralled, and excepting Darl, never a talkative man, and who this night kept close to Madeline, they clustered around Phil with praises of her furniture, her sandwiches and punch, her playing, most of all herself. Madeline was affable when addressed, but scarcely flirtatious, for she was thinking. Miss Hoffman, though she might have been enjoying herself, maintained a turtle's reserve. Phil had the boys to herself.

Madeline was not at all times sure whether her hostess was condescending or whether it was a pose. Marvin Hart had fought Jack Root in Reno a few days before, with the retiring champion Jim Jeffries as referee; and the talk about this Phil smilingly encouraged, because, she said, she wanted them to feel at home. Hart had won by a knockout in the twelfth, and officially at least was being acclaimed the champion. Most of the D.M.s disputed the validity of this title.

Phil cried: 'But I don't understand! The champion certainly has a perfect right to retire, if he wants to, hasn't he?'

Well, they supposed that he had. All the same——

'And you say he himself named these two men, and agreed to confer the championship on the winner?'

Answers jostled one another. Hart and Root were second-raters! What about this man Tommy Burns? And for that matter, what about the Negro, Johnson? It came down to this: that a champion could retire but he was still the champ. He was the champ until he was knocked out.

'But what if he doesn't want to fight?'

'He's got to fight!'

'I don't see why. I don't suppose you're implying that this man Jeffries was *afraid* to fight either of these other two men?'

Laughter. Derision. Why, Jim Jeffries could pick up Hart in one hand and Root in the other and bump their heads together!

'Well then, all I can say is that as far as I can see, this man Hart is the champion.'

'He can't be! A man isn't the champion until he's knocked out the champion!'

Puzzled, though smiling, Phil shook her head. 'I'm afraid it's too deep for me.'

Inevitably the talk slid into an immediate groove, the asininity of trying to dig a canal from Washington. There were always stories about this. Carmichael, addressing Phil—for the others all knew it— told about the boilermakers.

'They sent a cable for twelve boilermakers needed in a hurry. After a long while, when they got no answer, they sent another cable asking what had happened, and they got a *letter* back. A *letter*! It said "Concerning your requisition for twelve boilermakers, beg to report that twenty applicants have been examined but none was found physically qualified. They were all deaf!"'

Everybody but Phil laughed. Carmichael waggled his hands.

'Don't you see? You ever hear of a good boilermaker who *wasn't* deaf?'

'Oh' said Phil. 'I'm so sorry. You must think me very stupid. But the fact is, I never knew any boilermakers.'

Ward Wright, of an age with these D.M.s in countable years, but in experience much older, nevertheless fitted in. Few had previously met him, though they'd all heard of him, and in the beginning there was a certain reserve, more than a touch of awe, in their attitude toward the soldier of fortune. But he smiled, and talked as they talked, and even laughed at their jokes, until they came to forget that he was famous.

'What *do* you do, Captain? A bunch of us were talking about it only the other day.'

Blandly: 'I look mysterious. I hover in the background with a sinister sneer. I act as if I might start shooting at any moment. That's how I make my living.'

'But you've got to fight sometimes, don't you?'

'Not often. Not any more. Get a big enough reputation and you never have to even frown.'

He said this half playfully; nor would he say any more about his business, but only smiled and shook his head.

It was Phil who brought Captain Wright more generally into the conversation. After the empty sandwich trays had been carried away Phil said that they ought to have a discussion on some current topic. She suggested the canal itself, as something they were, surely, all interested in.

'Suppose we start with the oldest. That is, I mean the one who has been *here* longest. I think that would be you, mademoiselle?'

Madeline shook her head.

'I fear I have not any opinion. Being French, it is proper that I am sorry that my own countrymen did not succeed in building the canal. We only got about two fifths of the digging done, I understand. But that history has passed. And since we could not finish it ourselves, I am glad that the United States have decided to do so.'

'You believe it *will* be finished then, mademoiselle?'

'Oh yes, I think so. I know that many persons don't, but I do.'

'That's very interesting. Thank you, mademoiselle.' In fact it had hardly been satisfactory; but they all nodded. Phil turned to Captain Wright. 'And now, I suppose, you've been here *second* longest?'

On this subject he was not reticent.

'I think the whole business is a ghastly mistake and that the best thing we could do is admit it and clear out!'

He had everybody's attention. Anti-canal arguments were not new, but such blunt talk as this was seldom heard.

'I hope that doesn't sound unpatriotic? I didn't mean it to be. Matter of fact, I think it's my duty to speak up *as* an American when I see my country doing something I consider wrong.

'The first thing is the route. If we were going to build an interoceanic canal we should have dug at Nicaragua. And we *would* have, if it'd been left to us. Until a few years ago practically nobody dreamed of building here. The French had tried, with some of the best engineers in the world, and they'd failed. We were going to build at Nicaragua, if we built at all. That was taken for granted. But then the lobbyists began to go to work. They began to whisper to the politicians. After all, the French people still had a big stake here in Panama, and if we built at Nicaragua they could kiss every single franc of that good-by.'

He made Madeline a grave bow.

'I'm not saying anything against the French company. They'd put a tremendous lot of work and money into this place, and naturally they wanted to salvage what they could. So they hired the smartest lawyer they could find. William Nelson Cromwell. He saw the President, he saw the Secretary of State, he saw everybody—and he kept on seeing them! He certainly represented his clients well! Among other things, he made a sixty-thousand-dollar contribution to the Republican campaign fund—and the next thing you know Senator Hanna was in favor of the Panama route. I don't say there was any connection! After all, sixty thousand dollars couldn't mean much to a man like Mark Hanna. What I do say is that that contribution should never have been offered or accepted. It didn't come out of Cromwell's own pocket, naturally. He charged it to expenses.

'Well, there was more like that. They weren't interested in the engineers' reports. They were only interested in saving all they could. And eventually they got forty-two million dollars.

'All right. Then we were going to build here. We dickered for a contract with the Colombian Government. And what happened?' He gave a tight smile. 'You'll probably think it's funny for a man in my line of business to be criticizing high-pressure politics. All the same, I had nothing to do with that revolution, and I still think it was a dirty

99

trick. It's one thing for an individual like me to sell my services to this country or that, but it's a totally different thing for the Government of the United States to act like a cloak-and-dagger conspirator.

'Colombia didn't think we offered enough, and their Senate threw out the treaty, which they had a perfect right to do. Colombia had just finished a long, expensive civil war, and the country was bankrupt. The canal rights on Panama were the biggest thing they had to sell, and what could be more natural than that they should try to get a good price? But no, we couldn't wait. We'd been fumbling the whole idea for almost fifty years, but now all of a sudden we couldn't possibly wait a few more months. A couple of dozen men here in Panama stage a revolution—nobody else knew it was happening—and you'll never get me to believe that they hadn't had a promise from Washington!— and instantly, before any investigation could be made, U.S. battleships are at Colon and Panama, and Colombia is forbidden even to land her own troops in part of her own country! Well, what could Colombia do? Fight the whole United States? So our State Department, right off, recognizes this brand-new Republic of Panama. No conferring with Colombia or anybody else first. No investigation. No stopping to estimate what the effect might be on the rest of the world. We just up and recognize a new nation—and sign a canal treaty giving ourselves everything Colombia had hesitated about and a little more besides. That's a fine how-d'-do, isn't it?'

Prendergast somewhat darkly asserted that the politicos had been trying to blackmail us. Teddy himself had called them a pack of bandits.

Ward Wright: 'One of the oldest tricks in war or politics is bashing a man too small to hurt you and then screaming that he'd been about to stab you in the back. What did Teddy know about those men in Bogota? When did he make an effort to *find out* anything about them? I was mixed up in that civil war which had just ended, and I happen to know more than one of those Colombian senators who voted against ratification. They're not blackmailers or bandits. They're men who were trying to do the best they could for their country. Who is Teddy to call them names, when he never even tried to dicker with them? Don't you see that *they*'re calling *us* bandits—and with darn good reason, if Mrs Kellems will excuse my language? Even if they did want to hold us up for a few millions more, we could have conducted the business in an honest, straightforward fashion. What's a few millions to a country like ours, considering all we've spent here already—and all we're going to spend before we finally learn we can' finish the job? Why, we'll lose those few millions a hundred times over, a thousand times over, in good will! Do you think, after the way we acted, that anybody in this part of the world is going to trust us again? Years from now we'll still be wondering why we can't persuade Latin-Americans that we mean what we say. I contend we ought to quit,' said Ward Wright, 'before we waste any more money. We ought to admit we're wrong—and get out.'

There was a considerable silence. Somehow they all looked at Harry Kellems, who stared at the floor.

'There's a lot in what you say, Captain' Harry admitted at last. 'Maybe we did start it wrong. It certainly sounds like it. But all the same, we *did* start it. And so we've got to finish it.'

'I think you're mistaken there. I think the canal will never be finished anyway.'

'It *will* be finished! It's *got* to be!'

'You can't stand there and tell me——'

'I can stand here and tell you that this job's been started and it's going to be finished, and that's all there is to it!'

Harry's head was up now. His arms were stiff at his sides. He took a step toward Ward Wright.

'Why, darling, you don't have to be so serious about it!' Phil cried. 'Why, anyone would think you were protecting me from some insult, the way you look!'

Harry's arms relaxed, and he managed a sheepish smile.

'Sorry. No hard feeling, Captain. I did get pretty excited.'

'Why, that's all right' the soldier of fortune cried. 'Perfectly all right! Everybody's entitled to their opinion.'

'Let's have some more music' somebody suggested.

They sang livelier songs, 'Give My Regards to Broadway,' 'Meet Me in St. Louis, Louie,' 'I May Be Crazy but I Ain't No Fool.' They sang 'Only a Bird in a Gilded Cage,' most of them singing it straight, though Harry T clowned it, saying 'boid' for 'bird' and twirling imaginary mustachios when he referred to the old man's gold for which the repining narrator's body was sold. Phil vamped 'Sweet Adeline' and the cry went up for Harry K to give them a solo, but he refused: the truth was, he no longer felt like singing. They sang 'Yankee Doodle Dandy' and 'Ida, Sweet as Apple Cider.'

They had fun. Time after time, between numbers, somebody would exclaim that he hadn't had such a good time since he'd come down to this gosh-darn place—'this d-dash place' Harry T called it. The punch bowl stood empty but forgotten: nobody was drunk. Their faces gleamed with perspiration, despite a breeze which had set the palms furtively atwitter. Soon it would rain, and they'd slog back to the barracks and crawl under their mosquito bars; but now, singing, they were happy. Tomorrow morning they could sleep; and tonight, for a little while, they were not in this filthy land at all but back in White Plains and Coshocton and Flatbush and Lincoln, Neb., and also in Paterson, N.J.

Even Harry K relaxed and relented and ceased to glower when Phil, glancing up at him with an appealing smile, vamped for 'Jest Alongin' for Your Smile.' That of course he could not refuse her.

He sang slowly but not dramatically, not holding the end notes. It was almost a singsongy rendition, perhaps because Harry all the time could smell the earth and the growing potted plants in that vast dim conservatory and could see Phil in her blue dress.

They were all seated. Madeline, who had been seated all the while, Darl Winter stubbornly rather than solicitously by her side, watched Harry while he sang, as she had watched him singing before. This music, all this music tonight, excepting the Chopin, meant nothing to her; it seemed frivolous and bang-bangy, and either oversentimental or else raucous, either too slow, so slow as to resemble a wail, or else altogether too jumpy and fast to have any form. Yet she saw that it pleased the others and meant something to them. Even Darl, by her side, the most self-contained man in the house, obviously was moved by some of the numbers.

> 'When the clouds drift o'er the sky,
> When the moon comes peepin' shy—
> Still there's only sadness, dear,
> In a place where you ain't near——'

Harry, she thought, did not sing well. He lacked skill and training. He should have sung as he went about some work, not knowing whether anybody listened, not caring. *Then* his voice would have been at its best; for it was a careless, warm, and lovely voice. Standing before them, the center of attention, head up, one foot forward, he seemed like a man who had first said 'I am now about to sing.' That was the wrong way to do it. For Harry's performance was not artistic. It was pleasing; it was warming; but decidedly it was not artistic. But the voice itself was fine.

> 'I'm alongin' for your smile
> Jest to make my life worth while.'

Madeline was not ordinarily smug, but she was smug now. She had something to be proud of. 'I can always say that I loved him before I ever heard him sing' she told herself.

Lightning flitted across the sky and there was a mumble of thunder as the party broke up, but even this sounded familiar. At least the rain gave warning. A summer night at home was suggested, a clean and cleansing shower that would leave the air cool.

'I've had a delightful time' Madeline said.

'It was so good of you to come. And you too, Mr Winter. You must do it more often, now that you know the way.'

Captain Ward Wright followed them out—Phil had stepped outside the front screen door in order to get the benefit of the breeze, and Harry was elsewhere. Madeline, at the step of the carriage, and not knowing why, looked back.

The two were in silhouette, and there was nothing that was wrong, nothing anybody there excepting Madeline would even have noticed. Phil said that it had been so good of him to come, and he answered with just the proper note of friendliness that he'd had a delightful time, and they shook hands. No, nothing wrong. Captain Wright was sure of himself as he leaned over her hand; but then, he was always that. What Madeline remarked in her mind was that Phyllis was not sure of herself. Phil stood straight, and doubtless—Madeline couldn't see her features—she smiled the right smile. But her legs were jelly.

'Oh' said Madeline.

'What's the matter?' asked Darl.

'Nothing.'

But when Madeline settled back in the carriage, smiling politely at Darl, who had helped her in, she knew that she could afford to wait.

'You might at least have thought of *me*' Phil said, unhooking. 'The idea of flaring up like that, over nothing at all!'

'Honestly I'm sorry.' He was already in bed. 'I don't know what came over me.'

'Why, you acted as if you were practically going to *fight!*'

'Well, I guess I practically was, for a second there. It just made me so—— Ah, I don't know, darling! You're right, of course. He didn't say anything offensive, and as a matter of fact it was pretty straight turkey, all things considered. But I got to thinking about all the boys who had worked here, and the ones who still do, and all they've put up with, and then some of them like Georgie Walsh. . . . I used to like him a lot. We used to argue baseball. He was a Pirates fan. And Art Crowell. You didn't know him.'

'He died too?'

'Yeah. And they hurried him off at night, as if he'd done something nasty. They practically rushed him to his grave. Nobody went along except me. Me and the spiggoty who drove the wagon. The spiggoty was a gravedigger, besides being the driver, and there weren't any other gravediggers when we got there. There were *graves* all right! Five or six of them already dug. But nobody but this one man to fill them up. I had my prayer book, that I'd won for learning my catechism in Sunday school, and I read the burial service the best way I could—though as a matter of fact I didn't know whether Art was an Episcopalian or what: we'd never talked religion. The spiggoty didn't know what it was all about, not understanding English, and he went right to work shoveling dirt onto the coffin. It was raining, of course. And the rain and the wind were making such a racket I could hardly hear the sound of my own voice. After a while, when I'd finished the service—which I hope I got right—I could hardly see the page—then I figured I might as well help the spiggoty. So I picked up another shovel, and after we'd finished the job we drove back to town. I went to bed. I suppose that that spiggoty just went on carting other bodies out there all night. Poor Art! He came from Kansas, and he wanted to be an architect.'

Out of her corset, Phil undressed slowly. She wanted Harry to get away from this. He was a moody man. She had not remarked it in Paterson, even in all the years she'd known him; but here, living with him, sleeping with him, she knew it.

He was watching her.

Her back to him, she pulled her shirt off over her head. She reached swiftly for her peignoir, fumbled, dropped it, and with a little cry snatched it up and pulled it on.

'I'm sorry about him' she said. 'I can see how you must have felt, dearest. But I still don't see what that has to do with the way you behaved in front of everybody tonight.'

Harry didn't say anything.

'All the same, I think everything went off nicely. I think it was a very nice party and they all enjoyed themselves.'

'No question about it! And *you* were the hit of the whole business!'

'Do you think so, darling?'

It was all right now. She took her time. She got herself naked under the peignoir, and carefully put everything away, hung everything up looked around observantly, nodded, and went to the dressing table

Her skin felt a little damp, but not soppy. She started to brush her hair.

'You certainly waste an awful lot of time doing that.'

'It isn't a waste of time, dear. It's good for it.'

'It isn't good for me!'

'*Harry!*'

She brushed and brushed. The reflection was good; because after all she did love Harry. After all, he had greeted everybody just right, he'd been becomingly deferential to the Gorgases, he'd dished out the lunch and passed the sandwiches. He was a good husband. He was a nice-looking husband too, firmer in the way he stood, darker of face, brighter of eye than the man she had married. And he was going to be a very *surprised* husband, soon. She remembered how she had felt when she said good night to Ward just outside the screen door. That *helplessness,* disgusting! A body matter. And a bad matter because it was like that feeling she had had when she saw Ward on the balcony. A dirty, not-decent matter. But after all, she was perfectly certain that she'd done nothing wrong. Her thoughts were her own, weren't they? Yet even her thoughts, as they'd been then, when she said good night to Ward, she did not like. She brushed her hair.

'You go on and on. You spend hours doing that. Every night. Hours.'

'Precious, I don't mean to scold you. But honestly, don't you think you're being vulgar?'

'I certainly don't! Neither would any man who had a wife as beautiful as you are! Ah, darling, come on! That hair can wait.'

'That hair can't wait. It must be done just right.'

'Why?'

'Why? Why, because I have such a nice husband, and I must look my very best for him. That's why I want to brush it a little more.'

The reflection all but chortled at her. And why not? Why couldn't there have been some other women to see what a sweet husband she had? That Miss Hoffman, poor dear, probably had never been so thrilled in her life before. And of course that French girl. . . . The French girl hadn't seemed to know anything. Phil had watched her. No feeling. A cold fish.

'Do you remember how we used to sneak away and go up to that place on the third floor—the maid's room—that you said a maid wouldn't come along to, and we could lock the door anyway? And all the people downstairs used to talk and talk, it sounded like somebody dragging a stick along a picket fence all the time we——'

'*Harry!*'

'Well, we're married now.'

'Yes, we're married, but that still doesn't mean that you have to treat me as though——'

'You're taking an awfully long while.'

'Well, all right. I'm finished.'

He was not going to go to sleep this time. She smiled quietly, and walked back and forth, as though not certain where she had hung her nightgown.

When finally she got the nightgown she held it low, and looked at Harry, and said reproachfully: 'I don't think you ought to stare at me like that.'

'What do you think I'm made out of? Celluloid?'

'I don't like it. I'm a lady, and I feel that——'

'Can't a lady take her clothes off?'

'Well, I don't like it. I think I'll go into the next room.'

'The dining room, or the kitchen?'

'Harry, it would be nicer if you had manners.'

'I don't want manners, after what I'm going to have a look at.'

'Well, you're not going to have a look at anything! So there!'

She snatched her nightgown and sped into the kitchen. Smiling to herself, she changed. Just before she pulled the nightgown over her head she stood nude a moment, enjoying the feeling, enjoying the air against her flesh. It was a good body. Oh, Lord! she thought. Oh, Lord, after all, *this* is what marriage is! This is it, and I like it!

She was humming as she came out of the kitchen, and she folded the peignoir over a chair, and patted her cuffs, and touched her all-down hair, and then deliberately she smiled at him.

'Well, honey?'

'There's been an awful lot of this-and-that' he said. 'Why not come on in here, here where I am?'

She kept the smile on her face, walking toward him, and wondering why she had ever felt that way about Ward.

'Don't forget the light.'

'Why, so I have!'

'It's better with the light out, don't you think?'

She retreated two steps, the smile in place, and jerked the light cord, and then waited, laughing inside of herself; and she said aloud 'Oh, *my* . . .'

'Oh, *my!*' answered Harry from the bed.

Very quietly she got in next to him. He wasn't hasty when he took her in his arms. He got his lips next to one of her ears.

'Phil, darling——'

'It isn't that room on the third floor, dear. We have plenty of time.'

'We have the rest of our lives, darling.'

'Yes, we have the rest of our lives.'

He released her and propped himself up on an elbow.

'What was that?'

'What was what, dearest? Come back here.'

'It sounded like a mosquito.'

'Well, maybe it was a mosquito. Darling, you aren't going to——'

'Must have got in when we were saying good night to those people.'

'When *we* were saying good night? Half the time you weren't even there!'

'Excuse me, darling. It shouldn't take me more than a minute to——'

'Harry! You aren't really going to get out of bed now? Because of a *mosquito?*'

He was. He was fumbling around. He warned her about the light, and she shut her eyes hard and pushed her face into her pillow.

'You see, after all, I'm sorry, dearest, but if we don't——'

'Is a mosquito more important than me?'

'It isn't that. It's only that if—— Don't you understand that unless we—— Wait! It must have gone over toward—— Wait, I'll have it in a second.'

'Don't hurry for my sake' Phil said with weighty sweetness. 'Would it be an ano-whatever-you-call-'em or an aedes-whatsis?'

'*Phil!*' He stood there in his nightgown, waving his hands, in one hand the flyswatter. 'You don't get the idea! It was one of these little things, a tiny little thing like this, that—— Well, darling, I told you about Georgie Walsh and Art Crowell and——'

'Good night, dear.'

'If you think I'm wrong because I'm doing my duty . . . I'm doing my *duty* right now!'

'Good night' said Phil, pushing all her face into the pillow. 'And I may say,' turning a little, 'that I hate to even think of seeing you again, and I hate to even have to wake up in the morning and see a man like you—and I hate to—did I say a man?'

'*Phil!*'

'Good night' she said.

7

TO THE MEN who worked on the canal the indifference of the rest of the world was astounding. Nevertheless there were some visitors.

Harry remembered the Secretary of War and his party. Not long after Harry's arrival Mr Taft had come. Large and genial, his eyes almost closed in happiness as he thrust out a great fat clean hand for you to shake, a man who even when he was silent seemed to be guffawing inside himself, who was interested in everything and remembered everybody's name, he saw this person and that, talking English, talking Spanish, smiling—and getting a lot of work done. In ten days he had settled the principal immediate small hard-feeling problems, matters which should have been arranged in advance anyway. He'd been everywhere, beamed at everything, attended all sorts of fetes and banquets. He'd bowed repeatedly. He had danced like a tireless huge faun. 'Look at him' Dr Gorgas was heard to mutter. 'Why, I couldn't do that if I lived to be a thousand!'

Mr Taft's most intimate attendant was one who might have been selected to point up the Secretary's affability, as vain queens are said to insist upon older and uglier ladies-in-waiting. Not that he was unattractive! He was decidedly handsome—erect, a pink oval face, a twinkling fast-whitening mustache, violet-blue eyes. But he was a soldier, who wanted everything in its place; and he was pained at the aspect of Panama late in 1904. Those features were granitic: only dynamite or a smile, you would have said, could cause them to crack. Something invisible, something with an everlasting bad smell, might have been suspended just underneath the chiseled nose.

'Who is he, dear?'

'Colonel Goethals. The engineers. Dutch ancestry. A West Pointer. They say "goet-hals" means "stiff neck."'

'Perfect!'

Yet it was noted that neither Secretary Taft nor any junketing senators stayed in the Zone overnight. Back to the ship as soon as possible after the coming of darkness was the rule; and that ship, in the case of the Secretary of War, had been anchored far out in Limon Bay. They might romp in daytime, poking their noses here and there, trying to see everything; but for sleeping purposes they preferred their bunks on the vessel. It was all very well for men like Dr Carter and Dr Darling and Dr Gorgas to say that you were safe nights if you stayed behind mosquito netting. The visiting statesmen—it was a fact much commented upon—preferred to take no chances.

'Bet Teddy won't do that, if he comes! He's got gumption!'

'*If* he comes!'

'Well, they say he might. They're going to try to get that hotel finished in time for him if he comes in November.'

'Go on! November's practically the worst month down here! Besides, how can he leave the country when he's President? Isn't that against the Constitution?'

'I don't know. Is it?'

'I don't know.'

'Well, I don't know either. But anyway that's what they say.'

'Well, I *think* it is against the Constitution.'

About a year after the Taft visit the visit of Harrison Clyde Hillis created almost as much talk. Hillis was a small man—small all around, short, with a small head, small hands and feet—and he spoke in a high, almost girlish, almost lisping voice. He was white-haired, white-bearded, and had a priestlike mouth and priestlike eyes. In appearance benign, he carried a gold-headed walking stick. He did not smoke or drink. He had never held public office. He rarely gave out any public statement.

He came unattended, protesting that he just wished to see the sights, and he stayed about as long as the Secretary had, some ten days. He drifted here and there, shyly smiling, meeting people, looking at things. There were those who contended that his visit was 'sneaky,' though the man neither hid nor thrust himself forward. Nobody could make a definite complaint about his conduct; yet wherever he went he caused uneasiness; and more often than not after he had shimmered out of an office or away from a drill or steam shovel, murmuring thanks, the man interviewed would scowl after him: 'Now what *was* that guy getting at, anyway?'

Famous, or call it notorious, surely at least Hillis was well known. He was not a member of the firm of Somebody, Somebody, Somebody, Somebody, Somebody, and Somebody Else: he was simply Harrison C. Hillis, a man who maintained one small office in Wall Street and employed one secretary-typist; and perhaps this in itself, this showy lack of display, made him the more mysterious. It was certain that his fees were enormous; it was not certain how he earned them. A criminal lawyer was a man who represented criminals, and criminals were men who wore caps and turtle-neck sweaters; yet it had been said of this fastidious whisperer that he was a sort of criminal lawyer for corporations; that he took cases nobody else cared or dared to touch; and that despite his appearance, his avoidance of pomp, the circumspect life he led away from the Street, he was cleverly, quietly, and very gainfully employed in shoveling dirt. This is what they *said* of him. *He* said nothing, in Panama as elsewhere—except that in Panama from time to time he denied with blushes that he was working for any client and asserted that he had simply come to sightsee. Of course nobody believed this. In the bars, in the offices, out along the Line, they discussed him fervently, arriving nowhere out of breath. This mild-mannered little man was watched as though he were a celebrated jewel thief or an anarchist who might be expected to have an infernal machine hidden beneath the tails of his coat.

Harry met him in Simpson's office.

'Oh, sorry! I didn't mean to——'

'Don't let me interfere with anything' cried the lawyer in that high mincing voice. 'If I'm in your way——'

'Sit down, Mr Hillis. Wait a minute, Harry.'

Simpson was recovering from his third bout of blackwater, and he showed sadder and incongruously fatter than ever. His shirt was plastered to his chest. There was no color in his face. His skin rolled and flopped without plan, as though no nerves held it.

'Harry, this is Harrison C. Hillis, the shyster. This is Harry Kellems, Mr Hillis. He's one of our field superintendents. Isn't that what you are now, Harry?'

'More or less. This week, anyway.'

'Yes. Harry gets around. He knows a good deal about the work here, and he has the greatest faith in it.'

'That's fine! Just fine!'

'Harry believes in it so strongly that when a couple of months ago a guest at his house said he thought we ought to pull up stakes, Harry was so sore he almost slugged him. And this is particularly interesting, Mr Hillis, because the man in question is a professional killer, a thug whose services are available to the highest bidder.'

Harry cried 'See here, you're talking about a friend of mine!'

'Ach, Louie! I wouldn't admit it, if I were you. The man I mean happens to be at the bottom of humanity's scale. Or maybe he's even lower. Maybe he's dug a hole in the bottom and's climbed into that. Well, I wish somebody would shovel the dirt back over him. He's a skunk and a rattlesnake rolled into one. Only difference is, the skunk and the rattler were born that way and can't help it. Would I say this to his face?' Simpson asked sadly. 'Certainly not! I'd be afraid he would tear me to pieces if I did. All the same, he knows what I think of him.'

'I don't know how you learned about that fracas in the first place, but anyway it's a purely personal affair!'

'You live in a whispering gallery, Harry. Matter of fact, I knew about it the day after it happened. So did practically everybody else.' He examined first one moist palm and then the other, as though he suspected them of playing him a mean trick. 'A whispering gallery. . . . Everybody here knows everything about everybody else. Except that none of us know anything about this distinguished visitor, Mr Hillis. That's why I'm taking him out along the Line. To see if I can find out anything.'

He rose, shaking his head, so that his cheeks and chins swung limp in discouragement, as though to sympathize with him, and even his ears seemed to flap like sails in a scanting wind.

'What's that? Report on that place out at Corozal? O.k. Just toss it into the basket there, will you? Thanks.'

Wearily he worked into his coat. He took his hat from a knob, his umbrella from the rack.

'You're not in very good shape to be traveling, are you?'

'See here, there's no reason why you should take this trouble, Mr Simpson! I'm nothing but an idle rubber-necker——'

'Wouldn't miss the chance for a million. Harry, I knew there was something I wanted to tell you. The Chief's going to drop by. He's just going to pick up a report, but I happen to know that he's very anxious to see you about something.'

'What could that be?'

'I don't know, but them's orders. Something important. Why don't you hang around? He'll be along any minute. All right, Mr Hillis?'

He waddled out, shooing the small elfin lawyer before him.

Two minutes after they had gone the telephone rang. Thinking that it might be Dr Gorgas, Harry answered.

'Hello?'

'Hello. Listen, this is Enrico. Listen, about that nigger they picked up the other night, who was all beat up and one of his eyes practically gouged out. Well, I just wanted to tell you that——!'

'I don't know what you're talking about. This is Mr Simpson's office, but Mr Simpson isn't here. Could I take——'

'*Holy Jesus!*'

Harry's ear rang for a long time afterward with the sound of the receiver at the other end.

Dr Gorgas's eyes were gleaming, and his face was flushed. He seemed glad to see Harry, eager to talk.

'Simpson gone? Oh yes. With that Hillis man. You meet him, Harry? What do you think of him?'

Harry shrugged. 'What does anybody think of him? He seems very quiet. What's he doing here?'

'Um? What's he doing here? I wish you could tell me, Harry. But that wasn't what I wanted to see you about. You know, I've just come from the hospital, and they were getting ready to autopsy that yellow-jack patient we lost last night. Poor devil, it was a pity he had to go. Anyway, do you know what I told them? "Better take a good look, boys. It's the last one you're going to see."'

'Holy smoke! Do you really think so, sir?'

'I don't know, Harry. I hope so. I certainly hope so! But I don't know. The longer I'm in this business the more I realize how much guessing we have to do. I only said that to encourage them, really. There's been a low tone up there lately. If there aren't any more cases, then they'll hail me as a wizard. If there are, then they'll call me a fool. But I figured they had some word of encouragement coming to them, the way they've been working.

'It *ought* to be the last one' he said, as though to convince himself. 'We certainly can't kick about the way they've been treating Sanitation lately, can we? That man Shonts doesn't like me for peanuts, and to be frank with you I don't care much for him, but he does get things done. "How many men you got, Colonel?" he asked me, soon as he came. He always calls me colonel. "Two hundred and fifty." "How many you need?" "Two thousand, and I could even use twenty-five hundred." "I'll see that you get twenty-five hundred." Now I like a man who behaves that way. I may not want to introduce him to my wife, but I like to do business with him.

'But I don't know. . . . If something slips up, Harry: if one little thing is allowed to slip . . .'

The gleam was gone from his eyes, and suddenly he looked tired. You seldom saw him look tired like this. Never in the wards.

'But *that* wasn't what I wanted to see you about, either.' He brightened. 'It sounds frivolous to bring it up right on top of yellow jack and Harrison C. Hillis, but I've been wondering about it ever since that housewarming party of yours.'

'Why, what in the world——'

'Oh, I could have asked you long before this, but then I always wanted to try to figure it out for myself. But I've never been able to. And it's got too much for me, Harry. I just *have* to ask! If only Marie hadn't come along . . . You know what I'm talking about, don't you?'

'I'm beginning to.'

'It was a beer limerick, and the two first lines were about a young girl from Anheuser who swore that no one could surprise her.'

'The rest goes like this:

> *'But Pabst took a chance,*
> *Found Schlitz in her pants,*
> *And now she is sadder Budweiser.'*

'Oh say, thanks so much! I knew you wouldn't let me down, Harry. "And now she is sadder Budweiser," eh? My, I wish I dared tell Marie that one! How is your wife, by the way? Fine, fine! You'll give her my kindest? We've thought a lot about you, Marie and I. Well, I must be going. I only want to pick up this report. Now just once more, to see if I've got it straight.'

He repeated the limerick. He chuckled.

'You know, I needed something like that. Does a man good sometimes. Well, nothing else, was there?'

Then there was Lord Chudit, who was an Englishman.

Harry had received a note from Madeline that there could be no lesson because her father wasn't well, and he had gone around to ask if there was anything he could do, and Madeline had assured him that it wasn't fever but only a coughing spell, accompanied by restlessness, when her father would behave strangely.

'He probably *will* run a temperature when he learns a Yankee was out here talking to you.'

'Oh no. I'll tell him it was you. I think he likes you.'

'Maybe I'm not very American?'

'You're American all right.'

'Darl Winter told me he fairly yelled at him, last time he was here.'

'Yes.' She looked curiously at Harry. 'Darl confides in you, doesn't he?'

'Sometimes. A little. He's a quiet guy.'

'Yes. I—I haven't seen much of him lately. Father never did like him. I don't know why. Darl's a nice boy.'

'Comes from a very rich family. I suppose you knew that?'

She nodded.

'He had some run-in with his parents, which I never got clear. He doesn't talk much about it. He's—sort of proud.'

'I know.'

'He quit college. I don't know why. Anyway he's bound and determined he won't go back unless and until he's in a position to walk right up to his old man and spit right in his eye. That's the way he puts it. Sounds foolish to me. I figured he'd soften up after a while, but he never has, and I've known him almost two years now.'

'It's a horrid way to feel about one's own father' Madeline remarked, glancing toward the door.

'Want me to go?'

'No, no! It is all right!'

'I ought to go anyway. Think I'll go home instead of eating lunch in town. Little surprise for Phil.'

'How is Phil? I've hardly seen her since the night of that fete. That was so pleasant, that night, 'Arry.'

'I'm glad you liked it.'

'You will give her my regards? Someday maybe I will go up and play your piano, as she invited me.'

'She'd be tickled to death to see you. I guess she gets pretty lonesome up there sometimes.'

So he had climbed the hill and gone through the Cemetery. The Cemetery didn't look so bad these days. The flowers were gone forever, but some of the flowering shrubs and the border bushes, the tough ones, oleander, hibiscus, bougainvillea, were thrusting shoots right out of the hacked-off stumps. This would yet be a lovely spot again, when Sanitation got everything in order, when flowers could be trusted.

Phil wasn't home. Rosina, who had been scrubbing the parlor floor, rose with a series of amazed giggles and made a fuss about getting lunch. Rosina said, as nearly as he could make it out, that the Señora had gone shopping and would not be back until the afternoon. Rosina concocted coffee, much too strong, and a ridiculous sandwich.

'If my better half could see you using her bacon like that'—there was a lot of uncooked canned bacon in the sandwich—'she'd have the hide off you, kiddo.'

Rosina giggled, goggling.

'We'll just keep it to ourselves, huh? This tastes terrible.'

Rosina giggled. It was good to talk to her, knowing that she didn't understand. He did not feel like speaking Spanish. It was April, and a lovely day, clear sky, utterly blue, with becoming puffs of white cloud, and sunlight that got everywhere without blasting its way: it was a day to make you happy.

He handed the cup and plate back to the hunchback.

'Little chicken, that's the third worst cup of coffee but positively the God-damnedest *very* worst sandwich I ever had! Thank you.'

Rosina giggled and retired to the kitchen.

Harry walked around, humming. They were to get out of this place soon. Harry was high on the list of those entitled to married quarters, which were being built. They had a house all picked. It was up on stilts, like this one, but it had a parlor and bedroom in front, a bathroom with a shower, and a kitchen, besides a large veranda, all, of course, screened. They would be expected to furnish their own linen, china, and kitchen utensils; but the government was to supply them with a range, two kitchen chairs, a kitchen table, a double bed with mosquito bar, two pillows, a mirror, a bedroom table, a mission or perhaps fumed-oak chiffonier, a mission dining table, a mission sideboard, a towel rack, a dresser, one parlor table, three wicker rockers, and two porch chairs. All the forms had been made out, there couldn't be a slip. There was even a chance that they might rate golden oak instead of mission.

They wouldn't have this view, he reflected, looking through the front window. Still, they'd have a pretty good view.

There would be no ice; not yet.

There would still be no rugs on the floors.

The grounds would be Desolation.

But—running water! A toilet that toiled! A shower! If Phil seemed a shade distressed at the prospect, it was only, he reasoned, because she had made such an amusing fuss about this queer place they lived in now, and had borne it all so gallantly, saying 'Be it ever so humble' and laughing. Well, the house they would move into, soon now, in another two or three months, would not be anything compared with what Phil would have expected in Paterson; but it would be better than this.

Dr Gorgas had told him that they would even have a telephone instrument, a business telephone, in case Harry was needed some time for some emergency job; but there was no reason, Dr Gorgas had said, why Phil, and for that matter Harry himself, shouldn't use it now and then for personal calls—in case they knew anybody else who had a telephone instrument.

He felt pretty good. He called adios to Rosina, who giggled, and he walked down the hill. It was not too hot walking at this season, and it was pleasant not to have to tote an umbrella.

One of the first things Big Smoke Stevens had done was to shift Construction's G.H.Q. from Panama City out to Culebra, to a big new administration building. Sanitation's G.H.Q. meanwhile had been moved up the hill and into the hospital grounds, a good place for it. Still, Simpson stayed in the city. Harry never understood that. Simpson was a curious duck. Several times Harry had told him about that extraordinary telephone call, about the man who'd said he was Enrico and who had started to tell about a Negro beaten up and with one eye almost gouged out; and each time Simpson had said wearily that he hadn't the faintest idea of what Harry was talking about. Harry had gone over as much as he could of the Spanish parts of the Panama *Star,* and he'd read all the English parts for several weeks back, and he had asked in an offhand way at the hospital, without learning anything about any such Negro.

'If there's nothing you want me to do this afternoon——'

'There is something I want you to do' Simpson interrupted. 'I want you to look around, after this, when you come into my office, and if you should spy any stray bits of English nobility floating here and there, I want you to more or less come to attention.'

'Oh say, I'm sorry!'

'Not at all. Lord Chudit, this is Mr Harry Kellems, one of our field superintendents. We think a lot of Harry. He shares that opinion, judging from the way he busts into offices. Harry, meet the Earl of Chudit. Both members of this club.'

Harry told friends afterward that he might not have even noticed Lord Chudit if he hadn't been reprimanded into it, for the man was as medium as a man could be—medium height, medium build, somewhat brownish hair, rather brownish eyes, a so-so nose, an unremarkable chin, an in-betweenish mustache. His clothes were vague.

'How do you do' he said, and extended his hand.

Harry had met Englishmen before and he knew what was expected. He shook the hand with great vigor.

'Say, I'm sure pleased to meet you, Lord!'

He could almost hear Simpson swallow. He turned to Simpson.

'Or should I say "your lordship"?' he asked.

'Say what you damn please' grumped Simpson. 'Only, don't start organizing a papa-spank on *me* right in front of a nobleman.'

Lord Chudit was amused and said so.

'All right. Only you have to watch this guy, your lordship. Let me warn you, every time he thinks he sees a Goliath he starts looking around for a stone. And as for telephone messages——'

Simpson sighed. 'Well, Ferocious, what do you think of your Marvin Hart now? You saw what Burns did to him?'

'I never said I thought Hart was the champ! I don't think Tommy Burns is either, for that matter! Old Jeff could still come back and wipe the floor up with both of them!'

'Um-m. And when he'd done that, then *you'd* come along and wipe the floor up with *him*, I suppose?' Simpson turned tiredly to the visitor. 'I'm a little worried about entrusting you to this guy, your lordship. He's a tiger eater. He eats tigers.'

'Tigers?'

'Not the kind you have in India. He wouldn't even turn around to stick his tongue out at *them*. He only gets tempestuous when he faces a real tiger. I mean, the kind our novelists make heroes out of. You got heavy shoes on? Boots, I mean?'

'Oh, quite! I'm prepared for that sort of thing!'

'Good. Harry, here's your job. You're going to take Lord Chudit out to the Cut and give him a look at all that isn't happening there. He'll be dumfounded, and he'll ask you *why* it isn't happening, and you'll tell him you don't know. That clear?'

'I'll tell him whatever I please!'

'Sure you will, tiger eater. That's why I'm giving you the assignment. Incidentally, what do you think of Philadelphia Jack O'Brien's chances?'

'Why, if old Jeff wants to come back——'

'Oh well. Old Jeff. All right. Old Jeff. He's o.k. as long as he keeps away from you, I know.'

He heaved himself to his feet.

'All right. God bless both of you, and you'll excuse me? Never mind the tigers, your lordship. And Harry won't take you back into the bush where the snakes are. Though even if he did, you'd be safe. He eats fer-de-lances and cascabels and timbos just as easily. I *guess*'—he looked at Harry—'I *guess* you're in good hands. We'll stand back of any answers Harry gives you. Unless it's something about the Giants. He's not to be trusted there.'

'The, uh, the giants?'

'But there aren't any of them out where you're going now anyway. So you needn't worry. Good-by, your lordship. 'By, Harry.'

Lord Chudit turned out to be all right. At first he seemed silly, thanks to Simpson's somewhat elephantine Americanisms; but in the carriage he chatted twirkily, and twinkled at Harry.

'I say, this is a downing place! Dare say you're thinking earls are downing blokes to meet, far as that goes, what?'

'I don't know. I never met one before.'

'Ah, of course. Quite. Once I get a catch on your slang I shall be quite all right. Eh, eh? No flies on that, eh?'

'Hell no' said Harry, liking him.

Harry finger-jabbing points of interest, they rolled and rattled into the Cathedral Plaza, where Harry saw Phil emerge from a shop. He excused himself and yelled a halt.

'You don't mind? My wife.'

'Why, see here! Why, of course! Let's have the chap turn back!'

'No, that's all right. You wait here. I won't be long.'

As he walked toward Phil, who had seen him and was waiting for him, he glowed with the thought of how delighted she would be to meet an earl. It was pretty large monkeyshines, at that. Here he was, Harry Kellems, whose glee club had had to chip in to get him a dress suit when he was at Stevens, and now he was riding with an earl. It would certainly make a hit with Phil. *She* used to stew about why he didn't get to know the British consul, Sir Claude Coventry Mallet, a baldish popeyed laughing little gent with mustaches you could have hung a couple of towels on. Harry had been introduced to the British consul twice, but he hadn't said more than a few words to him, and he felt that it was better to keep this to himself. But now a lord! An earl!

'Hello, darling. Where in the world are you going in a carriage?'

'Government's expense, dear. Another visitor.'

'Colonel Gorgas gives you a lot of those, doesn't he?'

'Well, I sort of know the layout by this time. This man——'

'Darling, look. I bought a table cover I thought Mother would like, in this Chinese store just now. Here——'

'Well, say! That's pretty wonderful!'

Quickly she said: 'Now you're going to ask how much it cost?'

'Well, as a matter of fact, I was thinking about that.'

'Well, as a matter of fact, then, it was very cheap. I got it for only sixty-two dollars.'

Then he looked at her, O-ing his mouth.

118

'Well, it's for Mother. Is there anything wrong with that?'

'Nothing at all, dear. The only thing is——'

'Well, of course I'm not taking it out of our money.'

'Oh.'

He knew that there would be trouble. He looked at the sidewalk, while people passed, men in white suits, sometimes a bulgy black-clad woman, and the carriages, and the boys with lottery tickets.

'Now you're going to ask me if I'm still getting that allowance? Well, of course I am. And why not, pray?'

When she said 'pray' he knew she too was sore, edgy.

'Even though you're married to me?'

'Harry, you're being foolish. There is no reason under the sun why my father can't send me an allowance if he feels like it.'

'Even though you're married to me?'

'I wish you'd stop saying that.'

'Why? You *are* married to me, you know.'

'Well, all right. I know that, of course. But I still don't see any reason why my father can't send me an allowance. It isn't so much. It's just that he wants—well, he's always felt that way. He wants his daughter to have something extra, something special.'

Harry said slowly: 'We're not going to do this all over again, are we?'

'No! And certainly not here, anyway! And as far as attracting attention is concerned, it might be better if you stopped holding onto my wrist as if you were going to drown!'

'I'm sorry,' releasing the wrist. 'I hadn't imagined that I'd have to have all this all over again.'

'We're not *going* to have it all over again!'

'Phil, maybe we were wrong when we got married. I don't know. But we *did,* and as long as you're my wife I'm not going to stand——'

'As long as I'm your wife I'm not going to stand for you standing right here in the middle of the sidewalk practically *screaming* at me! It's my money, and I'll do what I want with it!'

'Well,' he said, 'I'm sorry.'

'Well,' she said, 'you should be.'

'I don't like it. I still don't like it. And I never will.'

'Maybe sometime you'll——'

'Yes, maybe sometime I'll make money like your father does. Maybe I'll be a big engineer and laugh at thousands of dollars—and then you can buy things that cost as much as this.'

'But Harry, sixty-two dollars isn't much!'

'It is to us. If maybe you'd come and asked me——'

'If maybe I'd come and asked you to learn some decent manners sometime, then maybe I'd have been crazy! You've got my wrist again.'

'I'm sorry.'

'Well, all right. I think you ought to go back to that person you're rubber-necking around with. He isn't a congressman, is he?'

'No, he isn't a congressman.'

'Well, I think you'd better go back to him. That's better than having you stand there screaming at me. With all these people passing. . . . No, that's all right. Never mind. I'm sure the Chinaman will be glad to wrap it up again for me without screaming and trying to grab my arm.'

'Well, all right.'

'And your friend in the carriage there, whoever he is, he's been leaning out and looking back and just dying to raise his hat to me, and I suppose that's because he figures that any woman you stop a carriage for to talk to and yell at her and grab her arm——'

'Oh, *all right!*'

Lord Chudit observed, but very quietly, that Harry might have introduced his wife, who was a very handsome female.

'Yes, she is nice-looking.'

'Is she occupied? Or could we perhaps go back and——'

'No, she's pretty occupied.'

Phil watched them go; and while she watched, and without looking at it, she rewrapped the Chinese table cover. She had to look at it, however, when she made the knot. She gave the cord a violent yank.

'Well' she said.

'He thinks I'm some kind of a slave' she said.

'Well.'

She lifted her chin, wondering whether any passer had noticed her eyes, which hurt. She looked at the package; tucked it under her arm. She drifted over toward the Café de los Dos Diablos.

Acting as guide for distinguished visitors was no new job for Harry. He was familiar with every foot of the way and acquainted not only with all the Sanitation personnel but also with many of the Construction superintendents and assistant superintendents and foremen. He had a good memory for figures, and his college training helped.

Lord Chudit was as easily entertained as any other Englishman. Harry had learned that they liked to have you speak all the slang you could remember or invent, and that they were delighted when you laughed at their own slang essays. Ordinarily Harry did not use much slang—Phil disapproved—but you couldn't give an Englishman too much of it.

Long before they got to Culebra—already a city, with houses, paved streets, electric lights, a water system, where a few months before there had been jungle—Lord Chudit was guffawing.

'"Pasteboard puncher!" My word, what a name for a guard! I knew old Simpy would see I got somebody amusin'!'

'"Simpy," sir?'

'Yes, quite. Old Simpy. Ah well, uh, "Mr Simpson" I daresay you're expected to call him, eh?'

Harry swallowed. He had assumed that Lord Chudit bore a letter of introduction to Dr Gorgas, who had turned him over to Simpson, who in turn had put him in Harry's care. Harry had never pictured Mr Simpson with any friend away from the Isthmus.

'You know him, then, sir?'

'Simpy? Oh, rather! Thick as thieves! I've had him up in Scotland for the shootin' and he's had me at his house in Long Island, New York. A bit lost sight of him these last few years.'

'What—well, what did Mr Simpson used to do?'

'Do? Why, uh, do? Why, nothing. Nothing except get into all the trouble he could find, that's all.'

'Trouble?'

'Quite. Always risking his neck. Went to Cuba some years before your Army did. Grampusing around with the revolutionists. Spaniards had him prisoner once, and they were going to shoot him. Truth. Up against a wall. It was only his family got him free, through some chaps in Washington. Then when the real war came, the Army wouldn't have him. Too fat. So he went after animals. Never did care for just shootin'. Grouse were no sport, he'd say. He went after grizzly bears, out there in your Rocky Mountains. Wyoming, I believe. Would that be it?'

'Well, it could be.'

'Ah yes. Bagged a good few, I hear. Then he went in for those gasoline-engine carriages. Last time I visited him, his place in Long Island, New York, he had no less than three of the absurd contrivances. Made a frightful racket. Went into all the races. Mad, sheer mad. Why, I've seen old Simpy tearing along a road like a cannon ball, forty, even forty-five miles an hour. Never did get killed. Can't understand why.'

'Well, I'll be damned!'

'Eh?'

'I mean, I'll be hornswoggled!'

' "Hornswoggled!" Oh, I say, that's delicious! "I'll be hornswoggled!" Must remember that!'

Harry said slowly: 'There's something I don't get: Mr Simpson called you "your lordship" and he even stood up when you were getting ready to leave.'

'Pulling your leg, old boy. Nothing else. Why, Simpy's got no more respect for my title than—than—well, than I have myself! Not that it's such a bad title. Understand it cost my grandfather a very large sum, back when money meant more than it does these days. He could afford it, though. Rich bloke. Opium.

'What I simply cannot understand,' Lord Chudit, gabby now, went on, 'is why old Simpy clings to a post like this. Can't be he needs the filthy. Family has packets of it. Huge estate. Oh, his coming *out* here, quite! Like one of our lads going out to Singapore. Adventure, color, all that. Just the sort of thing old Simpy would do. But—oh, I say! Been here three years, I understand?'

'Almost that. He was one of the first.'

'Oh, I say! In that ghastly office all the while, too?'

'Yes, all the time.'

'Don't have a gel somewhere? None of my affair, of course.'

'Not that I ever heard of. Come to think of it,' added Harry, 'I've never even heard of Mr Simpson going to a ball game. I invited him to our housewarming, as a matter of form. He was polite, but he just said he never went to parties.'

'Never was a drinker. I remember that. I say. I gather from him that you're the lad who all but tackled some sort of pugilistic champion, is that right?'

'Oh, that! Why, it wasn't anything. Just a misunderstanding.'

'Well, I daresay he was a bit of a battler, the way old Simpy described him. And Simpy should know. Did a good bit of sparring himself before he took on so much weight.'

'Say, I sure am learning a lot about my boss!'

'Curious, ain't it? You two working together all this time, and you never knew him. But then, I daresay all you chaps out here are—well, a bit odd, eh? I don't mean to be offensive! But don't you think it possible that all of you are a bit mad, looking for something you can't find, or running away from something?'

'Well, as far as I know we're just an ordinary bunch of guys.'

'Oh, I say! You yourself, now? Used to box a bit, I'll wager?'

'I never did. Always wanted to, but I never had the time.'

'Ah. But polo?'

'Hell no, your lordship!'

'Really? Sailing, perhaps? Or do you hunt?'

'Never fired a shot in my life. And the only boat I was ever on, outside of the Hoboken ferry, was the tub I came down here on. As a matter of fact, I can never even remember which side is port and which is starboard.'

'Odd. Odd. Still, I say, there's *some* reason you're here?'

'Oh yes. There's a reason' Harry smiled. 'But it hasn't anything to do with sport.'

It was pleasant walking from the station up to G.H.Q. This might have been a spring day at home.

'You know, your lordship,' Harry said just before they went into the divisional engineer's office, 'you're a funny guy.'

'Oh, quite' said Lord Chudit, lost in thought.

He did not seem interested in the personages to whom Harry introduced him. He expressed a proper astonishment at the figures they quoted, um-m-ming portentously. You'd have said that he was unaware of the fact that his title was creating some stir.

'If your lordship would care to have us set off some dynamite charges, to show you how——'

'Oh, see here! Dynamite? My word!'

'We have to. It's soft rock here, but not soft enough to scoop. Black powder would be cheaper, but it's too wet here. So we use dynamite. We happen to have plenty of it on hand, so if you want——'

'Very decent of you, really. But the truth is, Kellems here said something about taking me up some sort of hill?'

'I thought we might try Cucaracha' Harry explained. 'It's the best view. That is, if you could rustle up some transportation?'

'Hell yes. I'll fix you up with a set of Bims.'

'See here——'

'It means cockroach' Harry explained.

'"Bims"? Odd.'

'No, no! Cucaracha means cockroach. That's the hill. Bims means darkies from the Barbados. Your people. British objects.'

'Ha! British *objects*? I say, is that what you call them?'

The divisional engineer, a shade alarmed, whispered: 'Is he always this way?'

'As a matter of fact,' Harry whispered back, 'he's a good guy.'

Lord Chudit remembered his manners and asked how the various

British West Indian Negroes shaped up as laborers. The divisional engineer looked at the ceiling while Harry answered.

'Mr Dauchy, who isn't here now—he was Mr Wallace's assistant and then later he was in charge out here in this division——'

'Oh, quite.'

'Well, it was Mr Dauchy's considered opinion that the average British *object*, whether he came from Jamaica, as most of 'em do, or the Barbados, or Trinidad, actually accomplished about one fifth of the work that would normally be expected of a white American laborer.'

'I say, that's not much, is it?'

'No.'

'Rather bad, really. One fifth.'

'They quarrel a lot. They've always got some bellyache—their wages or their hours or their food or the way they're treated.'

The divisional engineer gave a huge nod.

'Sometimes it seems as if somebody must be poking 'em up' he said. 'Doesn't seem natural that they could kick so much all by themselves. Doesn't seem as if they could *think* of so many ways to take offense. It gets so that again and again we have to call in Sir Claude to straighten things out and make sure their rights are all protected and everything. In the meanwhile, the work isn't getting done.'

Lord Chudit deliberately asked Harry: 'That would be Mallet?'

'Yes, Sir Claude Coventry Mallet' the divisional engineer answered. 'A smart hombre! Get him here a few minutes, and everything's hunky-dory. He talks long words to them, and they eat it up.'

'By the bye,' Lord Chudit said to Harry, 'I'm having a spot of whisky with Mallet when we get back. Simpy'll be there. And they wondered whether you wouldn't join us, Kellems? Do you mind?' he asked the divisional engineer. 'Just remembered it.'

'Not at all.'

'Well——' said Harry.

'See here, Simpy particularly asked me to ask you, if I liked you.'

'Well, in that case——'

In a handcar manned by six disgusted Bims they went to the foot of Cucaracha.

'Well, come on' the white assistant foreman said wearily; and wearily, with him and Harry and even Lord Chudit helping, they lifted the handcar from the tracks. The Bims crawled beneath it and curled into a puppyish pile and went to sleep. The white assistant foreman lit his pipe.

'Going to be long?'

'We don't know' Harry answered crisply. 'An hour perhaps.'

'Oh hell.'

'You might try to exhibit a little more politeness in the presence of visitors' Harry snapped.

'Why?'

Lord Chudit had been looking around, nodding absently.

'Tell the truth, Kellems,' he said, suddenly facing Harry, 'I can't remember myself which side is port and which is starboard!'

'Well, it's a good thing we're not adrift at sea' said Harry.

Bland sunshine lit up rock and earth which had been violated for no apparent reason. The air held only silence. The rails of the one line of track occasionally met the sun and flared, but most of the time they were merely steel. The sky held two immovable clouds and no bird, not even a buzzard. The Bims snored. The white assistant foreman, a kid, Harry decided, who ought to be spanked, contemptuously puffed his pipe.

'It isn't much here. But from the top——'

'Ah yes. Quite. And, uh, which way do we go?'

'Up' said Harry.

His lordship was wiry. His medium-sized feet dug with vigor into ripped reddish earth, and his medium-sized legs gave no hint of tiredness as they toiled upward. Toiled? Lord Chudit, bless his heart, truly seemed to enjoy the exercise. Harry had taken other visitors up this hill, and previously he had permitted himself a certain smug feeling of pleasure, a purr of pride in his own condition as compared with theirs, the poor sissies. However, Harry had not been accustomed to chat as he climbed. Lord Chudit never stopped talking.

'You will come and have that spot with Mallet and the rest, won't you? Simpy did ask. I say, that's the jungle up there?'

'Yes, sir, that's the jungle. Used to be all over this place.'

'I say, it'd get here again in a moment if you chaps weren't watching it, eh? Beastly stuff.'

The jungle glowered over the lip of the Cut, leering down at them. It was not tall, nor was it pretentious, but it looked evil.

'Odd sort of gully. Why do they call it Culebra, d'y' suppose?'

'Culebra's Spanish for snake.'

'Oh, quite. I say, Simpy said something about snakes. About you and snakes, that is. You, uh, stuff them or charm them or something, eh?'

'Snakes? I hate them!'

'Why d'y' suppose he said that, then? Something about snakes.'

'Well, one nipped me the other day. He was probably kidding me about that. It was a tamagas. Got me in the face.'

'Oh, I say, not in the *face?*'

'It's a tree snake. Bright green. Very vicious. No rattling, no fooling around. Just strikes. It puffed my cheek for three-four days.'

'But see here, you mean it reached out from a tree——'

'Well, I was up in the tree too.'

'You were—— Now see here! Damn it, I knew you were a footballer or something! You, uh, climb trees, eh?'

'Not ordinarily. I just went up this one because I wanted to pick a flower.'

Then for a little while even Lord Chudit, that chatterbox, was silent. He did not cease to climb; and indeed, astonishment lent push to the shales and dirt that slithered under his feet. When he spoke again it was a whisper, as though his throat were parched.

'You were—I say!—you were picking a bloody *flower?*'

'That's right.'

'Up a—see here!—up a bloody *tree?*'

'It was an orchid' Harry explained. 'The flower, I mean. Not the tree. Quite.'

(I shouldn't talk that way to an earl, he thought.)

'And, uh, the snake objected?'

'Sure did. Bit me in the cheek. I didn't see the gol-darn thing until it was writhing away. Then I grabbed it. Don't know why.'

'And, uh, what did you do with it?'

'Dropped it right away, as soon as I realized that I was holding a snake in my hand. I don't like to hold snakes.'

'Well, uh, of course. Yes. I can readily understand that. But see here, Kellems, you flabbergast me. May I—I say, do you mind?—may I ask, please, old boy, *why* you were in the tree picking a flower?'

'Sure. I had a party of people from Washington, and I'd taken them up here, up where we're going now, and they were oh-ing and ah-ing and all that. And there I was, and there was the jungle right behind me, and so I walked back there looking for a flower.'

'But, uh, why a flower?'

'For my wife, of course, you half-wit!'

Nothing happened. The sky stayed right where it was, with those

126

two cotton-batting clouds snugged into it, and the air smooth and clean, and below them the suspended effort of digging a canal. No, nothing at all happened. Except that Lord Chudit giggled.

'See here, old boy——'

'I'm sorry I spoke that way, your lordship. What I meant——'

'Nonsense! When you called me a half-wit you probably gave me credit for much more brains than I truly have. All I was *trying* to say, old boy, is that you must be really frightfully in love—or else a frightful fool.'

'Well, I guess I'm both, more or less.'

'I knew there was *some* reason why you were out here. Ah well! Is this the top, Kellems? Is this where we look around?'

There was no sparkle or glitter, no challenge to the sun, whose rays were taken swiftly and expunged by jungle among the hills and by shards and ripped earth in the Cut itself. The earth was not bright, not a laughing yellow, but a dull yellowish red, and unresponsive. Only the two demure white clouds, which refused to be budged by a breeze, lent any note of daintiness. Nothing whatever lent a note of strength. It was a desolate scene.

'That's Contractors' Hill over there, and this one behind us is Gold Hill. They're the two highest points along the Line.'

'Ah' said the Earl of Chudit. 'Um-m, yes. So this is Culebra Cut?'

'This is the lower end of the Cut. It goes about nine miles up that way. This is the toughest part, right here.'

The world's greatest ditch-to-be? It was absurd! The obstacle had been but nibbled at, ripped, grooved, shoved back and forth, it would seem aimlessly. What was glorious? Four large excavators were in sight, but they were idle: they had the aspect of things that drooped, tired. Two shovels were in sight, and only one of these was operating, its arm swinging, swinging faithfully but scarcely with hope, a sliver of steam rising halfheartedly from its safety valve. Along the sides of the Cut, here and there, as though placed by a giant's child who had made room for them by drawing a finger horizontally along first one bank, then the other, were greenish-grayish buildings with red roofs, with white trim.

'That's Culebra, the place we just came from. And up beyond that, where those buildings are that aren't painted, that's Empire. Place where the French had their G.H.Q. We're using it for machine shops.'

'Ah, quite. This, uh, roughly will be the bottom of the canal?'

'Oh no! There's heaps of digging yet! We don't know how much, because we're not sure yet what the level of the canal's to be.'

'But didn't that, uh, that international sort of body——'

'They studied it. There were eight Americans, two Frenchmen, one Englishman, one Prussian, and one Dutchman, all canal experts. Finally, a few months ago, they recommended a sea-level job. Every one of the foreigners and three of the Americans recommended sea-level. Eight for sea-level, five for locks. It went to Big Smoke.'

'Eh?'

'Mr Stevens. He's chief engineer here. Big Smoke we call him, because he smokes big cigars.'

'See here, that's a thought! Won't you, uh, have one of these?'

'Thanks.'

'Then it's to be sea-level, eh? Sounds sensible.'

'No. Big Smoke favors locks, so I think we're going to have locks.'

'You mean you've taken all the trouble and expense to ask all those distinguished foreign experts to study the situation—and then you throw their recommendation away?'

'That's about the size of it. Mr Stevens thinks an eighty-five-foot lock canal would be right, and the rest of the I.C.C. said o.k., and Teddy —President Roosevelt, you know—he always believes in one-man control—and he o.k.'d it too, and he's recommended it to Congress. Congress hasn't done anything yet.'

'Ah, I see. That's why there's so very little work, eh?'

'No, that isn't the reason. Not the real reason, anyway. This cut's got to go deeper, even if we're going to have a lock canal. That's why the French, even when they weren't sure of their own plans, what with the bankruptcy and reorganization and everything, at least they figured they could dig, dig, dig, dig, dig here. Get it?'

'Quite. But in that event, if I may ask, why don't you chaps dig, dig, dig, dig, dig here, as you express it?'

'In the first place because right off the bat everybody at home wanted us to do exactly that. I mean, they wanted to see the dirt fly. That was the expression they used—see the dirt fly.'

'Well, you Yankees, I understand, can do just about anything?'

'Yes, we can' Harry answered soberly. 'Let's get this straight, your lordship, because I don't want to insult you or anything——'

'Certainly not, old boy!'

'I *do* think that we can do just about anything. I *know* we can! If I questioned that I wouldn't really be an American. Do you catch my drift, your lordship? It's kind of hard to explain.'

128

'Your, uh, your drift? Oh, quite! You've made it perfectly clear. Only, I say, feeling like that, then this sight must depress you dreadfully?'

Harry smiled and shook his head. 'It isn't very inspiring, that's true. I'm sure it isn't what you expected. Truth is, the French did most of what excavating you see done, before we took over. They removed about eighty million cubic yards. We haven't done one tenth of that, yet.'

The shovel finished its work and raised its arm; a high-piling column of steam rose from it, and on Cucaracha they could almost hear the shriek. A loaded train started down the Cut toward them—one of those dinky swaying European locomotives and about twenty flatcars loaded with dirt and rock. The train crossed from the west to the east banks just before it reached the foot of Cucaracha, and it chuffed past the derailed handcar and the white assistant foreman and the slumbering Bims. Dirt spilled negligently from the sides of the cars. From the stack smoke rose in identical black balls exactly spaced, for all the world like the smoke from a locomotive in a child's drawing. After a long while the train fussed out of sight, down toward Pedro Miguel. It never had seemed a real thing. The Cut was silent again.

'I would be discouraged' Harry said 'if I didn't happen to know what's going on. That railroad, that's our big problem right now. We can't do anything without it. There's no sense shoveling dirt unless you know where you're going to put it. The original plan called for two years of surveys and preparation, but the people at home weren't willing to wait. They wanted action! Sure!

'But Big Smoke knows. And Mr Shonts knows. One of the first things Big Smoke did was to stop practically all the digging here. And one of the first things Mr Shonts did was to give us Sanitation men enough money to really get things cleaned up. No sense bringing thousands of workmen down here if they're going to die off like flies.'

'Ah, quite.'

'That railroad was a good railroad once. It's American. It was built back in the days of the California gold rush, and for a while it made a heap of money. After that it was allowed to go pretty much to pot. It's got a swell roadbed, ballasted in gravel and rock, but it's single-tracked, there are practically no sidings or way stations, no good round-houses, no good terminals, the telegraph hardly works, the locomotives and the rolling stock are twenty years out of date, and there isn't enough of them anyway, and the warehouses, which were falling apart, were jam-packed with stuff that'd been there for years—with a lot of the shipping papers and freight records missing.

'Well, sir, you might as well say we're building a new railroad. We're double-tracking it clear through and tearing out the old fifty-six and seventy-pound rails and putting in ninety-pound ones. We're building sidings. We're building stations. We're building new terminals. We're getting in bigger locomotives, a lot of them, and we're getting in forty-ton flatcars and boxcars. Those flatties you saw on the train that just passed—they're the ones we inherited—they're ten-tonners and twelve-tonners. You can see the difference? It's not easy to get these things fast, either, because of course we have to buy all the equipment at home, where the standard railroad gauge is four feet eight and a half inches, while this railroad happens to have a five-foot gauge.

'Also, remember this: All that heavier equipment means that every foot of the roadbed has to be widened. And every culvert and trestle and bridge—and you can imagine how many of those there are in a wet country like this!—they all have to be widened and strengthened.

'When all that's done, and when the right dumps for the spoil have been established, *then* you'll see the dirt fly!' He pointed. 'The way it is now, that shovel we just saw stop work is likely to stay idle like that for an hour or even an hour and a half before it gets another train to load. Is that any way to build a canal?'

Lord Chudit smiled at him.

'Yet I gather that you're confident of finishing the thing?'

'Oh sure! You know,' thoughtfully, 'I've had an idea lately, and I think lots of us down here have, that maybe the rest of the world is sort of laughing at the way we're handling this job.'

'Oh, now see here, I wouldn't say——'

'Never mind being polite! Maybe they're not, but I suspect that they are. Well, that's just the sort of thing that will get us sore. You know, your lordship, I think we're beginning to *get* sore now!'

'Good chap!'

'You come back a year from now and stand right where we're standing, and I'll bet you'll see something!'

'I'm sure of it.' Lord Chudit did not sound sure of it. He harrumphed. 'When the, uh, water, when the *canal itself* comes through —assuming that it does—but I'm sure it will!—then there'll be a bridge down there, where the track crosses the Cut?'

'No. When we get ready to let the water in we'll have to pick up the whole railroad and move it to another place. What it'll amount to is that we'll be building a *third* railroad. Most of this line as it is now will be under water. You see, they're going to dam the Chagres and create an enormous lake, the biggest artificial lake in the world, and we'll get our electric power from there, to run the locks, *if* Congress says go ahead. The Chagres is a tricky stream. It has sudden terrific rises that you can't predict. So we've got to do something radical to it. This lake will cover a hundred and fifty square miles, and it'll mean we'll have to move fourteen or fifteen native villages. We probably won't move them, really. We'll probably just build new ones.'

'My word, there's nothing petty about you chaps!'

'We're not a petty nation' Harry said soberly. He pointed below, to where an empty spoil train was chuffing back from the direction of Pedro Miguel. 'Here the railroad won't have to be moved so far, here in the mountains. The plan now is to carry it along on a forty-foot berm along the east bank here, this bank we're on now, about ten feet above the water level. Though we may have to take it clear around Gold Hill back there. It all depends on slides.'

'Uh, landslides?'

'Yes. And we're likely to get more of them from now on. They can be bad. I was talking the other day to Mr MacDonald, who's our geologist, and he says there are all sorts of reasons for expecting slides along here—right in along here, particularly.'

'Ah?' Lord Chudit looked at the ground under his feet.

'Mr MacDonald said that the chief reason is because the earth along here consists of a top layer of porous clay, anywhere from ten to forty feet deep, and underneath that there's a stratum of much harder rock which is *not* porous. Well, you've heard how hard it rains here? Well, the rain water seeps through the clay, but it can't get through the rock, so it forms a sort of heavy soapy surface on the upper part of the rock. And then something happens—a dynamite charge, a train passing, practically anything—and the whole top mass begins to slide.'

'You don't say!'

'Yes. Right along here particularly.'

Up toward Culebra a cloud of dust rose twenty-five or thirty feet from the floor of the ditch, and as the dust thinned, shimmering in the sunlight, they could see that there were rocks in it, rocks arching to fall; and to their ears came a dull far *boo-oom!* Soon afterward they saw a man approach the brand-new crater, winding something on a big spool as he walked.

'See here, this place is sportier than I'd thought.' Lord Chudit drew a turnip and consulted it. 'But we mustn't forget old Mallet.'

'Oh, absolutely!'

'Shall we, uh, shall we join the gentlemen, then?'

Harry was late for dinner, and ordinarily Phil would be angry; but he had a brilliant excuse.

'Now don't start scolding me because there's scotch on my breath, darling! Wait till you hear about it first!'

She was seated at the front window, looking down a hillside gaudy with sunset, down over the bay, the islands, the pelicans. She did not even turn her head when he entered.

'All right, but listen! I've been detained by the special request of my pal the Earl of Chudit, with whom I've been spending all afternoon. Lord Chudit, darling! Does that mean anything to you? *And I've been having a few drinks with him and Mr Simpson and Governor Magoon and a few others at Sir Claude Coventry Mallet's house. Matter of fact, Sir Claude and Lady Mallet urged me to stay for——'*

She rose, turning, and because her face was shadowed he did not at first see that there were tears in her eyes.

'Harry, we've got to leave this country! We've got to! I refuse to live here any longer!'

8

THEY STOOD facing Las Bovidas and the bay, though they could see nothing beyond the sea wall, which itself was not always visible. They'd been caught without umbrellas.

'It's early for this' he shouted.

'Yes, isn't it?' Madeline shouted back.

Others who had taken refuge under this same balcony stood around them, women with bundles, supercilious men.

'Can't have a lesson tomorrow' Harry shouted after a while. 'Have to go over to Colon. See Phil off.'

'Oh?'

'On the *Havana*. She's going to take a vacation.'

'Isn't this sudden?'

'Well, yes and no. She only decided last night that she'd catch the *Havana*, and I only made the reservation this morning, by the telephone. Easy to get reservations now. More coming down than there are going back. Not a single case of yellow jack in more than six months—that's what does it!'

'But she'd been planning a vacation for some time?'

'Well, yes. Matter of fact, she wanted for us both to go—not simply on vacation but to quit and go back to Paterson.'

Madeline caught her breath.

'I couldn't see that' Harry shouted on. 'She was set on it. Kept after me morning, noon, and night. Seemed sort of desperate. Then she wanted me to at least take a vacation with her. Well, I rate one, as far as that goes. I've been here two years now. But I didn't think I could afford it.'

He frowned. Phil had gone so far as to offer to help finance the trip with her allowance money. She'd made this offer with as much tact as she could; it had angered him, all the same.

'We've been having it out for weeks now, regular hammer and tongs. But finally she decided to go alone.'

'You must say good-by to her for me.'

'I'll do that.'

There was a break in the rain, and the group was stirred to action. Madeline and Harry hurried two crossings toward the center of the city, dodging from balcony shelter to balcony shelter, reluctant to leave the safety of each for the next, for all the world like a couple of kids playing going-to-Jerusalem. However, when the rain did come again they were safely placed.

'Phil deserves it. She's been here a whole year now, and she's been a good sport about everything.'

Madeline wondered. Madeline had wondered a great deal about Phyllis Kellems in this past year. The American woman's endurance, admittedly, amazed her. Madeline after the housewarming, after glimpsing Phil in the seemingly innocuous act of saying good night to one of her guests, had given her three months. But Phil remained. She might be restless, but she was holding on.

'Tell the truth, I guess this place is kind of getting on her nerves, the way it does with a lot of people.'

'Yes.'

'It's never bothered me that way. I guess that's because I haven't any particular home to think of, anyway. Not since Dad died. I'd been three and a half years in college, and working summers, when I came down here. But I can easily see how it would be different with ordinary people.'

'Yes.'

'Do her good anyway to see a few shows and buy herself some new hats and so forth.'

'How long did you say she would be gone?'

'About six weeks altogether. It'll do her good. I'd been trying for a long time to get her more interested in things here. I've talked about how the work's going. I've urged her to study Spanish. I've even suggested that she come down here more often and just walk around and look at things. After all, it's the oldest city in the Western Hemisphere, even if it is pretty dirty. Now that the water's turned on and so many of the streets are paved it isn't too bad. And there are the churches, and the Cathedral, and places like this'—he waved a hand to indicate the sea wall, a blear, illy defined thing through the rain. 'Why, you couldn't find a more picturesque place! And then the ruins. I did take her out there once, one Sunday, in a carriage. But she didn't seem interested. Gosh, I could poke around that Old City all day!'

'Could you? I love it there too.'

'I tried to talk her into a trip to Nombre de Dios or Porto Bello. It'd be uncomfortable, but I'll bet it would be worth the trouble. I'd sure like to see that fort! And if you don't see it soon there may not be another chance. If they do build that big dam at Gatun they're talking about, then they might have to establish a quarry at Porto Bello. They're thinking of that. We've been notified that there might be a sanitation station needed there. There's a lot of good rock at Porto Bello, and a pretty good harbor. They could lighter the stuff down to Colon.'

'You mean they'd destroy the old fort?'

'Oh, I don't suppose they'd go as far as that! I certainly hope not! Matter of fact, that's just the kind of thing your father's always expecting us to do. But even so, it wouldn't be as much fun with cranes and lighters and laborers' quarters and all. Right now, the way it is now, there's nothing but a few Indians there.'

The rain stopped suddenly, and he lowered his voice, feeling, as he always did on such occasions, rather foolish because of having been caught in the middle of a shout. They scurried along the promenade, stepping around puddles.

'Well, maybe she'll feel different when she comes back.'

Maybe, thought Madeline.

'This place does act that way on some people. The heat and rain and so forth. And most of all, nothing to do. You and I, we have jobs. That is, you practically have a job, taking care of your father and teaching Spanish. But Phil just hasn't anything to do. No theaters, no concerts, nothing. I heard somebody say the other day that what this place needs most of all is a Coney Island. You know, there's a lot of truth in that!'

'A—a what, 'Arry?'

He explained. 'Oh, they'll get around to it. They're building club-houses right now in several places, with bowling alleys and so forth. And of course it'll be good when they get that big hotel finished. But right now it's pretty hard on Phil. I—I was kind of hoping that maybe you'd drop in to see her now and then, mademoiselle.'

'I am so sorry, Harry! I have meant to, many times. But——'

'I understand. Sure.'

Rain again, and again they stopped.

'What you say of the monotony here, and the heat and rain, and people acting queer sometimes . . . 'Arry, it is very true.'

'Yeah, that's just the way she's been lately—queer.'

'Another who has been acting queer, 'Arry, is Darlington Winter. It is of course not for our interference but—have you seen him?'

'Darl? No, not in some time. He always was a quiet cuss.'

'He is now quieter than ever, and when he does speak he says strange things.'

'Such as what?'

'Oh, I do not remember. It isn't so much what he says as it is the way in which he says it. It frightens me.'

In an effort to be playful: 'Maybe he's trying to screw up courage to pop the question?'

'It is—what?'

'To propose to you.'

'Oh.' She looked up. 'I do not know why you should have been expected to know this, 'Arry, nor why I should wish to tell you now, but—Darl Winter has already proposed to me.'

'No kidding?'

'Many times. And each time I have refused him.'

Harry felt like asking why. Darl had a good job.

'All the same, I like him very much and sometimes I worry about him. He always liked you so much, 'Arry. Do you suppose that you could find a chance to speak to him and see what the trouble is?'

'Well, you know he had some sort of nasty fight with his parents. Particularly his father. Maybe he's brooding about that.'

'Maybe. Or it might be something about me. If it is about me, 'Arry, and if there is anything I can do to help him or comfort him—short of marrying him—I'd like to know about it.'

'Well, say, that's mighty white of you! I'll get hold of him. Soon. Matter of fact, I think I'll go up to the old place right after lunch. Darl'll probably still be hanging around.'

'You will be discreet?'

'Watch me. Ambassador Kellems.'

They had reached her street, and she extended a hand. The French, Harry reflected, are certainly great on shaking hands.

'Adios, señorita.'

'Adios, mi amigo.'

'Hasta mañana.'

'No, no! No hasta mañana ahora! Hasta *la vista* ahora!'

'Oh, that's right. Well, hasta la vista then.'

He started along Las Bovidas, but turned back, he didn't know why. As he so often did, he watched Madeline's retreating form. He loved to see her walk. When at last she was lost in a crowd of those released by the pause in the rain, he turned away with a sigh.

A thin saturnine Panamanian in white was watching him from beneath heavy slitted lids. The Panamanian glanced in the direction

Madeline had taken and nodded ever so slightly. He looked again at Harry, and again he gave a slight nod. He almost smiled.

Seared by anger, Harry was about to tell him to mind his own damn business; but this passed; he relaxed; and indeed he even answered the almost-smile.

'Si, señor,' he whispered.

The man took the cigar from his mouth.

'Si, si, señor' the man said, and sighed, and put the cigar back into his mouth, and after glancing once more in the direction Madeline had taken, and after one final almost-smile, he walked on.

Harry seldom visited the D.M.s these days, because he knew so few of them. The original gang had long since been broken up; at one time or other, for one reason or another, they had all gone home or died—all excepting Harry T, who had been transferred to Cristobal, and Darl Winter, the least sociable of the lot.

The place had been improved. The steps had been strengthened; the whole building, inside and out, had been painted; steel lockers had been installed, and iron cots had replaced the wooden bunks, and best of all, there was a bathroom. Yet it looked much the same. The long table still was strewn with silverware and bottles of condiments, with boxes of powdered and tablet-form quinine, and salt and pepper jars (you couldn't use shakers in Panama, of course), and all the other articles forming the familiar debris which Bertram was forever promising to clear up. There were still muddy shoes under the beds, bottles behind pillows, crumpled towels on the chairs. There was an electric light dangling from the ceiling, but somebody had taped above it the green shade from the old pressure lamp, so that it looked much the same. And there, as always, directly in front of the door, where everybody would be sure to stumble over it, was the old kerosene tin, mounted on a rusty tripod, in which charcoal was burning; and around this, as though the original Disgusted Millionaires still were here, were the chairs on the backs of which hung steaming drying shirts, socks, underdrawers. The place still looked like a college dormitory and stank like a combination rathskeller and laundry.

Bertram emerged from the kitchen.

'It is a pleasure to envisage your countenance again, Mr Kellems.'

'How's it been going, Berty?'

'It has not been going well, sir.' It never went well with Bertram. 'I find myself in the grip of circumstances over which self-control lies virtually dormant.'

'That mean you're going to resign again?'

'I have decided to expediate my departure. I have been subjected here to unessential domestic inconveniences.'

'Boy!'

'Besides, I've got another job.'

'You don't say! I hope it's one that doesn't involve so much work. You know, Berty, I always felt that you were overworked here.'

'Thank you, Mr Kellems. Your understandment is gratifying.' Bertram went so far as to bow.

'What are you going to do?'

'My services have been engaged by the Sanitary Department, sir.'

'Say, I'm in Sanitation myself. We'll be co-workers, eh?'

'I tend to the belief, Mr Kellems, that my services will be directed largely along the lines of research. The nature of my duties-to-be was presented to me in that light, sir.'

'Research, eh? Well, that's very interesting. The boys'll miss you, Berty. None of them here right now?'

'Only Mr Winter, sir.'

Darl came out of the bathroom. His feet were bare, and he wore an undershirt and his best cheviot trousers.

'Hello. Thought that sounded like you. Say, I'm glad you came. Gives me a chance to tell you something before I go.'

'Go? Where? You're not going home, are you?'

'No. I don't know where I am going, but it's not home.' He hauled a suitcase from the top of a locker. 'I resigned this morning, to take effect immediately, and I got a reservation on the *Havana*.'

'Say, Phil's going to sail on that boat too!'

'That'll be nice.'

'What's the matter, Darl?'

'Everything. I'm glad you dropped in. You're the only one I can talk to here. The rest of these kids don't know their elbow from a hole in the ground. And then you're a friend of Madeline's too.'

'It's something to do with Madeline?'

'Yes. Only I don't want her to worry about it. She won't marry me, she's refused me more times than I care to count, but all the same she's the kindest-hearted woman in this world and I wouldn't want to think of her worrying about me—when something happens.'

Harry ignored the dark threat. 'Say, this is fine! Phil will be tickled to death to have somebody she knows on board, and I'm certainly glad to hear you've made it up with your folks.'

138

'I haven't made up with my parents' Darl answered coldly. 'And I'm not going home: I told you that.'

'Then where are you going?'

'That's something nobody knows.' He seemed for the first time to become aware of Bertram's presence. 'What are you hanging around for? Get a move on and get back to that damn kitchen of yours!'

'Don't you dare expurge language of a blasphemous basis to me! I'll have you know that I just resigned!'

'Wonderful. If you'd only stick to it.'

Bertram retreated, angry, as Harry knew from the back of his neck and the set of his shoulders. Harry said that he didn't see any need for acting that way. Darl was instantly repentant.

'This darn heat, I guess, and all this rain. I'll apologize to him.'

He went into the kitchen.

'It's all right,' a minute later. 'I not only told him I was sorry, but I tipped him and said good-by. He was so pleased about this new job he's got that he graciously forgave me.'

Darl dressed. He took shirts from his locker, folded them, approached the table with them, frowned.

'Of course he hasn't cleaned up. He just about never does '

Yet in spite of himself Darl grinned a little. That table did not mean food to him; for the less you thought about food here the better off you were. There were no fresh vegetables, there was seldom any fresh fruit. Fresh meat was often obtainable these days, but it was extraordinarily tough meat, for it had to be eaten within twenty-four hours of the slaughtering. No, meals were not what that table made Darl think of. Not meals, poker. He and Harry had been the two best poker hands among the old D.M.s, Darl a plunger, opening every other pot, boosting, boosting, while Harry, who needed the money, had been careful; yet Harry had always been a hard man to bluff, and he could be reckless too, just as Darl on occasion could be canny.

'I'll be leaving that to you, Harry. Why don't you come over here now and then and remove some of their mazuma? They're begging for it.'

'I might, at that. A little poker would be nice.'

'Your better half draws the line at it, does she?'

'No. No, on the contrary she urges me to go out any time I want. But I can tell from the way she says it that she'd be hopping mad if I ever *did* go. Anyway I have to leave her alone up there enough as it is. I feel I ought to stick around as much as I can.'

'Well, you be sure to get over here now, anyway. I'll feel better about things, when I go from Cristobal to nowhere, if I figure that you're taking these kids to the cleaner.'

Harry stood up, scowling. 'Hey, listen! You've implied several times that you're thinking of committing suicide. Is that right?'

Darl was putting underwear into the suitcase. He looked up deliberately 'That's right' he said. Then he went on putting underwear into the suitcase.

'They say that a man who talks about it first never does it.'

'They can say anything they want. You know me better than that.'

'Yes.'

'I shouldn't have told you. I haven't told anybody else, and I'm going to do everything I can to make it seem an accident. That's why I'm actually going to sail on that ship tomorrow. The reason I'm telling you is because of Madeline. Like I said before, I don't want her to think she had anything to do with it. I expect you to take care of that, Harry. I mean if you ever even hear about me again. Or if Madeline does.'

He was closing the bag.

Harry said 'The *Havana* doesn't sail until noon tomorrow.'

'I know. But I'm clearing out now. That way I won't have to do a lot of explaining to these nitwits I live with. I'll have dinner in Colon tonight and spend the night there in the hotel.'

'Not even going to look anybody up to say good-by to them?'

'No. I did mean to look you up, but now I don't have to.'

'Not even Madeline?'

'Madeline least of all. I'd go all to pieces. Don't you understand? As long as I can snarl at myself this way I don't feel too bad. But if I were to see Madeline, even for a second, I'd be blubbering and slobbering all over the place.'

'Well? Maybe that would do you good?'

'Maybe it might do some people good. Not me.' He took his glasses off and wiped them.

'Look, Darl. It's none of my business, but all the same——'

'Don't apologize, for Christ's sake! I—I—— As a matter of fact, I'm sort of touched that you're taking such an interest, Harry.'

'But look, why *sneak* away? You haven't done anything *wrong!* Look, you've been here almost two years now, and you mean to tell me you're going to just slip off without saying good-by to anybody?'

'I just now said good-by to Berty. He's enough.'

'I'll go over with you' Harry decided. 'I can take the afternoon off. Simpson won't mind.'

Darl looked at him. 'They're pretty good to you, aren't they, Harry?'

'Well, I do a lot of extra work I don't have to do.'

'I know. Well, suit yourself.'

He lifted the bag and strode out with no backward glance. Harry followed him, and they walked down the hill.

They sat in a hovel unexpectedly called the Transatlantic Gardens and had rum with water. Harry knew that the trip had been a failure. He'd hoped that the click of rails, the jolting of the car, the landscape's dreariness, and his own discreet silence would cause Darl to talk and talk. However, Darl had talked very little.

'It comes to this' Darl had said once. 'I appreciate your interest, Harry, and it's darn decent of you, but it comes down to this: that I'm just so much in love with that girl that I can't live without her. And she won't have me. So there you are.'

'But that's so *old-fashioned!*'

'Yes, I guess it is, at that. But it's the way I am.'

'Maybe if she got to know you better——'

'Don't be silly. She knows me as well as anybody can. After all, this isn't any sudden infatuation. I've been mad about her ever since I first met her. And Madeline isn't a person to change her mind, any more than I am. Besides, she's got somebody else she's in love with.'

Harry had sat upright. 'How do you know that?'

'She practically told me, the first time I proposed to her. That was the night you and Phil gave that housewarming, last year. I took her, remember? And when we were getting ready to say good night, in front of her house, I proposed to her. She was very sweet about it. She always has been. But when I asked her—like any other dizzy-flat who's lost his head over a girl—when I asked her if there was anybody else, she told me frankly that there was. That should have been enough for me. It wasn't. I tried again and again.'

Harry had gazed uneasily out of the window. 'Did she—I mean—have you any idea——'

'I didn't ask her, of course. That's her own affair. There's no sense being jealous, even if I knew who it was. I'd only make an even worse fool of myself.'

'But I've never noticed—I mean, Madeline is always so——'

'She's not demonstrative, that's a fact. And as I say, I never tried to find out. But my *guess* is that it's that man Wright.'

'Ward Wright!' Harry had wheeled on him. 'Why, what in the world makes you think that——'

'Why not? He's known her longer than any of us, and you've got to admit he's handsome. I don't like him personally, never have. But I do remember this: That night of the housewarming, when I was helping her into our carriage, she turned around and saw Captain Wright standing just outside your door and saying good night to your wife—and it gave her a jolt. I can't exactly explain it, but it made some difference to her there and then. She was much more thoughtful even than she'd been before. If I'd had any sense I wouldn't have proposed to her that night, but I just couldn't hold myself in any longer. I figured later that maybe she was jealous for just a split second there, when she saw them together. I don't mean that she thought anything was *wrong!* I certainly don't mean that, Harry! There was nothing that could have been more innocent than the way they were standing there saying good night to one another! But maybe it made Madeline just a little jealous even to see that man Wright talking to a woman as pretty as your wife. That's all I meant.'

'I see what you mean.'

'It certainly gave her a jolt. I can't exactly explain. She didn't say anything, but it had some powerful effect on her and made her quieter than ever. When I proposed to her that night, and she refused me, I asked her if she was going to marry this other man, whoever he was. It was the first and last time I ever asked her anything like that. And what she answered was kind of funny, Harry. "I don't know" she said. "But I think I can wait, now." That was all.

'Another thing. You don't see her around anywhere with Captain Wright, no, but haven't you run into him there at her house when you go to pick her up for your Spanish lesson? I know I have. Four or five times. And sometimes at night, too. He usually isn't talking to Madeline, he's talking to the old codger. He's the only American I know, except you, who can get along with Desmoulins for more than five minutes. You're different. Everybody likes you. But that man Wright is doing everything he can to make a good impression. Why? He can't speak a word of French, there's nothing he could have in common with a man like Desmoulins. Yet he hangs around there. Why? Well, it's my opinion that he's trying to talk the old man into something, or else out of something. Why couldn't it be Madeline? The French take their family relationships seriously, you know, and Desmoulins may be batty in some respects, but he certainly rates that daughter of his mighty high—as he should. Maybe Wright's trying to get the old man's permission.

'Anyway,' Darl had finished, 'she doesn't want *me*. I'm sure of *that* much! So I'm taking a ship to nowhere.'

That had been the end of the talk on the train, as far as Darl Winter was concerned. Harry had tried to argue, tried to kid him, to make him laugh, or cry, or even get sore. Darl had stared stolidly ahead.

Now they sat in the Transatlantic Gardens sipping rum and water. Harry would have preferred straight water, but in Colon you had to play safe. They used to say that when you first came to the Isthmus you'd put a little rum in your water to kill the germs, but that after a while you'd find yourself putting a little water into your rum instead. This was not true of Harry Kellems, who had never developed a taste for rum. Whisky, yes; but not rum. Besides, he didn't feel like drinking now.

He finished his drink and rose, putting a palm on the table.

'All right, if you won't listen to reason, I'll go straight to the steamship people and tell them there's a passenger booked on the *Havana* who's threatening to commit suicide on the trip!'

Darl's answer was dispassionate. 'If you do that I'll go to them and say the two of us have been celebrating and that you're talking through your hat. It'd be your word against mine, with both of us smelling like a distillery. Suppose they'd put me in irons on any such say-so?'

Harry shrugged, defeated for a moment. Then he brightened. 'Tell you what—here's a notion! Why *don't* we get drunk? They say men lots of times get flashes of insight and so forth when they're drinking, and maybe if we just went on a good bat——'

Darl had risen and was staring at him, and almost smiling. Darl slowly shook his head, in refusal but in amazement too.

'No wonder people like you so much, Harry. If there were more guys like you in the world I might not be so anxious to get out of it. But there aren't. Anyway the answer is no, of course.'

'Why not? Say, we could just sit here and swill ourselves and talk about any old thing we happened to feel like and——'

'And all the time you thinking of your wife over on the other side of the Isthmus, the last night you'll have with her for weeks.'

'Well, I could get a message to her by the telephone. Dr Gorgas's Tranquilina would take it. And then we could——'

'No. I never did like being drunk, and I'm sure you don't either. And I don't talk when I get drunk anyway—just grow quieter and nastier. Say, you've only got a couple of minutes to make that train.'

'But—isn't there anything at all I can do?'

'There's nothing at all, except to go home.' He put a hand on Harry's arm. 'All the same, thanks for that offer. Coming from you, I know what a hell of a lot it meant.'

Harry laughed, not joyously. 'Oh well, I just thought we might——Well, let it go. You'll feel different when you get on that ship. I'll be waving you off, remember. I'm bringing Phil over. See you then, huh?'

'I doubt it.'

Phil was angry, but not because of his late return, nor yet because of his breath: she was angry because she had so many things to do and she didn't see how she could possibly find time to do them all, and she *certainly* couldn't if Harry just *stood* there!

'I've been with Darl Winter, dear, and there's something I want to tell you about him. He's sailing on the boat with you tomorrow.'

'Is he really? That's nice. Now look, darling, I know you've been working all day and everything, but I don't often ask you to do much around the house, and right now Rosina isn't being a bit of help, and so do you mind——'

'Well, that isn't all I wanted to tell you about him. What I wanted to say was that he——'

'Darling, *please!* Rosina's been doing practically nothing all afternoon but just standing around *gawping* at me, so couldn't you just *try* to make yourself a little bit useful and hand me down those shirt-waists that are hanging at the end there?'

He thought: Well, she has got a lot to do, at that. He thought: I'll tell her later.

They were late for dinner because they finished the packing, and Rosina glowered. Phil, however, was no longer snappish. Her eyes shone with excitement, and she smiled at Harry.

'I'm sorry I was cross, darling. I'll make up for it. I'll play you some music tonight.'

'Ah, you'll be too tired.'

'No, I won't. I'll play for you. The only thing is, you must promise me you won't do too much drinking or poker playing while I'm away, and I don't want you to get too frisky with'—she swerved her eyes kitchen-enward—'with our friend inside there.'

He laughed, loving her. 'Go on! I'll be in bed by nine o'clock every night. Be all worn out every night, trying to cut this meat.'

'Poor Harry! And pretty soon I'll be eating filet mignon and Chateaubriand steaks and all sorts of things. Oh, won't it be grand!'

'I'll bet it will.'

'And won't it be nice to go out without an umbrella, and to be able

to go into a store where they actually have something to sell! I'm going to go into every shop on Fifth Avenue, if it's only to price things
or try things on. Except Vantine's. I don't want to see any more
Chinese articles again, even good ones. I do wish you were coming
along, dear.'

He shook his head. 'Just can't afford to. But look, about Darl
Winter.'

'Oh yes. So he's going on the same ship? You know, to tell the
truth I can't even remember—is he that tall dark-haired one?'

'No, that was Ed Carmichael. He went back two-three months ago.
No, Darl's quiet, never says much. Middle height, sort of stern-look-
ing, glasses.'

'Um-m . . . wears glasses. Oh, anyway, I'll know him when I
see him.'

'Sure you will. Here's the point: he's pretty broken up about something, and I wish you'd kind of try to be extra nice to him. You know,
jolly him along any time you get the chance.'

'Why, of course, if you want, dear. What's the matter with him?'

'Well, it's something sort of personal.' He prodded the dessert,
canned pears, a treat. He hated to lie to Phil, but he knew that she'd
fly off the handle if she thought he was keeping something from her:
she was so high-strung. 'He didn't tell me, and I didn't ask. But I did
think that maybe if you'd make a special effort to be nice to him . . .
He thinks a lot of you.'

'Well, of course I'll do whatever I can.'

She didn't ask him anything more about Darl, thank God. Her mind
was too full of her own affairs.

After dinner, with a fine smile, she went to the piano.

'You see, I haven't forgotten!' She murmured thanks when he pushed
the stool under her. 'No, no notes, please. I'll just play things I know
from memory. That is, unless there's something you'd particularly
like?'

'No, dear. Anything you feel like playing.'

Rosina came in to say good night and good-by, and Phil said good-
by and good night graciously, adding with a smile, in broken Spanish,
that she hoped that Rosina would take good care of Señor Kellems
while she was away. Rosina giggled, and bobbed, and went.

Harry sat in a chair at the end of the piano, so that he could see
his wife in the light from the dining room. His throat was one lump,
not only because of the music, not only because he loved her so much,
but also because he had lied to her. Yet if he'd told her the truth—

that he knew what was the matter with Darl—she would be sure to try to worm the story out of him. Not that he had specifically promised to keep Darl's secret; there had been no mention of secrecy; but the implication was there, and Harry felt that even a hint would be a betrayal of confidence. If Phil suspected a tragic love affair, she would make matters just that much worse by trying to pour sympathy all over the poor man.

She rippled out the last lingering chord and lifted her fingers from the keys. She was smiling at him.

'Like it, darling?'

'I loved it!'

'I wanted you to remember our last night together. Our last night for quite a *while*, that is!'

She sat with her hands in her lap. She lowered her head.

'It was sweet of you to realize that I'd be tired, Harry. But I don't want you to think—— Well, it will be quite a while before I'm back, and I don't want you to think that——'

She rose and went to where he sat, her head still down, though her arms were out. She slipped her hands behind his head, slid her fingers upward through his hair.

'After all, I'm not so *terribly* tired' she whispered.

'*Darling!*'

He squeezed her tight, pressing his face upon her abdomen, feeling her corset stays harsh against his cheek.

She was up soon after dawn, not humming but as brisk and birdlike as Harry had ever seen her. Soggy with sleep, while she started to work on her hair he tottered into the kitchen and got the charcoal stove going and put on coffee water. Phil would have nothing but coffee, said she was much too excited to eat anything, but he was hungry and he boiled himself a couple of eggs. By the time he had dressed, Phil had her hair up and was packing her toilet bag. The wagon came at eight, and Harry helped the driver out with the trunk and bags. Afterward Harry went down the hill to be sure that the baggage was properly checked. He returned with a carriage.

'Rosina came while you were gone. A good ten minutes late. She's been very careless lately, dear. I do hope that you won't spoil her while I'm away. I'm sure you will, though. Do I look all right?'

'You look perfect!'

When they got into the train Phil said that there was one other thing she hadn't told him.

'Yes, dear?'

'I just wanted to ask you not to point out all the different steam shovels and excavators and drills as we go along, and tell me about how much they load and all like that.'

'There aren't very many steam shovels and so forth along the Line anyway' Harry answered glumly.

'Well, I don't want you to talk about whatever ones there are. Do you mind, darling? I just don't want to even *think* about the Panama Canal for a little while.'

They were aboard the *Havana* by ten-thirty, but there had been some trouble about the trunk, and Harry was obliged to run back and forth between ship and dock several times after installing Phil in her stateroom with the bags. Though he kept a sharp lookout, he saw nothing of Darl. This cheered him. The previous afternoon he had left Darl in the Transatlantic Gardens waiting for a break in the rain. That rain had kept up clear across the Isthmus—though this did not mean, necessarily, that it had kept up all the while in Colon. Yet Darl *could* have ordered another rum, absent-mindedly or impatiently or to justify his loitering. He could have fallen to thinking about Harry's proposal that they go on a toot. He might have ordered a third drink, a fourth. . . . It was just barely possible that he was sleeping in the hotel now, having missed the ship.

When the trunk was accounted for, he and Phil went up to the boat deck. The sky, for the moment, was clear. Phil went over the things she wanted Harry to be sure to remember to do, and she recited again the things she wanted him to be sure to remember *not* to do.

'But most of all, darling,' and she glanced up sideways at him, smiling coquettishly, 'I want you to be very, very lonesome. You will, won't you?'

'Why, of course I will, dear! The only thing is——' He was looking around.

'Is there an exception, darling?'

'No, it isn't that. Oh, I'll be lonesome for you! But I just wondered, right now—I mean, it's not very long before sailing time, and I thought it might be a good idea if I took a quick look around and made sure Darl Winter's aboard all right.'

'Harry! Why must you always be bringing him up? *He's* not the one you're coming to see off, is he? I thought it was your wife!'

'No, no, it isn't that! Only—— Excuse me just a minute, dear. I'll be right back.'

'Harry!'

But he sped away.

The purser was busy and the assistant purser was rude. The stewards were occupied with bags. Harry got the number at last and raced up one corridor and down another until he found the stateroom. He knocked.

'Come in' a strange voice called.

Harry opened the door. A little thin-haired man, bellied like a Bonheur horse, and who smoked a cigar, stood in the middle of the cabin unpacking a bag. He wore only underclothing.

'Hello. Anything I can do for you? I thought it was the steward.'

'Oh, I'm sorry. I understood Mr Winter had this cabin?'

'Maybe he has.' The little man motioned with head and cigar. 'Maybe that's him over there? Ain't introduced one another yet.'

Darl was lying in the upper bunk, his face to the wall. He did not move. Frightened, Harry went to him, touched his shoulder.

'Are you all right?'

'I'm all right. Thanks, Harry.'

'Listen, why not rush ashore with me? There's time. We could——'

'No.'

The whistle blew. It was extraordinarily loud. The water glasses and the carafes in their metal racks leaped and rattled.

'Holy smoke!' the man in underwear cried around his cigar. 'They sound like they mean business!'

'Listen, Darl——'

'Harry, I appreciate your coming, but you're wasting your time.'

'Listen, I only wanted to say that Phil's on board. Stateroom A 22, on A Deck. I know you always liked her, Darl, and of course you know how I feel, and I'm kind of worried about her traveling alone like this, and I just wanted to ask you if you wouldn't kind of keep an eye on her, for my sake, huh?'

'I'll do what I can' Darl muttered. 'As long as I'm here.'

The whistle was blown again, imperiously stopping thought for an instant. Then somebody went along the corridor beating a gong.

'*All ashore that's going ashore! All ashore that's going ashore!*'

Harry gave the shoulder a little shake.

'You'll be all right, kiddo. You get some of that swell sea air and you'll be feeling fine.'

'He seasick already?' asked Underwear. 'Some people are like that, I know. Man in the same cabin with me coming down, he got into his bunk right off the bat and——'

'Excuse me' Harry interrupted. 'Well, you remember what I said about Phyllis, Darl? You'll be all right. I'm sure you will.'

'Oh, he'll feel better when he just gets up and walks around the deck a little' said Underwear. 'And another thing you want to watch out for, is you want to not eat any *greasy* food. That's what gets you, that *greasy* stuff. Now you take me. When I came down——'

'Good-by, Darl. Have a good trip.'

Darl didn't answer.

There were tears of rage in Phil's eyes. She *did* think, she started to exclaim—but Harry got his arms around her.

'I'm so sorry, sweetest! I thought there was more time than this!'

'Darling, please! My hat——'

'*All ashore that's going ashore!*'

The whistle blew again. Harry could feel its force clear through the kiss.

There was a wait of five minutes on the dock before the *Havana* finally pulled out. Harry could see her, up there on the boat deck, and he smiled without pause, and repeatedly waved his hat, but he knew that she couldn't hear what he called. He knew too that there were still tears in her eyes. He shifted from foot to foot, and waved his hat, and yelled cheery farewells, feeling like a skunk when he permitted his eyes to scan other parts of the rail and other decks in the hope of seeing Darl. He shouldn't be thinking about Darl! He should be thinking only of Phil! It was a pity that poor brave Phil should have to leave like this with only him to wave her off! A girl like her ought to have dozens of friends . . . But it would be better soon. By the time she came back it would be better. More white women than ever were coming down to join their husbands. Pretty soon there would be clubs and dances and all like that: this new commission understood that you can't expect people to just work, work, work all the time. And then their new house would be ready by the time Phil returned. He'd fix it up for her as fancy as possible. And he'd be nicer to her personally, too. He had been cranky and cantankerous quite a bit of the time this past year, but he'd be more thoughtful about her when she came back. After all, it had been hard for her in this place. *He* thrived on it, but he couldn't expect her to.

No, Darl was not anywhere in sight.

There was a last-minute flurry of waving and screaming. The hawsers were cast off and struck water with resounding spanks; and sailors began to haul them in. The *Havana* shuddered, sidling away. The whistle was blown yet again—and as though obediently and promptly answering an awaited signal, the rain came. By the time Harry got his umbrella up and could peer under its brim, the *Havana* was an immensity of blurred outlines and he could see nothing that he knew was Phil. It was as though a curtain had been drawn between them.

9

FROM THE BEGINNING there had been something ominous about that summer. The people at home were not much interested, having nearer catastrophes and thrills—the reconstruction after the San Francisco earthquake, Harry K. Thaw's murder of Stanford White, the furore about simplified spelling, Montgomery and Stone in *The Red Mill,* short skirts, Oscar Hammerstein's plans to open another grand opera house . . . and of course baseball.

As to baseball, the season depressed Harry Kellems from the start and filled him with foreboding. The Giants should have had everything their own way. Under that bad-tempered pouter pigeon of a genius, McGraw, they had moved from last place one year to second the next and then to the top; and when they'd consented at last to recognize the American League by playing its pennant winners, the Athletics, for the world's championship, they had, thanks largely to Christy Mathewson, won. In 1906 they should have been invincible. But Mathewson came down with diphtheria. Harry had never seen Mathewson, but he worshiped him from afar and felt his illness as a personal hurting thing. Well, Mathewson was scarcely back on the job when Turkey Mike Donlin broke a leg; and soon afterward McGann got a broken arm; and Roger Bresnahan, with Donlin the club's best slugger, was beaned with a pitched ball. Out of the nowhere came a hitherto insignificant team, the Chicago Cubs, with Joe Tinker, Johnny Evers, Frank Chance, Three-fingered Brown, Jack Pfeister, Wildfire Frank Schultze, and that great catcher Johnny Kling; and the Giants were shoved off the summit. As a matter of fact, the way the Pirates were playing, it did not seem a sure thing that the Giants could even hang onto second place.

On the Isthmus the wails were louder than ever. The old-timers knew that they were living, comparatively, in the lap of luxury, though conditions still were not what they were supposed to be; but the turnover among white workers was tremendous, and newcomers unhesitatingly broke into howls. The meat was rock. Prices at the commissary were much too high—kerosene was jumped from eleven cents to twenty-three cents in July of that year—you paid eight dollars for a pair of shoes which at home would cost you three—and there was precious little choice. A monopoly, was the complaint. Graft, was the allegation. The ice plant in Cristobal still wasn't finished. Few of the promised living quarters had been built, and the newcomers didn't get what there were. Servants of any kind were difficult to get. Not much digging was being done. The double-tracking was not yet completed, and the train service was execrable. There were labor troubles of all kinds, pesky at best, some of them dangerous.

True, there was no more yellow fever. But there was a smallpox scare in July, and two distinct bubonic-plague scares. As for malaria, it was worse than ever.

Not Aedes aegypti but the more hardy Anopheles was what Harry now sought and slaughtered.

Aedes aegypti is a small dark mosquito, but the white strips on its legs and the white lyre-shaped figure on its back lend it a silvery sheen. Seemingly shrewd and clever, it stays indoors, plies its trade by day as by night, never buzzes or hums. It favors such places as the underside of the wrist, where a swift slap is difficult. Moreover, it is wary and does not thrust its proboscis in so far that it can't get it out in a hurry: it is singularly alert to any movement on the part of the person it is biting.

First they screened and fumigated. They screened every government building as fast as they could get the screening. They double-screened the hospital doors and stationed a man inside of each vestibule to eliminate with chloroform whatever mosquitoes might have drifted in. They screened each yellow-jack patient additionally, putting him, literally, into a copper cage. Meanwhile they fumigated the house from which that patient had been taken, and the houses on either side, or, if they could afford it, all the houses in the block. With the coming of the second Isthmian Canal Commission, which threw out of the window Admiral Walker's cheese-paring policy, Sanitation, properly manned, did a *complete* fumigating job. Harry had participated in a good part of this, as a supervisor. They had fumigated every house in Panama City. The job took a month. When it was finished they had started all over again and fumigated every house a second time. Then they did it a third time.

This had been grinding, thankless labor, with householders screeching in protest, accusing the fumigators of theft, threatening to bring suit, sometimes bringing suit. . . . Night after night Harry had returned to Phil stinking of the chemicals they'd used.

Formalin was no good. On a special occasion, or when they couldn't get any pyrethrum or sulphur, they'd use one part camphor to three parts carbolic acid in a tin dish set over a vaporizing spirit lamp. This made dense white fumes which killed the mosquitoes in three or four hours; and it did no harm to the furnishings; but it was too expensive for every day. So they used sulphur or pyrethrum. They'd put some into a sort of Dutch oven, in a box of sand, so that a leak or overheating would not set fire to the house, and pour a little alcohol over it, and ignite this. It only stunned the mosquitoes, made them drunk, and the bodies had to be swept out afterward and burned: the floors had to be swept, the walls and ceilings as well, and every article of furniture brushed carefully. Sulphur stained fabrics and corroded metals, so they had to remove all of these before a job, and examine them, killing the mosquitoes by hand. For this reason pyrethrum, which did no damage to property, was preferred—when they could get it. Dr Gorgas's first requisition had been for eight tons of pyrethrum, and the Walker commission raised Cain about this extravagance! The first year after the second commission was in power, when Sanitation had been taken care of, one hundred and twenty tons of pyrethrum was burned—it was all they could get in the United States, and they were not allowed to buy anywhere else. That same year they used three hundred tons of sulphur.

A mosquito is a very small animal which breeds unbelievably fast, and had it not been for Aedes aegypti's lack of adaptability Sanitation might have failed to kill every one. However, Aedes aegypti, for all its appearance of cleverness, is as stupid as any other mosquito. A home body, it is set in its habits. This very fastidiousness caused it to commit race suicide in the Canal Zone, as previously it had done in Havana.

Aedes aegypti will have no truck with muddy pools, and certainly not with swamps (nasty places!) when some man-made contrivance suitable for breeding is handy. A basin it likes, preferably a metal one, nice and clean; or a shallow cement depression filled with clean water. In Panama the Sanitation men, after fumigating, amiably provided such receptacles. The Sanitation men examined those receptacles; and when not too much time had passed, cleaned them out. Eggs, all right. Larvae, all right. Even the pupae couldn't hurt anybody, though the Sanitation men did not take the chance of permitting the process to go that far. The imago, however, the dainty silvery killer itself, never developed. Aedes aegypti, not having sense enough to change its habits, simply ceased to be.

Well, you can stamp out yellow fever, as they'd proved, and by means of scrupulous inspections and a stringent quarantine you can keep it out. Malaria is something else again. You don't catch Anopheles being persnickety about where it lays its eggs. Any old splash of water, provided it be shady, will do. A forgotten calabash, a tin can, a rain-filled hollow between tree roots, and behold! the makings of a biblical plague! Anopheles is rugged, vulgar, and always thirsty. It is noisy and tough and plain, and its persistence discourages. The only thing really distinctive about Anopheles, aside from the fact that it spreads malaria germs, is its manner of biting: instead of taking a stance like an ordinary mosquito, its body more or less parallel with the surface upon which it has alighted, it stands on its head, an idiotic position and one by means of which it can be identified (usually too late) by the layman.

Screens were inspected for holes; but the keepers of rum shops, gambling houses, and brothels in Colon and Panama City could not be forced to screen their establishments, any more than the bored and weary workers could be prevented from patronizing such joints, or even made to roll down their sleeves and button high their shirts if they did go out of an evening. Sanitation—which had become a full bureau and not merely a department of another bureau, so that Dr Gorgas could address himself directly to the members of the Commission—was generous with advice as with quinine, both of which were distributed without charge; but you can't cram common sense into the heads of men who prefer to be fools. The thing to do was to get rid of Anopheles, or rather, since this was impossible, to keep him down to a harmless minimum. Sanitation carried the fight to the swamps; and Harry Kellems, who at first had been engaged with sharp disinfectants in Panama City, now found himself spending most of his time in the field.

They released millions of minnows. They spread Paris green. The Canal Zone extended five miles on either side of the ditch-to-be, but the Gorgas gangs actually started by working one mile on each side, a big enough job on a fifty-mile stretch of mountain, swamp, and jungle. They cut grass and underbrush. They dug almost two thousand miles of ditches, and regularly inspected these, and with portable pressure burners burned out of them the swiftly growing grass. They used arsenic; they used chloroform; they used a larvicide concocted in Ancon by Sam Darling and consisting of carbolic acid, resin, and alkali. They spread crude oil, some fifty thousand gallons of it a month, by hand from pump-tanks slung on the backs of Negroes—since the terrain was not suitable for any kind of wheeled vehicle. They inspected and inspected, and scolded, and pleaded, checked and trimmed, oiled, cleaned, sprayed, cut, making pests of themselves, while they obliterated tens of billions of mosquitoes.

Harry was not confined to any one of the twenty-five sanitary districts. As before, his status was uncertain and shifty. He kept a general check on oil consumption along the Line. He witnessed field experiments and reported on them. He supervised the establishment of new substations, as the changing work called for these. He broke in fresh assistant district inspectors and occasionally substituted for inspectors who were themselves felled by Anopheles. A liaison man between headquarters and the bosses along the Line, he was also a trouble shooter. He carried information about new technics. He listened to complaints.

Often he slept somewhere out along the Line. In such cases he would be doubly tired when he returned to the Cemetery the second night for a dinner warmed over by the solicitous Rosina. He played poker with the new D.M.s only once, and then listlessly, sleepily, and, to the amazement of the kids (for his reputation was great), at a loss. Nights usually he moped at home, doing nothing, glad that he was so tired that he'd be able to sleep.

He had intended to do a heap of studying while Phil was away. It would be a good opportunity, he thought, to bone up on some stuff he might have forgotten, to go ahead with some stuff he was still going to need. With this in mind, he had borrowed several engineering works. But it was no use. You can't study when you are tired. You just can't force your mind to work. He'd poke at the books sometimes after dinner, while the troubled Rosina, watching him sideways, cleared the table; and once he inaugurated a routine in which he was obliged to read so many pages each night he was home; but he gave this up when he realized that the reading didn't mean anything to him. So he would just sit alone, though he was too tired to be truly lonesome, and look out the window.

Even talking with Rosina wasn't the fun it had previously been. The hunchback clearly was worried about him, but she was afraid to start a conversation. When Rosina finally did move to stir him from his lethargy, however, she came right to the point, using no halfway measures. After dinner one night, after Harry had collapsed into the Morris chair, Rosina, who should have been doing the dishes, appeared suddenly with her cousin Manuelita.

'She is for you, señor.' Rosina spoke hastily, blushing, looking at the floor. 'Her name is Manuelita. I thought that perhaps you did not know where—— Señor, forgive me, but Manuelita is my cousin and she will be good to you tonight, if you want her, and she will not charge you much. She is my cousin.'

Manuelita was tall and young and buxom. Her clothes were 'noisy,' her bosom deep, and she held her hands on her hips as she smiled a fixed mechanical smile at once mincing and a shade defiant, like the smile of an acrobat or ballet dancer: there were many gold fillings in her teeth. Her face, vaguely Negroid, was white with rice powder. Her lips were a shrieking red. The hibiscus in her hair, the lighted cigarette between two fingers of her right hand, showed as last-minute-remembered stage properties, without which she would have felt uneasy. Even when she spoke, saying juicily and lingeringly 'Buenas noches, chico,' she did not seem real.

Harry was less concerned with this apparition than with Rosina, who continued to mumble in deep embarrassment that she hoped that the señor would forgive her but she had guessed that he didn't know where to look for—— Manuelita was her cousin and would be very good to him and had agreed not to charge very much and—— The señor must forgive her, but surely it was not good for the señor to be so many nights alone, and if he would——

Harry rose. He started to swear, and started to laugh, but he did neither. He bowed gravely to Rosina.

'It is very good of you,' in Spanish, 'to think thus of me. I am touched by your kindness. But you must not think harshly if I say that I prefer to sleep alone. There are reasons for this, Rosina.'

The hunchback said nothing, nor did she look up. The whore continued to smile.

'It is very good of you' Harry said again. He looked at Manuelita, resisting a temptation to giggle. 'It was good of you, too, señorita, to come. You must permit me to give you some little token of my appreciation.'

He found a couple of pesos and held them out to her, his hand palm down. She simpered as she accepted them. Harry bowed. Rosina, her head still lowered to hide the blushes, then led her inexpensive cousin back to the kitchen.

Some minutes later Rosina reappeared.

'I have made a very bad error, señor. I am much sorry.'

'Don't let it worry you for a second.'

'You—you will dismiss me, señor?'

'Fire you? Absolutely not! I wouldn't let you go for anything in the world! The only thing is—it might be just as well not to mention this to Señora Kellems when she comes back.'

'Oh, I will not! She—she is very good, the señora, but I do not think she would understand.'

'No, I'm afraid she wouldn't.'

'Buenas noches, señor.'

'Buenas noches, Rosina.'

Neither of them ever mentioned the incident again.

Running down false rumors of epidemics and issuing prompt, detailed, official denials was another big job at Sanitation that summer and fall, when there were more of such rumors than ever before. This was Simpson's work, not Harry's; but Harry was included in the junket to the San Blas Indian territory. Dr Gorgas himself headed the party. They were all curious to see what the San Blas Indians looked like, and the rumor that yellow jack had broken out among these mysterious survivors—a rumor Sanitation had to investigate, since the Indians roamed uncontrolled over a quarter of the Republic of Panama and their territory at several points touched the Canal Zone—was checked with alacrity.

The San Blas Indians didn't like white men. Once there were millions of them, but the Conquistadors killed them off with unrelenting fury; and not since those days had the remnants, excepting a scant few who were sailors, quit their jungle for the white man's cities. The less they had to do with civilization, the better. Nor would they permit the white man to roam in their territory. The San Blas Indian country had never been properly surveyed—for the simple reason that surveyors and explorers who went there never came back. There wasn't anything you could do about the San Blas Indians, a law unto themselves.

The Gorgas party went by steamer, and by appointment, it being the understanding that they could spend the whole day, though not the night, in a certain village—the old chief had decreed that in no circumstances could a white man spend a night in his domain.

The sick were lined up on the beach, and Dr Gorgas and Dr Carter and Major Lyster and the nurses did what they could for them. There was no yellow jack, though there was a good deal of pneumonia. Harry had no work to do; and indeed he and the several other non-medical employees were convinced that Dr Gorgas, who wouldn't admit it, had asked them along just for the trip, to give them a change of scene and a chance to see something very few white men ever had seen before. It was an eerie experience. A close group, they wandered about the village, peering into huts, smiling at the children, and being scrupulously careful not to approach any of the flamboyant glowering women. They were watched by stolid small-eyed men, every one of whom was armed in some manner: most of them had bows and arrows, but there were a few old muskets. Nobody got close to them. Nobody smiled or spoke a greeting.

There was no evidence of fire in the glum villagers, even slow-smoldering fire. There was no touch of dash in them. They looked not solemn, not poetically sad, these members of a doomed race, but only disconsolate, discouraged, tired—and in the case of the men, sullen and somewhat suspicious. Excepting Old Oxheart the Cimarron scout, and Sitting Bull, and Chief Rocky Bear, and other dusky members of the troupe of Buffalo Bill's Wild West and Congress of Rough Riders when it visited Paterson, Harry Kellems had never before seen an Indian. *Those* Indians had been glamorous in the tradition of war paint, feathers, grunts, horsemanship, gay blankets, and pride. *These* were only dingy. They might have been unconquered, but they were colorless all the same.

The women stole the show. The men, sullen, erect, watchful, wore drab clothes often of a semicivilized nature—odd shirts, odd pairs of trousers, in a few cases overalls—though most of them were naked or nearly so. They sported few ornaments. For the most part they were bareheaded, and their straight black coarse hair hung around their shoulders; and where one did wear a hat, it was a derby. But the women were bright in polychromatic skirts, with red sashes over their shoulders, and they fairly clanked with nose rings, earrings, anklets, arm bands, bracelets, all of pure gold. You couldn't call them pretty, but they were picturesque. They wore many ropes of beads or pearls around their calves and sometimes around their upper arms—ropes around the outside of which the flesh bulged hideously and which must have been fastened there in childhood. Best of all, the women smoked cigars.

Now Harry and the others had seen women smoke cigars, Indian women who came to the markets in Panama City and Colon, and sometimes part-Panamanians too. But these San Blas women put the *lighted* end of the cigar into their mouths! Phlegmatically they drew in air through the outthrust *cut* end, and after a moment drew the thing forth and exhaled wearily, smoke dribbling from their nostrils. Then they would put the lighted end back into the mouth again. It gave the visitors a queer sickish feeling each time they saw it happen: it almost hurt, almost pricked the skin, to watch it.

'Marvelous, isn't it? I wish I had the courage to try it. I'd love to go back to Marie tonight smoking that way. Little things like that every now and then keep our wives from taking us too much for granted, eh, Harry?'

The great sanitarian had ranged alongside of Harry at the rail as the steamer was pulling out. He stood at attention, facing a shore lined with population, and lifted his hat again and again in solemn, formal farewell; but there was nothing formal about the way he talked to Harry from a corner of his mouth.

'It looks dangerous' Harry objected. 'What if you forgot to hold your tongue back?'

Dr Gorgas chuckled, while he waved, saluted, lifted his hat.

'Dangerous, eh? Not half as dangerous as what we've been doing today, Harry! Say, they're a wicked-looking outfit, aren't they? My heart was in my throat. I understand they make pretty strict demands on their voodoo doctors here, these fellows. Cure or kill. That is, if the patient doesn't get cured, the doctor gets killed. Well, some of those pneumonia cases are sure to die, for all the sugar pills we gave 'em. There wasn't anything else to do—since we can't stay. So remind me never to come back, eh?'

'That chief looks as if he would cut your throat any old time.'

'Order it cut, Harry. Order it cut. I doubt that he'd stoop to do the messy deed in person.'

A member of the crew, who had an accordion, started to play 'Where Did You Get That Hat?' and provoked laughter. Dr Gorgas swiveled worried eyes in his direction.

'I hope the chief isn't familiar with our ragtime.'

The chief, in the center of the group on shore, was a massive aged man, from the hips down naked except for a loincloth, but who wore on his upper body a splendid silk-flowered gold-embroidered tail coat presented to him by the President of the Republic of Panama as a token of his—the chief's—sovereignty. The coat, befrogged, was mostly red. The chief's hair hung straight down, all around, and on his head also was a bright gray derby several sizes too large. Two wives behind him held over him a gold-headed umbrella, another gift from the President, who had been permitted to visit this country but not to stay overnight.

'Gilbertian, I'll grant you. All the same, I feel a lot safer now that we're leaving, Harry.'

He made a final bow to the chief, and then, the vessel being far from shore, turned to Harry, proffering a cigar.

'I don't suppose *you* were worried? A daredevil like *you!*'

'Huh?'

'A motorman's holiday for you, eh?' But the colonel's manner was no longer jocular. 'Did Simpson ask you to help him in that work, or did you find out about it yourself and volunteer?'

'I found out about it myself, sir. I sort of figured it out.'

'Had an idea that's the way it was. You know, Harry, I don't want to be an old scared cat, but you *could* get into a lot of trouble on that job. It's all right for Simpson. He loves danger the way some men love liquor. He gets listless without it. But you're another matter. You're young. You plan to finish college someday. You've got a pretty wife. When's she coming back, by the way?'

'Well, she *was* coming back the end of this month, but in her last letter she said she'd like to put that off a few weeks because she wanted to visit some friends. But about that other business: I don't think it's so very dangerous, sir.'

'It's not too safe' Dr Gorgas said soberly. 'I'll admit that it's got to be done and that we're in a much better position to do it than the police, and that you're an ideal man for the job, speaking Spanish and being able to get in anywhere as a result of that fumigation-squad experience. But still . . . There's a lot of money back of that crowd, Harry. You—you take care of yourself.'

'I will, sir.'

'You've got your wife to think of, remember. And a friend or two here and there, eh?'

'Yes, sir.'

Dr Gorgas nodded somberly. Still nodding, staring at the now distant shore, he slowly lifted the cigar to his mouth. At the last instant he reversed the cigar and thrust the lighted end between his lips, which he closed upon the middle. Almost immediately he withdrew it, but he blew out smoke as he did so.

'It isn't hard, at that!' Delightedly: 'You try it, Harry!'

'I will like hell try it, sir.'

Dr LePrince was currently the most unpopular man in the Zone. He could summon sufficient affability in any personal encounter, but his conscientiousness dismayed his victims. In charge of Sanitation's field work, he was always ruining gardens.

'You'll be seeing Dr Gorgas tonight, won't you, Kellems? Good!

Then suppose you let me take you around now, so you can see how the work's going. I'll stay on out here for a few nights.'

'Yes sirree!'

There had risen some question as to how far the Anopheles could fly. Malaria was getting worse, not better; and perhaps they weren't clearing and ditching and oiling far enough back.

'You see, we put 'em in this cage and spray 'em with aniline solution. Makes 'em bright blue. Giddy, aren't they? But you've seen all this. . . . Now the point is, we release them in the same place every night, and we keep a record of the wind direction and velocity that night, and how much rain there was, and so forth. Instead of doing what you fellows did in town, releasing them from different places and looking for them in one place, we reverse the process. We've got our sleepers scattered all over this part of the Isthmus, you might say. Seventeen of them.'

Harry grinned. 'I bet you don't have any trouble getting volunteers?'

'Say, you have to have *pull* to get a job sleeping for us! Let's go out and look at 'em. Haven't had a case yet. You know how these Jamaicans are. They hardly ever get malaria anyway. And we keep 'em loaded. Thirty grains a day—*and* we see that they swallow it, too!'

'I should think their ears would ring?'

'They probably do—when they're awake, which isn't often. Now you see, here's a few here. And further up the slope.'

There was one bed in each tent, one Negro in each bed. Each bed was equipped with a mosquito bar which was left open at night, to be closed, trapping mosquitoes, just before dawn. After dawn the trapped mosquitoes were examined, to see if any were blue. It was a simple matter. What happened to the mosquito bar during the day was the Negro's own business. These men drew full laborers' pay. It was a wonderful job.

'Good afternoon, Mr Kellems. I trust that your espoused wife is well and in salubrious health?'

'Oh, hello, Berty! So this is the research job you got, eh? Well, it looks pretty nice. Must give you a lot of rest.'

'It does, sir. Yes, sir.'

'All you have to do is sleep here or wherever the tent is every night, eh?'

'That comprises the sum total of the duties involved, Mr Kellems. Yes, sir. I sleep at night. That's what I do.'

'Then you have all day to yourself?'

'Yes, sir.'

'What do you do then?'

'Well, mostly I just sleep then too, Mr Kellems. They awaken one at periodic intervals, to take more quinine or because they are moving one's experimental habitation to another location. That routine can be disconcerting, as a person of your perspicacity can readily perceive, Mr Kellems.'

'I guess *so!*'

'But on the whole, I find that the disadvantages of this employment are notably outweighed by its advantages.'

'Well, I'm sure glad to know you're all right. I'll tell the other boys when I run into them. Don't strain yourself, now!'

'I shall endeavor to avoid that contingency, sir.'

He was avoiding it with overwhelming effectiveness when Harry left the tent. In fact he was sound asleep.

Harry was walking through the malaria ward at the Colon hospital one afternoon, on his way to the superintendent's office, when he was hailed in a voice which though weak was familiar.

'Harry *T!* Say, what are you doing here?'

The bony horsy face was drawn with suffering, but its grin was clipped into position.

'What do you *spose* I'm doing here, Chauncey Olcott? I spend most of my time here. Why, they couldn't run this place without me! My fourth session. I've gotten so now that I shiver and sweat anyway, even between bouts, just from habit. How's Phil? She back yet?'

'Well, no. It looks now as if she wouldn't get back until November. Had a letter only the other day. She's postponed it several times already. So much to do, so many friends to visit.'

'Ah, there! You want to watch out, kiddo! Remember what they say —absinthe makes the heart grow fonder. But maybe she's only buying a lot of these fancy new French low-neck dresses. Oh-oh! Bet you'll boil over when you see 'em—and when you see the bills! Did I tell you that one about the man who went to a fancy society dinner and when he came home his wife wanted to hear all about it. "What did the ladies wear?" she asked. "I don't know," he answered; *"I didn't look under the table!"'*

He laughed; but the laugh changed to a cough, and he shook under the force of it, and in a moment he began to vomit a dark green bilious fluid.

'I'll be all right, don't bother the nurse' he gasped.

'You're not all right. That sounds pretty nasty, Harry. Glass of water? When Phil does come back, you must get over the other side of the Isthmus and see us some time.'

'Will—if I ever get time between bouts. If I ever get a chance to miss the am-bul-ance. See? He's a poet and doesn't know it!'

'Four times' Harry muttered. 'Say, look, you old horse thief, maybe you don't take enough quinine.'

'Stuff gives me terrific headaches—when I can keep it down.'

'Then you really ought to go home, Harry.'

Harry T looked reproachful.

'I mean it' said Harry K. 'You've got to think of yourself.'

'People who live in glass houses shouldn't take baths. I don't see *you* quitting, Little Nemo.'

'I'm different—Flip. I haven't even been touched by malaria. Must be the pure life I lead.'

'You're crazy with the heat! Fact is, you Sanitation boys don't know how to kill mosquitoes.'

'We do the best we can.'

'Say, speaking of mosquitoes, did I tell you that one about Pat and Mike and they'd come to this country—well, that is, I mean God's country——'

The United States of America was habitually referred to as God's country by workers on the Panama Canal, even in the presence of Panamanians, and perhaps *especially* in the presence of Panamanians. The meaning was as clear as Home with a capital 'H' as spoken by Englishmen who aren't there, and even more offensive.

'—and they got this job in a labor camp, and the first night they were almost eaten alive by mosquitoes and they tried to hide deep under blankets in their tent, and after a while Mike sticks one eye out and looks around and he sees a lot of fireflies—you know, lightning bugs we used to call 'em—and he turns to Pat and groans and says "Begorra it's lost entoirly we arre, Patthrick, whin they come lookin' forr us with *lanterns!*" '

He tried to laugh, but he was shivering before he finished the story, and his teeth had begun to chatter. His face was pale, his hands were dead pale, and the nails were blue.

'Here we come again, kiddo' he managed. '*Early* this time!'

When the nurse arrived Harry T was delirious, his face more taut than ever in pain, his skin glittering with sweat, while he shivered and wept, not even knowing Harry Kellems.

After his business with the superintendent had been completed, Harry asked about his friend.

'Him? Oh, say, he's a card! He keeps everybody in the ward in stitches. It isn't exactly that he's funny—I mean *witty*—because he isn't—but it's just that he seems to be having such a good time *himself*.'

'I know' Harry said.

'You never hear a kick out of him. Laughs at everything. He's been fine for the other patients' spirits. Told me one the other day, for instance. Seems this man said his wife had very carelessly left her bracelet on the washbasin when she went to wash her hands, and the other man said "Oh, that's nothing. Every time *my* wife takes a bath she leaves a ring in the tub!"' The superintendent slapped his knee. 'I swear, I don't know where he gets them all! We're certainly going to miss that fellow when he's gone.'

'He's going home, then?'

'Oh, he'll have to! Man like that can't stay in a place like Panama. Why, he can't keep quinine down! He'd simply be in here again and again, getting weaker and weaker each time.'

Harry *T* was still shivering and sweating, twisting, squealing, with shut eyes and with clenched teeth, when Harry *K* went back through the ward on his way out.

'A few more like this, and we're going to lose another case' the nurse said.

10

MADELINE WALKED BACK AND FORTH. She walked out before her father, who in dressing robe and slippers, in his tiny black skullcap, still sat at breakfast.

'Do you like it, Papa?'

He lifted his eyebrows, shaggy white platforms, and lifted also, later, his eyes. He stared at her a moment, trying to be stern: his mouth at least was stern, a steel trap of a mouth.

'Do I like what? The lavaliere? Pity it had to be named after a trull. But since it is on you I do like it. Yes.'

'Now Papa——'

'Oh, the shirtwaist? Oh, this is what they are wearing, hum, in New York, is it not so? Ah well, it seems a bit *revealing* to me. All those, hum, apertures . . . And then must you have the neck boned up to your ears? I can't help thinking it's uncomfortable.'

'The shirtwaist is not uncomfortable, Papa. You get used to it.'

'Yes, yes, no doubt you get used to anything.'

'And I didn't mean the lavaliere. Of course I've always loved that! You gave it to me! But what I mean now is—listen——'

Head high, a hand on a hip, she walked to the other end of the parlor and turned, almost pirouetting, only with an effort keeping herself from a swiftness of motion which would have caused the skirt to whirl up.

'There!'

'That is very lovely, my little one. What I see is a beautiful woman. What I do *not* see is how it makes any difference what one wears, when one can walk like that and look like that. Granting, of course, that one wears enough of it.'

'Papa, you are vulgar!'

'Oh no,' mildly. 'No, I'm not vulgar.'

She smiled at him. As always, the thought of accusing him of vulgarity was amusing. He could be disagreeable sometimes, and sarcastic, and even shrill; but he could never be common. You needed only to look at the fragility of his face, and especially the nose, and the dry smooth unworried knowingness of the eyes, to be sure of this. Papa might be, Papa *was* a little touched in the mind; but he would never be uncouth. She sometimes wished that she too possessed that serenity of countenance, that fine-drawn, exactly right, aristocratic visage that couldn't be concealed, couldn't be mistaken—and could not be imitated with success. Madeline on the whole was pleased with her looks. There were a few things she would have changed, and those by not much. But she didn't have that breath-taking delicacy that was found in her father's face. Her mother, she supposed, must have lent her a brush of coarseness, which no doubt was all to the good. She did not know much about her mother. She had seen a few faded photographs, but these told little, and they were not ordinarily open for her inspection but kept somewhere in Papa's own chest. Papa never talked about his dead wife.

'No, I am not vulgar. But I am not blind either, my cabbage. What was it that I was expected to praise? The skirt?'

'No, no, no, no! The skirt is very old. It's falling apart. But the *swish*—listen.'

Again she walked the length of the room, a long one, and again she turned, birdlike, lightly, smiling.

'Hear it? Isn't that wonderful! It—it sounds just like silk, doesn't it?'

'Truly it does' he admitted in amazement.

'Well, some of the ruffles actually are silk, scattered around near the bottom. I sewed them on last night.'

'Is it possible? I did not hear it thus when you went out to listen to the band concert with el capitan.'

'I didn't wear this petticoat last night. I wore an old one. It was after I'd got back that I sewed on the ruffles.' She turned one hip in his direction, then the other. She had an almost irresistible desire to turn her back and flirt out her bottom toward him; but of course she refrained. 'Hear it? Isn't that wonderful?'

He made a smile which seemed astounded to find itself in so austere a place as his mouth.

'You should have worn it last night. But you see el capitan again today also?'

She frowned. They never referred to Ward Wright as anything but el capitan. Madeline did not dislike him, for she found him entertaining; and when he asked her out, as he had done last night, she was glad to go; but she distrusted him. She was not afraid for her own sake. Some years before, on a moonlight walk, he had made unmistakable advances, which she unmistakably turned back. There hadn't been any suggestion of marriage. When it came to marriage, el capitan wanted somebody with money. Afterward he had seemed amazed that Madeline continued to treat him with good humor, and even a whit affectionately: he must have been accustomed, a refusal over, to be ostentatiously snubbed. So they had continued as friends—until recently Madeline had become distrustful of el capitan's interest in her father. Madeline loved her father. When he was in excellent spirits, not tired or too worried, and when his liver was good, he could be marvelously the teller of tales. He had a pawky humor; his speech was bright and varied; his voice, except when he was angry, was a delight to hear. He could talk by the hour, never repeating himself, never wearing any subject to its last flappy thread, but giving to everything something new and bright. But Papa's English, while grammatically good, was halting and uncertain: all too clearly Papa was not at home in that language, and could not think in it. His Spanish was even weaker. El capitan, on the other hand, knew scarcely a dozen words of French. Why were these two so often together? Even the previous night, Madeline, though glad enough to have somebody take her out to hear the music and get the air, had sensed that she was being asked only out of politeness to her father.

'No, it is not with el capitan' she replied. 'I go to the church.'

He settled his coffee cup and looked at her. A lifelong freethinker, he did not hate churches but only ignored them. As for his daughter, since her emergence from the convent, since, that is, the death of his wife and sons, he had never spoken to her on the subject. Here in Panama for a little while she'd gone to Mass in a perfunctory way; then, when she realized that she didn't need to go, she had ceased going. She'd passed her religious period; that had been earlier, when she was fourteen-fifteen. She had been almost hysterically devout, for a little while. Her inherited common sense snipped that phase short —her common sense and the toilsomeness of the convent where she'd had *too much* religion thrust upon her. Now she was not an atheist! She believed in a God who was not unlike the God described in the sermons; but she believed too that her worship of that God, and indeed all her relations with Him, were His and her own business. She thought that this was the way her father felt, too. He had never questioned her about her faith. A sharp and watchful critic, in matter of behavior a martinet, quick to scold and even to curse if he thought that she was not conducting herself physically and socially as became a child of his, nevertheless in matters religious he stayed in his own enclosure and permitted Madeline to stay in hers.

'You go to Mass in that finery? You'll be stared at, my cabbage.'

Saucily, for she felt saucy: 'I am usually stared at. But I don't go to Mass now, Papa. I climb the hill to go to the Americans' ceremony. It —it is Protestant.'

Now astonishment really had him. Twice he opened his mouth to speak, and twice he closed it, though his eyes never left his daughter.

'Very good' he whispered after a while. 'If they consent to admit you in such finery——'

'In this Protestant religion it is different, Papa. Besides, it—it is not really a church. It is an office.'

'Now this is very fitting! This is good American worship—in an office! You must note the details well, my cabbage, and report them to me. Do the choristers have pens behind their ears, then? Is it that in place of candles they have form-spikes and in place of the chalices telephones and typewriting machines? The priest, whom I suppose they call the boss, does he elevate not the Host but a bag of coin?'

Severely: 'Papa, you are being not only vulgar but sacrilegious. Also you're wrong. The Americans have much feeling.'

'All the same, you must remark these things and place them in your memory. I shall be eager to hear of them. The antics of primitive peoples have always interested me.'

'And there aren't any choristers. Everybody sings, as I understand it, except sometimes when Harry sings alone.'

''Arry?'

'Monsieur Kellems. One of my pupils. He has not been around much lately, he's been working so hard because of the malaria. But you have met him, Papa, and you like him. He has grave eyes but a beautiful smile, and he always looks straight at you when he speaks.'

'Ah yes.' The old man nodded. 'Yes, I remember him. Far better than most of his kind, yes. But'—he looked up—'he is married, is it not so?'

'Yes, he is married. But he invited me to the church. There is nothing wrong with that, surely?'

'His wife will accompany you?'

'His wife is on a visit to the United States. She was to have returned last month, but then it was to have been early this month, but she has written each time that she delays the return.'

'Ah?'

'There is nothing wrong with this, Papa! Anybody who knows Harry knows that he is good. I wish to hear him sing, that's all. And in the afternoon he will be here to take me to visit the ruins of the Old City.'

168

An eyebrow-platform went up.

'But you have already visited the ruins of the Old City. Twice. Three times, it may be.'

'It does me no harm to go again, Papa. These things are very instructive.'

'Ah yes. I had thought for a moment when you spoke the name 'Arry that you meant that ugly fierce boy with spectacles. I have not seen him in many months, heureusement.'

'Darl Winter? He's gone home.'

'I think that that is a good place for him.'

'Oh, Darl was all right.'

From time to time she was troubled by the memory of Darl. Harry was troubled too, she believed. She knew that Darl had departed suddenly and by coincidence on the same ship with Phyllis Kellems; but Harry, telling her about this, had been singularly evasive. Harry had not read aloud to her Phil's first letter, but he had made a point of mentioning that it contained no word about Darl; and this clearly puzzled him, as it puzzled Madeline. He had replied, asking specifically about Darl; and when a couple of weeks later he received Phil's answer to this, he had made a special hurried trip to the Desmoulins home (he didn't have time, that day, for a lesson) in order to read one section of the letter aloud.

'He has the manners of a pig!'

It startled Madeline, though it was not the first time she had heard her father say this. It startled her now because it was, in French, the very words of Phyllis about the same man. Though Madeline could not see why, Phil had evidently been irked by Harry's query about Darl, and she declared that she'd scarcely even seen Darl the whole voyage. He had, she reported, skulked in his stateroom, seldom appearing on deck even for a few minutes. Thinking that he was seasick, she had even taken the trouble to dispatch a note by the steward, asking if she could be of assistance; and the note had been returned, the same note, her note, with just 'Thank you, no' scribbled on it—the *same note!* Phil reported that she had not even glimpsed Darl the last day, and that she couldn't be bothered putting herself out for such louts again. 'He has the manners of a pig!' she had written. Madeline could see Phyllis Kellems getting off the ship in New York (she could not see New York itself, for she never had ventured to picture that city in her mind), holding her head high and sniffing loudly whenever she recalled to memory that returned note with 'Thank you, no' scribbled on it, indignant, trembling with rage, never for an instant guessing that behind the breach of etiquette there might be an emotional war so intense as to make even that much of an answer an effort. Why did such a woman get a man like Harry?

'But he too' her father was saying softly 'was not married. I would surely not urge el capitan upon you, my little one, though I believe that he is a clever man and will go far. But between a man who is married and one who is not married, a wise young lady should know how to choose. I mean no harm. Often I scold you, but you do as you wish. You're not stupid, my little cabbage. But you are not the wisest person in the world either: remember that.'

She stooped to kiss him on the forehead. She fairly skipped to her own room and pinned on pancake and veil, pulled on gloves, picked up a parasol. In a moment she was back, standing upright for his inspection.

'That is, hum, *all* the hat?'

'That is all, Papa. Now do not start to grump about the Americans! I tell you, they are wearing just such hats as this in Paris too!'

'They are likely to wear anything in Paris. Well, until we meet, my dear. Is it that you have a shorthand pad with you, in place of the prayer book?'

She swung along the sidewalk of their narrow little street, conscious of the petticoat's sound, conscious too of a persistent desire to roll her hips. It was a beautiful morning. The air was clean and odorless, and it was not too warm. In the middle of the strip of sky that she could see there was one clump of small clouds huddled together with no distinguishing separation, like small white rabbits huddled in a corner of the hutch; but the sky itself was brilliantly blue.

She passed, as she so often did, under the balcony of a house four doors from her home. She did not know what the place was called, but the nature of its business was patent. It was curious how she had learned to take such places for granted. Though she had never attempted to peer through its door when that door was opened fleetingly, she never crossed to the other side of the street because of this establishment, nor stiffened.

Now as she approached the balcony she did something she had not done before. She looked up and smiled at the girls. There were three of them lounging on the balcony, and they jumped when Madeline smiled. They were sullen slovenly girls, in scarlet, magenta, and orange kimonos, and their unpainted faces were pale and lined in a light that wouldn't flatter; and one smoked a cigarette. When Madeline

170

smiled two lumpishly gave no response, but the one with the cigarette removed this and made her mouth into a simper, calling 'Buenos dias, señora.'

'Buenos dias, señoritas' Madeline replied.

She did not grit her teeth at sight of these women. Why should she? She despised them, but certainly she did not hate them; she did not in her mind call them 'unfortunates'; for she believed that they were up on that balcony not because they had been betrayed by lovers in whom they'd trusted—an explanation which had always seemed silly to Madeline—but rather because they were lazy, vain, poor, stupid, and morally slack. Well, despicable as they were, they were not as bad as their clients, the furtive men Madeline had seen sidling into or tottering sheepishly out of this maison de tolérance—or, having been about to enter, walking sternly past the place when they saw a lady.

Madeline wondered now, as she passed, whether the tarts up there heard the petticoat. She wondered why she cared whether they heard. She wondered what had come over her today.

Well, whatever it was, it had been a long while on the way. Here was no mere mood of exuberance induced by the weather, her clothes, the prospect of hearing Harry sing and of going out with Harry in the afternoon. Here was something, she vowed, which had come to stay! She had waited too long. She had played the game unwisely, not misreading Harry's wife but rather overestimating her own patience. Today she felt impetuous and was glad of it. Today, somehow, she would cause Harry to embrace her.

Oh, she knew that she was doing wrong! He should embrace her, and be brought to love her, while his wife was near at hand—not while his wife was two thousand miles away. Madeline would not concede that Harry was a prude, but she did know that he had a firm and possibly overstuffed sense of honorableness. Good! It was one of the reasons why she loved him. Only—when he embraced her, with his wife far away, then afterward he would feel ashamed of himself and perhaps for a little while even hate her, Madeline. But only for a little while, Madeline believed.

Anyway Madeline didn't care. Twice already the wife had postponed her return, and perhaps that too meant something? She had a lover in the States, maybe? Or maybe she was afraid to return to Panama where she'd be sure to encounter el capitan again? Was she el capitan's mistress? This Madeline did not know. The previous night, very cautiously, and lightly, while walking around the Plaza on el capitan's arm and listening to the music of the band, twice she had tossed out hints; but el capitan, suave and knowing, had pretended that he failed to understand. Madeline *believed* that they were not lovers—not yet.

No matter. This afternoon, while she and Harry walked among the romantic ruins, a perfect setting, something would happen.

It *must* start soon! It should start now. Otherwise—well, you could go mad with boredom, and Harry would not want a mad woman.

This was not the proper way of thinking for one who went to church, but she couldn't help it. Actually she was happy. She even realized, from the way men looked at her, that she was smiling. You never should smile in public in Panama—unless you were a man, or ugly, or one of those who lounged on such a balcony as Madeline had just passed. She straightened her face.

Another thing she came to know, soon, was that she was climbing— and climbing too fast. At this rate, by the time she reached the hospital's main office, that is to say the church, she would be out of breath and her face would be damp. No, no! She raised a gloved hand.

'Coche!'

Madeline was accustomed to being stared at, as she'd honestly told her father, but that was in the street, where men's eyes were direct. In the main office of the Sanitation Bureau in the Ancon Hospital grounds this Sunday morning, it was not stares but rather the throbbing effort others made *not* to stare which unsettled her. Naturally demure, Madeline had never before made so many persons conscious of her presence.

A church to her, previously, had been a public place, like a square, though darker, quieter. You went in when you pleased, by any door that chanced to be unlocked, and you genuflected, if you felt like it, finger-dipped the holy water, possibly dropped a coin into the poor box. You might wander around, looking at the windows, or perhaps stand in front of the altar to study it and its appurtenances. You might lean against a pillar, meditating. You might slip into a pew to sit or to kneel. Others came and went, but you paid them no attention, nor did they pay attention to you. You stayed a little while or a long while. You rested your eyes and ears, and the coolness was good on your face; and it may be, if you prayed, that you rested your soul as well.

When she went to the service in the office she felt that she had invaded a private club.

Oh, they were polite! Everybody was kind! But they seemed startled by the sight of a stranger, and uncertain what to do about her. Without mouthing them, they made swift plans to get a good look at her outside, after the service, when they could do so without being rude. They whispered to one another with extreme cautiousness and out of lips almost squeezed shut, being careful not to lean toward one another the while.

A young man with spectacles greeted her at the door and after a preliminary jolt of amazement fairly beamed upon her. Not in a whisper but in an ordinary voice he asked her if she would prefer to sit over near a window—'He could be a maitre d'hotel' she marveled—and when she said yes, he gallantly led her to a chair and drew it back for her, and even pushed it under her. She all but reached for the menu.

Others appeared, saw her, quickly recovered from their astonishment, and accepted seats more or less assigned to them by the young man with spectacles. Some smiled to her, and to these she smiled back. The smiles were large and firm, not stingy. One man came over with extended hand and said in a low kindly voice 'I am glad to see you here, very glad, very, very glad, yes.' Madeline, shaking his hand, thanked him.

They smiled at one another, these people, and spoke to one another, but they were thinking of her. She sat quiet, hands in lap. She had come to hear Harry sing, that was all. He knew that she was coming —in fact, he had invited her—but these people had not known it.

Papa would have chuckled at the office, which was even plainer than Madeline had expected. The pews were rows of uncushioned wooden-chairs, most of them folding chairs, which faced only a cleared space in which there were two plain wooden tables. The smaller of these tables, which was set to one side, held two shallow baskets and a pile of books. The larger, centrally placed, held a Bible, a vase containing oleander sprays, a pitcher of water, and a glass! Not only was there no altar, no altar cloth, no altar rail, not only were there no candles, but the single vase of flowers was the only decoration. However, the desks, which had been pushed against the walls, were all rolled down, and there was not a spike, inkstand, coil-spring penholder, sponge container, letter basket, paperweight, or blotter in sight. There was a telephone on the wall, to be sure; but this it would hardly have been convenient to remove.

The Gorgases came in and recognized her and smiled, nodding brightly. She was flattered that they remembered her, for she had met them but briefly at the Kellemses' housewarming more than a year ago.

A man passed out the books from the side table. They were exactly alike and utterly unadorned. The type was hard, harsh, black. Though few of the hymns bore titles, each was conspicuously numbered.

These people were oddly alike in appearance. None were peasants, none aristocrats. The men outnumbered the women about two to one, and some, Madeline knew, were physicians and engineers, some were office executives, while others were clerks or foremen; more than a few had callused hands, but all wore clean white shirts and stiff white collars, and to a man their shoes were shined. The women's clothes all looked as though they had been bought from some mail-order house and accepted without demur and worn without alteration. The women weren't perfumed, and none wore or carried flowers.

Though they greeted one another in lowish voices, and sometimes passed a few remarks, they did not strike up conversations, nor did they, after they were seated, speak at all except in whispers. Ordinary voices, after all, she realized, for Americans were *extra*ordinary. In any other such assemblage of Americans—it was one of the things she did not like about them—people would have started to talk in ordinary voices, perhaps, but soon the men would have been shouting, the women screeching, each trying to make himself or herself heard above the others. It was a curious custom: if you did not bellow (a man) or cackle (a woman) without pause, you were guilty of discourtesy. Here however, all was decorum. Was this because, despite the homeliness of the surroundings, these worshipers truly believed themselves to be in the presence of the Almighty God?

Harry was beside her, smiling, telling her how glad he was that she had come, how sorry he was that he was late.

'It'll be a pretty simple service' he warned. 'Sometimes we're lucky enough to get a minister, but most of the times we aren't. And we haven't got one today. So there'll be no sermon.'

'And what will you sing, 'Arry?'

'"Rock of Ages" and "I Love to Tell the Story," I think. Those are the ones I want, anyway. That's why I've got to leave you now. I promised Mr Harris I'd help him select the hymns.'

'Oh. He is a—a lay brother?'

'No, no! We haven't anything like that. I thought I'd explained, mademoiselle! There isn't any one denomination. It's all different denominations—Methodists, Baptists, Episcopalians, Lutherans—all scrambled together.'

'But if you can meet and scramble so well, then why are you different at other times?'

174

'Well, that's kind of hard to explain. . . . Of course, this is different from anything you've known before, I suppose?'

'Well, yes.'

Two men, one of them the bespectacled usher, went up the aisle toting a harmonium, and this they placed to one side of the table holding the water pitcher. They opened it. A firm-faced woman went to it, unsnapping a rubber band from a bundle of music.

'You'll have to excuse me now' Harry whispered. 'They're practically ready to start. I'll see you afterward, won't I?'

'But of course.'

Harry walked up the aisle, smiling right and left to acquaintances. He conferred, to the slap of pages, with the firm-faced woman and with a squat benign man who Madeline assumed was Mr Harris. A moment later he nipped back to the front row. The firm-faced woman sat at the harmonium and ominously spread her skirt. Mr Harris went to the big table. The service began.

The service began with no blare of trumpets or roll of drums, indeed without even a chord from the harmonium. Mr Harris beamed at those assembled, glanced at his hymnbook, looked up again, still beaming, and mumbled something Madeline didn't catch. *Then* came furiously a chord from the harmonium, and this was followed by a vast rustling of pages, and immediately everybody stood and started to sing.

Madeline too stood. A woman beside her, a stocky red-faced woman, who saw her confusion, sidestepped close, offering Madeline a look at her book and pointing to the hymn. 'Thank you' Madeline murmured. She sang a little because it appeared to be expected of her. She didn't know the melody; but neither did any of the others, she gathered; they sang against one another as they sang against the harmonium, which carried on with harsh reedy squeals.

Madeline was appalled by the noise they made, all singing gustily, determinedly, as though by the very strength of their vocal cords they could chase evil far away, so that the windows rattled and the dust danced on the floor. Madeline had a good speaking voice, low, even, slow, direct, but a poor voice for singing, an uncertain contralto she couldn't control. Knowing this, she sang only when she was in a group, and then but moved her lips to indicate that she was following the music. However, the other worshipers here imposed no such restraint upon themselves. They loved to sing. And sing they did—loudly and with enthusiasm, sharping, flatting, in all keys, to sundry times; heedless of the harmonium's strident attempt to guide, they sang a variety of melodies all at once. The hymn had five verses, and they sang all of them.

Then Mr Harris called for another hymn.

The stocky woman flipped over pages, smiling shyly at Madeline. As soon as she found the hymn she straightened, looking directly ahead, as they all did, and lifting her head. She was rigid with expectation as she held a corner of the hymnal while Madeline held another corner. The stocky woman's eyes were glittering, and a muscle in her lower jaw quivered. No sooner had the first chord come crashing from the harmonium than she started to sing, lifting and lowering her whole head in vigorous emphatic rhythm as she did so. Madeline noticed that most of them sang in this manner, staring straight ahead, their necks stiff, their eyes bright, their chins ponderously, thumpingly keeping time.

There were six verses in this hymn.

Afterward, at no command, they all sat. Mr Harris cleared his throat and smiled and announced that it had proved impossible for them to obtain the services this Sunday of Dr Somebody nor yet of Dr Somebody-else, whom they all remembered so well, *but* they did hope that *next* Sunday they would be led in worship by one who could and would deliver to them a message they'd long remember. In the meanwhile, for just today anyway, they would have to get along with him, with Mr Harris himself, unfortunately. He laughed, a nervous laugh. At the same time he happened to know, he told them, with a twinkle in his eyes, that a certain young man had promised to sing for them two of the hymns that were *everybody's* favorites; and it might be that *this* would go a long way toward making up for the weakness of his own, Mr Harris's, poor efforts. He *hoped* so, anyway.

Then abruptly, and with no change of voice or expression, he said 'Let us pray' and averted his head.

'Dearest Lord our God, look down upon us humble people who are gathered together here in Thy sight this beautiful sunny Sabbath——'

When she realized what was happening, Madeline instinctively started to slide off her chair; but she saw that nobody else knelt, so she stayed where she was, bowing her shoulders a bit, as the others did, and averting her face. Nonetheless, throughout that long and incredibly monotonous prayer she continued to use her eyes, peering here, peering there under far-lowered lids, studying the men and women around her and wondering about them.

She wanted to know them. They were Harry's people, and she wanted to understand them.

Assuredly they were naïve. Even more naïve than she had estimated previously. But she believed that they were good. They were kind. They might do wrong, but they wouldn't *mean* wrong. By what process of reasoning, or by what emotional handsprings, they had reached the belief that such impromptu prayer, such informal undisciplined caterwauling, could be acceptable to the God of the Israelites, she could not guess; but the truth was evident that they did have this belief and were happy in it. They were enjoying themselves. They thought that by this singing, howsoever discordant, they were somehow cleansing themselves.

And they were *strong* people, she divined, watching them slant-eyed, first on this side, then on that. They were not stupid—to be naïve is not necessarily to be stupid—but they thought well of others, being themselves persons of good will, and assumed that all were straight and clean and without evil unless distinctly marked by hooves and horns and bathed as well in the acrid odor of brimstone. They were *strong*. They had strong faces. Should their faith be violated, or advantage taken of their kindness, their rage, Madeline suspected, would be terrible. She had always been a little afraid of Harry, even while she loved him. Now she was more afraid of him than ever.

'—we ask it in the name of Thy Son, Our Lord Jesus Christ. Amen.'

There was a straightening of shoulders, a lifting of heads. Palm-leaf fans rattled. Mr Harris named a hymn; the belligerent harmonium spoke; and they rose and sang. Afterward they sat down. Mr Harris then, mincingly, like a wine steward who produces one of his most treasured bottles, announced that Brother Kellems would favor them with 'Rock of Ages.'

Harry did not go to the organ, nor did he turn to face his audience. He simply stood in his place, in the front row, with feet a little apart and hands clasped behind his back.

'*Rock of Ages, cleft for me,
Let me hide myself in Thee!*'

It was effortless and exquisite. He sang as Madeline had wished to hear him sing, as though he were alone. Even the harmonium could not slur the golden graciousness of his notes. Madeline saw only the back of his head, but she enjoyed every moment of the hymn. He sang it better than he had sung the ballads at the housewarming. The ballads were fancy small things, beribboned, self-consciously quaint. This hymn was simple and lovely.

Afterward—and it was a mistake—they all rose and sang another hymn, in any old time, their heads bobbing, their eyes fixed, to chase away the last echo of the solo.

Then they sat down, and Mr Harris read some verses from the Bible. He read them in a low, almost unintelligible monotone—he had explained in advance, smiling apologetically, that he was no minister—and without even looking up. His exhalation was audible when he closed the Bible, and again he made it clear, 'as I don't need to tell *you*,' that he was no minister. However, he said, we all have to do the best we can. He took a drink of water. He said that he was certainly glad to see such a nice turnout, even if they didn't have a real minister, 'and not every one of them a familiar face, either.' Everybody pointedly refrained from looking at Madeline. He said that half the collection today was to be used to buy new hymnbooks, while the other half was to go to the lepers at Palo Seco, and he hoped that they would all be generous. He was going to ask Mrs Mitchell, who had charge of that work, to tell them something about what was being done to brighten the lives of those poor unfortunates at Palo Seco. Mrs Mitchell rose and spoke. Madeline was not able to hear anything she said. Then Mr Harris asked if Brother Kellems and Brother Westcott would be so kind as to pass the collection plates.

Madeline would have liked to whisper a word of congratulation to Harry, who got her side—Brother Westcott turned out to be the bespectacled usher—but it was the red-faced woman and not Harry directly who passed her the plate. The plate in fact was a basket, one of those which had been on the side table.

In time the baskets, with the money in them all unblessed, were thrust back upon the table, and Harry and Brother Westcott, as though ashamed of their association with them and anxious to get away, hurriedly returned to their seats.

Harry sang again. He stood in the same position, feet apart, hands behind his back, needing no hymnbook; but this time his voice was even richer. He *enjoyed* singing: Madeline was sure of that.

'I love to tell the story
Of Jesus and His glory,
To tell the old, old story
Of Jesus and His love.'

178

There were tears in Madeline's eyes, and many a woman worked her palm-leaf fan with unwonted vigor. Nevertheless, and as though to shoo away the memory of not-nice beauty, they rose and sang the last verse over again together. Then they sang another hymn. And Mr Harris muttered a prayer. And it was over.

Some time was needed for Harry to get clear of the thankers. Madeline did not push into that group, but waited for him at the door. There was a great deal of talk, which was not now measured and comparatively subdued, as it had been before the service. The worshipers were flushed, as though they had witnessed an exciting race, and seemed happy; and their voices rose, the women screeching, the men tending to bellow. At least seven or eight, men and women both, approached her at the doorway with extended hands and introduced themselves and told her how glad they were to see her there and asked her if she didn't think it was a glorious morning and also if she didn't think that Mr Kellems had sung divinely. She would smile and say 'Yes.' They really did seem glad to see her, and their faces made her feel good.

At last, Harry.

'Thought I'd never get away. Let's wriggle out of here before somebody else grabs me. Let's take a little walk first. Have you got time? Or do you have to go home and get dinner ready?'

'No, I have time for a walk. You—you were wonderful, 'Arry.'

'I'm glad you liked it. I enjoy it so much myself. I'd like to start singing again right now.'

'Why don't you?'

He laughed.

She had never loved him so much, and she had great difficulty in keeping herself from staring around and up at him adoringly as they walked. She was proud to be seen with him. She smiled and bowed when passers called greetings to Harry and lifted their hats to her.

They strolled out of the hospital grounds but stayed high on the hill. They passed a row of one-family wooden houses, finished but not yet painted. No one worked on them today, Sunday. There was only a watchman, a Jamaican, who of course was asleep. No grass had been planted before or between the houses, each of which looked exactly like its neighbor, as though they had all been cut out by the same gigantic cooky cutter. The parts surely must have been interchangeable; even the debris left by workmen, the chips, shavings, cones of sawdust, chunks of molding, bits of glass and of screen, seemed arranged the same around each house.

'This is where Phil and I are going to live, pretty soon.'

'Oh?' She looked at the houses. 'Which one?'

'I *think* it's this one we're in front of now, the third one in' he answered slowly. 'But it *might* be the fourth. I'm not sure.'

'I see.'

'If Phil had come back when she planned, it wouldn't have been ready for us anyway, as it turns out. They should have been ready a month ago, but they've been using every workman they can get on that hotel they're building around the other side of the hill. You've seen it?'

'Yes. And it's certainly shooting up! Every time I look at it there's a new wall or a new floor.'

'They've got more than a thousand men on it, all at once. They're trying to get at least one wing done in time to accommodate Teddy. The President, you know.'

'Oh, he really is coming then?'

'Yes, he's coming all right. It's definite now. Week after next. Phil won't be here for that either. A pity.'

Vexed, she twirled her parasol, forgetting to be pleased that it *was* a parasol and not the usual umbrella. She did not want to talk about Phil. She wanted to talk about him, Harry, and herself. True, they would have the whole afternoon together at the ruins; but it was a shame to lose even an instant of a day like this.

'You said a little while ago that you still felt like singing, 'Arry. Well, why don't you?'

'Eh?'

'Sing me something. Something special for me. Don't you like to sing out-of-doors?'

'On the contrary, I like it better.'

'Well, sing me one of those hymns again then. Or anything.'

'All right.' He didn't face her, but looked down the hill toward the bay. He smiled a little as he sang, and she smiled up at him, standing close.

Afterward he walked her down the hill and to her home, but now he was still, and when she made a reference to the afternoon he blurted that he was sorry about that—he was afraid they'd have to postpone it.

It was a knife into her, and the pain was hot and made her dizzy for a moment. She hoped that she did not miss a step.

'Oh? I am sorry.'

'I have to do some work' he explained. 'It—it's something that has to be done this afternoon. I didn't know about it until this morning.'

180

'Poor 'Arry! They make you work Sundays too now?'

'Well, this is—— Well, it's something sort of extra. Hard to explain. But we could make that trip some other Sunday, couldn't we?'

He must have known, certainly she knew, that they were not likely to get another Sunday like this one until after Christmas; and by then Phil would be home.

'Well, if it can't be helped it can't be helped.'

'I'm afraid that's the way it is. It's something special. I hope you don't mind too much?'

'Well . . . Thank you for taking me home, Harry.'

Papa was offensive, asking her sarcastic questions, striving, good-naturedly enough but with elephantine humor, to poke fun at her and at Harry's friends. She was curt as she moved about, helping Conchita to prepare and serve dinner. It was a good dinner, and that quieted Papa, who loved to eat. Madeline herself ate little.

'Don't you want to take a walk with me?' she asked over the coffee. 'We're not likely to get another day like this for a long while, and a walk would do you good.'

'I thought that you were going to the Old City?'

'That's been postponed. Now I'm just going to walk along the sea wall for a while.'

'I shall read,' he decided, 'and smoke.'

Her mirror told her that she looked as well as she had looked when she left, earlier, for the service on the hill. She simply did not believe the mirror. Nor would she walk as well, she knew. She felt no spring in her step. The ruffles on the petticoat swished, but not gaily.

With the door half open she stopped short. Had she reached a stage of emotional silliness, in which she had hallucinations? Harry was coming down the street.

She did not step out on the sidewalk, but only stood there, breathless. He had got out of his extra work! They'd have their trip to the ruins after all!

Four doors away, before the maison de tolérance, Harry paused. He glanced furtively up the street and down the street, not seeing Madeline. He sidled to the door and rang the bell, and the door was opened and he went in.

Papa's shaggy eyebrows rose. He was lighting his pipe.

'You will not walk after all, my cabbage?'

'The sun is too warm' replied Madeline. 'I think I'll rest.'

She went to her room.

11

THE LIGHT LANDED BALEFULLY upon Simpson and all his rolls and bunches of fat, his sagging tiredness. He was an immense agglomeration of white balloons of different sizes, each balloon straining to burst; and the light glistened upon these, but especially on the ones that were smeared with sweat. Simpson was a sad man, whose sigh was frequent. He sighed now.

'*Why* do you think somebody's going to shoot him?' he asked.

'With all this crowd around, in a place like this, just before he's going to go away——'

'Listen, he's been here three whole days. He's hurled himself hither and yon at the God-damnedest rate of speed even *he* ever showed before. Through mud. Through goo. Through some of our most luscious and perfervid rains. Harry, he's been in places that even you and I don't get to very often. He's bounded just about practically everywhere. Can you think of any place he hasn't been?'

'No, as a matter of fact I can't. But still at the same time——'

'He's *hurtled!* That's what he's done—*hurtled!* By Jesus, I never saw a man move so fast or so emphatically!'

'You don't have to talk like that, do you?'

'Harry, I always have been an irreverent bastard. I'll talk any way I please. But getting back to cases: Why, if nobody's taken a crack at him so far, should anybody take a crack at him *now?* Can you answer me that?'

'Sure.'

'Oh?' Simpson's eyes lolled sideways. He put thumb and forefinger to the cigar in his mouth, but he didn't take the cigar out. Rain slashed off the edge of a corrugated-iron roof at his left, giving him, for Harry, a sheer silver background. The light hit him here and there, touching up his balloons. 'Why?'

'Because anywhere else there would have been parties, and no real crowd, like this tonight. Except the other day in front of the cathedral. I was worried there. I was scared stiff.'

'You scare too easily, Harry.'

'I don't like that remark!'

Simpson sighed. 'I didn't mean that you get frightened for your own skin. I didn't mean that. Don't be so tempery.'

'I'm trying to tell you that——'

'And I'm trying to tell you that just because there's a crowd here tonight, and just because he's about to go away, and just because nobody knows quite what the hell is going on, and it *would* be a pleasant spot for an assassin—I'll grant you *that*!—just because of those things, you and I don't have to jump around like a couple of kids that have peed in their pants, do we?'

He did take the cigar out of his mouth then, and he emitted an unbelievable amount of smoke for a long time. He gazed at the smoke.

'Here's the point, Harry. You and I aren't bodyguarding him. He's got secret service men to do that. We're audience, that's all we are. We listen. And I suppose we'd better applaud.'

'You mean you don't *like* him?'

'He flabbergasts me, Harry, I wouldn't say I don't like him. I often wonder what this ditch-digging would have been like if he hadn't happened to be President. But he is. And he flabbergasts me. He dumfounds me. My relatives say he's a traitor. Personally I think I sort of admire him. Though I understand that he actually isn't a very good shot, after all.'

'You know him personally?'

'Used to. Fact is, we're cousins. I'm not going to remind him of that right now, he's got too much to do. He didn't have so much to do when he was Assistant Secretary of the Navy and the war broke out. I went to him then and asked him to arrange it for the Army to take me. *Me*—when they later took *him,* who can hardly see three feet in front of his nose! But I was fat. That's the trouble. Never get fat, Harry. Well, we had lunch. Twice. Bully! he kept telling me. Why, of course, Simpy! Good old Simpy! Showed his teeth, hooted, burbled, chortled, made all kinds of noises. Fed me fairly well, not too well. Why, of course! Dee-lighted! Did I get the commission? No. No, he was busy sending the whole Pacific fleet to the Philippine Islands, for some confounded reason, and then he leaped right out of Washington and became a lieutenant colonel, and then a colonel, waving a sword and writing round-robin letters. And then he became a governor. Wasn't that wonderful, Harry? But meanwhile what happened to good old Simpy? Nothing. And yet I don't dislike him' Simpson went on. 'Whatever else you might say of him, you've got to admit that he's in a class by himself. As for anybody taking a pot shot at him tonight, Harry, forget it. They're not that stupid, even if they were that desperate. Matter of fact, killing my esteemed cousin would be the worst mistake they could possibly make. Nobody likes to commit murder, in the first place. Or rather the second place. The *first* place is that if T.R. were slaughtered here, the Panama Canal would be as good as built, no matter *what* else happened.'

'There's something in what you say.'

'There's a great deal in what I say. He does the job mighty well, Harry, alive. But *dead*—killed *here!*—why, he'd be unbeatable!'

'At the same time——'

'Harry, I've never had such a subordinate. Stop contradicting me.'

'All right, I'm your subordinate, but I'll contradict you all I please!'

'Tut, tut. I told you you ought to watch that temper.'

'Well, listen to this then: He's not here!'

'He'll be here. Keep your shirt on. What are we waiting for?'

'I'm not talking about President Roosevelt. You know the man I'm talking about. He's not here.'

'Oh. Well, all right. He makes a show of having no respect for Teddy anyway, doesn't he?'

'That isn't the point. Respect or no respect, he'd come have a look at the President, wouldn't he? Of course he would! And listen, what's more, he is not only not here but he arranged a poker game in his flat at least a week ago, and he invited some pretty important Panamanian politicians. What'd he do that for?'

The rain was worse than it should have been, even in Cristobal in November. It slashed across the roof edge so fiercely that it sent a mist over the two of them, and they had to shout at the top of their lungs and hold their faces close together.

'Harry, there's something in what you say.'

'There's a great deal in what I say!'

'I thought of that first, Harry. Stop joshing me. Anyway, how'd you get that interesting snippet of gossip?'

'I've got my own connections.'

'All right. Simpy's squelched. And I'll give you credit, Harry: you know our friend well. He never *is* in on the act itself, is he?'

'Has he ever been?'

'Not that I know of. I wish that the son of a bitch *would* be, one time.' Simpson toothed the cigar, then lifted it away without smoke. 'I just wish he *would* be! Well, your argument makes sense, Harry. For a change. But as I see it, there's nothing we can do.'

·   'If we got to him and told him that this man is playing poker very carefully with some picked companions——'

'Wouldn't that sound sweet, Harry? Wouldn't they just throw their arms around us and kiss us, if we rushed up to them at this stage of the game and told them something like that? No, come off it! As a matter of fact, if you ever *could* convince Teddy that there was such a possibility—then you'd never keep him *off* that platform! Well, anyway, it's too late now. Here he comes. Cheer, Harry. Cheer. Why, you're not a *Democrat*, are you?'

There were the glasses, which themselves, shattering and hurling back the light, challenged you. There were the cheeks beneath them, a strident red. There were the teeth.

A great filling roar had been in the place previously because of the rain, which always makes thunder on a corrugated-iron roof; but the roar now had the world to itself. On and on it went. The man grinned, standing at the edge of the platform; and the roar was even louder. When at last the crowd was quieted, the rain sounded a weak tinkle, the loudest Nature could arrange perhaps, but thin, far, compared with what had recently been. The man grinned again; and again the electric light bulbs were shaken in their sockets.

After a while he talked. They all heard him, for he talked loudly and very clearly, hasping each word shut before he shot it out of his mouth; but Harry at least remembered little of what he said.

He was fighting, that much was clear. Just standing there, addressing a crowd which whooped at his every syllable, he was fighting. His glasses fought, furious. His teeth flashed. His voice was Stentor's voice, and his very cheeks and forehead were truculent, and his body trembled with the force of what he so vehemently said.

No one could stop them, for they were doing a bully job. Did the world want to fight? *He* would fight it! *They* would fight it with him, wouldn't they, if it chanced that he needed a trifle of assistance? But that was absurd! His glasses glittered; he waved his fists.

He would remember them, he swore on the wet hot dock. He would not forget what they were doing. In fact, he thought that for what they were doing they deserved medals, as soldiers got medals for bravery under fire. Weren't *they* under fire? Weren't *they* soldiers? He believed, he told them that he believed, that they should be rewarded as brave soldiers were. They should have some evidence of their heroism, something they could show to their children and grandchildren. He would arrange it. He grinned. They cheered.

He was not fulminous now. His chafe was past. In great earnestness he raised his arms, the hands no longer fisted.

'I do not pity you because you have before you a hard task. I would feel ashamed of you if I thought you wanted pity. I admire you. I wish that any one of my boys was old enough to take part in the work. I feel that to each of you has come an opportunity such as is vouch-safed to but few in each generation.'

Simpson said: 'See? I told you he knows how to do it!'

Harry said: 'Shut up!'

Unkilled, the President got aboard the U.S.S. *Louisiana* and started for home; and Harry started for home aboard the Teddy Special. All windows were closed on the Special, for the rain threw itself now this way, now that, and the conductor's cap and shoulders were wet when he came along the aisle, and smoke swirled languidly around the Pintsch lamps.

'Heroic, eh? Sure, we're heroic as all-get-out!'

'Well, you got to give him credit, he stayed on shore!'

'Yeah, he never stopped long enough for a mosquito to catch up with him!'

'Wishes his sons were old enough to come down here, eh? Well, I wish they were too. Maybe if they had to eat the garbage we have to eat they'd tell the old man something about what it was like.'

'All the same——'

One by one they got out at the different stops, each turning up his collar, pulling his hat down, and drawing a long breath to run for it in rain where an umbrella wasn't going to do you any good at all. One by one. And each, swearing dispassionately, hoped that that bastard of a nigger had had sense enough to keep the charcoal going so that there'd be some dry clothes to put on in the morning.

Harry sat in a far corner, not speaking, not listening much.

'Medals he's going to send us! Why the hell doesn't he send us some *cows?*'

'They got them in town. Two bucks a jump.'

'Listen, I mean *real* cows! I'd rather have some honest-to-God milk than all the pieces of tail in the world!'

'Brother, that's a big statement, but I don't know but what I'm with you. He can keep his medals.'

'Well, why don't you quit gassing? He *came* here, didn't he?'

'Yeah, he came here. And he's gone away again!'

'Well, what'd you expect him to do? Stop all his work and just sit here and hold your hand?'

'Well, he might send some cows, at that. He can keep his measly medals, but I could use a cow.'

'Ah, there!'

'Or a hen.'

'I'd like to see you trying that.'

'Well, anyway, he *came* here!'

'Ah, shut up!'

'You know, I got an idea.'

'Keep it. You might need it sometime.'

'Listen, Teddy said we were like soldiers in a lot of ways, didn't he? And that this is like a war we're fighting here, didn't he? Well, if it's a war, why aren't there some war correspondents? If we had some of *them* I'll bet we'd get action! Yes, *sir!* The way it is, the folks at home don't know what's going on here most of the time—and as far as I can see, they don't care.'

'Yeah, the newspapers don't seem to care either.'

'That's a fact! Do they have anybody to report this war regularly? No. Now and then some magazine might send a fancy dude down here who shakes a lot of hands and gets bought a lot of drinks, and inside a few days, without having really seen anything, he goes back and says the situation is very grave. Or else somebody like that squirt Poultney Bigelow drops in and wanders around in the rain a little while and then goes back and thinks he spills the beans—only it turns out they weren't beans but rubber balls, and they bounce back and smack him in the puss.'

'He had that coming.'

'Sure he did! Because he didn't know what he was writing about. Why don't they assign some good reporters to come down here and live with us and find out what's really going on?'

At Bas Obispo several more got out; but the man with the idea—he sat two seats ahead of Harry—developed his theme all the same.

'This job is a damn sight more important than the Spanish War, no matter how you figure it. It involves more money and more men, and in the long run it's going to make a much bigger difference in the whole history of the world. Isn't that right? Well, when we fought the Spaniards you saw Richard Harding Davis and Stephen Crane and all the others trooping down there to Cuba, didn't you? Dozens of 'em, hundreds! And they didn't take one look and then turn around and run back, either. They went right up forward. As a matter of fact, if the Spaniards had wanted to contact us they'd have had to wade through a lot of newspapermen first before they could even find our advanced patrols.'

'Was you in that shindig, brother?'

'I was in it, yes. I was laid up with diphtheria in a hospital in Tampa practically the whole time. But at least I knew what was going on, even there, because I could read the papers. Why, the generals in the field practically had to send back home to get the newspapers in order to find out what they were doing or ought to do! Well, all right, why don't we get service like that here? I was one of the first ones down here, came down more'n two years ago, when things were really bad. But then the folks back home seemed to think that everything was o.k. *Now,* when things are getting so much better, why, they seem to have the notion that we're dying like flies and wasting millions. There's even talk about giving up the whole job—just when we're beginning to get started! Well, whose fault is that?'

'If we had a lot of reporters around here——'

'If we had a lot of reporters around here,' the Spanish War veteran broke in, 'you wouldn't have all these crazy rumors floating up to God's country, and you wouldn't see all these labor troubles. American reporters'd get down to the truth, come hell or high water! And you can't tell me that the truth wouldn't be one of the most sensational stories they ever had to print! You can't tell me that somebody isn't behind all those fake rumors, starting 'em in the first place maybe, or at least spreading 'em as fast as they can, trying to give us a black eye down here. You can't tell me that those Bims and Jamaicans are kicking up all this fuss and making all these complaints just because they can't think of anything else to do. Why, there isn't one of 'em's got gumption enough to start a damn thing by himself, unless maybe it's a nap. There's somebody behind 'em.'

'Who?'

'How should I know? I got to work on a dredge all day. I ain't got time to go around finding out things like that.'

'Well, *why,* then? *Why* should anybody want to try to spike this whole job?'

The Spanish War veteran looked with disgust upon his questioner. The veteran was a small man with the beak of a hawk and a pump-handle jaw and a fan of wrinkles at each end of his thin bloodless mouth. Harry, leaning forward now, studied him.

'Brother, even looking at you I find it hard to believe that you're so brainless you never heard of the Cragin-Grace-Eyre syndicate. Or the Atlas people. Or the Atlantic and Pacific Navigation Company. Or the Canadian Pacific and the Union Pacific and the Southern Pacific and for that matter every other transcontinental railroad there is. If the railroads can even *delay* this job of ours here they figure they're making millions. If old man Astor and old man Grace and the rest of that Nicaragua outfit can get the public so disgusted that Congress won't appropriate any more funds for us, and the thing's dropped *in Panama,* then *they* got a chance of making *billions.* If it comes to that, what reason have you got to think that there mightn't be one or two European governments that've got plans for a war and that wouldn't want this canal opened up too early? And you musn't forget the French gang. Most of those Frenchies were honest, sure, but some of them were the cleverest God-damn financial crooks the world has ever seen—and they're still out of jail, and so how do you know what monkeyshines *they* might not be up to?'

Harry Kellems nodded slowly, approving.

'What are you, a socialist or something?' somebody asked.

The Spanish War veteran answered slowly: 'No, I'm not a socialist. But I'm not an idiot either. And it stands to reason that when a guy sees the possibility of a million dollars dangling in front of him he forgets some of the things he was taught in Sunday school when he was a kid. Oh, he doesn't have to put his cards down! He's never called! That's one of the big advantages of being rich. You don't command any dirty work to be done. You just drop a hint to the guy underneath you, and he makes it a little stronger to the guy underneath *him,* and so on, until finally the word gets to a guy with brass knuckles. The gent in the high silk hat, he reads where somebody was picked up from a gutter with a cracked jaw, and he says it's terrible the way these criminals act and something ought to be done about it, and he probably never even really does know that he was the one who started the ball rolling. If you got a million dollars you not only don't have to let your right hand know what your left hand doeth, but you don't even have to let anybody else know what either of 'em doeth—and the nicest part is that you don't even have to know it yourself!'

They had reached Panama City.

'Well,' said one of the men, as he yanked his collar up, 'I hope those medals are nice and heavy. I could use a good paperweight.'

It was the third house from the corner, not the fourth; and though in every way it was superior to the Bridal Suite, Harry had not felt contented there; it was not a friendly house to come home to.

He crossed the veranda and let himself into the parlor and stood a moment without turning on the light, his ears alert for the sound of mosquitoes. There were none. He turned on the light.

He went to the kitchen, where Rosina, bless her heart, had banked plenty of charcoal in the stove. He undressed, hung up his clothes before the stove, toweled his shivering body, squirmed tiredly into a bathrobe, and lit a cigar. He was smoking too much, now that Phil wasn't here. . . . There was no sense lighting a cigar at this hour. Of course, he could put it into a receiver when he went to bed, and it would go out promptly, so that none would be wasted. Unless you kept puffing, cigars in Panama always went out.

Rosina had made him a sandwich, and he eyed this without enthusiasm. Rosina had her points; he was fond of her; but she never would learn how to make sandwiches. This one would have frightened the appetite out of him, if he'd had any appetite in the first place. Yet her feelings would be hurt, he supposed, if he didn't eat it.

He wandered through the dining room, wandered into the parlor. Here was all the government had promised, and a handsome layout it was; but Phil hadn't lived here yet, and so it seemed wrong. There was the mission dining room set, but he had managed through wire-pulling to get fumed oak for the bedroom and parlor. The Bridal Suite had seemed bare? Um-m. Well, this place surely was not overfurnished, even with the government things added to their own. *Their* own? Phil's own!

Her several things were here, including the piano, but they were only Phil in a hotchpotch. He had hung the Maxfield Parrishes in the places he thought she would like; but he was not sure. Her pillows he had not put out. She'd always been fussy about the placement of pillows.

Lonesome, lonesome, he wandered, a dirty guy playing a dirty game, and worst of all he wasn't really thinking about Phil at all, he was thinking about Madeline.

It had seemed to him, when he sang for her, two weeks ago, exactly two weeks ago tomorrow noon, that she leaned toward him and looked up at him. He hadn't moved! He'd sung as firmly as well as he could. Sure, he had probably been mistaken when he thought that he felt her arm pressed against his arm. Madeline was a very exciting woman; but no matter what they said about her she wasn't a woman who would deliberately *flirt*. Yes, he had been wrong. Had he been possessive afterward? Had he taken her arm too tight when they went up places and down places, so that she'd been offended? She was not a woman who would let you know when her feelings were hurt. But she could let you know by not seeing you. Since that day, that Sunday two weeks ago tomorrow, he had seen her only once. Twice her father had come to the door, saying 'Monsieur? 'Ow are you? My daughter is—'ow is it said?—not dispose'. Forgive me, monsieur.' And the old man had bowed, and Harry had bowed, and Harry had gone away with a thousand things, all bad, electric-sparking back and forth across his brain. The one time Madeline herself appeared had been even worse. 'Harry, do you mind much if we don't have a lesson today, please? I am tired.' Naturally he'd said sure. Naturally he'd been wounded. His chest had ached for a long time afterward.

What in hell was *this*? He was in the parlor, and it was Phil's parlor, and Phil would be back soon! He got out Phil's latest letter. He was sore at himself.

Somebody has said that the only interesting part of a woman's letter, as it is the only important part, the only previously *thought-out* part, is the postscript. This time Phil had made no more than a skimpy effort to be entertaining. It was a duty letter, pure and simple. She had seen Henry Miller in *The Great Divide* and thought he was wonderful. She had been to the Kepplers', in East Orange, and Connie Keppler was crazy about this new auction bridge, which was different from whist, much harder, but Phil herself was trying to learn it. She had seen Fritzi Scheff in *Mlle. Modiste* and she was wonderful, and he, Harry, would have been crazy about the music. The Corbins had tickets for the debut of this Geraldine Farrar at the Metropolitan, who they said was so wonderful and had made such a hit in Berlin. Phil wished she could go, but tickets were hard to get. She and Mother were going in to New York again tomorrow, shopping; there were still three or four things she needed to get. Mother, Father too, had been after her all the time, morning, noon and night, to stay on over the holidays, since she'd stayed this long already; they kept saying that they had missed their little girl so much last Christmas, the first Christmas in twenty-two years that she hadn't been with them; but of course she told them that she had to be with her Harry, she wouldn't dream of anything else. Clara Hedgepath sent her best. So did Joe Hedgepath. *He* had a job with the Snodgrass upholstery people now, which didn't amount to much.

There was more like this, most of it petty gossip about people Harry either knew slightly or not at all. The letter was carefully calculated to fill three pages and most of the fourth, the balance of the fourth being allotted to signature, to x's, and to the postscript:

'I suppose you're not in the old "Bridal Suite" any more? Do you remember how you used to get into bed first, and how after I had brushed my hair and everything I would turn out the light, and then I'd stand there in the dark, in the middle of the room, and call: "Oh, *my!"* and you would call right back *"Oh,* my!" You *do* remember that, dearest? Never mind, we'll be doing it again pretty soon. P.'

Sure, he remembered. He remembered the time, too, when a letter from Phil would have been *mostly* like that postscript, which here, honestly, looked dragged in by the heels, an afterthought, as a post-script was supposed to be but so seldom was: this one was a filler, somewhat more elaborate than another few decks of x's but hardly written with any more feeling. 'There!' he could almost hear Phil saying, when she finished the letter. 'There! I've got *that* done!' And she'd go off on another party somewhere, or another shopping trip.

He wondered whether Phil was going to like this new house. She wouldn't be able to laugh and fool about it as she had done about the Bridal Suite, but there was a lot to be said for running water. Yes. Remembering, he suddenly put the letter down and went to the bathroom and washed his hands and wrists vigorously and hard for a long while. Then, he didn't know why, he took off his bathrobe and got under the shower, and turned it on, and just stood there for a long while sucking in his breath, for the water was cold and bit all parts of his skin. She was sore, maybe? But about *what?* What had he done? Phil would get sore from time to time about almost anything or about nothing at all—just because it was time for her to get sore—but Madeline had always been so *dependable.* He shouldn't think of Madeline. It was not decent. Especially when Phil wasn't here. He shut the water off and finger-slapped many drops from himself and then used the towel. It was a big Turkish towel. He put his bathrobe on again, and ambled into the kitchen, where that sandwich confronted him. Hell. He went to the bedroom and turned down his bed. Then he wanted his cigar, and he searched a long while before he found it—in the bathroom. He lighted the cigar again. Uneasily, the cigar jutting high, he went to the parlor.

Never mind about Phil! Never mind about Madeline! Legs spread, he stood in the middle of the parlor and tried to make himself review what that Spanish War veteran had said.

No fool, that guy. Sure. He had been absolutely right. Harry remembered his face, and remembered too that he had said he worked on a dredge. You couldn't tell: Simpson might be able to use him?

Be careful, Dr Gorgas had said. You've got a very pretty wife.

Yeah. And where was she?

And where was *he?* He was standing in the middle of the parlor floor, trying to get some smoke out of a damp cigar and wondering why a certain French girl had not been amiable. Now here certainly was a fine way for a man to be, wasn't it? Why didn't he go to bed? Well, he would. He turned out the parlor light and felt his way to the bedroom, where he remembered the sandwich.

He went to the kitchen and got the sandwich, and he looked at it. If he dropped it into the garbage can Rosina would find it. He went out the back door and climbed the hill a little way, in his bedroom slippers, and threw the sandwich as far as possible.

When he was in bed he thought: Hell, I should have scrunched the thing a bit, to make crumbs.

And, rolling over: Hell, I hope Madeline'll be at the service tomorrow.

She was not at the service. Discouraged, he sang 'How Firm a Foundation' and 'Blessed Be the Tie That Binds,' neither a favorite of his; and despite the congratulations, he knew he had not been in good voice.

He ate no lunch. He moped, after making his own bed, after straightening a few things. He had to admit that he was thinking of Madeline all the while. Had he hurt her in any way? Not the hymns of the morning but that new ballad, 'Love Me and the World Is Mine,' was what hung in his head, leaving only when, forcing himself, he mentally brushed it away, but returning to the attack again and again, and again and again, with the pauseless, senseless persistence of an unwanted insect. He was still humming it, in spite of himself, when he walked down to the city a little after one o'clock.

He was tempted to go past Mama Margery's and put the question straight up to Madeline—*was* she sore about anything, *had* he hurt her in any way, or was she truly feeling bad and if so was there anything he could do? He sighed. After all, he had no claim on Madeline, who, truth to tell, had been a great deal kinder to him than he deserved. And in two or three days Phil would be boarding the steamer to return. In only a little over a week she would be back. *That* should take his mind off his troubles! If nothing else, at least Phil would give him a lot of work moving furniture around until it was where she wanted it.

So he didn't go on. But he did look up and down the street pretty carefully, as he'd done last Sunday and the Sunday before; and only then did he push softly on the bell of Mama Margery's door. He hated to think that somebody might see him enter a place like this.

The door was opened immediately, and he slipped in.

12

NO WISE MAN would have tried to guess Mama Margery's age, or her weight, or her nationality. If she was not young, there was nothing decrepit about her. She was huge, but didn't waddle: here was no mass of loose fat, but a solid and tough core of uncertain size, wrapped, you would have supposed, in layer upon layer of skin, of hide rather, each of which, though it added to the general bulk, was drawn and laced firmly into place, leaving no flaps. As for complexion, she was a rainbow cocktail, she was a pousse-café, with the colors gone sour. She gleamed like putrescence and glowed unpleasantly, without flame or smoke. Her hair was dyed; her face was painted; her eyes were perhaps black, perhaps a very dark blue or dark green. She spoke at least five languages, all badly. Nobody liked her. In her line of business she could be expected to be hard and exacting; but Mama Margery did not even make a show of delight and bigheartedness, as madames are supposed to do—at least when a customer appears.

Now, arms akimbo, she greeted Harry with accusations.

'You are here again!'

'So it would seem. Aren't you glad, Mama? How're the girls?'

He smiled at them. All five were there, loafing in wicker chairs, dressed in gaudy well-worn evening gowns, their faces painted ready for business but with sulky sleep still sticking to their eyes. But they brightened when they saw Harry.

There was also a small baldish man, apparently an American, who was composed of a great round ball of a belly into which a thin chest and absurdly skinny legs had been stuck. About forty, and a little drunk, he beamed.

'You come here one Sunday, you come the next, each time you take Lolita to her room—and you do not do anything!'

Lolita giggled sharply. All of the girls giggled. Harry felt himself blushing, but he made himself grin.

'I paid her, didn't I? What are you griping about?'

'I think that you are looking for somebody! I think that——'

'Ah, pipe down! How 'bout some wine?'

'How do I know, maybe you are the police?'

'Don't be silly! You ever know a policeman to *give* you money?'

Not notably intelligent, nevertheless Mama Margery could see the validity of this argument. The man held out good American gold. The wine she had was homemade wine poured into French bottles with their original labels intact. Profits on this were great. A good drinker, provided he didn't get nasty—and this man never had—could be persuaded to spend a lot on wine. Also, the girls didn't get a centavo of that, which was Mama Margery's own.

'Well . . .' She looked around. 'For everybody?'

'Why not?'

'Well, you can take your coat off' she conceded.

'Oh, I'm not hot.'

'I think you are never hot' Mama Margery grunted as she made for the kitchen; and this stirred a fresh wave of giggles.

Mama Margery, however, had not intended to be witty. She was angry, uneasy: she sensed the approach of trouble. In ordinary circumstances this Amazon was her own bouncer. Bouncers were low crude men who had to be paid, and who insisted also upon free drinks and free women, a great deal of both. Mama Margery knew that they were likely to cause more trouble, sometimes, than the clients they were hired to control. A bouncer could get too interested in one of the girls and raise hell every time anybody picked her. Or, drunk, he could be too quick about chucking out a good customer who might have been quieted by such a tongue-lashing as Mama Margery was capable of giving.

Nevertheless, even Mama Margery was a woman, if a formidable one, and even she knew that a strong man was sometimes needed. She saved herself expense and trouble by keeping this personage, one Riaz, as a call-in for emergencies. Riaz lived up the street.

Mama Margery said to the Indian maid, now: 'Take off your apron and go up to Riaz. Tell him he must hold himself in readiness. Tell him I expect him to take no more than a minute, if I do call. And I expect him to be sober. Otherwise—no pay.'

'Si, señora.'

Harry picked a settee, draped, for grandeur's sake, in a rotting Spanish shawl from Canton, and sank into it. He was not displeased with the way the visit was going. Mama Margery was bellicose, true; but then she usually was. He did not think that she was unduly suspicious of him. It must have been obvious that he was looking for somebody, rather waiting for somebody who might appear; but it was equally obvious that he was not a policeman and that his manners were quiet. Besides, he had a pocketful of the best possible answers to Mama Margery's objections.

Parlor A, where he sat, and where he hoped to continue to sit, was separated from the entrance foyer only by a curtain of painted beads, a Japanese curtain, through which it was easy to see. So long as Harry remained in Parlor A nobody could enter or leave the house without his knowledge. Oddly enough, considering the nature of the business conducted there, Mama Margery's had no back or side door. Had there been such a door, he reflected shamefacedly, he himself would have used it.

Parlor A stank of tobacco, steam, dirt, rum, and cheap perfume; but so did Lolita's room. Four of the girls had their beds upstairs, but Lolita's room was on the ground floor just off Parlor B, which was exactly the same as Parlor A and which also was separated from the foyer by a tinkling Japanese curtain. From Lolita's room, if you left the door ajar, it was possible to command a view of the entrance hall; and here was the reason why on his previous visits Harry had selected Lolita from among her sisters. Why Lolita rated the ground-floor room he didn't know. She was neither better- nor worse-looking than the others, about whom there was a curious sameness, so that Harry had trouble telling them apart. Perhaps Lolita could claim seniority of service? At any rate Harry had spent about an hour there—all he dared —each of the previous two Sunday afternoons, sitting on the edge of the bed and now and then looking through the slit of the door he'd left ajar.

It was not a prepossessing room, though it had its points of interest. The one window admitted little light and no air at all: it was covered by maroon drapes. There was a straight-back chair; a washstand on which reposed a slop jar and a basin containing dark purple potassium-permanganate solution; there was the bed, which was immense; a wardrobe, bigger still; a grass rug; a hand-painted china thundermug; and the things on the walls. Lolita was not much to look at, even after she'd slipped off her evening gown—she wore no underclothes—and so, while she lay, indifferent, studying a mole on her knee, Harry had sauntered around the room looking at the things on the walls. There were all sorts of fans, most of them cheap Chinese. There were messages and pictures, mostly salacious, penciled by patrons. There were strips of colored paper, tacked or pasted in knots and bunches, or, in the case of many, simply hanging as paper ribbons: they suggested the decorations in a nursery, except that they were pathetic, telling as they did of a childish taste, a dread of bareness, and uncountable hours of boredom. There were bits of verse, which Harry, who was nowhere near as good with the written Spanish word as with the spoken, had not been able to read. There were some pictures cut from magazines, mostly of women flashily dressed. There was a faded oval chromo of a young French naval officer, giddily braided, clutching a sword. There was a photograph of President and Mrs Amador, at the foot of the bed; while facing this, over the head of the bed, and draped with the American and Panamanian flags, as well as a rosary, was a large handsome photograph of Theodore Roosevelt.

From time to time Harry had gone to the door and peered out across Parlor B to the entrance hall. From time to time, too, a suspicious Mama Margery had peered through Parlor B to Lolita's room. Once, possibly because her sense of decency was outraged, Mama Margery had crossed Parlor B and quietly but firmly closed the bedroom door; and Harry, just as quiet, every bit as firm, had reopened it. You get some queer customers in a whorehouse, as Mama Margery should have known. She had not tried this again.

Now, today, it seemed silly to spend an hour or so in that close chamber. He wasn't deceiving anybody. He could pay Lolita anyway —with government money out of an expense fund. Here in Parlor A he was surer of his coverage. Also he would be nearer to Enrico if Enrico did come. There was a chance that Enrico might try to bolt: he must have known that they were looking for him (assuming that he really was back in Panama, as the tip had it) or he wouldn't be lying low.

'Here comes your wine.'

Mama Margery, she of the huge round gutta-percha body, strode into the room and deposited upon the table a tray holding three already opened bottles and a large variety of glasses.

'It is ver' good wine' she informed. She leered at him: 'Maybe it *make* you hot, eh?'

Harry laughed, refusing to be insulted. He filled all the glasses. Mama Margery snorted and returned to the kitchen. It was her practice, a wise one, not to hang around when there were customers. She was shrewd enough to know that it was hard for anybody to feel merriment in her presence.

The very smell of the stuff gave Harry a headache. He'd had a headache on each of his other visits. The air alone, without the wine, would do it. From the way that they sealed the windows in this dump, he reflected bitterly as he handed glasses around, you would think that their vice was a different one, say opium, which might betray them to the nose of any passer.

'You have one too?' he asked the bald man.

'Now I don't mind if I do. It looks mighty nice. Cigar?'

'Thanks.'

'Well, mud in your eye.'

'Here's looking at you' said Harry. And to the girls at large: 'Salud!'

They drank.

'Say, that's pretty nice stuff! Strong, eh?'

'Have another one?' said Harry, and filled his glass.

'Well, I don't mind. Say, while we're at it,' he extended a hand, 'my name's Landis.'

'Mine's—Jones.'

'Well, mine really *is* Landis!'

Landis lowered himself into a wicker chair over which scraps of imitation oriental rugs had been thrown.

'Say, now this isn't bad! All the comforts of home, eh? If I didn't happen to be broke I'd—— Come over here, sweetie. You can squat down on Gus anyway. They don't charge anything for that' he explained to Harry.

He had waved to the nearest girl, who came to him without question and sat on his knee and put an arm tentatively around his neck. It happened to be Lolita. He clinked his glass against hers.

'How do you say that—salute?'

'Salud.'

'Salud, then. Down the hatch.'

He drank. They all drank. Afterward the girls, excepting Lolita, redistributed themselves on the various couches and settees with which the parlor was overcrowded, in attitudes at least technically seductive. They were quiet and appeared contented; and in fact the atmosphere was incongruously cozy. With Mama Margery out of the room—that is, when they were not obliged to simper and smirk—the girls looked pleasant enough, lazy, comfortable. They were stupid girls, not at all brazen. Understanding little English, but wishing to learn more, since the tongue would be an asset in their profession, they listened attentively, shyly watching Landis as he spoke, smiling only when he looked at them, which he seldom did. Landis felt chatty. He addressed himself only to Harry. The others, including Lolita, who had put her head on his shoulder, he ignored.

'Say, now this is real nice! I was just about getting ready to leave, being broke, but this is swell. I had my little hop. Not this one. It was'

—his eyes strayed across them—'it was that one over there.' The girl smiled. 'We went upstairs, to a room upstairs. And say, you know what?'

'What?' asked Harry.

'She had a big picture above her bed of Teddy Roosevelt!' He chuckled. 'Wouldn't Teddy boil over if he was ever to find out about *that!* Dee-lighted hell! All the same, it's fair enough. They have a lot to thank that man for.'

He was within reach of the table, and without disturbing Lolita he put his glass down and poured himself another drink.

'So you're a married man, eh?'

'Certainly not!'

'Don't get sore. It's a cinch any man you meet in a fish market like this, and he tells you his name is Jones, he's married. That's all right. Matter of fact, I'm a married man myself. You got to look at these things philosophically. Now you take me, I been married seven years, and I'm devoted to my wife. Fact. Wouldn't do anything to hurt her feelings for anything in the world. But I don't know. . . . You got to look at these things philosophically, that's the way I figure. Gracie and me, for three-four years there we were as happy as a couple of goats. Well, we're happy now too, as far as that goes, but you know what I mean?' He looked right at Harry. 'Sure, you're a married man yourself. You understand. I guess it probably always has to be that way, with everybody. You have a hell of a good time for a while, and then after a while maybe you go right on having a good time—only not that way. Catch on?'

'Yes.'

'Not in bed, is what I mean.'

'Yes, I understand.'

'Naturally you do. Well, that's the way it was with us. I just worship the ground Gracie walks on.' His eyes swam, and he took a sip of wine. 'Only thing is, after a while it just wasn't the same. The way I see it, it wasn't her fault and it wasn't mine. We just both sort of lost interest, that's all. She got fat, for one thing, and I happen to like skinny girls. But it wasn't only that. . . . Anyway she just couldn't put her heart into it any more. And I'm a man. If I don't get it I might grow crabby and snappish, and then we'd both be feeling terrible, isn't that right?'

'I suppose it is.'

'You know darn well it is! But this way, I go out once a week to some nice quiet place like this, and it only costs a couple of bucks, and what's the harm? I suppose Gracie knows I do it. We never mention it. Well, we don't have to. It would be different if I was to go around trying to get some on the sly, pinching every woman I'm introduced to, or chasing around on the streets to see what I could pick up. I wouldn't do *that* for anything in the world. That would make her feel bad, naturally. But this way it's different.'

He looked at Lolita, as if something had suddenly reminded him of her. His left arm was around her waist, and the fingers of his left hand were cat-creeping up to her breast, which sponged under their pressure. She smiled fixedly at him. He bent down and kissed her, at some length. He beamed at her for a moment, then turned to Harry with a look of delight and amazement.

'Say, this is a kind of cute little chicken at that, ain't she?'

Harry smiled.

'For a guy that only came downstairs a little while ago—— Hey, I guess I better clear out! Once-a-week Georgie is getting ideas.'

He kissed her again. She wriggled, pressing herself against him. The other girls and Harry watched gravely.

'Ah, there! This is no place for a minister's son! Sweetie, get up off me before I start trying to take the gold fillings out of my mouth for security.'

His face was damp with perspiration, his breath came short.

'See here,' said Harry, 'if it's only a couple of dollars you're worried about, why, have one on me.'

'Ah, say listen, I couldn't do that! Hell, I sit here and drink your wine and—— Say, for a married man you got a lot of money there, brother. Gracie never allows me much. If I only hadn't stopped to snatch a little firewater before I came——'

'Go ahead. I don't happen to feel like it myself, right now.'

Fine words, he thought, to be coming from a man who a few hours earlier had been in church! He was certainly doing things he would never have dreamed of a little while ago. He wondered whether it would be right to take this two dollars out of the expense fund. He decided not. A man's got to have *some* conscience.

'Listen, brother, if you really mean it—I could get it back to you. Save it out of my allowance. You just give me your name—your real name—and where I can reach you——'

'Forget it' said Harry. 'You don't owe me a cent. Have another drink before you go?'

'Ah, there! Couple more of these and I won't be able to manipulate those stairs! Well, here's looking at you.'

'Mud in your eye' acknowledged Harry.

He gave the two dollars to Lolita, who disentangled herself, hitched up her left dress strap, and, humming, went out to the entrance hall, where the figure of Mama Margery had loomed as though by magic. Presently Lolita returned, and smiled at Landis, and extended her arms, wriggling the fingers.

'You bet I *will!* Little old Johnny-on-spot himself!'

The girls and Harry heard them cross the entrance hall, heard them started across Parlor B.

'What's this? We don't go up those stairs after all, eh? Oh, you're going to let me in on the ground floor, eh?'

The voice stopped, the footsteps too. Then Landis roared with laughter, a sound amazing from so small a man. He yelped back at Harry.

'Say, you hear that, what I just said? She's going to let me in on the ground floor!'

Harry hauled out the turnip his father had left him. A quarter past four. He was to stay here until seven, the assumption being that if Enrico hadn't appeared by that time he wouldn't appear at all. Enrico's habits were well known by Simpson, who knew everybody's habits; and before Simpson had started to look for him in order to ask him some questions, before he had glided out of Panama City, Enrico was wont to visit Mama Margery's every Sunday afternoon. He had been regular about this, a creature of habit. He'd never failed.

Harry knew the man by sight. Enrico once had worked on one of Harry's fumigation squads. He was tiny and mild, a mouse; but like a mouse too he was alert, he was cautious. To wait for him in some nearby doorway would be futile. Even if Enrico did not send a friend to reconnoiter in advance, he himself would be sure to spot a loiterer and to scamper away. Besides, there was a part-time bouncer, a giant named Riaz, who lived a few doors away, whose duty it was to scout along the street now and then, and who would infallibly accost and shoo away any suspicious character. To ask for Enrico at the cat house itself would be to give Mama Margery a chance to ingratiate herself with an old customer by means of a tip—or, if she didn't know where he lived, by turning him away at the door with a whispered word. The police? The police had nothing to do with the matter. There was no charge upon which to arrest Enrico. Besides, Simpson didn't want him arrested. Simpson only wanted to ask the little fellow a few questions—questions somebody else didn't want asked.

As for Simpson himself: 'I'm too well known. They're leery of me. I've been around those places too often. They don't think I'm cops, but they do know that I represent the law in some capacity, and the moment my sylphlike figure floats over the horizon they're clams. You know I wouldn't ask you to do a dirty job like this if I could possibly do it myself.'

Harry closed his eyes, which throbbed, as his temples were throbbing, for his headache was worse—and would grow worse still before seven o'clock. How could anybody *live* in air like this?

He didn't know what he'd do if Enrico appeared. That would depend upon the circumstances. Harry carried no weapon or badge. In fact, what he proposed was a kidnaping. He believed that a former boss could overawe Enrico and march him outside before the little man knew what was happening. He hoped that he could hustle him up to the Plaza de Santa Ana, if necessary twisting an arm behind him. Then a hack. Simpson's house. Harry felt a little sick already. It wouldn't be fun to play the bully.

One of the girls was strumming a guitar she had drawn from under a couch, and they were all looking at Harry. He shook his head. He didn't feel like singing. Besides, it would make him conspicuous. A fresh customer would be almost sure to look, to see who belonged to the voice. It was not likely that Harry would know anybody who patronized a place like this; but such a person might know Harry, at least by sight.

But the girls brought their chairs closer; and while the others hummed, the one with the guitar played a Spanish song they had taught him the previous Sunday. It was a catchy little number, now sad, now gay; and soon, as they began to sing instead of hum it, pronouncing the words carefully so that he'd know them, he too found himself singing; and he sang louder and a little louder, until the girls, delighted, fell silent, only urging him on with eye-applause.

They sang that song several times, and then they sang another, low at first, repeating the words for him carefully, and then louder, laughing. This second was a rollicking number. It made Harry feel good to sing it. He *shouldn't* feel good, he thought, in a place like this. There was something traitorous about such a feeling. But the girls sang a third familiar song, and he sang it with them.

The doorbell rang. Mama Margery, on her way through the entrance hall, glanced in at them. They were finishing the song, and the girls would have started it over again, but Harry shook his head.

Mama Margery opened the door, admitting two men, neither short enough to be Enrico. She called sharply to the girls, who trooped out, while Harry went to the table and turned his back to the entrance, filling glasses. Soon there were steps on the stairs. Two of the girls came back, one being the guitar player. They started up where they'd left off.

'Hey, that was sure a humdinger! I mean the song!' Landis returned, buttoning his vest. His face was flushed, his eyes bright. 'Jesus, you're a regular Chauncey Olcott! Do you know "Slumber On, My Little Gypsy Sweetheart"?'

'Well, the girl wouldn't know how to play that.'

'Ah, she can accompany you with just chords like. Come on! I love that song. Slum-ber *on*, my lit-*tul* gypsy *sweet*-heart . . . Let's have it the way it ought to be done, huh?'

Harry sang it, the guitarist doing well enough, the girls listening attentively, striving to understand the words. Lolita, smelling of disinfectant, rejoined them. Landis asked for 'Good-bye, Dolly Gray,' and Harry obliged. A man came, Mama Margery called, and the girls romped out; but the guitarist was spared, and with Lolita she hastened back. Landis, who had been helping himself to the wine, begged for 'In the Baggage Coach Ahead.'

'That would be pretty hard for her' Harry demurred.

'Ah, she can do it all right. Just like she's been doing, kind of strumming. Come on, let's have it. I absolutely *got* to go—should've gone an hour ago—but I won't go till I hear that.'

So Harry sang 'In the Baggage Coach Ahead' clear through and with feeling, while oily pear-shaped tears streamed down Landis's cheeks. Landis indeed was too overcome to speak for a while afterward, and when he did speak emotion made a whisper of his voice. He vowed that that had been the loveliest thing he ever heard. He vowed that he would go home now, right away. Only thing was, if Harry would just sing him *one* more. Just one short one.

'Now listen, you said you were going to——'

'I'll leave, absolutely I'll leave, if you'll just sing me this one. No other one, just this one. It's my favorite of them all. You must know it. Everybody knows it.'

'What is it, then?'

' "Jest Alongin' for Your Smile." You know that, don't you?'

Harry lowered his head as though to take a sip of wine, but he couldn't drink it. He turned away, pretending to cough.

'No, I'm afraid I don't know that one.'

'Ah, you must know it! Everybody knows it! It goes:

> *'Jest alongin' for your smile,*
> *Jest to make my life worth while.*

'Ah, it's *beautiful*! Not the way I sing it, no! But if *you* was to—— Ah, say, you *must* know it!'

'I don't,' curtly.

'Listen, it's easy to learn, and I know all the words, so maybe if we could get a paper and pencil in this dump and I could write 'em all down for you, and then maybe——'

'*No!*'

Mama Margery, hearing Harry's voice raised not in song but in anger, came promptly to the entrance hall and leered beyond the beads of glass like a fat foul fiend from a tinseled hell. The girls were silent. Landis put a hand on Harry's shoulder, lightly at first, but soon he was leaning his weight upon it.

'Don't get sore' he whimpered. 'Ah, I've had such a swell time here this afternoon, and all because of you, practically. I wouldn't want to think of you being sore, after we had such a good time. Honest, I can't think when I've had such a good time before.'

'All right. Don't cry. I'm not sore.'

'I'm not crying! What do you think! I wouldn't *cry!*'

'All right, don't *you* get sore now!'

'I'm not sore. I'm not sore and I'm not crying either. Only thing is, we've all had such a good time together, and I hate to go away thinking maybe you feel bad about something, at the end of such a good time we all had together.'

'I feel all right' said Harry, whose head was splitting. 'You'd better get moving, hadn't you? Your wife will worry about you.'

'I'm all right. Jus' need to get a little air.'

Air! thought Harry.

'Only thing is, if you'd only be philosophical you'd be all right. Like I am. You got to be phil'sophical.'

'I am' Harry assured him. 'I'm very philosophical.'

One of the girls brought Landis's coat, and they helped him on with it, while Mama Margery watched grimly. He was shaking his head.

'No, you're not' he blubbered. 'I know. I'm smart. I could see right away you're a man that isn't happy about something. But if you'd only be phil—— What you ought to do is not worry about it, because after all you *got* to do it sometimes, an' if your wife——'

He was put out gently, Mama Margery giving him a slight push between the shoulder blades to help him off the doorstep. For a little while afterward he rang the bell, but nobody answered. Then the house was quiet.

Six o'clock. Sundays were always like this. There had always been a hushedness about Sunday, which when he was a kid had frightened him, and later it had embarrassed or irritated him; and even now he didn't like it. Sunday was the Lord's day. It was clearly written that six days shalt thou labor, and all that. Yet Sunday never fulfilled its function, Harry thought. Certainly it wasn't a day of rest. It might be a day of doing-nothing, but not of rest. As a kid he'd not only had to dress up and go to Sunday school, which was worse than ordinary school, and then to church, but he'd had to be guardful of his clothes for all the rest of the day. Father usually had been tired that day, and cross. Nobody had been allowed to really play. There had been no quick music. Not only you but everybody else had been all dressed up and looked unhappy. You hadn't been allowed to yell, which was as bad as not being allowed to get dirty. 'You ought to see what it used to be in my time' Father would tell him when he'd whine. 'Now run along and play. But be quiet. This is Sunday, remember.' This was Sunday, remember. This was Sunday, remember. As if you were ever likely to forget! Harry sometimes thought that if he'd been cast upon a desert island for years, without any way of knowing how the calendar went, he would still somehow *feel* Sunday. He'd straighten up. He'd brush his fig leaf or his nakedness, whatever he had. He would make an effort to comb his hair. And this not because he liked it, but because he'd know deep in his bones, in the very marrow of his bones, he'd feel across the fathomless sea, the millions of acres of waste, that it was Sunday, when people must dress up and go to church, and when taking a walk was expected to be the total of your fun, and you should remember to be quiet. Yes, he was sure that he'd feel it on a desert island—not once, twice, three times, but for years, every single solitary seventh day.

Well, this was Sunday. Even in college, when the other fellows said they did, Harry had never enjoyed Sunday. He doubted that *they* had enjoyed it. They'd loaf, grunting. They'd talk big. But he sensed an uneasiness, an embarrassment. Nobody was ever exactly himself on Sunday. Could it be that they had a feeling that God really was looking at them, that day? Harry, who had worked in a laundry all day Saturday and until eleven o'clock every Saturday night, and had been obliged to sing in church each Sunday morning, had not enjoyed the afternoons. He'd been too tired to sleep, as he had been too tired to study. Tom Sawyer had thought of Monday morning, the beginning of a whole new week at school, as the most dismal time of all the week, the most depressing, the lowest point in a kid's life. Harry Kellems had always rather liked Monday mornings. Well, no doubt he was crazy. Tom Sawyer was what you were supposed to be like, everybody said. Would it have been different if Tom Sawyer had lived in Paterson, N.J., had gone to college in Hoboken, and had had to work until eleven o'clock every Saturday night in a laundry?

Mama's was singularly quiet. He drank some more of the wine—there wasn't much left—in order to get out of his mouth the taste of that cigar Landis had given him. Then he lighted another cigar, in order to get the taste of the wine out of his mouth.

Six o'clock. No, it would be five-ten minutes after six by now. He thought rather wildly that, assuming Enrico didn't come, he might go from here straight down the street to Madeline's house, and *beg* her to talk to him for a little while. He could tell her that he was sick. There was nothing that wasn't kind in Madeline, and she would be good to him. And after all, he *was* sick! Something—something he had said that Sunday two weeks ago?—had annoyed her. She didn't like him, right now. But if he told her he was sick she would be the old Madeline. She wouldn't ask questions, he was sure of it.

No, no! Christ, no! He couldn't go to her smelling the way he must smell now. Not only the wine and the cigars, but even more the insistent rank stale stink of this place, surely would cling to him and to his clothes for a long while. He couldn't possibly, leaving here, go into the presence of a clean person like Madeline. No, he'd do as he had done the other two times—go home and take a long, long shower. And sit in the window a while. And wash his clean hands once more before he skulked to bed.

It would be better if he didn't think so much of Madeline. This was the way it had been last night, after he'd returned from hearing the President—the way it had been so many nights lately. Thinking of Madeline, and at the same time thinking that he ought to think of Phil. . . . Perhaps he was rotten himself, with a mixed mind like that? A man ought to know what he wanted. Perhaps all the stink wasn't a stink that soaked into him from the air of Mama Margery's: some of it might have come out from inside?

The bell rang, and Mama Margery was going to the door. They should be applying thick and fast now. This was the time when he would do well to retreat to Lolita's room after all. What was an extra two dollars? He looked up, realizing as he did so that he'd been sitting with his elbows on his knees and his head between his hands. Well, Lolita wasn't there. Neither were any of the other girls. He had Parlor A to himself.

Mama Margery hissed for a moment, while somebody gruffed. The girls were out for the line-up? He turned his head. No, they weren't out there. Only Mama Margery and the newcomer were there, and the newcomer was a man much too tall and thick to be Enrico.

Harry put his head back into his hands. That was where it belonged. He wondered whether Mama would scream if he vomited.

There were heavy steps, and he looked up. The understanding about Parlor A was that when you bought wine you had it. If you bought even one bottle, the parlor was supposed to be yours. Harry had bought three bottles. Never mind why he'd bought them! Never mind on whose money! Mama Margery was taking liberties.

'Usted perdone, señor. I mean ex-cuse me.'

'Well, you should say that!'

He had swallowed no more of the wine than he thought was needed for the part he had to play. It had been too much. This was sharp stuff! His vision was not clear, his brain was not right up there keen against his memory, when he lifted his head. A full moment passed before he felt his skin go cold all over.

'I will speak in English, sir. I think that you are here too long.'

He knew the man. Riaz didn't know him, but he knew Riaz. Hadn't Simpson showed him Riaz? A gorilla, Simpson had informed. A gorilla which thinks it is a man. If it talks to you it will try to talk to you like a man at first, Simpson had pointed out. Only at first. Do not stir it, Harry, Simpson had said.

Yes, his eyes were perfectly clear now.

Mama Margery thought she ought to call *this* in, then, did she? Harry turned his head. Mama Margery was between the bead curtains, glaring malevolently. She had thought it all over, this astute old fat bitch, this unwieldy but fearful woman, and she'd decided to summon Riaz.

What the hell did they think he was?

He tried to keep his voice low.

'Will you have some wine, perhaps?' He spoke in Spanish. 'Mama, please bring another bottle.'

Mama wavered, but Riaz was firm.

'I think not, señor. I think that you should go.'

Harry shook his head, which movement sent pains crashing back and forth. He tightened his lips, looking down lest Riaz see how distressed he was.

'No,' still quietly. 'No, I wish to remain.'

He looked up.

Riaz was a very large man, large hands, large feet, a huge rubbered-out mouth. He had salacious protuberant eyes to tell of his weakness. He liked to hurt people physically. He liked to feel himself hurting them. He had been easy-spoken up to now only because Mama Margery had insisted that everything possible be done to make this exit quiet. Mama Margery was a fool! The exit would be quiet, oh yes! But still Riaz held himself in.

'Señor, I must tell you again.'

'No' said Harry.

Riaz reached out, and with a hand that was a Westphalian ham he took Harry by the arm, lifting him. Riaz was gentle, for an ape. He was doing well.

'Señor, I tell you——'

All right. Simpson had told him something too, hadn't he? Simpson had told him: keep in that temper of yours! No matter what happens, keep in that temper! Harry took a deep breath. The hell with Simpson, and of course the hell with Riaz. He pushed Riaz back.

'Get your God-damn hands off me!'

Riaz smiled; for this was all he would have asked for. Riaz was filled with joy. He stepped back.

Harry saw the blow coming. To retreat would be to sit in the chair again, to go forward would be to go into the arms of Riaz. Harry let his knees undo.

Just above the left ear. He felt the arm of the chair wham his right side, he felt his head go down, and he felt the floor, and for a split second, foolishly, he tried to hit the floor with his fists. Then he rolled.

'Caramba! This fool will not——'

He rolled again; and somehow he rose. If only he hadn't had that wine! He found himself half facing Mama Margery, who scowled ferociously. Harry twirked up one end of his mouth.

'Sorry, Mama, but I'm staying.'

She started to raise something she was holding.

'Don't worry, I'm not going that way. I'm not going out. The job isn't finished yet.'

Riaz, smiling heavily, though his throat veins worked, shuffled toward him.

'All right' said Harry. 'Let's see if you're as good as you think you are.'

There were only two blows that he remembered afterward. Both were misses. Neither made any real difference in the fight. Yet they hurt. They stung. One slished across his lips, not even jarring his teeth but bringing blood hot and fast into his mouth. The other was an uppercut which tore open his left eyebrow (of all places!), and it burned like a white-hot iron.

'If *that's* the best you can do——'

It was not the best, for many of Riaz's punches had been firm and exact. They *felt* dull. Once Harry went to his knees; and then he was astounded, for all he'd felt was a warm wet push against his jaw. Had he slipped? No, he hadn't slipped. As he rose he tried to step back—but he might have saved himself this trouble. Riaz, panting, puzzled, bleeding too, could have polished off the thing then and there; but Riaz was no longer sure of himself. Harry grinned with lips that were crackling with fire.

'I thought you were supposed to know how to fight!'

Now that was a boast without insides, and no more than a thing he'd said in rage. For Riaz did know how to fight. He knew very well. He came in swiftly, not hooking, his fists before his face, chopping, blocking at the same time, so that Harry tried to sidestep—and struck a chair. Harry, panicky, ducked. He hadn't been hit hard this time; but he knew he couldn't last much longer. He grinned—and stepped forward, swinging his fists.

It wasn't any punch of Riaz's. Of that he was sure, afterward. Yes, afterward. . . . Riaz had somehow pushed him. Anyway he felt the tinkling glass bead curtain at the back of his head; and then he felt the floor against his cheek; and he wasn't able to move; and he even felt Riaz's feet, first one, then the other, harsh, cutting his face; yet he couldn't get his hands up there. He even remembered feeling the fingers under his armpits.

13

THE LIGHT IN THE BATHROOM shone through into the bedroom, making triangles and parallelograms and trapezoids and rectangles in varying shades of gray on the ceiling and walls. Harry stared at the ceiling, all he could see. Something clammy and wet was over his cheeks just under the eyes, but the eyes themselves he could open. The clammy stuff pressed down as though to smother him, and he shivered. Frightened, with a terrible exertion he turned his head.

Beside the bed was a great upwelling of shapes which, in contradistinction to the shapes on walls and ceiling, were all curves: it was a mass here elliptical, there round, with no straight lines. It was white and wet, and it gleamed in the glow from the bathroom. It flapped a palm-leaf fan.

'How did *you* get here?'

'In a hack.'

'Oh.'

'I was summoned by telephone.'

'Well then, how did *I* get here?'

'In a hack also. Not the same hack. You were here first.'

'Oh.'

'You were lucky. A friend saw them putting you into the coche and went up and insisted upon taking charge of you. If the Cro-Magnon Man you grappled with hadn't been so mad, if he'd taken the precaution to get the vehicle *first* and *then* hustled you into it, what they'd have done, naturally, would be to pay the cochero to dump you out in some back alley, where the police would find you.'

'That Cro-Magnon Man you mention is going to be——'

'We'll take care of him. Officially we haven't any such authority in the Republic, of course, but we've got ways of exerting pressure. The joint'll be closed. And Riaz will depart, hastily. *He* doesn't look so pretty himself, from what I hear.'

'He'll look a whole lot less pretty if I ever——'

'Temper, temper! It's all in the line of business, Harry. Actually, as I said, you're lucky. Your friend brought you straight up here, before anybody saw you, and got in touch with me right away, and as soon as I got here I got Dr Bliss, and now you're not bad at all.'

Lying still, Harry had the feeling of opening his eyes very wide, though he was not sure that he did this: the cold wet mess pressing against them might have made it impossible. It was odd that he felt no pain. He did not even feel much interest in anything.

'They must have conked me from behind' he muttered. 'That madame . . .'

'It seems likely. You could hardly expect them to be sportsmanlike.'

'I don't feel anything there.'

'You don't feel much of anything at all. And you'll feel even less, in a few minutes. You're about to pass back into shadowland, Harry. Dr Bliss gave you a really big shot.'

Yes. . . . That's what his amazement had been about. Dr Bliss. But he was groggy and couldn't keep one thought long. Dr Bliss! Why, he was the most distinguished surgeon they had down here!

'There will be no report' Simpson said soothingly. 'Nothing happened. You're on leave now. You're on leave till you look all right again. About two weeks, I'd say.'

'Good God! My wife will be back before that!'

'I am a bachelor, so I wouldn't know, but I'd always assumed that you married men had an armory of excuses for every occasion. Well, you'll be backed up officially in any story you care to tell. And maybe Dr Bliss can make you presentable in less than two weeks. He can if anybody can. There won't be any bill, of course.'

Harry thought about this, but his thoughts, which wouldn't stay still, were unsatisfactory.

'I don't feel very good' he murmured.

'Wait'll you wake up in the morning. *That's* when it'll really hit you' Simpson said cheerfully. 'Right now you're not bad. You're actually falling asleep. You're falling asleep.'

'Stop trying to imitate a hypnotist! What's this stuff on my face?'

'Ah, don't call it "stuff," Harry! You ought to be more appreciative. You know yourself how hard it is to get an honest-to-goodness beef-steak here these days—much less *two* of them!'

'I shouldn't think Dr Bliss—I mean, a man like him——'

'He didn't approve, of course. But I told him positively that the *first* thing is beefsteak. I don't care how good a surgeon he is, I'll bet I know more about black eyes! But from now on you're in his hands. For a while. Until I give you another assignment.'

'You and your assignments!'

'You and your beefsteaks! Well, they're of more use on that mug of yours than they would be on a plate, anyway. They're probably tough as leather.'

Harry wasn't listening. 'What will the next assignment be, by the way?' he asked.

'The next assignment is to get so that you can face somebody without causing the poor bastard to faint. *Wait* till you see yourself, sweetheart!'

'Don't call me sweetheart!'

'There is no official record' Simpson said again. 'We'll arrange it any way you want. And as to where I'll send you next——'

'Listen! It just occurred to me! If you're going to close that place, how can we ever expect to get hold of Enrico?'

Simpson, that sighing man, sighed. He flapped the palm-leaf fan like one who performs an unpleasant duty.

'I was afraid you'd ask that. And on account of I'm always honest, Harry, having been brought up that way, I'm going to answer you the truth. The truth is that we got Enrico. We got him, actually, before you and the ape started trying to kill each other. I was just on the point of racing over to Mama Margery's to relieve you.'

'Oh . . .' Yes, he was going to sleep. But he was interested in this subject now. He wanted to know more. He wanted to keep his brain working until he could have something to wake up on. 'Did—did he admit he was the man who——'

'He didn't admit anything.'

Fiercely, if feebly: 'What's the matter with you? After all this trouble, you get him—and you can't make him talk!'

Simpson sighed. He rose and lumbered bearlike around the room, making no sound. His head hung as low as the chins would permit.

'Harry, you don't get the idea. Only God could make that man talk now.'

'You mean to say he's—— You mean——'

'Yes. Knifed back and forth, and up and down, and around in circles. My! They must have been mean men! Yes, Harry, it turns out that all the time you were waiting for him at Mama Margery's he was lying on a slab waiting to be identified.'

The ceiling, with all its triangles and rectangles and parallelograms, was descending; it was descending slowly; but it wasn't far away, and it was going to be right on top of him soon. He thought he couldn't hear any more. He was not sure that he could speak.

'That—that's—— I'm tired.'

'Go to sleep, Harry. Go to sleep.'

'Will you stop acting like a God-damn hypnotist!'

'Now, now!'

'That's—— That poker party——'

'Yes, Harry. That's the reason for the poker party. Another beautiful alibi. And as for us, we're right back where we started from. Discouraged?'

Harry tried to say that he wasn't discouraged. He was not sure whether he had said it. He tried again. He didn't hear anything.

Then he heard: 'Go to sleep, Harry. . . . Go to sleep. . . .'

Very cross, he said: 'Oh, shut up!'

It was not full morning when he woke, though the windows were dawny. He woke suddenly, almost with a start. The house was dim and silent. Lying there flat on his back, the way he had fallen asleep, as though he had not stirred through the night—perhaps he hadn't? —he was singularly clearheaded, and the events of the previous afternoon sprang instantaneously before him, not in a stream or succession but all at once, popping up like pasteboard figures worked by one string. He must have groaned. His throat was dry and hot.

He got up—he had to—and his bones seemed to squeal at the movement. Something slithered off his face and plopped on the floor. Yes, one of those beefsteaks. Angrily he tore the other off and threw it down. He fumbled his way to the bathroom.

Afterward he could not leave the bathroom without looking at himself. It was an instinct which compelled him: it was more than a mere impulse or mere morbid curiosity: it was a force he couldn't resist, though it shook him and made him feel sick. He snapped on the light. Leaning on the washbasin, he stared into the mirror.

It was worse than he had expected. Black eyes? No, they were dark purple and a dark dirty red, rather; and the skin around them was hideously puffed, so that the eyes themselves, which were bloodshot, appeared tiny and vicious and weak. Driblets of the juice from the beefsteaks slid slowly down his cheeks. His lips were enormous, and they were split in several places, where they showed red. There was a splotch of court plaster over his left eye, another on the left side of his chin. He shivered, swallowed. He thought he had never seen anything so revolting as this face with its great outthrust battered cheekbones and the mass of dark smudged bruises around each eye.

Those eyes hurt now, stinging him with their water. He did not

213

weep copiously: he did not seem capable of many tears: could a creature like this *have* an honest emotion such as grief?

More than his stomach, the very soul inside of him seemed convulsed with nausea.

An ordinary fight would have been bad enough, a street brawl would have been bad enough, but to be set upon and pulped (while drunk) by the bouncer of a third-rate whorehouse, and then thrown out upon the sidewalk . . . Phil would hear of it, of course. She'd have to. She would be coming home in nine days—no, eight days now—and even Dr Bliss wasn't going to be able to make this face a clear clean face in eight days. But Phil would hear of it anyway. And he couldn't explain. People were forever making jokes about husbands who were trying to *explain* something to their wives, trying to give plausible *excuses* for things. It was not a joking matter. It was a damned serious matter.

Yes, of course she'd hear of it. Everybody in Panama would hear of it, and no doubt many had heard of it already. A good laugh! Harry Kellems, eh? That boy who had such a nice voice and sang in church? Yeah, sang in church in the morning and then crawled into a fish market in the afternoon and got ossified and beaten up and chucked out. That was really very, very funny.

Whoever the friend was who had picked him up and brought him here—and he had many friends, he had friends everywhere on the Isthmus—*he,* though he might like Harry personally, could hardly be expected to keep such a hilarious event secret. And it was too late to get him now, whoever he was. Simpson would be quiet, sure. Dr Bliss would say nothing. But Panama would soon know about it.

He had tried mighty hard, too, to make this marriage a success. They wouldn't think of that, about how hard he'd tried, when they talked of what had happened to him and laughed. And of course Phil wouldn't stand for such a thing. Why, he wouldn't want her to! He wouldn't want a wife who would cravenly forgive an episode like that!

Well, it didn't make any difference what he wanted anyway. She wouldn't. Not Phil.

He drank two glasses of water, and scrubbed his teeth, and gargled, and very gingerly swabbed his face with water. His throat still hurt. His face hurt now too. The effects of the narcotic had worn off. When he drew even a moderately deep breath the pain in the lower part of his ribs was almost unbearable. He thought to take a shower, but he was too tired, and he drank another glass of water instead.

Back in the bedroom, in the dark, he placed a bare foot upon some thing wet and cold and squoshy. He screamed. Then he wept a little more, angry at himself and at his twitchy nerves. It was only one of those beefsteaks, of course. He crept into bed.

He couldn't sleep, and he wished that he couldn't think. He faced the wall, which grayed and gradually whitened as day came.

After a while he heard Rosina. It seemed to him that she entered by the front door. Not that he gave a hang. She was wearing shoes too, which was unusual. Her steps clacked toward him.

'Morning' he gruffed. 'I'll have some coffee, that's all. And bring it here, please. Just black coffee, that's all.'

The steps came on. Not until they'd reached the bed's edge did they stop. A hand touched his shoulder.

'How do you feel, 'Arry?'

He leaped at the sound of her voice and sat bolt upright, gasping, trembling. He forgot about his face. Afterward he recalled the fact that *her* face didn't change when she looked at him. She only smiled, a slow fond smile. She kept her hand on his shoulder.

'What are *you* doing here?'

'Why, I came to take care of you, 'Arry.'

She was still smiling. She gave his shoulder a little squeeze and turned away. She took her gloves off, carefully took the pins out of her hat, and put gloves and hat on a table. She patted her hair back, smoothed her skirt.

He did not move.

'But how in the world—— How did you ever know—— I mean——'

'Who do you suppose brought you home? And got you undressed? And put you to bed?'

'Good God! do you mean to say——'

'It was fortunate that I was returning from a walk then. 'Arry, you must be quiet! And you must not worry! I tipped the cochero to keep his mouth shut. And Mr Simpson was very thoughtful, for when he came, after I telephoned him—you didn't know who I was, 'Arry, but you blubbered "Get Simpson, get Simpson"—and when he had learned about it, then he paid me back all the money I had used. Is it that the United States Government gives that money, 'Arry? But it does not matter! Now you must be quiet.'

Swiftly, remembering, he put his hands before his face and threw himself back upon the bed.

'Oh, it is not bad today, 'Arry. It is beautiful—to what it was last night.'

He turned his face to the wall. He had been trying for some time to talk and not to sob.

'*You've got to go away from here! You can't be here!*'

She picked up the beefsteaks, one between each thumb and fore-finger, and gazed at them, shaking her head.

'Nonsense, 'Arry. You need somebody.'

'*You've got to go right away!*'

'No, no, no, no,' patiently. 'I am here, and I stay here. Now be still. I will get you that coffee.'

Simpson returned late in the afternoon, and with him was Dr Bliss, who washed Harry's face, examined it in a strong light, hm-m-m-ed, gave him some salve, left a sleeping powder, told him not to worry. Did Dr Bliss think that the face could be cleared in ten or eleven days? No, frankly, he didn't. Harry was a healthy man with a good spring-backy skin and good blood, and he'd heal quickly; but nature was nature; call it three weeks, certainly no less. Dr Bliss nodded affably, shook hands with Madeline and even bowed a bit, again told Harry not to worry and departed, quite as though this were an ordinary routine visit.

Simpson did not stir. He asked few questions of Madeline, who assured him that Harry had been quiet: Harry, in fact, had spent most of the day lying on his side with his face resolutely turned to the wall

'He was very hungry, but he refused to eat when the cook and I were in the room. He would not even let us fasten the napkin around his neck. So we left the tray each time and went out into the kitchen, and he ate everything.'

'He wasn't delirious?'

'No. He was silly sometimes, but never delirious.'

Without turning, Harry cried: 'When was I silly?'

She answered tranquilly: 'When you kept trying to persuade me to go away.' To Simpson: 'I read to him. The light hurt his eyes, so I sat over here and read him the *Estrella de Panama*, the Spanish side and the English side both.'

Simpson gravely inclined his head. He seemed not at all shocked, nor even mildly astonished. A bear in the office, irascible and impatient in all matters of routine, he was calmed by that which was startling, and he always seemed to take the unexpected for granted.

'You can keep on reading that, day after day,' he promised, 'and you won't find anything in it about this, uh, this unhappy affair.'

'I'm sure of that' said Madeline.

'The other gladiator's left town. Mama Margery is already in Colon, but she can't do business even there. Neither can her employees. The whole kit and caboodle of 'em are taking a schooner to Cartagena day after tomorrow. As to the cochero, I checked up on him this morning. I'm never convinced of the efficacy of bribery once the bribe's in pocket. Well, the cochero's all right. He could be sent back to Jamaica just like that'—thumb and second finger, for all their doughiness, gave a crisp crack—'for something he did not long ago. And he doesn't want to go back to Jamaica.'

Madeline took it up. 'The servant will say nothing. I talked with her. She is deeply in love with Mr Kellems. She swore silence.'

'The neighbors?'

'I shall play' Madeline said. 'They'll hear me play, after 'Arry's headache is better. Mrs Kellems very kindly invited me to come up here and practice on her piano any time I wished.'

Simpson nodded massively. 'Ah, that's good. And music will help him. I—I wish I might hear you play myself some time, mademoiselle.'

'If you come early enough tomorrow. That is, if the patient feels like it then.'

Harry cried at the wall: 'You're not coming here tomorrow!'

Neither paid him any attention. They sat in silence a little, while shadows tip-tilted over the mountain with such speed that if you watched you could see them move, as you can see the movement of the minute hand of a clock. In the kitchen Rosina slished about on her bare feet. Joe Casey came home next door, greeting his wife boisterously, as he always did.

When Simpson rose it was as though a statue of Buddha had reluctantly come to life. When he spoke again it was in French, and Madeline answered in French.

Harry boiled. This was too much! Not only did they treat him as though he were a baby, or contrariwise a senile invalid, but now deliberately they talked a language they knew he didn't understand.

'You can both get out, as far as I'm concerned' he snarled. 'I don't need anybody to take care of me.'

They walked to the door. Harry propped himself on an elbow, turning, and glared at them—the hall door was open—and he saw them smile thoughtfully at one another, standing close together, and then he saw fat sad Simpson take her hand and lift it, and bow over it, kissing it. Simpson did this very naturally.

'Au revoir, mademoiselle.'

'A demain, monsieur.'

Harry remained on his elbow while the door closed and while she walked slowly back to the bedroom, smiling at him.

'You can't stay here!'

'Just for an hour or so longer' she said soothingly. 'I want to see that Rosina gets you dinner and that you take your sleeping powder.'

'But—but—you can't *do* a thing like that! Even if nobody else find out, what will those men think, Simpson and Dr Bliss?'

She stood before him, arms down, her right wrist in her left hand and she was lovely. Her warm dark eyes were lovely in the dim room and her face was an exquisite oval. She stood exquisitely, too: she stood straight, but there was nothing ramroddy about her. She still smiled.

'Why, they'll think I'm your mistress' she answered. 'Is that so terrible, 'Arry? Would you be ashamed to have two gentlemen think that?'

He all but got out of bed and threw his arms around her, she looked so beautiful standing there, and her voice was such music. Slipping sunlight from the windows came across her right shoulder and touched her right cheek and the right side of her neck. The left side of her face he could not see at all; but he could see both large glowing eyes.

But he remembered his own face. He threw himself back upon the pillow and again turned to the wall. His throat hurt.

'I would be ashamed to have anybody think I was unfaithful to my wife—when I wasn't!' He had a hard time saying it. 'And I don't think —he caught and gulped a sob—'you ought to try to be funny about it.'

She sat beside him; he felt the bed give. She put a hand in his hair and moved the fingers around and around, being careful, however to avoid the bump in the back.

'I'm not trying to be funny, 'Arry. Somebody must take care of you. Rosina is not enough, and I happen to be here. To get anybody else would mean explanations. If Mr Simpson and Dr Bliss think what I said—and I'm sure they do—that will not hurt us. As far as your wife goes, she need never know.'

She never called Harry's wife Phil, but always either 'your wife' or 'Mrs Kellems.'

The next sob Harry couldn't conquer, nor the next. They'd been right in treating him like a baby, for a baby was what he was! All at once he felt helplessly weak, watery gelatine inside, with nerves that dangled and jangled, short-circuiting one another, so that he couldn't control either his emotions or his tears.

'I—I'm sorry. I've got no right to talk to you like this anyway

F-forgive me.' Crying like a kid! Making the pillow wet, while her fingers gently rubbed his scalp as though it were a kitten! 'What gets me most, though, is why anybody as nice as you even talks to—to a man who's been kicked out of a place like that.'

The fingers never paused. They were comforting, not flirtatious.

'I was angry at first' she said. 'That was two weeks ago, the first time I saw you go in there.'

'You saw me——'

'We were going to visit the ruins that afternoon, remember? I'd looked forward to it so! But you said at the last moment that you had some special work. And a little while later I saw you going into—that place.'

'Good God! You actually saw me going *in*? Do you suppose anybody else did? I looked up and down!'

'I don't think there was anybody else in the street. Not then, or last week either. Yes, I saw you last week too. I was watching for you, hidden in my doorway. I saw you go in the same way you had before. I went back to my room and thought about it. I have been thinking about it all week, as I had all the week before, but with more sense. I told myself that men sometimes did things like that, they thought differently about such things. . . . I could imagine you going to a place like that when your wife had been away so long. I hated it, but I could imagine it. But I could not imagine you being *sneaky*. I could not believe that you would *lie* to me. You have a very fierce temper, 'Arry, and I think that perhaps you might kill a man if you were angry enough. You might do many bad things. But you would not be sneaky and a liar. I thought and thought about it, until I couldn't stand it any more. I knew that you would tell me the truth if I asked you. I wasn't starting out for a walk yesterday afternoon, 'Arry, when they—when they treated you like that. Not just a walk. I was going to come up here, to this house, and if you weren't in I was going to sit and wait for you and ask you. I didn't care what the neighbors said, or your servant. I was going to wait for you. I had to! And then it happened. And thanks to le bon Dieu I was there when it did happen, and I could help you. And you kept calling for Mr Simpson, so I telephoned to him. When he came I knew from the way he acted and the way Dr Bliss acted that it was nothing wrong you had done. Men like that do not take such trouble for viciousness. I knew that it was all right, whatever it was. Mr Simpson told me a little just now, just before he left. Not much! It was when we spoke in French, and he only told me that you were doing a work that was very important, but I should not ask questions and I should not talk to others, and he added, very kindly, that I must not doubt you. Well, I don't.'

It was utterly dark. In the kitchen Rosina slished back and forth.

'It meant that much to you, mademoiselle?' he whispered.

The fingers in his hair stopped only for an instant, for the skip of a heartbeat.

'It—it means very much to me, 'Arry.'

The mirror and a calendar were what he looked at mostly when she was not there; but when she was there he would face away from her, looking at a wall, unless he forgot himself. She never mentioned his discoloration, but only asked him how he felt. She would come in the morning, about nine o'clock, breezy but quiet, and take her hat off as if she belonged there, chatting, being careful not to look at him when he was looking at her; she would bring him things he wanted from the city, little things, and gravely hand back the change from any money he had given her the day before. If there was mail for Harry at the office, personal mail, Simpson would sometimes bring it up in the afternoon, sometimes send it to her house for delivery: Simpson telephoned every morning and (when he wasn't going to be able to get there) every afternoon as well. Madeline would stay for perhaps an hour each morning, but for two or three hours each afternoon. She never stayed for a meal, though she had long, animated discussions about food with Rosina, who from the first adored her. Dr Bliss said that it might retard recovery if Harry used his eyes too much, so Madeline would read to him a little each morning. Sometimes too they'd talk. But most of the time she was there she was at the piano. 'I should play' she'd say cheerily. 'I should be heard. I'll play for Mrs Casey and —who's the one on the other side?'

'Name's Watts.'

'And Mrs Watts. I hope they like it.'

'They'll be fools if they don't.'

Hell, they would certainly have been fools if they didn't! Madeline played without tiring, usually softly, sometimes with vigor, always well. Harry at first was not sure about the music. He knew that it was classical, and this frightened him a bit, for he didn't know anything about classical music. He thought, listening, that he would never understand this, but that he'd always like it.

Also, he had never seen anybody, man or woman, sit at a piano without any apology for being out of practice. Madeline never addressed herself to the instrument. She didn't even seem to straighten her skirts, and she never tried the pedals or arranged her hair before a piece. She just played. She would not turn to him until she was finished. She never waited for him to say that it was wonderful, but went from piece to piece, sometimes with notes, sometimes without. She brought her own music with her. He had been brought up to offer always to turn the sheets when a lady was playing the piano, but when Madeline played he did not even stir. She flipped the sheets herself, nimbly, with a swift and accurate hand, never missing a note. Well, he couldn't have done it anyway, with this music. There were no words. He had always turned according to the words or when the player had nodded her head in signal. There were no words to the music Madeline played. Sometimes she played dreamily and slowly, but even at those times she did not seem tired. Sometimes when she played without notes he didn't believe that she was doing it from memory: he believed that she was making it up as she went along, and that in fact she *was* the music. He got over feeling uncomfortable because of the nature of the music. He ceased to wonder whether he would make a fool of himself if he asked politely what that last number was. He did ask it sometimes, from habit. 'Oh, Grieg,' she'd say. Or Rubinstein, or Brahms. He had heard of these composers. It was odd to get to like them without being able to understand them. He might have been a man in a strange land, listening to talk in the streets and cafés and markets, loving the sound of it without making out the sense. He recalled a story about some Hungarians or Finns or something, who, not knowing any English, had had recited to them carefully certain words and phrases and had been asked afterward which they liked best: and every one of those Finns or whatever they were had preferred 'cellar door.' Well, that wasn't a bad choice. He did not know what the other words and phrases had been, but 'cellar door' was pretty lovely when you said it quietly to yourself and tried to believe that you didn't know what it meant. This was the way he listened to the music Madeline played.

Another curious thing was that he never felt it incumbent upon him to clap or even to say something nice when she was finished. Sometimes, if a piece had been notably brilliant, he might murmur 'Say, that was swell,' and then she'd flash a smile over her shoulder; but mostly—he was sure of this—silence was the loudest applause he could offer.

The music was not interrupted, except a few times by Simpson. Nobody else ever came knocking while Madeline played. There were in fact few callers at any hour. Dr Bliss came each morning at eight, but it was unlikely that his calls attracted attention, for Harry had no more than a nodding acquaintance with his neighbors in this new street of brand-new houses. Dr Bliss, though he'd stay only a few minutes, was never abrupt, never curt; he was impersonal, competent, thorough, perfectly polite, and as careful as though this were a life-or-death case of the greatest professional interest. All their friends knew that Phil was on vacation; few of them knew where the Kellemses' new home was anyway, so quietly had Harry moved out of the Bridal Suite, out of the hospital grounds, to this other part of Ancon Hill. Harry K worked so hard anyway, and was working that much harder now that his wife was away, poor guy, that it wasn't worth while climbing up to see him, even at night, unless you telephoned first—and not many of Harry's friends had telephones, for these instruments were difficult to get. When anybody did phone, Harry, thinking it might be Simpson, always answered. If it was an invitation, he refused, pleading that he'd been about to leave the house for some work along the Line. This happened seldom. When anybody but Simpson came knocking—Simpson had his own knock—they behaved like well-trained conspirators in a basement. Madeline, if she was there, would go swiftly and silently to the kitchen; Harry would go to the bedroom; and Rosina would go to the door, where, with a bland directness amazing in one who ordinarily seemed without guile, she would tell the caller that nobody was home and that she didn't know when to expect Señor Kellems back. Harry used to rally her about this. 'I think all women are born liars, Rosina. Men have to study and practice for years, but it comes natural to women.' Rosina would giggle. 'Do you confess those lies when you go to confession?' he'd ask. 'They are not lies, señor. That is my duty. Not lies.'

At first Harry wondered why Dr Gorgas did not call. Despite the quadrupling of his department's personnel, Dr Gorgas kept intimate track of the old-timers. He might go a week without actual contact with Harry, but he'd certainly know if Harry was ill. When Harry thought it over, however, he decided that the great sanitarian was only being his old polite self. Officially he'd know nothing of the doings of Simpson and his snoopers; but unofficially no doubt he was up on this work: he'd admitted as much to Harry coming back from the San Blas Indian village. And he knew Harry, and knew that Harry would be horribly embarrassed to entertain callers, knew too that to try to comfort Harry would only be to embarrass him further, while to pretend to ignore his bruised face would be the rudest behavior of all. So he stayed away, that gentle man. And kept his wife away. And others, too. Sunday afternoon nobody came to ask why Harry had not appeared at church; nobody even telephoned him. Undoubtedly Dr Gorgas, the congregation's most distinguished and best-beloved member, had quietly passed out word that Harry Kellems was working night and day on highly important departmental business and was best left alone. Dr Gorgas could do that sort of thing. He could lie, the honest man, when a need rose, as blandly and convincingly as hunchbacked Rosina herself.

They had a set of habits, an arrangement of conventions, all their own.

Immediately after entering, Simpson would take a long, deliberate look at Harry's face; he'd lean close, his eyes in a squint—for most of the shades were drawn and it was darkening at that hour; then he would nod absently, ask a few questions, 'What'd Bliss say today? . . . Good!' and settle in the Morris chair, and look at Madeline, who'd smile; and then Madeline would play. Now and then Simpson would ask for this selection or that: they must have been familiar, the pieces he named, for Madeline always knew them without recourse to notes. Most of the time Simpson sat motionless in the twilight, his body slow-settled fold by fold into and around the chair, pudgy hands limp over the ends of the chair's arms, his face the face of an idol. How, Harry marveled, could the tender delicate stuff affect this hulk? How could it penetrate the thick soft rolls and slabs of flesh to the place inside where beauty counted? Yet he knew that it did. Simpson would not stir, would not even swing a forefinger when there was lilt in the music. He spoke seldom, to request her, meekly, to play something— usually some part of something or some 'movement'—a word strange to Harry—and when she was finished, and rose, he never urged her to play more, as Harry had been taught that you should always do, even when you had not enjoyed the performance. He would simply say 'Thank you,' and she'd smile. These two seemed to know something Harry didn't know. It must take years, he supposed, years of careful training, to reach a real appreciation of such music. He was frightened in the presence of this mystery; but he wanted to know more.

When Simpson was there Madeline used to leave with him—Simpson lived in the city—and they'd walk down the hill together in gathering darkness, not speaking. Once when Madeline had gone into the bedroom to pin her hat on, Harry asked Simpson in the hall: 'Is she really as good a player as I think she is?'

'She is very good' Simpson said soberly. 'Very, very good.'

Harry knew that he was missing something important. He enjoyed these sessions and knew that they were precious, that he was greatly favored; and he tried to make himself think only of the music itself, to let it sink into him; but in spite of his intentions his mind wandered, and again and again he found himself marveling at the flexibility of her hands and at her absorption, also at Simpson's iconic immobility, and at the absence of fuss and applause.

'It just doesn't seem possible that you can play so well when you haven't had any practice' he cried once. 'Do you mean to say you haven't played since you left France?'

'I never said that, 'Arry. No. Why, I brought my piano with me when I came here—the way your wife did.'

There was no piano in her house, he knew. It was a small house.

'I sold it three years ago' she explained.

Horrified, straight-spined: 'Why in the world did you do that?'

'We had to have the money.'

A simple statement. No apologies or excuses, no show of shame at the confession of poverty.

'I sold it to Señora Amador' Madeline went on. 'She was very kind. She begged that I go to her house and play it any time I wished. And I do, sometimes. So you see I still have practice.'

This was Tuesday, and Phil would arrive Thursday on the last ship before Christmas. They both knew this, and even Madeline was uneasy. Madeline had brought him a letter from Simpson's office— Simpson could not come that afternoon—and it was in Phil's hand-writing, as Madeline knew or guessed. Harry had not opened it, though Madeline gave him two clear opportunities by talking overlong with Rosina in the kitchen. The letter lay on the table now, on the leather throw-over Phil herself had burned.

'I should play for them tomorrow afternoon too, 'Arry. The señora has asked me, and she has been so kind. You don't mind?'

Of course he did, and of course he said that he didn't.

'Play something for me now' he begged.

He would go back to work in a few days. And the day after tomor-row he would greet Phil, in Cristobal; and Phil would know from one good look at him that he'd been beaten in a fight. This would be a hor-rible time. He'd contracted marriage, it was his promise and his career, it was the thing he should do; but when Phil saw his face, he believed, it would mark failure. His features were clearing well, but they still blabbed. Thanks to Madeline, he had not thought of this often in the past ten days. It was there, and it would have to be met; but mean-while——

224

'Play something for me.'

As she turned, smiling, he felt again an impulse to run to her and throw his arms around her and hold her very tight, not trying to say anything, not even trying to kiss her. He believed that she knew he felt this way. He believed that, though certainly she wasn't flirting—the very idea of Madeline Desmoulins flirting was absurd—she would not have resisted him. But did she want him to do it? He didn't think so. This after all was Phil's house. The fact that Phil had not yet seen the house, which when Phil left had not even been started, made no difference. It was hers. It was her furniture too, and Harry had spent many hours arranging the Maxfield Parrish prints, the piano, the Navajo blanket, the Spanish shawl, the books, as he thought she'd like them best. It was her place, Phil's. It was not right to feel, here, the way he felt about Madeline. *She* knew that too. He knew she knew.

She would not play long. It was understood that when Simpson was not there she would leave before dark. She was, after all, discreet.

He was no longer conscious of his face in her presence; and he wondered why he had ever been. From habit he kept the house dim; but he did not twist his head when she looked his way. He felt as though he had known her for years, as though he knew her better than he knew Phil. This disturbed him. It was disloyal? While Madeline played, now, he sometimes glanced at Phil's letter on the table. He did not really think of it, or of Phil, while he looked at it; nor did he think of the music, as he should have done. He only knew that everything was wrong. He wasn't doing what he should do—or else he was doing what he shouldn't do. Phil was coming back at last, and Phil was his wife. He loved Phil. Hell, of course he loved her! Then why hadn't he opened her letter? The *Havana* had been late and had arrived only yesterday at Cristobal: that was the reason for the letter. Phil herself was on the high seas now. She would soon be here, among her own things, and they would spend their second Christmas together.

Christmas in Panama would not be what it was at Phil's square shiny Paterson house. Well, Christmas had never been the same day to him that it was to most other people. No, not a day, a time. For weeks before, for more than a week afterward, ever since he could remember, people had thought of and talked of and *been* Christmas. They talked of kindliness, and meant it; but what were they likely to know about orphans? Orphans at Christmas—provided they were in asylums—were children to be feasted and pitied and plied with not-expensive gifts. Yes, provided they were in asylums. Provided they were properly grateful. Christmas was a time of families, of cousins and aunts and uncles and such, of presents and old friends, of everybody-being-happy, and of open house. His father had tried hard, Harry reflected, remembering Christmases. His father had spent more than he could afford, and they'd always had a tree. But where had the relatives been, and the fun of chasing from house to house and seeing friends you hadn't seen for a year? That preposterous little overdecorated tree they used to have, the two of them. . . . Oh, sure, his father had tried. A gallant gent, in a way, his father had been. His mother he didn't remember.

His father had died just before the first Christmas at college. That hadn't been a good Christmas. Even the miserable little tree had not been there. Harry had had just so much insurance money, and he had known that this must take him through four years—with help from the laundry job. Friends had invited him to their houses each year at college after that first terrible Christmas without a tree. They'd meant to be nice; they had felt good, and naturally they'd felt sorry for him, and he hoped he had appreciated their kindness; but it was not the same for him as for them. Christmas had never been a time he liked, though it was a time he could not ignore. A night, a prom, a party— you could stay home, not being able to afford it. You could feel blue for a little while, and then it was over with. But Christmas took so long! His first Christmas here in Panama, two years ago, had been spent with the D.M.s, the original group, not one of them here now— unless Harry T was still battling malaria over on the other side of the Isthmus. The others had gone, some of them under the earth. They had all wanted to go that night. Most of them had got drunk, pushing away the meal of canned food Bertram lackadaisically provided. After a while Harry himself had got drunk, for that had seemed the only thing to do. And the next day they'd gone back to work. *Last* Christmas Phil had been here. He'd loved her very much then. He had realized what it meant for her to be away from home on such a day, and he'd tried hard to be jolly. Phil had been good about it, no tears, practically no sniffling, nor any mention of the big house in Paterson. Phil had received lots of gifts beautifully wrapped, and there had been a few too for Harry—from her parents—and though there had been little enough in the shops in Panama City, they'd bought one another more than they could afford. They'd even had a tree, being brave; but she was braver than he was, for she was further from Christmas. No spruce was obtainable, but they had found a little pine which they'd decorated with ornaments of paper Phil herself cut out and stuck together.

No candles. A Christmas tree wasn't a real Christmas tree without candles; but Phil hadn't said anything. A pine tree is not a Christmas tree, anyway. All the same, in their fashion they had been happy then. Phil had been quiet, but determinedly smiley. She had cried that night in bed—but only after she thought he was asleep. He wasn't always a fool! He had not tried to comfort her. He'd gone right on pretending that he was asleep.

This Christmas? Well, they'd have a proper tree anyway, and candles, and ornaments. He had ordered them long before; and they were ready now, the tinsel and balls in their boxes in the kitchen, the tree in the kitchen too: he'd been taking the tree every few days into the bathroom and holding it under the shower for a little while, in the hope of keeping it fresh.

'It's getting dark, 'Arry. I should go.'

Startled, he looked up; and there she was, swung around on the piano stool, watching him.

'I am sorry about tomorrow night' she said. 'Señora Amador will have some friends and she asked me so nicely. . . . She has been so kind. I go to the Palacio whenever I please, and I should sometimes say thanks in the only way I can, no es verdad?'

The Palacio? He blinked.

'Say, this isn't Mrs Amador, the wife of the President, you're talking about?'

'Oh yes. She is the lady who bought the piano.'

She went to the bedroom for her hat, and he lumped to the front door and leaned against it, his hands in his pockets, feeling bad; but when she came, he brightened.

'Good-by, 'Arry.'

She had put out her hand. The French did that. He took it. He really wished that he could kiss it; but of course he'd look positively loony trying to do anything like that.

'Thank you' he said.

He heard her cross the porch and he heard the screen door closed. He went into the parlor, to a window, and watched her go down the hill for as far as he could see her. From this window there was not a view, as there had been from the storehouse in the hospital grounds. The slope was less spectacular, and you couldn't see the bay. Beyond the mussy lawn the road curved and dipped without enthusiasm; and then there were more houses, each exactly the same, with the same corrugated-iron roof. Madeline was a beautiful figure, all nasturtium in the last glorious slam of sunlight, walking erect, her hips swinging a little, her feet missing the puddles, an umbrella under her arm, and her little head resting just right upon her neck. She did not turn to wave back to him. He thought that she wanted to do so but was afraid of hurting him.

The letter from Phil said many things, but what it chiefly said, and what his eyes slid down to find, was that Mother and Father had at last persuaded her to stay over Christmas. She felt simply *terrible!* She didn't know how she'd ever be able to face him again, because after all he was her husband—and her lover too, wasn't he?—that's the way she looked at it anyway—but Mother and Father had made such a fuss, and it had seemed to mean so much to them, and after all she knew that Christmas had never really meant so much to him, Harry, and so even though she did feel simply *awful* . . . But she had consented to only that, only Christmas. She wouldn't stay a day longer than she had to, after Christmas. She wasn't even going to stay for New Year's, even though there were all sorts of parties all sorts of people were just simply *pleading* with her to go to. No. She'd told them that she had her Harry to think of. She was taking the *Panama* exactly three days after Christmas Day itself, the first ship after Christmas, and she'd be with him again—and *hugging* him and *kissing* him!—January fourth. It would be funny to spend New Year's Eve and New Year's Day itself on a ship at sea, and especially a ship like the *Panama,* which wasn't the one she would have picked if she'd had her choice, but she thought that the *least* she could do after leaving poor him alone on Christmas Day was to be with him just as soon after that as she possibly *could,* and she was going to make it up to him in ways that she wouldn't care to write about in just a letter like this but he knew what she *meant?*

Sure, he knew what she meant.

He went to the window again. The lady all tinted nasturtium, the friend of the Amadors, was not in sight; and he could scarcely see, now, the houses she had passed around. The brand-new houses. They seemed stiff and unreal in what was left of the daylight.

He went to the kitchen, where Rosina looked up anxiously. The boxes were piled in a corner, and the Christmas tree. The Christmas tree looked sad. He had been neglecting it. If only he had freshened it with water more often this past week or so perhaps it wouldn't sag. The needles were touched with brown, and no longer pert. Well, probably that was his own fault.

'The supper is ready, señor.'

He felt like saying, You know what you can do with it, don't you? He did say: 'Thank you, Rosina. I'll get washed up right away.'

14

SHE SMALL-STEPPED DOWN the gangplank, laughing, on a sunny day so different from the day on which she'd first arrived in Cristobal, and to a covered pier, and from a ship much superior to the old *Allianca*. She was holding something to her breast, and with the other hand she upheld her skirt, but she smiled and laughed greetings as she descended. She wore an Alice-blue traveling dress frogged in black, and a teetering fur boa, and instead of the pancake of a year before an enormous straw heaped with ribbons, ruchings, hatpins, and a bird, and tipped far back on her head.

'Darling!'

He put his arms around her, and the kiss was good, though it was brief, being interrupted when something under his chin squealed hideously and yanked Harry's necktie. He jumped back.

'Holy Jesus!'

'Harry!'

'Sorry, but—— Well, after all, I hadn't expected an assault!'

'I'm sorry, darling. I was so excited at seeing you again that I forgot all about Dorothy. But don't you think she's cunnin'?'

'Oh.'

Dorothy was a pug, tiny, beige in color, with a wet black pushed-in muzzle, small floppy ears, dark-brown venomous eyes. She stuck her tongue out. She growled.

'Oh, she isn't pretty, I'll admit that! But she's got a sweet disposition.' And when Harry put his hand to what had been his best necktie: 'Well, of course she doesn't know you yet. But she'll get used to you, darling.'

'Well, did you have a nice trip?'

'Oh, fine! That is, the weather was perfect, and the food was all right. The service wasn't too good: some of those stewards don't know their place. And the other passengers were pretty common, most of them. But I met one girl—— But wait. I'll get somebody to watch Dorothy a minute. I want a *real* kiss.'

Dorothy was on a leash, and Phil soon got an acquaintance to hold her, and then Phil returned, her eyes bright, her arms out.

'Now!'

He heard himself mumbling that she was more beautiful than ever. And hang it, that was the truth! Because her hat was tipped so far back, her hair showed in front, and it was the color of honey in a reddish light: he thought that he could stare into it for hour on uncomplaining hour, as he might stare at the sea or into a fire in a grate. Her face below his own was the deftest triangle ever drawn, her little mouth pouted provokingly, and her huge dark brown eyes, wide open except at the very instant when he kissed her lips, shone wet with happiness.

She dipped her head and pushed her face against his breast. Then she stepped away, laughing, crying at the same time.

'Oh, it's so good to be with you again! Did you miss me *terribly?*'

'Terribly.'

'I'm going to tell you later, when there aren't so many people, how I missed you. It was more than you think! You think I was running around to stores and shows and parties—— Look, darling, I must get Dorothy back. She's so small, and she's not used to crowds like this. Do you know a Dr Lemming?'

'Huh? Lemming? Well, I know of him, yes.'

'Reason I ask is because it's his wife who's minding Dorothy over there, and I want you to meet her. She was the only *real* person on board, all the way down. We got to know one another very well.' She took his hand. 'Come on.'

'Don't you think you'd better pull your hat forward first?'

'Silly! That's the way it's supposed to be. Come on. You'll like Mavis.'

Harry was not sure whether he did, or would. Meeting this Mavis was an unsettling experience. She was tiny, a toylike woman in her middle twenties, who no doubt thought of herself as vivacious: Harry thought her a jumping jack. Granted that she was 'interesting,' he could not decide whether she was very ugly or very pretty; and the reason for this indecision was the lady's failure to keep her features in one place. She twinkled and twittered, and her hands were panicky. A brunette, she had a long mouth, a sharp nose, very large dark eyes; but how agreeably these organs were related to one another he could not even estimate, for the face behind the veil fluttered like a caught bird.

She was *so* glad to meet Harry, the real Harry himself, at last! She had heard so *much* about him! He couldn't *imagine* how much that lovely wife of his talked about him, and in fact raved and *raved* about him, so much so that if it was anybody else but Phil doing it you'd get tired of *listening!* But she shouldn't tell him any more! *Other*wise he'd be getting a swelled head!

'Oh, I say——'

'No, I really mean it, Mr Kellems! It's funny to be calling you "Mr Kellems." All I've *heard* of you, all the time, all the while coming down, was "Harry"—Harry this and Harry that. My, I'll bet your ears must have been burning!'

Lemming was there too, though the fact did not seem of importance. He was a pallid sarcastic young physician with weak eyes which seemed always to be screeching: 'All right, insult me! Go ahead and insult me! I dare you to!' He touched Harry's hand and said something about how good it was to have the fraus back again, eh? 'You know what they say about women' he offered. 'You just get to thinking that you can't live with them—when you find out you can't live *without* them!' They all laughed.

Dorothy growled ominously at Harry's left trouser cuff, and Phil pulled the beast away.

'She'll be all right when she just gets used to you, dear. Now look: Don't you think it would be nice if we all took the same train over to Panama? The Lemmings live right in Ancon, precious! Right in the hospital grounds, where we used to. Isn't that a coincidence? And it's so funny to think that we don't live there now. I'm dying to see the new house. Is it as nice as the other one?'

'Well, in some ways it's better, and in other ways it isn't.'

'You're so *indefinite*, darling! I never *could* get anything out of your letters, about what it was like! Look, let me call the coche, just for old times' sake. A coche is a hack, my dear,' she told Mavis, 'and the hackman you call a cochero. You'll soon pick up words and expressions like that.'

Harry suggested that they get the baggage together first, but she ran unheeding to the street end of the pier.

'Isn't she beautiful, though!'

Dr Lemming had wandered in search of bags, and Mavis Lemming was standing very close to Harry, at his elbow, gazing after Phil. For a split second, as Harry looked down at her, Mavis was not grimacing. Adoration had stilled those leaping features; awe made a whisper of the gabble-gobble voice.

'I think she's the most beautiful person I have ever seen. You must be very proud of her, Mr Kellems?'

'Well, I am, I guess.'

Neither the sharp chin nor the nose quivered, the lips were motionless, and the eyes shone with tears of admiration. But the lady became a bluejay again almost immediately and leaped about, emitting sudden scritches of sound.

'Oh yes, that's what you *say!* But I'll just bet, Mr Man, that you were staying out late every night and drinking highballs and playing poker all the time when she was away!'

'No' said Harry. 'No, I didn't do that.'

Phil came back, having hired a cab, which they kept for an expensive half hour while baggage was being found. On the way to the station Phil exclaimed upon the comparative cleanliness and dryness of Colon's streets, some of which had been partly paved. It hadn't been like this in the pioneer days—oh no, sir! Then it had been something unspeakable. Hadn't it? she asked Harry.

'It was pretty bad.'

'We'll be living practically in the lap of luxury here now' Phil told her friend. 'But you should have seen it when I first came out! You wouldn't believe it if I told you!'

'You have told me' Mavis reminded her gently, not maliciously.

'Do you suppose it'll be all right to take Dorothy in my lap, darling? I simply refuse to put her in the baggage coach! She'll behave herself, I know she will.'

'I don't know what the law is about that.'

Dr Lemming didn't know either.

'Well, if the conductor does have the nerve to say anything, precious, I know you'll know how to handle him.' She wheeled upon her shipmate. 'Did I tell you how when I first came down here there was a conductor who was rude to me on this very line, it might have been this very car for all I know, and Harry told him where to get off at?' Phil giggled. 'If you don't mind my slang.'

She had told this story, as Harry saw by glancing at Mavis's face, but she told it again. Anyway Dr Lemming had never heard it. She told it halfway to Panama.

The conductor didn't say anything about the pug.

Phil even brought them home, up to the new house, straight from the train. 'Oh, you two want to be alone!' archly. 'Why, of course we do! But there's no reason why you shouldn't come over and take a little look around, so that you'll know what to expect when you get to your own palatial establishment. It's right on your way, practically. Isn't that right, darling?'

'Absolutely.'

'And I'd even go so far as to hold out the temptation of a little drink of port wine, except that, knowing Harry,' slyly, 'I'm afraid there might not be any left.'

'There's plenty left' he said.

Lemming, listlessly but without spoken complaint, helped to get the trunk and bags to the porch, while the women flew from place to place, uttering little cries.

'An icebox! Isn't it *wonderful*?' 'I'll bet you didn't have anything like that when you first came out?' the envious Mavis said.

'Well, we certainly didn't! And real running water, a real bathroom, almost like home! My, they're *spoiling* us, Harry!' She did not, however, approve of what she saw from the windows, and she was loud, if laughingly loud, in her condemnation of the arrangement of the furniture. '*Darling*! For such a sweet person you have the worst taste in the world! *Look* at the angle of that piano! and where those prints are!'

'What's the matter with 'em?' he asked mildly.

'Dear, if you don't understand now, I certainly won't be able to explain. But just look at them! And that Indian blanket, the way it is! Oh, I can't stand that for one second longer! I must change a few things right away! Will you help me, dear?' she asked Mavis Lemming. Of course Mavis would help her. Mavis would have done anything for her. They worked, in fact, harder than Harry and Lemming did.

Phil even arranged the books on the shelf, putting them in what she took to be a more logical order. She did not add to them the books she had brought with her. These she scattered on tables and taborets. They were all brand-new. There were Jack London's *White Fang* and Rex Beach's *The Spoilers*, which she averred she had really brought for Harry, who ought to read more than he did; *The Conquest of Canaan* by a man named Tarkington, of which she had read almost half on the voyage down, and which she liked, so far; and a novel called *The Jungle*, which instead of being a tropical romance, as she'd supposed, turned out to be all about the Chicago stockyards, and was absolutely disgusting, so that she'd refused to read more than a few pages of it and would have thrown it overboard except that she hated to do that with something she'd paid good money for, and after all she might be able to use it as a bridge-whist prize.

'But don't you tell on me, if I do!' she adjured Mavis.

'Not bridge whist, dear' Mavis reminded her gently. 'Auction.'

'Oh, of course, auction! You'll love it, Harry! Everybody gets a bid, all four. And the scoring's different. It's more complicated, but it's a lot more fun. I learned it at the Kepplers', and Mavis here is a perfect *wizard* at it——'

'Oh, now!'

'—and I understand that you play it too, Dr Lemming?'

'Well,' with a smirk, 'I play *at* it, a little.'

'Oh, I'm sure you're being much too modest!'

Harry too was sure of that; and he decided not to play with Lemming if he could possibly get out of it.

Phil had a fifth book, a copy of *The Future in America,* by H. G. Wells. It was a serious-looking book, and she put it in a conspicuous place. Harry was a shade grim when he asked what the author, an Englishman, had announced about the future of America. Phil replied that she hadn't read the book yet, but she intended to, and she'd heard that it was simply fascinating.

'I used to love to read' she told the Lemmings. 'And I still do—only somehow nowadays I never seem to have the *time!*'

There was a lot she could and did do about the rearrangement of the furniture, but there was nothing she could do about the view from the parlor windows. She stood there, hands on hips, the corners of her mouth drooping in comical mock anguish. The naked new houses were bad enough; but the lawn was a disgrace. The grass, so recently planted in bunches that it hadn't had time to spread, admitted to sight the color of the earth, and looked obscene, like a triangle of pubic growth which had been shaved for an operation and was just beginning to grow back in again: there was still chips in it, and sawdust, and scraps of cement and of screening.

'Well, I suppose we can't have everything' she said courageously. 'When we were in the Bridal Suite—I've told you how we used to call it the Bridal Suite, Mavis—I'd tell people "Well, of course the roof leaks, but on the other hand we get a lovely view of the bay." Didn't I used to say that, Harry?'

'Yes,' replied Harry, 'often.'

When he fetched the wine Phil reproved him in a whisper for not having Rosina serve it, 'though I suppose she still hasn't learned to wear anything on her feet?' No, she hadn't, Harry whispered. Aloud Phil exclaimed in apology about the glasses. 'I can see where it's a good thing I came back!'

'They're lovely glasses' Mavis murmured.

'When they're clean they are. They've been in our family for—oh, I don't know how many years. But it's a pity they have to be so dusty.

'Oh, well,' Dr Lemming cried with sudden unexpected jocularity, 'it won't show through port wine—not the way it would through gin.'

'George!' cried his wife, whose mouth flapped like a speared fish.

They drank standing in a small circle, each, at Phil's suggestion, looping his left arm through the right arm of his neighbor. Phil herself squeezed close to Harry.

'There aren't really many people here you'd care to know well' Phil announced. 'You'll find that out, dear,' she told Mavis. 'So I think we ought to just drink to us ourselves, the four of us.' She raised her glass. 'I propose a toast to a better acquaintance in the future, all around.'

They drank to a better acquaintance in the future, all around.

When the visitors started to leave, Harry insisted upon paying for the coche. Lemming's objection was brief and not forceful.

In the house again Phil whirled, holding out her arms.

'Darling! It's been so long! Kiss me!'

He did kiss her. Then he kissed her again, and again, with mounting enthusiasm, until she broke away, laughing softly.

'My, I thought they'd never go!'

'Well, after all, you asked them in.'

'I know, but they didn't have to stay and stay and stay! They knew —Mavis certainly knew anyway—that it's been almost six months since we've seen one another, even. Ah, precious, I've been so lonesome for you! And not coming back for Christmas—that was cruel of me! But you know I did mean to, but Father and Mother kept after me, day after day, and everybody else was the same way. . . .'

He went to the porch to get the bags and her trunk. The trunk was a lot of work. When finally he got it into the bedroom he was panting and sweating in the close hot air: there was a storm on the way. The bedroom was unnaturally dark. Phil must have pulled down the shades, he thought, as, wiping his forehead, he looked up. Phil was standing by the side of the bed, and when he saw her he gasped.

'Do you like it, darling?'

He didn't answer. He couldn't.

'It's all hand-done, too. And this lace around the top, I had a terrible time finding it, and I won't tell you what it cost, but don't you think it's attractive?'

She had not let her hair down, but she'd performed a miracle of speed in undressing; for it was apparent that she had nothing on underneath the nightgown.

'Well, you haven't said what you thought of it?'

'Well—well, say, it's galloptious, of course! Only——'

'Only what?'

'Well, I certainly hope nobody else ever sees you in it!'

She smiled roguishly. 'Nobody else ever will, Harry. I bought it specially for you, and this is the first time I've had it on.' With a mischievous smile, then, as he approached: 'And something tells me that I won't have it on very long, either!'

Breathlessly, a moment later, she whispered against his cheek: 'Don't you think you ought to lock the front door, precious?'

He released her and started for the door. He stopped. 'Rosina——'

Phil was getting on the bed. 'I sent Rosina downtown. She won't be back for at least an hour. You see, I *do* think of you sometimes, darling.'

He was soon sick of that expression, 'in the pioneer days,' which Phil appeared to have acquired in Paterson. He'd thought she was kidding when she first said it, on the pier. Later for a little while he had supposed that she was using it to impress the Lemmings—Dr Lemming had been in Panama only a few months, his wife had just come—though why anybody should try to impress Lemming was more than Harry could understand, and as for Mrs Lemming, Mavis, she needed no impressing by Phil: she was Phil's already, and fairly wallowed in that subjugation. Yet even later, again and again, in any sort of company, Phil could be heard referring to the pioneer days or the 'early days down here,' and she was prouder than Harry himself of the fact that he was an Inca, a charter member of that society, the Zone's Cincinnatus, which consisted wholly of charter members, being open only to men who had gone to work in Panama during the first year of construction, 1904.

Well, it was true enough, when he thought about it, and looked around, that things had changed. Things were cleaner, and were running smoother. There were more men, more women too: the Dr Lemmings were sending for their wives a few months after arrival, and some even brought the wives with them. New houses, whole streets of them, were springing up everywhere. Yes, malaria was still on a rampage, but the garroting atmosphere of fright was a thing of the past, and only the worst scaredy-cats even whispered about yellow jack and the bubonic plague. You didn't see the funerals you used to see. Nor were there any more hasty midnight burials. The government had guaranteed to every American worker who went to Panama that if he died there, of whatever cause, his body would be shipped home at no expense to his folks.

236

Sure, everything was improving. Everything except the weather, and you got used to that.

There was even, for the first time, an official awareness that all work and no play would make Jack go right home again. Harry had told Madeline once that what the place needed was a Coney Island. The government did not go as far as that, but it did do certain sensible things. Somehow, and in spite of everything, there had been baseball teams from the beginning; and now there were leagues. The Knights of Columbus had organized a council in Ancon and were talking about one in Cristobal, where the Socialist party was about to open a reading room. The Improved Order of Red Men, the Woodmen of the World—these were names you were beginning to hear along the Line. There were some Odd Fellows, too, who were getting together. Somewhere, somehow, people said, an outfit was incorporating or thinking of incorporating under the name of the Independent Order of Panamanian Kangaroos. Harry had heard of two Masonic lodges. There was talk of converting the sanitarium for convalescents on Taboga Island into a hotel, a short-vacation place, if the malaria ever let up. Washington was sending down Y.M.C.A. secretaries trained to start things recreational, who were put in charge of the new clubhouses scattered along the Line. Getting drunk, though it continued to be favored by many, no longer was the only thing to do on Saturday night.

Women's auxiliaries were mentioned; and there was a rumor that the government, as part of the process of becoming human, was thinking of sending down a *female* professional organizer.

'Lord, I hope not!' Phil said.

Harry said: 'I thought you said you were bored here?'

'Not as bored as all that!' Phil cried.

More important, from Phil's point of view, and certainly more immediate, was the Tivoli Hotel in Ancon. Teddy Roosevelt was a Catherine of Russia for this huge building, and at one time a thousand men—some said twelve hundred—had worked upon it in a fevered effort to get it habitable by the time the presidential glasses glittered there and the presidential teeth shone. If the job was not quite done, on the occasion of the Visit, it is doubtful that the Visitor knew this. *His* suite was finished; and the members of his entourage at least were bedded, at least had a roof overhead. The Tivoli Hotel (tarantara!) was opened. It was closed again immediately after Teddy's departure, and the carpenters and plumbers and plasterers and roofers and cabinetmakers swarmed back into it. But not for long. Another six weeks—a little more—and triumphantly, on New Year's Day of 1907, the Tivoli was fully and definitely and indisputably opened. That was a remarkable event. You could walk into a lobby—an American hotel lobby, damn it!—where there were potted plants and fairly deep rugs and large upholstered chairs with arms. The garden would have to wait; but you could go into the dining room and order a meal, or go into the sunroom, rentable for social affairs, or the ballroom, where there actually were balls every other Saturday night.

'You see? I *knew* I was smart when I brought my evening gowns this time! I'll have Rosina air out your dress suit.'

'Aw——'

'There will be no "aw"s! I tolerated all that rough-and-ready business, back in the early days, and now I'm going to have you look nice!'

'Well, I suppose that's only fair, at that.'

'It certainly is' said Phil. 'And you see that you get a haircut tomorrow, too.'

The telephone would have been a boon to Phil if there were only somebody she could call. Telephones were business instruments, which your friends, her friends anyway, didn't have. That Harry rated one pleased her, for it was a mark of his high standing; but you couldn't call any tradespeople, for even if there had been any tradespeople they wouldn't have had telephones; and the Lemmings did not have a phone either. 'I can't understand that. He's a doctor, isn't he?'

'Well, yes, but not a doctor who takes care of people. He's a kind of chemist. Works in the laboratory under Sam Darling.'

'Oh. . . . Well, any doctor ought to have a telephone, anyway.'

She could not even call Harry—and expect to catch him in. She could leave a message, for he stopped at the office each afternoon before climbing the hill; but often he was so late that the message meant nothing.

She complained: 'It seems to me that you get busier and busier. I thought you said you had it under control now?'

'Well, there's still a good deal to be done.'

She no longer displayed any interest in his work. Once it had been romantic. Once he had been part of Men against Disease, a hero, and the danger and dirt had held a bright glow. But the crisis had been passed, and now Harry was only a man who supervised the spreading of oil in ditches and the cleaning out of rain gutters. It wasn't romantic any longer, and if the truth be told it wasn't always even decent.

In this attitude she was not altogether wrong. Most of Sanitation's first big job had been done: now it was largely a matter of holding the gains made. Only the trained workers knew the importance of this holding on. Only Harry himself, and Simpson, and a few others, knew that Harry, as a matter of fact, had practically nothing to do with it. There remained some routine duties, for show purposes; but most of Harry's work, the work he enjoyed, and which kept him in Panama, was as one of Simp's snoopers.

They had no standing. They were not cops, and they were not Secret Service. They were men who saw trouble, trouble which really threatened the whole project, and who met it in their own way. They knew they'd never get any praise for their work, though, win or lose, they might catch hell.

Most of it was prosaic enough, this work. It was chiefly a matter of checking—checking on this man and that man, and whether this man had been seen in the company of that man recently, and whether still another had been spending more money than his job would normally permit. To go at the matter from the top would be the right way; but they knew that the top was not to be dislodged without evidence, detailed evidence; and so they nibbled on the underside. They had to work secretly, they had to work hard. Anybody who had talked to Harrison C. Hillis, on that lawyer's visit more than a year before, might have helped them. They still sought out such men. Enrico could have helped them tremendously—but Enrico was dead. There was a Negro, too, who had been about to tell something—but he'd been killed even before Harry got into this work.

Nineteen out of twenty jobs Harry did for Simpson were dull. The twentieth would sting and scare, sometimes.

'Old Johnny-on-the-Spot!' Simpson said one afternoon when Harry entered the office unexpectedly. 'We're off for Paraiso. Hat. Hurry.'

On the way to the station he said: 'I suppose our friend's playing poker again?'

'No,' promptly, 'but he's sitting in full sight in the Pacific Café, and has been for two hours.'

On the train Harry asked what it was all about.

'The long-word boys again. They beat up an assistant foreman, don't know why. And they won't come in. Mallet's on leave. The D.E.'s away and so's his assistant, and the man in charge lost his head and telegraphed for the Marines. I heard of it and got Magoon to countermand the order. Now no Marines. Just us. Do you have a revolver?'

'No.'

'That's good. When you have a revolver you never know when you might get excited and use it. One of the Jamaicans has one.'

The scene was peaceful enough, at a glance. Up the Line, up toward Contractors' Hill, at the entrance to the Cut, steam shovels swung, the drills were working, now and then a dynamite charge was set off, and the dump trains chuffed back and forth. In the repair shops at Paraiso, several hundred feet from the station, there were at least forty men. They were all white men. The Jamaicans who had struck, who had beaten a boss, were grouped near a steam shovel, itself deserted, and they were silent, swaying uncertainly. There were eight or nine of them, and they simply stood there. They could have sheltered themselves behind the steam shovel. They could have hit out for the jungle. Perhaps they had sense enough to see that if they ran away they would be chased, despite the pistol, and torn to pieces. More likely they were simply too scared to move.

'Don't go out there! One of 'em's got a revolver! We're waiting for the Marines! Pretty soon you're going to see some dead niggers!'

'Uh-huh' Simpson said.

'They can't do a thing like that! Some of our boys have gone back to their houses, and pretty soon——'

'Do you know which one it is?'

'No, I don't, but what's that got to do with it? You just can't trust 'em when they're that way. When some of our boys——'

'Come on, Harry. We'd better fix this matter up before these pinheads start exploding in their own gas.'

'Say listen, mister, I don't care who you are, *you can't go there! Didn't I tell you one of them's got a gun?*'

'Yes, you told me that' said Simpson, walking toward the Jamaicans.

Harry followed him. It was a walk Harry was not likely ever to forget. Simpson, waddling a little ahead, thumbs in suspenders, his straw hat tipped back, seemed never to glance at the huddle of Negroes. Harry, on the other hand, looked right at the Negroes, who glared at him, puzzled, twitchy. 'Let's hope they don't bolt' muttered Simpson. 'It'll mean lynchings all over the Isthmus if they do.'

The group had no leader or spokesman, and it swayed, uncertain. When Harry and Simpson were about thirty feet away somebody called: 'Don't you come a step closer or you will be exterminated by gunfire!'

'Thanks for the tip' Simpson drawled. He pointed to a boulder a few yards ahead. 'No objection to my sitting down there, though, is there?' Without waiting for an answer he walked to the boulder and sat. Harry moved up next to him. Simpson took his hat off and fanned himself.

'Now tell me all about it' he called wearily. 'What crazy story sent you off this time? Why did you slug that man?'

'It was his fault!'

'That's something to argue about later, before a magistrate. What I want to know now is, why are you all off here, shaking in your boots? Why don't you give yourself up to justice?'

'Those men might kill us, if we go in!'

'They might—but that's because one of you has a revolver. Get rid of that, in such a way that they're sure you *did* get rid of it, and you won't get hurt. I'll take you in myself.'

They mumbled and bumbled, shuffling their feet.

One said: 'I was here in the French days, and we didn't make as much money, no, and we had to work longer, yes, but we didn't have to work as hard. These foremen now, they *kill* you working!'

'How many do you know who have died from that cause? Surely you've kept track of them, a veteran like you?'

'Even so, sir, in those days a man who wanted to make money could get himself put on piecework, loading, and take in as much as thirty-five dollars a week sometimes. An ambitious man of color could get to be a timekeeper or checker. Not now! You Americans don't treat us colored personages fair.'

'I agree with every word of that' Simpson responded cheerfully. 'But on the other hand, you've got to admit you're getting better food and quarters than ever, and better medical care, eh? And you're making three times as much as you'd make at home.'

'Yes, and what good does that do when something that'd cost us a shilling in Kingston costs us a whole dollar here?'

'Your return fares are posted' Simpson reminded them. 'If you don't like the contract, all you need to do is go home.'

'Yes, an' that's another thing: government want to drag down our pay, so they're bringing in Chinamen that are heathens and work for five cents an hour—and they're going to make all of us work for that or else get out. And the Chinamen all have leprosy.'

'That's a lie' Simpson said quickly, coldly. 'Where'd you hear it?'

Nobody answered. Simpson leaned forward, an elbow on a knee. 'I'll tell you the truth about that matter right now, and I'll prove it to you on paper when we get to Panama—because I know you can all read. Well, the I.C.C. has been dickering for twenty-five hundred

Chinese on two-year contracts, with the privilege of increasing this to fifteen thousand if needed. I don't know about their religion, but every single one of them would be examined by doctors before he was allowed to put a foot on shore. They would get between nine and eleven cents an hour. But this *positively would not make a penny of difference in your pay!* Anyway I don't think the request's going to be granted in Washington. Too much opposition from the California congressmen. So there's your answer. But I still want to know who told you that, uh, malignant falsehood.'

'We don't feel called upon to elucidate the matter at this particular juncture' one of the Jamaicans said.

'Quite right. I perfectly understand. Besides'—Simpson looked back toward the repair shops, where the crowd was increasing—'it would perhaps be advantageous to push on to matters of more immediate significance in the interim, don't you think?'

There was a murmur of approval. He was talking their language now. He had ceased to wipe his face, and his voice was cool and friendly; his eyes were friendly too; and his manner, though he did not rise, was one of great dignity.

'Let us discuss this interesting subject in my office in Panama, where we can be more comfortable. I apprehend that you are all British subjects, who find yourselves in a most embarrassing situation. Nevertheless, keep it in mind that as long as you have that gun you're likely to be mobbed! It is my avowed purpose to extricate you from your unfortunate predicament, but I can't do this while you retain possession of your firearms. I am sure that you perceive with alacrity the soundness of my ratiocination.'

'Masterful!' whispered Harry.

'Wait' whispered Simpson.

'And now,' continued Simpson, 'my assistant Mr Kellems will go among you in search of artillery, and I hope that he will meet only your most cordial co-operativeness.'

To Harry, in a whisper from a corner of his mouth: 'There! If that didn't sound like the spiel of a mind reader on the Keith Circuit—— Do you know which one it is?'

'No. How do you know?'

'The way he acts. The one with the blue shirt. Don't go straight to him. And another thing: Stop nipping the end of your tongue with your teeth. It dimples your cheeks, and they might see it and know you're scared half to death. You are, aren't you?'

'Of course I am' muttered Harry.

Here was the hardest part of the walk, the last few yards. But Simpson, who knew best, had had some reason for asking it of him. Perhaps if Simpson himself went nearer to them it would break the spell? Harry put one foot before the other with agonizing effort, yet evenly. He held his head high. He felt rivulets of sweat running down his chest and belly, running down his legs too; and his shirt stuck with chill to his back. He could have been without a heart. He stopped before the man with the blue shirt, stepped a little to one side, and held out his hand.

'Will you give me the weapon, please? That would—it would considerably expedite our disinvolvement.'

None of them looked at him, and it seemed to him that none of them breathed. Most were looking at Simpson. The one with the blue shirt looked at the ground; but after a long while he reached into a hip pocket and drew, very slowly, a tiny shiny revolver. All the sweat was cold on Harry now, and it no longer ran. The Negro, still not looking up, handed Harry the revolver, holding it by the butt between thumb and forefinger as though it were a loathsome animal. 'Thank you,' said Harry, and took it.

'My prisoners' Simpson said airily to the group at the repair shops. He flashed some sort of badge. 'Tell the D.E. he'll get a report in the morning. We're going to Panama.'

On the train he made no attempt to question them. That could wait until he got them in his office. He might be questioning them all night then, in an effort to learn the source of that story about diseased coolie labor designed to force down the Jamaicans' wages—a familiar story and here troublesome by no means for the first time. Instead Simpson sat quiet with Harry.

'How is Mademoiselle Desmoulins?'

'Haven't seen her for some time. Not since my wife got back.'

Immediately he thought that this sounded pointed, as though there were a connection between the two facts. Well, come to think of it, there was! Simpson only nodded.

'Say, did you know' asked Harry 'that she often goes to the Palacio and plays for the Amadors and their guests?'

'Sure I knew that. She's been friendly with the President and his wife for years. Didn't you know that?'

'Not till the other day.'

'There seem to be a lot of things about Mademoiselle Desmoulins you don't know.'

'I'm beginning to think so.'

'She's not all on the surface, that girl.'

As they were drawing into the Panama City station Harry took out the revolver. He held it as the Negro had.

'You want to take this, for evidence? You won't be needing me to-night, will you?'

'No, you can go on up. Thanks.' He pocketed the pistol. 'Well, he handed it over all right. I thought he would.'

'And *I* thought he *never* would! It took him about ten minutes!'

'It took him about ten seconds' Simpson corrected mildly.

'He might have shot me' Harry grumbled.

'Oh no.' Simpson leaned forward, so that nobody but Harry could see what he slipped out from under the left side of his coat. It was a lean, small, dark blue revolver with a very long barrel scarcely thicker than a pencil. Simpson leaned back, and there was nothing to show where the thing had been put. 'No.' He placed hands on knees, pre-paring to rise. 'No, he wouldn't have shot you, Harry.'

Phil's enthusiasm for her new clothes bewildered him. They *were* new, yes, and some of them, in some ways, probably were better than the old ones; but on the whole, except for the absence of hips, which might have been slashed from Phil's garbed body, and the fact that the hats all were tilted so far back that they would have slid off except for the pins, he saw no notable difference.

'I'd like to see you wear that blue dress again. You know, the one you had on that night when we went into the conservatory—and afterwards we got married. Say, that was a beaut!'

'Don't be ridiculous, darling! Why, I'd look a perfect fright if I put that on now! People would laugh at me!'

'I don't see why. *I* wouldn't.'

'Well, I've given it away, anyway. Long ago.'

One feature of the wardrobe he did admit was brand-new, and maybe it was even revolutionary. Phil had four peekaboos, three Georgette, one crepe de Chine; and the sight of them rocked her husband. Never mind, Phil told him, delighted. He needn't apologize. Nobody else on the Isthmus had seen anything like them before either. But they'd catch up to things here, after a while. This assurance did not make the shirtwaists any the less disconcerting.

'Why, they're all—they're all *holes!*'

'Yes,' and she was smiling fondly at his embarrassment.

'They show your underwear right through them!'

'Well, it's pretty underwear, isn't it?'

244

With mock weariness, then, but graciously, she reminded him again that she had always insisted upon colored silk underwear, and had been wearing it for years, no matter what her mother or anybody else said.

Well, what *had* they said? he asked.

'That it isn't respectable. That only—well, only a certain kind of women—they were the only ones who'd wear such things. But I said no. And now you see I'm right.' She was as pleased as though she had made a brilliantly successful investment. 'So you see? Where would I be if I had nothing now but old white cotton underthings? Why, I wouldn't be able to wear these peekaboos.' Look at Mavis, she said.

Harry asked how could you look at Mavis when she wouldn't stay in one place long enough to let you see her? Phil ignored this stupid remark.

'Look at Mavis. She's got one of these shirtwaists, but she's only got one corset cover she'd dare wear with it, and even that doesn't really look very nice.'

'I see' said Harry. 'The only thing is——'

'Yes?'

'Well, I always sort of had an idea that nobody but you yourself ever saw your own underclothing, except the washwoman, and of course your wife or husband, as the case might be. I always thought underwear was something private.'

'In a way it still is' Phil said, 'but not as much as it used to be.'

'I guess not' said Harry.

'I *know* not' said Phil. 'And after all, darling, you know nothing whatever about women's underwear.'

Now this was true. Though he would not have confessed it to any of the boys, any of the old D.M.s, say, his own wife's was the only feminine underwear Harry had ever seen. Here was something droll, he thought. The man who had patronized Mama Margery's, and had eventually been thrown out of that dive, couldn't have told you, until now, whether women wore white garments inside, or pink, or red, white, and blue. As far as that went, the gals at Mama Margery's hadn't worn any underclothes at all. They'd just had evening gowns right over their skin.

There was never a phrase or word, and never a look, to suggest that Phil had heard of that terrible Sunday. For more than a week before her return, his face had been clear of the marks Riaz put there: he could not even find them himself, in a mirror. He knew his wife well enough to be sure that if she heard any whisper of what had happened to him, she'd confront him with an accusation; and as day passed into day, and she made no mention of it, he breathed more easily.

Indeed she was singularly incurious about his behavior during her absence. Sometimes, usually in the presence of others, she would make a playful reference to something 'back in the days when you were having a high old time for yourself here alone' or she'd declare that it was certainly a good thing she had come back when she did, to straighten him out; but the very playfulness made her faith patent, as she meant it to do. She was sure of Harry. Whatever else happened, even if the heavens fell, Harry wouldn't do anything wrong.

Yet there was the time when she asked him about Christmas. *She* started it, he didn't. He had been careful to avoid mention of Christmas; but one night in bed Phil introduced the subject.

'Precious, I've thought about it so often, and I feel so ashamed of myself, about the way I didn't come back here in time to be with you Christmas. I was a mean girl to do that.'

'Ah, that's all right' he said.

'Well, it isn't all right. I should have been with you. That's where I belonged. But it was so hard, with everybody around me there at home, all the people I'd always known and everything, and naturally they were all talking about Christmas, and the parties there would be and all that, and Mother and Father kept after me. . . . Naturally it meant a lot to them to have their only child with them at a time like that, Harry.'

'Naturally it did.'

'But all the same, I shouldn't have stayed. I think it was because I remembered the Christmas before. You remember that, darling? We were in the Bridal Suite then, and it was the only time I'd ever spent Christmas away from home, and our tree was a measly little pine, with paper ornaments I'd made, looking so woebegone, and no candles. . . . *You* were as sweet as could be, precious, but I don't mind telling you that I cried that night after we got to bed, after you'd gone to sleep. I cried for a long while. I wouldn't let you know, of course, but I did feel terrible.'

'Ah, poor thing!' he gruffed, hitching himself closer to her.

'And I couldn't help remembering that time. Course I knew it would be different the second year, because we'd have so many more comforts and everything, not like in the early days. But all the same, there I was, already home, right there in the house with Mother and Father, and seeing all my old friends every day . . . and all the store windows and everything . . .'

246

'I think you did absolutely right' he said.

'I don't. I think I was a mean, nasty girl. I think I should have come straight to you. You did miss me, didn't you, darling?'

'Why, of course. Naturally I missed you.'

'What did you do? Drank too much, I suppose, trying to forget?'

'Well, no. I drank a little, but not much. It was wine.'

'Wine?' In the dark he heard her move her head. 'Not champagne?'

'Oh no. Nothing fancy like that. But it was nice. Beaune wine. I think that's the way you pronounce it—like the bone you give a dog. Say, did you take Dorothy for her walk, by the way?'

'Yes, I did. Yes. Beaune. Yes, that's right. It's a Burgundy, I think. Or maybe a Bordeaux. Anyway I've had it.'

'It was nice.'

'But this is very mysterious, darling. How did you ever happen to get hold of a bottle of Beaune? You must tell me.'

'Well, it was old man Desmoulins gave it to me. You know, Madeline's father.'

'Oh yes. Your Spanish teacher.'

'Yes, her father. He gave it to me. Well anyway, he didn't give me the whole bottle, but it was his and he opened it and we all had a few drinks. It was very nice. We had it with the dinner, a little bit at a time while we ate.'

'Oh, you had them up here?'

'No, no! This was at their house. They invited me there.'

'Oh? How did that happen?'

'Oh, I don't know. I guess they just heard somehow that I was going to be alone, and they just thought they'd ask me to dinner, that's all. The French don't make much of Christmas, the way we do. It's just a church holiday with them.'

'Yes, I know, dear.'

'They don't go in for a tree and candles and Santa Claus and stockings hung up and so forth. It's different with them.'

'You don't have to tell me all that, Harry. I know something about the French. I've been there.'

'Sure. Well, that was all. We just ate and talked about things, and drank this bottle of wine. The old man talks very good English, except that you have to go a little slow with him sometimes.'

In her basket, Dorothy Vernon of Haddon Hall stirred, whimpering a little.

'Who else was there?'

'Nobody else. Just Madeline and the old man and me. He used to be a pretty cantankerous old customer, and I guess he still is, ordinarily, but he was very nice that day. Talked about all kinds of things, and never a word about the Americans or the Canal. It was—it was fun. We didn't give one another presents, of course, but we had the tree and all.'

'Tree? I thought you said the French people——'

'Well, this was a tree I brought there myself. Thought it might make things jollier. I had it here, you see. I'd been saving it, and I'd managed to get some tinsel and balls and candles. But then when I got your letter about how you weren't coming——'

'Poor sweetest! But what I can't understand is, how did they ever happen to ask *you*?'

'Well, I don't know. I guess they heard I was alone up here and they felt sort of sorry for me, that's all. Just between you and me and the lamppost, I think it was very nice of them.'

'Yes, it was very nice of them.'

He got up on an elbow. 'Well, it *was* very nice of them!'

In the darkness, though her head was only a blur against the white blur of the pillow, he could almost feel her eyes opening.

'Why, of course it was nice of them, Harry! That's what I said, and that's exactly what I meant. There's no reason for you to shout.'

'I wasn't shouting.' He settled back. 'I only thought maybe the way you said it——'

'Why, I don't know how you could be so silly! I said it was very nice of them to have you for dinner that day, and that's exactly what I meant.'

'You're not sore, are you?'

'Sore? Why, dearest, what are you talking about? As a matter of fact, I'm glad to hear it. It makes me feel a little less guilty about not having been here, that's all. I think it's fine you were able to enjoy yourself. You *did* enjoy yourself, didn't you?'

'Well, yes.'

'Well, there you are. I think it's fine. Poor darling!' She patted his hip, but she withdrew her hand when he reached for it. 'And you had a tree and everything ready for me, too!'

'Well, that's all right' he mumbled. 'It was probably better the way it was. Christmas is a time when you really ought to be with your family, I guess.'

'No, I was a mean, disagreeable girl. Kiss?' She leaned across and kissed him, and then turned on her side. 'Now go to sleep, precious.'

'You—you mean that, Phil? I mean, that you're not sore?'

'Oh, stop being silly, darling! Of course I'm not sore!'

'I just sort of thought that maybe——'

'Ah now, darling! You know I've had an awfully long day, and I've got to get up early in the morning because I promised Mavis to take her down to see the native market. So you go to sleep, like a good boy, and forget about it.'

'O.k. Good night, then.'

'Good night, Harry.'

In her basket, Dorothy Vernon of Haddon Hall began to snore.

15

PHIL SHOWED Mavis all over Panama City, doing a different section every day; and they both enjoyed it. Mavis was so much help. She listened to everything Phil had to say, and exclaimed with flattering astonishment.

Other times Mavis was at the house. Phil saw nothing wrong with this. If Dr Lemming didn't complain—and he didn't—she could not understand why Harry should. Not that Harry wasn't polite when Mavis was actually there; but afterward he made it clear that he didn't like her.

'Well, it isn't that I don't like her, exactly. She's all right. Kind of funny-looking, but I guess she's all right.'

'She's very clever, if you must know!'

'But the only thing is, she gets me jumpy. Why doesn't she sit still now and then? For that matter, why doesn't she stay home now and then? She's got a husband of her own, after all.'

'Harry, if you're intimating that——'

'I'm not intimating anything. I'm just telling you that I'm sick and tired of coming home practically every night and finding a woman here who keeps *fawning* on me. Oh, she's very nice! She's too damn nice, if you ask me! With her eyes always opening and shutting, and her mouth hurling itself back and forth——'

'She's all right, dear. She's a little hard to get used to, but you'll like her after a while.'

'Like Dorothy, eh?'

'Never mind about Dorothy! And Mavis is a superior person, even though you haven't gotten around to understanding her yet. She comes from St Paul.'

'What's that got to do with it?'

'Well, nothing. I just said that she comes from St Paul.'

'Sure you don't mean St Vitus?'

'Harry, there's nothing funny about that!'

'No, I don't suppose there is. I'm sorry.'

'You *should* be sorry! There's never anything funny in talking about another person's nervous affliction.'

'Well, she's my nervous affliction, all right.'

'*Harry!*'

With Dorothy he was unexpectedly lenient. Phil had worried all the way down about how he would react to Dorothy; and she'd conceded to him, in her own mind, in advance, some cause for resentment. Nor had the first meeting been a remarkable success. Yet Harry had laughed it off. With her, alone, he sometimes grumped about Dorothy, but in company he was impeccable. In company Phil would put her arms around Dorothy and press her cheek against Dorothy's wet black muzzle and goo-goo absurd little love phrases, and Harry, without being told, would sigh and say 'Oh, for a dog's life!' which always made everybody laugh; and when somebody, watching her pet Dorothy and listening to her coo, would murmur 'Beauty and the Beast,' Harry invariably, with a quizzical smile, would say 'She *is* lovely, isn't she? Look at that tail! And those floppy ears!' Once he added 'The only trouble is, she snores. The dog, I mean.'

'*Harry!*' But she enjoyed that sort of thing.

Yes, he could be very nice when he wanted to be. She wasn't worried about Harry. She'd be silly to worry about Harry. He knew still, as he always had, that he was lucky to get her. In one sense, she admitted to herself, she was lucky to get him. There weren't many wives who had husbands as reliable. Often he was companionable too, and made her laugh. She liked him. It made her feel good to have him around. Why, it was Harry who had brought her down here in the first place—and got her away from that prison, the house where she was born. It was Harry who had brought her down again, in the second place. If only he had gone back with her, when she went back! In Paterson, among the right people, and with the background they had now, talked about, pointed out, they could be happy. Why hadn't he left this place when she did? Or, afterward, why had he not despaired of living without her, and quit his job, and raced north? Some of her postponements had been made in the hope of this. *Some* of them. But she knew the reason for most of them. Not Harry, no, no! Ward Wright.

She did not love him. Ward Wright—she did not love him. She was, by now, fairly sure of this. She was even more sure that she was afraid of him and that she wanted to see him again. Possibly if she could just see him enough times, watch him walk around, listen to his talk, she might get over it. This, too, she had thought of a long while before, when she first came to Panama. Then she had hoped that Ward and Harry would be friends, and that Ward would come often to their house, and that sooner or later she would tire of the sight of him. It would be all right if there was always somebody else around.

She knew how she felt, and she wasn't happy. She knew why she had kept poor Harry waiting, with letter after letter. *Why* couldn't the two of them get along together, Harry and Ward? With Harry in the same room she would feel strong—or strong enough. For she did love Harry, after all. He was a nice husband.

And the way it was, she felt like a bad woman.

The way it was, she was not at all amazed to find herself, on the fourth sightseeing trip, in the Café de los Dos Diablos.

'It's quaint' said Mavis, unfolding her napkin. She was quiet, and didn't twitch. With Phil she was usually this way, if they were alone. It was only in company that Mavis was jumpy. 'It's quaint' she said again. 'And it's familiar. Why, *I've been here before!*'

'No, dear,' absently, trying to remember Spanish for when the waiter came, 'we've never been here before.'

'Oh yes, dear, we have.'

It was not often that Mavis contradicted or corrected her, even playfully; and Phil looked up with sharpening eyes.

'Don't you remember, dear, the night when we both had three glasses of that crème de menthe after dinner, and then we went up on deck and sat down in somebody else's deck chairs, and after a while . . . Which is his balcony? Oh, I see it! With the yellow curtains!'

Canary-yellow, yes; and there they still were, not quite as bright as when Phil had last seen them, six months before, but the same curtains. Phil until now had very carefully not looked at them. Her eyes hurt with heat, and she was choky, but you couldn't be angry with Mavis—not with someone who loved you that much.

'I could kill you!'

'Oh, dear, you aren't——'

'You have the memory of—of an elephant!'

'Oh, my! Think of me—poor little me,' whimsically, '—an elephant!'

They both giggled at that, they had to; and they felt better. Phil, trying to be severe, but still giggling, told her that she ought to learn how to *forget*.

'I always meant to learn that,' Mavis said humbly, 'but whenever I do get the time I never can seem to remember what it is.'

They giggled again.

Mavis asked, would French do here? And Phil, picking up the menu, said of course not. Phil explained that while they were a great deal alike, in many respects, you just had to know Spanish in places like this—places off the beaten track.

Mavis spoke French, and this was one of the bonds between them. Mavis had not been abroad, no; but she had learned French in school, and they used to toss French phrases at one another. But here, Phil insisted sweetly, only Spanish would do. Not, she apologized, that *she* knew much of it! Harry was the one who knew the Spanish. Most Americans here didn't take the trouble to learn it, and just called it the spiggoty talk, and she didn't blame them, by and large, Phil explained; but Harry had studied it very hard, and he spoke it very well.

'Nice teacher?' Mavis asked absently.

Phil bristled. 'What makes you ask that?'

'Oh, dear, I'm so sorry! Why—was there anything wrong about that? I—I was just trying to be funny. Oh, darling, you aren't annoyed, are you?'

Her distress was genuine; and Phil smiled, clicking the menu upright.

'Sorry, dear. I just wondered if—— Well, anyway, we'll get something very exotic to eat, and I have to think of all the names I can remember, and goodness knows what he'll bring even when I do order. We might get almost anything. Now let's see——'

At her shoulder: 'Señoras?'

'Uno momento' Phil said primly, squinting. 'Uno momento, mozo.'

At her shoulder: 'Que va Ustedes a tomar, señoras?'

'All right! Now give me just a minute. Estudio la lista. Uno momento, favor. If I can just remember——'

Something made her look up. Mavis, agoggle, had eyes that were ping-pong balls, and her mouth leaped this way and that.

'Que va Ustedes a tomar, Señora Kellems? And while I'm at it, may I add that I've never seen you looking lovelier?'

She turned; and there he was, solicitously bending over, his face close to hers, his teeth a white long flare, his mustache as trig as ever, in his small brown eyes quick-shifting flecks of red. He was laughing, but laughing with politeness.

'You didn't let me know that you were back. It's so good to see you! You'll forgive my little trick, I hope?'

'Oh' said Phil, not moving. 'Oh' she said again, after a moment. 'What—what are you doing here?'

'I live here' he said without reproach. 'Up there, where you see those yellow curtains. It's my home.'

'Oh' said Phil.

Mavis coughed, and Phil turned swiftly, bubbling with apologies.

'Now isn't this nice, dear? Isn't this a coincidence? It was only the other day I was mentioning Captain Wright to you, who came down on the ship with me the first time I came here, in the early days. And here he is! Let me introduce you: Captain, this is my friend, Mrs Lemming. Mavis, I want you to meet Captain Wright.'

Mavis was perfect. You could always count on Mavis.

'Captain—Wright, was it? I'm so glad to meet you, Captain.'

He clicked his heels and bowed, and Phil, looking at him, almost wept. Phil looked too at Mavis. Mavis's nose jerked; her mouth swung back and forth eagerly, anxiously; her eyes remained ping-pong balls. Phil thought: She knows what I meant, now!

'See here, you two were going to have lunch? Well, why not come upstairs to my place and have it with me? Keep a poor lonesome bachelor company. They always serve me up there anyway. I don't want to boast, Mrs Lemming, but Mrs Kellems will tell you I can speak Spanish fairly well, and I'm sure I could order you a better meal than you could get for yourselves. More breeze up there, too.'

'I don't think——'

'Oh, come, come! In this day and age, surely there's nothing wrong with that! We can't quite eat *on* the balcony, it's too narrow, but we'd be right there in the french windows. And then before we start we can have a—well, I won't say a cocktail, because I know Mrs Kellems doesn't care for cocktails, but that French word—what is it?'

'Apéritif' said Phil.

'That's it! We can have an apéritif. I have some vermouth.'

'I can speak French too' Mavis said.

'Can you really? I wish I could. But you will come, won't you? We'll have wine, too. I have some Beaune.' He asked Phil: 'Isn't that the way you pronounce it?'

'Yes, Beaune' said Phil. 'Like a bone you throw to a dog.'

'Yes, that's right' said Mavis.

'Well,' smiling winningly, 'why don't you two ladies throw this poor dog a nice bone by coming up to his apartment and having lunch with him? I'm sure nobody could possibly see anything wrong in that. It's no spider web, I'll promise you. And anyway, who would ever take you two for a couple of flies?'

'I'm sure you don't mean anything wrong by that, Captain. Ah-ha, you see I know you too well! But still, at the same time——'

'Nonsense! It would be practically eating out in the open anyway!

254

Why, look—you can see the end of the table through the windows right up there now.'

It was the longest table, Mavis declared, she had ever seen. It went the whole length of the parlor. One end, as Captain Wright had pointed out, virtually thrust itself through the open french windows. Mavis said she couldn't understand why anybody would want such a long table.

'Do you give banquets?' she asked innocently.

'I give poker games sometimes.' Ward Wright turned politely to Phil. 'I have heard, incidentally, that your husband is a very keen poker player, Mrs Kellems.'

'I've heard that too, but frankly I don't know about such things.'

'You must ask him to come here and play with my friends some time.'

'I'll tell him. He's frightfully busy, though, these days.'

At a knock on the front door, the one leading to the Calle de San Martin stairs, Ward frowned fleetingly and excused himself. They could not see the man in the doorway, the host so loomed above him, but his voice was insistent. Ward's answers, angry, were whispered. As near as Phil could make out—they spoke in Spanish—it was something about a bill. After all but pushing the visitor downstairs, Ward returned, smiling in apology. When he went for vermouth and glasses, Mavis, unable to restrain herself, twirled out of her chair.

'My dear, I've simply got to look around!'

'It is sort of—masculine.'

Crisscrossed from the ceiling, strung on a string, were, alternately, purple cigarette boxes and scarlet cigarette boxes. A cashmere shawl was thrown over a Spanish mission chair. On the wall was hung a saddle, stunningly polished leather set with silver. Opposite was a guitar, from which ribbons dangled. Dullish brown blobs, resembling onions gone bad (though they had no odor), hung everywhere. These fascinated Mavis. 'What are they?' 'How should I know?' asked Phil. There were many Indian rugs and blankets. There was a rack of dueling sabers, there were three fencing masks and a couple of leather elbow guards. There were four matched decanters, square, made of crystal, with little half-moon silver tags hung by silver chains around their necks: PORT, SHERRY, RYE, SCOTCH. There were pistols enough, on tables and shelves, or fastened to the walls, to furnish a museum— old weapons, most of them, double-barreled pistols, ball-and-hammer pistols, dueling pistols, rim-fires, pepperboxes, huge forbidding horse pistols with fishtail butts, Colts, Ketlands, Derringers, Floberts, Comblains, Collison Halls, Delvignes. . . . On the long table there was but one article—a skull in the form of an ash receiver, or perhaps it was an ash receiver in the form of a skull. At the end of the table, the far end from the french windows, stood a silver tripod holding a silver champagne bucket. There was another and more ornate tripod near the couch, and this supported a shallow copper basin containing a tiny triangular wire dingus. 'For incense' Mavis whispered. Comforting, fairly tut-tutting, was the Morris chair, though it was upholstered in purple leather. Next to the Morris chair was a pipeless pipe rack, which, too, was comparatively homely: the burned words were 'Wine,——? and of Course Song Too!'

The couch was enormous. It was square, and with its huge Chinese overhang it became not an article of furniture but part of the architecture, a nook in itself: it was as separate as a bay window or a Moorish corner—though indeed the whole room was something of a Moorish corner. The couch, then, was a tangle of polychromatic throw-overs and pillows. From the center of the ceiling above it hung, by brass links, a stupendous brass taper lamp which when lighted would surely cast a mysterious glow. The links by which this lamp was suspended were themselves monstrous chunks of brass, though because of the draperies they could not be seen well. Through them, through the links, entwined among them, the semblance of a green and scarlet snake wound upward, its colors in the faint light and its poise giving it an oddly realistic look.

'You'd have to lie down there to really see it' Mavis breathed.

'I think I hear the waiter coming' said Phil.

'It must sort of—*Dear!* That's really his *bed!* This is really his *bedroom!*'

'Sh-sh! It *is* the waiter. Try to act all right.'

'But how *bohemian!* And I don't think it's right! Why, I wouldn't have come up here if I'd known he was going to entertain us in what amounts to practically his *bedroom!* Why, he must use that to *sleep* on!'

'Yes, I suppose he uses it for that too.'

'*Phil!*' Yet she was too excited even to giggle. She could not keep her eyes from the couch-bed and from the big-linked chain and snake which wound its way up that chain to be lost in the shadows of a ceiling itself invisible because of the drapes. 'But I think we really ought to—— Do you suppose if we called him and explained that we hadn't understood that——'

'Sh-sh!'

The waiter was small and bald, a resigned gnome who paid no attention to them as he set three places. He had finished and was about to depart when Ward Wright opened the green baize door of what, glimpsed, appeared to be a pantry lined with shelves loaded with glasses.

'Aqui, Pedro. Favor.'

'Si, señor.'

The waiter went into the pantry, and the door swung closed, and simultaneously with that motion Mavis leaped from her chair and hurled herself on her back across the couch-bed.

'I just couldn't help this! I've got to see where——' She scrambled back to the table. 'Do you know what, dear?' breathless. 'That snake goes right on up through a hole in the ceiling!'

Phil was staring at the green baize door.

'Yes, I know' she said without thinking.

Immediately she felt the blood surge to her face, and her cheeks flamed. Hastily she framed an excuse, that she'd stooped and stolen a look under the red-and-gold canopy a few minutes before, and she was opening her mouth to say this—when she found the courage to glance at Mavis. Mavis was straightening her hair as though nothing had happened. Either she hadn't heard or she was pretending that she hadn't heard. The excuse, shoved clumsily forward, and clumsy enough in itself, might make matters even worse. Phil closed her mouth.

Ward came out with the vermouth.

It was a good meal, well served and piping hot; and the wine was excellent: Phil knew what Beaune tasted like now. The conversation was lively, amusing, but not hilarious. There was no sniggering reference to two young married women dining in a bachelor's apartment. They might have been in the patio below. Nor was Ward indiscreet. He spoke always to Mrs Lemming and Mrs Kellems, never to Mrs Lemming and Phil. He laughed often, showing his teeth, and when he was thoughtful he ran his thumbnail along his mustache. They told him where they had been, and he proposed other places to see, giving them the names of caretakers, secretaries, curates.

'Captain Wright is all mixed up in Panamanian politics. You can never get him to talk about it, though.'

'Mrs Kellems makes it sound too glamorous. All I am, in point of fact, is a sort of hired thug—hired to stand by for emergencies.'

257

'Oh, I'm sure that you do yourself an injustice when you say that' Mavis cried earnestly. 'Why, I've heard of you for years. Ward Wright, the great soldier of fortune. They say you're the one who gave Richard Harding Davis all his ideas. Oh, you're famous in the States!'

He laughed deprecatingly. 'People exaggerate things. . . .'

There was an unfortunate episode, when they feared that Mavis was going to faint or be sick. She had asked him, make-conversationally, what were those small round reddish-brown objects which hung in strings from so many places in the ceiling, and he replied, as glibly as though discussing a deal with the grocer, that they were heads, shriveled mummified human heads, brought back from the upper Orinoco country by a friend of his, an explorer. He seemed to see nothing gruesome or even out-of-the-way in this; but he was attentive and sincerely distressed when he saw the effect of the answer upon Mavis, who swayed, turning pale: he went to her, held her shoulders, pleaded for forgiveness, regretted that he had no smelling salts, offered her brandy, filled her wineglass—and afterward assiduously talked of other things.

Even after the meal, after they'd had coffee, and after Ward, with their permission, had lighted a cigar, Mavis looked shaky; and when she expressed an interest in a cushion cover made of hundreds of cigar bands, Ward was especially eager to please her and to explain. She was getting her husband to save his bands for her, she said, and she had always meant to make him a cushion cover with them sometime, and that's why she was so interested in this one. Ward, who had made the thing himself, went into details. He showed her how the bands were arranged on a sheet of leather, how they were pasted into place with a kind of cement—he gave her the recipe—and how afterward a square of colorless sheer transparent silk was stitched over the whole thing, so that the edges of the bands couldn't work loose: this permitted the colors to shine through, and yet it prevented the whole business from being too garish, 'too advertisementy,' as Ward put it.

'Take it out on the balcony, where you'll get a better light.'

She took it out on the balcony, and Ward immediately grasped Phil's hand and led her, almost yanked her, into the pantry. He did this swiftly. Before she knew where she was, he had his arms around her and was kissing her, while the green baize door clack-clacked itself shut, and on either side, only half seen, in long gleaming rows, were the glasses—the wineglasses and whisky glasses, cobbler glasses, highball glasses, cocktail glasses, old-fashioned glasses, merrily, pertly peeping.

'Oh, Ward, we can't! Not with her right out there——'

She had known that this was going to happen, yet it gave her no feeling of comfort, of come-homeness, as Harry's first embrace on the pier had done. It did not quiet her, it troubled her. It did not delight her, didn't even please her physically: it only filled her with panic, causing her temples to throb and her lungs to hurt as though scorched by the air she inhaled.

'You didn't tell me when you went away, and you didn't tell me when you returned. . . . And oh, you beautiful, beautiful creature! all this time I've wanted you so much!'

'Please, Ward! She might turn around and——'

His face came close again, and she felt his mustache, then she felt his lips. She did not turn her mouth away, though for a little while she did continue to push, with a kitten's strength, against his chest. The kiss was a long one, however, and at its end she was limp, dizzy, weak.

'You must come here to me again—soon, soon, you adorable thing! If you only knew how much I love you and how much I want you!'

'Ward, we can't—I don't think it's right to even talk about—— If Mavis——'

Holding her with his left arm, with his right hand he uncorked a bottle she didn't see. He held the mouth of this bottle under her nose for a moment. It was whisky or brandy, she didn't know which, and very strong and pungent. She coughed. He swung open the green baize door and half led, half carried her through.

Mavis was still on the balcony. Mavis really was interested in that cushion cover.

'You know, I think it's amazing that a man like Captain Wright, who does so many masculine things, can still order a delicious meal like that—and make a cushion cover like that too, with his own hands!' cried Mavis as they issued into the Calle de San Martin. 'He's a remarkable man, in a good many ways, isn't he?'

'Yes, he is' said Phil.

Phil was pettish going up the hill and paid little heed to Mavis, who chattered, that letterslot her mouth never closed. Well fed, they took a hack; and when Mavis insisted upon paying, Phil did not object; nor did she invite Mavis in—which was just as well, in view of the dead rat.

Harry, unexpectedly, was home. He was in the kitchen, guffawing

259

about something, while Rosina giggled. Phil went there. In the middle of the floor, immensely proud of herself, a rat dangling from her black slobbering mouth, stood Dorothy Vernon of Haddon Hall.

'Atta girl, Dot ol' Dot! They'd have to get up pretty early in the morning to get the best of you, wouldn't they?'

Dorothy put the rat down, but stood over it and wagged her preposterously twisted pig's tail. When she saw Phil she picked the rat up again and started to bring it to Phil, who screamed.

'Take that away from her, Harry! Don't let her come here with that horrid thing! Where did she ever get it, anyway?'

'Outside. I should think you'd be proud.' Harry was stalking the pug, which, without suspicion, supposing this to be a game, backed away, watching him, retaining a firm bite on the prize. 'That's pretty smart for a pup her size.'

'Harry, *please!* Can't you get that thing away from her?'

'Well, it isn't going to be easy. It's her first one, and you can't blame her for wanting to hold onto it.'

'I certainly *do* blame her! I blame her for catching the horrid thing in the first place! How did she ever happen to be out?'

Too angry to speak Spanish, she glared the question at Rosina, who with timid looks from time to time over her shoulder was trying to aid Harry in the pursuit of a pug now openly coy.

'Well, Dotty's got to be taken for a little walk now and then.'

'She's supposed always to be taken on the leash! And don't call her Dotty!'

'You figure I don't know her well enough for that, eh?'

They had cornered the pug, which now, only kidding, growled. Harry was still laughing, still having a fine old time, when he reached down for the rat. Phil fled.

She was at her dressing table, trembling, re-doing her hair with aimless hands, when Harry stuck head and shoulders into the bedroom.

'Sorry I missed you at lunch. I didn't know I was going to make it, or I would have telephoned. Rosina fixed me up, though.'

'I hope you've thrown that filthy thing away!'

'It wasn't filthy. Not for a rat. It was practically clean, compared with the ones down at La Boca when we had that plague scare, year and a half ago. We burned down three whole blocks of barracks, and we were going to electrocute them as they came out, but something went wrong with the current, and so we used clubs instead. They just poured out, hundreds of 'em. We all wore heavy rubber hip boots, and there was a time there when we were practically up to our knees in those dead bodies, and if you think this one today was dirty you should have seen——'

'Spare me the grisly details, *please!* I asked you if you'd got rid of this one, that's all.'

'Yes. I buried it.'

'And I hope you washed your hands afterwards?'

'Why, of course.' Frowning a little, frowning at her reflection, he edged into the room. 'You shouldn't be so sore at Dotty for a thing like that, dear. Why, it's just part of her nature. There'd be something wrong about her if she *didn't* catch a rat every time she got a chance. You don't want her to grow up to be a fat spoiled nasty-tempered lap dog, do you?'

'Please leave the care of Dorothy to me, darling.'

'Well, sure. The only thing is——'

'I can smell that filthy thing on you still!'

Harry had been walking toward her, meaning to kiss her, but now he stopped. He turned, shrugging.

'You can't, but all right. I can take a hint. See you tonight—maybe. I might have to go over to Colon. I'll call.'

He did not slam the door. He was not as sore as that.

Not that she cared how he felt. She did marvel, though, sometimes, how all the vulgarity inherent in a person will come out sooner or later. Harry was clever, and he could put on a very good show of refinement sometimes, and there were probably plenty of people who supposed that he came from a perfectly nice home. They ought to be married to him for a little while! She supposed that there was a streak of commonness in every man, anyway, or almost every man; but there were times, times when he laughed, when she thought that Harry had more than his share, and she would link him in her mind then, for a little while, with those most loathsome of all human creatures, still real to her, who used to loaf in front of Donnelly's Livery Stables, chewing tobacco and spitting in long sparkly squirts and making remarks about her when she passed on the way to school: there were even times when Harry's person suggested the same wet smell.

She made a face at her reflection, which dutifully made a face; and she wrinkled her nose, despising all men; and when Dorothy, not a whit repentant but simply lonesome, came scratching and whimpering at the bedroom door, Phil said sharply: 'Go away! You have disgusting habits!'

16

THE MAN WAS SMALL and square and gray, his hair gray, his eyes too, and the suit he wore. If each was taken by itself, the features of his face said strength, strength: he was handsome. Clearly he was intelligent. He might have been forty-seven or -eight. Well, he *should* have looked sure of himself; but instead he gave the impression of being scared.

'What can I do for you?' asked Harry. It made him feel like a clerk in a store. 'Sit down. Swell weather we're having.'

'It is. I—I'd supposed it would be hotter down here.'

'It gets pretty hot sometimes. Just arrived?'

There was something familiar about this man, about his square face, his unsmilingness.

'You're busy, Mr Kellems?'

'Not particularly. Just waiting for one of the stenographers to bring me in a sandwich.'

'Oh' said the gray man, and a smile appeared on his mouth and instantly sank from sight, like a drop of water on arid ground. 'Do you know why a man could not starve on the desert?'

It would not have been any more unexpected if he'd started to recite dirty limericks.

'I give up. Why can't a man starve on the desert?'

'Because of the sand which is there.'

Where had Harry seen him before? I've never visited a lunatic asylum, Harry reflected, or otherwise I'd figure it was there. And why single *me* out to chuck those chestnuts at?

'I was instructed to be sure to ask you that question and give you that answer, by the man who sent me here. But if I'm intruding——'

'Not at all. Who was it sent you here?'

'A Mr Thompson, whose first name is the same as yours.'

'Harry *T*! Say, why didn't you say so before? How is he? You come from his home town, I suppose?'

'Well, no. I don't really know him very well.'

He sagged. Everything about his body sagged, refusing to make the effort to live up to the clothes. Had he tightened the skin of his face with a smile or with a good old-fashioned frown he might have looked authoritative: certainly he would have looked strong. But something had recently been taken out of him. The central core, the marrow of some nerve, had been drawn stringlike from a vital place. In a photograph he would have been a bank president. In Harry's office he all but sniveled.

And why didn't he come out with what he wanted? Grinning only inwardly, Harry knew what Harry T himself would have shouted here: 'Come on, don't keep me in suspenders!' But Harry K was attentive.

'No, I just met him a little while ago. Just this morning.'

'You mean to say the fool's still here?'

'I don't think he'll be here long. He was very sick. He had a chill while I was there, and they hustled me out.'

'Ought to have his ass kicked! Absolutely! Well, excuse me. Here's my sandwich. You don't mind if I eat it now?'

'Certainly not! By all means!'

'We forget to be polite down here, sometimes. It's a sort of rough-and-tumble place.'

The square gray man hitched himself forward.

'It's just because you are one of the old-timers that I've come to see you, Mr Kellems. I've been told—well, as a matter of fact, I was told by Mr Thompson, whom I looked up, after asking around for a while —but he was too sick to tell me much—but he did say that if anybody could help me, you could.'

Harry nodded gravely, eating his sandwich, wondering what was coming next. It was a lovely day; and somehow, in spite of the way things were going at home, he was in good spirits. He munched, affable.

'He said—Mr Thompson said, that is—he said that you had probably known my son better than anybody else down here.'

'Oh' said Harry, and stopped eating. 'Yes' said Harry. 'Well, now I know who you are. When you say that.'

'Oh, I'm sorry! Didn't I introduce myself?'

'No. But it's all right. I know now. I was wondering where I'd seen you before. Though of course I never have, really.'

Not only had he stopped eating, he had taken his hands off the sandwich, which sat, a twisted violated thing, on its paper napkin.

'See here, I'm sorry I forgot to introduce myself. I am Darlington Winter. And you did know Junior, didn't you?'

'Darl? Sure. Knew him well. Very fond of him.' Harry looked up with a jerk of his chin. 'How is he? What's he doing?'

'Oh. . . . You didn't know, then?'

'Know what? What is this? What's the matter, Mr Winter?'

The gray man made his mouth go around the words several times before he forced them out.

'He—he's dead, Mr Kellems.'

Well, that shouldn't have been a jolt. Darl was dead, eh? Harry was sorry to hear it, but not astounded. Darl had always been a guy who went in for tragedy. He'd worn gloom like a favorite coat.

All the same, it made Harry uneasy to look at this man.

Junior had left here—when? About six months ago? Yes, Harry confirmed. 'I saw him off, matter of fact.' Had he ever mentioned his parents? Mr Kellems would forgive the personalities, and if he wanted to, why didn't he just tell this gray man to mind his own business? No, no, that was all right!

'Mr Thompson did tell me,' plaintively, 'that you probably knew Junior better than anybody else here knew him, Mr Kellems.'

'Well, I suppose I did. But nobody knew him very well.'

'Yes, he was always quiet. And—rather fierce.'

Harry was startled by the word. He looked hard at his sandwich.

'But I just wondered if you could tell me—I wondered if you remembered whether he sometimes mentioned me or his mother.'

'Well,' said Harry, 'I don't know that he ever did. Course I knew that he had a father and mother, and I knew they were still living, so I guess he must have said something about you at some time. But if he did, I'm afraid I can't remember it.'

The gray man's gray eyes were touched with hope.

'You say you saw him off, on the ship, Mr Kellems? Did he—was he —well, did he act all right then? I mean,' hastily, 'did you think that there was anything unusual about him?'

So it had happened. . . . But why hadn't he heard of it before? Hell, Phil herself had been on that ship!

'Did you—suppose I put it this way—did you get the impression, when he sailed, that he was going home?'

'Well, yes, I suppose so.'

'He didn't like me, you know. In fact he hated me.' The gray man said it sadly. 'I don't think he really did, because after all I am his father. But he *thought that* he did.'

'Oh, nonsense.'

'Well, Junior had strong feelings. You know that. But what I wondered was whether he'd ever said anything to you, or to anybody else here, about me—about his father and mother.'

264

'Well, yes and no' Harry said, hating himself. Why did he always have to lie so much? This poor punctured man, you couldn't give him added hurt. 'Well, what I mean is that I always sort of had the impression he'd had trouble of some kind at home. But you know how it is down here: we don't ask about things like that. How did he die?'

'We don't know. That's just the trouble. That's what brings me to Panama, Mr Kellems, and it's the reason why I've taken the liberty to come and bother you like this when you probably——'

'No bother at all!'

'We're not even sure he *is* dead. Though he must be.'

'Where'd he go when he got off the ship?'

'He didn't get off. That's the whole point. It was from the steamship people that we heard about it, in the first place. We didn't know where he was. He never wrote. But the steamship people got in touch with us and said that Junior had been a passenger on this boat, the *Havana,* and that when the boat got into port, in New York, they couldn't find him. Well, actually they'd missed him before they docked. They missed him when the immigration men and the quarantine men came on board. They had to account for him then, so they searched the whole ship, high and low, absolutely everywhere. They were quiet about it. Nobody else knew about it. They learned that Junior had had dinner the night before, and he'd eaten a regular healthy meal, as far as that goes, but he didn't show up for breakfast. He'd been seen on deck the night before, after everybody else had turned in. He was walking up and down, alone. There wasn't any entertainment of any kind that night, and the other passengers had gone to bed early because they were to be in first thing in the morning, but Junior, it seems, stayed up very late. He hadn't been in the bar. A sailor, a watchman of some sort, said that he saw him leaning over the rail away back by the stern. Saw him there several times. Then, the next time he came along, Junior wasn't there. The sailor just took it for granted that he'd gone to his cabin. But his bunk hadn't been slept in, and his roommate said he hadn't seen him.'

'A little man in underclothes' murmured Harry.

'Eh?'

'His cabin mate. What did the steamship people do?'

'Searched everywhere, as I told you. Turned the whole ship upside down. Quietly. They assured me afterward that there wasn't any possibility that my son was aboard. He—— They figured he must have got dizzy watching the wake and somehow fallen overboard.'

'I see' said Harry.

'That's all we know. That was the official report—death by accident. None of the other passengers knew. There wasn't any publicity afterward. But then you know how steamship lines are. They'd do everything possible to get out of admitting that—— Well, people are superstitious about that sort of thing. It could hurt business.'

Harry interrupted. 'Listen, Mr Winter. Let me get this straight. Are you implying that you think maybe Darl committed suicide?'

Here was a terrible word, and the man winced.

'Because if you do, then all I can say is you're crazy! Darl may have been a quiet guy—he was—but if he'd ever had anything like that in his mind I'd have known about it.'

He had been looking at the gray man, but he did not dare to look at him any longer. It hurt his heart to see the gladness in that face. He got up, instead, and went to the window.

'If you say so, Mr Kellems. . . . I came down here just for that, just for that reason. And Mr Thompson—he was very sick——'

'Harry Thompson ought to have his ass kicked!'

'—but he did manage to tell me that anything you said would be the truth.'

'Why, of course it's the truth!' Harry wheeled on him, glaring. The man was twice his age, and a gentleman, and certainly rich; but Harry glared. 'Do you think I'd stoop to telling you something just because I thought maybe you might——'

'I'm really very sorry! I never meant to suggest that——'

'O.k. I'm sorry myself. I shouldn't get sore like that.' He walked to the gray man and put a hand on his shoulder. He pressed down, briefly. Then he slipped the hand back into a pocket and strode to the window. 'My fault. Been working too hard, I guess. Actually, Mr Winter, I'm terribly broken up to hear that Darl's dead. Maybe that's why I was so nasty just now. Don't mind me. The only thing is, you're just plain crazy if you're thinking anything like—well, like what you just said.'

Rosina did not have to confess lies like these. All the same, lying wasn't any fun. The silence behind him was terrific.

'You have made me—very happy' the gray man breathed at last. 'You've made Junior's mother happy, too. I'll send her a cablegram. It was wrong of us, of course, to even think of such a thing. But if it *had* been—— You see how it was, Mr Kellems? If it *had* been—and with anger in his heart——'

'Forget it' Harry said rudely.

266

'There wasn't—there wasn't anything here?'

Why didn't the man go away? Harry couldn't stand forever looking out the window.

'Good God, no! I won't say that your son was the most popular man who ever came down here, no. But, as far as I know, everybody liked him. Yes, and admired him. He was reserved, sure, but you always knew where you stood with Darl. He was honest and—and straightforward.'

'Yes,' simply. 'I—I hate to bring this up, Mr Kellems—you've been so kind already—but Helen—that's my wife—Mrs Winter and I, we wondered if by any chance—— Well, there wasn't any sort of woman, or anything like that, was there?'

'Huh! Why, there weren't any white women down here then anyway—or practically none. Don't be silly!'

'Yes, you're right, Mr Kellems. I'm sorry I brought it up.'

Harry heard the man rise and heard him come toward the window.

'You've been very kind, and you have made me feel much better about the whole thing. And my wife, she would thank you, if she was able to. You've made us both very happy. I—I asked about you, before I came here. Everybody seemed to know you, and everybody I spoke to said that if you said a thing, then it was right—you were always completely honest.'

'Well, o.k.' growled Harry.

'That's why I feel so much better. I—I came down here just to talk to somebody like you, and to have you say something like what you just said a little while ago. So—so thank you, Mr Kellems. I'm not going to cry. I just want to say God bless you.'

Harry's two hands were as deep into the pockets as they would go, and he scowled through the screen at a siesta-time Panama street where nothing moved.

'You finish your sandwich. I—I think I'll just take a little walk and then go back to the other side.'

'Well, you might as well look around. I can't go out with you myself, this afternoon, but I can give you a few notes to divisional engineers along the Line, and they'll see that you get taken care of. Naturally you'll want to see some of the work.'

'No, I don't think so, Mr Kellems. Thank you. You've been very kind, but I think I'll just take a walk and send that cablegram to Helen —to my wife. And then I'll go back over to the other side and get that same ship home. But thank you just the same.'

'You mean you don't even want to look at what we're doing?'

Harry began to feel sore. There was no reason why he should, and he kept looking out the window; but he was feeling sore.

'No, I'm sorry. I'm sure that it's wonderful work, and very interesting. But I'll just go. I won't bother you any more.'

'No bother' Harry said disagreeably.

'Good-by, Mr Kellems.'

'Good-by.'

Harry shook the hand, then dropped it, and turned back to the window. The square gray man went out. After a while Harry pitched the rest of the sandwich into a wastebasket and went out himself.

He went to Madeline's house. This was not because he had been reminded of Madeline: he thought of her often, though he had not seen her in almost two weeks. The Spanish lessons, increasingly irregular of late, appeared to have come to a full stop with the return of Phil. Harry didn't like that. He felt a touch of panic, now and then, at the thought of losing track of Madeline.

Certainly he was not going to the Desmoulins' in order to tell Madeline about Darl Winter. Not that what had happened was her fault! Darl had killed himself because of something more than unrequited love. Darl had killed himself because he was lost, he couldn't grasp and hold on to anything, he couldn't find his way out of lonesomeness. There was more to it than Harry ever would understand; but he was at least sure that Madeline wasn't to blame.

He just wanted to talk to her now. He was disturbed, low in spirit, and he wanted to see her for a little while.

Ward Wright opened the door.

'Hello! Why, here's the man who's trying to get me kicked out!'

'And we're going to' Harry said quietly. 'You're looking pretty seedy, even now. They're not funneling the blood money through any more? It'd be a pity if you actually had to work for a living.'

'You're ambitious.' Ward Wright's eyes laughed, though the smile on his mouth was fixed, waxen. 'Ambition should be made of sterner stuff, Kellems. Sterner than you, anyway. And in this case, a whole lot tougher too.'

Madeline came down the hall.

''Arry! It's good to see you again. You've been avoiding us.'

'No, honestly I haven't. I've been—busy.'

'Too busy' said Ward Wright, his eyes laughing.

Papa Desmoulins was in a bad mood. His politeness was so formal as to show a sheen of ice. A man less reserved and in such a turmoil of mind would have muttered to himself. Papa Desmoulins said the proper things; but under mossy white platforms his eyes were spurts of vinegar; and his mouth was a steel-toothed trap. Oh, he was not angry at Harry, nor at his daughter, nor at Ward Wright, nor even at the humble Conchita, who worried in from the kitchen at his call. It was something inside of himself.

'Enchanté, monsieur. You have not often honor' us lately.'

'Been busy' Harry muttered.

'Ah? The Canal goes well, I 'ope?' Only, he didn't hope that. On the contrary he hoped that the Canal was going very badly. His affability was habit.

'It's getting on.'

'I am glad. Coffee?'

'Thanks, I will.'

Conchita already was handing him one of those tiny cups the French take after meals. Harry never refused coffee at the Desmoulins'. The place might be threadbare, as was the old man, as were the clothes of even Madeline herself when she was at home—clean but worn, overscrubbed, thinning—but the coffee, like the wine, was always good.

None of them sat comfortable, though Ward Wright pretended to, while Papa was unaware of his position. Papa was growling inwardly. Something had happened just before Harry came.

So they talked of this and that, Madeline and Harry frankly troubled, Ward Wright with his affected flippancy, Papa from some hidden inherited reservoir out of which words were sent exactly forth without need of the brain as intermediary; Conchita had gratefully scuttled back into the kitchen.

The ring was a crash of relief and rescue, a sound welcome to all of them. The doorbell was one of those knobby things you yanked, and which, after a long while, and as you were about to yank again, set in motion far away a whirligig apparatus which waved a small bell more languidly than any schoolmarm ever would have done; and then the bell went on and on, slowing, slowing, getting mixed with its own echoes, so that nobody knew just when it stopped.

Madeline rose. 'I'll go. I'm sure it's Arthur Price, for his lesson.'

As he got up, Ward Wright murmured 'Still another? The place gets crowded.'

Harry too was rising at this time, and he could not see her face, but he could *feel* her eyes rake Ward Wright.

'You are not in a café, Captain.'

'Oh, say, I'm sorry!'

He *was* sorry, too. It had not been scalding, the rebuke, and certainly it hadn't been prim; but it had hurt him. He swung around with her as she passed, and started to make further apology; but she disappeared into the hall. Harry smiled.

Harry knew Arthur Price, and had indeed sent him to Madeline in the first place, two months ago, when Price appeared on the Isthmus fresh from his internship. 'D-do you know of a p-place where I could learn Spanish?' It wasn't a stutter, it was the slightest halt in speech, scarcely perceptible. 'They tell me you j-jabber it swell.' Harry had grinned up at Dr Price, who was his own age but seemed younger —though, coming to think of it, most of the newcomers seemed young to Harry. Long, Arthur Price was. Long and pleasant and careful. He had humor that was not rubbed on like an ointment but came plenteously from inside of him. He didn't talk much, he was shy; but Harry had liked him instantly, all awkward six feet three of him. Harry had given him Madeline's name and address.

Arthur came in. He had dressed carefully; his clothes were always good anyway—he was somebody with money.

'Hello. Am I interrupting anything?'

He was uneasy. Sensitive, he knew that this was a bad place—now. Harry swallowed the last of his coffee.

'I was just about to leave anyway. Just dropped in to say how do y' do. Work at the hospital o.k., Art?'

'Oh, it goes along.'

'Say, excuse me, you've met Mr Desmoulins, haven't you?'

Yes, they had met. Nevertheless they bowed. Arthur Price actually bowed; and hanged if he didn't bow well!

'Enchanté, monsieur.'

'Enchanté.'

All the same, Art Price was uneasy.

'I hate to leave' Harry said heartily. A lie. Always he was lying, these days! 'But—you know, relentless duty.'

'Ah, but to be sure, the Canal' said Papa Desmoulins. 'You are so— loyal, monsieur.'

'Well, it's my job. Good-by, Art. I mean, adios. Learn a lot.'

The old man would have accompanied him to the door, but Madeline took Harry's arm.

'After all, it was to see me that he came, Papa.'

'Ah, that is so true!'

It must be nice to be able to bow.

'So long, Jack' Ward Wright said rudely.

'You mean the one who killed the giant, of course?'

Now that was good; it was witty, and exact; but Madeline pushed his arm firmly and led him out into the hall, saying as they went: '*You* are not in a café either, 'Arry.' He heard Ward Wright chuckle.

At the door, which she unclicked without opening it, she looked at him seriously.

'You are well, 'Arry? Everything is well?'

'Everything's all right' he muttered. 'Sure.'

'You will give your wife my regards and ask forgiveness that I do not visit her?'

'Well, if you feel that way.' He looked hard at her. 'You don't usually kid anybody, mademoiselle. What do you really mean?'

'Are you happy?'

'With Phil?'

She nodded. She had a hand on his arm, but they stood far apart. She was rigid, looking at him.

Was he happy with Phil? Why, of course he wasn't! He had known that for a long time now, for days, in spite of all he had done in his mind while she was away—he'd known that they were not right together. He felt sneaky and wrong about this. Phil after all had trusted him; she had married him; she had come down here to join him, in the worst days of the yellow-jack epidemic; and she had come back, to be with him again, after the firm solid happiness of the old life in Paterson. What amounted to a hell of a lot more, Phil was his wife.

He answered steadily: 'Why, of course I'm happy.'

Another lie. It seemed you always lied. People expected it of you.

The corners of Madeline's mouth went up twitchingly, and when she smiled that way it was a false smile, not her real smile; she squeezed his arm and then released it, still making that smile.

'It was rude of me to ask, 'Arry. But I worried.'

'Well, that's all right, I guess. After all,' he told the floor, and his voice was very low, 'she's my wife.'

'Yes.'

'Remember that.'

'I am not likely to forget it, 'Arry. Well, good-by.'

'Good-by. I mean—adios.'

'Yes, of course—adios!'

Phil was showering, so he went right into the kitchen. On the way up the hill he had been thinking too much about himself and Phil, and he was wrenching himself into amiability, knowing that he'd have to play auction bridge tonight; and it was because Rosina could be a lot of help when he felt that way that he went to the kitchen.

'Buenas noches, chica! How goes the dinner?'

'Monsieur?'

An enormity confronted him, an immensity of black skin, garbed in a tent. Protuberant eyes tried to reach right out and touch him, though the rest of the mountain didn't move. There was a turban on the head. The feet were bare.

'Oh, I'm sorry. Rosina here?'

'Monsieur?'

'La cocinera, Rosina. Esta elle aqui?'

'Monsieur?'

Poe's raven only had one word. Poe's raven, Harry reflected, must have been much, much smaller. And also, he reflected, gayer.

His eyes slapped the surfaces of the kitchen, and there was no Rosina. The Immensity, solemn as Fate, would have croaked 'Monsieur?' again; but he cut her short. A substitute, no doubt. Pity. What a curious substitute though! Couldn't little old Rosina have sent somebody less terrifying? Well, you took what you could get here.

'Let it go' he said pleasantly. 'It'll all come out in the wash.'

'Monsieur?'

He undressed, wondering about the look Madeline had given him in the hallway there. He got into his bathrobe. Phil came out of the bathroom.

'Hello, darling.'

'Hi!' He lolloped with his head. 'What's the black menace in there?'

He had been starting toward her, meaning to kiss her, but she stood very straight and still; and he stopped. There was something wrong, and he knew it. There was usually something wrong these days.

'Her name' said Phil, as though she expected a jeer to follow the announcement and was prepared against it, 'is Célestine.'

'Well, that's nice' said Harry.

He stood looking at her. She had that blue wrapper on, and it clung to a body still damp after the shower. She had taken the towel from her head, and her hair fell soft and smooth around her, caressing her. She looked damn nice—except that in her eyes there was that challenge he was getting to know too well, that same look Dr Lemming habitually had in *his* eyes, the look that kept iterating senselessly and passionately: 'Well, go ahead and insult me! I dare you to insult me!' It was not a good time to kiss her. He tried jocularity.

272

'From Martinique?'

'Yes, she comes from Martinique,' still challenging.

'One of the back-pay mamas, eh?'

It was a joke going the rounds, and admittedly not a very funny one, and a dirty one, dirty enough so that a man really shouldn't mention it even before his wife. Harry was instantly sorry.

A shipload of Martinique women had recently arrived, several hundred of them, black, stolid, extraordinarily stupid, speaking a patois nobody understood. Some were wives of Martinique workmen already on the job, and others were sisters, daughters, mothers. All were needed —as washwomen, as cooks, or wives. Yes, the need of them had been clear enough, the shipment had been sensible. But a New York reporter had got his grimed talons into the tale. Why not a good reporter? Why, as that man on the train had asked, didn't the papers send trained correspondents down here to Panama and cover the building of the Canal for what it was, a great fight? Well, no. This reporter presumably had never moved far from a Park Avenue bar. His story was a sensation. WHY, prithee, did the United States Government, under the august leadership of that screeching cowboy in the White House, feel itself obligated to import COAL-BLACK PROSTITUTES? Had IMPERIALISM IN WASHINGTON gone so far that the transference of hundreds of professional native females from a French colony was felt to be necessary for the carnal accommodation of Our Boys? Question mark, question mark. That sort of thing. The story itself, the original story, and the stories that followed, as wax-legged as the first, and the stories that had fitted around that first story, and bumped into it, and embroidered its flamboyant absurdities, and even more the stories by word of mouth which these printed stories had inspired, were truly funny to Our Boys who heard about them some weeks later. All you had to do was look at one of those Martinique monstrosities to see how very funny the whole idea was. The usual view was from the rear: they were, ordinarily, bending over washtubs. Each pair of buttocks—it was perhaps due to the climate in Martinique—was even larger than those of the average unenticing Negress. COAL-BLACK PROSTITUTES, for Christ's sake! 'It's easy to see' some local wag had remarked, with no notion of how his words would be snapped up, 'that they are here for their "back-pay"!' This was often repeated, and the women from Martinique—when white women weren't around— were referred to as back-pay mamas.

All of which was no reason why Harry should have said such a thing before his wife, as his wife with no hesitation pointed out.

'Gosh, I really am sorry' mumbled Harry, who really was.

Just the same, he couldn't help wondering where Phil had heard the expression.

'Well, you should be!'

At least the I-dare-you-to look was gone from her eyes, now that she knew she was possessed of righteousness.

'Well, it slipped out.' He shuffled into the bathroom, encircling her. 'I was just surprised not to see Rosina, that's all.'

'You go straight to the kitchen to see Rosina, of course?'

'Ah, cut it out, Phil! You know perfectly well you were taking a shower when I came in. I could hear it.'

'To the kitchen right away, and afterwards to your wife, so that you can be as nasty and common as you know how!'

He left the door ajar, in case he was called upon to defend himself. He took his bathrobe off.

'Well,' still trying to be light, still denying the tension, 'this one doesn't wear any shoes either, I see.'

'She'll learn to. You can't expect everything, at first.'

'At first?' He had tentatively turned on the shower, but now he turned it off. He went to the door. 'Say,' he called, 'how long is Rosina going to be gone?'

'I discharged Rosina this afternoon' said Phil.

'*What!*' He stamped out of the bathroom, waving his arms. 'Why, you can't do a thing like that! What did she do, anyway?'

'Harry, I refuse to talk to you while you're standing there in that condition. Put something on, if you expect me to answer you.'

'Well, you've seen me before, as far as that goes. But listen, what's the idea of treating poor little Rosina as if——'

'Harry, *put something on!*'

She rose, holding the wrapper tight around her, and scooped up clothes, as though preparing to go into the parlor to dress.

'Well, all right! Wait a second!' He got his bathrobe. 'Now will you please tell me why in the world you fired that poor kid?'

'That "poor kid" means more to you than your wife does, I suppose?'

'Oh, stop talking nonsense! Listen, you're not actually *jealous* of Rosina, are you?'

'Of course I'm not!'

Yet she was. Harry saw it. Nor was the discovery as startling as it would have been a few months ago. He had learned that you could be jealous of a person without suspecting any physical connection between that person and another. As far as that went, he wouldn't dream of any infidelity on Phil's part! But there were lesser degrees of jealousy, not the grandiose thunderous eloquent rage of an Othello, but nippy small-nuisance jealousy as persistent as ants. Harry himself indeed was jealous of Mavis Lemming. It was ridiculous. You didn't suspect your wife of doing anything wrong with a frizzy-haired jumping jack; but in spite of yourself you resented the way your wife loved to have her around. Another thing—why so suddenly all this sight-seeing? In the more than a year Phil had spent here before her vacation he had repeatedly proposed a little sight-seeing—proposals received with scorn. But now she must be gadding about all the time, peering, peeking, triumphantly practicing her Spanish, emitting ohs and ahs about so-quaint buildings which earlier she had thought only grubby —and always in the clinging, cloying company of Mavis, who had never been abroad, didn't speak Spanish, and nursed no memories of the pioneer days.

'Jealous of a ratty little cripple like that? You must think I'm crazy! Or else it's just that your smutty mind automatically——'

'Well, I didn't exactly mean——'

'If you must know, I discharged her because she was impertinent.'

'You mean she wouldn't wear slippers?'

'The girl simply didn't know her place, that's all. I wouldn't have a servant like that in Paterson, and I don't see why I should here.'

'You wouldn't *get* a servant like that in Paterson! The best you could do there would be some Swede or Polack you'd have to pay twenty, twenty-two, maybe even twenty-five a month to. *And* you'd have to feed her, and give her a room! *And* let her have every other Sunday afternoon off!'

Phil, ladylike, was combing her hair.

'Célestine' she said 'is receiving the same wages. Eight dollars.'

'I hope you at least *paid* Rosina before you bounced her out?'

'Of course I paid her. As a matter of fact, I gave her her whole month's wages, though they weren't really due until the day after tomorrow. I just couldn't be bothered' said Phil 'figuring out how much those two days would have amounted to.'

As she talked she often closed her eyes and opened them slowly. She tipped her chin high, very Gibson Girlish. She put down the comb and picked up a brush, her fingers daintily crooked.

He glared at her. Was it inherited from her father, this streak of meanness? Phil had a childish fondness for grandeur—he sometimes saw loomed behind her that massive square four-story house in Paterson, with its curlicues and gingerbread, with the gilded finial that topped its tower, and with its plate-glass windows, its hardwood floors, its matching stable, the brightly painted iron carriage boy on the block in front. She would spend all the money she had on clothes—for him, admittedly, as for herself. She had bought him this bathrobe. She'd bought him the swank velvet smoking jacket he was never going to wear: he was certainly never going to *smoke* in it, anyway! Just because there was no Panamanian tariff on such things, she bought herself any amount of fancy French perfumery. But in matters of the immediate household, more specifically in matters pertaining to the kitchen, Phil was niggardly beyond belief. She'd pay fifteen or sixteen dollars for a hat, even though she had already had three or four of them; but she would refuse to speak to anybody in the family of a grocer she suspected of once having overcharged her by four cents. She wouldn't ask the price of a muff or a pair of gloves she meant to buy; the Chinamen in Panama knew that they could ask almost any price from her if the article hinted of the Orient; yet she would haggle by the hour with a huckster. Possibly that was one of the things that made her so irritable these days—the fact that there weren't any hucksters on the Isthmus and that it was impossible for even the cleverest and most determined white woman to go to the market and get anything for less than twice its worth? You sent your servant, of course. Everybody did. Possibly Phil had resented Rosina for this reason, among others? Phil had tried the market more than once, to come back fuming. Rosina, meek, ugly, slow-moving little Rosina, would come back with her basket overflowing, with a few extra pieces of fruit thrown in, her pocket full of change, and flowers in her hair.

'What are you staring at, dear?' asked the perfect lady.

'Nothing.'

She began to brush her hair. Harry stamped back into the bathroom and turned the shower faucet on. He was so sore that he had stepped under the shower before he realized that he was still wearing his bathrobe.

When he returned to the bedroom he was amazed to find Phil still there. He had expected her to be gone; but she sat brushing her hair.

'Harry——'

'Yes?'

Her eyes were downcast. The hand with the brush scarcely moved. There was nothing repentant in her attitude; but her voice wheedled.

'I—I'm sorry if I hurt your feelings about Rosina, dear. But I considered it my affair entirely.'

He did not answer. He had begun to put on his union suit.

'Harry, please come here a minute.'

Glowering, he went to her. She kept her eyes averted, but she put down the brush and reached up toward her shoulder, wriggling the fingers, seeking his hand. The V of her wrapper fell open.

'Harry, I wish you could see how I feel sometimes when——'

'It's easy enough to see how you feel. Your friends the Lemmings are coming, and you want me to behave, so you figure that if you can just maneuver me to where I'll be looking down at your titties—why, you'll get me excited and then I'll do anything you ask.'

She sprang to her feet, recoiling from him, with both hands holding shut the wrapper. Rage blotted the blood from her lips.

Inexorably: 'You know perfectly well that whenever you've done something you think might make me sore, you try to get me to forget it by coming up close and rubbing against me like a cat.'

She found voice, though only, at first, as a wordless squeal. She snatched up her clothes, and she was in the bathroom before he could make sense of her fulmination.

'. . . filthiest thing I've ever heard of, and if that's the way you feel, well then I can tell you right now that you needn't worry about *that* any more!'

She stepped inside and slammed the door. The next instant she swung the door open.

'Not *ever* again! No matter *what* happens!'

She slammed the door a second time.

'I'm sure of it' muttered Harry.

He fished his cigar from an ash receiver, relighted it, and began to button up his union suit.

The auction bridge was not a success.

This was the second time they had played together, and Harry had not enjoyed the first time either. He faced Phil, who ever since a wordless dinner with him had been smiling brightly. 'Families' Mavis explained. The stake was to be a tenth of a cent a point. This meant little to Harry, for the scoring was different from that of bridge whist; but when Lemming suggested that they make it a little higher, Harry swiftly said no. Lemming looked sideways at him and grunted. Lemming was on Harry's left, Mavis on his right.

Well, when you play poker people don't keep offering advice. When you play poker people don't keep telling you that you can't do this because of that, which means some other thing, and what it comes out to is so and so, don't you see? You don't see. You could have seen, no doubt, if there had been less conversation and a little more chance to think—and not so many rules.

'You play your cards perfectly, dear, but the only thing is——'

'Sure does, yes' Lemming granted. 'Plays 'em swell.'

'You see, dear, the *bidding* is so important! No matter how well you play the cards, if you *bid* wrong——'

'It's your deal' said Harry.

Probably Lemming didn't do anything else well. Harry had heard that he did not amount to much in Sam Darling's department. Any mirror could have told him what everybody else knew: that he was about as unattractive a guy as it was possible to imagine. He had given evidence that he could not carry an intelligent conversation; and it seemed likely to Harry that he didn't even know enough to come in out of the rain. But he did know how to play auction bridge. At least, he knew about the bidding; and from the high place of his expertness he was willing to help beginners begin.

'Down four, oh dear! And we were doubled too' said Phil.

'Yes, I doubled' said Lemming. 'Now *that* time, Kellems, you had a doubleton in the suit I'd opened the bidding in, you see?'

'Sure I see' muttered Harry.

'Now if you'd had only a *singleton*——'

'Well, we had simple honors anyway' Phil said, scoring.

'But even a *singleton* would have been too much, really, considering that my partner——'

'Want to cut these?' said Harry.

Harry did not even like the way Lemming treated the cards. In poker you don't bulb-of-the-finger your hand, and shove cards here and there, and haughtily pluck one from among the others, to thrust it between two strangers, and shift your tail this way and that way, and squint, and then start mistreating those pasteboards again, slip-slapping them everywhere as though you thought you could by that motion change the spots on them. In poker you look at your hand like an honest man and decide what to do, and then put your hand down again.

He tried not to look at Phil. His wife, uh-huh. His wife who was going to be his wife no longer. Well, he didn't blame her. He had insulted her as much as a man could do; and he was sure that she had meant it when she said 'no more.' All right. He meant everything he had said, too.

'Up to you, Kellems.'

'Well, four clubs.'

278

'Double' said Lemming.

Phil looked at her cards very earnestly, tut-tutting. She didn't know whether she ought to try to rescue him, she said.

'You can't rescue me' Harry said grimly.

Lemming, who didn't need to, coughed. He put his cards down.

'Now of course this is all friendly, and families, and all that,' Lemming said, 'but just as a technicality——'

Phil cried 'Oh, I didn't mean to do anything wrong——'

Mavis started: 'George, you really don't have to——'

'We're playing for money, aren't we?'

Harry's voice grated like some heavy object hauled across stones: 'Just on a technicality, then, I'll make it *five* clubs.'

'Double' said Lemming.

Harry did not even like the man's face. He tried to concentrate on the faces right and left, rather than on the one straight in front. Mavis's face was too familiar. The yes-yes-yes-yes girl, all raptures, waiting for you to turn your back. Oh, she had her function! She did help Phil to burn. But did Phil need such help? Not now! Phil was fully lighted, uncrackling but harsh, not like the flame on a Bunsen burner, where you could pick out and all but finger the separate cones of color, but like the flame right at the needle point of a welder's stick —but no sparks! Not yet!

He tried to concentrate on Lemming's face.

Well, Harry T would have said that Lemming had a face that only a mother could love. It was a smooth long face—in its proportions, but not otherwise, suggesting that of a horse. What Harry saw was mostly cheek; for the man's eyes went cards-ward, and he had no nose worth mentioning, while the chin showed overeager to get back into the mother countenance and be lost. The cheek was a slab saying No, no. It was a shutter put up at nightfall by some shopkeeper afraid of robbery—though there could have been little in the place worth stealing. The cheek said, Go away! All right, the cheek didn't need to say that. Nobody in his right mind was going to get very close to Lemming. How did Lemming ever happen to snare Mavis, by the way? Well, how could *anybody* ever do that? By waiting, tense, a wedding ring in both hands, and by leaping at just the right moment? Jesus, Harry thought, his eyes swerving to the female Lemming, if Pavlowa could only see the tip of that nose!

'The lead's in your hand, Kellems. Sorry.'

'No, it's from out there.'

'No, it's in your hand.'

Harry tapped the card he had taken from the dummy.

'That's the one. And I'm playing this on it. I don't care what you play, only don't hold up the game.'

Lemming put his cards face down on the table, not mad, just sighing. He spoke only to the women.

'Do you mind? I don't think there's much sense in going on.'

'There's a lot of sense in going on!' cried Harry. 'What are you going to play on that?'

He realized that he was shouting, and he tried to bring his voice down. He realized, at the same time, that Lemming was right and that the lead should have been from his own hand.

'Play it out, dear' Mavis cooed.

Phil: 'Harry, I do think that perhaps you ought to——'

'Why don't you do what your wife says?' asked Harry.

Lemming said 'When it gets to the stage that——'

'What stage?'

'Play it out, dear' Mavis begged.

'All right' said Lemming. 'Here you are.'

'Down three' Phil cried cheerily, a moment later, through splintering silence. 'Did you double, you—you wizard?'

'Yes, I doubled' said Lemming. 'But it should have been down four.'

'Well, make it down four then' said Harry.

'I don't intend to play any more' said Lemming.

Harry thought of getting up and asking him to take his coat off, but after all you couldn't slug a thing like that. Phil was suggesting that perhaps they were all too tired to play any more, and Mavis said they might as well finish the rubber, but Lemming declared flatly that he was through and that was all there was to it.

The good nights, the women chirruping, were overloud. At last the door closed. The carriage wheels gritted away. Phil turned.

'Well, what I said before dinner certainly applies a thousand times more now!'

She swept past him to the bedroom.

17

THE CAFE DE LOS DOS DIABLOS had a day dress and a night dress. In the daytime it was a tolerably smart restaurant and respectable; but with the coming of darkness the roulette wheel and the keno and faro setups and the poker chips and the dice were brought out, and the tables, so innocent a little earlier, were pushed together and covered with green felt. A new set of waiters appeared, stronger, bulkier, less agile and at the same time less friendly than the daytime waiters. Dapper men in white, whose fingers were all rings, took their places at the tables, lighting panatelas. Along with the first of the customers too came the girls, hands on swinging hips, their scarlet-slippered feet moving with deliberate provoking languor, muddy faces powdered to the color of coffee-with-cream, their lips painted, flowers in their hair, pearls in their ears. The girls fascinated Phil.

Quickly, especially when the awning had been slid into place at a threat of rain, but quickly anyway, the patio would fill with blue slow-swirling tobacco smoke, through which rose the click of chips, the slip-slap of cards, the ball's frantic clittering when the wheel was spun. There were not many other sounds. For example, there was very little laughter. Not often were men's voices raised in anger, and never long: the waiters saw to that. No, it was not rowdy, nor was it noisy, this nighttime Dos Diablos; but this very fact, emphasizing the rapt religious attention of the clients, and making even uglier the pawings of the girls, caused its evil to gleam the more, like scaly decay. Phil, looking down at it through the smoke, might have been looking into hell—not an orthodox sulphurous hell bright with flames and loud with the hissing of brimstone, but rather a place where sin was studied, weighed, and concentrated upon with an intensity which to the outsider seemed grotesque. The men did not smile, not even when they won; but the women never ceased to smile. The methods of the women were direct to the point of brutality. They did not try to charm and ensnare by flirtation, for which perhaps they didn't have time—or perhaps it was because the men would pay them no attention; they did not roll their eyes; they didn't whisper honeyed invitations; they used their hands. They got right down to the point, sitting on the man's lap if permitted to do so, one hand fondling his cheek or neck, the other hand more secretly though more directly engaged. If rebuffed—and Phil saw many rebuffed—they turned away with no slackening of the smile, to address themselves to the next man. They worked hard for whatever they received. Not often did one slide from a lap and, with arm hooked into his, and hastily, before he could change his mind, lead her conquest out through the door, assumedly to some nearby apartment. The man would soon hurry back, his lips moving as he calculated percentages, his hand in his pocket for money, and throw himself again upon the game that had brought him; and the girl would saunter in later, a fresh cigarette between her lips, her eyes alert for another man.

Poor unfortunates! How could they ever have sunk so low as not merely to accept shame but go out and seek it, in front of all sorts of people? And how could men, having seen such women, and been accosted by them, ever again respect the sex? Phil shuddered, turning away from the french windows when she thought she heard Ward's step. As it happened, it was not Ward but somebody else; but Phil did not return to the balcony windows; instead she started to walk.

The room was long, and there were no side windows, nor was there a skylight, so that even in daytime it was dim there. This was only the second time Phil had been there at night; but it was like night afternoons, and often, leaving, she was startled by the sunshine in the street.

However, she knew every inch of the room, and knew too that despite its appearance of masculine disorder the furniture was arranged with great care and never changed. She walked slowly but with confidence, taking long strides, sometimes rubbing her hands under her breasts, and enjoying there and all over the touch of silk against her skin. She had nothing on under the kimono, not a stitch. The kimono was a lovely thing, and she thrilled to wear it. The Chinaman had said it came from Canton. She had bought it from her allowance, and it was expensive: she would never have dared to wear it at home. Not full and sacky, like so many of them, it offered no resistance when, in walking, the curves and outbulgings of her body touched it. In front and along the edges of the sleeves it was stiff with gold brocade, very rich; but the silk of the inside, without ornament, was an unceasing caress.

She stood at the Calle de San Martin end of the apartment and closed her eyes, there among the swords and bottles and pistols, gently inhaling the darkness. It smelled of wine, saddle leather, eau de cologne. Opening her eyes, she decided to burn some incense. He would be here any minute now, and she thought that incense would be nice. She found the tripod with her hands and placed it near the head of the bed, so that the fumes would be carried by the draft between the hangings and across the bed, in the light of the altar lamp, the only light in the room. She resisted the temptation to look out over the balcony again at those poor painted females as with unspeakable smiles on their faces they plied their unspeakable trade. Instead she got on the bed, and piled cushions, and lay there on her back, listening to the faint sounds of gambling from below, listening for the step of her lover.

Cozy, warm, she all but purred. She wriggled a little, to feel the kimono's silk and to hear its braiding scratch the cushions. She smiled up at the snake, so convincingly iridescent in the light of the altar lamp, as it squirmed forever among the links of the chain and through that hole in the ceiling—smiled, and then giggled, because it reminded her of the time Mavis had been on this bed for a squealing instant.

Mavis was so much help, such good company, better company than Dorothy Vernon of Haddon Hall herself. Dorothy (a sigh) had been a disappointment. Her dainty glossy body, her sensationally ugly face once had delighted Phil; but Dorothy's disposition was not all it might have been. She had coarsened. Not often, any more, was she content to snooze in Phil's lap or to permit Phil to press a cheek against the wrinkles of her own beswagged profile. Dorothy had become restless and—and naughty. She barked too much. She was bellicose. Since that first rat, she had been overeager to get outside; and she slavered, and leaped about. Harry had spoiled her. He'd box with her, punch her gently in the chest, and wrestle her with his hands, so that his very appearance caused her to go into a frenzy of belligerency, yapping and dodging and charging.

'She's all right' Harry would say. 'Old Dot's all right.'

Phil did not think so. 'She was bred through—oh, dozens of generations. The pedigree only gives five, but you can tell by looking at her that——'

'O.k., but they raised 'em to fight! They didn't raise them to be mantelpiece ornaments! Did they, Dotty?'

'Wurff' said Dorothy Vernon of Haddon Hall, gleefully bull-charging.

'I'll show you the pedigree.'

So she'd got it out.

'You've showed it to me already. Why not show it to Dot?'

Without stopping to think, Phil had thrust the paper before the dog's nose. Instantly it was snatched; and Dorothy had romped from room to room, ferociously shaking the paper, tearing it, while Phil screeched 'Oh, *get* it, Harry! *Get it away from her!*'

Harry, laughing uproariously, at last had cornered the dog. 'Here it is. Not very pretty, I'm afraid. Looks like a lace valentine. But you can always get a duplicate' he had added coolly, with no sympathy, no feeling for the way she felt. And he had grinned at the panting quivering pug. 'Now, *there's* a real aristocrat for you!'

Well, that scene itself had been amusing; and even Phil had laughed afterward; but it wounded her to watch Dorothy go all Harry's way.

But not Mavis. Mavis would always be faithful, almost fiercely faithful, with an every-second fidelity which occasionally made it hard for Phil to get here to Ward's apartment. Mavis doted upon every little thing about her friend; and it might be that keeping a secret like this from her was unfair; but after all, Phil was married and couldn't be too careful: she felt guilty sometimes, in the company of Mavis, but she played safe. Mavis, bless her heart, with her twirky face up-tilted—she was even shorter than Phil—would listen when Phil talked, and talk the rest of the time, not seeming to mind whether Phil listened. Anything Phil was worked up about, she was worked up about; and when Phil laughed, she laughed. Would she weep if Phil wept? It did not matter. Phil didn't need that sort of help. What Phil needed was a companion who'd agree with her. Harry, these days, never did seem to agree with her. They differed about everything; and sometimes she wondered whether he didn't oppose her only out of sheer cussedness. Well, if it came to that, very quietly sometimes she wondered whether she didn't do the same thing to him. Not as often as he did it to her, of course, but maybe she did do it. The other night, for example, when he'd slumped in with the news that Harry Thompson was dead, over in Colon. Then she might have cried out in sympathy, for she herself was fond of the gawky, grinning, horse-faced Harry *T*, as she remembered him. She might at least have preserved silence. Instead, she had lashed at his mooniness. 'Well, from what you tell me, that's the best thing that could have happened! You've said yourself that he was a fool to stay here! Why in the world didn't they *send* him away?'

'They couldn't. He had a civil service job.'

'Well then, that simply means that he wanted to commit suicide!'

'No, I think that he just hoped to survive long enough to see the Canal get going. I think that's all he had in mind. He was a funny guy. . . . I don't mean those jokes he was always telling. But if you got to know Harry T the way I did for a while there, you'd see he was romantic. I know that sounds silly, but it's right. He was romantic. When he came down here I think he more or less fell in love with the whole job—with Panama, and the ditch itself, and the life, and even us D.M.s, who were probably the first guys who had really laughed at him and with him at the same time.'

'Aren't you making some of this up?'

'No. Harry didn't talk often, not straight out, I mean, but a couple of times there he did. . . .'

She had cried: 'It's absurd! Imagine a man being in love with a construction job! If you ask me, I think you've been down here too long yourself! You're getting crazy with the heat! He certainly wasn't *helping* your beloved work, was he, when he stayed on and on, even though the doctors told him he would never be any good here?'

'Well, on the other hand——'

'Let's talk about something more cheerful, *please,* Harry!'

'Well, the only thing is, I did like that guy.'

She should have been more responsive and said something nice. But it was difficult to be nice to Harry. A little while ago, before she left, it would have been easy; but he was so abrupt with her and so inconsiderate these days; there were even times when he was insulting. It would be a long while before she'd forget what he had said that night the Lemmings came over. She hadn't forgiven him yet, though she would soon. In a little while. She giggled, snuggling low. It would do him good to wait a little longer.

Sometimes she wondered, as she did again now, whether being with Harry had coarsened her. She was worried about this, and examined herself again and again as an actress might examine her face in a glass, watching for the telltale saggings, the wrinkles, the small but so important uglinesses. Phil had been considering this problem, off and on, for a long time, since even before she had made up her mind to have Harry propose to her. She had decided, then, that in her hands, in or somewhere near Paterson, or some place like Paterson, he would gradually build up acceptable manners. He had natural charm: practically everybody liked him at first meeting. All he needed was polish; but he did need a lot of that, as she had known when she made up her mind to lead him to the conservatory that night. She had not known then, of course, that he would not finish college and that in a few months he would be embarking for a strange hot country like Panama. One of the many things she disliked about Panama—she had felt this from the beginning, but the feeling was especially strong since her return—was the way it affected Harry. Oh, it didn't run him down! Physically at least it had seemed to build him up! He was sunburned, his eyes were clear, he stood firm and strong. More significant, from Phil's point of view, was the fact that he seemed to like it here. He really seemed to enjoy Panama. That wasn't right! Nobody, not even a Panamanian, should enjoy a place like Panama. But Harry seemed to fit in. He was never homesick, the way Phil was.

In Paterson he would have been the boy Edwin C. Harmey's daughter had married. In Panama she was the wife of Harry Kellems.

This would have been all right up to a certain point, or for a little while. Phil had told herself many times that she was willing to take a back seat to Harry, and in these circumstances even glad to do so, for she was proud of the respect he commanded in Panama. But for how long? And how commendable was it, after all, to have the respect of such people? There were a few nice ones, now and then, but they didn't stay. There was always Dr Gorgas, and Mrs Gorgas, a lady; but Harry saw more of them than Phil did; and anyway they were much older. The rank and file of the white people, even the rank and file of those in the upper salary brackets, were perhaps good workers, as Harry insisted, and no doubt loyal and courageous; but they were common.

She didn't mean to be snobbish, she reflected, gazing up at the snake. She hated snobs! But all the same, if you were settling down to live in a place you had the right to expect that there would be at least a sprinkling of neighbors who talked your language and with whom you could mix without strain. In the beginning it had been different, for then it was new and held the excitement of a camping trip or slumming trip. But when it came to be an everyday matter . . . You could say what you liked about them, and Harry could say what he liked, and so could Big Stick Teddy; you could call them heroes, trail blazers, even martyrs; but they were—it couldn't be blinked at—they *were* ordinary. She hoped that the life was not coarsening her. She had dreamed of something better. She had dreamed of going to exotic places with Harry, yes; but Harry was to be a real engineer, an important man, an executive, suave, urbane, in riding breeches, sought out by the consuls and ambassadors of European nations and by the president and cabinet secretaries of the exotic country itself. She felt that she was equipped to help Harry in such a position. She would try hard,

286

in that case, and be thoughtful and clever; and her looks and the way she wore her clothes would help, and her knowledge of French too, as well as the fact that she had traveled abroad. But—here! She shrugged.

The shrug felt good, and she smiled at the snake and shrugged again.

Something happened in the Café de los Dos Diablos, and a swirl of voices rose, some of them the shrill voices of those unfortunates, which made Phil stiffen and feel a little sick. It did not last long. Hell had boiled over for only an instant. How like Ward to live like this, so tranquil and assured, on the very edge of such a place! She smiled, relaxing as the sounds relaxed. After all, *she* was all right. And the light was all right; and her hair, let down, must be enthralling. She glanced at the tripod. The ribbon wandered groggily between the hangings to the darkness of the other side. When she moved, the ribbon swung her way, and then it was too sharp, and stung the back of her throat and hurt in her eyes; but when she lay still, it was exquisitely and lazily right, sauntering past. Everything was right. There was no need to think about those poor depraved women.

She heard his step. This time it *was* his step! She heard him coming up the stairs. She moved her head very carefully, so as not to break the incense ribbon; and she let the Chinese kimono slip a little more open; and she released her hands from her breasts, slowly spread-eagling her arms. . . . She heard his key in the lock, the mate to the key he had given her. She drew a breath. She began to smile, and smile.

He was in no festive mood. He got out a bottle and asked her permission to smoke, but he did not appear to find pleasure in either cigar or wine, and he paced the floor, very handsome in his sleek silk dressing robe and turkey-red slippers. She reflected, watching him, that he looked more pantherine than ever—perhaps because now he seemed confined. Still, panthers don't show worriment.

'Something's wrong, dear?'

'Oh, business.'

'You're always so mysterious about your business!'

'I've explained that,' frowning. 'The mysteriousness is part of it. I wouldn't have any business if I wasn't mysterious. It's politics, of course. But politics are different down here.'

'You're not in any—trouble?'

He smiled. 'Not exactly. I'm having a little trouble keeping *out* of trouble, that's all. Oh, I could find work! I could go up to Costa

Rica, for example. But that isn't what I want. I'm tired of fighting. You can get awfully sick of war. Besides, if I go into battle again I might get killed, and I don't want to be killed—not now,' smiling at her again, 'now that I have you.'

She yessed sleepily, feeling warm, turning her wineglass around and around.

'So I try to keep out of revolutions' he added, cocking his head, regarding the tip of his cigar. 'On the other hand, I'm afraid I was never cut out to be a politico or a businessman. Anyway things aren't going well right now. And while we're on the subject, that forty dollars I borrowed from you last week——'

'Don't worry about it.'

'But I do worry about it! I thought I could easily pay you back by this time. Makes me feel like a fancy man, owing you that much.'

She laughed. She reached out with a bare arm, jiggling her fingers. 'Imagine you a fancy man! Come over here, darling, and kiss me.'

'All the same, forty dollars is forty dollars.'

'I can get more,' carelessly. 'My allowance is due any day now, but I can get more anyway. Some securities Daddy gave me for Christmas —all I have to do is put them up at the bank, and they'll lend me money. But never mind that. I want the kiss.'

He smiled, put his glass and cigar down, and strode to the bed. As he had done when he entered the apartment, he placed one knee on the bed and leaned low, expertly scooping her up in his arms. He was very strong. His mustache was stiff.

'You may be a poor businessman, as you say. But you're a wonderful lover.'

'If I am, it's because I've got so much to love.'

'You really could qualify as a fancy man, at that. If only—— There! I shouldn't have said that, even teasing! I didn't offend you, did I, darling?'

'You couldn't offend me when you talk in that voice. It goes back and forth across me like one of your hands on my chest.'

'Dearest!'

They kissed again; and he rose, and resumed his cigar, his pacing. She watched him. He stopped before her, looking down.

'You do love me, don't you, Phyllis?'

'You know I love you!'

He went to one knee. He took her hand. His face was close to hers, and he was so handsome it almost made her cry.

'Phyllis sweet, you have made me very happy. Happier than I

288

thought anybody could ever be. Won't you go further and make me the happiest man in the world?'

'Again, so soon?' she asked roguishly; but her remorse was prompt, for he all but frowned.

'I didn't mean that. I meant—Phil, will you marry me?'

She giggled.

He did not let her hand drop, but he did put it down quickly, and he got to his feet.

'Oh, I'm sorry, darling! But I thought you were trying to be funny!'

'No. I proposed to you. I didn't expect that——'

'But dearest, I *am* married. Now. Already.'

He didn't answer for a moment, but stood with chin on chest, looking down at her, and looking rather noble, rather like a statue.

'D'you remember, Phyllis—but of course you must, we've said it so often—d'you remember how we've talked about what it would have been like if you and I had only met before—before you married?'

'Of course, dearest! But the point is, we *didn't!* And I was young and flighty and didn't know my own mind'—she gave him a warm full smile—'the way I do now.'

'There is such a thing as divorce' he said quietly.

She sat bolt upright with such force that the bed shook and the rich gloomy hangings swayed: the million points of green and scarlet light reflected upon the hangings from the snake seemed to move back and forth listlessly.

'But—— Oh, I couldn't do that!'

'Why not?'

'Why, Harry's my *husband!*'

'That's just the point' he said, smiling.

She was not certain whether she wanted to laugh or to cry, but she thought she would be afraid to laugh. Ward was smiling, yes; but it was his hard smile, which he put on or took off as easily as another man might put on or take off a pair of glasses, and which gave no clue to his real feeling. But his eyes were narrow as he stared at her, and his temples throbbed, and the blood was dark in his cheeks.

Of course he did not understand and she could not explain. She loved him, yes. She couldn't keep her eyes from him when she was here, and when she was away she thought of him a good part of the time. Now more than ever before, when she met him she felt as though all the inside parts of her softly and swiftly melted and ran away. When he held his arms around her, and kissed her, she was exquisitely happy. But he was not Paterson, as Harry was. Though technically an American, Ward was a piece of this country, of Panama, of all this part of the world. He was love, oh yes. He was excitement and danger. But she had no fondness for danger. Risk was a man's thing, for which she would never develop a liking, any more than she would develop a liking for—well, chewing tobacco! But Harry was Paterson. There were many things about Paterson she didn't applaud, things she even despised. It was an ugly city, she'd grant that. She had not always been happy there, even though she was Edwin C. Harmey's daughter. Paterson was— well, limited. But it was home.

She could not explain this to Ward. She wasn't even clear about it in her own mind. Ward was furious; and she must put the refusal in another way.

'Consider, dearest. . . . You have paid me a great honor. But it's impossible, what you suggest.'

'The hell it is!'

'If you're going to talk like that——'

'Now wait a minute. You know I mean no disrespect. I'm used to the company of men, that's all. Mine has been a man's life, such as it is. I'm not used to ladies.'

'You do very well in the presence of ladies, as far as this one knows.'

He was looking into his glass. She cuddled her buttocks and shifted her shoulders, so that she felt the kimono. She hoped that her voice was as silky as that. She was frightened.

'It isn't a matter of forgiving you, Ward dear. I love you too much ever to hold anything against you. But let's be sensible.'

'Why?'

'Because we have to be sensible, dearest. Because that's the way the world is. *We* didn't make it that way. But that's the way it is, all the same.'

' "Ah, love, could you and I conspire to grasp this sorry scheme of things entire——" '

'Please, dearest! You know what that does to me!'

'Why shouldn't it do it, then?'

'We must be sensible. We must! We are not like other people, Ward, and if the——'

'We could be like other people, if you'd marry me. Ah, darling, you know I want you! Really want you! All for my own, really!'

He had his back to her now, standing there. Small hot javelins pierced her heart, finding no obstacle. Tears burned on her eyes. She had all she could do to keep from getting up and going to him.

Softly, tenderly: 'I know, I know, dearest. But here's just the hard, harsh, cold world we're up against. It would be nicer, and we could talk about it, if Harry had wronged me—if he had ever been even in thought unfaithful to me. Then we could talk about what you want to talk about. But the way it is——'

'Even in thought you figure he's all right?'

'Dearest, you know Harry. Or if you don't, I can't tell you. It's my fault, I suppose, for marrying him. I didn't know, then. And I felt so sorry for him. I—I didn't dream then that I was going to meet you. But there it is. And don't delude yourself, precious. My husband is the faithfullest person in this world.'

'Is it in the Bible where it says about pride goeth-ing? Or is that Shakespeare?'

'You misunderstand. This isn't pride. This is just common sense. Please believe me! If there was ever the slightest *chance*—— But you don't know him.'

He straightened his shoulders, lifted his head.

He whispered 'Sometimes I wonder whether *you* do.'

She laughed. She tried to catch the laugh as it welled up inside of her and to smear it with sadness.

'You don't know him' she repeated. 'He's been in love with me ever since we were children. He's never known anything else. He never *could*. It's the way Harry is. Darling, I'm not trying to sing the praises of my husband. But we must be fair. We must' she said evenly, in a low voice, 'face the facts.'

'Why don't you, then?'

'What?'

'Face the facts.' He started to walk, but he didn't look at her. 'See here, I'm no tattletale. The last thing in the world I'd want to do is to squeal on another member of my sex. But after all—— Well, you were away for a long time.'

'Ward dear, I'm afraid you're just being wishful.'

'I'm afraid I'm just being treacherous.'

'The cook?' She asked it lightly. 'That little hunchback?'

'Oh. No. I see you have a different one now, though.'

'I could never have trusted Rosina to carry my messages here to you. She adores Harry. But Célestine is different. And Harry can't speak French.'

Ward said, syllable by careful syllable: 'He speaks very good Spanish, now.'

She stretched. She wished that he would get out of this mood. She did not enjoy gloominess.

'That's silly, dear. A pretty woman, oh yes. I'd be the first to admit that. But she's looking for money.'

He shrugged.

'Well, isn't she?'

He shrugged again. 'Maybe she's looking for money too. But—— Well, I can't tell you. It's a matter of honor.'

'Ward, you mean that——'

'It was before I had even met you' he said quickly, not turning.

'I see.' It injured; but after all, it was past; the French would call it a fait accompli. But they had been talking about Harry. Harry was a fait accompli, too. 'Dearest, you can't make me think anything like that. If there was a chance—— Ward darling, please believe me when I say that I'm trying to think of a way out for us! But just to slander poor Harry—that isn't enough.'

Walking: 'It seems to me he's out a lot. He isn't often home. It seems to me that you have plenty of chances to get here.'

'Aren't you glad I have?'

'You know I am! But is his work so important, all the time?'

'*He* believes that it is. He works very hard. He works too much, I think sometimes.'

'I sometimes think that myself.'

'What do you mean, Ward?'

'Where is he now, for example? Where is he, that you can feel so safe about coming here tonight?'

'Don't you want me here?'

Explosively: 'Of course I want you here! I want you here all the time! But as my *wife!* I don't want us to have to sneak around like this. I want us to face the world, with our arms around one another, and say: "Here, here we are, Mr and Mrs Ward Wright, and what are you going to do about it?" Is it wrong of me to think that, Phyllis darling? Or perhaps you meant it when you suggested that I had the makings of a fancy man?'

'*Dearest!*'

He walked up and down, the empty wineglass in his hand. He'd forgotten his cigar, from which blue smoke rose in an unhurried straight svelte column. He stopped before the french windows and threw them open. The curtains tumbled in, touching him. The light from the Café de los Dos Diablos touched him too, here and there, tentatively, like the finger tips of a blind man.

'You haven't answered my question. Where is he tonight?'

'You're being silly.'

292

'Well, where is he?'

'Over in Colon. On some business. He told me he wouldn't be able to get back before the midnight, and that means he can't be at the house until almost two, and that's why I sent Célestine.' Tremblingly: 'Perhaps I did wrong?'

He was looking down at hell, from whence, now that the windows were open, the gambling and soliciting sounds rose. Sleep-slup went the cards. The girls twittered. The wee ball raced high and thin. Occasionally somebody scratched a match. A quiet place, hell.

'There is nothing you could do that would be wrong, Phyllis. You're afraid that I'm offended? You belittle me.' He stood there, looking out, looking down, his hands jammed into the pockets of the dressing robe. 'I love you too much to be offended, Phyllis.'

Her lips were quivering, and her hands, and her eyelids; her very heart quivered. Ward meant it! He did love her! Unmoving, his voice low and deliberately toneless, he went on:

'Come and tell me that you love me. Tell me that again.'

'Ward, you know——'

'Come here.'

She rose with speed; she almost tripped at the edge of the bed, and hurried to him. She slid her arms around him. The kimono had fallen open, and she fumbled with one hand to hold it across her.

'Nobody down there can see' he whispered.

He kissed her for a long time. He put a hand under the kimono and ran it up and down, pleading.

She let the kimono stay open like that. She let him half turn her, and was glad of his arm strong across her shoulders.

'Look down there. That's where I belong. Except for you, sweetest Phil, that's where I would be—in some place like that. Darling, d'you suppose it's any accident that we are *above* that place, you and I? Or d'you suppose it was meant to be that way?'

Sobbing, both breasts brashly loose, she looked down.

When she saw Harry it took her some time to believe it, and even when she did believe it it took her some time to cover herself.

Harry was not aware of her. Nobody down there was conscious of what was up here. As a matter of fact, nobody in the café could have seen anything anyway. But nobody was looking. The various games, the cards, the dice, had their attention. They all looked down. Even the girls looked down. Even Harry.

Ward was kind about it. He did not sneer. When she whirled, gasping, and ran from his arms, he made no protest. She was whimpering. While she dressed he emptied the ash receiver.

'I—I don't understand it!'

'Must you go home? Now that you know? Why don't you stay here the night and brazen it out?'

'No. . . . No, no!'

'I had hoped—— Well, I won't bother you, when you feel this way. I'll get a coche?'

She was dressing, slamming the clothes onto her body.

'If you'll be very sure——'

'The only thing is, I'm a bit short of change and if you could——'

'In my purse, dear. Oh, please, please hurry! And you mustn't come with me! I'll go alone! And you *do* know that the cochero——'

'It will be all right, the right one. Don't worry.'

She lay straight, her legs straight out, for a long time. Where was he? Nothing could be more natural than his position, as he sat in the café, as he leaned over the box from which the man with rings on his fingers was taking cards. He had been entoiled. One of those women —even in the little time Phil saw him this had happened—one of those women had slithered hands across his shoulders and tried to sit in his lap. And Harry had brushed her off. Exactly as you'd brush off a fly. With no more feeling than that.

Well, he hadn't wanted those things anyway!

But he had had a strangely intense look, as he bent over that table. Oh, if he'd just been standing there and carelessly making one bet, it would be different! Then she could figure that on the way home, perhaps for some business reason, he had dropped into that place to waste a little time. Of course he knew about it. Harry knew everything in Panama City. And she had no objection to his gambling a bit now and then, if he felt so inclined. She knew Harry. He wouldn't waste money. He wouldn't——

Did she know Harry?

She lay, straight, stiff, listening. She heard only the snores of Dorothy Vernon of Haddon Hall. If Harry had——

She got up, hands wobbling, and hoisted Dorothy from the basket, and carried her to the kitchen door, and put her outside. 'There—now.' She had to do *something!* Dorothy, clogged with sleep, slumped to a sitting position and looked up, wan and cross. 'Now, please! Try! Because,' whispering, 'I'm nervous. *Try!*' Dorothy whuffed and slashed at the screen. 'I think I hear him coming. Why don't you——' Yes, he *was* coming! She ran back to bed.

He entered quietly, less quietly though when he saw the light. He was humming. He said ''Lo!' and from the bed she murmured ''Lo!' He started to undress. She turned on her side.

'Hard work, dear?'

'Not bad. Why?'

'I just wondered. You always seem to work so hard.'

'Oh, well. It's only hard when you think it's hard.' Unnecessarily: 'I'm sort of cheerful tonight.'

'Why?'

'Oh, I don't know. Things are going all right.'

'I'm glad you think so.'

He kept undressing, humming while he did so. He looked at the basket.

'Hey, how 'bout old Dotty?'

'I'm sorry, dear. I forgot. I left her outside. Do you mind getting her? Were you gambling tonight, dear?'

'Sure. I always gamble. Out the kitchen door?'

When he came back, laughing and romping with Dorothy, the two of them making a great game out of nothing, Phil just grunted, turning her face a little further into the pillow.

'Gambling Kellems they call me.'

'You're feeling pretty good tonight.'

'I've had a few drinks. Sorry,' earnestly. 'You're not sore?'

'Why should I be sore, dear?'

Gurgling, he got into bed. 'You know, I've been thinking, old wife, old wife——'

'How many did you have, Harry?'

'Never mind that patience-is-a-virtue voice! I had a few, no more. What's so wrong about that?'

'Nothing's so wrong about it. What was it you wanted to say?'

'Well, I figured this. I figured we've been fretting and fussing and stewing and not getting anywhere——'

'Oh, you figured that, did you?'

'Now wait a minute! Can't you listen to me? I figured that this being the time of year it is——'

'And you being as drunk as you are.'

'I'm not drunk! Ah, now listen, Phil! It's going to start to rain pretty soon. It's going to rain and rain.'

'I'm perfectly aware of that fact.'

'Sure. You know that. But now here we are, with everything nice, everything beautiful, and even the weather is beautiful——'

'Harry, if you don't mind I want to go to sleep.'

'Now, wait!'

'Well, all right. Now what *is* it, dear? Now what sort of funny idea have you got? The North Pole, is that it, Dr Cook?'

'Please don't act that way, Phil. All I thought,' hitching the covers up, 'all I'd thought was that maybe we could go up the Chagres some time. They say it's very interesting.'

'No doubt it is.'

'At this time. Right now. Don't you understand?'

'No, I'm afraid I don't.'

And right there the nastiness overtook her, and put the ends of fingers possessively into her, and *had* her. So she said:

'If you like this river of yours so much, dear, if you like it so much, and if you're just dying for companionship, why don't you go there with that French friend of yours?'

'All right, I will' said Harry.

18

CLOUDS OF TINY WHITE BUTTERFLIES resembling fluff, as unsubstantial as that, as unsubstantial as milkweed balls, tumbled across the slit of sunshine from the jungle on one side to the jungle on the other, silently, confusedly carried by a breeze too gentle to feel against your cheek. There were billions of them. Some would collide with the muck-smeared roots and flutter there, helpless. Some flew too low in the corridor, and when they touched water instantly ceased to fly: these floated without struggle on the surface, turning and turning, looking like petals shaken from a grand white bouquet.

The banks were mostly roots, and the roots were fantastic. Roots should be under the earth; but these reared high and angular, as though the trees, clutched by a fear of collapse, were striving to lift first this foot and then that, and put them back in different places. You couldn't collapse! Once you were down, in this jungle, in this damp, hot, black land, you were finished: the ants, the rot, the minute busy grubs swarmed upon you—and good-by. So the trees, panicky, tottering, stepped here and there, trying each spot, finding it unsafe like the last. This was the bottom; and a foundation should be firm; but the trees lived in terror. The roots lifted knobby elbows and knees, grotesque joints, on which mud was caked. The roots twisted and squirmed in agony.

Over the roots and mud the jungle hung, implacable. The agony below was silent; but the jungle was not silent! Screeches and scritches and high-singing sounds came constantly out of it, and birds you couldn't see wrangled and scolded. Once, like a splatter of spots against the green-black of the foliage, the faces of monkeys appeared; they blinked, startled, and then with a thin squealing they left this corridor of sunlight, all the faces disappearing at once, as though by signal. Orchids nodded. Wet moss hung lank. The insects were furiously at work.

This was the terrible Chagres—this absurdly low tame creek, the color of milk chocolate, speckled with the rotting ends of logs, this creek which ambled here and there, purposeless, to be turned by any opposition—this negligible halfhearted unimpressive stream. The

Chagres!—which laughed at men, which could change in an hour, rising high, churning, killing, sweeping everything before it. For many years the Chagres had baffled the Spaniards. Since then it had driven the French to desperation: their plans for a canal might have been put into operation if the Chagres hadn't, every now and then, decisively said no.

For this river was treacherous. You could plot to fool it in the rainy season. Plans had been laid by the Conquistadors; and plans had been most carefully laid by the Aspinwall crowd when they built the railroad, and by every group that aspired to cut water through from one ocean to the other. For the rainy season, such plans were; and even then the Chagres, outrageously unpredictable, had smashed everything. In the dry season no man of experience ever even tried to predict the Chagres. The dry season was dry where you knew it, where men were or had been; but how could you guess what would happen far back in the mountains? The lazily meandering Chagres, that ornery stream, in a matter of hours, and when no drop of rain had fallen that you could see, might rise eighteen, twenty, twenty-five feet—a creek now, and now a loud malicious torrent.

So—the roots outelbowed and outkneed from the muck and black jungle, and the water drifted along, and the native in the stern poled while the native in the bow paddled.

It was not like being out of doors. It was like being in a tunnel.

'I saw Art Price yesterday.'

'Oh?'

'He—he seems pretty dippy about you.'

'Well, he asked me to marry him.'

'Yes, he told me that.'

Something large and long slid off the bank on the right a little ahead and blupped softly into the water, leaving mud bubbles where it had been. Another cloud of butterflies came, tumbling, tumbling, getting caught in things.

'Are you going to?'

'Well, I don't know, 'Arry. I'd like to. But I thought I'd wait and ask you, today.'

'Ask *me*?'

'Well, it seems natural to turn to you and ask you things.'

Her back was to him. There wasn't room in the cayuco for them to sit side by side.

'That's a funny thing to say' he muttered.

298

'No. I don't think so. You come to me when you're worried about something, don't you, 'Arry?'

'Well, I always *want* to, anyway.'

It was just as well that she could not see him. He was fairly blushing, and he knew it. The native boys, who understood no English, paddled and poled on and on.

'Well, I feel that way about you, too. You see?'

'Sure I see.'

'You have seen for a long while, haven't you, 'Arry?'

'Let's get back to Art Price. Are you going to accept him?'

'I told you I don't know. I like him.'

'Well, he's a nice guy. He's about as straight and honest a guy as I've met.'

'Yes, I should want honesty.'

'Are you laughing at me, mademoiselle? I can't see your face.'

'No, I'm not laughing.'

From Bas Obispo upstream to Venta de Cruces was only fourteen miles, but they were taking many hours. A good part of the time the cayuco was stuck on some mudbank or snag. The poler and paddler worked steadily enough, if without enthusiasm: they looked bored.

'Naturally I wouldn't dream of butting into your private affairs.'

He wondered if that sounded priggish. He hadn't meant it that way.

She said 'And yet the answer rests with you, more than with anybody else.'

'So Art told me. It—it confuses me. I'm flattered, of course, but I'm confused. It doesn't seem right to talk about such things right out like that, to other people.'

'Not to other people. Just among ourselves. What did Arthur tell you?'

'He asked me my intentions about you. He wanted to know whether they were dishonorable. He smiled when he said it, but he was deadly serious, all the same. I was flabbergasted. I asked him what I had to do with it, if he wanted to marry you, and he told me outright that you— well, he said that you——'

She helped with: 'He asked if you'd either do something about me and get it over with, or else step to one side, isn't that it?'

'Well, just about.'

'Yes, he told me he was going to put it up to you that way.'

'I wasn't sore. I like him so much, and he smiled all the time.'

'What did you say to him?'

'I told him it wasn't any of my business.'

'In other words, you refused to answer him.'

'No, not at all! I just thought that——'

'It comes to the same thing, doesn't it?'

He bit his lower lip, frowning at the back of her head. He wasn't shocked so much as embarrassed. He still thought that they shouldn't discuss matters like this. He said so.

'I don't see why not. We'll never find out how we feel about one another if we don't speak up. And whether we like the idea or not, the way we feel about one another is an important matter.'

'But I'm a married man!'

'And not happily married. You were for a little while, 'Arry, but not for long, and you haven't been happy at all since your wife came back. Oh, I know what you told me when I asked you that question the other day! But you were only trying to protect your wife, and yourself too. You thought that the whole matter was none of my business, and you thought I had a nerve to ask you. You lied to protect your wife, and also because it isn't quite proper to be unhappily married—and admit it.'

'Well, I still don't think my attitude's so very wrong there.'

'With me it is, 'Arry. It's not kind on your part, and it's not sensible either, to treat me like a stranger. You have a duty to your close friends, just as you have a duty to your wife.'

'Well, I suppose that's so' he mumbled. 'I certainly shouldn't have lied to you, the way I did. You took me so by surprise. . . . Of course I'm not happy with Phil! We've been squabbling for a long time, and it gets worse every day. I—I'm appalled sometimes at the meanness that comes out of us! It just seems as if everything in the world had turned sour. We aren't even really *sane* at those times, I suppose. I've tried to straighten things out. I think I've tried. I've meant to. But I'm tired when I get home, and I just can't get interested in auction bridge and the new novels and the fashions in magazines. Why, the other day—— Well, there's no reason for me to go into details. But the way I figure it is that there's nothing can be done. And I don't see why anybody else should be made to suffer. It's bad enough the way it is.'

She was silent for a while, watching the rise and fall of the paddle.

'As an interested party, 'Arry dear, I shouldn't be saying this, but all the same—hasn't it occurred to you that maybe you *can* do something about it?'

'A separation?' he asked. He shook his head, forgetting that she could not see him. 'Phil talks about it sometimes. She says she's going to leave me. Well, she's said that a lot lately—and she's still here. One thing she's got into her head, and that is that if we went back to Paterson together everything would be all right again. I can't see why, myself. But she's convinced of it, and she's forever after me to quit this job. I've saved money enough so that I could finish college.'

'But you won't go?'

'No. I can't quit at a time like this.' Glum, he shook his head. 'No, I'll stick it out. If Phil wants to go home I can't stop her, but I don't think that I ought to do anything to make her go. After all, I can't help blaming myself for the whole business—except when I'm actually quarreling with her, and *then* I'm sure that she's the wrong one. But the rest of the time, when I get to thinking it over, it seems to me she's sacrificed an awful lot, and if she hasn't turned out to be quite as perfect as I thought she was, well, I ought to keep it to myself. It isn't—it isn't as though she had done anything really wrong! If she'd done anything really *wrong*—you know what I mean?——'

'Yes, I know what you mean.'

'—then I could get sore. But of course Phil wouldn't act like that.'

With a great effort of will Madeline kept herself from turning. Yet she didn't need to look at him. His voice was enough. He was not vainly boasting, nor was he trying to talk himself into something. He was stating it as a fact that Mrs Harry Kellems would not look at another man. A fact—just like the fact that water was wet.

Butterflies fluttered past, futilely batting with their wings, or got caught in the boat, or fell into the stream.

Well, there wasn't an older story. He *would* be the last person in Panama to hear about it; and it was going to hurt, when he did. Already her heart ached for him, and she yearned to comfort him.

The pretty Mrs Kellems herself, Madeline believed, fondly supposed that her affair was a secret. She was most careful! Before she would turn into the Calle de San Martin she would glance around, head high, to make sure, as she thought, that nobody was looking; then, very proper in bearing, nevertheless she would all but scamper down the alley. Madeline herself had never witnessed this scene; but many others had; it was much snickered about. It was well known too how Mrs Kellems sent that extraordinarily stupid Martiniquaise of hers with notes to el capitan. Whosoever cared to intercept Célestine and ask her questions could learn. The waiters and all the help in the Café de los Dos Diablos were likewise aware of the arrangement. They often saw Mrs Kellems peer out through the windows of el capitan's flat, and they were amused by her air of breathlessness, as by her assumption that they knew nothing about her. Among themselves, and among such of their patrons as they gossiped with, she was called la Señora Wright; but the leer seldom was there when they spoke this joke today, for they were already tired of it: things like that, being common, are funny only for a little while. El capitan himself never made mention of it, even obliquely, Madeline understood. But then, el capitan told only when he thought that the telling would stir admiration; and he was first of all interested in feathering his somewhat shabby nest. The Señora Wright, all knew, had money. In such circumstances el capitan could be a clam.

Madeline watched the butterflies. She waited for Harry to speak. When he did it was in a hesitant uncertain voice.

'Since we are talking so much about one another, since we're going to be so frank . . . Well, listen, mademoiselle, was Art Price right? I—I never thought that you disliked me, but I certainly never thought that you—— Well, was it right, what he said?'

'It was right.' She swallowed, feeling the sun on her face. '*He* could see it, of course. Everybody could see it but you. You are not blind, 'Arry, except in things that have to do with yourself. You know my situation. I have only marriage to look forward to, and I don't get younger. It should not be difficult for me, though the choice is not great. But Arthur, he is good. I am sure he loves me very much, even though he knows the way I feel about you. He has money of his own, for I have asked him. Why do you gasp? Is it not a thing worth learning, when you think of marrying a man, whether he has money?'

'But—but do you love him?'

'No, 'Arry, I love you. I have loved you almost from the first time we met. And it hurts! But I have a stomach as well as a heart. And Papa, he has a stomach too. And we must buy hats for our heads and shoes for our feet. For *you*, 'Arry, I would wait. I would wait and wait, if you asked me to wait. I—I will be your mistress, if you wish. You are shocked? But why is this so shocking? It is impossible, yes. We could not live that way, here in Panama, where everybody knows everything, and where you Americans look upon love as a dirty evil thing. No, we could not do it. But nothing can keep me from thinking about it, 'Arry. I have thought about it so much!'

There was no answer from behind her, so after a moment she went back to his question. She told him, quietly, how she loved him, how she had first felt that way, how she had fretted when his wife was to come, how when she had seen his wife she'd decided to wait. . . .

'It is not pleasant, waiting. It makes me feel like one of those vulture birds, what do you call it? A buzz—buzz——'

'Buzzard.'

'Buzzard. Yes, thank you. Buzzard. I feel like that, often. Perched with my bald head, my skinny white neck pulled back into my shoulders, sitting watching for somebody to die. No, it is not nice, 'Arry. But I want you.'

She told him, she told the roots and mud, and the twisted trailers, the bright birds, the monkeys that blinked down with small wrinkled aged faces, about how she had thought and thought of him, and had contrived to see him as often as possible; and she even told him about how she had determined, when they were to have gone to the ruins that Sunday afternoon, to make him embrace her.

'I came away from that thought, 'Arry. It was not a clean thought. When I went to your house each day, when you had been wounded, and I played for you—then I did not reach out to touch you, ever. But it was hard to keep from doing it. Had you touched me, at any time then, you would have had me.'

She told the orchids and the snags and butterflies, she told the strip of blazing blue sky, how she loved him. She didn't stammer. She kept her voice low and slow, making something of a chant of it, but an inspired chant, making it almost rhapsodical, as they drifted.

When they reached Cruces and got out of the boat they did not directly face one another, but Harry noticed, even then, that there were tears in her eyes. In *Madeline's* eyes! Simpson had been right: there were many things about this girl he did not know.

Now she slipped an arm into his, informal, friendly.

'Before we look at the church, let's squat right here, eh, and open the basket? So much emotion has made me hungry.'

Venta de Cruces the Conquistadors had built at the top spot on the river for navigation. Those Spaniards, they were stubborn. After years and years they still believed that they could make the Chagres behave! Disagreeably they fought that disagreeable stream; and the stream won. The stream was bound to win. The Spaniards, as far as Cruces was concerned, went away—rather, they faded: they dissolved into certain black slaves they had brought from Africa, and into natives who had been there all the while; and as for the Spaniards who didn't do this, they had other things than Cruces to think about, and they hurried off.

Venta de Cruces had been the second city in Panama, and Panama had been the pivot of the New World, the pivot around which turned the silver and gold which kept a king on his gold-and-silver throne, and supplied his armies, and antagonized those who were not his allies, and played ducks and drakes with all European currencies, so that farmers could no longer live on what their farms produced, though sailors could always get jobs.

It was a foolish idea they had, those Spaniards, that they could run half the world by mulcting the other half. Up from Peru and down from the west coast of Mexico came the gold and silver, and in Panama City it was loaded on asses, and the asses were beaten, and this was what the Spaniards called a recua. Sometimes it might be miles long. The Rio Chagres chuckled in its dark brown throat and said no. The Chagres kept saying this; and after a while the Spaniards understood; and so then the Spaniards began to make the asses carry the stuff clear across that narrow and uneven path grandiloquently designated as the camino real—which was fine, until Frank Drake and his thugs intervened. Oh, the Spaniards were stubborn! Cruces lasted for a long while after Frank Drake, a knight, had been wrapped in canvas and let go over the side. Cruces was not to be put away by a thing like that. It lived, and lived. Why, it had never died!

'There will always be chumps like us' Harry observed.

They had to walk a long way. Cruces was on the banks of the Chagres? Like hell it was! Cruces, by this time, had more sense than to be on the banks of the Chagres. They walked and walked, a damp black curtain of foliage on either side of them. It was not swamp, but it was wet; and Harry, craning his neck, sometimes saw quilts of silt and mud through which silently ferocious plants pushed. The river came up here sometimes, then? The river was likely to go almost anywhere.

'Gives you the creeps, doesn't it?'

Huts made of palmetto thatch and bamboo, no doors, no floors, no chimneys, not even a hole in the roof. Primitive? That San Blas village hadn't been further from civilization! The natives seemed friendly enough, but tired, or perhaps bored; none of them was able to speak Spanish, and they only smiled sheepishly when addressed. Naked children trailed the visitors, but even the children showed little real interest. Madeline and Harry had come alone from the river; the two boatmen, curled in sleep, remained in the cayuco.

'I don't believe in mixing personal affairs with sight-seeing, and certainly not right after lunch, but will you answer me one thing, 'Arry, before I explode from curiosity?'

'Well, I wouldn't want to have that happen.'

'What did your wife say when you told her you wanted to invite me out on this jaunt?'

'I didn't. I didn't even mention you. *She* brought you up. All I said was that I wanted to make the trip, before the rains came, and she suggested that I ask you along to keep me company.'

'Oh.'

The air of the church engulfed them, and it was cool and felt good on their skin, still prickling after the sunlight. There were no steps, for this church was scarcely more than a large hut, and there was no floor, though the earth had been barefooted as hard as cement. No provision had been made for windows, but in many places the wall had crumbled away or had been knocked in. There were no pews, there was no holy water font, nor was there a poor box. The altar was a wooden platform, scarcely more than a table, and on it stood a candleless candle branch, while above it hung a wood-and-silver crucifix over which a rosary had been looped. There was a woman kneeling before this altar, pressing her forehead to the ground, but she was so still, and so like the earth in color were her clothes and skin, that they didn't notice her at first: it startled them when she rose and pulled her shawl over her head and went out. The children did not even come close to the church doorway—there was no door—but stood in a scattered thumb-sucking row halfway across the square.

Of all the original Venta de Cruces, with its wharf and stables, its fort, its inn, its celebrated warehouse, its offices and smithies, only this broken church remained.

Some priest must visit it occasionally and hold services there; for the roof at least was almost new: it was a corrugated-iron roof.

The priest, it could be assumed, was too lax a man, or perhaps too wise a one, to object to the little wooden images the natives had hung around the perforated walls; or it may be that he was nearsighted and truly believed these to be the likenesses of saints. But they were not. They were ancient half-forgotten gods, still to be propitiated if you wanted to play safe. Some had been stained, some colored with dyes. They were of various sizes. All were crude and all grotesque, and a few were obscene.

The rain announced its arrival curtly. There was a low far heavy drumming as it beat on palms, sweeping nearer, so that the sound swelled. Harry lifted his head. They had been about to leave the gloomy church.

'That'll be here soon. Couple of minutes.'

It arrived, however, almost as he spoke. There was no lightning, and there was no thunder except the thunder of the drops on the jungle, but that was a tremendous roar; and everything outside was blotted from sight.

They backed away from the doorway, through which came a rainbow drizzle, the pulping and smashing of the bigger drops beyond.

'From the north, too' he shouted, leaning close to her.

She nodded. She knew what that meant. A rain here, a rain even down along the Line, at this time of the year—it was still March—was not without precedent but was not to be taken seriously. But nobody knew what that rain might amount to back in the Santa Rita Mountains where the Chagres had its start.

There was nothing to do but wait. Talking was difficult, all shouts. They moved back toward the center of the church, and then, as spray bridal-veiled in at them through holes in the walls, back toward the altar: the back wall was unpunctured. The noise on the roof was deafening; and sometimes a palm frond slashed down, and now and then a tree was snapped, making a far high thin *skeek!* through the drumming; but the wind was not strong, and they were safe if they stayed where they were.

They stood close together, before the altar, sweating a little, for it was hot, yet shivering at the same time.

Madeline thought: Could that woman have named my name for the purpose of getting him into trouble? Could she have guessed that something like this might happen? Mon Dieu, Madeline thought, could *she* be waiting too? Did she love el capitan so much, and was she so much in his spell, that she thought to *marry* him? Did she hope to compromise her husband, in order to clamor self-righteously, afterward, for a divorce? Eh, she would not need to make plans (if she was making plans) aimed at the entrapment of Harry by another woman. She, Madeline, would supply the cause! That Mrs Kellems was a fool. She, Madeline, should perhaps speak to her, and reason with her, and point out that here was a thing over which they need not pull opposite, the two of them? She was not sure of this. She thought, though, that she might visit Mrs Kellems soon and talk with her. For the woman, though not clever, no doubt was logical when she was not in a rage. If she thought that somebody was trying to take 'Arry from her—here was the trouble—if she thought that, she would overwhelm poor 'Arry with possessiveness, she'd burn bright with loyalty. Well, there was more than two of them. 'Arry himself would have something to say. She looked up at him now, smiling, nodding her head to show that she agreed that it would be stupid to shout. He did not smile; but he did shout. He jerked a thumb toward the altar.

'It's a funny time to think of this,' he yelled, 'but would it embarrass you if I made a prayer?'

'Not at all' she screamed back. 'Go right ahead.'

He got to one knee.

'You're sure you don't mind?' he shouted anxiously.

'Not a bit! In fact, I think I'll even join you.'

This was not at all what he'd intended, and indeed he had wanted to get away from her for a little while, but she knelt so close to him that, thinking of what she had said, thinking that he could have her with a touch of his hand, Harry trembled and was not able to pray for some time. He could smell her body. . . . Not until she had crossed herself and risen, and had quietly moved back from the altar, was he able to feel himself really pray. He asked for strength to do the right thing and even more fervently for wisdom to see what the right thing was.

When he was finished he rose and joined her near the door. The rain had slackened and would soon stop, and it was no longer necessary to shout.

'I'm not very religious' he explained. 'But it does make you feel better, now and then.'

'I know just what you mean.'

As soon as they could they hastened down the path to the river. They did not have so far to go, this time. They came upon the cayuco much nearer to the village than the place where they had left it, though it was still at the edge of the river, and the two boatmen, soaked and peevish, were pulling it further up on the bank.

The Chagres no longer meandered. Still satiny, though a little more yellow, a little less brown, still without ripples, but fiercely now, it moaned on, sucking with sullen lips at the roots which previously it had merely brushed from beneath. It caught ropes of liana and dangling hanks of moss and ferns, and curved these, tugging and tugging at them. It no longer broke deferentially against a snag, to go right and left; now it took snags along with it: even as Madeline and Harry appeared at a rapidly moving bank, a tree at least thirty feet long, branches and all, went whirling past.

'No, no, señor. Not today we go back. Mañana, perhaps. Not today.'

'But listen, we've *got* to! Don't you understand?'

He knew both boatmen well, had been friendly with them for a long time, and generous with them; but now they shook their heads, unwilling to look him in the eye, but firm in their refusal.

'Not this day. No, señor.'

'You're getting your feet wet, 'Arry.'

Sure enough! Already the water had risen another three or four inches. He stepped back.

This couldn't have been caused by the petty rain which had fallen upon Venta de Cruces. The answer, of course, was a serious tropical disturbance over the Santa Rita country.

Harry fobbed out his turnip. They had not been here long, but they'd taken a long while coming up the river: it was already half past four. It was too much to expect a flood like this to subside in a few hours. The down trip even now would be dangerous: after dark it would be suicide.

Water was edging closer and closer to his feet. Another tree went whirling by.

He put the watch away. He had made up his mind. If they stayed all night, even if they slept in separate houses—and they wouldn't—everybody on the Isthmus would know it by noon tomorrow.

He whispered to the boatmen for a while, earnestly. He addressed Madeline:

'There's only one thing to do. I'd like to stay. I'll be just as honest as you were this morning. I'd like to stay, and I'm perfectly sure what would happen if I did stay, and it's not to save your reputation that I'm going. It's because I made a promise.'

'Oh, you promised your wife to get home for dinner?'

'There's no need to be sarcastic, mademoiselle. I'm not having any fun being noble. I'd rather go ahead and be bad, any old time.'

'I'm sorry, 'Arry.'

'What I meant was that I made a promise when I got married. Phil made one too, and she's living up to hers, and it wouldn't be right of me to break mine. I—I'm sorry that I take such things so seriously, mademoiselle. It would be more fun if I didn't. You—you look very lovely there.'

He turned and began brushing the boatmen away from the cayuco as though they were flies. He didn't dare look at her any longer.

'Have you thought of this, 'Arry: Have you thought that perhaps your wife *wanted* us to stay here all night?'

He shook his head, picking up the pole. He got into the boat.

'No. Not Phil. I see what you mean, but it can't be that way. Phil doesn't like you, and she certainly wouldn't give me up to anybody she doesn't like, not even if she hated me, as I sometimes think she does. It's the way she is, that's all. She didn't propose you for this trip deliberately. She said your name with spite. Why didn't I take along my French friend, if I was looking for company? she asked. When I said right away that all right, I would, she didn't like it a bit—but she wasn't going to back out then.'

'I see.'

'I feel like a coward, but as a matter of fact you'll be perfectly safe here. They're gentle people. And I know both these boatmen well. They're utterly reliable, and they've both sworn to watch out for your comfort. I'll have a bigger cayuco sent up first thing tomorrow.' He pushed with the pole. The boat fairly sprang away from the bank, for the water had been shoving it and sucking at it.

'You'll be safe, all right!' he yelled.

'Assuredly I'll be safe' she replied, immediately behind him.

In the stern, she had already picked up the paddle. Going downstream it was customary to reverse the upstream arrangement and put the poler forward, a pole being better for warding off snags.

'Though I won't be safe, at that,' she amended, 'if you keep staring at me and allow us to head right for that big log.'

There wasn't any chance of putting back. The river had them, and it meant to hold them for a while. Harry might have landed the craft, but by the time he had caused them to miss the log they were already several miles downstream, and to make the trip back to Cruces through the jungle would take many hours.

They didn't talk much. They couldn't. Madeline sat pale, frightened, her face gleaming with perspiration, but ready to smile whenever he glanced back at her. It was not necessary to paddle. Her job was that of keeping the stern from swinging around when Harry, standing in the bow, poled them away from some obstacle. Fortunately she was kept busy, as he was. They didn't have much time to think. And they moved with amazing speed: the boat fairly leaped through the furious water.

The roaring behind them increased. Harry was afraid that it meant a small tidal wave was racing down the river. This happened sometimes, at the beginning of a Chagres flood. Uprooted trees, torn scraps of creepers, moss, masses of leaves would catch onto some temporary holdout among the snags and pile rapidly, forming for a little while a small or even large dam, which the increasing weight of water would smash very suddenly, to roll on like a great brown wall inches, even feet, high. If anything like that caught up with them, they were as good as dead. He tried not to look back. The roaring was louder.

Blessedly, much sooner than either had dared to hope, it was all over. They squodged into a mudbank within sight of the trim gray-

and-white red-roofed government buildings of Bas Obispo. He was laughing as he helped her out, and she laughed too, but they held one another rather more tightly than was needed. They did not look at one another. They hardly spoke until they were back in Panama City, at her door.

She put out her hand.

'Thank you for a very nice time, 'Arry. Well, a very interesting time, anyway.'

'Have you made up your mind about Art Price?'

Softly: 'The decision wasn't up to me, it was up to you.'

'I—I don't see what else I could do, Madeline.'

'You could say good-by to me.'

'Well, I guess that's—I suppose that's what we're doing now, really.'

'You could kiss me. That wouldn't hurt anybody, and I'd enjoy it so much.' She stepped back through the doorway. 'In here, 'Arry. Where it's dark.'

A minute later he was stumbling past what had lately been the brothel of Mama Margery, sobbing, his head down; and it was like this that he walked all the way up the hill to his house, where Phil greeted him with the news that the Lemmings and the Wattersons were coming over after dinner—not for cards, but to hear her play, and she *hoped* that for once he was going to stay home.

Passing her, making for the bathroom: 'Got to work a few hours.'

'What's the matter with you, Harry? You sound strange.'

'I'm all right.'

'Was the trip interesting?'

'Yes,' spluttering through water, 'it was very interesting.'

'But you will come back early from the office, won't you, dear? You will get back in time for at least a few ballads, won't you? The Wattersons have never heard you.'

'I'll do what I can' he muttered.

19

HARRY WAS TALKING BASEBALL with Burt Waterman when the call came. He had been on his way out, and if he had not stopped to argue with Burt, a Cubs fan, he would never have received the call.

'So they're dropping McGinnity, eh? Guess he was too good for them, eh?'

'Guess he was too old for them' Harry said somberly. 'McGraw's lining up a lot of youngsters this season, from what I hear.'

'He ought to get a whole new team!'

'All the same, the old Iron Man was a great chucker in his day.'

'Why did they call him the Iron Man? Because of what he's made of above the neck?'

The telephone rang, and Harry, suppressing an indignant retort, went to the wall. It was Simpson, drawling, sounding fat even over the telephone: you would know he was fat, just to hear his voice.

'Hello, Happy Hooligan. Are you there?'

'This is me' Harry replied. 'Where are you?'

'Gatun.' Simpson sighed. 'And I'm catching a train in a few minutes for Cristobal, and I wish you'd do the same.'

'The old story?'

'The old story. Only black this time, instead of brown. The big pier. I'll leave word that you're following me.'

'I'll come lickety-split.'

An affectionate chuckle. 'The Candy Kid himself, eh?'

Harry was never to forget those words, though at the time they meant nothing. He hung up, and glanced at the wall clock, comparing this with his watch, to learn that he had a full nine minutes to get to the station. He knew every train.

Burt picked up a sandwich and a cup of coffee somebody had brought him. He looked quizzically at the sandwich.

'As for your Jawn McGraw, you know what I think of him? I think a squirrel could run up one of his legs and run right down the other, without stopping for an instant. Only don't tell him I said that, if you should ever run into him.'

Harry grinned. 'Well, he's more than a thousand miles away.'

"Thank God for that!' cried Burt, and bit into the sandwich, loudly humming 'Down Went McGinty to the Bottom of the Sea.'

'The Iron Man's name is McGinnity, not McGinty' Harry corrected.

'His name is mud' mumbled Burt around the sandwich.

'Just the same, these youngsters are going to show you something, you Cubs that think you're so smart!'

'What youngsters?'

'Well . . . well, you take this Larry Doyle, for instance.'

'What Larry Doyle? Never heard of him.'

'He's a second baseman, I think. Or a shortstop. Anyway they say he's pretty good.'

'Who says so?'

'Why, the sporting-department reporters that were sent out there, out to Los Angeles, to look over the spring training. They all say that this Larry Doyle—— Ooops, got to beat it! Sorry.'

'Not at all, old chappie, not at all!'

'But anyway, you wait until the season opens!'

'I'll wait' Burt promised. He put his feet on the desk, and waving his sandwich in one hand, the cup of coffee in the other, he started to sing 'Down Went McGinty to the Bottom of the League.'

On the train Harry lapsed into gloom. He no longer thought of Burt Waterman and baseball, nor did he think of the job ahead, which he supposed would be another bit of routine, the quieting of another group of Negroes whose minds had been poisoned. He thought about Madeline and Phil.

Though it hurt, the thing was simple enough. He loved Madeline, and he was married to Phil. He knew that many another man had found himself in the same position; but this knowledge didn't help Harry a bit. His problem was not one of a choice between the two women. He could not have Madeline anyway, except in a sneaky, underhand way; and such an affair, even if he were to consent to it, would not, as Madeline herself had pointed out, remain a secret very long. No, that was unthinkable, and unworkable besides. His problem was whether to let Phil go home without him.

She was going home, she was going back to Paterson. She'd made this clear. A few days ago—and he believed that she meant it this time —she had actually begun to pack. She had stopped packing only when she received the letter from her mother.

Mr and Mrs Harmey were about to start for Panama. Edwin C. had been working too hard, and the doctor had recommended a sea voyage; and instead of Europe they had decided to go to Panama, to visit their darling daughter. They would arrive the week after next.

'I'll wait for them' Phil had said, in a dead voice. 'I won't make any further arrangements until I've spoken to them. But I'll promise you this right now, Harry: I'm going to go back with them, whether you come along or not. If this silly, dirty job is more important to you than your wife is——'

'What else did they say? How long are they going to be here?'

'Just four days.' She had looked hard at him. 'And I expect you to behave yourself while they're here.'

He had swallowed, glaring. 'What did you think I might do?' he had asked at last, with laudable moderation. 'Get soused and flirt with Célestine?'

'That isn't funny, Harry.'

'No, you're right,' bitterly. 'It isn't.'

Now Phil was unpacking, but not very much, just enough so that the half-packedness would not show; and at the same time she was airing out clothes, and getting her gloves and dresses cleaned, and putting fresh laces into her shoes.

'I have a hunch that Father is going to offer you something, back home' she had told him.

'What makes you think that? Your mother write anything about it?'

'Not exactly. But I just sort of have a hunch. They're pretty smart, after all. Or Father is. Maybe they've sensed the situation.'

Yes, he'd thought, and maybe you've told them about it in your letters. Maybe that's why they're coming down.

Well, he would know soon.

He would have to make up his mind soon.

When the train pulled away from Paraiso he started to look out the window in earnest. They would be in the Cut presently, and the sight never failed to thrill him. For things were humming now. Shovel arms were really swinging. Drills rattled, and deep dynamite charges shook the earth, loosening rock into which the great five-ton steel sun-bonnets dug powerfully. At the rate they were going, it wouldn't be long before they were tearing out a million cubic yards a month. That was *digging!* Even the French had never done anything to compare with that!

'Now you'll have to promise me one thing, before I consent to ride with you, and that is that you won't keep pointing out cranes and derricks and so forth!' Phil invariably said this when they started for any point along the Line. Only once had he pointed out anything to her, and that was the first time they'd crossed together, when she had just come, his bride, and he was nervous and excited. Ever since then, however, she had made a loud mention of it, and it made no difference to her if others were present. 'He's like a small boy at the circus' she would explain. 'You might think that he'd get tired of it, seeing it as much as he does. Mais non. But not *now*, Harry dear.'

After Cucaracha, his favorite spot, and when the train had crossed to the opposite berm, in the shadow of Contractors' Hill, he moved to the other side of the car, so that he might keep the Cut in sight.

Theodore Shonts had removed his dynamic unpleasant personality to New York, where he was to have charge of building the subway. He had left behind him a large crop of enemies—and an efficient organization. Well, that's all he had promised: to get things going right. He had promised Teddy that; and he'd done it; and he was through. Teddy, they said, was fuming.

Magoon had been sent to Cuba, where his tact was needed.

Big Smoke Stevens, one of the many who had disliked Shonts personally but worked with him beautifully, was chairman of the commission now, as well as chief engineer—Big Smoke, that blunt, affable, quiet genius who more than any other man was responsible for the way those dump trains ran back and forth out there beyond the window—but it was common knowledge that Stevens too was about to resign. Like Shonts, he had promised to stick to the job only until it was running right; and now he would leave the Isthmus, and in the White House Teddy would fume some more.

The assistants too, Dauchy first, then Sullivan, had quit.

They knew what they were doing, those men. They had faith in the Canal. So they went on to other things.

Dr Gorgas could not quit, for he was an army officer assigned to this post; but his work had become chiefly a matter of holding the gains made.

Would it be so wrong to go now? Simpson's work, that inglorious dirty work about which the others knew so little, if they knew anything—*it* was not finished. Enemies of the Canal lingered, and were active still. But Simpson had the situation well in hand. Simpson had perfected a technique so efficacious that it remained unknown: the very fact that so few men knew what he was doing was proof that he was doing it well. He didn't really need Harry now. Not the way he had.

Twice Phil had come down here for Harry. Well, maybe he ought to go back once for her. If he refused to do so, he doomed her to the life of a woman separated from her husband—in Paterson, and especially in the circles the Harmeys moved in, a terrible fate. She would be pointed out, whispered about. She would be only coldly tolerated by her parents, who had told her so. She'd have neither the freedom of singleness nor the security of marriage. She'd be giggled about, sometimes tongue-clucked about; and she would not often be invited to parties. Hers would be a life, then, of crunching, grinding humiliation. She wouldn't even have anybody to scold.

He was no longer in love with Phil, but you could feel sorry for a woman without loving her.

As for Madeline, he couldn't have her anyway. Any thought of divorce was absurd. Phil would never consent to that. A woman who had left her husband was bad enough, but a divorced woman was a leper. The Harmeys had climbed high, in their way; but they were by no means in the Four Hundred, in the Newport-Fifth Avenue set, where divorce was accepted and by some even applauded as fashionable. Such standards were not for Paterson.

And if he stayed here, Harry thought, louring at a dump train on a siding, it meant inevitably seeing Madeline and Art Price every now and then, and such meetings would embarrass them, as they would embarrass and pain him.

Well, he was not the only one in the world. You had to think of other people. It would probably be best for all concerned, he thought as he got off the train, if he did go back to Paterson.

The hacks were quickly engaged, all but one, and he climbed into it, giving the direction. The dock was not far away, but Simpson had asked for speed.

The cochero turned, gravely shaking his head.

'My disinclination to accommodate you, sir, is very pronounced.'

Harry climbed out. There was no time to argue. 'Trouble, is there?'

'Sir, I would not consent to go to that pier, or anywhere in close proximity to it, for all the money in a bank!'

So Harry went on foot.

This was new, this pier, a great corrugated-iron shed set upon concrete, the very place where four or five months ago Teddy Roosevelt had promised medals. The trouble was not on the pier but on a ship alongside, and Harry heard strange noises as he walked back to the gangplank, where sunlight slammed in at a slant. There was a great stamping, there were shrill high screams of terror, and most of all there was a pauseless, accentless jibber-jabber—the sort of sound a pack of apes in the jungle might be expected to make. Harry quickened his step.

At the foot of the gangplank three Canal Zone policemen stood with drawn revolvers. There were three or four ship's officers; there was an immigration official; there were three quarantine men—two doctors and a clerk. Harry nodded to the quarantine men, acquaintances.

'What's up?'

'They're waiting for more cops. To go aboard now would be as much as your life was worth.'

The gangplank proper, covered by the revolvers, was deserted. Beyond that was the hubbub.

'From Martinique, eh?'

'Yes. And I wish they'd stayed there. We started to vaccinate them, and they went wild. Seems somebody had told them that we were planning to poison them through the arm, or put voodoo signs on them, or something. Anyway they went wild.'

Wild they certainly were. Great black men, jabbering, gesticulating, they ran back and forth on the deck. They were bareheaded, barefooted, and dressed in any old thing. Their eyes rolled; their teeth flashed; they never left off screaming and jabbering, sometimes among themselves, sometimes to the men ashore. They were in a frenzy. None seemed to hold weapons, but they shook their fists at the men on the pier, and waved their arms, while shrieking defiance in a language nobody understood. There were hundreds of them. They leaped about as if the deck were hot under their feet. Again, and more forcibly, Harry was reminded of gorillas and orangutans: he would not have been amazed, nobody would have been amazed, if these yammering Negroes had lifted their arms, grabbed rigging or pipes, and begun to brachiate.

'What's that they're trying to say?'

'God knows! I'm supposed to understand a little French, but I can't make out a word of this. Mr Simpson couldn't either.'

'Where is Mr Simpson? I meant to ask that.'

The doctor looked at him sideways. The doctor was young and frightened, and he was trying to cover the evidences of his fright with a cynical, the-hell-with-it sneer.

'That's right, you work for him, don't you? You're Kellems, aren't you?'

'Yes. Where is he?'

'Well, he *was* here, a little while ago. He was trying to talk French to those missing links up there. But he couldn't get to first base. Anyway, he said, he hates to shout. So he went on up.'

'You mean he's aboard? Now?'

'Unless they've torn him limb from limb and cooked him in a pot and eaten him already, which I'll admit is quite possible.'

'Why didn't you say so?' Harry pushed past the cops. 'Please keep those pistols down for a minute, if you don't mind. I dislike the feeling that somebody's pointing a gun at me. It makes me nervous.'

'You're not going up there, mister.'

'You're not going to stop me. I've got a pass in my pocket signed by George Shanton himself' lied Harry. 'Now remember what I said about those guns, won't you?'

The men from Martinique did not fall away, but neither did they block or menace him. Most of them indeed seemed unaware of his existence. A few glanced curiously at him. A few tried desperately to talk with him, getting in front of him and windmilling their arms, while sweat gleamed on their faces and from their mouths came torrentially great gouts of sound in which he could only detect 'an occasional 'Monsieur.' They did not seem to be threatening him. Rather they seemed to be pleading with him.

'Big man, fat man, where he go?'

They never stopped talking.

Harry made movements with his hands, to indicate a great belly, but he stopped this when they fell back, cringing, as though they thought he was casting a spell on them.

He went from place to place, jostled by the great sweating black men, peering, squinting. All cabin doors were locked, and the hatches were still battened down. The men from Martinique all were outside, it appeared. The decks were crowded, but Harry saw no sailors, no white men.

He found Simpson at last on a little afterdeck, lower than the main deck, on which Harry stood, and which did not go clear to the stern. Simpson stood against a rail gate, and he was pressed by excited blacks. The whole deck down there was crowded, and for a moment Harry thought that Simpson had been cornered and was being threatened; but Simpson looked up and waved.

'Come on down, Happy Hooligan! I think we've got something at last!'

To vault over the rail would be to land upon somebody's shoulders. Harry ran forward, seeking a stairway. He had found a stairway and was halfway down when he heard the scream. It was Simpson's scream, a very loud one, carrying even above the raised voices of the Negroes, a scream of stark terror.

Harry squirmed past and shouldered aside scared Negroes to reach the rail. The gate hung open, the pins dangling on little chains. He leaned over. In the oily, refuse-littered water, a great white body, all balloons, rose to the surface, rolled lazily like a cask, and sank again.

It was at least thirty feet down there, three times as high as Harry had ever dived before.

'Just what' asked Carter 'did you think *you* were doing?'

He was an intern at the Colon Hospital, and an acquaintance. This was in the emergency room. Harry sat up, his ribs aching.

'Water' he whispered.

'Suit yourself. Here. Only thing is, if I were in your position I don't think I'd ever even want to see any water again, much less drink it. We certainly pumped a heck of a lot of Limon Bay out of you, Harry, before you came to. Hurt you to breathe?'

Harry nodded.

'Listen, you rate a dollop of brandy too, on the house, if you think you can keep it down.'

'Sure I can keep it down' Harry said crossly.

The brandy felt good, though it made him cough. He rose from the cot. He was naked.

'My clothes?'

'They're drying. Don't be in such a rush. What happened, anyway?'

'Where's Mr Simpson? They got him out all right, didn't they?'

'Oh yes. They got you both out. What were you trying to do, rescue one another? Or were you just showing off?'

'Where is he? I want to speak to him right away.'

'He's—— Well'—Carter rolled his eyes—'he's in the next room there.'

Slowly, getting scared as he did so, Harry remembered that the next room was used as a morgue. The fear sat hot in his chest, it stung him behind the eyes. He felt his fingers tremble.

'Did he—— Was it—— Listen, he wasn't drowned, was he?'

An intern on emergency duty gets pretty hardhearted. Carter looked the other way.

'No, he wasn't drowned. He never had a chance to drown. He was killed when he hit the water, just like that.' He snapped his fingers. 'Broke the neck.'

Harry walked up and down the room, trying to thrust his hands

318

into pockets, remembering that he had no pockets because he had no pants. He scowled.

'God damn it, he was pushed! I didn't see it happen, no, but I heard him scream when he must have felt himself falling. Somebody slipped those pins out and released the gate, purposely. It'd be easy enough to do, in all that confusion.'

'Don't get yourself too worked up, now.'

'I'm not worked up. But I tell you he was pushed! He was murdered! He had a way with colored people, and he'd just learned something about who had panicked those niggers by telling them that vaccination was black magic. That's the first thing he said to me, when he saw me up there on the higher deck. He yelled that he thought he'd got something at last. And then they murdered him.'

'Maybe you'd better lie down for a while. You might as well take the afternoon off anyway. I'll certify that you need it.'

'Go to hell. Where are my clothes? I tell you that man was murdered, and I'm going to get the son of a bitch who did it if it takes the rest of my life! Get my clothes for me, God damn it! And you might pour me another drink of that brandy, while you're at it.'

When he got home he found Ward Wright there. The pantherine captain, as trig and debonair as ever, stood in the middle of the parlor floor, fixedly and insistently smiling. Phil, also standing, faced him; but Phil had not been smiling.

'No poker party this time, eh? Got a new alibi this time—you were calling on my wife.'

'Harry, you look so strange! So—so sort of wild. Has anything happened?'

'Yes. Mr Simpson was just murdered.' Harry did not look at his wife. He stared hard at Ward Wright. 'By one of your hired hands, I'm sure. Don't worry! I probably won't be able to prove anything.'

'I don't know what you're talking about, Kellems.'

'You know perfectly well what I'm talking about. And don't pull a solemn face and say that you're sorry to hear about Simpson, because as a matter of fact you're tickled pink. If you didn't actually order his assassination you certainly hoped for it.'

The smile evaporated. The dark brown eyes showed flecks of black.

'Now see here, Kellems. You're making a pretty serious charge.'

'That's right, and I can't back it up either. Simpson's death will go down as an accident. But he *is* dead anyway, which is all you care about.'

'I don't pretend that I liked your Mr Simpson——'

'Wouldn't expect you to, when he was the man who's been working for years to get you run off the Isthmus, as you ought to be. He was pretty close to it, too. Even your politician friends wouldn't have been able to do much for you if Simpson had assembled all his evidence and placed it before the right parties. Oh, don't worry. None of it's documentary. Which means that I'll practically have to start all over at the beginning again. But don't think for a second that I'm not going to! Simpson may be dead, but Simpson's work is going to be done, all the same!'

'Bravo' murmured Ward Wright.

Phil cried: 'Harry, what in the world's come over you? Are you drunk? I can smell brandy.'

'No, I'm not drunk. I'm just announcing that I don't want men like this in my house, now or ever.'

'I can take a hint' drawled Ward Wright, but he was sore.

'Now see here, Harry, Captain Wright is a friend of mine——'

'Well, he's no friend of mine!'

'—and I won't have him treated like this, here in my own house.'

'I won't have him treated in any way in this house. I don't want him here at all.'

'Harry, if you're jealous just because Captain Wright happened——'

'Jealousy hasn't anything to do with it! The man happens to be poisonous, that's all. He's a snake, and he's poisonous, and I don't want him around. If we had a commission down here with any real authority he would have been booted out long ago.'

'Harry, it isn't right for you to go around talking like that!'

'Why not? It happens to be true. This shining hero, this Captain Macklin, do you know why he's here? He tried to sell his services to the revolutionists just before we took over, but they wouldn't listen. Then he tried to sell them out to the Colombian Government. Made a special trip to Bogota. But his reputation was too shady—they don't read Richard Harding Davis down there—and they shoo-flyed him. Then, when the first diggers came, he went up to New York and got in touch with the lawyer he figured would probably represent the interests opposed to the Panama route. Well, he figured right. It was Harrison C. Hillis. And our Galahad here saw him several times, for long sessions. This much we can prove. That's where the deal was made, and when you met him he was on his way back here to spread lies and try to start strikes and race riots. He was to give the whole project a black eye. He would *rather* have had the job as chief of the Canal

Zone police. He tried to get that job, which would have been steadier, but Teddy Roosevelt had an old Rough Rider friend picked out for it —George Shanton. So our hero moved into the opposite camp and settled down to throw filth.'

'A very interesting recitation' said Ward Wright.

'It gets better as it goes on' Harry promised. 'I just want my wife to know what sort of vermin she calls friends. Now the funny part about it is that the job's petering out. He just can't seem to deliver the goods. That's what Mr Hillis came down here for. He wanted to see why his clients weren't getting more action for their money. He and Sir Galahad, they were very careful not to be seen together. They wouldn't even nod to one another if they passed in the street. All the same, they managed to meet a few times, on the sly. Hillis was meeting all his hirelings on the sly. He's a very sly man.

'Well, we don't know for certain what they talked about, but we've deduced that our valiant captain here sold himself to Hillis as a master spy. Centralization. Instead of being only one worker, though maybe the most important one, he became the head of all the forces in the field. Quite an appointment. The trouble was, if he ever did manage to succeed in the work, then he wouldn't have any job left. So I guess he wasn't too anxious. It must have been like those revolutions he used to be in, where he didn't really want to win—not right away, anyway. He only thrives on misery and trouble.

'But they began to put the screws on him. They cut his expense account. And they're just about at the point now where they've decided that he not only isn't worth as much as they've been paying him but he isn't worth anything at all. In other words, they're thinking of firing him. Or have they done that already, Captain? Maybe it's to try to borrow a little money—is that why you came here today?'

Phil gasped, gazing wildly at her husband. Had he overheard anything as he came in? She was less concerned with the charges against Ward—charges which didn't make much sense anyway—than with the prospect of an immediate fight. If they fought, Harry would certainly be beaten: he might be killed. Or Ward might prefer to use other weapons—he might talk. He was angry with her because of her refusal. He was even angrier, however, with Harry.

Ward brushed the left side of his mustache with his left thumbnail, the right side with his right thumbnail. He no longer pretended to smile. His anger came up slowly, in wider clouds, enlarging, expanding, thinning out as it did so, until at the surface it was no more than a filmy discoloration. Stick a stick into the mud of a still clear pool, and move the stick a little, just a very little: it was like that. His anger made no sound as it rose and roiled. All the same, the pool was not what it had been.

He said 'Your work isn't dirty too, I suppose?'

Harry turned the stick again.

'Yes, but I only clean out privies—*you* live in them!'

Phil fled to the bedroom, closing the door behind her. She would not have been astounded to hear a shot: she was not sure that she would have been frightened. A shot might clear the air. All she did hear was the slamming of the screen door, and when she looked out the window she saw Ward striding down the hill. She hurried to her purse, took out all the cash it contained, not as much as he had demanded. She scribbled a note: 'Please—please! I'll get more.' She took note and money to the kitchen, and soon Célestine was lumbering after Ward Wright. Not until then did Phil permit herself to weep.

20

TO GLANCE AT THEM, not having had a chance to study them, not seeing their grimaces—say to look at Phil's photograph of them— you would suppose that Mrs Edwin C. Harmey bossed her husband. Persons meeting them for the first time often made that error.

The photograph showed him standing, her seated, against a back-drop of wan groves, roads, and somewhat dusty cataracts. She looked determined, and she had disapproving eyes, a thin thorned smile; whereas her husband, droopy, slack, mustached like a walrus, showed as vague as a figure in a dream you didn't remember well. Her voice was sharp, and she'd speak rapidly; but Edwin C. Harmey's accents were honeyed and unhurried. Every movement she made was decisive —or seemed so, at first. He slouched and slumped, and even his most characteristic manual gesture, a jiggling of the chain across his vest, was lackadaisical.

Nevertheless Father wore the pants in that family; nor was this only because there was money in the pockets of those pants. Father, who had started with nothing, knew what he wanted. He also knew what Mother was to want. Mother's movements were soon seen to be bird-like, no more than swift dartings, which landed her back where she had started from; whereas Father would murmur a suggestion, and this, for all the nectared voice, was a command. Mother might skitter here and there, might do the packing, buy the tickets, even call the hansom; but it was Father who decided where they were to go, and when, and how long they would stay. Father looked a melancholy man, for he had watery blue eyes, swagged cheeks so loose and low as to suggest burnsides or even dundrearies, and a brow of such unnatural paleness that it reminded you, with its wavy wrinkles, of a charlotte russe, and you believed that you could puff into it a hole which would stay. He harrumphed a great deal, but apologetically, not impressively.

He was nobody's fool! Harry, watching him across the table, re-membered how this man had taken the news of the marriage. Mother had fluttered in all directions, sometimes weeping, sometimes screech-ing, upbraiding now Phil, now Harry, never proposing a solution; but Father had grunted, staring long and curiously at Harry, and afterwards had offered Harry a job in the bank, and had nodded without protest when Harry explained that he wished to finish at Stevens. Father hadn't approved, probably still didn't approve; but he was no man to waste effort.

That first look, however, that early morning when they came back from Passaic married—that had been a hard one. It was the only time Harry had seen Edwin C. Harmey look that way, and it had frightened him. He fancied that others had seen it. A man might see it who was trying to do Edwin C. Harmey out of money, for instance. The blue eyes, ordinarily so watery, became dry, and their blueness was that of mountain ice silhouetted against a wintry sky; and the mouth under the preposterous hay-colored mustache went straight and thin, the blood leaving the lips.

Harry chuckled, remembering a story about a banker. A man had been pleading for a loan, mentioning his sick wife, his undernourished children, the struggle he'd had; but the banker, who did not like the collateral, continued to say no. However, it was the banker's birthday, and after a time he said 'See here. I've never done this before, but I'll make you a sporting offer.' He looked straight at the applicant. 'Years ago one of my eyes was put out, and I traveled to Vienna and got the finest substitute the finest surgeon could provide. I'm very proud of that operation. Practically nobody knows I have a glass eye. If you can tell me which one it is, I'll grant the loan.' 'The right,' promptly. 'You win.' The banker, disgruntled, picked up the collateral. 'It was a guess, of course?' 'No, not a guess. I'd thought all along that that one looked softer than the other.'

'What's the joke, darling?'

'Eh?'

'What were you laughing at, just now?'

Mother and Father got after him, too. Yes, what was the joke? They were polite, trying to bring him into the conversation: clearly they had predetermined that they'd show him there was no hard feeling.

Harry felt his face grow hot. 'Oh, just a story I heard the other day. But it wouldn't interest you. It's about the work.'

Father leaned forward, saying that anything about Harry's work would interest *him*, at any rate, and adding that, while they were on the subject, he hoped Harry would find time to show him around a little.

'You see, we'll have to sail the day after tomorrow, in the afternoon.'

'Yes.'

Their ship had been late.

'And of course I'm anxious to see all I can of the work in that time. Though from what Phyllis tells me, you may be very busy. She says the head of your department died the other day?'

'He—— Well, he died, yes.'

'What a pity!' cried Mother. 'Does that mean—— Well, I wondered——'

He did not grin. He shook his head. 'It doesn't mean that I'll get his job, no. I haven't my engineering degree.'

'But you're doing the work?'

'Sure. But I'm not drawing the pay.'

'I see' said Father, and tapped his mustache with his napkin. 'It may be that—— Well, you see I'm particularly interested in the work here not just because you're engaged in it, Harry, and have been engaged in it so long——' He harrumphed. 'But I became extra interested on the voyage down, when I had, harrumph, several opportunities of discussing it with your new governor.'

'I was going to ask if you'd met Goethals' said Harry. 'What kind of a guy is he?'

'Well, uh, "guy" isn't precisely——'

'You really met him, Father? Well, I do hope I'll get a chance to! I've been down here two years now, except for the time I was home, and I never have met one of the big heads. Mr Wallace just came back and turned right around and went away again——'

'He sure did' muttered Harry.

'—and Mr Shonts and Mr Stevens never did go out anywhere. Not even when the dances were started at the Tivoli. Harry knew them, and he could have introduced me, but they never went there.'

'They were too busy' Harry explained.

Edwin C. Harmey smiled fondly upon his daughter.

'I hardly think you'll find Colonel Goethals any more sociable than those others you mentioned. He too will be busy. The—uh—that man in the White House, I understand, has lost all patience with civilians who quit before the job's done. That's why he has given the Army charge. Goethals *can't* leave until he's ordered away. And he'll have plenty to do.'

'Yes siree, sir!' cried Harry. 'We've all been wondering how it's going to affect us here. Whether we'll have to get out of bed when they toot a bugle, and whether we'll have to salute——'

'I assume that you're joshing, Harry. It is true that Colonel Goethals has been appointed not only civil administrator here but also chief engineer, chairman of the commission, and president of the railroad which runs the commissary and owns the warehouses and docks and ships and so forth. It will be a government far more despotic than any other in the world, more than China or Russia. But I don't think you'll find Colonel Goethals any stickler for etiquette. *I* never even saw him in uniform, on the way down. He's a West Point man, yes, but if you'd ever met him——'

'Matter of fact, I have.'

They all looked at Harry.

'Well, it was just for a minute. That was before you came down in the first place' he explained hastily to Phil. 'He was Secretary Taft's military aide on a trip down here only a few months after the work had been started, and I met him then, at a reception. But as I say, it was just to shake hands.'

'This is, harrumph, most interesting. And did he make a good impression, would you say?'

'Well, Taft stole the show, and nobody paid any attention to Goethals. He didn't look as if he thought much of the place. He wouldn't. I don't blame him. It was even worse, then,' he said to Phil, 'than when you first came.'

'Ugh! I don't see how it could be! Why, in the pioneer days——'

'He struck me as a cold fish, personally.'

Edwin C. Harmey smiled. Edwin C. Harmey handed over a cigar. He had previously given Harry a whole box of cigars and a bottle of brandy, as Mrs Harmey had given her daughter piles of handkerchiefs, stockings, and dress material.

'A guy? No, I hardly think so. A cold fish? No, not that either. Cold he may be, yes. And gruff. And certainly not likely to put on epaulettes and buckle on his sword and ask Phyllis here for the honor of a dance.'

'I waltzed with a man who was wearing a sword, once, in Paris' Phil said. 'It wasn't so hard.'

'But a fish, no. No, I'd hardly say a fish. A fish isn't intelligent, and I think you'll find that Colonel Goethals is, harrumph, *very* intelligent. A tireless worker too, I should say.'

'He'll need to be' said Harry.

'I have, harrumph, something else to tell you about Colonel Goethals, Harry. Something which might interest you and Phyllis very much. But first, suppose we hear that story of yours?'

He beamed, and without asking permission he cut and lighted his cigar. He jiggled his watch chain.

Harry was ready. He had expected Edwin C. Harmey to come back to that story. Phil's father was not a man to forget anything.

'Well, it's a story Mr Holcombe told me, but it'll be hard to explain it to anybody who's never seen our Negro workers. Most of them come from Jamaica. Lately we've been getting Armenians, Greeks, Rumanians, Italians, and especially Spaniards—Gallegos they call 'em, don't know why—but even now the biggest majority of the workmen are Jamaicans, and whatever else you can say of them, they certainly don't kill themselves! Do less than half as much as these Gallegos, for instance, and *they* don't compare with what Americans would be.

'Well, Mr Holcombe—he's a divisional engineer—he was showing a visitor around and they were somewhere on the bank of the Chagres when they came across an ant run. Millions of ants, *billions* of them, big ones too, in a column as wide as your hand, and every one of them staggering under a load three or four times his whole size and weight, running just as fast as they could, working, running, struggling, carrying all this stuff. . . . Well, the visitor was fascinated. He'd never been in the jungle before, so he'd never seen anything like it. "Goodness," he said, "where do they all come from?" "I don't know," answered Mr Holcombe, "but I can tell you this much anyway: *They don't come from Jamaica!*" '

Father laughed benignly, Mother politely. Phil, who knew the story, did not laugh at all, but turned to her father:

'Now, what was this about Colonel Goethals?'

A harrumph. 'Well now, you did say that you'd like to meet the colonel?'

'Certainly I would.'

'And I'm sure that Harry would like to meet him again too, and get a little better acquainted. Never does any harm, you know.'

'You mean you've invited him up here?'

'Well, hardly that.' Mr Harmey looked around. He was polite enough, but it was obvious that the Kellems house had disappointed him. 'Not exactly. Fact is, it was just the other way around. *He* asked Mother and I if we wouldn't call on him tomorrow night after dinner, and I mentioned that we were coming to visit our daughter and son-in-law, and he said why not bring them along? So there you are. You'll like Mrs Goethals, Phyllis.'

'Oh.'

'Aren't you pleased?' asked Mother.

'Why, yes, of course' answered Phil. 'Why, naturally! Is it—— Will it be a reception?'

'Well, no. There'll be a few others there, people who were passengers on the ship with us. But nothing formal. I'm sure we'll have a chance, you and I,' he said fraternally to Harry, 'to speak to the colonel about that, uh, matter you mentioned a while ago.'

'That's mighty nice of you' Harry said. 'But from what I've heard of Goethals it won't do any good. They say he's all regulations.'

'Still and all, matters like that can, harrumph, sometimes be arranged, if they're properly explained to the proper parties.'

'Is it much more, Harry?'

Mrs Harmey swung her sweetest smile; but her pinched face, Harry thought, was as malicious as that of an old monkey. He had never liked her. He suspected that even Phil didn't like her. The woman's eyes now were avidly counting money.

'Well, quite a bit, yes. But I can't seem to think——'

'Edwin is very good at arranging things like that' she said sharply.

Edwin tut-tutted. 'Ah well, no promises, of course! Harrumph! But still and all, no harm trying, is there?'

'I—I may have to work tomorrow night' said Harry. 'In fact, it looks now as if I would have to.'

Mrs. Harmey's eyes were cocked pistols aimed at him. Mr Harmey blinked bluely through the blue of cigar smoke.

'Is it, uh, *that* important, Harry?'

'It's pretty important.'

Edwin C. Harmey turned to his daughter, but she was ringing the bell for Célestine.

'*We* have a little surprise for *you*, too' she said brightly. 'Colonel and Mrs Gorgas are going to drop in tonight.'

'You'll like both of them' said Harry.

That first night Mother had not been offensive. It was late afternoon by the time they had crossed the Isthmus and climbed the hill, and what with bringing the bags in, and apologizing for the absence of a view, and distributing the gifts after the bags were opened, and needing to go into the kitchen to straighten out Célestine—that woman was impossible!—there was not much time for comment on the house. Mother had been tired then, anyway. And Harry and Father had been there.

'My!' was all Mother had said, in a smothered voice.

'Well, of course it's no *palace*. You didn't expect to find us in a *palace*, did you? But it's not bad. You get used to it.'

'My!' and that had been all.

In the morning, however, and after Father and Harry had gone off on a tour of inspection, Mother, who said she hadn't slept well, was a jangle of nerves, darting here and there, her every exclamation an exclamation of dismay.

'I don't see how you can *stand* it, Phyllis! I didn't like to say anything while your husband was here, but, my, it's so *small!* I'd had no idea that it was so *small!* And so *bare!'*

'Well, we've got enough furniture' muttered Phil. 'Right now it even looks pretty crowded to me.'

She did not mean this to be personal. She had been thinking of the borrowed Murphy bed on the porch. It took up a lot of room; and it had been necessary to bring two of the three porch chairs into the parlor.

Too crowded? Well, it was not necessary to explain, for Mother had not heard. This was the way it was with Mother. She could pay attention when she wanted to, when a man or some woman more formidable spoke; but when Mother herself started rattling, her words went ahead of her thoughts, so that her mind was a blank when she paused, and she almost never caught the beginning of a reply.

'Why, you poor thing! Having to live in a place like this!'

'It isn't so bad. Down here in the tropics it's different.'

Phil kept an even voice only with difficulty. She did not want to evaluate the house; and she *did* think that since Mother had come all this distance to see her, and they were alone together for the first time, Mother could think of something to do besides cascading on in pauseless cavil, picking at this, picking at that, always picking, picking, as if she were a hungry hen. Come to think of it, Mother did resemble a hen. Phil had never liked her much. But Phil felt the need of somebody to talk with—if she'd had time she would have looked up Mavis, who would understand and be sympathetic—and it did seem a pity that Mother couldn't listen to her own daughter once in a while. Phil wanted to ask her advice on how to approach Father about the News. Phil was afraid of her father, and always had been. Mavis of course couldn't be any help there. Dear Mavis! she was so sweet and sympathetic!

Mother kept turning and turning, turning her head faster than her body, giving plaintive little cries of despair.

'Why, if I'd known you were living like this I could have sent you some things!'

Outside, Phil was prepared to admit, their home was depressing. Inside, she was prepared to argue, it wasn't bad. She had done a lot to it. But Mother refused even to glance outside, as she brushed off Phil's suggestion that they take a stroll over to the hospital to see the grounds.

The hospital garden, which Harry once had dutifully demolished, was a show place now—now that the need for pottery rings had been banished by the discovery that vaporized bisulphid of carbon, pumped into the nests and there exploded, killed all umbrella ants. You could boast about the hospital grounds.

Mother was not interested in the hospital grounds, or De Lesseps Park, or the Old City. Mother flew here and there, appalled by the squalor in which she found herself.

'Why, you can hear the dishes rattle in the kitchen when you just walk across the floor!'

'That's never hurt us.'

'And it's so—— Why, I should think you would *make* him buy you things! If I'd ever thought——'

Her head moved faster than her body, and her eyes moved faster than her head, and she remarked again and again, usually aloud, the floor spaces where the rugs did not reach, the ceiling from which hung a solitary black-corded bulb, the gaping corners, most of all the walls, which were decorated with no more than a few prints.

'My!' she whispered.

'Now listen,' losing her temper. 'This isn't Paterson. I've told you that! Things around here go bad. They run, or stick to one another, or get covered with mold. You haven't seen it when it rains every day for months on end. You've got to take that into consideration.'

'I've got some things up in the attic I could send down.'

'I don't want them' Phil said.

'Don't *want* them?' Mother wailed. 'But Phyllis, how can you say that there's *anything* you wouldn't want when all you've got——'

'Listen, Mother. Maybe I'd better put it this way: What would you think if I said I may not go on living here?'

'Oh, my!' said Mother, who hadn't heard. 'If I'd only known about this when we were doing spring cleaning! There were so many things I gave away or even threw away then!'

I'll bet you didn't *throw* away anything, Phil thought grimly: and I'll bet you wished many a time that you didn't have such a houseful of junk! Spring cleaning, eh? She thought: I haven't faced that in two years, I'd forgotten how horrible it can be!

'And not even any portieres between here and that hall! Goodness only knows what your father is thinking, Phyllis. I haven't dared to speak to him about it. But couldn't you——'

'Mother, speaking about speaking to Father, there's something I thought you might bring up with him this evening, if you get the chance. Well, maybe not this evening. Well, no, it would *have* to be! You see, I figured that I won't be here any longer.'

Célestine had shuffed in to clear the breakfast table, and now for the first time Mrs Edwin C. Harmey noticed the bare feet. Phil might have been saying anything at all, in any language.

'*Phyllis!*' when the maid had shuffed out. 'Do you mean to tell me that that woman always—— Do you mean to say——'

'I never have been able to get her to wear shoes.' Phil rose and went to a window and stared at the obscene lawn. She was ready to cry. 'Maybe you think we ought to have an iron deer out there, Mother?'

'We might be able to find you one, but I think you ought to consider the *inside* first. And anyway, I can't bear the thought of you being in such a place, even if there were some nice things you could put around here and there. It would still . . .'

She went on and on, while Phil, with lips squeezed shut, with nostrils squeezed until they almost touched, stood at the window and thought about spring cleaning.

For days in advance, for weeks, the whole household knew It was coming. Mother would talk of nothing else, and Phil herself would pout, and Anna would all but snatch the dishes from under their noses, and Father would make arrangements to eat dinners downtown once It had started. On the terrible day itself Mother would get into gingham and wrap a towel around her head, and the two men would come from the Salvation Army agency, and Anna's friend Christine would come, and Phil would have to go home immediately after school and get into *her* gingham and wrap a towel around *her* head. Many of the carpets and rugs would already be up by the time Phil returned, and one of the men would be in the backyard hanging them over the clothesline and beating them with small switches, making a persistent swift whap-whap-whap, a sound fated to carry all through It. Whap-whap-whap-whap-whap-whap. Where the carpets and rugs had been removed, Anna's friend Christine would have scattered torn-up wetted newspapers. They made a damp gooey mess when you swept them into a dustpan.

'. . . and I happen to know that your father is going to speak to Harry, and if you ask me, it's about time somebody did! He thinks this is no place for you, and I must say I agree with him!'

The other man from the Salvation Army would take down the chandeliers, which had to be cleaned and polished, all the glass and gilt on them. And he'd take down the curtains, two sets at each of the downstairs windows, excepting of course the kitchen windows; and the shades; and the drapes in the parlor and dining-room windows; and the portieres. Whap-whap-whap-whap, relentlessly. Anna and Christine would brush the green-satin overstuffed chairs, and work on the legs and arms, and polish all the other wood on all the rest of the furniture with polish that was sharp against throat and eyes. While one of the men started on the windows, Anna and Christine would take down the pictures and scrub and oil the intricate gilt frames and polish the glass; and Phil and Mother would polish the mirrors. The curtains would be washed and taken out back and fastened to stretchers. Whap-whap, the man beating carpets. The whole house would stink of banana oil and ammonia and polish and paint. You couldn't eat: it all but made you sick. Father was wise, and lucky, having lunch and dinner downtown. He used to say that he ought to go the whole hog and sleep in a hotel. He complained of headaches at breakfast, the only meal he ate at home while It lasted. For that matter, they all had headaches. They had headaches for three or four days, even, after It was all over.

'. . . and if he's so pigheaded as to turn down a real good offer, in a bank where his own father-in-law is the president of it—and when *here*, where he works for three years and then can't even get a promotion when his own boss dies . . .'

Saturday, the last day, was the worst for Phil. Then, with no school, she had to work all day. It didn't make any difference that Father was getting ahead at the bank. There were certain jobs you just simply couldn't trust a servant girl to do, or even Anna. Until she was sixteen and actually at finishing-school, Phil had been obliged to go through the whole hysterical business once every year. Whap-whap-whap-whap. You couldn't breathe right. You couldn't find anything you wanted. Whap-whap. You could never dress up in anything nice. You couldn't take a real bath because one of the men the Salvation Army sent had painted the bathtub. You couldn't sleep well, nights. Whap-whap-whap-whap-whap-whap.

The last things that happened were when Anna put the final shine on the figure of the woman, the mahogany figure upholding a yellow twisted electric bulb, at the foot of the staircase, and when one of the Salvation Army men painted the iron Negro, the carriage boy, which held a ring at the curb. These two jobs marked the end. It was a sort of tradition. But even when you watched that work you could in-breathe no sense of relief, knowing as you did that you'd have a headache for days, and that tomorrow you'd have to go to church with your hands and hair looking simply awful and everything about you smelling of banana oil.

'There are couples who've had an application in for almost a year for a house like this' Phil said.

'Well, I certainly can't see why! Now about your husband, as I was saying—if he doesn't think enough of his own wife to——'

'I hope he turns it down' muttered Phil.

'What?'

'Nothing.'

'By the way, what was that you started to say to me a while ago—something about that maybe you wouldn't go on living in this house much longer anyway? Did you mean that——'

'I don't know what I meant' said Phil, who was lonesome.

It was a blazing clear day of no breeze, and Harry felt swell when he got to the top. He spread his legs and hooked his thumbs into his suspenders.

'Now that's *something!*'

There were more than fifty shovels in the Cut, the big ones, the ones that took up five or six tons at a scoop, and you could see most of them, and they were working, working, swinging and lifting and dumping as lightly as dancers dance. There were thousands of men, not in groups but scattered, all working, working. There were dozens of strong big American locomotives, pulling hundreds of strong broad American cars, coming, loading, going away. On the opposite side, the west side, a compressed-air main went the length of the Cut, nine miles, and out of it snaked scores of pipes connecting with drills: the drills made a frenzied far rattle, like a rat-a-tat on a window, heard through the chuff of the engines.

'I feel as if I'd led you to the top of a high place to show you the whole world, and tempt you' panted Edwin C. Harmey. 'Only, *you* led *me*. And I don't suppose I look like the devil anyway. Or do I? I certainly feel like it.'

Harry grinned. When he remembered how he used to be scared of this man, he had a hard time to keep from laughing. The grand shiny house with the slate roof, with the iron fence, the stupendous staircase, the hardwood floors, and electric lights—it seemed not only very far away (as indeed it was!) but very long ago; and its master, Edwin C. Harmey the banker, cut a sad figure atop Cucaracha. His collar had wilted and was soppy with sweat. His fedora had been tipped far back. Pain lit his watery blue eyes. His face, ordinarily so pale, was red, true, but the redness was not bright and healthy: it was a dirty purplish color, wavering, pulsating. His mustache drooped more woefully than ever. His breath came in gasps.

Well now, it was unfair to look with scorn upon a man twice your age, an indoor man, just because a climb had winded him. Harry was ashamed of himself. At the same time Harry was astonished. Scorn for Edwin C. Harmey! Still, it wasn't fair; and he cried out.

'I'm sorry, sir. I guess I took it too fast.'

'I'll be all right in just a minute. But something tells me that the tempting isn't going to go off any too well.'

'I usually take it straight up from the Cut, instead of around by the way we came. It's shorter, straight up. But of course it's steeper. And more dangerous. The shale's pretty loose. Last time I came up, last week, a big rock came bounding down and missed me by inches. It started a small surface slide.'

Edwin C. Harmey looked around.

'I don't see any big rocks.'

'That's just what I thought when I hurried up the rest of the way.' Harry scowled a little, looking at that black haven, the jungle: a man could get down the far side of Cucaracha and into the jungle much faster than a man could climb halfway up the Cut side. 'There hadn't been any rains, either.'

Edwin C. Harmey wiped his face. He fanned himself with his hat. He sighed and with a trembling hand jiggled his watch chain. He nodded slowly, while admiration swam into his eyes.

'It *is* something' he conceded.

Harry had been liking him all day. This was not the man of the mansion, not the one in the bank either. Away from women, he had less of the air of Santa Claus crossed with a senator: he seldom even harrumphed. He had not been confidential, he'd been dignified; but he had asked many intelligent questions, as Harry took him through Sanitation's offices and around the hospital and out to Engineering headquarters at Empire; and he had listened carefully to Harry's answers, and had not been condescending with the men to whom Harry introduced him. Oh, no hail-fellow-well-met! But a pretty decent guy, at that.

'You know, Harry,' he said now, 'even in these few hours I've got a much different impression of this place than I expected. Why—everything works!'

'It sure does.'

'Why, at home, from what you hear about it and read about it you get the idea that this is a graft-ridden pesthole inhabited by ex-convicts and the inmates of an insane asylum!'

'I know' Harry sighed.

A Lidgerwood train crossed the Cut and started south, just below them. Harry pointed to it. They used to have to sidedump the old French cars, he explained. Half a manual job. Now:

'Twenty, twenty-one cars there. About six hundred tons of fill, it would amount to. Well, they'll clear that in four or five *minutes*—and be ready to start back!'

'Go on' said the banker. 'Before I start my tempting I'd like to hear more about this. Besides, I'm still out of breath.'

'I'm out of breath every time I come here' Harry said. 'Every time I think back on what it was only a little while ago. You can't see it as sensational unless you knew what it was before.'

'Looks pretty sensational to me right now.'

'The big part's practically done! Well, I mean it's started right. Course we still have to take out something close to a hundred million cubic yards of rock—and it might turn out to be a lot more, if we keep getting slides. But the important thing is that it's started right, at last! You see, it's really a railroad job. It never was anything else. And Big Smoke Stevens, *he* was the man who figured it out! Look—up that way—up near where that dynamite charge just went off? That's Lirio, just about halfway up the Cut. Now the whole thing's so planned that that's the high point, and the dump trains roll more or less downgrade all the way from there, whether they come this way or go north toward Colon. When they go the other way they coast to the dump at Tavernilla or maybe all the way to Gatun, where the fill's being used to build the big dam. When they come this way there're different places, but most of them right now go clear out over the trestle to Naos Island—which isn't an island any more—and that makes the harbor just so much the better. And then of course they come back empty, when it's easy for them to make the grade. You know how many trains there are now? *One every three minutes!*'

'Um, yes' said Edwin C. Harmey, watching Harry, not the Cut.

'That's the whole point. We know where we're going now. It doesn't make any difference how much stuff we have to haul out of here. We know where we're going to put it, and how we're going to get it there, and how we're going to use it when we do get it there. I tell you it doesn't make any difference *how* much work there is, we can do it! We're headed in the right direction now. It's just a matter of time. And nobody can stop us!'

'You speak as though you were the chief engineer himself.'

'Gosh, sometimes I think I am—when I stand up here! Sorry. I didn't mean to boast. I mean, not about myself.'

'That's all right.' The watch chain was jingling. 'It's been very interesting, it really has. I'll have a lot to tell the folks back home. And speaking of back home, why don't you?'

'Why don't I what?'

'Come, come, Harry, you know perfectly well what I'm talking about! Why don't you come back to Paterson? I could find work for you that would be half-time, so's you'd be able to finish your course. I don't mean at my bank. Not even in Paterson, if you don't want to be there. Nearer college, perhaps? Now wait a minute! Don't shake your head yet! Listen to me a little further. I want to explain something. . . . This isn't like the other time I offered you a job. You were pretty sore then. And now that I think it over, I don't blame you. I probably wasn't too diplomatic about it. You had just got married to my daughter, out of a clear sky, and I was sore myself. I might have sounded scornful, the way I offered to find some work for you? Well, I'm afraid I was, when I think back about the way I felt then.'

Harry said nothing. Hands in pockets, he stared up the Cut.

'All right, I was wrong. I didn't know you very well then. Neither did Mrs Harmey. All we knew about you was that you were a college kid with no money and no connections and—a beautiful voice. Because you do have a beautiful voice, Harry.'

'Thank you, sir.'

'Might be nice if you sang us a few things tonight, before we go over to Colonel Goethals.'

'I'd be glad to. But as far as Colonel Goethals is concerned——'

'I know what you're going to say! That I haven't got any chance of getting you your boss's job, just because I happen to be a bank president and happened to have met Colonel Goethals socially. You haven't got an engineering degree, so it can't be done. Why, of course! I knew that as soon as I met Colonel Goethals. You didn't take me seriously at dinner last night, did you?'

'Well, I——'

'Harry, you've been married for three and a half years, almost, and you ought to know better. My wife *expected* me to say that. If I hadn't said it I would hear about it for weeks, months. And after all, it didn't *hurt* anybody, did it?'

'No, naturally not.'

'Well, there you are. But getting back to what I was saying——' He

336

harrumphed, for the first time in a long while. 'Understand me, Harry, I'm not making a speech now. I'm not enjoying what I'm going to say. I don't suppose anybody ever enjoys admitting he was wrong. Well, I was wrong. I took you for a kid who had a chance to marry a rich man's daughter and naturally jumped at it. And even when I offered you a job and you refused, even then I figured that you were just trying to get me to go higher. That was my mistake. And I'm sorry. I really am sorry. Will you believe me when I say that?'

'Why, sure. I'm glad to believe you.'

'Will you shake my hand?'

They shook hands, not looking at one another for longer than an instant.

'All right. I was wrong. I know how you were even sore about Mrs Harmey and I sending an allowance to Phyllis—which was pretty silly of you, but still and all I can understand it. I know how you're wrapped up in your work here. And I suppose that when I come along and make you another offer, you feel sore all over again?'

'No, no! No, I don't really, this time!'

'I hope not. Because it's different this time, Harry. I've had a good look at you on your own home grounds, as the baseball fans would say. I've got to know you through Phyllis's letters to her mother, but I've got to know you even better, much better, since I've been down here. I was watching you just now when you were telling about those dump trains. I watched the men you introduced me to today, and I could see what *they* think of you. They know you. They've worked here with you for years. I'm no mind reader, Harry, but I'm not half-witted either. So you see, it's different from the other time. It isn't a question of me asking some friend of mine, as a favor, to find some place for a kid who ran away and married my daughter. When I ask somebody to take care of you now, I'll do it not only with a clear conscience but knowing all the time that I'm really doing *him* a favor. You get the idea?'

'Hell,' muttered Harry, 'I hadn't expected this. If you'll excuse the language, Mr Harmey.'

Mr Harmey jiggled his watch chain. He said 'You and Phyllis haven't been getting along very well, have you? As a matter of fact, she's thinking of leaving you and going home, if you don't agree to quit this place, isn't she?'

'Has she spoken to you along those lines, Mr Harmey?'

'No. But I've read her letters. No, she hasn't said anything to me. And as far as I know she hasn't said anything to her mother either—

though I shouldn't be surprised if they were talking it over right now. But it's true, isn't it?'

'Yes.'

'Well, of course I don't know the reasons. I couldn't—not even if you both tried to explain. You don't look like the kind of a man who would do anything—well, wrong. You know what I mean?'

'I haven't,' tonelessly.

'And I think I know my own daughter well enough to assume that *she* wouldn't do anything of that sort.'

'Why, of course she wouldn't! Listen here, Mr Harmey, I don't care if you are her father, you can't stand there and——'

'Now cool down, Harry. Cool down. I wasn't accusing anybody of anything. All I was doing was pointing out that a marriage is something only two people besides God know about—and God usually keeps the confidence.' He paused. 'In that connection, Harry, uh, have you tried praying?'

'Yes. I prayed. Yes.'

'It didn't do any good?'

'No.'

Edwin C. Harmey sighed. Down below, thousands of men strained under loads, made hose connections, moved throttles, threw switches, hacked and picked and hammered, and grumbled a great deal, sweating hot in the sun; but up here, these two stood motionless.

'Let me put it this way: She's my daughter, and you must admit that I have some right to say something about it?'

'Yes, sure. Of course you have.'

'Well then, let me put it this way—admitting always that I can't know the real causes—admitting that, you understand? Well, here it is: She's lived with you in your place, so why don't you come and live with her in her place? Is that too much to ask?'

Harry stared up the Cut.

'Is it?'

Harry stared up the Cut. He shook his head. 'Yes, I'm afraid it is, Mr Harmey.'

'Um. Well, I thought I ought to bring that point up, anyway. I just thought—— Harrumph! Well, it's been most interesting, Harry. Most interesting. All this you've told me about the clever way they get rid of all the dirt, and all that. Shall we, harrumph, shall we be getting down again?'

'All right' said Harry.

338

Phil had not undressed, only taken her shoes off. She lay listening to Mother and Father go out, and she heard the screen door slam and heard the scree of carriage wheels, the crack of a whip. Harry was not with them. He had gone out immediately after dinner, excusing himself, disregarding Father's hurt look. Father did not understand Harry. Father could not understand (Phil couldn't either, but it was so like Harry!) a man who would conscientiously go about some extra after-hours non-paid-for work when he had a chance to meet, socially, his high boss. Neither Harry nor Father had talked much about their day, except that Father had repeatedly exclaimed upon what he called Harry's grasp of the situation. All the same, underneath their talk, Father's talk for the most part, Phil had read a clear report of what happened. Father had offered Harry a job, probably a mighty good one too, and Harry had turned it down.

Phil snickered into her pillow. Perversely, forgetting all the times she had upbraided him for this very stubbornness, she felt like cheering Harry. Bless him, he wasn't afraid of them! She had never liked Mother, and just now she felt that she didn't even like Father very much—or at any rate, didn't admire him as fervently as she had. Father was used to getting his way. He was hurt now, his pride was hurt. And on top of it all, Harry had not only turned down the offer of a job—Phil was sure of this, *sure* of it!—but he had politely refused to let his work slide in order to go out and meet Colonel Goethals. Father had shown no anger: here was the very proof of Harry's victory. Father had simply looked hurt, and very, very puzzled. And Harry had made excuses and waved aside his dessert and said good night.

And Father had stared after him, baffled.

While Mother had looked this way and that, shaking her head, clucking her tongue. Mother and her spring cleaning!

Phil slipped off the bed. It was their own bed, which Mother and Father were using. She glided out to the porch, where the borrowed Murphy bed had already been lowered: Harry had done this chore, laughing, because Célestine was afraid to go near the contraption. Phil sat on the edge of the Murphy bed, knowing that she could not be seen through the screens, and watched the carriage depart. Lights were popping up in windows.

A headache, she'd explained. Father, who could sometimes be nasty about such excuses, had gravely acceded to her request. Mother, aflutter, had got her aside after dinner and asked why she hadn't told her. 'I hadn't expected it until next week' Phil had coldly replied. She could not remember ever telling Mother, outright, that she had the curse. Mother thought it was a dirty word. The nearest Mother ever came to it, whispering, was That; and she hated to say even that.

The truth was, Phil didn't have the curse. She hadn't had it for two days.

When the carriage had gone she hurried back to the bedroom in her stockinged feet, and got her shoes, and put them on, trembling. Lacing up shoes took such a long time! She went to her dressing table. She did not dare to turn on the light, but there was light enough from the Caseys' windows to show her her face; and she patted on the tiniest film of rice powder. She touched her hair in places, cocking her head now this way and now that. She rose, and in the darkness with thumbs and forefingers daintily lifted the shirtwaist out from her breasts, to which it had damply clung. She must have looked a fright. . . . She counted the money Father had slipped her. She knew that there were ten bills, but she counted them all the same. One hundred dollars. Would he still be angry? She'd tried to get this money for him, but at the bank they had said that while her securities appeared to be all right it would be necessary to send certain cablegrams to New York; and, panicky, she'd snatched the securities and run out. How did she know what that might mean, sending a cablegram to New York? To the bank there, or to the place in Wall Street or wherever it was, or would it be to her father? She'd taken them back, breathing 'Oh, never mind' as haughtily as she could.

He had wanted a hundred dollars, and he'd been very angry when she said she didn't have anything, and she would have explained to him—except that Harry had come in just then. Harry had been angry too, she didn't know why. She had sent Célestine after Ward with what money she did happen to have—twenty dollars. Was he angry, still? She had a hundred dollars now. Ten ten-dollar bills. If she gave him that, and laughed, and apologized glibly for having kept him waiting, and assured him that she'd never questioned his integrity . . . There was where the trouble was! He'd stormed that she was questioning his integrity. Probably he would kill a man who questioned that; and for a little while, just before Harry came, she had been afraid that he'd kill her: there had been clear straight murder in his eyes.

But now it would be all right. She had a hundred dollars in her pocketbook. A hundred dollars and the key. And if it was all right, she would stay in Panama. She was more than half inclined to stay anyway. Mother and her spring cleaning! Father and his sad stabbed look! Father had looked, for a little while there tonight at dinner, like a fish flipped into a boat and not understanding why there was no water: his eyes had looked that way, uncomprehending fish eyes.

Of course it would be all right! She counted the money again. Ten of them. She giggled a little. After all, he had asked for only one hundred, and she'd already given him twenty. She might need some excuse, some explanation, while she was accompanying Mother and Father back across the Isthmus to the ship at Cristobal. She'd have to be able at least to *offer* to spend something. She peeled off one of the tens and thrust it into a pile of corset covers where she was sure she could find it afterward. Everything was so topsy-turvy with Father and Mother here! She closed her pocketbook and tried to see herself in the mirror again, but the Caseys had pulled the shades down and the light was poor. She took an extra hanky. She knew she was sweating on the backs of her hands, on her face too. And she knew that she was trembling.

Halfway across the porch she paused. It was dark now, and she was safe going out the front way. All sorts of windows threw light, smeary at the close ones, sharp at those far away, but even the close ones were not very close. She drew a deep breath.

After all, a hundred dollars was what he'd said he needed, and she had given him twenty, and she had ninety now. She wouldn't dare take a coche down, and she could take one only part of the way back, and *he* could pay for that! She smiled in triumph at the thought.

He'd be so happy to know that she still loved him that he would be glad to pay for the coche.

He'd be so happy . . .

She would tell him about how for a little while she had thought of going away, going back home, and about how her parents were here now and visiting Colonel and Mrs Goethals, the new chairman—oh, yes, and she'd warn him that she had very little time, for she'd have to hurry back, she'd have to fairly *rush* back! And when she showed him that she still loved him and trusted him and didn't believe any of the stories that were told about him, he'd look at her and smile, and he'd put his arms around her, and she would whisper that after all they had *very* little time, no more than a few minutes practically, because she *had* to get back.

She giggled. She went to the bedroom and thrust another ten-dollar bill among the corset covers.

Before she came to the Calle de San Martin she slowed her walk. She glanced casually around, her head high. She drifted into the Calle de San Martin; but once there, among the shadows, she ran.

341

The alley door was always unlatched. Ward used to say that he liked to hear people come up. He used to say that he could tell from the steps, right off, whether it was friend or enemy. Not that he cared, he'd add.

Well, he wouldn't hear her this time. She was a cat.

He was there, too. She saw a light under the door. She crept up, laughing soundlessly. On the landing, her ear against the door, she listened a moment. After all, he might have a poker game, as he sometimes did. But there was no sound; and she smiled as she slipped her key into the lock and turned it.

'Wait a minute! Who is it?'

She threw the door open, smiling.

He wore that sleek silk dressing robe, mulberry in color, which she liked so much; and he wore the turkey-red slippers. But he did not look pantherine. He looked scared. He held a glass of brandy.

'*Who's here?*'

'Why, Phil, darling!' His voice was abnormally low. He put the glass down on a taboret and extended his arms and came toward her. 'Why,' still so very low! 'it's as though a dream had come true!'

'*Who's here?*'

Now he was against her, but she wriggled away from him and slipped inside the flat.

'Darling, you know how I'd hate to turn you away,' he whispered, and it was a whisper lower even than love demanded, 'but I expect some very important politicos. One of them's a cabinet minister. And while you know how I'd love to have you stay——'

'I'll find out!' she yelled.

He started toward her, but she was already running. The bed was empty, the glittery green snake crawled away from nothing into that hole in the ceiling. There was nobody behind the bed. But incense was burning in the tripoded basin.

'Now listen, I hate to have to——'

She ran to the green baize door, back of which he kept his wine and glasses. She kicked the door and then let it swing toward her, and she caught it.

Mavis simpered and twittered, her features jerking, her hair in disarray, while her breasts flopped this way and that, a couple of pendulous blobs no more accountable than her mouth. It was the first time Phil had seen Mavis's breasts. Mavis made inane small sounds.

Ward had grabbed Phil's arms from behind, his hands strong.

'All right,' scaldingly. 'I'm going out.'

342

The hands left her arms. She stepped away from the green baize door, which she permitted to close, so that she wouldn't have to see that naked squirming fool in there.

Ward made no attempt to stop her. He probably shrugged—it was the sort of thing he would do—and certainly he picked up his brandy.

'I just came to bring you something' she said from the doorway, and opened her pocketbook and put fingers over the money.

He was not so far away but that she could throw it into his face. And he was standing perfectly still.

She closed her pocketbook. She had decided not to throw the money.

'I just came to tell you, in case you're interested, that I'm leaving Panama tomorrow and have no intention of returning. Good-by.'

'Good-by' he said.

She slammed the door, her key still in it.

Harry went around to the side of the house before he went in, for he feared that the flushing of the toilet might wake somebody up. He did go to the bathroom, but he didn't snap on the light. He found the bottle of tincture of iodine by touch and took it into the kitchen, where he peeled off his coat and shirt and washed the slash on his forearm with plain water, keeping the faucet turned low. 'Sometime one of those sons of bitches is going to do it better than that, Kellems' he murmured. He couldn't see it well, and it didn't hurt now. But when he spilled iodine on it, *that* stung! It stung so hard that his tired heart leaped; and he held onto the edge of the sink for a moment, gritting his teeth.

On the way back through the hall he bumped a trunk. Oh? The Harmeys had left their only trunk on the ship. His hands went over familiar surfaces, finger-tipping each flamboyant label. They certainly plastered up your baggage, those hotels in Europe.

Well, that's it, he thought.

He knew that that was it when he reached the porch and stumbled softly over Phil's two suitcases. They were open. He could see Phil herself, lying on the Murphy. He could see her in the moonlight. The rains were late this year. . . . Sort of a pity that the last night should be in a borrowed bed, he thought. He knew perfectly well that she was awake. She lay motionless while he got out of his clothes and pulled the nightshirt over his head, and she didn't even stir or speak when he slipped in beside her. But he knew perfectly well that she was awake

343

21

THEY STOOD UP, all eight of them, and bowed ceremoniously, simpering, as he came in, and they said in unison, in a sort of chorus, falsetto, 'Good morning, dear boss.'

'You can go to blazes' he cried, sweeping past.

He paused before the door of the inner office.

'I'm sorry, Miss Wallace' he said.

He had not yet become accustomed—none of them had—to the presence of a woman in the office. Miss Wallace was not likely to be raped or insulted. She was a stenographer. She wore glasses and her hair was stuffed with rats and she certainly used some kind of powder on her face. She was no prude! She insisted upon being called Wally, and cried 'Oh, come on!' when anybody called her Miss Wallace, as everybody still did.

Now she dropped her eyes. Demure? She was about as demure as a mountain torrent.

'It's o.k., dear boss' she cooed.

'Well, you can go to *hell* then,' cried Harry, as they started to laugh; and it was with an effort of will that he refrained from slamming the door.

He threw himself into a swivel chair, which squeaked and swung. It was a big chair, and he did not fill it. Simpson had bulged and dripped over its edges, and for Simpson the chair had squealed on a less doleful note.

Who did they think he was? He had been acting head of the department for over a month, but everybody knew that a real head would come from Washington soon. Indeed such a head had come. He'd looked around, at Cristobal, at Colon, and refused to go further: he'd gone back, without even crossing the Isthmus to see what his office looked like. By this time, presumably, another executive was on his way. Meanwhile Harry did the work.

Well, the work was all right, though it involved more paper than he had expected: sometimes he wondered, as he checked and rechecked and signed and committed and requisitioned and denied, how Simpson had been able to do this and still do all that he did outside. He,

Harry, could do the work. Could he do the rest, too? That's what he was worried about.

And those people outside, he knew they weren't really laughing at him, but all the same . . . Just because three days ago a new typist coming in had forced Harry into Simpson's office—*that* did not mean he was trying to *be* Simpson! And if they thought it did——

Or was he too stewy? A month? Christ! He'd gone six months without Phil and never felt this way! No Dorothy Vernon of Haddon Hall, either. No more of those before-dinner romps. Amazing, the difference one pug dog could make. Sometimes he thought he missed Dotty more than he missed his wife. It was gloomy in the house now, gloomier than it had been when Phil was in the States the previous time. Then he had expected her back almost any time. Now he knew that she wasn't coming back. They were calling it a visit, a vacation; but that was a sop to respectability. Phil couldn't face the actual blunt fact that she had left him. Somehow that wasn't a decent thing to do. She had taken the prints and pillows and throw-over, but she'd left the novels —she'd finished them anyway, or at least read enough to know that she wasn't interested—and she had left the piano. She attached a great deal of significance to the leaving of the piano. 'Nobody who knows me will figure that I'd ever be apart from my piano very long. I'll send for it later—when people have sort of, well, gotten used to the idea.' But the piano remained closed, and it was gloomy in the house. He had tried some of the books, but without interest. Célestine irritated him. He had quietly instituted a search for Rosina, immediately after Phil departed with her parents, but he'd learned through Tranquilina, the Gorgases' maid, that Rosina was contentedly employed by eight bachelors who loved her and spoiled her, out at Culebra. She was being absurdly overpaid. It would be mean to lure her away.

Célestine, that ungainly hulk, that moist black cloud, kept the place reasonably clean, and she did make swell coffee. No other good thing could be said for her. She was sullen and uncertain of temper. She was ugly. She was either stupid or contrary: no matter what he said to her, she answered 'Monsieur?' and went on doing whatever she pleased. Harry had picked up a little French from Madeline and Papa Desmoulins, and, what was more to the point, he had picked up a little of the Martinique patois from workers along the Line; but he was never able to make Célestine understand or admit that she understood a word. Yes, she did make good coffee; but her cooking was bad. She fried everything, using too much grease. She put onions into everything, absolutely everything. Harry had once liked onions. He would never like them again. Worst of all was her stink. She must have used all her wages on French perfumery, or else she had brought a great supply with her from Martinique, where it was duty-free. She was drenched in it, at all hours. Very strong stuff, too. The scent did not drown her natural nigger sweat, but rather combined with this; and the combination was bad.

Yes, it was much harder this time. He had more work, which helped; but it was harder in every other way. He felt cheap and petty when he told those who asked about her that his wife was only taking a vacation. He knew perfectly well that she wouldn't come back; and sooner or later he would have to admit this; but she'd asked him to say the lie for her sake, and so of course he did. Sooner or later he would have to give up the house—there was a waiting list for married quarters —and go to live in a flat in town or else team up with some bachelors. He had hundreds of acquaintances; but since the dissolution of the D.M.s he was no longer intimate with any group, and the thought of dormitory life, these days, dismayed him. They were all such *kids!* He liked them, but they were just youngsters.

He sighed, and shouted for Burt Waterman.

'Hello, Giants.'

'Hello, Cubs.'

'You don't have to yell like that, you know. The push button's still working.'

'I always forget about it. Listen, what's the matter with that bunch out there? What do they think's so funny?'

'Can't you take a little kidding?' Burt sat on the desk. After five months in Panama he was virtually a veteran. 'They just think they're being clever, that's all. They'll get over it.'

'I hope they don't think that just because I moved in here——'

'Don't be crazy! They're just trying to have as much frolic as possible before the real boss comes along. They all hope he'll get shipwrecked on the way. *You* would be the boss, full-time, if they had anything to say about it. If this was like one of those volunteer regiments in the Civil War my old man used to tell me about, where the soldiers just got together and elected a colonel and announced that they wouldn't serve under anybody else—so that the government practically had to give him his commission—well, if this department was like that, you'd be elected unanimously, Harry.'

'You really think so?'

'I know so! Don't worry about them out there. They love you. But

I'll tell you somebody that doesn't love you.' He was looking hard at Harry. 'That man Ward Wright was here this morning.'

'What did he want?'

'You. He wouldn't say what for. Just that he wanted to see you personally. I don't like that man, Harry.'

'Neither do I. Never have.'

'Any idea what he wants?'

'Not the slightest. But I told him five-six weeks ago that I didn't want to see his face around my house again, and I suppose he realizes that I meant it, and he figures that if he wants to see me he'd better come here.'

'I still don't like it. That business at Ralston's Ritz the other night couldn't have made him feel any pleasanter toward you.'

'He could have hit me then if he'd wanted to.'

'Don't get it into your head that it was physical fear that held him back. That man may be a worm, but he's no coward! The reason he didn't light into you at Ralston's was because there were too many men around who knew you and liked you, and if he'd started to beat you up they'd have all piled on him. Well, he's no Samson, and if a whole crowd jumps on him he's going to get mauled. He knew that. And that was the only reason he turned away.'

The episode at Ralston's Ritz, two nights before, had been brief but dramatic. Ward Wright had been there, at the bar. Harry had been there too—not snooping, just having a few drinks before dinner: he was dropping into bars more often, now that he was alone. Ralston's had been crowded and noisy, and nobody had noticed Lemming's entrance. The first thing anybody knew, Lemming had whirled Wright around, and with his glasses in his left hand, and trembling all over, his long slab-sided face glittering with sweat, was shrieking all manner of curses at the soldier of fortune. The only clear part—and this had been perfectly clear—was that he was accusing Ward Wright of getting Mrs Lemming in a family way.

Lemming had interrupted himself passionately to punch Ward Wright high on the left cheekbone, a blow to which Wright easily rolled his head. Wright, utterly cool, had put his highball on the bar. The rest had been faster than any eye in that crowded place could follow. The only thing which had saved Lemming from falling was the fact that he ran or stumbled backward toward the street. Nearsighted, gasping, sobbing, he had tried to swing punches; but Wright was a pugilistic machine, hitting straight and sure, right, left, right, his fists splop-splopping into Lemming's face. Near the end of the bar, where

Harry stood, Lemming had tried to make a stand, and Wright had caught his chin with a clean cross. Lemming had whammed back against the doors, which swung open and let him fall out. Wright had started out after him—and Harry had stepped in the way.

'All right, he's had enough!'

'I'll kill the God-damn son of a bitch!'

'That's just what you will do if you hit him any more.'

'I'm going to tear him to pieces!'

'No you're not. Not unless you want to take me on first.'

Ward Wright had turned away, and Harry had gone outside to help the prostrate Lemming. Harry smiled a little now, when he remembered it. That made twice that Harry had faced the celebrated fighter down. This second time must have been the more bitter, because of the audience; but the first time could scarcely have been any fun for Wright. Harry had expected to be shot then, at the least to be beaten. He still couldn't see why Wright had tamely walked away. Because the scene occurred in Harry's own house? But Harry would gladly have stepped outside. Because Phil was in the next room, had until a moment earlier been in the parlor with them? Why should he consider Phil's feelings? And now the same thing had happened again, with the same result; and as Burt pointed out, it wasn't going to make Ward Wright love him any more.

'I tell you it hurts his prestige, and he can't afford that. He'll figure he has to make it up. It'll have to be something public, too. Nothing sneaky. He's just got to recover face, as the Chinks would say.'

He slipped open a drawer. 'You still got that—yes, I see you have.' He tapped Simpson's pistol, the long flat shiny revolver. Simpson had not had it with him that fatal day in Cristobal. Harry had inherited it along with the desk. 'Wouldn't be a bad idea if you carried that around, Harry.'

'Oh, don't be dippy!'

'Don't you be dippy! Trouble is, you've got to thinking that man's all bark and no bite. He can bite when he thinks he has to. You saw for yourself what he did to Lemming.'

'Yes.'

Harry had got Lemming into a coche. The man's eyes were closed, his broken lips were swelling, a cut had been opened over his left eye, and blood streamed from this; probably his nose was broken; Harry picked a tooth from the bloody pulp at his lips. It had been raining, and Harry tried to wipe the man's face with rain water as they started for Ancon, hoping to make him a little less hideous. Once Lemming had opened an eye and had seen Harry in the light of an arc. He had laughed sloppily, gurgling.

'You, eh? Of all persons, *you!*'

'Take it easy. We'll be there soon.'

'Of all the guys in the world! Taking me back to my wife, eh? My nice faithful wife! Well, I'll slug her when I get there.'

Mavis had been weeping. There were half-filled suitcases everywhere.

'Oh, has he—— What's happened?'

'Hello, you whore' Lemming had said, and swung a wide wild punch which Harry caught from behind.

Harry had hustled him to a couch, had held him there.

'I'm wrong. You're not a whore. Whores get paid for it.'

'Shut up' Harry had muttered.

'Coming from *you*, Kellems, that's pretty comical!'

Harry had sent Mavis out into the rain with a note to a friend, a physician; and not until morphine had been injected into Lemming's blood stream had Harry dared to leave.

'I'll sit here with him, if you want, and you can go up to my house. I don't like to think of you staying here.'

'No, no! I'll be all right. He'll get a good sleep and he'll be all right in the morning. We're leaving tomorrow anyway.'

'You're sure you won't——'

'No, thank you so much! You've been very kind. Much kinder than I d-deserve. Thank you, Harry. You go, please.'

Harry said now, his feet on the desk: 'You know, I can't understand it either way. Can't understand in the first place what he saw in her. How'd he ever manage to *get* there? How'd he keep her *still* long enough? And then, what did she see in him? He's good-looking enough, in a cheap theatrical way, but any woman in her right mind could see that he's three cuts below a rattlesnake as far as decency and dependability are concerned. He's nothing but an animated tailor's dummy with a reputation that's probably built on lies from beginning to end.'

'Now, that's just what I wish you wouldn't think, Harry! That's just what I'm afraid of! If you're going to underrate this man, you might find yourself doing what Lemming did and slamming your mouth against his knuckles. I tell you he's dangerous! And remember, he was here looking for you a little while ago and wouldn't say what his business was. Why, I shouldn't be surprised if——'

Miss Wallace opened the door and stuck her head in.

'Man to see you, Mr Kellems. Tall man with a mustache.'

'All right' Harry said, not moving.

Burt Waterman sprang to the desk, pulled open a drawer, took out Simpson's old revolver and held this beneath his coat.

'Show him in' he said.

Arthur Price, immaculate in white pongee, a silk umbrella hooked over his arm by its Malacca crook, blinked through gold-rimmed glasses. Clumsy, scarecrow-thin, he yet had the grace of his caste: he was every inch Boston.

'I d-do hope I'm not intruding?'

'Hello, Art. Not at all. Burt and I were just breaking up anyway.' Harry gave a malicious side glance at Burt, who held the pistol under his coat. 'Meet Mr Waterman. Burt, this is Dr Price.'

'How do you do, Mr Waterman,' with extended hand.

Burt somehow got his hand out: he was pressing his left arm against the pistol under his coat, holding it up that way.

'Glad to meet you, Doctor. Well, you'll keep in mind what we were talking about anyway, won't you, Harry?'

'Sure' drawled Harry. He had not lowered his feet. He nodded to a pile of reports. 'I wish you'd take those out, Burt, and look them over.'

It took some doing. Burt slipped his right hand back under his coat to catch the pistol, and he picked up the reports with his left hand. He manipulated the door with his feet.

'Glad to have met you, Doctor.'

'Don't fall down, Jesse James' Harry called. 'Sit yourself, Art. Glad to see you. How's Madeline?'

'Thank you. Why, she's all right. A little worried.'

'Would you say that you were engaged?'

'Not exactly, though I k-keep on hoping. I would say, though, that I think you're t-taking it like a gentleman.'

'Well, what else can I do?' Harry shrugged. 'I'm not going to pretend I'm happy. I go around all day feeling sorry for myself.'

'Nobody would know it.'

'That's good. You say she's worried? Well, can I do anything?'

'Yes' said Art Price. He hooked his umbrella over the back of the chair and spread his feet and put a hand on each bony knee. 'She's worried about two things, and they both involve this man Ward Wright.'

Harry sighed. He kicked a drawer and made himself swing half around; then he put a foot on the floor and swung himself back.

'This chair' he said sententiously 'is like an old war horse, and the knight who always rode it to battle is killed, and there's just a squire riding it home now. The chair can't get used to that. See?' He shook himself, wriggled. 'I'm not big enough for it.'

'What the deuce are you talking about?'

'Why, Ward Wright.'

'Oh yes. You mean that was Mr Simpson's chair?'

'Uh-huh.'

'You really b-believe that he was k-killed, Harry?'

'There isn't any doubt of it. Any more than there is any doubt that the investigating board turned in the only possible report—that it was an accident. Of course he was killed! I don't know who did it *directly*, and I never will. But I know who's *really* responsible, and I think I said so at the time.'

'You did. And you added that you'd get the son of a bitch if it took the rest of your life.'

'Sometimes I'm very outspoken.'

'Your w-words were w-widely quoted, too.'

'And el capitan resented them, eh? Well, it was nothing to what I told him later, when I came home and found him with my wife.'

Price's eyes popped half out of his head, and he slid to the edge of his chair.

'I figured it was a refinement of his usual method. And smart. He couldn't very well hold a poker game in the middle of the afternoon. So he dropped in on the Kellemses. I was feeling pretty bitter, and I didn't mince words, even though my wife was there.' Harry shrugged. 'Well, he backed out.'

Art Price took his glasses off and wiped them. He kept looking at them, wiping them.

'Harry, you should be more careful. There's something s-sinister about that man.'

'There's nothing sinister about him at all. He just tries to make himself look that way and sound that way. How's Papa?'

'That's one of the things Madeline is worried about.'

'Yes. I've known that for a long while. And I've worried about it too. He's around a lot, is he?'

'Yes, and it's n-not j-just that. It's the *intensity* of the man while he t-t-talks to P-Papa. Do you know what he's up to?'

'I wish I did,' morosely. 'The old man is—well, you're a doctor. Can't you certify he's crazy and have him sent away?'

'Then how would Madeline live?' Art Price asked quietly.

'Well, I have a little put aside. . . . But you wouldn't want that, I suppose. But *you* must have some dough, Art?'

'I have. But you know Madeline.'

'Um. But have you thought about it anyway?'

'Yes, I have. But he lives in the Republic of Panama, and an American physician would have no s-say in the matter. It would need two Panamanian physicians, and I doubt that you could find two Panamanian physicians who would testify that he's d-dotty. To be honest about it, I don't think I could certify to that myself. N-Not in the sense we're talking about.'

'So that brings us back to Ward Wright. You know, Art, I'm getting tired of that man. Some one of these days I'm going to lose my temper and walk right up to him and bust his nose.'

Price shook his head. 'He'd kill you, Harry.'

'Everybody's so sure of that! He hasn't killed me yet! He's known for a long while that I'm trying to get him run out. He knows what I think of him. I've told him so. Well, where's your terrible murderer? I'm still alive.'

'That's j-just what Madeline is worried about. That you don't t-take him seriously enough.'

'I take him seriously' Harry answered. 'Listen, Art, I'm not as dim-witted as I seem. I haven't been able to get anything against the man by the methods Simpson used. I think Simpson had it, or almost had it. But I can't seem to. I'm not as clever as he was. I told you I couldn't fill this chair.' He wriggled; the chair squealed. 'But I've got this one important thing on my side: Wright's let himself hate me. When a man gets that way he's likely to do something wrong. I tell everybody, every time the subject comes up, that I think Ward Wright is a strutting fool. I say he's an overinflated windbag. I say he's making a lot of noise about himself and hasn't got anything back of it. He doesn't like that.'

'N-Naturally!'

'He doesn't like it. He's getting sore. Well, he's been sore at me for a long while, as far as that goes, but he's getting really sore now. He knows I'm after him. He's afraid to move.'

'Yes. You d-do sort of investigate him, d-don't you?'

'That's a nice quiet Boston way of putting it. Investigate him? Why, I'm around him all the time! I do everything but sleep with him' said Harry 'and *that*, of course, seems to have been a privilege reserved for somebody else.'

Price sat aghast. He was afraid to move or to say anything.

352

'I hope I'm not spilling any secrets' Harry said quickly. 'It's certainly all over town by this time!'

'W-Well . . .'

'Lemming himself yelled it out, again and again, in front of a crowd the other night.'

'Oh yes, of course. Yes. I heard about that.'

'The sort of thing Wright would do' Harry said. 'Pick on some flighty married woman and break up what I suppose was a perfectly good home. I knew the Lemmings, both of them. I never cared much for them, as far as that goes, but what happened is going to make me even more eager to step on that insect. They might have been o.k. For all we know they were happy. And our great big brave gilded hero comes along and lures that little giggler into his bedroom. Oh, swell work! Dashing, wot?'

Art Price wiped and wiped his glasses. 'Calling him names isn't going to solve the problem, Harry.'

'How do you know it isn't? He's just the kind of guy who can't endure being called names and being laughed at. I laugh at him every time I get the chance. As publicly as I can. Well, he can't afford to let that go on. As Burt Waterman was saying, just before you came in —Burt said the man's prestige is the most important element in his business. If he loses that, he loses everything. And he *will* lose it, if I keep picking on him!'

'There's something in what you say. But have you thought of what he might do?'

'Sure. He might kill me. All right, he's got two ways of doing that. One is the way he likes to work—through some catspaw. That wouldn't be easy, now. He could arrange the murder of a Negro who was going to squeal. But that was back in the old days, when things were not so well organized, and when people here didn't know much about him. He could arrange to have a little Panamanian petty criminal stabbed in an alley. Never mind how I happen to know these things! He could even arrange to have somebody arrange with somebody to have a wild Martinique nigger pull those pins out and let Simpson fall off a ship. But would getting a man to kill me be such an easy job?'

Art Price put his glasses back on and stared and stared. 'He c-could fix it to l-l-look l-like an accident.'

'He could, that's true, and that's what I'm most afraid of.' Harry had not forgotten the rock which had tumbled from a rockless summit.

'And that's one reason why I hope to get him so riled that he'll try to do it himself. That's what I've been working for.'

Dr Arthur Price rose, unfolding too many joints, like a crane or a camel. He flopped his arms. He was a gentle person, and a very good person, not too much of a snob, intelligent and kind; but it came to him now that his must have been a cloistered life. He had thought that men who talked about slaughter as calmly as that were vicious men, or else fools. Harry Kellems certainly was not vicious. Was he a fool? Art Price wandered to the window, outside of which a handsome carriage was drawing up.

'Harry, you dumfound me. Do you really mean to say that you are trying to commit suicide?'

'Certainly not! I—I'm pretty miserable nowadays, I won't deny it, and I guess you know the reason. But I have no more intention of pushing my back into a knife than I have of flying to the moon. I'd much rather be alive than dead! But there's the situation. If he gets sore enough and loses his head and comes for me—well, he'll probably kill me. Everybody says he's a wonderful shot. My wife even told me—she was on the same ship with him when she first came down here—she told me about how one time on the afterdeck, with the ship rolling, this man Wright pulled out a revolver and without even seeming to take aim knocked off five sea gulls on the wing—in five cracks. Oh, I guess he's pretty good! But miracles can happen, and I'm praying for a miracle. And if he does get me, what does that get *him*? You've heard about John Brown's body, haven't you? Well, I've got no more desire to be a martyr than you or anybody else has. But there you are. If he does kill me himself, or even if he does it through somebody else—as long as I'm openly and unquestionably murdered—then you know how long Ward Wright will be allowed to stay on this Isthmus, don't you? I don't want to sound stuck-up, Art. I don't want you to get the idea that I think I'm a great man. I don't think that! But I mean it in all honesty and humility when I say that apparently a hell of a lot of other guys here *do* think so. Ward Wright won't kill me unless he loses his head—and if he loses his head I've got him licked.'

After a while Art Price said soberly: 'The funny part about all this is that you m-mean it. I think I'd better do some praying myself—for that miracle.'

'To a Unitarian God?'

'I'm not a particularly religious man, but as far as I can see, a Unitarian God would be just about the same as any other.'

'Say, I'm sorry! I was just trying to——'

354

'That's all right. I knew you were just joshing. No doubt when I've reported all this to Madeline she'll pray to a Roman Catholic God. And it'll come out the same, one way or the other. B-But do try to be careful, Harry. I mean, just for me, if for nobody else.'

Harry smiled, leaning across the desk. 'Sure. I understand. And don't think I'm not scared. I'm scared of standing up to a fight, if it ever comes, but I'm even more scared that it won't come and that I'll just stop living some time without ever having known when I died. That's what it amounts to.'

Harry leaned back. He put his feet up on the desk again.

'You tell Madeline that. As nicely as you can. Tell her all I can do is wait.'

'And if he——'

'If he stays away from me, then *he* might win. If he comes to me—*I'll* win.'

The door was opened.

'May I come in?' asked Ward Wright.

He looked perfect. His shoulders were back, his eyebrows were quizzically high, his suit hung on him without a wrinkle. His oyster-colored Ecuadorian hat was jauntily tilted. His mustache was trimmed to the last millimeter. He leaned upon a gold-headed umbrella. Oh, *he* was fine! Harry started to laugh.

Harry laughed and laughed, rollicking in the great creaking chair. His feet came down, and he swirled, laughing. He thumped his chest while he leaned far over.

'Don't hurt yourself' Ward Wright said coldly.

Art Price started: 'Harry, do you think I ought to get you——'

'Ugh-ugh-ugh-ooooo-AH!' Turning, he gurgled: 'I'll be all—all right—in a—minute.' Turned, he looked at Ward Wright; and he started to laugh again. Tears streamed down his cheeks.

Ward Wright looked at Art and said with his lips: 'Hysterical?' 'Well, I should certainly think so' Art Price said sharply, aloud. Harry rocked back and forth, trying to control himself, making flappy signs with his hands to beg that they excuse him for a moment.

'I—I'm very sorry' Harry gasped at last. He looked at Art. 'It isn't so much what I just told you—and—and him doing this up-popped-the-devil act so nicely.' He mopped his face with a handkerchief. 'It isn't that so much—though God knows *he's* funny enough!' He waved a hand to indicate Ward Wright. 'But it—it's his *escort!*' And Harry started to laugh again.

There they were, not actually in the doorway but just behind it, in the big office, tense, ready, all eight of them, determined that their boss should not be injured. Burt Waterman was the nearest, and he held Simpson's long-barreled shiny revolver. The others were not so well armed, but they'd done the best they could. Joe Saltis had an umbrella stand gripped in both hands. Georgie Law and young Horace had straight-backed chairs. They all had something. Even Miss Wallace held a huge glass paperweight—and she had it drawn back too, ready to throw.

'Well, I'll be pushed off a cliff' muttered Ward Wright. He lifted his eyebrows again, the quizzical lift, as he faced Harry. 'Your help protects you well, I see.'

'I think' Harry said solemnly, still trying to control his laughter, 'that it's the funniest thing I ever saw. You're funny enough, el capitan. But look at *them!*'

'They make me positively uneasy' Ward Wright drawled, uncertain of himself. 'Is this the routine here?'

'No, this is special for you, Captain. You should feel honored.' Harry went to the doorway. 'Shoo-fly, darlings. Go back to work. The battle's over, and everybody won, so go back to work.'

Burt Waterman started seriously: 'Now wait a minute, Harry——'

'It'll be all right. I'm sure Captain Wright will agree not to assassinate me right now, anyway. Won't you, Captain?'

He closed the door. He wiped his face again. Trying not to laugh, he went back of his desk.

'What was it you wanted, Captain?'

'Well, frankly, I was a bit worried about walking into the lair of such a fire-eater. But I got my courage up——'

'This is a public office, and you have a perfect right to come here if you have any legitimate business. It's not my home. And I'm not asking you to sit down. You know Dr Price, of course?'

'Yes, I know Dr Price.'

'Well, all right. Get your dignity together and tell me what you came here for. Should Dr Price leave?'

'It's not necessary. In fact, what I came here for doesn't need all this—well, this display of militarism. I'm sure I just dropped in in a friendly sort of way.'

'Of course, Captain. But the point is, you did come here. I didn't go to *you.*'

'Why, that's perfectly true. And what I came here for was to ask you if you wouldn't care to take a ride with me.'

'Eh?'

Wright said rapidly to Art Price: 'I'm sorry I can't include you in the invitation, Doctor. But four is all the carriage can accommodate, and Dr Obarrio and Senator Gomez are already there. You don't mind?'

'Oh, stop being fancy!' snapped Art Price. 'What are you doing?'

'Why, I was simply asking Mr Kellems if he wouldn't care to take a ride with us. With Dr Obarrio and Senator Gomez and me.' He nodded affably and turned to Harry. 'What do you think?'

'Of course he won't!' Art cried.

'Well, let's take a look' said Harry. 'If it's a nice comfortable carriage, I might.' He went to the window. Yes, it was a nice comfortable carriage. Indeed it was something special in the way of carriages, and belonged, obviously, to somebody rich. Dr Jose Obarrio and Senator Gomez, impeccably dressed, sat in back.

Senator Gomez, Harry knew only as a politico who spoke pretty good English and was at all times eager to be friendly with Americans. He was a hearty man, and Harry was inclined to distrust hearty men; but he knew nothing wrong about Senator Gomez. Dr Obarrio, Harry knew fairly well and admired. Harry had met him several times at Sir Claude Mallet's house—had been introduced to him, indeed, by Lord Chudit. Dr Obarrio had spent a considerable part of his life in Paris and London. His English was flawless, as were his manners. A scholar, he was a bit haughty, but unmeaningly so: it was natural to him. He was a brother or perhaps a cousin of Lady Mallet, herself an Obarrio.

'The company would seem satisfactory?'

'The company is quite satisfactory' Harry said, and went over and got his hat and umbrella. 'All right, Captain.'

Art Price waved his arms, a stork flip-flapping its wings.

'See here, Harry, you can't do this!'

'I don't know why not' said Harry. 'It was his bet and he made it, and now it's up to me to call. All right, Captain.'

Ward Wright, brushing back his mustache first with this thumbnail and then with that, looked almost affectionately at Harry.

'Will you promise me safe-conduct through your French Revolutionary mob out there?'

'Don't worry about them' said Harry. 'Come on.'

Madeline stood straight, with her arms at her sides but with her hands turned palms up.

'But didn't you do *anything*? Didn't you try to *stop* him?'

357

'I'm sorry. I argued with him all I could. But—you know Harry.'

'But even then you could have chased them! You could have got a carriage and gone after them, instead of coming here!'

'There wasn't a hack to be had. It started to rain right then. I kept hanging onto Harry's sleeve, and I kept begging him not to go, but he'd smile at me—you know that way he smiles.'

'Yes.'

'I don't see what else I could have done. I thought of following them. I'd thought of that even before I got outside. But the rain came, and everybody ducked, and there I was.'

'We must do something now! Let us get a coche and go out and ask where they went! People as prominent as that——'

'I'll do it, if you want. You know I'll do anything you want. But I think that by now——'

Stiff-legged, she almost fell against him; and he put his arms out and caught her. She sobbed and sobbed against his breast. She sobbed for a long while. When she stopped sobbing she still stood close to him, but she did not put her arms up. She held her face against him.

'Do you think he's dead?'

'No, I don't think he's dead. I don't think he'd have gone if he thought he was going to be k-killed.'

'It might be a duello.'

'I have more respect for Harry's intelligence than to think he'd let himself get caught in anything like that. No, he's not dead. He's finding out something. He was *happy* when el capitan came! He was actually *p-pleased* to see the man!'

She stood there, not moving, leaning her head against him but not otherwise pressing him.

'If he is dead, Arthur, I won't marry you.'

'There, there, dear.'

'I haven't been very kind to you, Arthur. You have been kind to me, and I haven't been very kind to you.'

'Well, we've had all this over, before. You know how I feel.'

'If he is dead, Arthur, I won't marry you.'

She took her head away from his chest, but she didn't lift her face, and she turned deliberately and walked away and sat in a chair and put her feet together and put her hands in her lap.

'You go and look, Arthur, please. Try to learn what happened. If he is dead——'

'Are you sure you're all right? Should I stay here, or maybe try to get somebody to come in and s-sit with you?'

'No. You go, Arthur. Please.'

'Madeline dear, maybe I ought to get somebody to——'

'Please go, Arthur. You have been very kind. And I have not been kind. I—I am sorry, Arthur.'

'Madeline dear, I'll do anything—anything under the sun——'

'Please go.'

22

WHEN HENRY MORGAN'S bearded cutthroats took it, back in sixteen-something, it was a pearl of great price, both in age and importance the first city of continental America. Morgan's men had lingered several weeks, torturing priests in order to learn the whereabouts of treasure. Oddly enough, they stayed sober. The artful Henry had told them that all the wine in Panama was poisoned; and they were so tired from battling the Chagres, hacking their way through the jungle, and at last conquering the Spaniards, that they believed him! It probably wasn't Morgan and his anything-but-merry men who set the city afire, the third day. *They* would have preferred to hold it for ransom. It probably was the Spaniards themselves; or perhaps it was an accident. At any rate, when at last the buccaneers marched off, driving a hundred and seventy-five pack animals that staggered under bullion and church ornaments, there wasn't enough left of Panama to bother about. It was rebuilt not on the same site but five miles nearer the bay. And the jungle took charge of the ruins—the jungle, the lizards, the snakes, and the monkeys and bright-tailed screeching birds.

Panama Viejo was it official name: that is, Old Panama. The Panamanians themselves had never displayed interest in it. More than a few Frenchmen, some archeologists, most mere sight-seers, had poked around the site, loosening the jungle's grip, peeling it back off a few of the grander buildings. They did little more than this, however. Now all that was visible of the Jewel of the West were some shaggy vine-draped towers and walls, parts, dimly glimpsed, of the cathedral and the San Jose monastery. If you knew where to look, though, there were still plenty of other buildings, blackened piles of emptiness, their steps and floors untrod by human feet since the buccaneers went swaggering away. It was to one of these that the party repaired after quitting the carriage—Gomez first, then Wright, then Harry, with Dr Obarrio in the rear: they were obliged to walk single-file along a path not easily followed. Harry heard the carriage being driven away. Nobody said anything. Nobody had said anything all the way from the city.

Gomez stopped. 'Señores, we are here' he announced, bobbing. He was a short stout man, very self-important, just now very excited too. He might have been a Boniface welcoming a party of distinguished travelers.

From the outside it was impossible to guess what this place had been. The lichened walls were shapeless now; the doorway was merely square; the windows were clogged with vines. Not a military building, certainly, nor a church. Call it a countinghouse; or perhaps it had been a grand private residence from which all ornamentation had long ago been stripped.

Harry turned. He had little faith in Senator Gomez, though the man was ambitious and made much of his fondness for Americans; but he was confident that Ward Wright would not lead his dearest enemy to peril in so public a manner; and he believed in the tall saturnine Obarrio.

'Would it be too much to ask what this is all about, Doctor?'

'It will be safe,' without expression. 'You can go in.'

'It isn't so much a matter of its being safe——'

'It would be better to go in.'

Harry went in.

Work had been done inside. The building was square, possibly thirty feet on each side; it was roomless and of course roofless. The walls, inside as out, were covered with mosses and lichen and hugged by creepers. But the center was clear. There was no litter of stones in the center, no roots, no vegetation. It had even been swept! The floor was unexpectedly smooth, consisting of some sort of flagstones so well cemented that no chinks were left for weeds, and the floor was as even and clean as it must have been when it was first laid, two and a half centuries ago. The space thus cleared, a large oval, was dazzlingly neat in the midst of the slovenly helter-skelter jungle.

A man was shaking hands with Wright, and presently he shook hands too, solemnly, with Obarrio and with Gomez. Harry had never seen him before. He was a thin severe man with a face the color of a lemon, a hairless face. He might have been fifty.

'We feared you might not be able to come, señor,' Wright said in Spanish, 'and this is why I brought another gentleman. But now,' in English, turning with a smile to Harry, 'it proves not necessary. Still, you will stay and see the sport, eh? And may I present Señor Arias y Avila? Señor Arias, Mr Kellems.'

Taken off guard, Harry nodded. He did not offer to shake hands. He said to Obarrio: 'Nobody told me there was going to be a duel. I don't think I'll stay.'

Gomez exploded into Spanish too rapid for Harry, though Ward Wright and Dr Obarrio listened gravely. Afterward Dr Obarrio said to Harry: 'Gomez is sorry. He thought that you had heard of the challenge, as so many others have. And when you came he took your silence for consent to act. He is desolated that you were under a misapprehension, but he thinks that since you *are* here you'd better stay.'

'Why?'

'Because there is no carriage, and you could get lost. There are so many who know of this affair and are looking for us! You left the city with us. If you are seen near here it might bring a crowd, and if there is a crowd the police might feel obliged to come. And after all, Señor Kellems, it *is* against the law.'

'I know it is, and I don't want to have anything to do with it!'

'Nor is there any reason why you should. You do not even need to look, if you don't wish. In case of trouble we'll all be ready to testify that you had no part in the business. I will answer for it that each of Señor Nuñez's party will make the same promise, when they come.'

He repeated this in Spanish for the benefit of Arias y Avila. They all agreed. They all bowed.

'All right, but I still don't like it.'

Dr Obarrio drew him aside, while the others walked over the cleared space, whispering.

'Indeed, Señor Kellems, you should be delighted to find yourself here.'

'I'm a little surprised to find *you* here.'

'I don't know why. You consider this a barbarous custom? We don't. There are certain things which cannot be settled in any other manner. We'll not argue it—but I do wish to assure you, señor, that I would not in ordinary circumstances lend my services to a minor meeting between politicos. This one is different. Not that I have anything to do with the causes of the quarrel! But I think it will be worth watching.'

'This Nuñez—is that Raphael Nuñez?'

'Yes.'

A friend of Simpson, Harry remembered. A young man, rich, arrogant, a leader of the opposition. Harry knew little of Panamanian politics, but he did know that Nuñez was in the opposite camp from Ward Wright and was trying to have Wright deported.

'It has to do with el capitan remaining here, Doctor?'

'Ostensibly, no. Actually, yes, it has everything to do with it.

Nuñez was pushing him too hard, and Captain Wright insulted. Oh, he did it very cleverly! Nuñez lost his head—and challenged.'

'Oh. That gives Wright the choice of weapons, then? Well, I hope Nuñez is a good shot!'

'As to that, I don't know,' carelessly. 'But he is a master with the saber. We who like the sport, we who attend the fencing academy, we consider him the best saber in Panama.'

'That's not going to help him much now.'

'On the contrary, señor, it should help him a great deal—since Captain Wright chose sabers.'

'*What!* You mean he deliberately——'

'He plays a bold game, señor. There are few men I know who would stand up to Raphael Nuñez with naked steel, and then only if they were in a rage. But el capitan is cold about it. He knows of Nuñez's skill. He knows the importance my countrymen attach to affairs like this. And I think he knows the meaning of the word psychology, too. Nuñez must be—— Ah, here he is!'

The party, entering singly, was as solemn as a funeral procession. One man carried what might have been a long violin case, another carried a Gladstone bag. With each Harry had a nodding acquaintance, no more.

The sight of Harry disconcerted them, and they paused, irresolute. Dr Obarrio bowed to them, and they bowed. Only one, however, the one with the violin case, bowed to Harry, who answered with a nod. Gomez hurried to them, and then Arias, and there was a whispered conference, from which Nuñez himself stood apart.

Ward Wright, who had bowed inclusively to the newcomers, now strolled the cleared space, humming a little tune. He paused before Harry and Dr Obarrio.

'We're lucky about the rain, aren't we?'

'Yes, it is most fortunate' said Dr Obarrio, politely glancing at the sky.

'He is an upstart, but his courage is great' Obarrio said sidewise after Wright had strolled on. 'I shall be scolded by the family for standing with such a man, but I don't care. I have never held with the aristocratic conception of the duello. If a man can *act* like a gentleman, for that one occasion, I think he should be permitted to fight. Do you not agree, señor?'

'Well, you know the way I feel. I think the whole business oughtn't to be allowed.'

Gomez came over and bowed to Harry. It was all explained and

363

agreed about Harry, Gomez said. He would have no part. As far as any of the others would know, he would not even be a spectator. Gomez spread fat palms, triumphant.

'You are—*invisible*, señor!'

'That's nice.'

'Dr Obarrio, it is thought that we should start promptly. The party of Señor Nuñez may have been followed. Will you be so good as to join with Dr de Morales in the sterilizing of the blades?'

'With pleasure, Senator.'

Harry, left alone, 'invisible,' was fascinated. It was not at all like the first time he had seen a cockfight, when he'd expected to be disgusted and wasn't; or the first time he had seen a bullfight, when he'd expected to be disgusted and was. There were no shouts, there was no betting. The silence awed him: the jungle outside was a noisy place compared with this ancient secluded court. The men held themselves stiff and spoke in low voices, even in whispers, when they spoke at all. No ring was pitched, no line drawn; apparently there were to be no territorial limits to this fight, other than those enforced by the walls.

The swords were taken from the oversized violin case. There were four. Two were long, heavy, straight, blunt-ended; their edges were taped with sticking plaster; they had massy brass basket guards. The other two swords were so bright that Harry blinked.

If ever Harry had known that childish norteamericano tendency to scoff at the institution of the duel as at something ludicrous—'Here's me cahd, suh!' 'Pistols for two and coffee for one, at sunrise!'—if ever he had thought of an affair of honor as a great bowing-and-scraping of imperialed Frenchmen in silk hats shaped like truncated cones, an Alphonse-and-Gaston riot—he changed his mind when he saw those swords. Oh, he had been nervous enough! The sight of the swords put him beyond nervousness; so that the rest of the time he stood rigid, and the only things about him to move were drops of sweat that formed on his face and body and delicately broke and rolled downward, an unceasing stream.

They were only slightly curved, the sabers. They looked razor-sharp. Their guards were of light smooth sheet steel, not burnished like the blades but dull—so that they wouldn't reflect light, Harry supposed. He had a hard time getting his eyes away from those blades. He watched them while the seconds hefted them one by one, and while the physicians, when the seconds were satisfied, swabbed the blades with cotton soaked in disinfectant. Dr Obarrio at least handled them lovingly, testing their weight not as the seconds had done, not to be sure that they were identical, but with a sportsman's interest in a beautiful thing: he might have been a fox hunter touching with approval the head of a superior hound or caressing the neck of a mare.

Ward Wright, at the far end of the clearing, had stripped to the waist and taken off his shoes and socks. He permitted Senator Gomez, a solicitous valet, to wrap cord around his trousers from the knees down. He had a belt around the top of his trousers, and now he tightened this, making his waist wasp-small. He was a fine figure of a man. He stood quiet, firm, sure of himself; and when he made even the smallest movement, the muscles of his arms ran easily back and forth. He was very strong, but his muscles were flat, not lumpy. There was not much hair on his chest. His hands and face, and his neck down to the collar line, were deeply tanned; his skin elsewhere was as white as that of a woman. There did not even seem to be any purple veins at his wrists. His belly—and he wasn't sucking it in!—was perfectly flat.

Nuñez, though he was nearer, Harry did not see so well. Nuñez was not as tall as Wright, and probably did not weigh as much, but he had fine broad shoulders and exceptionally long arms. Stripped for the fight, indeed, he showed chiefly shoulders and arms, from the armpits running down past a smallish chest, narrow hips, legs that were slats, to tiny feet. His skin was a dainty yellow-brown. Seeing him from behind, Harry could not judge whether the man was nervous or just impatient: he shuffled a good bit. He had not taken off his shoes and socks.

The two men were about the same age. Call it just under thirty.

It would have been uproarious to watch Gomez and one of the Nuñez representatives prepare themselves—if Harry had not first seen the swords. Gomez and the Nuñez man donned large brown fencing masks which protected not only their faces but their ears and the tops of their heads, and additionally there were huge brown thick bibs hanging over their necks. They worked themselves into plastrons. Each drew onto his right arm a gauntlet, stiff leather above the knuckles, which went beyond the elbow: it was as though they were preparing to spar with riding boots instead of boxing gloves. Then each stood to one side, presumably watching the other—Harry couldn't see their faces because of the masks—and they shifted this way and that until they were just right. They were Tweedledum and Tweedledee, bombasted, facing one another across the field, each holding, down-pointed, one of the swords made blunt with tape. The two physicians opened their cases on the floor and stood a little further back. By the side of each physician, on his left, stood an unpadded second.

Oh, it certainly should have been funny! It was so geometrically spaced! But Harry hadn't any laughter, and the sweat went rolling down him in tepid pear shapes.

Arias y Avila stalked to the middle of the clearing. He was in his ordinary clothes; and as for his face, it probably always did look like that anyway, like a yellow sheen of doom. He spoke quickly, in a Spanish too formal for Harry to understand, probably pure Castilian; but Harry could gather that he was delivering a cold and correct plea to the representatives of Raphael Nuñez to make some other settlement of this quarrel rather than the settlement by arms. He didn't speak long, and he didn't seem to expect an answer. He walked back to where he had been.

Click-click, fancy, precise—and fast! One of the Nuñez's seconds, the one who was not Tweedledum (or Tweedledee), strode to the center of the cleared space and made a similar speech. The answer, as before, was assumed to be no.

Undoubtedly some legal precaution, some technicality.

Senator Gomez advanced, bowed briefly to his double, who bowed to him. They could not bow all the way, they were so padded. Gomez took one of the bright swords and crab-walked to Ward Wright, and handed it to him. Tweedledee (or Tweedledum) did the same to Nuñez. Then these mattressed figures retreated. Then Gomez came forward again, and again he bowed. The bow he received in response was clearly on o.k. He lifted his head as far as he could, and cried in Stentor's voice: *'Gentlemen, you may engage!'*

Ward Wright started forward with a curious creep Harry had never seen before. His left arm, the hand fisted, was doubled against the small of his back. His chin was high. He moved slowly on his heels, his right foot advanced, his left foot directly behind it, a small step with the right foot, a small step with the left, heel-and-toeing it, a small step with the right, a small step with the left. Harry knew that if *he* tried to move like that he'd collapse. It must take years of practice and the development of muscles not ordinarily used.

After a moment Nuñez started forward in the same fashion. He soon stopped. He stood erect, and brought his feet together, lowering his point. He shook his head.

Ward Wright stepped back, standing erect.

Wright's non-padded second went to Nuñez, and there were whispers. There were further whispers among the others, though the doctors stood away. There was a great deal of glancing at Ward

Wright's feet. Harry's estimate was that Nuñez did not care to fight a man with no shoes or socks on.

It seemed to be decided Ward Wright's way. Nuñez, whispered to, shrugged. He retreated a yard or so. Wright, not shrugging, but always smiling, smiling, turned and walked back to where he had first been; and then he turned again. His blade went up. He dropped into that crouch.

Senator Gomez centered, and with his taped sword straight before him, he looked first right, then left. Then he looked at Tweedledee (or Tweedledum), who nodded.

'Gentlemen, you may engage!'

It was something like a cockfight then. Harry, before he had seen one, had thought of cockfights as pick-pick-picking on the part of a couple of roosters. He'd been unhinged when he saw his first cockfight. The cocks had been held, straining, and the main master had shouted the release command—and feathers, and it was over. It was all over. One cock limped fiercely around, an eye hanging out, and crowed and crowed, trying to find the other cock, which was dead. Crowing, crowing, it had found that cock; and then it had crowed until they took it fainting away. A fight? It had been! Harry had watched others, thrilled. They were much the same. They were not always as short as the first one, but they never lasted long, and he was never able to follow the spurs with his eyes. He never saw how one cock killed the other and was left to crow and crow.

This was like that. When Gomez had bellowed his permission Ward Wright started forward with that same velvety cat creep; but Nuñez flew at him. The blades slee-ed and cricked. Truly, the blades set off sparks. Seconds yelled, upraising their own swords. The fighters fell back.

There seemed no change in them. They were not sweating. The hair of neither was mussed. Arias said something to Ward Wright, who swerved his eyes to look at the elbow of his sword arm. Dr Obarrio said something sharp and walked with sure feet to the middle. Dr Obarrio looked at Ward Wright's elbow, and Harry saw now that there was blood coming from that elbow. Dr Obarrio touched the place the blood came from—a scientist examining, for the sake of form, a familiar insect. He sniffed and went back to his place.

'Gentlemen, you may——'

This time it lasted longer, but to Harry it was no more followable than the first engagement. The swords whirred and flared, and for a terrible instant the two men stood not moving, having met, with only

367

their right arms and their sabers at work. They stood as statues—except for their right arms and sabers.

Gomez and Tweedledum leaped in, lifting their swords, yelling.

By God, I wouldn't have done that for anything in the world! thought Harry.

Nuñez and Wright stepped back and straightened, holding their sabers down. The physicians walked into the field. Dr Obarrio stood before Ward Wright, stood with arms akimbo. He did not touch Wright, who smiled at him. He nodded and went back to his place. Dr de Morales fussed before Nuñez. He had brought his case, and he appeared to be touching Nuñez's body here and there: Harry saw only Nuñez's back. The Panamanian stood straight, not flinching. Harry saw blood at the top of his head, and the blood sopped down through Nuñez's hair and began to reach with wriggly fingers to his neck. There must have been a lot of blood.

Dr de Morales said something to Gomez, who bowed to listen. Then Gomez lifted his mask from the bottom and called something to Ward Wright. Blood that was dribbling off Ward Wright's elbow splapped on the pavement; but Wright showed unaware of it.

'You know your instructions' Wright said loudly, evenly.

Gomez said something to Dr de Morales, who shrugged and went to his place, though he glanced back at Nuñez.

Then stillness. And between the two men there was only a courtyard on which wavered sunspots shaped like eggs.

'Gentlemen, you may engage!'

They came together slowly this time. It was not like a cockfight now. They met near the place where Harry was.

No sooner had they met, and there had been scarcely the click of steel, when Ward Wright faded backward. He did not run. He did not even seem to step. It was as though he glided on ground under his control. Nuñez, snorting, went after him. Wright went back, moving a little to one side. Nuñez went after him.

Ward Wright began to laugh. It was not a loud laugh, it was a rich juicy inside-the-chest laugh, and what little of it was heard came between his smiling lips. He backed away, and backed away. Nuñez charged him—but Ward Wright glided back like an unreachable phantom, like a vapor in a nightmare.

The conscientious Tweedle-referees were lost. They jumped this way and that, holding their straight swords straight before them, willing to step in, but not sure of themselves.

Nuñez went to one knee, and both padded men got there, lifting their blades. Ward Wright stepped back, smiling still, but no longer making any sound from his chest.

Dr Obarrio strode to Ward Wright, who shook his head. Dr Obarrio put a forefinger upon a slash on the lower part of Ward Wright's cheek just above the jawbone: it might have been four inches long, and now blood was running eagerly from it and running down to the chin, from where it dripped off to the chest. Dr Obarrio pulled back a flap of the cut, shook his head, and let the flap fall into place. Harry could almost hear it splash. Dr Obarrio had brought his bag this time. Carefully, but swiftly, he dabbed the wound. Ward Wright stood smiling all the while. Dr Obarrio went back to his place.

Senator Gomez pouter-pigeoned his chest.

'Gentlemen, you may engage!'

Now this might have been a rule, that he shouted the command as loudly as he could. It was the only loud sound. Everything else was hushed. Even the jungle, leering over the walls—the jungle, usually so turbulent—watched silent now.

Nuñez retreated, sidestepping to the right, his back foot, his left, feeling for the stones and weeds which would tell him he could retreat no further. Wright kept after him, not striking, only feinting, and making that sound again in his chest.

The seconds stopped the fighting, for no reason Harry saw. Nuñez and Wright straightened, handing their sabers on demand. Was it over? Hell, Harry would feel sick as soon as he could feel anything! A nice honest-to-goodness slugging match when you'd got your Riley up, that was one thing. But these men were measuring rage. They were slicing by pattern one another's faces with the coldness of butchers handling meat!

Now the physicians were swabbing the sabers with disinfectant again. Each examined the other's work. Very professional they were, too, in order that this fight should be entirely antiseptic or prophylactic or whatever it was! Nobody must get any germs, anyway. Doctors must be careful about things like that.

'Gentlemen, you may engage!'

They were catercornered in the yard now, so that Harry, had he been an expert, could have followed every stroke. Harry was not an expert; but he knew that Nuñez was about to be hacked down.

It was Ward Wright who was moving sideways, with calculation forcing Nuñez to the center of the clearing, while he himself stepped to his own starting place.

The rest, though it was quick, was to Harry the clearest part of the

369

whole fight. Harry thought he saw each blade, each slash and parry, as the men came straight across the yard at him. He saw most vividly Ward Wright's face. The fight was over now. It had been over when Ward Wright worked himself back to his original place. After that Ward Wright went slashing forward, slashing, slashing ferociously—coming right toward Harry.

There wasn't anything Harry could do. He stood drenched in his down-crawling sweat and watched the face get nearer. The eyes were the eyes of murder. Blood bubbled out of the cheek wound and ran over the chin and down the neck. The lips were spread a little, showing nice teeth: they were spread in Ward Wright's favorite drawing-room smile.

Harry watched that face getting closer and closer. Smiling. A lightninged cloud of steel before it—but antiseptic steel! Oh, sure, antiseptic! Closer, Ward Wright, sure of himself, was creeping, not rushing. He wouldn't stop. He was going to kill a man, and he was enjoying it; and Harry stood there and watched his eyes.

As a matter of fact, Raphael Nuñez was not killed. This was not because of courage. Nuñez had courage. But Nuñez had just that much strength, and he had fought too long, and when he fell he fell directly backward, spewed out like a stamped-upon ant, his saber leaving his hand, his face up.

If his face hadn't been up, it wouldn't have been so bad.

The court-plastered stoppers got in then. Ward Wright stepped back, smiling, smiling. And the face of Raphael Nuñez, turned up, all blood, without a mouth, with only one eye, was not two feet from Harry.

He wasn't dead, the doctors said soon afterward. He would never *look* the same again, of course. But he wasn't dead.

Ward Wright did not glance at Señor Arias y Avila as he handed him his wet saber and as Dr Obarrio started to work on the cheek wound. Ward Wright kept looking at Harry. He didn't have to say anything. He just looked.

Dinner was a thing he did not want. He told Célestine to take it out and feed it to the birds, if she could find any.

'Monsieur?'

He went into the bathroom and for a while just washed; but he did not feel clean enough, so he took off his clothes and showered. It was raining outside now. We were lucky about the rain, weren't we?

He put on fresh clothes and went back to the parlor. Célestine, damn her, was there.

'Listen, I'm trying to say that I don't want to eat. No eat. Pas mange. Catch on? Now please, *please* get out of here!'

'Monsieur?'

He tried as best he could to get her to turn, but she couldn't or wouldn't understand, so he walked around to the other side of her and kicked her hard in a very large place where he had always wanted to kick her. When she fled he felt no comfort; except that soon afterward he was able to go into the bathroom and kneel on the floor next to the toilet and get up a little more. He hadn't supposed that there was any more to get up. He was sure he was not going to forget those faces, the one, irreparably mutilated, all slobbered with blood, right practically at his feet, the other, cut once, smiling at him with eyes that said 'Well?' He'd have to get over this business of vomiting, anyway. He certainly couldn't forget *either* face while he vomited. He scrubbed his teeth and rinsed his mouth and went into the bedroom and threw himself on the bed.

Perhaps he had slept? It wasn't likely. It was still light. He tried to ignore the knocking. But the screen door was opened.

'Harry——'

'Oh, it's you.'

'M-May I come in, Harry?'

'No.'

'Well, are you all right?'

'Of course I'm all right! As a matter of fact, I was never even threatened. Nothing ever came near me, except a face. I wasn't even there. I was invisible.'

'Harry, are you all r-right?'

'For Christ's sake, don't keep asking me whether I'm all right! Of course I am! But since it's you, and since I assume you're going back to Madeline, tell her not to worry any more about me not taking el capitan seriously. I've learned my lesson.'

'Harry,' dutifully from the hall, 'you m-mean he w-won?'

'He beat the other guy, but he hasn't beaten me yet' Harry answered. 'Now get the hell out, *please!*'

23

DR GORGAS WAS WHISTLING SLOWLY, very thoughtfully, and off key. The plop of ice, however, brought a smile to his face. He liked a drink with ice in it. You were getting all you wanted now, delivered. The combination icehouse-bakery-laundry at Cristobal was finished, and from it each morning went eighty tons of ice, twenty-five thousand loaves of bread, laundry for at least three thousand persons, and lots of frozen meat. By nine o'clock every white person on the Isthmus—every one, that is, with commissary privileges—had been serviced.

The meat wasn't bad, either. Not as bad as it used to be, anyway. Marie still complained about prices; but women always complained about prices—'*Forty* cents a dozen, and they're cold-storage eggs at that! Why, at home——' But anyway it was nice to have ice.

He went back to the veranda and picked up his cigar.

'Why don't you go to Mr X.Y.Z. with what you've got?'

'I'm surprised to hear you suggest that, sir.'

'You have me wrong. I won't pretend I like the man, no, though I don't dislike him as vehemently as'—he dropped his voice—'as Marie in there. But I certainly don't *distrust* him. Whatever else you may say about him, Harry, you've got to admit he's *fair*.'

Harry shook a sad head and gazed down the slope. It had recently been raining; but now the sun was out, not in sight, its rays not low, here, but still striking the bay itself, and striking too the tops of the palms, making them clusters of ruby, emerald, diamond, and amethyst, laying long shadows.

Everybody in Sanitation, all the old-timers at least, all who had been out more than a few weeks, thought that Dr William Crawford Gorgas could do no wrong. In consequence, youthfully, fanatically loyal, they thought that Colonel Goethals could do no right. In appearance, in point-at-able details, these two were curiously alike. Each was erect, pink-faced, white-haired, white-mustached, neat, handsome, distinguished of presence. Each was a colonel who seldom wore a uniform. Each was efficient—though Goethals looked efficient, while Gorgas didn't: Goethals was furiously, relentlessly efficient, but Gorgas, who never drove anybody but himself, would win obedience not with a scowl but with a smile. You couldn't help liking Gorgas; you couldn't help admiring Goethals.

Dr Gorgas was the best-hearted of men, and he had been in the Army all his life and was accustomed to disappointments. Yet even he, after three years of heroic work in the field, must have resented being at last made a member of the Isthmian Canal Commission—just when such membership became an empty honor.

That Man in the White House, who lost it so often, had lost his patience again. When the original commission of seven proved a failure, Teddy had asked Congress to authorize a commission of three. Congress had failed to act. Teddy had thereupon appointed another seven-man commission but with instructions that three of this number, as an executive committee, should have all the responsibility. This worked well; but it didn't work long enough. When Magoon and Shonts and Stevens severally resigned, President Teddy appointed a third seven-man commission, sticking to the letter of the law; but this time he had so instructed the appointees that only the chairman held any real authority. Dr Gorgas could sit in on the commission meetings; he could advise, as could the others; but Colonel Goethals ran the show, and each final decision was his.

From the beginning, they had not liked one another. Temperamentally opposites, they were predestined enemies. There was no open warfare! The clashes were quiet ones, behind closed doors. But you couldn't tell anybody in Sanitation anything good about this upstart Goethals—and expect him to believe it. The Sanitation crowd sneered at the 'Yellow Peril,' the yellow track motor which hauled the new chairman up and down the Line on his inspection trips each morning. They commented without approval upon his unsmilingness; pointed out that all he was doing, really, was following plans already laid by Stevens with the organization built up by Shonts; and derided his passion for exactitude. 'Mr X.Y.Z.' Dr Gorgas used to call him.

The Sanitation boys thought Sanitation a half-starved stepchild. Mr X.Y.Z., who knew about conditions in the old days only from hearsay, thought Sanitation a spoiled, overfed darling. The mosquito-cost story might have been concocted; or it might have been true:

The chairman had Dr Gorgas up on the carpet. 'Colonel, do you realize that every single mosquito your men kill is costing the United States Government'—he referred to a sheet of figures—'nine dollars and ninety-eight and three-fifths cents!' 'But Colonel,' sweetly, 'what if one of those nine-dollar-and-ninety-eight-and-three-fifths-cent mosquitoes was to bite *you*?'

Harry sipped his drink and gazed down a shadow-streaked hillside to the bay, where in the final glory of sunset thousands of birds wheeled and dived. Even the birds seemed to know what they wanted in Panama now.

'No, I wouldn't take it to him. I haven't got enough to *take!* He'd laugh me out of the place.'

'No, he wouldn't do that' Dr Gorgas said gravely. 'He never laughs.'

They drank and smoked. Dr Gorgas said something about how he and Marie didn't see Harry up there on the Highball Deck often. Harry smiled. He was enjoying himself now. Lonesomeness had gone away for a while. He stretched his legs. He lifted his glass—and saw with amazement that it was empty. He'd been drinking too much lately. He'd had two—or was it three?—at Ralston's before he came up the hill; and he hadn't yet started for home. Home? Well, you had to call it something.

'Another, Harry?'

'Well . . .'

Dr Gorgas took the glass, but he eyed Harry with a troubled eye from above. Dr Gorgas always liked to make his own drinks. It wasn't a thing you ought to expect your wife to do, he would say, and it wasn't a thing a servant was capable of doing. He went inside, whistling low. He made Harry's light at first, but when he held it up his conscience rang like a chime. After all, you didn't give a guest a drink that looked like the reflection of liquor in a chaser. He dumped in a little more whisky.

'I always feel a bit sacrilegious about calling this veranda the High-ball Deck,' he said as he went out, 'because I always remember that we hold our services downstairs in the office every Sunday. Now if we held our services up *here,* and you and I had a drink occasionally down *there,* Highball Heaven might be more appropriate now, eh?'

'It's nice up here.'

Dr Gorgas lowered himself into his chair. With no hurry he brought his cigar to his mouth.

'Speaking of tomorrow morning, what are you going to give us?'

'I've got to talk it over with Mr Harris. I thought of "Jesus, Lover of My Soul" and "Bringing in the Sheaves." '

'Um-m,' judicially. 'Yes, Marie would like that. Particularly "Jesus, Lover of My Soul." That's one of her favorites.'

'And speaking of tomorrow morning,' said Harry, 'is that your idea, sir, that I should go to Colonel Goethals then?'

'Oh no, no! You're too important for that!'

The czar heard complaints on Sunday mornings, in his office. Already this was an institution. He sat, that grave handsome man, smoking Three Castle cigarettes from a round tin, smoking one after another, while one after another he listened to complaints. He sat solemn and exact, flanked by interpreters; and workmen groused about their foremen, and foremen found fault with their workmen, and clerks found fault with their food, and nervous, twitchy young men asked for advice about getting married, and wives demanded to know what they should do if their husbands got drunk on Saturday night, and somebody alleged the existence of a jinx, while somebody charged bedbugs and somebody else charged favoritism. They were heard, no matter in what tongue, no matter how trifling the kick. Whoever they were, whatever they had to say for themselves, they were heard. The Gentile Solomon with the violet-blue eyes dispensed pure if cool judgment. Once, it was said, a delegation of prostitutes related that they were willing enough to refrain from crossing into the Canal Zone, as ordered, but asked the colonel a reciprocal favor—that married women from the Zone be prohibited from crossing into the Republic and wandering *their* particular streets. Stiff Neck imperturbably took care of the matter.

'No, you're too important for that' Dr Gorgas said again. 'Yours isn't any wait-in-line matter. But if you don't think you have enough——'

'I'll get enough, soon!'

'Bringing things to a head?'

'*He* is. I think he's losing his nerve. I've got a hunch that he's going to try something pretty wild in a little while.'

'Be careful now! As far as I know, there's no criminal charge against him at all, here or in the Republic. And his political position in the Republic, I understand, is firmer than ever. You hear about that duel he fought the other day?'

'I heard something about it.'

'They say the man's face was pretty well slashed to ribbons. Lost the sight of one eye entirely, and he's going to New York in the hope of saving the sight of the other. Not to mention a broken nose, and his front teeth out, and all sorts of cuts down his cheeks. A man who will do a thing like that is no man to fool with, Harry. I don't want to tell you your business; but after all, it stands to reason that you can't afford to carry on a private vendetta with somebody so much better equipped for such things than you are.'

'He's going to do something wrong pretty soon' said Harry. 'I can feel it coming.'

'You're not going to Mr X.Y.Z., then?'

'No, I think I'll wait for Mr Wright to make his misstep first.'

Harry rose. His glass was empty again, and he felt ashamed of himself for having drunk so fast. He glanced down the hill, which the shadows had almost won.

'Your wife isn't in?'

'She's lying down. We've got to go out tonight, and she wanted to get a little shut-eye first.'

'Well, you'll give her my kindest regards, sir?'

'I certainly will. I'm glad you dropped in, Harry. Does us old codgers good to get together now and then, eh?'

'And you tell her I'll positively sing "Jesus, Lover of My Soul" tomorrow. I'll make a point of it.'

'Thank you. I know she'll love it.' He had led Harry to the head of the outside steps. His fingers dug into Harry's shoulder for an instant. 'And take it easy, lad' he whispered.

'I'll take it easy.'

'Don't you finish up sadder Budweiser!'

'I won't, sir. And thanks for the drinks. Good-by.'

'Good night, Harry.'

A kick had not been enough to shoo Célestine away; and indeed that great damp black smudge was more definitely with him and more persistently monsieuring him than ever; and Harry even had the horrid thought, sometimes, that she was in love with him and was plotting to abduct him and carry him away to some remote spongy place and rape him. He liked Célestine less than ever, and he wished he hadn't rooted her with his good right toe that time. Now, it was clear, he would never get rid of her.

She simpered massively at him and held the screen door open. He snarled 'Hello!' and if that was churlish, then let her make the most of it: he *felt* churlish.

She was trying to tell him that somebody was waiting for him. This much he could gather from her mouthings on the porch. And suddenly he was afraid to walk into his own parlor.

Was it Ward Wright? Would he be standing there, smiling as he always smiled, theatrical but competent, and with a revolver?

If that happened, as he'd told Art Price, *he* would win.

But also, he would be dead.

There was no reason to assume that it was Ward Wright. The drinks? All right, call it the drinks! But it scared him right up to the roof of his mouth—right up, hot, to the back of his eyes. He knew his face was wet. He knew his heart was tight.

'Who's there?' he called. He swallowed and called it again, louder: 'Who's there?'

Jackson Smith came out, looking crankier than ever, his glasses fairly aflame in the light from the porch bulb, his jaw granitic.

'Mr Kellems, I believe?'

'Absolutely' Harry said, and breathed. 'This is an honor. What brings you here, may I ask?'

'You don't have to ask. I sent a man day before yesterday.'

'To my office, yes.'

'Yes, to your office.'

'Well, I'm flattered. Gosh, imagine talking to two members of the I.C.C. within ten or fifteen minutes.'

'Eh?' Jackson Smith shuddered with righteousness. Slab-sided his face was, and wan-brown and thin his hair, and his cheeks reminded Harry of the cheeks of poor old Lemming; but Lemming, gone now, was a weak man; Jackson Smith was anything but weak. Square Foot Smith! Was there ever a man who was hated more and cared less? Surly, hard-working, precise, unforgiving, he dominated fiercely the Division of Labor, Quarters, and Subsistence. He said: 'You can live here, or you have to live there.' He had worked out a plan—for he always operated according to a plan. You were allotted one square foot of furnished floor space in a government-built house for every dollar of monthly salary. Just that. If you were a married man and entitled to married quarters—that is, if your wife was actually in residence with you—you got the same number of square feet doubled. Not a breath more. Not a speck-of-dust-in-the-corner more. Unless of course you had children, children actually and in fact resident with you, under your roof (remember, it was the *government's* roof!), and in that case each child, regardless of age, entitled you to five per cent more of your original basic floor-space allowance. Up to the number of three! Either you weren't supposed to have more than three children, or else you weren't supposed to have them all living with you in a government house, or else you had to just take the straight fifteen per cent extra for all of them and make the best of it. There was much more to the plan, more detail, but nobody, probably, had ever understood it clear through—excepting, of course, its inventor. Oh, they kidded him, they cursed him, but nobody questioned that Square Foot Jackson was doing a wonderful job! Pull meant nary a breath of air to him. He didn't care who your boss was, or your congressman; and if you flourished a please-take-care-of letter—even maybe from a senator, even maybe from Teddy himself—Jackson Smith would tell you, in so many impolite words, what you could do with that letter. He certainly was not amiable. And he certainly was not crooked.

'The point is,' Harry temporized, 'you don't usually go around calling on people. It, uh, it sort of takes the breath out of me. Won't you come in and have a drink?'

'Thanks, I don't drink. I sent a man, day before yesterday?'

'Yes. And he asked me about my wife.'

'And you told him you didn't know!'

'Excuse me, Mr Smith. I told him I didn't know *when* she was coming back. I didn't say I didn't know *whether* she was coming back.'

'But you don't, do you?'

'Don't what? Don't know *whether* she's coming back? Say, listen here, Mr Smith——'

'Never mind the listen-heres! You know what everybody's saying, don't you? Now I don't care whether it's true or not. It doesn't mean anything to me. But I'm running a business, and I'm going to see that the married men who are really entitled to quarters—— Why, *you're* living here alone!'

You were not supposed to lose your temper with Jackson Smith. The man was always right. He was time and tide; he was inevitability; and your instinct was to placate him. Placate time, tide? Well, it was an instinct.

'You're living here *alone!*' accusingly, his glasses shaking.

'Do you expect me to have three or four concubines around?'

You can't insult God; and Jackson Smith, with his slide rule, was God. He nodded briskly, not offended. He started for the door.

'All right. You'll be closed out in fifteen days, beginning tomorrow noon, unless you can prove in writing that your wife is seriously ill and unable to rejoin you *but* expecting to rejoin you as soon as possible. That must be in writing, mind you!'

'Should I have it notarized, you bastard?'

Jackson Smith slammed the screen door; but he was a man who would slam the door when he went out of any place: he was that kind of man.

There was a face, still. There was a face which was not that of a member of the I.C.C. twisted in furious regulationism. No, this face had a blood-bubbling slash on the left cheek, but more immediately it had sharp bright killing eyes, and bright teeth, and it was coming toward him. . . . Then there was another face, which he'd seen an instant afterward. Gone to New York, Dr Gorgas had said, in the hope of saving the sight of one eye. But that second face, which had been right at Harry's feet, would never, at its best, from now on, no matter what surgeons did to it, be anything but a sight from which men would turn with a queer cold restriction inside the chest.

Sure, Wright had known what he was doing! He had planned very cleverly! He had placed himself so that he would go toward Harry; and when some misstep, some unanticipated move on the part of his victim had caused him to be out of position, he had righted the matter; and he had come in, and come in, his eyes blazing, his eyes on the man he was cutting down, but his mind on that other man who couldn't help seeing this. Flattering? No, no! You don't get flattered by the devil—at least, not to any good purpose.

It would be well if Harry forgot. But Harry knew that he wouldn't ever forget those faces.

Why, he was still scared, standing there on his own front porch!

'Monsieur?'

'Whisky' he muttered.

Amazingly, she understood. He supposed, when he was seated in the bathroom, and when she blandly opened the door and handed him the whisky bottle, that those were two things any foreigner, howsoever benighted, understood—that is, 'whisky' and 'o.k.'

'Get out!' he yelled.

'Monsieur?'

She would not go until he took the bottle, so he took it. *She* couldn't blush, of course! Even if she did, how would anybody ever know it? He drank some whisky, and showered, grumping; and afterward he drank some more whisky.

'I don't want dinner' he said when he came out of the bathroom. 'No dinner. Pas de mange. I'm going downtown. I've got a feeling something is going to happen, you dusky imbecile.'

'Monsieur?'

'No dinner.' Harry put on his coat. 'You see, I used to have a gal named Rosina here, and she could have brought up a gal named— well, I've forgotten her name. But anyway, *you* can't. And I'm going downtown. No dinner. I've got a creepy kind of feeling that it's coming tonight,' he told his face-in-the-mirror, 'and I'm certainly not going to stay here and wait for it.'

'Monsieur?'

'Good night.'

He thought as he walked down the hill that the *Havana* was due next morning, which meant that the mail ought to be distributed by Monday noon. He wondered whether he would hear from Phil. Not that he cared.

He thought as he entered the city that he didn't really like Panamanians. He didn't dislike them; but with the exceptions of Rosina and a few upper-classers such as Dr Obarrio and Lady Mallet he didn't like them either. He had tried to be sympathetic. He respected their prejudices, he hoped. Even in the most informal talk he never referred to them as spiggoties or spigs. He did not call Pedro Miguel 'Peter McGill,' as most of the boys did; and to him the Avenida Central was the Avenida Central, not 'Central Avenue.' But he decided now, walking, that he really didn't like the natives. Their *listlessness* irked him. They stood around, staring without expression at nothing and not seeming to care. He reflected that they were a race lost in their own country. The Chinese and a splattering of East Indians ran the more prosperous shops. Americans built sewers, constructed houses, ran the railroad, dug the canal. Jamaicans were the porters, hack drivers, house servants. The laborers were from everywhere but Panama—from Spain, Barbados, Martinique, Guadeloupe, Greece, Italy, Rumania. Even the whores, the better ones anyway, and most of the madames, were French or Brazilian. The Panamanians themselves were simply what was left over. Numerically they might have excelled; but you would not know it to walk their streets—streets paved by West Indians under American engineers and foremen. The sanitation of their cities was supervised by Americans. Their rich when ill, a great many of their poor too, went to American physicians in the Zone; and the corpse of any personage whose relatives or supporters esteemed him worth a big funeral—you buried soon in the tropics ordinarily—was embalmed by Sam Darling's assistants at the hospital, without whom there could not ever have been a state funeral. Their army and police, jokes, depended upon Americans to keep order. Their brave bomberos permitted Americans to put out the more serious fires. Their currency was riveted to U.S. currency; and indeed the very coins were struck in the States. Almost the only profession left to a Panamanian was politics. And even their politics . . . Well, Colonel Stiff Neck could intervene any time he wished. And back of Colonel Stiff Neck was That Man in the White House, showing his teeth.

Happy is the nation (goes a saying) which has a lot of geography but not much history. Switzerland was an example. Panama too was an example—yet Panama was not happy.

Harry turned into the Avenida Central, turned into a café. He ordered whisky and water at a low zinc bar, and he glowered over it.

A revolution usually unites a people: at least it gives them character and some new songs. Panama had won its independence, had spread its flag to the winds—and that very flag had been designed by a Frenchman with large holdings in the States. The average Panamanian, not knowing what had happened until it was all over, even then hadn't greatly cared. And not only the average Panamanian but just about everybody else in the world knew that the revolution would not even have been promoted without a promise of American battleships.

Harry looked at his drink. There was scarcely any left, just about enough to keep the bottom of the glass wet. He scowled. He shouldn't drink like this! To lean against a bar and meditate upon the relationships of the Latin- and North-Americans—that was all right. And he could pick up a little dinner later, somewhere downtown. But he had all but finished a highball before the bartender could wipe the space underneath. He shook his head in disapproval. He must watch himself! He would stay here awhile, and hold this glass, or rather turn it around and around, making a hooked series of wet rings, before he drained it.

Even so, they might at least be picturesque! There were times when you walked around the Cathedral Square at night, a Wednesday night or Saturday night, when the white-uniformed bandsmen played. . . . Everybody walked slowly, in stately procession, the ladies non-flirtatious, eyes earnestly down, the gents in dead white and very serious. . . . But even then, what was the music? *Poet and Peasant,* usually, or the *William Tell* overture! There were times, at carnival, for instance, when you watched them cavorting in costumes presumably nationalistic, the men in gaudy motunas, the women in polleras colored to knock your eyes out, each with four huge gold buttons at the waist, and pearl-studded side combs they wore at no other season, and their hair polychromatic with tiny bright jiggling jiggers looking like lightning bugs caught in a rainbow. . . . Those were unusual times. For the rest, he was bound to admit, they were drab, a people willing to be shoved aside. They were *listless,* and not concerned with life. That was it! They didn't look upon life as a gift, a thing to be made the most of. They looked upon it as a period of dullness imposed from above for reasons beyond their comprehension. When you tried to teach them the simplest hygiene, explaining how it would avert sickness, they shrugged. They didn't want to dodge death. Rather they seemed to look forward to it. Life was a sickness, and as such a bore; and only death was interesting. They must have thought often of death. You could see it in their eyes.

The bartender took more change and shoved another drink at him. Harry could not remember having ordered another. He had meant to study the end of the previous drink while he thought about the Panamanians. But he didn't like to make a scene. He pocketed the rest of the change and lifted the drink. Midway, he began to feel frightened again, and his hand shook.

The Panamanians thought often of death, did they? Well, *he* had been thinking a lot about death himself, here lately. Why, he had been frightened on his own front porch when Célestine made the mouth-sounds which said somebody was waiting inside! Well, was that so foolish? Hadn't he been as good as told that he was doomed if he didn't skiddoo? And would he skiddoo? No, he was damned if he would! And not just because he was drinking now, either! Nobody was going to bulldoze him! Not even though this night might be the night. . . . He did feel that. He felt that tonight was going to change his whole life, somehow. Perhaps by ending it.

'Tonight is going to change my whole life, somehow' he told the bartender.

'Señor?'

'No, I won't have another. Thanks. Gracias.'

'Buenas noches, señor.'

'Buenas noches, amigo.'

The avenue was crowded with slow-moving people, many of them Panamanians. And Panamanians loved to contemplate death. They would stand—being too lazy to sit down—and look at death. That's what the Panamanians did. You had to see them as much as Harry had seen them to know about them. They'd just stand and look at death.

Ralston's Ritz was crowded. Why had he come here? There were no Panamanians here! The men were of many nationalities, but none stood looking at death. They were too busy getting drunk to stand and look at death. Somebody grabbed his arm.

'Harry, old horse! Here, have a drink!'

'Thanks, I just——'

'Here, throw it into you! Keep you from catching cold!'

They talked and shouted, leaning on their elbows, bending across him; and he wished he had never permitted himself to be dragged here. He shook his head. They shouted into his face, something about a penny for his thoughts.

'Make it ten centavos' Harry suggested.

'You're faded, chico! Let's have it!'

Harry paused, his drink half up, and looked at the ceiling, where flies battered against and buzzed around the electric-light bulbs. He closed his eyes and opened them.

He was expected to say something amusing. He was supposed to be a pretty funny guy. He picked up the ten-centavo piece.

'Well, what's the difference between a poor marksman and a constipated owl?'

It brought silence. Nobody made silly guesses. All they did was gawp. All right, they said at last, what *was* the difference between a poor marksman and a constipated owl?

Harry finished his drink.

'I haven't the faintest idea. You asked me for my thoughts, and I was thinking about Harry Thompson. You guys didn't know him. He died of malaria, and that was the last question he asked, and he died before he could give us the answer. I just happened to be thinking about death, and that made me think about Harry Thompson, and so I remembered what it was that was the last thing he said, that's all. Don't ask me the answer! I've never been able to dope it out myself. Well, buenas noches.'

He walked out on them. He wasn't sure who they were. He knew he knew them, that was all.

The next place was quieter and better fitted to thoughts about Panamanians. Harry was getting frightened again. Fear was sweeping over him and shaking him as the fever did to men who hadn't taken their quinine. He would get very scared, and his hand would tremble. He didn't think anybody noticed it; but he didn't want to be where he knew anybody; and this place was all right. He sat at a table, by himself. He really did drink slowly now, looking at each sip before he took it.

It was like an explosion of dynamite when suddenly he remembered the dynamite explosion.

It had happened last week, Tuesday of last week, when he was out near Culebra, walking over to where one of the steam-shovel superintendents was, a man he wanted to talk to. He had been just walking along, not thinking of anything. It was only by chance that he'd looked up and seen a man with open mouth, a man starting frantically to shout. He had acted fast, throwing himself down. Pieces of shale had torn the back of his coat, and his head had been splapped with mud, and for two hours he hadn't been able to hear right out of the ear on that side. At the time he was only too pleased to be alive, and he had giggled when they picked him up and brushed him off and babbled apologies. Well, it was an accident—that's what he thought then. He had been daydreaming and hadn't seen the signals. He'd tut-tutted, himself apologizing, insisting that it had been his own fault and that nobody should catch hell for it.

It was only now, with a start, that he began to suppose that no accident had occurred. Daydreaming or no daydreaming, he must have been seen walking across that stretch. There had been nothing to hide him. And a man who sets off a dynamite charge doesn't close his eyes and look the other way.

Oh, it *might* have been an accident! Sure, and there might have been a rock on the top of Cucaracha which had somehow got itself dislodged. How? Ants? And who had lugged the rock up there in the first place? Ants?

He marveled that he had been so stupid. Was he walking around with the luck of a drunk, never falling into the holes he should fall into, never getting hit by the things that should hit him?

He began to tingle electrically, and sweat ran down his chest wherever his shirt did not stick to it. His hand wobbled the drink.

He rose and went out.

Not home, no. They might be waiting for him there.

Not to the Cathedral Square, where he had planned to walk around listening to the music. The Cathedral Square was too public.

He could not run to Madeline. No. She belonged to Art Price.

He wouldn't go to Dr Gorgas, who had already been too kind. The Gorgases wouldn't be home anyway. Dr Gorgas had said they were going out.

He found himself in a bar where there was a monte game, and he thought that gambling might straighten his nerves. He had almost a hundred dollars in his pocket. He wrinkled his nose at the professional, a man everybody knew to be a cheat, who shouldn't have been permitted to run any kind of game anywhere. Nevertheless Harry lost four or five dollars to him, out of sheer exasperation. The professional, scorned by most of the customers, fawned upon Harry—but didn't have sense enough to permit Harry to win for a little while. Harry walked out in disgust, leaving a half-finished drink.

At that, a little gambling was the right thought. He had always loved to gamble, chiefly because he had never been able to afford it. If he gambled he might forget about being afraid. He knew he *was* afraid! When he went out into the street again he felt that somebody was following him. He kept turning suddenly.

Well, for one thing, he'd had too much whisky. He knew that. But the fear went deeper than the whisky. He could take large breaths, and walk fast, swinging his arms, and the fumes of the whisky would be low for a little while; but the fear stayed right there back of his shoulder, reaching for him.

He wheeled around.

'Pardon, señor.'

'Oh, I'm sorry! I mean—pardon, señor.'

'Es nada.'

A very decent man, a Panamanian who probably was not thinking about death at all, with a lady on his arm. They all bowed.

A carriage stopped at the curb, and the cochero said something.

'You're darn right I will!' cried Harry, and got in. 'Go to some quiet place where I can——' He twisted thumb and forefinger, to suggest a roulette wheel; he followed an imaginary ball around and around with his eyes. 'Entende?'

'The intent of your purpose has been impeccably conveyed to me, sir. Be assured that I shall transport you to such a joint.'

'Fine' said Harry.

A girl sat in his lap and started to unbutton his fly, but he kneed her off, and when another sat there he paid her no attention—except to hand her a counter.

'I play, eh?'

'Do whatever you want with it' said Harry.

For no reason, except that it was near him, he selected seventeen. He put a dollar counter on seventeen each time, betting three or four dollars on odd, and sometimes a dollar or two on the middle twelve. It was good to watch the ball. He smiled, his brain clearing. He won a little, lost a little; and he kept betting a dollar each time on seventeen, winning or losing on the even bets. He had a highball, but it was very tall and weak, and he had a blue water bottle beside it, and each time he took a sip he would pour a little more water into the glass; and in this way, he figured, he would get less and less drunk. For he still felt drunk! But he felt less nervous. It was good to see the wheel spin.

'I have lose that, señor. You give me another, eh?'

'What for? For stopping the circulation in my leg? Well, all right. Here. Only—vamoose.'

Seventeen did not show up, but the number was often odd. He lost very little. He leaned back, pleased that the whore had gone, and he lighted a cigar. He smiled at his watery drink. He lifted his head to exhale smoke.

Hey! He must have been sure-enough drunk when he came here! Only now did he know where he was.

He saw the yellow curtains move. Why, he thought, I'm right underneath the place! Did el capitan have some other flighty female up there now? Those were the french windows out of which Jumping Jack no doubt had often peered. A pity, that business. Lemming hadn't acted right, screaming it in a barroom; but on the other hand, it must be a horrible feeling to know that your wife had been in bed with such an obvious posing fraud. There was something to be said for Lemming. How could anybody behave well in such circumstances? It must have been pretty bad.

'Señor?'

Automatically he pushed another counter on seventeen.

Now why, he asked himself, had he been staring at those windows so long without noticing that they were lighted, and without hearing, above the click of counters and the ree-ee-ee-ee of the swirling ball, the click of chips from there?

Again he felt the sweat on his chest. A hand out of an icebox reached inside of him and began to squeeze all that its fingers could find.

His own hand, his own right hand, reached the glass. He raised and lowered it.

'Señor? The whisky again?'

'No, thank you. It was only that I meant to ask——'

'Señor, **you** have——'

'Never mind that! What I wanted to know is whether el capitan has poker up there tonight.'

'Si, señor. You know el capitan?'

'We are intimately related. And there are politicos there?'

'Many, señor.'

'Thank you. Here.'

'Gracias!'

The croupier: 'Señor, it is that you mean to——'

'Of course' said Harry, gazing at the french windows.

It seemed that he fought darkness, pushing it back from him, gasping while he pushed it, struggling against it. What would Simpson have done? Do you suppose Simpson would ever have been panicky like this? Why, even the sweat didn't roll down his body now, but hung there. Everything hung. Everything waited.

Ward Wright was giving a poker party.

Yes, that had been an accurate hunch.

Here was to be his night. If he had waited at home—— But he *hadn't* waited at home! Ward Wright was giving a poker party; and Ward Wright would receive the news in the morning from hired killers, and he'd smile while he listened the son of a bitch! He'd smile, would he?

Harry thought: There is only one safe place for me.

He rose. His drink didn't matter, but if he had any counters left . . . Everybody was looking at him. Had he screamed? His upper lip twitched as he turned this way and that. The croupier kept pushing counters at him with a little hoe. The croupier kept pushing the pile off seventeen with more and more counters; and they were yellow counters. Everybody was looking at him.

What he would have done if this had happened at any other time, he didn't know. He saw what it was. One chance in the Lord only knew how many thousands, or millions. He could see it now—less from the piles of counters than from the faces of the others around the table. A waiter, accompanied by one of the managers, was emptying a tray of yellow counters before the croupier, who piled them neatly with swift hands and shoved them across.

It would have been wonderful at any other time. Here was the dream of the occasional gambler. Seventeen had come up, and Harry had been paid, and the counters had remained right there in front of him—on seventeen. He'd been watching the french windows, unaware of the fact that he'd won. And seventeen had come up again.

The sum would be staggering. Would it help a man who was marked to die tonight? Harry thought: There is only one place on the Isthmus where I'll be safe.

'It is correct, señor?'

'I suppose so.' Harry tossed a handful of counters to the croupier. 'Buy yourself a box of cigarros.'

'Muchas gracias, señor!'

'Champagne, señor?'

'Well, not for me, thanks. But you may buy it for the others. And send over that mozo with the tray, please.'

'Este momento, señor!'

Thirty-six times one dollar is thirty-six dollars, and thirty-six times thirty-six dollars is a lot of money. Harry didn't even watch the waiter with the tray of counters, who preceded him to the office. He accepted the cash with thanks, tipped here and there—all sorts of persons had appeared—and, declining a glass of the wine he had just purchased, asked for the services of a waiter.

'I think that Captain Wright is expecting me.'

'Ah yes, señor!'

'Not just in this form, but I think that he does expect me. And if the mozo could show me up the back stairs, to save me the trouble of going clear around to the Calle de San Martin——'

'But of course, señor! *Chico!*'

Ward Wright himself opened the door. He opened it carelessly, talking over a shoulder as he did so, expecting no more than some waiter from the café. There was a waiter, yes; buť Harry slipped ahead of him. Harry and Ward Wright stood chest-to-chest.

There was a long black sticking plaster on the left side of Ward Wright's face. It was crossed by narrower bits of sticking plaster. It twitched when Ward Wright saw Harry.

Cigar smoke came from the room, through a great pause.

'Hello' said Harry. 'You once invited me to come up here when I happened to feel like playing poker.' He started to pull masses of money from his pockets. 'Well, I sort of feel like it now.'

Cigar smoke sauntered past them. Nobody back in the flat so much as whispered. The sticking plaster twitched again; but Ward Wright smiled.

'Come in' he said, and stepped aside.

It was a high-ceiled room, with a great canopied bed which endeavored to dominate it. The light wasn't good, and there was a great deal of smoke. They played at an enormous table, a table big enough for fourteen men: there were eight, including Ward Wright, when Harry came.

'It would be presumptuous to introduce you to a man as well known as Señor Kellems' Ward Wright said in easy formal Spanish. 'I am sure that you are all aware that Señor Kellems is unsurpassed in the cleaning of sewers.'

Harry bowed. They all bowed.

'Yes, I do that pretty well' Harry said.

He felt slack and sure of himself. He knew he was all right now. Wright brought him a tall amber drink.

'We are playing very quietly, a friendly game' Wright said, still speaking Spanish. 'You will perhaps join us in the sport?'

'That's what I came here for' said Harry.

'Is there any special place you would care to sit?'

Now they occupied about two thirds of the rectangular table, at the head of which Ward Wright sat as host, his back to the windows which overlooked the café. The table was too big. There were four men down the far side, three down the side nearer to Harry. Each made some show of offering his chair; but Harry had already spotted Von Alvensleben, who, as a matter of fact, was third man down on the near side, exactly the spot Harry would naturally choose.

'I think right here will do me nicely' Harry said in English.

Von Alvensleben clicked his heels, bowing from the waist.

'Von Alvensleben!'

'Kellems' said Harry, sitting down. 'What's the limit?'

The German, reseating himself, said out of a corner of his mouth: 'I think that *you* are the limit, Kellems, for coming here at all!'

He guffawed quietly, pleased by his own use of American slang.

'I wanted to be safe' Harry explained mildly to him. 'And this is the only sanctuary I know of.'

'Safe?'

Von Alvensleben took a glass from his pocket and slapped it against his left eye as though trying to hurt himself. He turned deliberately. He did not screw up his face to hold the glass in his eye: it stayed there as though it were accustomed to obeying him.

'Safe?' he said again. Then he nodded. 'Ach, yes. I understand. That was very clever of you, and very daring.'

'Only thing I could do' Harry said. He called to Wright: 'You the banker? I'll buy—oh, make it two hundred dollars' worth.'

Von Alvensleben was stacking his chips. He did this with care: obviously he was a neat man. With his military haircut, his square face, the schmisses on his cheek, he *looked* the traditional East Prussian officer, especially when he had that glass in his eye. But his manners were mild enough, and his voice too was gentle. He and Harry spoke in English, and in undertones.

'You take it to be a matter of juxtaposition, I gather, no? If you are —how shall I put it?—if you are inside the mouth of the lion, then the lion cannot pounce upon you?'

'That's the idea' said Harry.

Von Alvensleben chuckled. The cards were dealt. The dealer ante'd.

The seating arrangement, the only one possible at such a table, had its disadvantages. Since eight of the players faced the ninth, like board members facing their chairman, or minstrel-show singers their interlocutor, that ninth, Wright, could see all of their faces well, as they could see his; but the men on one side of the table could scarcely be expected to lean far forward, turning, and to gaze into the faces of their companions on that side. Most unfortunate of all were the end men, Senator Gomez and Harry; for the tendency of the others was to turn a bit toward the occupied end of the table, toward the host. Harry, for example, was not faced with the back of his companion's shaved pink neck, but when he did glance at the German what he saw chiefly was a plump pink ear, the tip of the nose, the slope of a scarred cheek. This was all right. This pleased Harry.

Harry was feeling good, anyway. The first dive had been difficult, but now he found the water fine and wondered why he had ever thought of anything but swimming. He did not touch his drink, and he breathed deep for a while, concentrating on his cards, trying to clear the fumes from his head.

He talked a good deal with Baron von Alvensleben; they carried on an almost continuous conversation out of the corners of their mouths, like stage conspirators; but it was Ward Wright whom Harry watched.

Wright was a good player. He was no genius; but he was steady, intelligent, sometimes daring, always unpredictable; and his smile remained a fixed formal thing no more expressive than the mustache above it. Given an ordinary run of luck, and guests not overreluctant to try his liquor, he could expect to win—as Harry himself expected to win each time he sat down at a poker game. They played much the same game, these two. However, there was a great difference between them tonight: Harry had money, Ward Wright didn't.

Captain Wright bluffed sometimes, but not as often as he would have liked. Perhaps he didn't call as often as he would have liked, either. Necessity, the actual lack of cash, made him play his cards close to the vest. Harry knew the signs! All his life Harry had been obliged to play his own cards close to the vest—all his life until tonight. Now, even after buying two hundred dollars' worth of chips, more than he had ever had before, he still felt the press of money in his pocket: he didn't even know how much it was, perhaps a thousand dollars. Oh, he'd win tonight! Anybody who, thinking about something else, had failed to pick up his winnings from a number and then had seen that number come again—anybody like that was due for a killing. Harry played his usual game, except that his betting was stronger. He didn't stay in pots he wouldn't have stayed in had his pockets been empty. He never called out of bravado. But when he had the cards, now, he rode them.

He knew that Ward Wright, smiling from side to side, being the

perfect host—if a shade too mincing for this kind of session—in fact
was looking at him, Harry, every time he got a chance. He knew that
Ward Wright was envying him his ability to back good hands with
many chips: Wright was like a general in the field who commands a
stripped army of veterans, each of whom must be made to count, and
envies his opponent who can bring up fresh reserves all day and still
never have to look around for more.

'I hear that you attended the mensur the other day? The duel?'

'By design, Baron. But not my design.'

'Ah?'

'The lion was flexing its muscles then and showing its teeth. It
hoped that it wouldn't have to pounce. I don't think it enjoys pounc-
ing—except maybe on very small animals—like a mouse, say.'

Von Alvensleben chuckled.

'I'll stay.'

'There's your three and up five' said Harry.

'Call' said Senator Gomez.

Harry leaned back and lighted a cigar, still ignoring his drink. He
noticed Von Alvensleben glance at that drink, which Ward Wright
himself had poured.

'No, it isn't that I think there's arsenic in it' Harry drawled. 'It's
just that I don't feel thirsty.'

The German smiled. He was amused. Certainly he was every
inch the aristocrat, who wrapped arrogance around him like a cloak
and pulled it over his face like a mask; but when he met somebody
who didn't fawn on him, he could laugh and have a good time. He
was not quick-witted, but he did have a slow sardonic humor.

'How do you like it here?'

'Oh, I've always loved lions' mouths! They're so—cozy!' Harry
looked around, uptilting his cigar, waiting for a new deal. 'Not that I
think much of our host's taste in decoration.'

The room was big and it was dim, and he could not see far beyond
the light on the table; but all that he did see was what he would have
expected if he'd ever given any thought to the subject. One of those
dashing-bachelor flats—guns and swords and saddles, a skull ash tray,
a pipe rack (when had Wright started smoking a pipe?), decanters,
fencing masks, criss-crossed ropes of cigarette boxes dangling from the
ceiling. How could anybody, even a featherbrain like Mavis Lemming, ever be impressed by such a standardized array?

'After all, he *is* your host' Von Alvensleben chided.

'Not because he wanted to be. He was forced to invite me in.'

'Eh?'

The German turned, slapping the monocle into place, and his eyes and cruel big-lipped mouth were in startling contrast to the amiability of his voice. His English was perfect. He had served for some time as military attaché at the German Embassy in Washington. At present he was 'visiting' his 'friend' Herrdoktor Rundkopf, a fussy middle-class nonentity, an insignificant functionary acting—nobody knew why—as German consul at Panama. Rundkopf, overwhelmed, had turned over his best bedroom (and his wife with it, some said) to this high-born 'friend,' whom he 'baroned' assiduously, all but clicking his heels at each meeting. They made a comical pair when they went out, little Rundkopf and the massy firm-fleshed Junker. Von Alvensleben had been 'visiting' the Rundkopfs for several weeks; and though it was of course a high honor for the little consul, it must also have been a great expense.

'You mean,' the monocle gleaming, 'that you pointed a pistol at him in the doorway, like a cowboy?'

'Oh no. I didn't need to raise a gun. All I needed to raise was my voice. At least one or two of you men in here would be sure to recognize it.'

'Well?'

'Well then, how could he turn me away? It would look as if he was afraid of me, wouldn't it? It would certainly show him up as a poor sport—and in the eyes of most high Panamanians, just like with Americans, that's even worse than being a coward.'

It took Von Alvensleben a moment to get the point of this, but when he did get it he grunted appreciatively. From the end of the table Ward Wright, who was not in this pot, watched them. Von Alvensleben was stacking chips precisely, more interested in the talk than the game. Harry leaned back, smoking. He never stacked or sorted his chips: this was one of his few superstitions.

'But about the mensur, Kellems? the affair of honor?'

Harry said a harsh word.

'I spoke technically, of course. I do not understand how such a man as you happened to be there.'

'It was our host's idea, as I told you. He was eager to show me a sample of his ferocity and very great cleverness in making trouble. Has he offered to show *you* such a sample, Baron?'

Von Alvensleben's neck stiffened a little. His fingers, which had been aligning the tops of the chip stacks, became still.

'I feel sure that he has, Baron. I don't know what you've answered, but I hope you had sense enough to turn him down. His previous employers found him wanting, you know. I hardly think he's a good bet for the Imperial German Government.'

'I'm sure I do not know what you are talking about' said Von Alvensleben. 'I shall open for five dollars.'

'Stay' said Harry. 'Well, whatever your General Staff thinks about the chrome in New Caledonia—and if we do get the canal open by the middle of nineteen twelve, which is the dope now—well, I don't know. But you *have* consented to see Captain Wright many times, Baron.'

Gratingly, slowly: 'You have been spying, Kellems?'

'Why, of course! I thought you knew that! I didn't learn much, but my guess is that you're stalling him while you find out what Berlin thinks of the proposition. That's my *guess*. My wish is that you and your government would have nothing to do with the man. I tell you, Baron, he's a hopeless bungler.'

Von Alvensleben turned stiffly, and the eyeglass was in place.

'We will talk no more about this, please.' He turned back, raising his voice. 'Yes. . . . Now, who was it who raised? Ah. And it is fifteen dollars to me? Well, I shall make it thirty dollars.'

'Too steep for me' said Harry, and threw in his hand.

It was too steep for Ward Wright too, but he stayed another round before he learned this. He was not losing much; he might even have been making a little; but it was clear in his eyes and smile, and in the jerky way he handled his chips, that he had counted upon this game. To him as to Harry the situation was clear. They were the two best players. They were equals; but Harry had cash; Harry didn't have to care whether he won or lost—and so he won. Harry estimated that he was winning just about what Captain Wright might reasonably have hoped to win if Harry wasn't there. He leaned back, puffing at his cigar. He even took a sip of his highball, warm now. He wondered why he had ever felt anything *but* swell. He knew what he was doing.

Presently he began to talk to the German again. He made no mention of an agreement with Ward Wright, but instead talked about the duel. Graphically, slangily, in layman's language Von Alvensleben found deliciously funny, he described the duel, not as he had seen it, not as he remembered it, but comically. The baron ate this up. The baron was losing, but he didn't seem to mind. He scarcely noticed the game. He leaned closer to Harry, chuckling lecherously, delighted to hear confirmed his own conviction that one who had not belonged to the right corps in the right German university was inevitably a clown with a sword. Hating himself, Harry nevertheless did not spare himself. Von Alvensleben thought him a card! Von Alvensleben's neck and cheek quivered, and from time to time he stole merry side glances at the host.

When the game ended, long after the last sounds from the Café de los Dos Diablos had died, Von Alvensleben and this entertaining American were chattering and gossiping like schoolgirls.

Harry had won more than two hundred dollars—about fifteen hundred altogether, counting what he had won at roulette.

'You must come again' Ward Wright said, smiling, smiling, but a shade haggard, like an aging beauty in a harsh light.

Harry and the Baron von Alvensleben walked arm in arm to the Plaza de Santa Ana, where they got hacks. The arcades were packed with shadows still, but the middle of the square was all hard gray dawn, not in the least pearly. It would rain soon.

'Well, I'm out of the lion's mouth unscathed.'

Von Alvensleben actually thumped Harry's back. His hand was heavy. He had drunk a good deal of brandy.

'The lion and the mouse, eh?'

He laughed so hard that tears rolled down his cheeks. He was really a rather simple soul, Harry reflected.

'Well, I take it that you agree with me about the lion, anyway,' quickly, 'and that you're not likely to do business with it?'

'You may take anything you wish' Von Alvensleben said. 'But to you, Kellems—you need not worry. Of course I never said that!'

'Of course' said Harry.

24

THE HACK SQUEALED AND STRAINED, but Harry was watching butterflies tumble across the Chagres. His mood of exaltation had been succeeded not by one of dejection but by a sober awareness that all he had gained, besides the money, was a respite. It had been thrilling to win, but it had been merely a pause; for if Ward Wright had meant to kill him last night, Ward Wright was not likely to drop this plan because of a bad run of cards. True, Harry had had a nod from Baron von Alvensleben, who however had committed himself to nothing and at most had only hinted a confirmation of Harry's theory —that Wright, desperate for funds, cast off by his backers in Wall Street, had appealed to a German skilled in diplomatic dirty work, had been half encouraged, and now was about to be refused. Harry had reasons for thinking that Von Alvensleben had given el capitan money, probably not much, probably a mere sop, while they waited for word from Berlin. Why were those countries in Europe always talking about war? There was a scare that summer. Harry himself didn't believe anything would come of it; but it was true that great efforts were being made and vast sums spent in preparation; and it was also true that of Germany and France, the two snarlingest countries, France alone would get any war benefit from a canal at Panama.

This was a minor matter. What Harry really thought about was the butterflies. He had been thinking a great deal about Madeline for a long while, but he had never dreamt of speaking out until that afternoon on the river when she recited her own feelings; and indeed he might never have learned how much he loved her if she had not spoken first. Since then, however, and especially since Phil left, he had been more honest. He knew now that he'd been trying to ignore something which would not permit itself to be ignored. He had made a mess of the whole business, shying away. He had promised Art Price to keep from seeing her. No time limit was attached to the promise, which, however, Harry had taken to mean perhaps forever; but now, after only a little more than a month, he was cracking. Now that he had less than ever to offer her, now that he was a married man whose wife had left him, a man who was about to be turned out of his home, and whose very existence might be snipped off at any moment—now he was about to go to her on his knees. Well, he couldn't help it. He knew when he was licked. He supposed that love was like a liquid compound which must not be permitted to stay in a state of suspension: boil it, if you wish; agitate it, stir it vigorously; if you haven't the courage to drink it, uncork the bottle and dump the stuff out; but don't try to pretend that it isn't there—or it may explode.

He had half a mind to go to her now, though it was hardly light. Well, he'd go right after church.

He showered, set the alarm at nine, locked the bedroom door—Célestine never gave warning before entering a room—and threw himself down. He was very hungry, but too tired to browse. Even closed, his eyes hurt: they stung from the cigar smoke, and sometimes he saw the red and black spots on the cards, but mostly what he saw were the butterflies tumbling in fleecy swarms above the surface of the river, while the voice of Madeline behind him talked of love.

Joe Prendergast, who came from Nebraska, used to tell the D.M.s that nobody who had not lived out on the prairie could ever really appreciate a railroad train.

Well, nobody who hadn't lived on an island could ever really appreciate a ship. As far as communications were concerned, Panama was an island, an island fifty miles long and only about half a mile wide, and very crowded. The Panamanians themselves probably gave no heed to the matter; but the canal workers thought and felt like islanders, and, just as the prairie-town men drifted to the station when the five-something was due, *they* went to Cristobal as often as possible when a ship was to come in—even though they might have no friends aboard, even though they would have to return to the other side of the Isthmus to get their mail, if any. Mail was always the greatest topic of conversation, among newcomers and old-timers alike, in all seasons. Was it true that the ship was going to be late? Do you suppose it would be distributed before lunch? If it wasn't in until late afternoon, would the postmaster stay up through the dinner hour sorting it? Most of the postmasters were kind and conscientious men, and would go to work on the mail as soon as it was dumped off the special train from Cristobal, regardless of the hour, not pausing until they had boxed it or distributed it from the general-delivery window. You could always kick up a discussion as to whether it was better to get your mail through the office or to have your own box—assuming that you could get a box. Others said that even if you could get the box, general delivery was the quickest way; though still others pointed out that this depended upon the postmasters, who could hardly be expected to be good-natured every time. Everybody isn't Jerry Bliss, they used to say.

At any rate, the mail was the most popular topic of conversation. At the St Charles, before the service started, everybody talked about the mail. The *Havana* was due early the next morning (she was really the *Colon*, now that the Panama Railroad people had bought her from the Ward Line, just as the old *Mexico* was now the *Panama*; but they were often called by their original names). They said she wasn't going to be late.

Harry Kellems, like any islander, was interested in ships. He knew the *Havana* and the *Mexico*, as he knew the old *Alianca* and *Advance* and *Finance*, and the *Esperanza* and the *Seguranca*. If he didn't know every foot of them, he knew their passenger accommodations and their promenade and boat decks; he knew their skippers and officers, many of the stewards and sailors too. He had traveled on only one; but he had greeted friends, or, more often, told friends good-by, on all of these ships, which inevitably, and even though he seldom got over to the Atlantic side, played an important part in his life.

The mail was different. Mail meant little to him. He would talk with the others about it, but he really didn't care. Before Phil came he would look for her letters, and then too he had carried on a fairly considerable correspondence with friends in Paterson. Phil took over a good part of this correspondence when she arrived: she was a diligent letter writer and she wrote naturally to the friends they had in common, so that it was easy for Harry to ask her to tell so-and-so this-and-that. The other correspondence fell off—for no reason, it just fell off. This didn't seem to matter. In high school and college, what with the need for odd jobs, and especially the laundry job, and what with singing in church Sunday mornings and choir practice Wednesday nights, and the painful lack of spending money, Harry had never belonged to any fraternity or club excepting the glee club. Though anything but aloof, he had not gone around with any one crowd. And he had no near relatives. Mail day meant nothing to him.

He supposed that he would hear from Phil on this ship. He didn't much care. He wasn't thinking of Phil when the service started. He was thinking of the turgid Chagres and the butterflies.

They had a guest preacher, a Rev Mr Epwright, visiting the Isthmus for nobody knew what reason; but Mr Harris, as always, read the announcements, called the hymn numbers, and offered the open-

ing and closing prayers. It was Mr Harris who introduced Brother
Kellems and made known the fact that Brother Kellems would favor
them with 'Jesus, Lover of My Soul.' Mrs Halsey at the harmonium
thumped the opening chords.

There was somebody coming in, in back, and Harv Ellsworth was
showing her to a chair. Politely, to give her a chance to get seated,
and to give Harv a chance to get back to his own chair, Harry paused,
and Mrs Halsey played the first verse and chorus clear through. Only
when it came up again did he start.

> 'Jesus, lover of my soul,
> Let me to Thy bosom fly——'

The newcomer looked up and smiled at him, and it was Madeline.
Mrs Halsey was annoyed, and frowned openly, when Harry missed
several beats. Mrs Halsey was a straightforward woman who liked to
go right through with anything she had started, and whose musician-
ship, though thorough, was not supple. But Harry caught up.

> 'Hide me, oh my Savior, hide,
> Till the storm of Life be past——'

Madeline was no longer smiling. She was gazing earnestly at him.

There were the usual people to shake his hand and tell him how
beautifully he'd sung; and he smiled and fidgeted; but the presence of
a real preacher—though the sermon, Harry thought, had been uncon-
scionably long—relieved somewhat the customary pressure upon Harry
himself, who slipped away earlier than he had dared to hope.

Madeline was waiting outside. 'May I take you home afterward?'
he had whispered when he passed the collection basket to her; and
she had nodded. Now in friendly fashion she took his arm. You would
never have supposed that these two hadn't met in a month.

'I'm so glad you came. I was going to go right down to your house,
right after the service.'

'Were you, 'Arry?'

'I think I've been a fool, and also I think that you and I haven't
seen enough of one another.'

'Yes, I think that too. That's why I came up here today. But you
really were coming down anyway?'

'Yes. I wanted to see you and tell you that I'm ashamed of the way
I've behaved. I've been foolish and prudish.'

'Yes,' she agreed quietly, but without rancor, 'and presumptuous too, 'Arry. And so has Arthur Price.'

'You don't mean to tell me Art——'

'Oh, he's always a gentleman! But what is there that makes you two suppose you can divide my time as though you were sharing the services of a cook?'

She did not speak angrily, she didn't speak archly. She still held his arm and walked close to him.

'It wasn't that. It was only that Art asked me, considering that every time I was around—— Well, he thought it was only fair——'

'I see. That was very kindhearted, and very stupid. If you want me, why don't you try to take me? And if you don't want me, why do you care enough to stay away for the sake of another man?'

'But I do want you, Madeline! I—I've wanted you for a long time! I've had my dose of going without you. It was terrible. Oh, I've been so lonesome! And I *do* want you!'

Softly, 'You're hurting my arm, 'Arry.'

They had stopped. They were at the foot of the hill, near De Lesseps Park and the boundary line. A lot of people were passing, Sunday strollers, but Harry and Madeline paid them no attention.

'But I—I wanted to tell you. I'm not very good at this, I guess. What I'm trying to say is just about what you said that day in the cayuco. I mean, I love you. There isn't any holier-than-thou any more, or any wondering about what people will think, or any stewing about my duty toward my wife, or anything else. Madeline, I'm ready to give up anything or go anywhere or do anything in the world for you. You understand? I love you!'

'Y-you're s-still hurting my arm, 'Arry' she whispered.

They had been standing stock-still, side by side, each looking ahead rather than at the other, as though fear or amazement or perhaps horror had petrified them; but now he turned wildly.

'Why, you're crying, mademoiselle!'

'Yes,' her head down. 'Of c-course I'm c-c-crying!'

She leaned her head against him, and he got his arms around her and patted her back with large awkward hands.

'Well, I meant every word of it, and I'll tell you again, if you want. I'll tell you over and over again, if you want.'

'I w-will want you to, 'Arry. I've b-b-been lonesome too!'

She pushed him back a little, not lifting her face but turning her head. She dabbed her eyes with a handkerchief drawn from the pocket of her skirt, and blew her nose. Unexpectedly she chuckled.

'The idea of you two men debating between you which ought to have me! Did you draw cards perhaps, or roll dice?'

'Madeline, you mustn't say things like that!'

'I said something like that to Arthur last night when I told him I wouldn't see him any more. Only I made it stronger.'

'You told Art——'

'But he's coming tonight anyway. But let's not talk about it now.' She took his arm again. 'We haven't far to go now, and let's just walk along being happy. You are happy, aren't you?'

'Do you love me?'

'Yes, 'Arry.'

'Then I'm happy.'

She kept her head down, but her fingers dug into his arm, and her step was light: he could see the tips of her shoes, sometimes, peeping out from under her skirt in front: she seemed almost to be skipping.

Papa Desmoulins met them, his skullcap on his head, rag slippers on his feet. His presence dashed Harry, who had hoped for an embrace in the hallway. Harry sensed that Etienne Desmoulins too was displeased: he seemed to have expected somebody else. Madeline's father seemed thinner and even smaller than he had when Harry last saw him, and older too. His manners were correct; nor was he, as he sometimes was, distant and reserved; but he seemed excited, and there was a glint of madness in his eye.

'Ah! You have been to the church again, my cabbage?'

'Yes, Papa. And I do not wish dejeuner. I have no hunger. Conchita can serve you, n'est-ce pas? Monsieur Kellems and I, we would walk ourselves. Do you mind?'

'Surely not, my cabbage. You know that I have always a fondness for my own company.' There was something furtive about him. He opened the door. 'Only—I fear you might meet rain.'

'We will chance that, Papa.'

She disappeared into her room, and Etienne Desmoulins led Harry to the parlor.

'You 'ave not visit' us for a long time, monsieur. Is it that you work so hard on your canal?'

'There's been a lot to do.'

'You waste your time, monsieur!' The old man's voice was sharper now, and his eyes were brighter, though he sat quiet. 'That canal will never be finish'! I have the reason to know!'

Harry leaned forward, his face deferential. 'There is perhaps something in what you say, sir.'

'There is a great deal in what I say, I assure you!'

'Now if you would be good enough to tell me what it is that makes you believe——'

'I shall do nothing of the sort, monsieur!' He caught himself. He made a smile of great charm, drawing upon reserves built up throughout a lifetime's training. He waved a small hand. 'I only say, monsieur, that the canal will not be finish' by the men of your country. That is all.'

'You think France will undertake the work again?'

'I do not know,' gloomily. 'But it will not be finish' by Americans. I tell you that.'

Madeline returned, looking lovely, her face clear. She seemed poised on the balls of her feet.

'You are ready, 'Arry? Good! Let us go, then.'

They sat in the Café de Jesus, where the sudden rain had driven them, and though the rain itself forbade conversation they were absurdly happy, and sat close together, and beamed at one another, holding hands under the table; and indeed they were so disgusting that Jesus himself, who ordinarily took care of such norteamericanos as came to his place, sent Jose the stupid one to their table. Not noticing this, Madeline and Harry burbled on, as silly as kids.

They ordered coffee, which they didn't drink.

In a lull, one would start to say something—and then would stop, as the rain crashed down again; and the two of them would giggle, truly thinking that this was funny.

A coche came, its curtains flapping, the hoofs of the horse clop-clop-clop-clop-clopping on the pavement, and Harry whistled to it and when the cochero didn't hear ran out and stopped it. Inside, both a little wet, they clung together, kissing and kissing. Madeline's mood had changed. She was not gay, nor was she twitchy, as she'd been before. She kissed him very hard, pressing against him, and moaning a little, her eyes closed. After a while she disengaged herself.

'I want music' she said in a curious muffled voice.

She leaned forward to tug open a corner of the curtain, and shouted something at the driver through rain that sprang in. She sank back into Harry's arms; but she was quieter; and she no longer trembled.

They turned into a semicircular drive and stopped under a marquee. The plate-glass window in the door was backed by lace, and there was a Panamanian soldier who carried a rifle with bare bayonet attached.

'Uno amigo, Fernandez.'

He saluted her and smiled. He held the door open.

They went up a Turkey-red carpet spread over marble steps and opened another door, and then they were in the ballroom. Harry had been there once, soon after his arrival in Panama, when he'd stood uneasy in soup-and-fish, on this foot, on that, perspiring, shuffling gradually to the end of the room where the Presidente and his lady interminably shook hands. When it had come Harry's turn he muttered something in English, for he knew no Spanish then; but Dr Amador had replied in cheerful English. Then Harry had moved on, to swallow some punch, to munch a bit of cake—and to get out. He remembered little about this ballroom. Almost all he remembered was how hot it had been and how uncomfortable he had felt. The whole affair was staged, he had supposed, in order to give the white workers a chance to say that they'd met the President of Panama. That had been possible three years ago. *Now* if the Amadors were to essay such a gesture they would have to shake hands for days on end.

It was a square room. The walls were hung with maroon velvet, with here and there a gilt-framed oil painting of some Spanishy personage, male and female, but mostly male. The floor, all rugless, shone not like glass but rather like ice in a recently shadowed spot. From the ceiling hung two immense chandeliers.

'You don't mind, 'Arry? I feel I just must play a little while. And it has been so long since I played for you.'

'It's been too long.'

Tugging her gloves off, she went to the piano which once had been hers. She sat swiftly, and with no hesitation started to play.

She went from one thing to another, and most of it he had heard before, though there were times when he believed that she was improvising. She played with vigor, clearly, firmly. It was music that had gizzards, and it stirred him. He sat in one of the tiny gilt chairs that lined the room—unarmed gimcracks, the backs and legs of which were profusely Cupided and cornucopia'd, while the seats were of crimson satin. He leaned forward, elbows on knees. From somewhere behind him he could hear the sullen slap of rain on a window he couldn't see; but the hangings dulled this sound, and for all practical purposes the music had the mansion to itself. A servant came in, glanced curiously at Harry, bowed to Madeline, who didn't notice him, and went out. The rest of the time they might have been alone in the house—for that matter, alone in the whole world.

Madeline finished abruptly, with no thumped finale, with no drib-

402

bling-drip. She rose and went straight to him and put a hand on his head.

'Poor 'Arry! You were not thinking of the music, were you?'

'I was thinking of you.'

'Of us, n'est-ce pas?'

'Well yes, of us. I was thinking that there is only Célestine at the house, and I could arrange to send her downtown for something.'

'Don't hold your head low, my 'Arry. Naturally you thought that! Is it that you suppose I hadn't thought it too? That was one cause why I came here to play—to quiet myself. *No!*' as he rose, reaching for her. She touched his chest, drummed it with her fingers. 'You see, 'Arry, it is not yet to be. Not quite yet. I told you that Arthur Price is to call on me tonight. When I sent him away, last night'—she was whispering now, and he leaned over to catch the words—'I told him that no matter what happened, or what you thought of me, I must go to you. I told him that I liked him too much to be his wife. He cried out that he knew how I felt about you—we'd talked it over many times—and he was willing to have me even then. But I said I could not go through with it, I liked him so much. I could marry a man I didn't like at all, if he was rich and seemed kind. But to marry Arthur, it would be like incest. We know one another so well. Not the way you and I know one another, 'Arry! But we do know one another well, and it would be like that, like incest. But he was very earnest. He pleaded with me, and he asked me at least to take another day to think over it. Give me until tomorrow night, he said—that is, tonight—and he begged and pleaded so, 'Arry, with his long sad face, and I think he was weeping a little behind those glasses, and I felt sorry for him, so I said that very well he could call tonight. You see? It might make him feel a little better, somehow. He is very sensible and logical, and he thinks that I will see reason. He thinks the French are sensible and logical too, like him.'

'Aren't they?'

'Not when they are in love.'

She raised her face and kissed him quickly. With shortened breath, when he tried to hold her, she led him toward the door.

'No, not here! We—we can stop a little while in the foyer.'

The guard saluted, smiling upon them. 'It was very beautiful, the music, señorita. I listened whenever I could hear, when there was not too much rain.'

'I'm glad you liked it, Fernandez.'

The rainy season was with them for sure. It used to start tentatively, hesitantly, reconnoitering with breezy loud showers the land it meant to smash, gathering its strength, drawing in its breath; but now it had fully come.

There was rain, off and on, all that night. There was a great deal of rumbling bumbling thunder, especially between rains—or so it seemed, though this might only have been because when it was raining you could scarcely hear the thunder. The rain was immediate and obstreperous, all around you; but the thunder seldom came nearer than the top of the hills out Corozal way. They were getting it worse over on the Atlantic side. They usually did.

After dinner Harry went into the kitchen and definitely, unmistakably fired Célestine. He did this with all the gentleness he could command; for he felt kindly toward the big black slob, as indeed he felt kindly toward everybody in the world. But he did make it clear to her. He explained, or tried to, that it was necessary for him to quit this house and that he would hereafter live in a flat and eat his meals in cafés. He gave her two months' wages as bonus.

It caught his throat when she wept. She stood shaking, wailing, while great round tears rolled down her cheeks.

I shouldn't have kicked her that time, he told himself.

Feeling like a scoundrel, he made it plain that she was not to come back in the morning. It seemed brutal to thrust her out in the rain, and he squirmed and fussed, and was about to give her his only umbrella—when it occurred to him that she might use that as an excuse to return. It occurred to him at the same time that a coche would be cheaper; but he could think of no office in the city which would be open on Sunday night, nor could he think of a café or barroom where there was a telephone; so he called the hospital.

'Hello, hello? Is this the hospital? . . . This is Harry Kellems . . . Can you hear me? . . . Look, I wonder if you'd be kind enough to——'

'Hello, Harry.'

'Oh. Hello, Art. You're working late, aren't you?'

'Emergency operation. But I'm through now. I'm just about to start down the hill.'

'Yes. I—I wanted a hack, Art, and I didn't know how else——'

'I've got one waiting for me. I'll stop around for you.'

'No. Tell you: you take it on down and then send it back here. That'll be all right. Anyway, I suppose you're in a hurry to get to wherever you're going.'

You know where that is, Harry.'

Art Price's voice was clear, his accent precise; but he was suffering! It did not seem right to listen to a man suffer, even over the wire of a telephone connection.

'Harry, are you still there? Can you hear me?'

'Yes.'

'Do you want to wish me good luck?'

Harry heard the rain and the far thudding thunder. He looked at the ceiling. His hand around the receiver was all sweat.

'I can't exactly do that, Art. But anyway it's nice of you to send the coche. Good night.'

'Good night, Harry.'

He paced the parlor, troubled. Art Price always had a low exact voice, a careful pronunciation, an assuredness . . . Art was a man who hefted each word he was about to speak, and tapped it, and considered its relationship to the words just gone and those to come, before he released it from his mouth. As Madeline had said, he was a sensible and logical man. Just now, over the telephone, he had not sounded worried. Well, was he being his usual self, or did it mean that he had something up his sleeve?

In the kitchen Célestine blubbered, tears streaming down her face, while her shoulders and all her torso shook, shook. She did not wail, but she made a low wailing sound. The light in the kitchen was out, and the sound coming from there was eerie.

'Not when they are in love' Madeline had said, and had kissed him. But Art Price was a smart man, and he wanted Madeline. How much money did he have? Nobody on the Isthmus knew or would guess, but it was agreed that he was rich. His clothes were expensive. He had the air of a person accustomed to fine things. He had gone to some fashionable prep school—Harry forgot which one—and he was a graduate of Harvard. He never tried to show off. But he was stubborn, for all his careful politeness, for all the swell quiet grin.

Here! What was he doing? She had said she loved him, and she'd kissed him, hadn't she? Well then, why was he questioning? That's what it amounted to—*doubting* her! He was practically calling her a liar in his mind!

Why, he could not remember ever having doubted Phil this way!

The exercise, just the walking around, made him feel better. After all, he was the luckiest man in the world. He should be riding his luck, as he would do in poker. He didn't know how the game would end—you never do—but he knew that he was ahead, right now. He couldn't figure how he and Madeline would manage to get married; but he knew that she loved him—she had said so—and that tomorrow morning he would bring her here. They'd not have a long time! Jackson Smith the infallible would see to that! But never mind the future. Tomorrow was practically here now.

Tomorrow!

He found himself facing the piano, which had not been dusty since he kicked Célestine. He smiled with fatuous fondness at the pleated silk behind the lyre shape. Phil had taken the throw-over with her, but still the thing didn't look too bare. What would he do with it? It was Phil's; and he supposed he would store it somewhere and eventually send it back to her. Madeline must have a better piano than this, which was tinkly and thin, and not fitted for grand music. He opened it. Even the keys were clean, though it had not been played since Phil left. Standing, he started to one-finger. Soon he sang.

The rain beat down, the thunder rolled; and in the kitchen Célestine wailed on a higher note, like a dog baying at strange music. These sounds, crowding into the house, struggled for supremacy. Yet Harry sang.

When the carriage came he took her out, holding the umbrella over her, holding too one fat thick wet black elbow, while she sobbed. The cochero, too wet to care, and always mannerly, as became a British *object,* gazed sideways at them. Harry thought that he caught a glimpse of one of the Caseys at a window. He grinned. He gave the cochero money and instructed him to take Célestine wherever she cared to go. He kept the umbrella.

From the porch, afterward, he heard Célestine's wailing until it faded and was sunk in the rain sounds as the hack went down the hill.

It was fortunate that he was so tired. He'd had less than three hours' sleep the night before. He was rich, for him; he was tired; and he was in love. He lay on his back in bed, stark naked, and softly sang different ballads over and over, smiling as he sang, knowing that soon sleep would come.

The morning was garish. There wasn't a cloud in the sky, and the sunshine was sheer braggadocio. All the same, it was sultry; and the air you breathed tingled an electric warning in your nostrils. To the north and east, snuggled in clouds not seen, thunder spoke ominously: it was as though there were war, a bombardment, far away and out of sight; while in Panama City the puddles gleamed clear and innocent.

They were all talking about the mail, and when they could expect it, but they leaped to their feet when Harry entered.

'Good morning, dear boss,' the high chorus.

'Hello, dizzy-flats!' He smiled right and left, and nodded, and went into his office, leaving the door ajar. He was half humming, half singing. 'Oh, Burt!' he fairly caroled.

'Feeling pretty good today, huh?'

'I shall be very busy, Burt. I'll be outside somewhere, inspecting. I don't know just where you could get me. No sense trying.'

'Say, that boat's in. Came alongside more than two hours ago.'

'That's good. If any letters come for me, you can just leave them here on the desk. Don't send them up to the house.'

'Listen, Giants. That wasn't what I meant. I meant that the sure-enough engineer is supposed to be on this boat. Don't you think it would be a good idea if you stuck around the premises, in case he decided to start to work right away? Don't you feel like gazing at the melody?'

'It's all right, Burt. If he comes you can show him around. Tell him to just make himself t'home.'

'If I didn't know you better, Giants, I'd say you were shellacked.'

'But you do know me better, don't you?' with a smile. 'All right. If the new boss does come, just let him take over, and explain that I'm very busy today—outside.'

'Doing what?'

'None of your business, Burt. Well, you know where everything is——'

'Everything except you.'

'—and if there are any calls on the telephone, you can take care of them.'

'Back pedal, bobolink! Emerge! You can't throw so much responsibility on me! This is a day when you ought to stick around the shanty!'

'Good-by, Burt. And be sure to keep everything neat.'

'Hey, hold your horses! You saw what happened to your friend Larry Doyle last week, didn't you?'

'Larry Doyle?'

'Yes, Larry Doyle—that you said was going to prove such a lulu! Muffs a straight liner that practically walks up and tries to cuddle into his glove, and the White Sox bring in two men who're——'

'Good-by, Burt. Remember what I told you now. And be a good boy. Ta-la-la-lo-loo!'

Burt, baffled, followed him into the big office and stared after him. 'Not pifflicated,' decided Burt, 'daffy.'

These were the streets, these were the narrow streets of Panama, but they were fields of daisies; and the sun shone bright. Here was the stench, and it had become perfume. Somewhere thunder spoke, trying to scare people; but Harry and Madeline walked springily.

'Was Art all right?'

'He was gentle. He always is.' She held Harry closer and actually pressed her face against his shoulder. Anybody could have seen them. 'That was last night. That's the past.'

Their bodies appeared to move together; they took the same length of stride; there was no real difference between walking like this and dancing.

'The future will be wonderful, 'Arry. We will—the word you would say—we will *fix* it.'

Reverently: 'We'll fix it.'

They passed under the balcony of what had been Mama Margery's house, closed now and empty. They issued into the Plaza de Santa Ana.

From here, ordinarily, they would have turned toward the waterfront for a stroll along Las Bovidas, along the sea wall, to watch the gulls. Now they looked at one another. They smiled, and almost kissed. They started for Ancon.

They were through the park, and climbing, when the first drops whapped on the ground. These were fat drops, warm and round, and they hit with a casual juiciness that was pleasant to the ear. There were not many of them. They fell with no plan, haphazardly, anywhere.

Madeline and Harry looked to the left, and the clouds were coming, yes. The war was no longer a distant bombardment; it was getting near; the clouds, dark cavalry, had raced halfway across the heavens to claim the sky over this land.

Madeline giggled.

'We're going to get wet' she said.

'Yes' he said.

'And you forgot to bring your umbrella.'

'Yes' he said.

'I am glad because of that, 'Arry. I would not like to think that you remembered your umbrella when you knew that you were coming for me—for——' She stopped, turning to him, turning him. She looked up at him with eyes that did not blink. ''Arry, we know what we're doing, don't we?'

'We know what we're doing' he said.

'If you want to stop now——'

He drew her close and kissed her lips slowly. Oversized drops of rain plopped on the ground here, there.

'Oh, I am so happy, 'Arry. Let's run. We will get wet anyway, but let's run.'

Laughing, they ran.

The sun might have been stepped upon. The trying-out showers, the attack of the advance cavalry, passed lightly and without malice, like that many great sheets of paper being flipped across the hillside.

They had too little breath for laughter when at last they sprang up the steps and Harry opened the screen door and they reached the shelter of the porch; but they had enough breath to kiss. Damp, shivering, panting, they squeezed one another. Presently Harry held her a little away and put a hand against the side of her neck and slipped the thumb up through her hair to touch the lobe of an ear he couldn't see. The hand was wet, the neck was wet. Her hat and dress glistened with raindrops. She raised her face, her eyes open; and she was weeping.

'Madeline, Madeline my sweet, mademoiselle, I love you!'

'' Arry, I love you!'

He let his hand slip lower. She gazed at him, tears welling out of her open eyes; and her lips were open too. The rain swung in easy sheets against the screen door; and minute drops, a spray, besprinkled them.

Tin, tin, tin, went the piano. Tiddy-tiddy-tin. High and fancy, and with refined upswings, with grace notes. Jest alongin' for your smile, Jest to make my life worth while. . . . There were ripple-offs. There were dramatic pauses. Still there's only sadness, dear, In a place where you ain't near. . . .

'Excuse me a minute' said Harry.

He crossed the porch and opened the door, and Phil turned on the piano stool, reaching out her arms. She had taken her hat and veil off, and her gloves: these were on her suitcase in the middle of the parlor. She was wearing a blue dress. Her eyes were half closed, and her arms were straight out, and she wriggled her fingers, inviting him.

'Darling, come here and kiss me. I tried, darling, but I can never live without you. I know that now. Come here and kiss me.'

25

SHE SAT WELL CURVED, this woman, this wife of his. They were shapely arms that she reached out, and her buttocks spread with daintiness on the stool, and her knees were together, her feet were together, the tips of the toes peering out from under the skirt. It was a pretty face too—the face of a doll in distress. The forehead, a shade too broad, though not bulgy, made the chin seem even smaller than it was. This was a somewhat pointed chin; and Harry remembered that Mrs Edwin C. Harmey had a pointed chin. That exquisite trifle, the mouth, pouted. The hair, the finest feature, no longer was pompadoured: caught in a huge Psyche knot now, it drew to itself whatever light was in the room, and glowed a deeper, darker honey-yellow, even showing teasing glints of red.

She moved nothing but the coaxing fingers.

'Darling, darling,' her eyes half closed, 'I've been waiting so long for this moment. I was wrong to think that I could ever live without you, darling. Come and kiss me.'

Harry was a statue.

Phil's head had been back; but now she lowered it a little, and she began to open her eyes very wide, popping them, pouting even more, to give her face the babylike expression she knew became it.

'Harry, dearest,' a whisper, 'have I surprised you? I thought it would be fun if—— Darling, don't you know who this is talking to you? Don't you know that this is your wife?' The eyes were enormous, as wide open as she could stretch them. 'It's your wife, who loves you, Harry. It's me. It's your Phil.'

He did not stir.

The fingers ceased to wriggle, and she drew her hands toward her face and shut her eyes and lowered her head. Her shoulders sank.

With a stifled sob: 'Dearest, you mustn't stand and stare at me as if you were seeing a ghost. Come to me, Harry sweet! Come and kiss me! I can't bear seeing you just look at me that way!'

Her breast, back of the peekaboo, rose and fell. She began to rock from side to side.

'No, you mustn't look at me that way, darling, darling! You *mustn't!*

I—I've been a bad girl, Harry precious, bad and foolish because I thought I could live without you. But all the time I've wanted you so much! I've been bad, and I'm humble now, dearest, and you can scold me, but don't stand looking at me like that! Take me, Harry! Take your wife! Tell me afterward that you hate me for the silly way I've acted, but take me now——'

It was then that she rose from the piano stool, lifting her head with a passionate toss, throwing her arms wide—and seeing Madeline.

'Oh' she said.

'Good morning' said Madeline.

Thunder bounded like great boulders on the roof. From the north there came a crash of lightning like the splitting of thin but resistant wood; and the windows leaped momently in light; and the air twanged, taut.

It was difficult to breathe. Phil rose on her toes, and her arms were stiff at her sides, the fists clenched; and she raised her chin a little, as though she was about to scream. However, she didn't scream.

Feels she can't make any headway against the thunder, Harry thought. Well, she was the same. The rest of the world might change, and Harry with it, but Phil stayed the same. For an instant, when he first saw her sitting on the piano stool, he had been stabbed to the heart by pity and love. After all, and no matter how well you knew her, she was a woman of beauty—of a very feminine beauty too, gentle, warm, soft, touchable, kissable. She had looked contrite, and this must have wounded her, who had no stomach for humble pie. She had kept her eyes downcast, so that her lashes showed well.

Just a gasp, a swallow, a dizzy moment, and then he was clear-headed. He was disgusted with her tricks and gestures, her theatrical-ism. How had he ever been fool enough to fall for that stuff? She wasn't even original with it: she behaved like a third-rate actress in a fourth-rate play. And her flirting! her coquetry! Why, this spoiled daughter of a rich man, accustomed to getting whatever she asked for, knew how good-looking she was and never hesitated to turn on a smile, as readily as you'd turn on an electric light, when she wished to wheedle something out of somebody. She was wheedling Harry now. She was flaunting her charms, her curves. She was confident in her ability to make any man tremble, and she was sure, had always been sure, that Harry at any time, with a little teasing, could be made to trot just behind her left heel like a well-trained dog. He could imagine her saying it, smiling as she said it: 'Heel, Harry! Heel now!' It had worked once, it had worked often, it would work again—she thought.

Once he would have gone to her with no hesitation. But he saw through her now. She had decided to take him back, as better than nothing. Afraid that he might reply to a cablegram with a curt refusal, she had simply sailed. She was ready for him now. She had probably sat up half the night getting primped. She had been posed at the piano. A little playing, a little weeping, she had figured, and a few kisses, and she'd have him on the bed. Once she got her clothes off she could do anything with him.

Well, God damn it, he thought, looking at her, it's going to be different after this! The next time I perform on that bed it won't be with her!

'Harry,' in accents icy, 'please send that woman away.'

'No.'

'Harry, I did think that in my own house——'

She stopped, a baffled Bernhardt, for the thunder's rocks once more slammed the corrugated-iron roof. Lightning flared at the windows, and went out, and flared again, and went out again.

'In my own home,' she pursued with dignity when she could be heard, though even then she had to shout above the rain, 'I *had* thought I might be free from—from women like that.'

Madeline only smiled a little.

'Women like what?' asked Harry.

'Harry, after all I've been to you, and all I've done for you——' It was not only to overcall the rain that she raised her voice: she was beginning to scream. 'And now you have the nerve to stand there and tell me I have to receive this—this foreigner! And when I've just come back to you too, disregarding everything my own mother and father said, and all my friends. Here I've just come back—and this is the way you treat me.'

'I didn't expect you' he pointed out.

'Well, that's clear enough. You wouldn't be having visitors if you did. And I must say you haven't shown any pleasure at *seeing* me back, after I've come all this distance. You almost look as though you didn't *want* to have me back!'

'I don't' said Harry.

The thunder bumbled, then burst into the greatest noise of all; and its echoes were cut by the slash and patter of rain.

Lightning lit her eyes, and even in that instant he saw the bewilderment they held. She had flirted, she'd been imperious, she had scolded; and still he would have none of her. Perhaps she would have wept then—sincerely, not for effect—but Madeline must have moved behind

Harry; and when Phil looked at Madeline she knew only rage. She ignored Harry's presence, or possibly even forgot it.

'*You told him about Ward Wright!*'

Had Madeline smiled in that slow Mona Lisa way? Was that what Phil had seen? Madeline was not smiling now, when Harry turned to her.

'No' she said.

'You told him, you—you stuck-up adventuress!'

'No, I didn't tell him. Nobody told him.'

'And a fine thing, coming from *you,* of all persons! Why, you were his mistress yourself, before I even met him!'

Madeline shook her head.

'He told me himself that you were!'

'Then he lied' said Madeline. 'He often does lie. You should know that.'

The realization of what they were talking about rose inside of Harry: it rose in thick dark slow clouds, like smoke from a smudge pot, and there seemed to be no fire connected with it, and no sharp pain, though it did sting his eyes and throat, so that when he spoke, turning to his wife, he had to say the words twice over in order to make sure that they were audible.

'Is—is this true, that you and—with that man——'

'Yes, it's true! As long as your French friend told you!'

'Nobody told him' Madeline said again, without anger, without raising her voice. 'Everybody in Panama knew it, but nobody told him —until you did yourself, just now.'

Harry said, shaking his head, coughing a little: 'But a cheap—a cheap show-off like that——'

'Yes, I went to bed with him! Not once, but a lot of times! Why shouldn't I? He's a better man, that way, than you will ever be! Isn't he, my dear?' she snarled at Madeline.

Madeline shrugged.

Phil began to weep.

'Oh no, I shouldn't have said that, Harry! I didn't mean it! I didn't know what I was saying!' She stumbled toward him, her hands over her face. 'Don't listen to what I said, Harry darling, darling! Put your arms around me and say you forgive me! Do anything you want— beat me, kill me—I deserve it—but forgive me first, darling!'

He put out an arm, stepping away from her. He tried to be decent about it; but he really didn't want her to touch him.

She grasped the hand and covered it with kisses, crouching like a whipped dog. He shook the hand free, again gently; yet she went staggering back as though shoved.

'Oh, oh, you've hurt me!' She dropped upon the piano stool. 'You struck me!'

'I didn't do anything of the sort' Harry muttered.

They might have been hearing the scratches for some time, between thunderclaps, but it was difficult to be sure in the pauseless thrum of rain. Harry, when he first became conscious of them, believed that they had been going on for several minutes. It might have been a dog or cat at the front screen door; though why in a rain like this a cat or dog should be there, instead of under the porch, he couldn't guess.

He didn't like to look at Phil. He went out on the porch and opened the screen door.

Conchita, soaked, trembling, her eyes rolling, tumbled in. She must have run up the hill, and she was scarcely able to breathe. She'd lacked either the strength or the wit—she was not bright—to knock at the door. She had only scratched, animal-like, to attact attention. Now she knelt; and even when Madeline went to her and spoke sharply, the poor stupid wet girl could only whimper for a while.

When words did come, however, they came with such a rush that Harry had to strain both his ears and his Spanish.

Papa had said that he would not go to work. This was not unusual. There was little work for Papa to do, few records still to be translated; so that there was nobody to press him. His health had not been of the best, and sometimes, especially when the rain was heavy, he preferred to stay home of a morning. Either Madeline or Conchita was always there; and if anything happened when Madeline was not there, Conchita knew that she was to get in touch with her mistress as soon as possible.

Well, not long after Madeline and Harry left, el capitan had arrived with a package for Papa. Papa had sent her, Conchita, to the kitchen, and he had closed the door, dropping his voice to a whisper. He had seemed excited, and Conchita had been frightened, sensing trouble. Conchita had looked through the keyhole. She hadn't been able to see the things in the box, but one had fallen to the floor, and afterward she'd picked it up, and here it was. El capitan had gone. Papa, who had put the box away but still hadn't noticed the fallen object on the floor, paced up and down, looking at his watch. Suddenly he had clapped on a hat, taken an umbrella, tucked the box under his coat, and sallied forth.

'You didn't stop him, Conchita?'

'Señorita, he went so fast! He was out before I knew it!'

She had, at least, pursued him. Not daring to accost him—the look in his face was fierce and strange, and she was afraid—she had trailed him to the railroad station. She had seen him buy a ticket, she didn't know to where. She had hurried back to the house, picked up the thing which had fallen, and run up the hill.

Harry took the thing from her hand.

'What is it?'

'A detonating cap for dynamite.' Harry pocketed it. 'I think I had better go after Papa.'

'Yes, yes!' Madeline spoke hastily to Conchita, commanding her to go home, change into dry clothes, and wait there on the chance that el señor would return.

Harry was looking at his watch.

'Hasn't been a train in three quarters of an hour, but the eleven-five will leave in a few minutes.'

'Can you make it, 'Arry?'

'I can try.'

Madeline nodded and turned. Phil, still on the piano stool, no longer wept. It might be that Phil had heard or sensed the departure of her audience. She stared through the open door to the porch.

'And you?'

'I will stay here, 'Arry.' Hands on hips, she started for the parlor, for a fascinated rabbit. 'I would like to have a talk with Mrs Kellems.'

He knew the ticket agent, but he had no time to ask about Papa Desmoulins. He had no time to ask anybody anything. It was only by sprinting that he made the last car—and almost jerked his arm out of joint. In a down swirl of cinders he grasped the rail, panting and panting, while his heart thumped, his chest heaved.

It was then that the pain began to come. It came bobbing atop a flood of memories and half memories of hushed conversations, embarrassed looks, sudden silences, puzzled eyes, astonishment at the mention of Ward Wright. . . . Oh, it was perfectly clear now! Even if Phil had not blurted it, Harry would have known. He needed no proof. All he had needed was suspicion, and his memory. He recalled to mind the way waiters at Dos Diablos had treated him, the way Jackson Smith had sneered, the way Madeline had fallen silent that afternoon on the river when he pointed out that Phil, of course, would never do anything *wrong;* and how men he liked would look down or look away, changing the subject, when he made any mention of wives. So they all knew it? Most of all, he remembered now, clinging to the rail of the back platform, how Lemming had screeched: 'You, of all persons!' Yes, Lemming had known too.

The door was opened, and the conductor appeared, and the pain went away. Did he know? Harry laughed.

'Say now, you're not allowed to stand out here! You ought to——'

'Shut your mouth, sweetheart' said Harry.

It was the same conductor with whom Harry had had a tangle the day of Phil's first arrival.

'All right,' backing into the car. 'You stay out there and I'll get a cop somehow! You know perfectly well that——'

'Don't burst into tears' Harry advised. 'I'm coming.'

He went through coach after coach, not walking backward but turning for a back glance at the face of every oldish man. There were not many. This was a young man's job, this Panama Canal.

Now and then somebody would call to him, invite him to sit down and have a cigar; but he'd say 'No, thanks.' He kept moving up, looking at the back of every head, at the front of a few. It was close and hot in the cars, with all windows shut: it was steamy, smelling of wet clothes. Between cars, each time, he'd be caught in a strong down draft which pelted him with soot.

They had passed Pedro Miguel, they were pulling into Paraiso, when he reached the foremost car. Papa Desmoulins was not there. Puzzled, Harry went to the brakeman.

'Say, Clarky, have you seen a little thin old Frenchman?'

'Papa Desmoulins?'

'That's the guy.'

'Sure, he's here. 'Scuse me. Got to call the old all-aboard.'

The train had come to a stop. Clarky sprang down, looked back and forth, waved his arm, sprang back. In a moment he was again beside Harry.

'Yeah, he's here somewheres. Didn't get off just now. Only three men, and they were all big guys.'

'Yes, I saw them through the window.'

'He was sitting up front here. . . .'

They started forward, and they were near the middle of the car when they saw Etienne Desmoulins—or at least the top of his hat. He had been on the front steps, by the side of the furthest-forward platform, just behind the tender. Instead of getting off on the platform at

416

Paraiso, he had waited a little until the train started, saving himself a hundred yards, before he jumped. Men who were going to work up the Line a little might do that—but it was not what you'd expect of a small frail aged aristocrat.

Harry ran to the platform. He was starting down the steps when Clarky, who had run after him, grabbed his arm.

'Let me go! I want to——'

'You can't jump now, you fool! Not when it's here!'

He was right. Even with the train picking up speed, Harry might have done it on a level expanse without breaking a leg; but the train had swung left to start across the Cut on a narrow wooden trestle. Cursing, Harry climbed back. Through a window, when the train was all on the trestle, he could see back toward the Paraiso station, between which and Cucaracha, making for the hill, trudged a small figure in white.

'Is it that important?'

'It's pretty important.'

The train reached the northern bank and left the trestle to go upon the berm. It slowed considerably for the turn; besides, Culebra, a stop, was just ahead.

'Here I go now.'

'All right, but don't ever tell anybody I let you!'

'I won't.'

He landed on the edge of the berm, running, and slipped and went over. The bank was not sharp at this point, and below the berm it was not high. He cut himself on some stones; but for the rest the trip down, though messy, was swift and not notably uncomfortable: he made it on the seat of his pants. He rose and started to run.

Such a thing as a cloudburst made no difference to the workers— unless it made them more disagreeable. Scores of drills, hundreds of them, tripod drills and well drills, rat-tatted into the soft stubborn rock. Compressed air hissed. A Lidgerwood train crossed the trestle, dirt and small stones spilling from its sides. A foreman strode back and forth, waving a red flag, shouting for everybody to stand away: he had to shout very loud to make himself heard. Another Lidgerwood train started out of a siding to the main track, where still another, empty, awaited it. The shovels dipped steel sunbonnets and raised great steel arms. . . . Harry scampered around the end of the compressed-air main and ran toward the trestle. He heard the blast the foreman had flagged against, but in sound it was no more than a cough behind him, though he felt as if somebody had pushed his shoulder blades and he saw small stones and splaps of mud land near his feet: a dynamite blast meant little here in the Cut.

He stayed on the upperside of the trestle, the far side from Cucaracha, on the chance that Papa Desmoulins might have seen him or might be looking for him. When he had climbed to the berm on the southern side of the Cut, at the foot of the hill, and was back on the railroad, he looked up. Madeline's father was a white speck on the muddy yellow hill, a toiling wavering speck.

It was a dark enough day at best, and even when there was no rain there was a good deal of thunder and lightning, and the clouds hung low. Now the rain came again, sweeping in sheets like masses of driven fog across the face of the hill, alternately blotting and rediscovering the small white figure. Papa Desmoulins was about half-way up when it began to rain. He did not raise his umbrella, which he seemed to find more useful as an aid to climbing.

Harry started after him.

Twice Harry yelled, but if the man ahead heard he gave no sign. Thereafter Harry saved his breath.

This was a bad slope. The Cut side of Cucaracha was shaly, but there stretched underneath it a stratum of rock which got slime-covered when the stones above let rain through: this was the worst place in the Cut for landslides. While Harry climbed, small stones and shards dislodged by Etienne Desmoulins tumbled and bounced past him, and rivulets of pebbles formed cones like plaster dust when you have knocked a hole into a wall.

At one time Cucaracha had been peaked, but its top now was a ridge some sixty feet long, not razored: indeed, there was a path, a path Harry had walked with Lord Chudit, with Edwin C. Harmey, and others.

Desmoulins made for the south end of this ridge, and when he reached it he seemed to collapse. Certainly he fell to his knees, and his head was bowed far over: he might have been doubled in prayer to some oriental god.

He sprang to his feet nimbly enough. He turned—no, whirled—with the umbrella lifted. Perhaps he had heard Harry, who was climbing fast, or perhaps he had known all the time that Harry was behind him. His mouth was open. He threw the umbrella. Without waiting to see where it landed—it landed a few feet from Harry—he leaped along the ridge. Such agility and speed would have been amazing in anybody. In Etienne Desmoulins they pointed straight to madness.

Twenty feet from the first place he dropped into another oriental prostration of obeisance.

Harry had changed direction when the man leaped along the ridge, but now Harry swerved back for the first place.

There was a tin can, opened side down. It looked like an ordinary food can, except that it was unlabeled and the sides had been punched with holes. Harry kicked it—and all but fainted.

Dynamite may be wet, it will explode in water; but a fuse, to burn, must be fairly dry. The can had protected the fuse, which must have been capped into place and lighted by Papa Desmoulins. The stick of dynamite to which the cap had been fastened was wired to another stick about two thirds of the way down, and the second was wired to a third, and there could have been and probably were more.

Harry remembered afterward that his back hurt as he lurched forward to one knee. Was that the muscle to resist, in such a case? But he did get down. He ripped out the lighted fuse and threw it somewhere behind him.

There was a crash of thunder, as though in applause, or derision.

He rose, running toward Papa Desmoulins. He saw another tin can at Papa Desmoulins's feet, and another beyond that, and another. . . . He tried to run very fast, but he tried too hard. His legs might have been in steel braces, like the legs of some unfortunate crippled child. He fell, nose and mouth and forehead lacerated by stones. When he looked up, trying to get up, he was glad he had fallen.

Etienne Desmoulins stood between the second and third cans, facing Harry; and his right arm was straight-stretched toward Harry; and he had something bright in that hand. Harry heard the shots, which were not loud: but they were clear, distinct. Rain whammed him, as he pushed his face into the mud and wet stones.

Well, I'm dead, I suppose: this was what he thought.

Well, maybe it's just as well: he thought.

He lay for what seemed to him a long while. Should he think of Madeline? That was what he wanted to do, if he was going to die. . . . After all, Madeline meant more to him than anything else in his life. His *useless* life, damn it! Why, he'd just begun to live, just really started to feel things as he knew now he ought to feel them. He didn't *want* to die! There were no shots. He listened with absurd fussy care; and still there were no shots. He could remember the quick sharp sound of them—a small sound, not loud, a trifle to anybody who'd roamed the Cut below and heard real noises.

He looked up, and at the same time got up. Papa Desmoulins was there, a white erratic figure in the rain, leaping up, down, up, down, but no longer facing Harry with that bright thing in his hand.

With no hesitation now, Harry ran to the next can. He kicked it over. He threw himself on his face again, as again he snatched a spluttering fuse.

This couldn't continue. The mud was good. He wanted it on his face like this, and he wanted to dig right into it with his nose, dig and squirm in, and try to get himself as far below as——

He made himself lift his head.

Papa Desmoulins was rising, a hunched mad figure, from the place where the third can was. Papa Desmoulins looked down; he looked around; he began to windmill his arms.

Something had gone wrong. Harry didn't know what it was. Harry only knew that he pushed his face back into the mud. He held his face there, squeezed it there.

His ears hurt hard and harsh, as though somebody had stuck sticks into them. His temples were pushed. He felt nothing against his back until, lifting his head, he felt the rain.

Papa Desmoulins after all was a fragile man. His little bones, you thought, could have been broken with a flick of your forefinger, no more strength than you'd use to send a spitball across the room. Yes, he teetered, a shadow, a white wavering, on the edge of Nowhere; and it seemed an hour before he fell.

The earth gurrumphed. Harry felt as though somebody were slapping a wet towel across his shoulders very hard. He got up, somehow.

Etienne Desmoulins did not get up, but turned over and over, a silly scarecrow, over and over, his limbs stiff, sometimes covered with stones and sloppy mud, sometimes with an arm sticking straight out, and sometimes his thin fine face appeared as a flashed thing.

Harry got out of where he was. He began to run downhill.

Etienne Desmoulins had not rolled beyond the tracks, though the spew of earth which had carried him was there: it was a stoppage a dozen Bims could clear in half an hour. Somebody had seen the fall, and there were five or six men there when Harry reached the body. It *was* a body, one of the men said.

'He's as dead as anything can be. I'll promise you that. I used to work in a hospital.'

'He must be very carefully taken care of' said Harry, sliding to the spot. 'He was on a special mission for Dr Gorgas.'

'Are you hurt? You look pretty bad.'

'I'm all right. Only thing is, I must get to a telephone.'

420

'What in hell happened? I looked up and I saw——'

'Never mind the gassing! I said I want a telephone!'

'Now keep your shirt on, snooky-ookums! The Yellow Peril's on the siding over there, and I guess the colonel will know.'

'I'm not talking about *that* colonel! I said Dr Gorgas! Whose hand-car is that? Are you dizzy-flats going to help me, or will I have to pump it myself?'

A foreman said: 'Mister, I don't know who you are, but this here's a pretty serious accident, and I figure——'

Somebody else said: 'Hey, it's Harry Kellems. I don't know what it's all about, Harry, but I'll help you pump that handcar.'

'Thank you' said Harry, who didn't remember the man. He looked around. 'Is there anybody who would like to stop us?'

'Come on' the man said. 'Nobody's going to stop us.'

Colonel Goethals was in the office at Culebra and had heard about the accident and was about to start out. Harry walked past him to a telephone. Harry spun the crank.

'Do you mind telling me what this is about?'

'I'm sorry, sir. I have an important call to make.'

Mrs Gorgas answered through the echoes of the gasp. She started to say that Dr Gorgas was not in—but she recognized the voice.

'Why didn't you say right away who you were? Harry, if you——'

'Excuse me very much, Mrs Gorgas, but could I have the doctor right away?'

'Why, certainly!'

Harry said that of course Dr Gorgas remembered the assignment he'd given to him and to Etienne Desmoulins out at Cucaracha. When Dr Gorgas started to speak, Harry said the same thing again in a louder voice.

'Not a very good connection, sir. Did you hear me?'

'Yes, I heard you.'

'You see, Colonel Goethals is here, and I think it might be better if you were here too, sir, to explain to him about that special assign-ment. Could you catch the one-nine?'

'I'll catch it, Harry.'

Violet eyes were close, and they were eyes you couldn't laugh at. Dark violet eyes in a dark pink face.

'Perhaps I had better speak to Colonel Gorgas myself?'

'I'm sorry, sir, but I think he's in a hurry.'

You didn't say such things to the master of the Yellow Peril. The violet eyes were steady, but there was a film of uncertainty over them: the very boldness of the speech made this man wary.

'You're certainly not questioning my *word*, Colonel?' The line had gone dead: it was a dead piece of mechanism he held to his ear. 'Possibly you'd rather have Dr Gorgas tell you?'

Nobody likes a showdown; and the eyes wavered.

'Very well' Harry said into the mouthpiece, into nowhere. 'Colonel Goethals agrees that it would be proper for you to catch the one-nine. He will meet you here, and I'll be in Panama to meet you first, sir. . . . Oh yes, sure. . . . All right. Good-by.'

He hung up.

'Now if I may have the services of that handcar——'

'Why?'

'Because Dr Gorgas asked for it, sir.'

'*I* didn't hear Colonel Gorgas ask for it.'

Harry couldn't think of anything else to say, so he walked past the man, walked past them all, and out of the office.

'You—and you—and you too! Colonel Goethals' orders, you're to take me to Panama City right away. There's a slight block, but we'll carry it around that. Well, *what are you standing there for?*'

By the time Colonel Goethals reached the porch of the office building, the handcar was far down the tracks.

Harry had four and a half minutes with Dr Gorgas, who listened up to the last split second, his hand on the platform rail. He was nodding as he swung himself onto the step. His cigar waggled. He had never asked Harry why Harry hadn't stayed out in Culebra. He was a gentleman.

She came toward him, straight, not smiling, arms at her sides, but with welcoming eyes. They kissed.

'Is he all right?'

He wanted her very much. He wondered if she could read his face.

'He doesn't need your help' he said simply.

They kissed again. They went into the parlor. Phil's bags were no longer there, and the piano had been closed.

'She's going back' Madeline said.

'What did you do to her?'

'Nothing. I only told her that if she did not permit us to marry I would kill her.'

'Oh, is that all?'

He could see into the bedroom, where the shades had been lowered and the bedspread taken off and the sheet turned down. He decided to say nothing further, now, about Papa Desmoulins. He had assured her that her father didn't need her help. He could explain this later—when she asked for the explanation she was apparently afraid to ask for now. They had both waited too long already. There must be no more delays.

'Or if I couldn't reach her to kill her, I said, I would see that everybody in Paterson knew what everybody in Panama knows now.'

'You fight dirty. What else did you tell her?'

'That she should go to that place—the place where Americans——'

'Reno?'

'Yes, I said that either she divorces you or you'll divorce her.'

'But I wouldn't do a thing like that!'

'I told her you had sworn to me you would.'

'But on what grounds could she——'

'I promised her that, 'Arry. If it is infidelity it is easy.'

'And we haven't done it yet.' He laughed. He turned her to face the bedroom. 'No, come to think of it, we haven't yet, have we?'

'No, 'Arry. Not yet.'

The thunder made a lot of noise.

26

THE COLONEL SMOKED one cigarette after another. He took them from a round yellow tin: Three Castle. He seldom said anything; and when he did speak it was with studied accuracy. He would not have made a good lawyer; he didn't know how to be dramatic; but God as well as Teddy Roosevelt had made this man a judge. His mouth told nothing but honesty. Even his eyes told little. Those eyes already were famous: the color of violets, an abashed flower, a flower habitually described as shrinking, they did not shrink, no, no!—but they didn't snap, either. For instance, when Ward Wright talked, the eyes were careful not to challenge. Wright spoke his piece with all the liberty he could have asked, and more surely than he'd expected: he was permitted to stride back and forth; he worked his smile without interruption; and when Harry, choking with indignation at a falsehood more than usually flagrant, rose and started for him, calling him a God-damn liar, the colonel, the man with the eyes, merely rapped 'Sit down, Kellems'—and Harry sat down. On the other hand, with Conchita the colonel was almost gentle. For Conchita, as for some of the others, there was an interpreter; but the colonel, smoking, smoking, regarded her gravely and with no unkindness, and appeared to be listening to the very words she spoke rather than to those of the interpreter. You must not suppose, however, that he didn't listen to the words of the interpreter too, and weigh them, and move them back and forth in his mind, testing their relative importance! But all the while the violet eyes were upon Conchita, telling her that she had no cause for worry.

It was by no means a public affair; but Harry was present all the while, as was Dr Gorgas. 'Because you two are really the ones on trial' the colonel explained.

Harry, not liking the colonel, cried once: 'If I'm doing anything to prejudice the position of Dr Gorgas——'

'That will do, Kellems.'

Dr Gorgas said: 'You don't have to say things like that, Harry.'

'I hope to hell I don't! I hope that Jesus Almighty over there understands that he wouldn't even get in the neighborhood of Panama, much less build a canal, if it wasn't for——'

'All right, Harry!'

'That will do, Kellems.'

'Well, I don't like your tone!'

The colonel said 'That's too bad.' He looked at the two of them with no sneer, but shaking his head. 'We're on very thin ice here, gentlemen, and a false move might send us all through. So let's be careful.'

The metaphor was a strange one on that sweltering day. This was in Engineering G.H.Q. at Empire, and the colonel wore his coat, a stiff collar, a necktie. Flies indefatigably batted the screens.

'I don't suppose there's any use calling Von Alvensleben.' He looked at Harry. 'He'd deny everything?'

'Not only that, but he'd raise Cain about being summoned.'

'Yes.'

'I don't really think he knew what Wright was up to anyway. I think Wright meant this for a show-off stunt, a sort of see-what-I-can-do-when-I-put-my-mind-to-it business.'

'Yes. Yes, Von Alvensleben will not say anything, even if he knows anything. Wright certainly won't say anything. Etienne Desmoulins can't. The servants and those others didn't know what was going on, really. The engineer you sent up to remove the unexploded dynamite, Colonel——'

'Utterly reliable, I can assure you, Colonel. That's why I picked him.'

'Well, that leaves us here, and Miss Desmoulins. What about her? She seems an intelligent young lady. Good-looking, too.'

'You won't have to worry about her' Harry said.

'She would naturally have every interest in protecting her father's memory' Dr Gorgas pointed out.

'Yes, or his pension.'

Harry started up: 'Now I'm not going to stand for any——'

'Be quiet, Kellems. I'll grant Dr Gorgas' point. She *would* have an interest in protecting her father's memory—if you go on the assumption that I'm going to dismiss all charges against the dead man and give it out that he was up there on Sanitation business and somehow stumbled over and set off a capped and fused stick of dynamite—the fuse, of course, being perfectly dry—perhaps with sparks from the nails in his shoes striking some perfectly dry rock in that rain?'

Harry and Dr Gorgas looked down.

'This is the part I can't understand. I can understand a man like

Wright going in for dirty work. I can understand the interests of the men who first employed him, whoever they were. I don't say I have anything but loathing for them, but at least I can see their motives. I can understand Von Alvensleben being interested. I can ever understand Desmoulins, a bitter broken man, being brought to think that his own nation—of all of them!—would benefit by a delay in the opening of this canal. If, as you say, Kellems, and as Miss Desmoulins said, and that maid intimated, Wright worked over him repeatedly, worked on his prejudices against Americans, and twisted his mind—*that's* clear, even though it's deplorable. What I can't get into my head is why a man of your position and standing, Colonel, could lend his backing to a cock-and-bull story such as Kellems here made up on the spur of the moment.'

Gorgas looked right at him. 'If Harry Kellems says it, I'll back it up.'

'No matter what it is?'

'No matter what it is.'

Colonel Goethals looked at Harry, who looked at the floor.

'You must have a lot of faith in this young man?'

'I have, Colonel.'

Colonel Goethals turned a pencil over and over.

'Now see here, if I give out your version of the affair, people will say I'm covering something up, but anyway nobody can *dis*prove it. All right. But why should I do such a thing? Wouldn't that be suppressing evidence? Wouldn't it be winking at attempted treason? Desmoulins is dead, and I have nothing against him, but after all he *did* enter into a conspiracy to destroy government property and to endanger the lives of government employees. He *did* try to set off a series of dynamite charges embedded deep in the top of a hill where they might easily have started a serious slide. You can't gainsay that. Now why should I make myself ridiculous in order to try to protect the memory of such a man?'

Harry, waggling his hands, said: 'If I get it straight, sir, a conspiracy has to involve at least two persons. One person can't conspire with himself, isn't that right?'

'That's right, as far as it goes.'

'In this case the conspirators were Ward Wright and Etienne Desmoulins—*you* say. Well, one's dead. You can't try him for conspiracy when he's not here to face his accusers, can you? Therefore you can't try Ward Wright on that same charge either.'

'I wasn't thinking so much about the legality of it——'

'What witnesses have you got against Desmoulins? Ward Wright you've already heard denying everything. The others are Mademoiselle Desmoulins, who certainly won't testify against her father, Conchita the criada, who won't do anything Mademoiselle doesn't first tell her to do, and me, who am committed to the story that Desmoulins went out there on an innocent mission.'

'The bar lost something——'

'Look at it another way.' Harry leaned forward, elbows on knees. 'You say an official report that the whole thing was an accident would make you look ridiculous. Well, I don't see why. Everybody knows that lots of official reports are more or less doctored for the sake of appearance. Nobody takes them too seriously. And listen: such a report wouldn't make you look anywhere near as silly as a report accusing a sixty-year-old French aristocrat of conspiring with an American soldier of fortune to cause a landslide that might delay the completion of the canal by months or even years. What would the public think of a story like that? Everybody down here would jump to the conclusion that you were covering up Von Alvensleben. Nobody's ever been able to figure what that man's doing here, and you can imagine for yourself the stories that are floating around. Well, it would be said that poor little Desmoulins was being made a scapegoat—a man who was dead and couldn't defend himself. The French would be wild. They don't like us too much as it is. And Papa Desmoulins was a well-thought-of figure. He'd lost a fortune in the Compagnie Nouvelle, and he lost his wife and two sons in a yellow-jack epidemic. There would be a lot of sympathy for him.

'And then Ward Wright. We three here, we know he's despicable, but how do they look on him back home? He's still the strong silent warrior who can do no wrong, there. He's a hang-over from the days of chivalry. He's Romance—and you can't accuse Romance of anything bad. Watch any of the new lads who come down, watch them when they hear that Ward Wright lives in Panama City—why, they're as excited at the prospect of seeing him as they might be if it was Ty Cobb or Jim Jeffries or Teddy himself! He's always had a way with newspaper reporters. It's part of his stock in trade. Now, you kick him out quietly, as I've argued for a long while ought to happen, and there isn't anything he can do except call you names. But bring charges against him, serious charges like treason—and incidentally charges you can't prove—and right away you've got a martyr on your hands. The newspapers have never been kind to our little effort down here. The newspapers aren't in the Army, you know, sir. With a ready-made grievance like that they'd go dippy.'

'I am not concerned with the papers,' coldly.

'I'll bet you Teddy is!'

Colonel Goethals shot him a violent violet look.

'Take another aspect of it' Harry said quickly. 'You accuse an American and a Frenchman of a conspiracy to delay the opening of this canal. Why? What sense does that make? Who pays them? If you drag Von Alvensleben's name into it you'd only make it that much worse. France would screech that Germany had committed an overt act, or whatever they call it. Germany would yell that the French were practically declaring war. Those politicians in Europe have made capital out of a lot of things less than that. You know how they are over there right now, from what the papers say. Ready to jump at one another's throats.'

Colonel Goethals stood the pencil on end and let it fall. 'There is a great deal in what you say, Kellems. One more thing strikes me, however. I mentioned it before, and you were rude. If Desmoulins goes on record as having died in the performance of his duty, then his daughter is entitled to draw a pension from the government. And *that*, it seems to me, is too much.'

'She wouldn't draw a pension if she didn't put in her application.'

'But she'd be entitled to put in such an application. We couldn't possibly stop her.'

'I'll answer for it that she won't.'

'You seem to know her pretty well.'

'I do.'

'But how can I be sure you'll be able to do this?'

'Listen: You heard what Dr Gorgas thinks of me, didn't you?'

'Yes, I did. Yes. Very well.' He pushed the pencil away and reached for cigarettes. 'We'll close the matter, on your terms. No charges against anybody, living or dead. It was all a ghastly accident. As for you, Kellems,' and he still didn't smile, 'if you were in the Army and you'd acted as saucy as this, I'd not break you but I'd give you a tongue-lashing which would all but take the hide off you. I might buy you a drink afterward—you'd need one—but I'd let you have some language first you wouldn't forget in a hurry.' He looked at Dr Gorgas. 'I don't know whether that's the way you do in the Medical, Colonel, but that's the classic procedure in the Engineers.' To Harry again: 'However, I'm not going to. You're not in the Army, and for another thing you did chase that man at the risk of your life and put out two fuses with your own hands. That could have been a nasty business if they'd all gone off more or less at the same time—the way you could see it was planned from the lengths of the fuses. You might have saved the government millions of dollars, and you won't get a word of credit for it, thanks to this "accident" report.'

'That's all right' muttered Harry. 'I'm not looking for credit.'

'Just as well. You should get a medal, or at least a raise. As it is, you won't even get the fun of telling other people about it—because you've agreed to keep your mouth shut. So I won't give you that tongue-lashing, Kellems. I'll give you my hand, instead. Remember: it's all you will get!'

Grinning, Harry crossed the office and shook the hand. 'It's more than I ever expected, sir. Thank you.'

Colonel Goethals leaned back, puffing a Three Castle. 'However, I still have an oversupply of profanity. Things have been going too well. I haven't had a chance to cuss in weeks. In my position, that can be a serious matter.'

He rang for his secretary. 'Send in that man Wright.'

El capitan did not bluster, at first. He listened in silence, attentively, respectfully, almost standing at attention, while the dictator, himself calm, made the matter clear: this had been no trial, though there was evidence; there had been no verdict, yet there would be a sentence.

'The sentence is this, Wright: That you get out of the Canal Zone and the Republic of Panama on the next ship. And that you never come back. Not while I'm here anyway, and I intend to stay till the job's finished. For your information'—he consulted a slip—'the *Havana* leaves tomorrow morning at ten from Cristobal. Either be on her as a passenger, or I'll see that you're on the next ship in handcuffs and leg irons. That's all.'

Ward Wright lifted his chin. 'Excuse me, Colonel, but that isn't all.'

'You have something to say?'

'I have a great deal to say. Principally that you have no right to give me any such command and that I refuse to obey it.'

'Stop trying to act like a soldier, which you're not! I have the right. The duly elected representatives of the several sovereign states conferred certain powers upon the President of the United States under the Spooner Act, which governs this place, and the President has delegated those powers to me. Your only court of appeal is the President himself, and I'll tell you right now that after he's read my memorandum he won't see you.'

'Yes, but you haven't any right to order me out of the Republic!'

429

'No, that part's as illegal as hell' Colonel Goethals said with alacrity, almost with cheerfulness. 'I haven't that right, but I'm taking it. Would you care to have me telephone to President Amador and tell him what I'm doing? You know what the answer would be.'

Harry, sitting a few feet from where Wright stood, on Wright's left, watched the man. Wright's neck was purpling, and then the face. The color rose in slow thick clotted waves. Wright's fists were clenched.

'Oh, and one other thing' Colonel Goethals said quietly, almost absently, almost as though he'd just thought of it. He looked straight into Ward Wright's face. 'When you go, please carry with you assurances that Panama and the Canal Zone are well rid of you, and that if it weren't for the fact that you're not worth the trouble I would see you in jail, where you belong, and where you'll end up, instead of permitting you to pollute some other neighborhood with your presence. I'll put it in another way, in case I haven't made myself clear' said Colonel Goethals. "Slops and filth we expect in the tropics, and garbage left to fester in the sun, but I had never thought to encounter, even in the tropics, anything quite as noisome as you. You flaunt a military title, sir, which I suppose you won in some dice game. It's a pity. Of course I can't ask you to drop it, because you haven't even enough decency to realize how you disgrace it. But it's a pity. The United States Army, at least, would have nothing to do with a man of your stripe—a posing, strutting, grimacing, underhanded scoundrel. See here: A streetwalker remains at least a woman, even though she fouls her own sex. But you never were a soldier, and you aren't now. You're a liar and a fraud. You're lower than a pickpocket, you're lower than a skunk. You don't even make a good traitor. Also, you stink. Please get out.'

Harry started to his feet as he saw Wright move. He thought that Wright was about to hurl himself across the desk. He forgot the accumulation in the man's bile. It was not forward he went, no. He whirled; and his right fist swung wide and clipped past Harry's chin, stinging it like a bee, and sank into the top of Harry's left shoulder. It took Harry entirely by surprise. It was a hard blow; and it spun him around and pushed him backward over the chair he'd been rising from, so that as he fell his head and shoulders were slammed against the wall. Ward Wright began to kick him.

The kicks didn't hurt, not at the time. Harry was chiefly concerned with the problem of rising while his back was against the wall: he was afraid that one of the kicks would catch him in the testicles. He glanced under a high-held arm to see Colonel Goethals coming from behind the desk. Dr Gorgas grabbed Wright's shoulder.

'You stay out of this' cried Ward Wright, and punched Dr Gorgas in the mouth.

That gave Harry his chance to get up.

Soldiers separated them. Harry's mouth was cut, but his tongue told him all his teeth were firm. His shoulder hurt.

'You may use that washbasin over back of the screen, Kellems, if you care to. There's a towel back there.'

Ward Wright's nose was bleeding, and his mouth was bleeding badly, and he spit out a tooth. 'Good' said Harry. Ward Wright tugged at the soldiers who held his arms, and he was strong: he yanked them back and forth. The sergeant looked at Colonel Goethals, who nodded. The sergeant drew his heavy service revolver, grasped it by its barrel, and deliberately struck Ward Wright on the forehead. Wright collapsed.

'Only way to do, with men like that' the colonel, Mr X.Y.Z., said. 'See that he's on the *Havana* tomorrow, Sergeant.'

Silence rushed into the office as though it were listening for echoes.

'And now that that little matter has been cleared up,' said Colonel Goethals of the stiff neck, the man who never smiled, 'possibly you gentlemen would care to join me in a drink, eh? Colonel? Kellems?'

'I should be delighted, sir.'

Harry was washing his face.

'Abso-blub-blub-lutely!'

27

THE SEA WAS SMOOTH and shamelessly blue when Mr Morrison plopped himself into a deck chair beside Harry.

'Well, everything's all fixed, and you can take it from me this is going to be a real show. It's going to be splendiferous!'

'That's fine' said Harry, watching the sun on the water.

'It's not going to be any ordinary amateur performance like you'd usually see on a ship. It'll be practically like something you might see at Hammerstein's Victoria. Remember the Victoria?'

'Well, it's ten years since I've been back.'

Mr Morrison was properly awed. He knew that Harry was an Inca, a man who had gone down in nineteen four. Mr Morrison had gone down three years ago.

'Whatever made you not take your vacations, Mr Kellems?'

Harry shrugged. 'Oh, there just wasn't anybody in particular I wanted to see.'

'Not me! I go back to God's country every time I get the chance! But you're really quitting now, aren't you?'

'Yes, I'm really quitting. I'd have quit before, only I—I sort of wanted to stick around and see the job finished.'

'What you going to do now?'

'Finish my engineering course. I've got a little money saved up. And then I'll try to get a job.'

'Well, I sure wish you luck!'

'Thank you' said Harry.

He did not need luck to get a good job: he had pull. He had letters to some of the biggest civil engineers in the country, warm letters of recommendation from General Gorgas, Colonel Goethals, Major Gaillard, Major Sibert, Admiral Rousseau, and even a couple from Dr Amador. Oh, he'd get a job all right. But it was going to be odd, not being on civil service. He went fluttery inside whenever he thought of it. Getting a job, after all, was just the start. Engineering wasn't politics. Pull might launch you, but it wouldn't carry you through.

'First of all, of course, we got you. That's going to be the high spot on the program, naturally. I wonder if you could tell me, so's I can get this all down'—he kneed a pad, poised a pencil—'just what you're going to give us, Mr Kellems?'

'Oh, I don't know. What do you think? How 'bout "In the Gloaming"?'

'Oh, swell! Galloptious! They'll go crazy about that! And do you suppose you could—I mean, do you know it?—an old favorite of mine that's called "I'll Take You Home Again, Kathleen"?'

'All right, "I'll Take You Home Again, Kathleen."'

'Say, swell! They'll love that! And won't I, though! You know, when I used to hear you sing in church I used to wish I could stand up right then and there and ask you for "I'll Take You Home Again, Kathleen" as an encore. But of course I couldn't.'

He wrote.

Sometimes a wavelet, a hair higher than the rest, or for some windreason canted at a different angle, caught the sun's great push and fleered and sparkled: it would be, for an instant, a rope of brilliant silver tinsel, even a string of diamond chips—and then it would be swallowed by the blue.

'Then we got your good wife, who has agreed to play some selections on the piano, which I'm sure will be wonderful. She wrote them down for me here, but to tell the truth, Mr Kellems——'

Harry swiveled lazy eyes toward him. 'Well, if she picked them they'll be all right.'

'She certainly knew how to pronounce them herself! Say, she could reel 'em right off like all get out. Incidentally—and say, I hope you don't mind my bringing this up, Mr Kellems—it isn't the sort of thing I'd ask ordinarily—but anyway the other day somebody told me your wife was a foreigner. Is that right?'

'She's French.'

'You don't say! Now, nobody'd ever know that! Why, you talk with her and everything, she's practically like an American! French, eh?' Confidentially: 'How do you think they're going to make out, yourself, Mr Kellems?'

Harry sighed. 'I don't know. I can't see what it's all about, as far as that goes.'

'Don't ask me! Russia's in it too now. England and France and Germany and Russia. But they say Italy says she's neutral.'

'Well, of course *we* won't get into it' said Harry. One of the diamond necklaces had been hurled into sight, and went. He smiled at where it had been. 'We don't have to worry about that stuff.'

'All the same—I got a copy of a paper the other day my aunt sent

433

me, and all over the front page it was nothing but war, war, war, war, war, war, except 'way down the bottom there was a little teeny-weeny bit of an article about how the *Ancon* had gone through from the Atlantic to the Pacific. Were you on her then, Mr Kellems?'

'Yes, I made the trip.'

'Well, that was certainly a historical occasion, if there ever was one! The opening of the greatest construction job the world has ever known —the greatest one that has any *use* anyway: those pyramids in Egypt you hear about, they were just fancy decorations for some old king's grave. But the Panama Canal hooks the two biggest oceans in the world together. And yet here this paper my aunt sent me—and it isn't the only one I've seen like that either!—it has just a teeny little article, because everything else is war, war, war. They're not interested in a big building job, those crazy politicians over in Europe. All they're interested in is to tear something down.'

'Um-m' said Harry in an agreeing tone.

Yes, what *was* wrong with the world anyway? Now that his first real job was finished, now that he could turn around and look at other things and places, he had a sinking, sickening conviction that everything was out of line. No doubt part of this was because he was no longer in civil service, he was setting forth not for high adventure but for work in a world of competition; but part of it too was a direct result of what he saw and heard.

There was a Democrat in the White House, a college professor; and his Secretary of State, a man who never drank anything stronger than grape juice, and who wanted a law to prevent anybody else from doing so, had actually apologized to Colombia for stealing the Isthmus of Panama—apologized and offered a thumping indemnity! Teddy had volcano'd, helpless in Oyster Bay, and the men who were putting the finishing touches to the canal had gasped and then swallowed hard.

And the baseball. Baseball after all was the only outside activity he had followed throughout those ten years when he was busy. Baseball meant a lot to him. And now what had gone wrong with it? The Pirates had started off at the head of the league but by the end of May the Giants were on top, with the Red Sox creeping up on the Pirates, and the Cubs and Cards moving up too: but the Giants still looked to have the pennant in their pocket The Boston Braves at that time were last. The Braves moved to seventh place by the middle of July, and by the end of the month they were fourth. Oh, they had a great team! Johnny Evers, Hank Dowdy the catcher, Rabbit Maranville, Lefty Tyler . . . On August 15, a Sunday, the same Sunday the

Ancon steamed from the Atlantic to the Pacific in nine hours and forty minutes, the Braves clicked into second place. On Labor Day, on the Braves' own home grounds, in the ninth inning too, the Giants went all to pieces. Their nerves must have been shattered; and since that time, more than a week ago, they simply couldn't pull themselves together. Nobody was calling Rube Marquard an eleven-thousand-dollar lemon any more, for he'd shown what he could do; but now the Rube blew up. Even old Christy Mathewson blew up. Bob Bescher, the best stealer in baseball, couldn't steal a base. Larry Doyle, Fred Merkle, Big Chief Meyers couldn't hit a pop fly.

Oh, of course it was silly to think that this had anything to do with the breaking out of war in Europe, and as a matter of fact Harry didn't really think so; but both catastrophes he faced with dismay, in a world suddenly gone dotty, when he turned from his job of digging a ditch. Dotty, sure enough! Anyway it certainly was not the world he had left in Paterson.

A couple of youngsters strolled past, arms hooked. They didn't look old enough to think of going to Panama in the first place, yet here they were returning on vacation. They were singing:

> 'O-riginal!
> O-riginal!
> When you say "Hey!"
> When you swing and sway,
> When you throw your shoulders right away
> To that O-riginal Rag!'

Mr Morrison shook his head. He said that he certainly didn't care much for this ragtime, which wasn't really music at all. Did Harry? Harry said he sort of liked it.

'I'm surprised to hear you say that, a man with the talent for really good classical music that you have.'

> 'Mom says nay,
> Pop says nay,
> But play, brother, play,
> Just moan and play——'

'You should see them when they do this turkey trot, or this bunny hug. It isn't dancing at all, of course. You'll see! Wait'll you get home!'

> 'That titillating,
> Captivating,
> Fascinating
> O-riginal Rag!'

'Now we got Elv Lancaster. He does card tricks, and I haven't seen him myself, but they say he's very good. Then there's Mrs Washburn's two girls that are going to dance. She's got dresses for them and everything. Very pretty. And then those two twirps that just went by, they're going to sing a duet. I didn't much want them, but they came and asked if they couldn't sing this duet, and I didn't know what else to do.' He consulted his pad. 'Song called "Can't You Hear Me Calling, Caroline." You know it?'

Harry shook his head.

'And *then*,' Mr Morrison said, uplifting a finger, 'what I just arranged for, and what I really came here to tell you, Major Wright's going to tell us about some of his experiences!'

Harry raised eyebrows at this and tipped his cap back.

'Well, congratulations. Ward Wright doesn't ordinarily consent to tell anybody about his experiences, not even personal friends. Didn't use to, anyway.'

'Say, do you know him, Mr Kellems? Why, if I'd known that I'd have asked you to ask him for me. I was nervous as a kitten, talking with an important man like that! But he was very nice, democratic. So you know him, eh?'

'Well, I hadn't even seen him for seven years, until I got on board and found he was a passenger from Cartagena.'

'Say, you know, funny thing about that. One of the stewards told me. This boat was there in Cristobal from Cartagena for three whole days—and Major Wright never even went ashore! That's what this steward told me. Says he walked around the deck the whole time they were there. Course you wouldn't expect a man like that to exactly go *sight-seeing*. It's an old story to him, naturally. But all the same, you'd think he might want to at least stretch his legs, wouldn't you?'

'It does seem odd.'

Dropping his voice, glancing up and down: 'Course, I'll tell you what I figure. I figure it was somebody laying for him. Men like that, you know, they got a lot of enemies. He's been mixed up in all kinds of revolutions, you know, and there must be a lot of these politicians don't like him.'

'It seems quite possible.'

'But anyway, don't you think it's pretty swell, him agreeing to give us a talk? He says he's willing to do it because he believes that us Americans ought to be more military-minded and we ought to have a lot bigger army, and now that a war's started up over there in Europe he believes in us getting ready to lick the whole bunch of them, if necessary. He says that's what he's going back to the United States for, to spread that ringing message. And that's why he was willing to start spreading it right now, here on the boat.

'Why, you know, he isn't just an ordinary one of these soldiers of fortune. He's an important man! There was a big write-up about him only a couple of months ago in the *Saturday Evening Post*. Said he was the Hero of All American Boyhood. And here right now he's coming away from a fracas down in Costa Rica or Venezuela or some such place. I forget just what it was all about, but anyway Major Wright led one army and practically all his men ran away and left him standing there, and he defended this bridge practically singlehanded against a whole company of the enemy, or maybe it was even a regiment. Anyway they finally captured him, but they let him go because he'd fought so well that he was a public hero. That's why he happens to be free now, instead of facing a firing squad.'

'They probably kicked him the hell out, like so many other places have done' Harry muttered.

'Eh?'

'Nothing.'

'Oh, he's an important fella! This thing's been in the newspapers all over the country, this thing that happened there on that bridge. And then there was this big write-up in that magazine. Oh, I bet there'll be flocks of reporters waiting to interview him when we get in, and photographers! They won't be interested in a lot of old ditch diggers like us, but they'll be mighty anxious to talk to Major Wright, especially now with a war in Europe and he can give them a professional opinion about it!'

'Yes, I suppose you're right.'

'Another thing, he's got a rich wife, you know. Daughter of a big millionaire. He wouldn't ever have to work if he didn't want to. He could just stay home and take it easy. But he comes down here every now and then, all the same. It's in his blood, I guess.'

'Yes, I suppose it is.'

'Well, anyway,' getting up, slapping Harry's knee, 'it's going to be a swell program, don't you agree with me, Mr Kellems?'

'Absolutely.'

The blue of the sea changed to a chill green, and they had their entertainment, which was a success, and they knew when they were off the coast of New Jersey, because gulls appeared.

Late the last afternoon Harry went to the cabin, a deck cabin, to relieve Madeline, who would eat at the first sitting. He met the stewardess backing out with a tray; and he appraised it. 'Doing well for herself, eh?' 'Oh, she'll be all right, sir.'

Madeline kissed him, somewhat absently, and Claire grinned up from the bunk. 'That certainly wasn't much of a kiss, was it, kiddo?' 'Not much, Father.' They had agreed that he should not be called Papa: they'd agreed on that even before Claire was born. 'Don't you think she could do better?' Madeline cried 'You two!' and turned in the small place, and got close to him, putting her arms around him, and they had a real kiss. 'Ray!' cried Claire.

'That's what I love about you, old nuisance. You don't forget you're American.'

'Beg pahdon, Father?'

Harry turned to his wife, recently released. 'Did you teach her that?'

'What's the matter with that, Father?'

'In America we don't say *beg pahdon?* We say *huh?*'

'Okay then—*huh?*'

'That's better.' He kissed Madeline again and gave her bottom a spank as he stepped out on the deck with her. She was breath-taking in a dark green sheath. He didn't approve that tight, following-the-lines business; but he had to admit that his own wife looked wonderful.

'You sang very well last night, 'Arry. It's late to tell you, but you did.'

'You didn't do so bad yourself, tickling those ivories. Shame you didn't stay to hear el capitan.'

'I was worried about Claire. Did he speak well?'

'As a matter of fact, he spoke very well. I found myself getting all excited. He's practiced it. And he's good! As Mr Morrison said the other day, with a war just starting over there in Europe, and everybody talking about fight-fight-fight, he's going to have a real audience when we bring up alongside.'

'In the United States, 'Arry.'

'In the United States. It will seem almost as funny to me as it will to you.'

'We'll see the Statue of Liberty?'

'Oh yes. And later we'll go to the Singer Building and the Flatiron Building and the Aquarium and so forth.'

'I think it will frighten me, 'Arry.'

'I'm sure it will. It will frighten *me*, as far as that goes.'

Ward Wright passed, walking easily, a white linen cap on his head, sundry no-accounts at his heels. He looked good. His clothes were old but smart. His smile didn't waver; and his teeth looked fine in the smile, except that one of them was too white. Harry wondered how much that tooth had cost Edwin C. Harmey. Ward Wright's eyes were slightly bagged: it was a pendulous blotchiness which would have waggled had he walked the wrong way. There was a sprinkling of gray at each temple, very becoming. His step was sprightly. His lips were a little slack. Nothing could possibly have been changed in his mustache.

He bowed, always smiling. Harry said 'Hi' amiably enough. Madeline made a good smile.

'Why do you suppose he's only a major?' Madeline whispered. 'I should think it would impress people more if he called himself a general?'

'He's too clever for that. Don't you see—a general from Latin America always sounds a little pompous and political, like a colonel from Kentucky. But "captain" or "major"—that sounds straightforward. Like a man who really does lead troops into battle. "General" or even "colonel" would sound as if he had won the title in some office.'

' 'Arry, there are times when I think you're stupid, but there are many other times when I think you are very clever.'

'I wish I could kiss you. . . . Well, have a nice time at dinner. I arranged to have the steward bring your coffee up here.'

Thank you, 'Arry.'

She stood looking at him very seriously. People were passing, taking a last turn around the deck before dinner: the gong for the first sitting already had been sounded.

'Are—is it that you are happy, 'Arry?'

He cried 'Now I *will* kiss you!' and he did.

She broke away and hurried along the deck. He looked after her a moment, wanting to enjoy the sight of her walk; but so many people were staring, after that kiss, that he felt embarrassed. He went inside.

'You have a very nice mother' he told Claire.

'I know that,' solemnly. 'I've got a fairly nice father too.'

He grinned and sat down and touched her forehead. She was no longer really sick, simply a little switchy-switchy inside. She was still afraid to get up—afraid she might vomit again. But this way, lying like this, she was all right.

'Well, how're you feeling, old nuisance.' He stroked her hair.

'I'm all right.'

'Want me to read to you?'

'Father, okay.'

There was still summer sunlight, so he did not switch on the electricity.

Madeline returned in a few minutes.

''Arry dearest—Claire, will you excuse Father for a minute, please? I want him to see something with Mother.'

'What?'

'Well, just something. Nothing that would interest you. I'll send him right back.'

He went out and went aft with her to the end of the promenade, and from there they looked over the deck below. There was a large group, mostly men. Gulls hung and slid in the air, and rocked idiotically sometimes, and sometimes swooped. The sea had no motion, except in the wake. The gulls hung in the air, nonchalant.

'They've been pleading with him, and I think he's going to—— Yes!'

Men fell away from Ward Wright, who smiled as he whipped out a long pearl-handled revolver. He spread his feet. He aimed rather carefully; and then he seemed to shift his aim a little. He began to shoot. He wasn't smiling now. He was frowning.

He fired five shots. The gulls held their pattern, not seeming to move, though they were speeding through the air. Now and then one would lazily flap its wings, crane its neck, make a scratchy high noise. One of them dived for a bit of garbage.

'He got *that* one!'

A gull squawked indignantly, and flapped sideways, and whirled half around, and then dived, and permitted itself to float on the water for a little while.

'He got *that* one too!'

The gull with the snippet of garbage rose, listlessly flapping its wings, working its long throat. The gull which had permitted itself to float struggled out of the water and started uncertainly, lumbrously, awkwardly, in the direction of New Jersey. It flew low.

Harry thought: He probably really did hit that poor critter. On the tip of a wing, I suppose.

Ward Wright smiled apologetically and blew a wisp of smoke from the pistol's muzzle and thrust the pistol back under his coat.

'The deck' he said. 'With the ship moving like this . . .'

'Say, you got one of 'em anyway, Major!'

Somebody else said, through the murmurs of uncertain applause: 'Say, Major, you didn't shoot them all out.'

'I always save one cartridge' Major Wright answered.

Harry slid an arm half around his wife's waist.

'Well, have a nice dinner. I'll go down after you've come up.'
Claire challenged him promptly through a thickening darkness.
'What was it, Father?'
'Oh, a man with a gun.'
'Why?'
'I don't know, dear. I never have understood things like that.'
'Like what, Father?'
He sat beside the bunk and touched her face. She had no fever.
'Want me to read to you again? I'd have to turn on the light.'
'No, don't read. Just sit here and talk to me.'
'All right.'
'Okay.'
'Okay, kiddo.'

It was not so much that darkness crept into the room as that the light crept out through the open door. The ship scarcely moved; it only creaked a little, far below; and they could hear the faint bored shee-ee-ee of creamed water at the bows.

He stroked Claire's head and touched her arm and squeezed it. There was never much need to explain things to Claire, who was like her mother. The ship shee-ee-d on and on, toward Sandy Hook, toward Quarantine. Harry saw through the doorway that the stars were spick-ing out, one by one. Not many people were passing now. Half of the passengers were eating, the other half were washing or dressing.

Harry wondered whether he would catch a glimpse of Phil on the pier when the Hero of All American Boyhood got a little advance publicity for his lecture tour; and he wondered how she had weathered the years, and what her parents thought of this second son-in-law with whom she had returned and whom they so seldom saw: likely enough Edwin C. Harmey paid him to stay away. It must have come as a pleasant shock to Ward Wright when he found that Phil was a fellow passenger on the *Havana* seven years ago. He was at his best on a ship. He would not of course tell Phil that he was broke and was traveling at the government's expense—and at the demand of a quiet man with violet-blue eyes who chain-smoked Three Castles. No, no, no! He would tell her that he'd heard at the last minute that she was aboard and that he simply couldn't live without her, which was why he caught the ship with nothing but the clothes on his back. He would tell that story very well. The thing had been arranged, no doubt, before Phil started for Reno.

'Father, we get to the United States tomorrow, don't we?'
'Yes, dear.'

'Do you think I will like it?'

'I think so, dear. You—you'll have to get used to it.'

'Why?'

'Well, it's kind of funny. The people all rush around, and they all think that they know everything, right away. They usually get everything wrong, at first.'

'Why?'

'I don't know. It's just the way they are, I guess. But they get things right after a while! They always do!'

'Always, Father?'

'Always.'

She thought about this for a little, or perhaps she didn't really think about it; for she was very sleepy. She yawned.

'You'll be there, Father?'

'Oh yes.'

'And Mother?'

'Oh, she'll be there.'

'Always?'

'Always.'

'All right' said Claire. Then, very sleepily, she said: 'I mean, okay.'

'Okay, kiddo' said Harry.